D0879675

Stiller's Pond

Stiller's Pond

New Fiction from the Upper Midwest
Enlarged Second Edition

Edited by
Jonis Agee, Roger Blakely,
& Susan Welch

NEW RIVERS PRESS 1991

P S
6 4 8
6 S 5
S 7 2
1 9 9 1

Stiller's Pond has been published with the aid of grants from the National Endowment for the Arts (with funds appropriated by the Congress of the United States), the First Bank System Foundation, and the Arts Development Fund of the United Arts Council (with partial support from the McKnight Foundation). Our special thanks to the Dayton Hudson Foundation for a generous enabling grant for this publication.

The Enlarged Second Edition of *Stiller's Pond* has been issued with the assistance of a generous grant from the Dayton Hudson Foundation.

New Rivers Press books are distributed by:

Bookslinger   The Talman Company
2402 University Avenue West, #507   150–5th Avenue
St. Paul, MN 55114   New York, NY 10011

Stiller's Pond has been manufactured in the United States of America for New Rivers Press (420 N. 5th Street/Suite 910, Minneapolis, MN 55401) in a first edition of 2,000. Second edition of 3,000, September 1991.

24357440

Contents

Acknowledgements

"Stiller's Pond" was published in *Mpls/St. Paul Magazine*.
"The Mai-Loan and the Man Who Could Fly" was published in *Great River Review*.
"Rufus at the Door" appeared in *Lower Stumpf Lake Review*.
"Taking Miss Kezee to the Polls" originally appeared in *City Pages*.
"Flowers in January" was published in *Groundwater*.
"At D'Ambrosia's" was published in a slightly different form in *The Iowa Review*.
"The Amazing Human Torch" was published in *Hurricane Alice*. It is excerpted from the forthcoming (Fall, 1992) novel *Running Fiercely Toward A High Thin Sound* (Firebrand Books).
"Trap Lines" was published in *Prism International*.
"Drinking" is from the book *House of Heroes* (Random House). © Mary LaChapelle.
"Conversation" appeared in an earlier form in *Free Passages*.
"Pigs" was previously published in *Vinyl Arts* magazine.
"Spring Concert" was originally published in *Twin Cities Magazine*.
"A Novel Theory of Extinction" was first published in *Minnesota Monthly*.
"The Lion. The Eagle. The Wolf." originally appeared in *Other Voices*.
"The Deerhide" originally appeared in *The Iowa Review*.
"The Privacy of Storm" originally appeared in *Minnesota Monthly*.
"Telling Uncle R" was published in the *Sonora Review*.
"On the River Road" originally appeared in *The Madison Review*, spring 1986.
"You Ain't Dead Yet" was originally published in *The Iowa Review*.
"Doña Baby" appeared in an earlier form in *Paunch*.
"The Time, The Place, The Loved One" first appeared in *The Paris Review*.
"And Say Good-bye to Yourself" appeared in *Minnesota Monthly*.
"The Natural Father" originally appeared in *Crazyhorse*, fall 1987. It was reprinted in *The Best American Short Stories 1988* (Houghton Mifflin, fall 1988) and in *The Best of Crazyhorse* (University of Arkansas Press, fall 1990).
"Bus Is Coming" was published in *Hurricane Alice*.
"An Apprentice" appeared first in *Minnesota Monthly*, then in the HarperCollins book, *The Tomcat's Wife and Other Stories* by Carol Bly.
"The First Indian Pilot" was published in *Farmer's Market*.
"The Ivory Comb" originally appeared in *Amazons II*. Copyright © 1982 by Eleanor Arnason.

Introduction

AS WE READ a new round of submissions for this enlarged second edition of *Stiller's Pond*, our goal as editors was to retain the openness to innovation, to new patterns of experience, that characterized the 1988 edition. We resisted approaching these works with a fixed notion of form. We didn't want the book to sound like some preconceived idea of what Minnesota or Iowa or the Dakotas or Wisconsin were like, so we tried to let the works tell us what we didn't know. Obviously, the process of choosing one work over another is a risky business, but often the stories simply chose themselves, because their truth and originality demanded publication —and by truth, we don't mean the factual exactitude journalists claim, because fiction claims another truth: of point of view, of experience, of bearing witness.

Since the first well-received edition of *Stiller's Pond* had been out of print for some time, and we wanted to keep it current as a text for readers and teachers of all sorts, we sent out a call for new manuscripts in the fall of 1990. Once again, we were overwhelmed by excellent material—far more than we could possibly use. Fifteen stories—all by authors who did not appear in the first edition—were added. As in the original, the editors arrived at a mixture of familiar and less-familiar names.

While we made our choices, we continued to consider the question that we'd asked ourselves when compiling the first edition: is there such a thing as an Upper Midwest literature? Do regional aspects define a body of work that could be compared, say, to Southern literature? Would any definition become so broad that it would be ineffective, or so narrow that it would disappoint readers outside the region? Would any attempt to locate the sensibility behind these stories ghettoize, suppress, or silence our authors' voices by placing them in a category that could be shelved and footnoted within American literature texts of the Eighties and Nineties?

This is the danger. However, in discovering for ourselves what our literature encompassed, we recognized some fairly clear characteristics. And this will hold true whether or not the artist approaches her or his work consciously with all of its intention predetermined—such considerations being the job of the scholar or critic after the fact.

First of all, the Midwest values silence. Not drawing attention to one's self is the ideal. A man from Thief River Falls told one of the editors about his dream of becoming a writer in a community that discouraged talk. "He's a nice guy," would be said of a neighbor; "he never says a word."

Even in corporate cultures of the Upper Midwest, "niceness" and "reticence" are key attributes for success. Being a person of "few words" is a positive quality. This makes the language act itself powerful: it bears consequences. Words are valuable because they are a sparse commodity to be carefully measured and preserved as part of the local economy.

"The Bert and Ernie Show" by Lon Otto, "Taking Miss Kezee to the Polls" by David Haynes, Wanda Kolling's "The Halfway House," and Mary Kay Rummel's "White-Out" show us the power of language here. In Otto's story, a lawyer confronts a deaf person whose problem is language, and later discovers through a nearly fatal experience in a snow storm that it is language itself that must be kept alive, as he dons the puppets to keep his hands from freezing, and makes them converse to keep his own mind and spirit alive.

In Haynes's story, a young black man takes an elderly black woman to vote—and in so doing, his attempt to grasp the complexities of her experience and the language it generates sheds light on his own limited perspective. And Rummel's "White-Out" documents the power of discourse of all kinds as her character is gradually stripped of its use in the noviate. Rummel's title, "White-Out," suggests the fear of ultimate disconnection from language, the need to recognize its importance and to use it with care and economy that characters in all these stories share.

Under the spell of silence, Upper Midwesterners so often turn inward that readers seem to eavesdrop on the self in a part-satirical, part comic or sad dialogue that opens momentarily on externally uneventful lives. What we discover is an ironic, morose or tragic vision out of which we earn wisdom. Thus William Meissner's "The Outfielder"; Will Weaver's "Sheetrock"; George Rabasa's "The Lion. The Eagle. The Wolf."; Judith K. Healey's "Flowers in January"; and, David Johnson's "Another Savage Day in the Belly of the Whale," to name a few, examine the consequences of a silence driving the self inward.

Even when the insularity imposed by the community turns a writer's voice ironic, the self can discover such extraordinary resources at the core of the psyche as self-reliance of the Emersonian sort, and self-rehabilitation. Thus survival might depend on the individual's ability to commune with self.

The quirkiness, isolation and dislocation induced by the struggle to survive emerge in an independent discourse that refuses to move with the centers of fashionable trends. Although the Twin Cities are a nationally recognized cultural center, the area as a whole remembers that life can't be expected to be easy or even interesting, and that culture and art are luxuries we cannot take for granted.

No matter how diverse their particular experiences, the characters in these stories often expect and suffer hardships to which they respond with stoical or comic resignation. Lives are intensely lived in small communities, urban neighborhoods, or even other countries. The protagonists of Jim Northrup Jr.'s "The Odyssey" embark on a journey to earn money for survival in a society that has taken away their natural livelihood and won't hire them because of prejudice; yet they rely on ancient skills of endurance, supported by their mythmaking and storytelling talents, to achieve a modicum of satisfaction. In casting the narrative against Greek epic, Northrup lets us view a world that has fallen from the ancient ideals of justice, and yet reminds us that such journeys are undertaken daily, despite social injustice, as a means of proving one's self fit to exist, as belonging inside one's own skin.

If our literature seems to lack the Gothic horrors of the South, a constant honing of spirit and character by weather and hardship underlies its imagination, regardless of setting. Being forced to pay attention to the land, to drought, to ungodly low temperatures of long bitter winters, leaves some of our authors obsessed by the notion of survival, of what it takes to endure despite all attacks. Conrad Balfour's account of tortures in South Africa, Marianne Luban's about a Holocaust survivor who must retell her tale like an Ancient Mariner, Dan Gadow's about an action that haunts a father at his son's football game years later, and Davida Kilgore's of a woman's addiction to bingo—all of these suggest the cost, quality, and risk of losing. In "An Apprentice," Carol Bly's heroic narrator, with a desperate innocence, struggles to maintain meaning amidst a dizzying series of insults—from a treacherous urban environment, from her own body, from inconstant human nature. She keeps her humor and her wits about her, the prototype of the engaged narrator who refuses to apply the clichés of the moment to what she's experiencing and insists on her own moral truth.

Opposite, but stemming from similar roots, are stories that attempt to recapture an edenic golden age of plenty, of wilderness, of infinite possibility, of dreams. Eleanor Arnason's "The Ivory Comb" and Cheryl Loesch's "Horse Story" belong to this group.

More often, though, stories show a fallen world where Eden and the dream of infinite resources have just slipped through our fingers. Life itself is discovered through the loss of something real and true that you can never recapture. Lyn Miller's "Fire Sermon," "What She Really Did" by Ellen Lansky and Jon Hassler's "Rufus at the Door" recall such moments. Often, too, this lost world is prefigured through the loss of animals, of the land, of the natural world itself, as in the dead pig of Anne Panning's story, the tanning of a deerhide in Stephen Rosen's, and John Solensten's illegal ducks.

Lacking the diversion of mountain chains, our terrain stretches horizon to horizon with no visual escape. Even densely populated cities lie only minutes away from the natural world. This very flatness may evoke a surrealism of the mind that can't locate itself in traditional space. Noise drifting from the metropolis dissipates across wide expanses. With nothing to hold them fast, even urban writers register the underlying threat of extinction. Therefore they turn anthropologist, researcher, explorer, trying to discover or invent forms of life and frameworks of experience solid enough to bear their weight.

Indeed, some writers seem to be visitors from another planet who study and catalogue the curious gestures of natives. Many of our writers have not always lived here; yet they do not intend to return home. Janet Shaw's "On the River Road," and Margi Preus's "A Novel Theory of Extinction" view the Upper Midwest as a land where the laws of behavior, even of science, are suspended, or waiting to be invented.

Finally, we hope these stories demonstrate a sense of place that is not limited to mere geography, but found in the way imagination seeks a location for itself. When the self is freed from such boundaries as mountains and oceans, traditions, customs and culture, long-established and codified laws of behavior and thought, and rhetoric that shapes and limits behavior, then it emigrates into imagination as a true homeland where anything is possible. The self as an exile on the landscape is free to observe, and free to imagine and create worlds within.

–The Editors
June 1991

The Bert and Ernie Show

Lon Otto

I T HAD BEEN a freakish winter, mild and rainy, and the light snow dusting yard and sidewalk, swing set and sandbox, seemed irrelevant to Burney, a half-hearted effort coming long after anybody could take it seriously. He stood looking through the glass panel of the back door, finishing a cup of coffee, while the baby tugged at the dangling belt of his trench coat. When the belt came loose, he turned on the boy and chased him across the kitchen. The baby squealed with play terror, his knees slipping and churning, laughing like crazy when Burney caught him and struggled for the belt.

Greta pushed her cereal bowl back and chanted, "We're going to make a snowman, we're going to make a snowman, snowman, bo bowman, fee fie foe mowman, snowman!"

"There isn't enough snow," he said. "Anyway, we've got to get going. Maybe this afternoon, if it keeps up."

The girl stopped. "You said! You promised, when it snowed, we'd make a snowman. God damn it!"

"Watch your language," Burney said. "Didn't Hal get a time-out for saying that at school?" The jargon of preschool discipline still felt odd in Burney's mouth, but consistency, he thought, was helpful. "You want a time-out now?"

Greta started crying. Laurel, fixing the baby his breakfast, groaned. "Let's not get too involved here," she said. "I've got to finish dressing and leave in a few minutes. Can you drop Ben off at day care?"

"Maybe. I guess, if he's ready soon."

Greta wailed.

"Look," he said, "let's run outside, make some snow angels, and then grab Ben and leave. There's enough snow for angels."

"Snow angels!" Greta shouted. "All right!" She ran for her coat and boots.

"What time do you have to be at Stillwater?" Laurel asked.

"Not for another hour. My guy didn't give me a chance to file an event letter, though, so I'll need some extra time."

"Are you going to take the appeal?"

"I don't know. Probably not. I don't know what he has in mind."

"That trial was awful for you, honey. You hate trial work. Wouldn't the appeal be just as bad?"

"I don't know. I've never done one."

"That's what I mean."

"Snow angels, bo bow angels, fee fie foe mow angels, snow angels!"

"In a minute, Gret."

"You know what I mean?"

Burney shook his head. "I really thought I could handle it," he said. "Somehow I kept missing something."

"It's not your thing, Burney."

"Snow angels, bo bow—"

"Okay," Burney said. "Okay." They went out into the backyard.

"How do you do this?" Greta asked. "I kind of forget."

Burney eased himself down into the light fluff of snow, stretched out, fanned his legs and arms, and then carefully stood up again. "There, it's easy." His angel's outline was faint at the extremities, dark in the middle. "Your turn."

Greta shrieked, "No way! Look at your back! You're all yucky."

He twisted his loose coat around. "Shit." There was a long smear of mud where he had lain down. When they got back inside, he gingerly removed the coat and scraped at the mess with a paper towel.

"Daddy gets a time-out," Greta announced to her mother. "He got all dirty, and he said 'shit.'"

Laurel laughed. "I'll take it to the cleaners, honey. Ben's ready to go as soon as I find his cap. Greta, check for Ben's red cap when you go upstairs to brush your teeth. I think I saw it in the hallway. The car seats are in the station wagon, Burney. You want to take it?"

He disliked driving the ungainly blue Ford and would have preferred to pull into the prison parking lot in something a little less conservative, but it was a pain cramming the baby's complicated seat into the back of the old two-door Datsun and then stuffing the baby in and buckling everything. In the station wagon, it was easy.

When the three of them stepped out onto the back porch, Greta started to take off her parka. "What are you doing?" Burney asked.

"If you don't have to wear a coat, neither do I."

"I'm wearing a coat," he said. "See, this is a coat. A sports coat, they call it. I'd wear my trench coat if it wasn't muddy."

"It's not a real coat," Greta complained, but grudgingly she zipped up her parka again.

"Anyway," Burney said, "I'm just going to be in the car and then run inside. You guys will play outside today. You need a coat."

"I know that!" she shouted. "Don't keep saying it! Don't you see that my coat is zipped up?"

"Okay," he said. "Fine." He got the baby strapped in, buckled Greta's seat belt, and then cleared out the crayons and colored papers and toys that had drifted onto the floor, threatening to jam the brake or accelerator pedal. This was another thing he disliked about the station wagon—the ever-present kid mess.

Greta sang songs all the way to preschool and kissed him passionately when he was about to leave. "That yuck will wash out," she assured him. "Don't worry."

"Good," he said. "Thanks, Greta."

Burney parked near the old warden's house and pulled his jacket collar up against the wind and driving snow that had been snaking across the roads ever since he left the city. Through the slanting whiteness, the brick walls looked softly blurred, and it took him a while to find the entrance.

With his hand stamped and three more heavy doors locked behind him, Burney entered the prison's old law library. Even this room was secured with a ponderous steel door. A young woman sitting at a table introduced herself as the interpreter, Jenny Marx. The only other person present was an inmate librarian, reading the newspaper. The room reminded Burney of his high school library, which had, in fact, been used as a place of detention, on the assumption that troublemakers hated books. This library, though, was a place of power, its donated collections of cheaply-bound advance sheets holding the secrets of the labyrinth. After a while, a guard brought in Walter Reilly, Burney's armed robbery appeal.

"They told me you've thought of a new angle for your appeal," Burney said, watching out of the corner of his eye as the woman translated his words into sign. She was graceful and relaxed, concentrating on her work, managing somehow not to be distracting, though she was effortlessly beautiful. Burney wished she had been the interpreter at the trial.

Walter Reilly was Burney's age, but his thinning blond hair made him seem older. He had the sort of blue eyes that are hard to face, hard to avoid, and he looked amused and comfortable. The interpreter watched Walter closely and translated, Burney judged, a few words behind his expansive signing. "I missed you," Walter signed. "You don't have a TTY anymore. How can we shoot the breeze anymore?"

"I borrowed the portable," Burney said. "I had to give it back. What's really going on?"

"I like you, Burney. Don't you believe me?"

"Of course I believe you," Burney said. "I'm your lawyer, I have to believe you."

Walter laughed with a sweet strange sound and smacked Burney's shoulder. "I love this guy," he signed. She smiled and translated. Then he signed, "This idea came to me. Tell me what you think, your expert opinion. See, we say that what the judge should have allowed for is the fact that the gun was unloaded, wasn't really a gun but a sign that said, "This is a robbery. Give me money. I'm serious."

Burney shook his head. "I don't get it."

"We have to stress the language problem. What could I do, go in there with an interpreter? Jenny, you go with me next time?" She interpreted evenly, unemotionally, not discriminating between comments addressed to her or to Burney.

"But it *was* a gun. We *made* the point about it not being loaded. It's still armed robbery."

Walter laughed, signed more slowly, emphatically, with more finger spelling. "No, to the hearing devils, it was a gun. For me, it was a word, a sign. Language, not weapon."

"Hearing devils?"

Walter laughed and waved him past the question. "What can I do, rob only other deafies, make sure they know sign first? See, this is what we base the appeal on. They ignored the language question. I was deprived of my rights of expression."

Burney looked at the interpreter and asked her, knowing it was a breach of decorum, "Are you sure? Does this make sense?"

Walter reached across the table and grabbed him by the shoulder, redirecting his attention. "It makes sense to me." He used his fierce beautiful eyes on Burney like the threat of a knife. "It makes sense. It can cut my sentence in half. Call the whole trial into question. The interpreter was a joke."

Burney had wondered about her, a woman who struck him as rather hesitant, less comfortable with legal terminology than he had expected from someone certified for court work. The interpreter he and Walter had used in preparing their case had seemed more fluent, and now, listening to Jenny, the contrast was striking. He nodded. "All right," he said. "I can't handle it, though. Appeals work is something else again. I've never done it. I'll help you find someone experienced." He looked out the heavily screened window at the driving snow. "I should have done that in the first place, Walt. I'm not really a trial lawyer. I told you that."

"No, no, I like you. You did your best. That was all I asked."

"Anyway, I'll help you find somebody really good."

"I have somebody good."

"No, I just can't do it."

"Andy Conlin."

"Andy Conlin?"

"Deaf lawyer from Washington, D.C. Very famous in the deaf community. You maybe saw him on 'Sixty Minutes.' Real deafie, profoundly deaf from birth. Young man, very brilliant."

"So," Burney said, "you think he'd take your appeal?"

"Yes. He'll take it."

"Well, great. That sounds great. You want me to write him?"

"Not necessary," Walter signed. "He's going to fly out next week. You can meet him then. Very famous, very brilliant man."

"I'll do whatever I can to help," Burney said, wondering how much he'd contributed already to an appeal based on the incompetence of a hearing world to deal justly with the nation of the deaf, how much his *pro bono* eagerness had laid the groundwork of Walter Reilly's real case. All right, Burney thought in the entryway of the prison before slogging coatless and gloveless to his car. Good luck to him. He's welcome to my mistakes if they'll do him any good. The law moves in mysterious ways.

He waited for the car to warm up a little, edged out of the parking lot down the long prison drive to the road, and slued out onto the barely visible highway. It was colder than it had been before, and the snow had grown harsh, grainy, and flung itself against the windshield as if blasted out of a firehose.

Now Burney was glad of the heavy car, which plowed through the storm in a stately and untroubled fashion. The half-hour drive would take at least an hour and a half, given the rate of the sparse traffic. Burney listened to the radio, tightened a window against the splinter of cold air that carried little bullets of snowflake against his cheek, sang, signed through the alphabet. He'd picked up a little American Sign Language and gestured now, "be cool," "see you later," "any questions?" "good luck," he signed, and while his hand was off the wheel, the car skidded a little, fishtailed left and then right, caught the edge of a drift, and slid nose first down a long embankment, gaining speed.

When Burney came to, it had started to get dark. Snowflakes still whirled around the top of the cracked windshield, visible in the few inches of glass not yet drifted over. Burney's forehead had bled a little and now was clotted and sticky. When he turned the ignition, the starter just whined and then stopped altogether. He sat there in the darkness, vaguely dizzy, examining by faint dome light the toys and papers spilled over the dashboard.

Burney knew enough to stay with the car. It was getting cold inside, though. He found an old receiving blanket in the back, which he wrapped around his neck and tucked into the front of his jacket. Then he shoved the door open to check the damage. The car was utterly stuck, he observed, standing with his hands thrust deep into his jacket pockets. There were no lights from the highway visible through the storm, but he thought if he could scramble up the embankment, he might be able to flag down a snowplow or something. After an almost snowless winter, they would be out in force.

He crawled back into the car and looked for stray gloves or mittens under the seats, but the closest he could come, among the toys and trash, was a pair of hand puppets, which Greta had been given for Christmas. He would need to use his hands to get up the hill, so he pulled on the two puppets and wiggled his fingers into the flannel arms and plastic heads. "Okay, Bert?" he said. "Okay, Ernie." The round-headed Ernie puppet fit his hand better than the narrow cone-shaped Bert, but both had long gauntlets that would keep the snow out of his wrists. "Let's go!"

Burney's leg bothered him a little, while he worked his way up the steep embankment, squinting into the blizzard, but it wasn't broken or even sprained. It worked. It kept moving, and he moved slowly upward, slipping, floundering in drifts, making pretty good progress where the wind had swept the weed bristle clean. At least it felt as if he were making good progress, but the embankment rose and rose, the highway always eluding him, higher in the darkness and slanting snow, the earth not yet leveling off. Gravity guided him, pulling him back. "Jesus, Bert," he grunted, pausing, "something's wrong here."

"You can say that again, Ernie. Hih, hih, hih."

And then the embankment crested. Burney staggered forward toward the road and slammed headlong into a wall that rose suddenly out of the night and storm. He stood again and felt cautiously ahead with his puppeted hands. He found the wall, glass, stretching out on either side quickly out of sight. It was a greenhouse. He'd climbed in the wrong direction, away from the highway. But this was better than he'd thought. He knew where he was. He'd find shelter here.

After creeping and patting his way completely around the greenhouse, he was unable to see any other building or light, and he was afraid to leave the greenhouse, fearing he'd get lost in a forest of arborvitae and blue spruce or in the simple open fields he remembered stretching out from the nursery.

He worked his way back to the entrance and again tried the door that he knew to be locked. He was starting to shiver wildly. He had to get inside, but it isn't easy to break a pane of glass with a hand, even protected by the plastic head of a puppet. The spirit holds back, softens the blow. Finally, using more violence than would have seemed necessary, he smashed a pane, reached in, and got the door open.

No smother of warm moist air met him as he stepped inside, no ranks of mysterious plants breathing in the darkness, only cold black stillness. He found a rag of burlap to stuff into the broken pane to stanch the blast of storm. He moved cautiously up and down the paths between the empty benches. "At least we're out of the wind," he said.

He found a bale of straw in the darkness, kicked it apart until he could pull the straw loose from the twine, and made a nest for himself to curl up in. The effort warmed him, and he was relatively comfortable for a while and even dozed, until he started to shiver again. He looked at the faint glow of his watch. It was only seven o'clock. The colon separating hours and minutes flashed steady as a pulse. He thought with longing of the car and the drifts of crayoned paper, which he could have used to start a fire. Straw would burn and the benches were wood. He could turn the frozen darkness of the greenhouse into a huge lantern, visible for miles, tropical and brilliant. If he had matches. If he smoked. He made another circuit of the building, gathering leaf litter and moss and rotten burlap, scooping it all up between awkwardly puppeted hands. When he tried barehanded, his fingers quickly stiffened and grew numb. His toes already had no feeling. He scoured the darkness, adding to his nest, until his head throbbed and he started to feel nauseated, exhausted from the work and the cold.

Nestled into the mound of debris, his knees drawn up under his chin, Burney smacked blood into his hands and sang some songs to keep himself awake. He clapped his hands again and then furiously worked his fingers inside Greta's puppets. "Well, Bert," he said, "we're in a fix now."

"You can say that again, Ernie."

Greta hadn't liked the puppets much when she first got them, her desire had been so focused on a stuffed bear she'd been promised. But when Ben reached the point of being susceptible to entertainment, his explosions of watery laughter themselves became objects of desire, and Greta found that the puppets set him off like magic. Locked in his car seat, he was a boundlessly appreciative audience for the shows she performed for him, with Bert and Ernie improvising long dialogues on the subjects of the day. She kept them always in character—Bert the straight man, a little slow, not getting the most outrageous pun at first, laughing tightly when he did, Ernie more confident and clever.

"Bert, bo dert, fee fie foe mert, Bert?"

"What, Ernie?"

"Why did the warden stop sending his shirts to the prison laundry?"

"I don't know. Why?"

"Because he could never figure out what to do with the extra button."

"Extra button? I don't get it, Ernie."

"Me neither, Bert. A guy told me that one today."

The storm crashed against the greenhouse, rattling the panes so violently that it was almost impossible to conceive that the spidery shelter could survive. Before leaving the prison, Burney had tried to call home, but either the lines were down or the circuits were overloaded. Laurel probably would assume he had stayed, waiting out the storm, drinking coffee and joking with the guards in the employees' cafeteria. She always overestimated his good sense. Even if she got through to the prison, it was likely that, without an event letter on file, nobody would be able to tell her when he'd been there or when he'd left.

"Extra button?" Bert said. "Extra button?"

Suffering as much from tedium and loneliness as from the awful cold, Burney painfully stood up, shedding his carefully arranged nest, and climbed blindly onto one of the benches. Edging forward, his hands raised high, he finally felt Bert's tall head graze against something yielding. Jumping as high as he dared, he caught a fold of the gauzy fabric that had been hung to protect plants against sunscald, and he gradually pulled it free. He felt his way back to the mound of debris and worked his way under it again, using the fabric to keep a little space clear in front of his face. He kept his hands close to his chest and wriggled down into the nest, allowing straw and trash to cover as much of the cloth as possible. When he stopped moving, he felt himself go lightheaded. His legs became leaden. Activity warmed him, but he hadn't enough energy to sustain it now. He'd have to stay put.

Imprisoned by glass and mulch, cold and exhaustion, Burney wondered how convicts endured separation from their families. He kept moving his fingers. "I want visitors," Bert moaned, absence aching like pulled teeth. "I want to hold my kids again. I want Laurel."

Checking his watch, Burney plotted like a mariner their various positions. Now the children would be getting their baths. Now they would be in the kitchen, Greta having a bedtime snack. Now, back upstairs, Laurel would be putting them to bed, and now Greta would be searching her out, wanting to be held while Laurel dialed and dialed, getting no answers. Laurel would be holding Greta now. And now. And now the baby.

Burney woke a little crazy, stupid with cold, the blood moving through his brain too slowly for the flicker and flash of thought. If he had not buried himself so well, he would have crashed out of the greenhouse and staggered toward home. He wanted to, willed it, but Bert held his right hand, and Ernie held the left, until the impulse grew quiet.

"*What* family?" Ernie whispered then. "Are you joking? Wife? Kids? *You?*"

And Bert put his arms around him and said, "It's a mystery, Ernie. I never meant to hurt you."

Invisible in the darkness, they wrestled. If a whirlwind had uncovered them, it would have revealed them in an embrace, locked like wrestlers or lovers, cone head and round head, and one carried hidden the stamp of freedom, and one did not.

It had stopped snowing, and the wind that scoured over the greenhouse roof revealed stars here and there and a half moon, blurred by whitewash. Without clouds to capture the small warmth left in the earth, it would grow truly cold now, heat leaping out toward the stars in unhesitating abandon. Snow was drifted against the walls too high to see anything but sky outside, but the thin light made the greenhouse itself visible, an icy uninviting web of crystal and lead, its benches stretched out like a banquet of emptiness.

They slept through the night the intent sleep of buried ones. In the morning, the state patrol would probably have found them, if the nurseryman's collie had not leaped away at first light from the valley where the farmhouse was sheltered and dove and tumbled through the crusted drifts up to the glass houses on the hill, if the dog had not been tracked by the nurseryman's daughter, clumsy on snowshoes she had been given for Christmas and never used till now, if the dog had not yanked the burlap rag out of the broken pane and had not howled ecstatically at the strange still mound inside, if the girl had not let the dog in, to spring in a fury of long blunt claws.

The dog found Ernie first, snatched him out of the mound's thrilling smells, and shook the puppet's body like a rat. When the girl shouted and wrestled Ernie away from him, he barked thunderously and dug again and this time found a man shrouded in white and went really wild, twisting and whirling until his long fur blurred.

The girl hauled the dog aside, brushed peat moss and bark from the man's face, and touched his cheeks, first with her mittens, then with her bare hands. His skin felt cold, stiff. Bert, hidden till now, jerked in his sleep. The girl stepped back. And then everything was pain and light and a shattering racket that thundered over Burney like an avalanche of roaring life.

On the River Road

Janet Shaw

K ELDA WAS CERTAIN that Larry was seeing another woman, so after she closed up the Cut 'n Curl she drove out to The River Tap, a roadhouse he used to go to before they married. That he'd be there was a long shot, but she wanted proof. He'd had a lot of time on his hands tomcatting around since he'd hurt his wrist at Illinois Storm Doors and been laid off. Their baby, Coco, was only two and a half; he said he'd babysit if Kelda went back to work, but now she heard from friends that often he left Coco with neighbors and went off on his own. They said he saw a blonde in East St. Louis, and a part-Indian girl up in Grafton. When Kelda accused him, he told her she was a fool to believe gossip. "Folks will always talk about me." He smoothed his curly brown hair with both hands, then slipped his arm around her waist. "I'm the kind of guy who stirs things up. I stir *you* up, don't I, sweetie?" Oh, she did love him, but his lies made her feel old and used up, although she was only twenty-two. If she could catch him outright with a woman, maybe she could find the energy to leave him and start over.

As soon as she reached the junction of the Edwardsville Road and the river road, she spotted Larry's pick-up in front of The River Tap. Finding his truck right where she'd hoped to dried her mouth and made her hands shake. It was like the meets in high school when she crouched on the track, the tips of her fingers pressed into gravel, her knees trembling, then the blast of the starter's gun—

inside her chest, it seemed—sending her hurtling forward. She welcomed the feeling that something would *happen* now.

Chocolate-brown mud spattered the wheels and fenders. He'd probably planned to alibi that he'd been fishing down on the levee. A lot of time he brought catfish home from there for supper. He said he left Coco on the bank and went out alone in a rowboat. "But she could fall in and drown!" Kelda said. "I tie her to a tree with a rope around her waist," he said, but he laughed so hard that Kelda didn't know whether to argue with him or to laugh, too. He had a million ways of throwing her off. Sometimes when she was angry he'd start fondling her while she was shaking her fist at him, or maybe he'd shove her against the wall in rage and reach up under her skirt at the same time. She short-circuited, so many different currents running through her. She thought he liked her confused. Then, he was in command. "What are you doing!" she'd say and he'd say *this, baby*. She was helpless when he made love to her. But now she wouldn't be.

She pulled into the narrow drive between the feed store and an abandoned garage, parked, and settled down to wait. Lights inside The Tap stained the greasy windows yellow. The big beer advertisement over the side door, "The River Tap," in swirly red neon like the patterns Coco drew in the air with her sparklers, blinked on and off. Country-and-western music whined when a guy in jeans opened the door and ambled out. Over the familiar animal stink of the Mississippi she smelled fish and French fries. The evening sky, the green of cheap turquoise, darkened quickly. She'd stay right here until she got what she needed.

In her lunch sack she found a few leftover chips and a plum. The chips were limp from the August humidity, but the plum was sweet. She wiped its juice from her chin, then tilted the rearview mirror to repair her lipstick. She saw one brown eye, the dark hair at her temple, the two pearl studs in her left earlobe. She smoothed her pink lipstick with her little finger, a trick she'd learned from her mother, who always marked her cigarettes with a crimson dimple. Now Coco had picked up that gesture and spread her chapstick with her plump little pinkie. How could you predict what a child would learn? And now Coco spent her days with Larry—what would he teach her?

Time passed harder than Kelda thought. After half an hour she decided to make her move. Taking her straw purse, she slid out, walked the half-block to the junction, and waited for the light to change. Her reflection gazed at her from the feed store window—a slim girl, her white blouse and blue madras skirt wrinkled in the heat, her purse clasped across her breasts. No one would suspect she was about to make a scene in The Tap, to scream at Larry, "I'm through with you!"

She crossed the road and walked slowly back toward the tavern. When she reached it, she stepped up on the sloped cellar door near the kitchen, peered into the window of the dining room, then quickly jumped down and pressed back against the wall. Larry sat right there. Coco stood next to him on the bench of their booth, and opposite him sat two heavy men in gray work shirts.

So he wasn't with a woman after all. Maybe there weren't any other women.

She was more relieved than she could have guessed. Though she knew he couldn't see her with the lights so bright inside, she stayed pressed to the creosote shingles. She studied him and Coco—it was like rejoining them after a long and painful separation. How darling Coco was with her chubby arm around Larry's neck, the hiked-up hem of her pink gingham pinafore revealing her panties and the butterfly-shaped birthmark on her leg. Strands of her white-blond hair stuck to her chin as she munched fries from his plate.

He leaned forward, his elbows on the table, and laughed the way men do when women aren't around, his mouth wide open, head tipped back, eyes slits of blue. He reached over the pitcher of beer to slap the white-headed man on the arm. The men all laughed. And she realized she was smiling. Maybe she'd tell him later that she'd seen him when he didn't know she was looking, that she'd fallen for him all over again. Any woman would notice the fullness of his lips, the square angle of his jaw, his uptilted nose. She imagined she could taste that sheen of sweat on his face. Once, she licked him all over his throat and chest like a mother cat grooming her kitten. They'd just made love, and, as she caressed him like that he fell asleep; how tender she'd felt toward him then.

Coco whispered in his ear. He rolled his eyes, made another joke that started the men laughing again, got to his feet and hoisted her onto his hip. As he turned away from the table the younger man emptied the pitcher of beer into his glass and picked up the check.

Kelda ran back across the road to her car. She'd wait until he pulled away, give him a head start, and drive home after him. The night was moonless and her car was hidden between the buildings. Cicadas rasped in the trees. The two men came out, a burst of music pushing at their backs, and headed for their truck. The younger man lit a smoke and flicked the match, a tiny falling star. They got in and the truck groaned away.

Larry shoved through the door. Coco hung on around his neck, her face against his white t-shirt. He scolded her, jostling her for emphasis. She squirmed, pointed down the road as though begging to be taken home. Kelda thought she heard Coco whimper, "Me!" Larry looked where Coco pointed. He stared hard down the dark road, spit into the dust, and said, "Bastard! That bastard!" Now he ran to his truck, shoved Coco in, loped around to his side.

What had sent him running? Beyond the jello colors of the neon sign, the night thickened into a wall. No cars approached. A moving shape on the white gravel shoulder of the road pulled her gaze. At first she thought she saw an injured dog, a big one, maybe a collie. Then she realized it was a man.

As she made out his splayed legs, outspread arms, lifted head, Larry passed in the pick-up, backing up so fast his tires shot gravel. Steering with his right hand, he leaned out the window. But until the man lying in the road twisted and rolled off into the side ditch, she didn't realize Larry was trying to run over him.

The pick-up skidded to a stop, pulled forward, backed up again, more slowly this time, rear wheels veering into the ditch where the man now lay, exhaust blossoming over him. "No!" Her cry startled her. Larry pulled back onto the pavement and gunned ahead. When he reached The Tap his headlights splashed on. He swung left onto the Edwardsville Road, the rear-end fishtailing, and was gone.

She gripped the steering wheel so hard her hands ached. She felt as though Larry had been after her as well as that man in the ditch. He'd tried to kill that man. Had there been a fight? Who was he? Was Coco in danger?

Trying to think, she sat frozen. Maybe she should call the police instead of an ambulance. The man's blond head was visible again now as he dragged himself back up onto the pavement. A sedan came down the road, slowed, stopped; a tall fellow in a plaid jacket climbed out and crouched by the man. So she didn't have to make any decision except to get out of there fast.

In darkness she backed the length of the alley and into the dirt road behind the feed store. When she yanked on her lights after she turned the corner, the faded white line, a strip of tire rubber, a dead cat, corn stalks coated with pale dust loomed before her. Her eyes hurt from staring after the sweep of her lights. Something terrible had just happened, but she didn't know what it meant. *Why* had Larry done that? Had that man dealt Larry bad dope, or squirmed out of a gambling debt? Whoever he was, he must be so dangerous to Larry that he had to be wiped out. She hadn't realized she knew so little of her husband's life. She imagined grabbing him by the shoulders, shaking him, demanding, "Who are you? Tell me!"

When she reached the little duplex they rented in Granite City, Larry was giving Coco a sponge bath in the kitchen. Traces of ketchup around her lips, her feet in the sink, she sat naked on the counter. He soaped her with the Ivory that bubbled around her ankles. "About time you're home," he told Kelda.

Coco cried, her face streaked. She held up her arms. "Mommy!"

"Okay, I had to spank her. She peed her pants is why," he said.

Coco wrapped her legs around Kelda's waist. Kelda kissed her bare shoulder, her arm, the top of her head. The warm, wet weight in her arms seemed the only certain thing in the world.

Larry wrung out the cotton panties he washed. "You're sure late."

"I had to clean up tonight." Because she didn't know how to invent what might come next, she said, as she always did, "How was your day?"

"Nothing to show for it."

"Anything go wrong?"

"I didn't win the lottery again, if that's what you mean." He half-smiled. "Get us some beers, sweetie?"

Nothing was different about the way he popped open his beer, stripped off his t-shirt and wiped his face and arms with it, switched on the TV to the baseball game. After she comforted Coco and put her to bed, Kelda sat by him on the couch.

Without glancing at her, he circled her nape with his hand, slipped his finger under the silver chain she wore. "I ran into Jim Koch and Al Herbert today. Haven't seen them since I was laid off at the plant. Jim says if I can't work the line anymore I should try for a job in sales. He says I could sell storm doors to Eskimos. What do you think, Kelda, could I sell you a storm door?"

"Did you have your supper?"

"We got burgers at The Tap."

His tug on the chain pinched, so she took his hand instead. His fingers laced through hers. "What went on at The Tap?"

"Like I said, the kid peed her pants. That's about all I can say for the action."

Now was the moment when she could say she'd seen him, beg him to explain, but the words wouldn't come. Maybe she was afraid; she wasn't ready for his answer. She pressed his knuckles against her teeth until he winced and jerked from her clasp.

"What the hell!"

"You haven't once looked straight at me since I got home."

He turned swiftly and pressed his damp forehead to hers. His eyes merged into one huge blue eye; it reflected her face like a pinpoint of light. "Now I'm looking. Now what?"

"Nothing." After a minute she got up, changed into her nightgown, and remembering she hadn't had any supper, made herself a bologna sandwich. She took it into Coco's room, closed the door, pulled the rocker to the crib and leaned against the bars. In her night diaper, Coco slept on her back, her arms flung up over her head. Coins of light from the streetlamp sifted through the moving branches of the honey locust and drifted across her face as though she lay under shallow, moving water. Kelda breathed talc and baby sweat. "What happens now?" she whispered. "Oh, Coco, what now?"

The morning paper reported a motorcycle accident the previous evening on County K at the junction of the Edwardsville Road. The injured man, Mason Brady of Alton, Illinois, was in serious condition at Memorial Hospital in St. Louis, Missouri.

She called the hospital from the beauty shop. Mason Brady's condition was described as serious but stable. He'd suffered multiple fractures to his leg and possible damage to his spine. His left leg had been amputated above the knee but he'd come through the operation as well as could be expected.

She decided to wait a couple of weeks. By then he'd feel well enough to talk. She didn't know what questions she would ask, but somehow she'd persuade him to reveal what he'd done to Larry, why they were enemies. Once she understood the situation she'd talk to Larry about what she'd seen and hear his side. If she learned the truth first, he couldn't evade or confuse her.

Luckily, her mom was on vacation from Lloyd's Finest Cleaning and Pressing. She agreed to keep Coco on the days Kelda worked. Although she didn't worry so much about the baby, Kelda slept less well all the time, and kept waking before it was light. Those mornings she wandered around the house, listened to the first squawking of the crows in the spruce trees. In the pre-dawn haze, the flower-patterned walls, dark floorboards, limp chintz curtains looked unfamiliar, as though she'd wakened in the house of strangers.

One morning she lay down on the couch under an old afghan of her mother's and fell back asleep. She dreamed she walked a highway shimmering with heat somewhere in the west. On the pavement by her feet lay a lizard pounded paper-thin by passing traffic. The lizard curled up like a dried leaf, its legs frayed ribbons where the feet had been torn away. As she gazed at the lizard it came to her that it was herself she'd found flattened there.

In Memorial Hospital she followed the signs to the east wing, then took the elevator, reeking of pot roast and disinfectant, to the fourth floor. At the nurses' station in Orthopedics she got the room number for Mason Brady. Without knocking she looked in. Through the dim light slicing from half-closed Venetian blinds she saw a slender, blond-headed young man in a wheelchair. Instead of a hospital gown he wore an Army shirt unbuttoned over a pair of red nylon running shorts. The stump of his left leg was heavily bandaged. Chewing on his fingernail, he watched a game show on a tiny TV, the sound turned so low she couldn't hear the voices of the men and women who laughed and clapped.

She smoothed the collar of her pink blouse. "Hey."

He glanced at her without turning his head. His yellow moustache was carefully trimmed, but he needed a haircut. "Looking for someone?"

"If you're Mason Brady, I'm looking for you."

"Well, I am."

"Can you have a visitor?"

"I could if one would come."

"I'd like to visit you. I'm Kelda Crownhart." She came down firm on her last name to see if he'd register that.

He smiled, showing white teeth with a gap in the center. "You're from some church, I bet."

She lifted her hair from her shoulders and shook her head. "I heard your story from a friend and thought I'd say hello."

"Won't hurt me none to talk to a pretty girl. Come on in." He wheeled backwards to reveal a path at the foot of his bed to a straight chair under windows which looked onto a narrow interior courtyard. She bumped the footboard with her hip as she squeezed by, then sat and faced him across the bed, which now concealed his stump. She realized he planned it this way.

As though he'd just remembered not to chew his fingers, he folded his hands and nodded to the pamphlets scattered on the window sill. "Some church folks stopped by yesterday, but for my part I'm not a believer."

When she saw he was trying to put her at ease, her face got hot. "No, me neither. I'm just here to wish you well."

"I can use a lot of that." He squinted against the afternoon light that entered behind her. His eyes were dark and down-slanting, with heavy lids. He'd probably been somebody with girls before his accident; maybe he'd gone after an old girlfriend of Larry's.

"I want to say I'm sorry for all that." She waved vaguely toward his leg.

"Can't help but feel sorry for a man so purely stupid."

"I heard a guy tried to hit you after you were smashed up." Because she blushed harder she traced the ribbon trim on her purse.

He leaned toward her slightly, his shirt falling open on his smooth chest. "Has that story got around the hospital?"

She nodded. What should she say now?

To her surprise he laughed. "I thought you meant you were sorry about me running my cycle off the road. *That* was purely stupid. I saw an oil spill and didn't even slow down. I thought I was beyond the laws of nature, you could say, as though I'd just float over trouble. A Harley makes you feel like that. But I slid off that road with nothing under my tires but air. Braking on air. Next thing I knew I'd slammed that pin oak and was laying there pinned. But maybe I'm talking too much."

She laid her purse on the bed so he'd see she was there for a while. "Were you on your way to somewhere special?"

"Just home. Had too many beers, I guess."

"You're married?"

As though her interest drew him, he inched a quarter turn on his wheelchair nearer the bed. "Wasn't even hurrying to see a girl, if that's what you're asking. Just feeling mighty powerful and mighty drunk. Then, whammo, I'm under all that metal."

Imagining it, she grimaced. "You must have been real scared."

"Your name is?"

"Kelda. Kelda *Crownhart*." But he didn't blink.

"Kelda, if it was you pinned under your cycle, you wouldn't be scared. That's one thing I found out. Shock numbs you. I began thinking real matter-of-factly, well, how do I get out of here? I looked around for help, but I was twenty, maybe twenty-five feet off the road and into a woodlot, so if you didn't look close at the swathe I'd cut you couldn't see me at all." He spread his arms, moons of sweat showing under, to describe the trail.

She judged by the ruddy flush that had come upon him that he was glad to tell his story, probably told it over and over to himself, marveling that he'd come through alive. "You've had a real tough time, haven't you?"

His eyes went brighter. But he said quickly, "At least they didn't cut off nothing *but* my leg," and winked at her. She understood he'd rehearsed that line, so she gave him back a smile.

"Want to hear more?"

"I want to hear it all."

He settled back in his chair as if, until her pledge, he'd been afraid she might leave as suddenly as she'd arrived. "It's all real clear to me, you know. Like my mind was working extra hard. I suppose I must have been drunk, but I felt cold sober. I began digging out handfuls of dirt from under my legs, thinking if I could make more space I'd be able to ease out from under, then drag myself to where I'd be seen. But even in that sandy soil digging was slow going and night began to come on. Now and then I'd see headlights sweep through the scrub pine, and I'd holler, but no one heard me. Or, if they did, they didn't stop. Then my hand hit on something sharp." He held it out for her to see the scar across the palm.

She touched the raised pink line with her fingertip. "You carry a knife?"

"Hell, no. I scraped my hand on my own thigh bone. By that I knew how bad off I was. The bone had come clean through the muscle and skin and I didn't feel a thing. My left leg was just some vegetable I had to pry out of the ground."

He motioned for her to pour him a glass of water from the yellow plastic pitcher on the bedside table by her. From nerves she brimmed the glass, the ice in the pitcher clicking against the spout like chattering teeth.

"Won't you have some? Or a can of soda?" He peeled the plastic wrapper from another glass and handed it to her. The water, very cold, tasted faintly of mouth-wash. She swallowed too fast and it burned in her throat.

When she got her breath she said, "I guess I would have despaired right about then."

As if to make sure he had her attention, he tapped her wrist with his damp fingers. "You don't know what you'd do. You can't prepare for such a thing. It just happens, then you find out. Once I ran into my grandpa's burning barn to save the milk cow. Afterwards, I couldn't remember doing it, but I stood covered with ashes, burns on my hands and arms, and there was Minnie. If you asked me would I risk my life to lead a cow from a barn fire, I'd say, I'm no fool. You see, you do what you do. Until you have a test, you don't know what that will be." He ran his hand through his hair that fell thick over his forehead. "I've had a lot of time to think things through lately."

She held her water glass to her hot temple. "I couldn't do what you did about digging out. I know myself pretty well and—"

"Hey, we don't know one thing about who we are! Not *that* much!" With his thumb and forefinger he measured a half-inch, then wiped his mouth with his wrist. "We don't know what we can or can't do until right at that minute. If I didn't have this accident I'd never know I could dig myself out from under, drag myself through a woods and then a mile, maybe more, to the junction. See, I found that out the hard way, but now I know."

She set her glass on the bed table crowded with ice cream cups, newspapers, sandwich wrappers, a razor.

When she looked at him again he was watching the open door. "Sometimes on Sunday night the aides bring the supper trays early so they can leave. Sure does make a long evening."

"It's only four-thirty."

"And you'll stay a while?"

"Yes." Then they were both silent. Down the hall a cart rattled, a distant radio played a big band version of "Yesterday." *Now*, she told herself, and her heart ballooned in her chest. "How about that man in the truck who went after you? Who was he?"

He laughed, gold flashing from deep in his mouth. "Lord, *him*."

She pushed forward in her chair, the hard edge pressing aginst the back of her thighs through her cotton skirt. "Why would he try to run over you?"

"I been driving a taxi, and thought I knew everything there was to know about folks, claimed I'd met up with every single kind of crazy, but I was wrong."

"Did you know him?" Her pulse thudded in her throat.

He took a deep breath and cracked his knuckles. "I haven't told this part straight through before."

"Would you tell me?"

He sighed. "Why not? I think about it often enough, can't stop thinking about it. There I was, dragging myself along the road toward the junction. Cars that passed me didn't stop. Maybe they thought I was a drunk, I don't know. After a while I quit trying to flag them down and just concentrated on dragging along. Once I passed out and woke up scared because I'd forgotten where I was. Then I remembered and startted dragging again.

"After a long time I came around a bend and saw the tavern up ahead, lit like Christmas, the door banging and cars starting up. I figured I had it made if I could get there.

"When I got closer I started in yelling again, but my voice cracked like static. Then *he* came out with this little girl in his arms. He didn't spot me, but she did. I heard her say, 'Lookee.' And he looked. I waved. As soon as he got a bead on me he jumped into his truck with the kid, and what do I see but he's backing up right at me! At *me!* Maybe twenty miles an hour, sighting me out the window. I couldn't believe it. Then I believed it and rolled down into the ditch.

"I was laying in the water thinking this man is going to kill me! When I looked up, his truck was right there. The kid stood by him, no seat belt or nothing. I thought, he wants her to see. Personally, I wouldn't want a kid to see me do something so shameful as run down an injured man. But he didn't care. Maybe he thought he'd teach her a lesson of some kind.

"He shoved into gear, pulled up, then here he come again, rear wheels aimed down into the ditch. Threw dirt into my face. I thought he'd hit me sure, then I thought he'd missed me. Turned out, they told me later, he ran over my left leg, but it was numb and I never felt it. Smashed it flat, the doctor said. Might have been able to save it except for how he smashed it.

"The wheels went by my head again. I looked for his license, but the plate was caked over with mud.

"By the time I had myself out of the ditch again a fella pulled up and asked me, 'Hurt?' I said, 'Hurt bad.' Then I passed out. That was good luck, wasn't it? I mean, that I didn't pass out until then. When I woke up I was in the hospital and my leg was gone."

He whooshed out a long breath and finished the rest of his water, his throat working around each swallow. "I sure would like a real drink about now. Bet you would, too."

She was afraid to speak, so she nodded.

He wheeled backwards to the locker, opened the door and pulled a fifth of gin out of a blue backpack. The bottle was half full. "My daddy brought me this. Best thing he ever gave me." He poured two inches into his glass, two inches into hers, and she added water. Quickly, he slid the bottle into a drawer of the built-in dresser. "Better than medicine, but *they* don't think so."

The gin tasted green, like freshly cut grass. "That's an awful story!"

"Want more?" He held up his empty glass.

She saw with surprise she'd drunk hers just as swiftly, and passed her glass back to him.

He poured. This time neither of them added water.

The gin made her lips tingle and gave her courage. "You didn't say how you knew that guy in the truck."

Tiny drops of sweat beaded his upper lip and the crescents beneath his eyes. "I never saw him before in my life."

"Never?"

"I don't forget a face, and I got a good look. Never, never."

She was suddenly as tired as if she'd run a long, long way, had been running for days to get here. "Maybe he wanted revenge."

"Revenge for what?" The gin brought up a rash on his throat as though he'd been in the sun.

"But why you?" Her voice shrilled in the echoing room.

"Now that's the exact line of thinking I follow over and over—why *me?* What did he have against me? No matter how I think it through the answer comes out the same."

"What would that answer be?" She realized they both whispered now, like conspirators.

"This is how I figure it. If the question is, Why would a guy try to run down an injured man, the answer is *why not?*"

The suddenness of his grin startled her. It was as if he'd discovered something that pleased him. "Why not?" she repeated, as though she'd never learned the words before.

"See, it wasn't personal. That's what I've worked out. That guy just didn't have any reason *not* to run me down—not the law, not right or wrong, not his conscience, not even his kid."

Her hand shook. She set down her empty glass.

He stroked the tautly folded blanket, then cupped his hand over hers. "That's how I've got him psyched."

His hand was very warm and lightly damp. Maybe he had a fever. Maybe he was hallucinating. There *had* to be a reason. She wanted to stand up now but the feeling had gone out of her legs as though in sympathy for Mason. She shifted her weight until her feet stung with blood flowing back into them. "A man might get angry."

He cocked his eyebrow. "Angry at a helpless stranger?"

"He might get carried away by feelings."

Holding her hand tightly, he pulled her toward him until her waist pressed against the bed. Their faces close, she smelled gin and mint on his breath. "That's what I've been telling you. That guy probably never guessed until right when he did it that he'd try to run down a man. He was probably as surprised as I was."

"Oh, Mason." She supposed she spoke his name because he held her hand so firmly, as though he had a claim on her because he'd told his story.

"He did what he did. It's like when I ran into my grandpa's barn. You don't think. You don't plan or judge. How you act at such a time is character, and you can't change character. The way I see it, the guy in the truck is a goddamned *weapon*."

As he spoke he turned her hand and opened it to stroke her palm with his thumb, meditatively, maybe reading her future there. She was dizzy, as though the air had been sucked out of the room. He'd described Larry to her so plainly she could see him: a shotgun pointed at her head, a rifle aimed at Coco's heart. It was only a matter of time until he exploded and blew them all to smithereens.

When she got to her feet she swayed against the end of the bed. He rolled forward to meet her and steadied her with his hands on her waist. "I've been talking too much, and you sure are a sweet girl," he said in that husky voice men use when they're lonely or horny, or both. "You are just so pretty and so nice. God, I'm glad you're here."

Because she thought she owed him, she leaned down to kiss him before he had to ask. His lips were hot and soft and his hand went to her breast.

"Why don't you go ask the aide for my supper tray so we can close that door and no one will bother us for a while," he said against her cheek.

On her way from the hospital to her parents' house Kelda drove along the river to think things through. Shafts of evening sun pierced the canopy of plum-colored clouds. Directly overhead she saw what she thought might be an eagle, but then recognized it as a turkey buzzard. With wide, powerful wings it thrust upwards through the still air. At the top of its climb it poised, then began to spiral slowly in descending arcs over the brown water. Maybe in a moment it would fold its wings and plunge after its prey. Once a turkey buzzard dove by so close she heard the air split around its path like a sigh. She wanted her plan now to be that swift and certain.

She and Coco would stay with her parents. She'd send her dad after a couple of suitcases and get along with that until she found out what Larry would do. And she'd buy a gun. If he came after her—and he might—she'd point the gun at him.

"Why?" he'd say. "What did I ever do to you, Kelda?"

She'd answer him right back, "*Why not?* Give me one reason why not shoot you?"

Maybe even Larry wasn't hopeless. He might say, "Because I'm a human being. You can't kill me for no reason at all."

If he said that, or something like that, she'd say, "Well, maybe *now* you understand. But I watched you that night on the river road, so just get out of here and stay out."

So close now that she could see the gray neck-wattles and the thrusting red head, the turkey buzzard swooped downstream ahead of her. Then the black wings thrummed, and it turned to soar back up above the bluffs to that height where, she guessed, it could see the whole broad span of the river, the road along the bank, and her blue car traveling fast now back towards the city.

Pigs

Anne Panning

"IVAN WILLIAM," Olive hollered at the house, "you get down here and help your mother. The damn pigs are loose." She saw his window rise. Ivan was her only son, actually her only child. Every day he fed the pigs and splashed fresh water in their trough.

"What's wrong, mom?" He stood in red pajamas on the cement steps, hand covering his eyes from the early morning sun.

"What do you mean, what's wrong? The pigs broke outta that damn fence I've been asking you to fix for the past three weeks. Now, get moving." She wiped her dirty hands on her dress and spat in the gravel.

Ivan stood there, rubbing sleep from his eyes. He was man of the house now and he hated that. Dad left when he was in grade school. Just like that. Mom had sent him into town to pick up some milk and buns and he never came back. People say he ran off with a young girl, Renee, the librarian. Ivan didn't know what to believe, only it felt like his dad was dead and now he had to run the entire pig farm at twelve. Oh, his mom helped some, but she was different after dad left.

Ivan ran up to his room and dressed. It was so hot he didn't need a shirt. In the mirror his chest caved in bony and smooth. He straightened, pulling back his shoulders. From the window he saw his mom running around the pig pen, shit smeared all over her legs. She was waving a broom at the pigs, trying to get them back into place. Instead, they wandered to the house, tearing up the green lawn to black. His mom raised her hands up to the sky, shaking her head.

Ivan felt a sinking in his stomach. He worried that she really was crazy, like people said. When he got his haircut at Hal's last week, he overheard them talking as he left. Yeah, the poor kid. Olive really lost it when Cliff left her, that's for sure. She's crazy as they come. Ivan had started watching his mom closer. After supper last night, he found her stuffing chewed-up corn cobs into cupboards, dirtying clean dishes. Why are you doing that? he asked her. She whirled around with wide eyes and hugged him hard. Then she sat on the floor and cried.

Now Ivan ran outside, picking up a thick branch of oak from the ground. Damn pigs! He saw his mom stooped over in the mud. He ran up behind her and there was his new pig, Chiz, bleeding and limp. His mom held it close to her chest, bloodying her dress and arms.

"Goddamn swine. They stomped right over her and now she's hurt." She was petting the coarse hair, smearing red into it. "Look at what happened, Ivan! You just stand there! Help me."

"What should I do?"

"What should you do? What should you do? Help me, Ivan." She started sobbing, rocking back and forth with the dead pig.

He stood there, empty. Chiz had been his favorite, named after his best friend, Tom Chizmadia. Now its stomach was torn and its skull was blue and purple and red.

"Ivan, go get the keys for the pick-up from the kitchen counter. Go, now."

"But— "

"Get them," she hollered, flopping the pig's head to one side as she turned. He found the keys and stood beside her, out of breath.

"Now get the truck started and let's get this pig some help."

"Mom, I can't drive. I'm not old enough."

"You're old enough if I say so. Now get going."

"No, I'm not. I don't wanna. I can't." He felt like crying.

"Then you're no son of mine, Ivan William Klaybur." She whispered his name right up to his face, dropping the pig in the mud. "Pick up that pig and bring him over to the truck."

Ivan stood looking at the carcass while his mom hobbled over to the truck. She had never had a license. He heard the motor start and gravel crunch under the tires. She pulled up next to him, dust from the road blowing in his eyes.

"Get in here before the damn thing dies. That's all we need."

"But it's dead, mom. Look, it's not even breathing."

"That doesn't mean anything. Let's go now."

He didn't want to, but he picked up the dead pig. It was heavy and reeked of shit and sour innards. A stream of yellow juice was trailing out of its gut. When his mom swung open the door, he climbed in. The truck was intolerably hot from being shut up for so long. He laid the pig over his bare legs, its mouth open and drooling blood. His mom's small hands gripped the big black steering wheel tight. They bounced down the narrow driveway and looking back, he saw the loose pigs watching them drive away. They seemed sad and apologetic to Ivan, like they didn't really mean to cause trouble. His mom was staring ahead, biting her lips and sweating. He let the wheat fields fade past in a blur. When they slowed into town, he saw his friends, Ron and Steve, buying pop at the gas station from a Pepsi machine. He looked down, suddenly aware of the pig on his legs, heavy and wet. His mom drove down Main Street past the barber shop and two grocery stores. Ivan looked at her, wondering if she would stop at the doctor's office, or the animal clinic, if they even had one. She kept driving.

When they were out on the tar-paved highway, Ivan started worrying. The blood from the pig was drying sticky onto his legs.

"Mom, where are we going?"

She didn't answer right away, just lit up a cigarette and flicked ashes out the window. "We're going to find your father. He's the only one who knows how to take care of these pigs and he's gonna do it."

Ivan swallowed. He kept staring at his mom. The dead pig was now crusted and brown from the air of the open window. Ivan laid it gently on the floor near his feet, half-expecting a protest from his mom. He stuck his head out the window, hair flying straight back. His face pulled tight and his eyes watered from the force of the wind.

The Odyssey

Jim Northrup, Jr.

D UNKIN BLACKETTLE, Luke Warmwater and Tom Skin were playing their usual game of finding work. They were out of employment and unemployment checks.

Just to pass the time, they were talking nostalgically about jobs they had in the past. TV was the only place they saw people working. They knew these things worked in cycles, but this last period of unwork was lasting too long.

Someone came by and told Dunkin he had a phone message. He went next door to his sister's house to use the phone. It was about a job.

"It's a one-day shot. Drive to St. Cloud, load up some furniture and drive back. Twenty bucks, each," said Dunkin.

"Not much job security there," Luke observed.

"It's twenty bucks more than you got now," Tom teased.

"What the hell, let's do it. You weren't doing anything this month, anyway," said Dunkin.

They bummed a ride over to look at the truck. The 15,000 pound monster looked like a bread truck or a SWAT team truck.

"Which is it?" Tom wanted to know.

"Depends. Do you want to eat or fight?" Luke deadpanned.

A pre-trip inspection of the truck showed a frayed fan belt, a broken bolt on the coil, shorting plug wires and an exhaust system that efficiently pumped fumes into the pasenger part of the truck. The wipers worked. When one was going east, the other was going west.

It was one of those cold, misty, foggy mornings. The kind where you wish it would rain just to get it over with. The gray clouds covered the sky, sometimes all the way to the ground, It was good that the wipers worked.

They got a map, trip money and a promise of more work. They got in and began the trip. Their first pit stop was three miles down the road. They stopped in Sawyer for jumper cables, a little food, coffee and smokes.

Luke was driving because Tom's driver's license was sick and Dunkin's was dead.

As they started off, everyone became the navigator. Each one knew the best way to the freeway.

"I'll take the tar road to the freeway," said Luke

"Three miles closer down the gravel road." said Tom.

"Highway Patrol doesn't go on the gravel road," observed Dunkin.

They went down the gravel road.

As they drove along, different places brought out different stories.

"This is the corner Georgie bragged about. He said he could take it at fifty," Luke remembered.

"He was half right," Dunkin laughed.

"Yep, rolled it over exactly halfway through."

"Here's the field the State game wardens chased us from."

"Yah, we got away clean that time."

"They could stay with us on the straightaways, but we lost them on the corners."

"Dunkin was really wheeling that night."

"He shut off the lights and passed that car that was waiting to enter the highway."

"The game wardens followed that guy. I think they got him stopped down by the Big Lake Road."

They laughed together as they invented conversations between the driver and the game wardens. They remembered the twenty-five-year-old chase as if it happened last week. By the time they were finished with that story, they were at the freeway.

They began to play like real truckers.

"10-4, back door," said Luke as he spoke into his imaginary CB mike.

He slid in behind a semi on the freeway.

As the men rode along, they admired a bridge that Dunkin had worked on a couple summers before. He told that story for a good five miles past the bridge.

It was blue inside the truck from the exhaust, but after experimenting with the windows and doors, they were able to make the air breathable.

The monotony of the trip was broken up by more stories.

By the time they got to St. Cloud, the back of the truck was full of them and their embellished outcomes.

There was a pile of guys in one corner, all knocked out with one punch.

There were seven deer in another corner, all killed with one shot from 500 yards away.

There was at least 700 pounds of wild rice, all knocked in one day.

The fish were so big, their tails were sticking out the back of the truck.

There almost wasn't room for the pile of ducks, all shot at impossible distances.

There was at least a year of jail time in the back of the truck. There were overnighters, some 30's and a couple of 90's.

The back of the truck contained four dogs that could dive deeper, come up drier and out-retrieve any other dog in town.

There was a parking lot full of great cars of the past. A '51 Ford, a '69 Chevy, a '75 Ford pickup.

There were so many stories in the back of the truck, they had to stop for gas. They were in St. Cloud.

After gas, they drove to the "X" on the map. They found the place right away. The furniture wasn't too heavy. They loaded the truck, and when Dunkin slammed the back door, it fell off.

He picked it up and threw it in with the furniture.

It was beginning to sprinkle as they left town. They found the right road and began the trek home.

The towns crawled by. It was starting to get dark. By the time they got to Moose Lake, it was completely dark. The rain was heavier, too.

None of the three Sawyer Indians knew it, but the fan belt was dying. It had stretched about six inches and was just occasionally turning the fan.

The engine got hot, so hot it started a fire in the engine compartment. The steam escaped from the radiator and drowned the wiring. The steam did not put out the fire.

The smoking, steaming truck coasted off at the Mahtowa exit. They all gave orders.

"Get the fire extinguisher."

"Stop the truck."

"Open the hood."

"Find some water."

The truck stopped, the hood opened, the fire was put out.

They found some water in the ditch and cooled the engine. The wires were dried and they were back on the road again, wondering how far they could make it without a fan belt.

The hot engine made them stop wondering about three miles down the road.

After the first time, it was just a standard roadside emergency—stop the truck, put out the fire, cool the radiator. This emergency was right by Otter Creek so they had no trouble cooling the radiator.

The trouble came when Luke tried to start the truck. The same belt charges the battery also, he thought.

Tom flagged down a passing motorist. The Good Samaritan gave them a jump and they were on their way again.

They made a dramatic, smoking, steaming entrance at the truck stop on Highway 210. They were seven miles from home and the trip was over.

Dunkin called the owner of the truck and told him what was happening. The owner asked if the fire was out. Dunkin asssured him it was.

He came to the truck stop, paid them for their labors and gave them a ride to Sawyer. He felt so bad about the truck and the trip, he offered them a three-week job.

Dunkin Blackettle, Luke Warmwater and Tom Skin found work again.

The Ivory Comb

Eleanor Arnason

I N THE FAR NORTH, there is an old woman. Her tent is in the sky. The walls of the tent are made of light, hanging in folds from the tentpoles, which are made from the bones of the original World Monster. How they got in the sky is another story, which I don't have time to tell. The old woman has a comb, which is made from one of the monster's teeth. It is ivory, as white as snow. She uses it to comb her fur. When she does this, she pulls creatures out. They fall to the floor and vanish, going through the floor into the world. All the animals in the world come into existence this way.

When the old woman combs the left side of her body, the animals that come out are good and useful: the bowhorns we herd, the birds we hunt and eat. When she combs the right side of her body, the animals that come out are harmful: lizards with venomous bites and bugs that sting. The people of the world sing to the old woman, praising her and asking her for help. This is one of the songs:

> Grandmother, be generous.
> Comb the left side of your body.
> Then we will be prosperous.
> Then we will be happy.
> Our children will be fat
> in our tents by the fire.

Grandmother, be compassionate.
Don't comb the right side of your body.
Leave the lizards where they are.
Don't send us
the bugs that bite and sting.

In the far south, there is a young man. He is tall and handsome. His eyes are yellow as fire. No one is certain who his mother is. Some people say, it is the great spirit, the Mother of Mothers. Other people say, it is a demon of fire.

The young man is called the Trickster. He is the one who comes to men in the winter, when they guard the herd. Each man sits alone under a tent that is made by stretching a cloak over the branches of a bush or tree. Snow comes down around him. The fire in front of him is low. The man sits and shivers, holding his arms close to his body. Then the Trickster comes. His voice is like the wind. He says, "Why are you doing this? Why do you suffer for the ungrateful women of the village? Forget your mother. Forget your sisters. Forget the sons and daughters you may have. Go off into the hills and live like an animal, without obligations, pleasing yourself alone."

Most men ignore the voice. But some listen. They go crazy and leave the herd, wandering into the hills. No one sees them after that.

The Trickster is the same one who goes to meet women in the spring, when it is mating time. He looks like the best kind of man, large and strong and self-confident. He establishes his territory close to the village. No other man dares to confront him. When the women come out, full of lust, they meet him. Some of them meet him, anyway. Each woman who mates with him thinks, "What an excellent father! My child will be hardy and resourceful, good-looking too."

But the mating produces no children. Or if children are born, they are sickly and bad-tempered. They cause nothing but trouble.

This is usually so. But the Trickster is never reliable, even in the evil he does. Once in a while, a woman mates with him, and the child who comes out is like her father, large and strong and self-confident, a true heroine.

One of these was our ancestor, the Ropemaker. But first I must tell how the Trickster stole the ivory comb.

He was in the far north, cold and hungry. There was nothing around, except the wide plain covered with snow. After a while, he came to the tent of the old woman. It shone above him, white and yellow and green. He took off his snowshoes and stuck them in a bank of snow. Then he climbed up into the sky. He entered the tent. The old woman was there, sitting in the middle of the floor. Her fur was gray with age. She was combing it with the ivory comb.

The Trickster sat down. He watched greedily. The old woman was pulling the comb through the fur on her left forearm. Out came animals. They were little and dark. The old woman shook her comb. The animals tumbled down. When they reached the floor, they vanished. They were going into the world, into the deep burrows of the builders-of-mounds.

"Grandmother," the Trickster said. "Give me some of your animals. I am hungry, and they look delicious."

The old woman stared at him. "I know who you are. The Trickster, the one who tells lies." She gave the comb a shake, then she caught one of the animals in midair. It sat up on her hand. Its tiny nose twitched. Its whiskers quivered. It looked at the Trickster with bright dark eyes. "These animals are part of me. I give them to people who treat them with respect. But you—oh evil one!—you misuse everything you get ahold of. There is no respect in you. I will give you nothing." She turned her hand over. The animal fell to the floor. It was gone.

The Trickster ground his teeth. "Grandmother, have pity."

"No," the old woman said. "You can starve for all I care. And let it be a lesson to you." She turned around so her back was to the Trickster.

He leaped up. "You will regret this, you old biddy!" He ran from the tent. He climbed down out of the sky and sat next to his snowshoes in a heap of snow. There he waited till the old woman went to sleep. The sound of her snoring filled the plain. The Trickster climbed back up. He crept into the tent. The walls shone as brightly as ever, and the tent was full of a pale flickering light. He saw the old woman stretched out on her back. Next to her was the ivory comb. He picked it up.

"But where am I going to hide?" he asked himself. "When the spirits hear that this is gone, they will search the whole world. What place is safe?"

Then he had an idea. He made himself small and the comb as well. He crawled into the old woman's vagina. She groaned and scratched herself, but she did not wake.

"This isn't the most pleasant place that I have ever been," the Trickster said. "I'd like more light and a bit less moisture. But no one will think of looking here."

The old woman woke and reached for her comb. It wasn't there. She let out a scream. All over the world, the spirits leaped up. "What is it?" they cried. "What is going on?"

"My comb has vanished!" the old woman cried. "The Trickster has taken my comb!"

Then the search began. Up and down, back and forth, in and out. The spirits searched everywhere. But they didn't find the comb.

"What will I do?" the old woman said. "The comb is irreplaceable. There is none like it, and without it, I cannot comb my fur."

The spirits had no answer.

Spring came. Vegetation appeared. The hills and plain turned blue. The people of the world noticed that something was wrong. In every village, they went to the shamans.

"What is going on?" they asked. "Fish thrash in the river, as they do every year.

But no one has seen any fingerlings. The birds build nests as usual. The nests are empty. As for the little animals, the builders-of-mounds, they puff up the sacks in their necks. They scream and moan and carry on. But they produce no young."

The shamans ate narcotic plants. They danced and had visions. They said, "The Trickster has stolen the ivory comb. Without it, no more animals will come into existence. We will all starve, because of that malevolent person."

All the people cried out. They beat their chests and thighs. They prayed to the spirits. But what could the spirits do?

Now the story turns to the Ropemaker. She was a woman of the Amber People. She was large with glossy fur. Her eyes were as yellow as fire. Her arms were strong, and her fingers were nimble. Most people believed she was a child of the Trickster. She had the look.

Her trade was making rope out of leather. She was very skillful at this. Her ropes were narrow and flexible. They did not stretch. They were hard to break, and they lasted for years.

In any case, the time for mating came. The women of the Amber People felt the spring lust grow in them. But this year, they were unwilling to go out onto the plain. "What is the point of leaving the village?" they said. "Why should we bother to go and find a man? The children we conceive will die of starvation."

But the lust grew stronger. Each woman packed the gifts she had made during the winter. Each woman saddled a bowhorn and rode out onto the plain. The Ropemaker was among them. In her saddlebag was a fine long rope. It was her mating gift.

Now the story turns back to the Trickster. By this time, he was getting restless. There was nothing to do in the old woman's vagina. He knew it was spring. He wanted to go out into the world and play a mean trick on someone. He waited till the old woman was asleep and crept out. He left the comb behind. Off he went towards the south. After a while, he came to the land of the Amber People. He found a territory close to the village. There was a man there already: a big man with many scars. The Trickster went up to him and said. "You'd better leave."

"Are you crazy?" the big man said. "I got here first. And anyway, I'm bigger than you."

The Trickster stretched himself till he was taller than the big man. He glared down. His yellow eyes shone like fire.

"Well," said the big man. "If you put it that way." He mounted his bowhorn and rode off.

The Trickster shouted insults at his back. The big man did not turn.

After that, the Trickster settled down and waited. A day passed and then another. On the third day, a woman rode into sight. It was the Ropemaker. The Trickster felt satisfied. This was an impressive woman. This was a person worth misleading.

As for the Ropemaker, she liked what she saw: a big wide man. He was standing on the plain with his feet apart and his shoulders back. His fur was thick and glossy. He wore a fine tunic, covered with embroidery. On his arms were silver bracelets. They were wide and bright.

When she got close, she noticed that he had a peculiar aroma. "Well, no one is perfect," she told herself.

When she reached the man, she dismounted. They lay on the ground and mated. Afterward, she said, "I have some bad news."

"Oh yes?" said the Trickster.

"The old woman of the north has lost her comb. Because of this, she cannot comb her fur; and no more animals will come into the world."

"So what?"

"If we have a child, it will die of starvation."

"So what? It's no concern of mine. As long as I am able to mate, I'm satisfied. Who cares what comes of the thing we do together?"

"I care. And anyway, if this situation continues, we'll all die. For how can we live without the bowhorns and the birds in the air and the fish in the rivers?"

"If you want to die, then go ahead and do it. I'm not worried. I intend to go on living, no matter what happens to the rest of the world." The Trickster rolled over and went to sleep.

The Ropemaker looked at him. His fur shone like copper, and there was a glow around his body. This was no ordinary man, she realized. It was a spirit. A nasty spirit. The Trickster.

She got out her rope and tied him up. Then she waited. He woke and tried to stretch. He could not. "What is this?" he cried.

"You are caught," said the Ropemaker. "And I will not let you go, until you give me the ivory comb."

The Trickster ground his teeth. He thrashed and rolled. One heel struck the land and made a hole. Water rushed up and made a lake. The lake is still there. It is wide and shallow, full of stones and reeds. Bugs like it. Birds like it. It is called the Trickster's Lake or the Lake of Bugs and Stones.

The rope did not break. The Trickster continued to struggle. He rolled away from the Ropemaker. He beat the earth with his bound hands. He made another hole, deeper than the first one. Hot mud rushed up. It seethed around the Trickster. He was boiling like a bird in a pot. But his magic was powerful. He took no harm. The rope, however, could not survive the heat and moisture. It began to stretch. The Trickster pulled free. He jumped up. He shouted:

I am the Trickster,
oh you foolish woman
I cannot be held.
I know no obligation.

I am the Trickster,
oh you foolish woman.
No one can hold me.
No one can make me stop.

After that, he ran off across the plain. He went north, back to his hiding place.

The Ropemaker watched him go. She bit her lip and clenched her hands. "He is a great spirit, and he may be a relative of mine. But I won't let him get away with this."

She mounted on her bowhorn and rode north. For a long time, she traveled, and she had many adventures. But I don't have time to tell you about them. At last, she came to the place where the old woman lived. It was midsummer. The plain was yellow. The rivers were low. The Ropemaker dismounted. She tethered her animal. Then she climbed into the sky.

"Grandmother," she called. "Will you let me in? I have come a long way in order to see you."

"Come in," the old woman said. "But I can't help you. I have lost my comb. I have nothing to give."

The Ropemaker entered the tent. The old woman was there, sitting in the middle of the floor. She was naked and scratching her belly with both hands. "I am going crazy," she said. "My fur is full of animals, and I can't get them out. I can feel them crawling in the folds of my belly. I can feel them in my armpits. I can feel them on my back. Granddaughter, I beg you. Be kind to me! Scratch me in between the shoulderblades."

The Ropemaker scratched her back. The old woman kept on complaining. "I can even feel them in my vagina, though I have no fur there. They stir from time to time and tickle me. Oh! This is terrible!"

The Ropemaker frowned. She remembered the way the Trickster had smelled. All at once, she knew his hiding place. "But how will I get him out?" she asked herself. "And how will I catch him and hold him, once he is out?"

She decided to go to sleep. She lay down and closed her eyes. The old woman sat next to her, scratching. Soon the Ropemaker began to dream. Three spirits came to her. One was a woman of middle age with a big belly and noticeable breasts. She wore a long robe, covered with embroidery.

The next spirit was a man. His fur was blue-green, and he had wings instead of arms. He wore a kilt the same color as his fur. His belt buckle was round and made of gold. It glittered brilliantly

The third spirit was a young woman. She was large and muscular. She carried a hammer, and she wore a leather apron. Her eyes were orange-red.

The Ropemaker knew them. The first was the Mother of Mothers. The second was the Spirit of the Sky. And the third was the Mistress of the Forge, who lives in Hani Akhar, the great volcano.

"Oh holy ones," the Ropemaker said. "Help me out! I know where the Trickster is. But I need a way to get him out of his hiding place. And once he is out, he will try to run away. I need a way to catch him."

The Spirit of the Sky spoke first. "I will keep watch. If he tries to run away, I will see where he goes. He won't be able to find a new hiding place."

The Mistress of the Forge spoke next. "I will make a rope out of iron, forged with magic so it will never break. It will be self-fastening and able to move. The Trickster won't escape from it."

The Mother of Mothers spoke last. "I know how to get the Trickster out of his hiding place." She leaned forward and whispered into the Ropemaker's ear.

In the morning, the Ropemaker woke. There was a rope lying next to her in a coil. It was dull-gray in color, and it had a peculiar texture—like the scales of a lizard. The Ropemaker took a close look at it. It was made of many tiny links of iron, fastened together.

"Good morning, grandmother," she said to the old woman of the north. "I've got an idea. You said that your vagina tickled, even though it has no fur."

The old woman made the gesture of assent.

"I don't think there's an animal in there. I think you need sex."

"You are crazy!" the old woman cried. "It's the wrong time of year. And anyway, I'm too old to feel lust."

"Remember," said the Ropemaker. "A woman doesn't grow old easily. The feeling of lust doesn't vanish all at once. Often, a woman becomes irritable and uncertain. Her behavior changes from day to day. She feels lust at the wrong time. At the right time, in the spring, she feels nothing at all. She cannot understand what is going on—any more than a young girl can, when she becomes a woman. I think this is what has happened to you."

"No!" cried the old woman.

"In any case, try sex. I will go and find a young man for you. If I'm right and you are feeling lust—a bit late, I will admit—then the young man will respond to you. And maybe you will feel better afterward."

The Ropemaker got up and left the tent. She took the iron rope with her.

The Trickster heard all this. He became uneasy. "If that crazy woman can find a man who is willing to mate with this old biddy—well, my position will not be comfortable. I am likely to take a terrible beating. I'd better get out of here."

He waited till it was night, and the old woman was snoring. Then he crept out. The comb was in his hand. He stole to the door. Out he stepped. The Ropemaker was waiting there. The Great Moon was up. It lit the sky and the plain. It lit the man, as he came through the doorway.

"This is it, you nasty spirit!" the woman cried. She threw her iron rope.

It twisted in midair. It wrapped itself around him. He stumbled and fell. The comb flew out of his hand. The Ropemaker caught it. As for the Trickster, he fell out of the sky and landed on the plain. He rolled back and forth. He yelled.

He struggled. But the rope would not break. After a while, he gave up. He lay still, breathing heavily.

Three spirits appeared around him. He looked up at them. "I can tell that you are responsible for this."

"Yes," said the Mother of Mothers. "This is the end of all your malevolent tricks. We are going to take you far from here and drop you in the ocean. You'll cause no further trouble."

"Don't be sure," the Trickster said.

They picked him up and carried him through the air. In the middle of the ocean, they let go of him. He splashed into the water. Down and down he sank. At last, he hit the bottom. Aiya! It was dark and cold! Deep sea fish nibbled on his toes. He twisted and tried to yell. Instead, he swallowed water. But he could not drown. His life was everlasting. He stayed there for more years than we can count. He gave his nature to the ocean. It became changeable and unreliable, impossible to trust. In the end, he broke free. But that is another story.

As for the Ropemaker, she went back into the tent. She woke the old woman and handed her the comb.

"Oh! This is wonderful!" the old woman cried. She began to comb her fur. Animals came out, hundreds of them. They tumbled out of the sky and filled the world. All the people rejoiced.

To the Torturor

Conrad Balfour

J OHN BREEDE was awash in thought. One moment he was a stranger . . . the next moment both of them were stripped naked before each other as if it was only natural, as if it was always that way. The ritual demanded a precise manner, a cup clearing its saucer, a demure glance even if he was not demure, a certain stance where he stood, a particular pose when helping or being helped on with shawl or wrap, then the proper stride departing the room, past other diners who as yet were not quite completed with their seductions. It's all so elegant if both carry it off well, not unlike the caterpillar's transfiguration to butterfly. Hold out a hand, step up, step into, cross over to his side and with a slight shrug crowd behind the dashboard. (To reveal eagerness is not to carry it off well.) A bit later he deposited his clothes separate from hers. On first assignations clothes are segregated. He accepted her body as it was. He studied her step upon the floor, her movement from the bed to another room, discreetly of course, his eyes on her outline, on her flesh, on her stiff nipples, on the fold about her waist and he reserved judgment, declined even a secret evaluation of her. She was not a poster nor a wallet snapshot for the men to give rating to. She was an equal of sorts. This stranger knew his scent now, the roughage of his teeth now, the body flab no longer secluded beneath his uniform. So he declined judgment and in a blind faith he presumed that in her heart she too suspended comparisons. Thus, due to, because of that discounting he possessed a repetitive familiarity to her fleshless thighs and a charming old-hat attitude to the awkward angles of her, angles he thought he'd known for a lifetime, and in the knowing he was transformed into that limbo of judgment, to that haze of myopia where in the eye of his heart an inch contracted to half an inch, a scar metaphased to a dimple, and a peculiar gait was now a model's float. Yet oddly, ironically, inexplicably, as John Breede stepped into his shorts, belted his trousers, buttoned his jacket, he grew distant to her. Each item of clothing he donned brought him to his reality, as if the layering of flesh with cotton and leather was his true identity, as if that layering gave life to an impulse within him to return to the poses and postures of formalities. John Breede was dressed now. John Breede was proper now, falsely elegant again, a stranger to the stranger who bedded him moments ago. And now John Breede was positioned to make his exit, to step briskly into the street, to walk erectly past the gardeners, to point his vehicle toward John Vorster Square and the quaint security building where he would check a mark by the name on the roster, his name, and receive duties from his superior, and for two hours until permitted a recess at the canteen, for that tenure of time that is no longer than the midday shift of a broadcaster, no longer than cakes and sex, he, John Breede, young, reckless, naive, impressionable John Breede would impose catastrophic pain upon the mind and body of a black detainee.

He was a Major but Breede thought of him as his superior and therefore referred to the Major as "the Superior." The Superior was gaunt with the trace of a blond mustache that evoked Breede's curiosity. He wondered why it didn't grow, why it wasn't allowed to thicken? It was barely visible with little substance to it, nothing there to trim or twirl. How did he manage it with his blade and bar? Likely it was to trap perspiration on his upper lip, its presence there during interrogation might, if he knew the Superior, indicate an emotion, a nervousness, even a weakness. He was of such erect posture, of such stiff backbone and sturdy legs, of a deceptive height that even when his peers looked down upon him they imagined that they looked up, of such intrepid repute, that Breede imagined he could ill-afford any badge of inferiority that beads of moisture might imply. That aberration, slight as it was, would compromise what the Superior represented.

Breede knew the Superior as a man with a stake in his public image. A man without temerity but ready to set examples. Without excesses yet loyal beyond question to the colors. Even without humor but not above allowing others theirs. There were some tales of this true soldier, stories of discipline, grace under pressure, the rescuing of a situation under the most arduous circumstances, but perhaps none more telling than that morning the Superior gestured to Breede to accompany him in his vehicle. There was a colored driver behind the wheel and the motor running and the Superior striding swiftly ahead. Breede was thankful to dodge interrogation on his shift yet wary at what was ahead of him. Soweto perhaps? Hardly that. There had been trouble in surrounding towns but Breede knew that the open vehicle wasn't safe for Lebowa or Carltonville. More likely

a family dispute here in town, or a foreigner with a complaint, a misunderstand-
ing by an international that someone of the Superior's authoritative demeanor
could straighten out. Breede thought himself fortunate that the Superior had
chosen him to share this assignment but the flash of pride was only momentary.
The Superior had been in a haste and Breede was the first officer he'd sighted.
Breede was young and much too inexperienced to accompany his commandant
on any but the most mundane assignment.

In minutes the vehicle stopped before a luxurious dwelling. Like so many in
its class it had a brilliant swimming pool and a tennis court. The driver remained
behind as the Superior led Breede over a pink-tiled walk past a gardener who
kept his back to them as he squatted over a non-existent sprout. Even so, Breede
detected a communication from the man. Actually it was the lack of greeting,
an indifference to their presence, as if the two visitors didn't exist, that tipped
off Breede that the gardener was in effect pointing out the direction to which
they should proceed.

They turned a corner of the house, walked past wicker chairs piled atop each
other, entered a screened opening, and as if the Superior had studied a map of
the house, or as Breede suspicioned, he had been there on other occasions, with
Breede in tow they padded silently but rapidly through a series of rooms until
one last door impeded them. With chin high and back straight the Superior pushed
the door with the heel of his hand and there before them was a man and a woman
wide awake and beside each other in a white bed. Not just a man nor just a woman,
but one with black skin and the other with white.

The woman was startled and like some silly charade in a movie scene where
nudity is implied, she clutched the sheet to her front which was already well concealed by it and which in turn exaggerated this occasion of danger into melodrama.
Rather than edge down further into the false security of the bed, she inched her
head upward so as to better view the intrusion and whatever was in store for her.

The man was also on his back. The sheet, due to the angle its hem covered
the woman, fell across his chest from waist to shoulder and with his skin and
even darker hairs gave him the appearance of a soldier in a cummerbund or a
sash barren of decorations. His chin rested down and his eyes were lowered as
if resigned to his fate. Because of this Breede could gather no insight to the character
of the man he being a staunch believer that to know a man instantly one must
see into his eyes. The man was inscrutable. He seemed inured to this intrusion,
appeared accustomed to them, and whether or not this unseemingly disruption
of his privacy was by the law or by an evangelical pastor or even by a burglar
was of no concern to him. His breathing was undetectable like one recovering
from a light sleep. The man displayed no emotion.

In contrast the woman exuded an inner frenzy. Breede half expected her pale
skin to leap from the bed leaving in its wake bones and matter. Her eyes implored

the intruders but it was obvious that she would wait them out, react to any words or actions forthcoming.

But the Superior did something strange, something entirely unexpected by any of them, including John Breede. He grasped a light dressing bench, planted it by the bed on the man's side and sat upon it. Then he dropped his visored hat on the floor as if a courtesy to them, crossed his arms and legs and peered down at the two reclining figures. Breede who was near the door, advanced a step, but only to observe the Superior's countenance more clearly. In any event he was responsible to hold his position by the only entrance to the room. The Superior cleared his throat, extracted a tan cigarette from a blue case and once lighting it declined to smoke but rather seemed to employ it as a timer like one does for eggs. Then in the most inconceivable moment of his young life Breede was witness to an extraordinary occurrence. The Superior lectured, calmly and soberly. One would have thought his words for the benefit of a small group of juveniles, or to enlighten candidates to his club, or even a soiree in the prime minister's residence. Breede was dumbfounded.

"Ahh, turning the other cheek—is that it? A virtue—no doubt, no doubt. And pacifism. Splendid qualities. However—place yourselves in this situation. You move to Prince Edward Island with other—lovely neighbors. You've fled there in order to avoid the troubles of Johannesburg or an East London. From, shall we say, Crozet Island a contingent of brigands descend upon you. They confiscate your valuables. And what do you do to retaliate? You turn the other cheek—of course." He brandished his cigarette. "Now they beat you, molest your daughters. You plead but you're ignored. Still you keep your hunting weapons concealed. You believe in pacifism. They take you away in chains, sodomize you—and soon your life seems pointless to you. But a friend reveals where knives are hidden beneath a floorboard. You have a chance to escape, but to accomplish this you must kill your guards. What do you do? If as a pacifist you make a go for it, meaning to accost your guards, then you must concede that violence is necessary to achieve your escape and that your action is an extension of what nations call war." He leaned forward. "What else can you do? Well, what WE do is gather ourselves to live. We launch a navy to protect ourselves." He uncrossed his legs, studied his cigarette as if the curling smoke pleased him. "Do you understand what I'm saying? When the call goes out to defend our blood, blood that through indifference so often remains unprotected, WE, rather than dodge the crisis, WE answer. We carry the weight, interrupt our leisures and give battle. It's as noble an act as is your turning the other cheek." He snuffed his cigarette stub against his boot and then tucked it into a pocket in his tunic. "Smoking—I pray that neither of you indulge." He paused. "This sort of—thing." He gestured to the bed and its occupants. "Petty thievery, dissent, consumer boycotts—Africans in—bed. Only irritants—but we must protect ourselves from even that." The Superior retrieved his hat and got to his feet. Addressing the man he said, "You do need time to dress and clean up a bit—get your business in order. I then expect you to report to security headquarters within the hour." And with a slight mocking bow to the woman he turned on his heels and with Breede following he left the room.

As much as that encounter impressed Breede he was even more amazed when the African entered the security building in the afternoon. From what source did the Superior's power generate to prevent that black man from fleeing? These Africans, he thought. Breede recalled the strange story of Burindi in East Africa where the Hutus comprised 85% of the population and the Tutsis only 14%. During independence the Tutsis feared they would lose their power to the majority Hutus so in 1972 they massacred every Hutu with an education or a government job. In a matter of months the tall Tutsis slew more than 200,000 of their rivals, tore down their schools and ignited their dwellings. In the capitol of Bujumbura scarcely a Hutu was spared. Unexplainably the Tutsis led their enemies as if they were sheep. They would order them to report to the town square and the Hutus reported. They commanded them to stand muster at the jail and they came. They directed them to the firing wall and they stood and they were shot. If the jail was crowded or the firing wall not yet cleared of bloody bodies then they were asked to return on the following day and on the following day they meekly returned to the jail and stood against the wall and made no outcry as the Tutsis leveled their rifles and shot them by the hundreds. If a more adventurous Hutu walked from the square on some sort of fantasy to freedom, all a Tutsi need do, and do without arms, was to hail the errant traveler and the shamed Hutu would halt in his tracks, turn about as if caught in the act of stealing a peppermint cane and return to the square and the jail and the firing wall for his execution.

And so too this African returned in his rumpled white shirt and his silver-gray trousers and his dusty sandals, trudged to John Vorster Square, past the refuse heaps and slag piles and the mines, past the orange and blue and white flags with their Union Jacks and its former Boer republic pennants reproduced upon them, past the American-styled drive-ins, walked methodically without a police officer laying a hand upon him and demanding his passbook, walked in a trance through white Johannesburg as if a star citizen, as if a flush tourist staying at the swank Landfrost, as if readying himself for cuisine at Cafe de Paris and a pink wine from the cellars of Franschhoek, this stubby African with the broad chest and curly hairs, this immutable, plodding non-citizen who mated like a whelping hog with the daughter of one of Johannesburg's finest, now surrendered himself to the security people not knowing or thinking or caring whether he would be banished or beaten. It was a mystifying thing.

The four walls were unadorned except for a graffittied AFRICAN NASHNAL CONGREZ. He sat in the center of the room with his hands clenched and on his thighs and John Breede sitting opposite and close to him, his hands folded in his groin. Breede was instructed to sit there passively. Of course sitting before this detainee could not be termed passive. Whether he interrogated the man or berated him or physically bruised him, whether he sat before him like a white buddha it was far from passive. Not in this room of heavy air and incessant intimidation. Not in this inner square of semi-light (semi-darkness would imply an entirely opposite mood) and its door that always opened suddenly as if to surprise its inhabitant, and always closed as suddenly and in its muffled shutting seemed to cut the umbilical cord of hope from without. Not that whatever was beyond the door indicated a freedom to whomever was imprisoned within the room. It didn't indicate that. It only symbolized freedom because on the far side of the door was natural light and that natural light was better than the darkness on this side. Nevertheless when the door did open, in that moment before it closed again there was a sliver of illumination and with it a sliver of hope and when it closed fifteen or more times a day, it cut away the hope as a clamp cuts away oxygen flowing slowly through tubing. Passivity wasn't an ingredient here in this room in the security building in John Vorster Square. So Breede sat there stiff and proper, emulating the Superior who was stiffer and more proper, sat there fresh and rested from good tea and ripe lemon and sexual gratification, fresh and rested and strong because of his youth and his freedom. He sat and stared at the bowed detainee who looked to the floor. What did he think? thought John Breede. Did he believe that at any moment the stern official would barrage him with questions or strike him with a switch? Breede wished to clear his throat but would rather have had the black man clear his throat first. He wished to rub his eye, to straighten his left leg, to loosen his crimped underwear beneath his trousers, to scratch a ghostly itch on his scalp. He could perform none of these minimal normalcies in the presence of an inferior. To subject himself to these hesitations was absurd, almost laughable. As these thoughts disturbed his head he measured two bothersome suppositions: in whose presence was whom? That alone gave him considerable debate with himself and though he arrived at no satisfying conclusion it did serve the purpose of whiling away the time of his two hour shift. He now turned to the issue of the throat clearing. He concluded that even if the detainee cleared his throat first Breede would not follow. To do so would imply imitation. Unless of course he did so in such manner that it mocked the prisoner. To mock an inferior was permissible, mockery a tool of the torturor, but to imitate was to display a subtle weakness, at least that's how Breede's thought processes worked.

So there they were. Two grown individuals with a particular accumulation of native savvy or with formal education or at least with a background of hands-on experiences, two adults with comparable muscles and like brain weight, two men with the same number of teeth, presumably, an equal count of fingers and an approximate frequency of bowel movements and gaseous expellings. They possessed similar gristle, joints, arteries, ventricles, a singular liver, one spleen and one sternum—here they sat facing each other, both unspeaking and both suffering in their individual way. They could have been poring over bishops and pawns or studying a beaker of clear liquid and though these sophisticated items were not present in this room, indeed there was a far greater force between them. Simply put they were enemies. And why enemies? Because there was a raging difference in them, that difference being that one man was white and the other black. And even if this detainee possessed a white caucasian face as was the face of the detainee in the adjacent room, by virtue of sitting in that specific chair before an interrogator, he was deemed black. Biologically black or sympathetically so, once in that chair, you were an African. An African knew absolutely that any black body meant that absolutely you were black, that many a white body could be black in a political manner, but under no circumstances could a black body ever be white. Not in South Africa.

As for the African, his name was insignificant, even to himself. He knew that. He knew that once arrested and subjected to the ordeals of the torture rooms he was no more than a routine to the workers there, someone who was worked upon by men coming on shift, men who saw him as a normal part of their work-day as they also saw a file of papers or a tray of paper clips. And when the paper clips were exhausted they petitioned supply for another bright box as they did with the unnamed prisoners and political malcontents.

As office workers often complain about the grain of paper goods or the brittleness of a new supply of pencils, so too interrogators at security headquarters were prone to register protests with the quality of prisoners. "He's insolent," they'd say, or "He's not like the last one we had," and even, "Where DO we get them from these days?" Yes, if not for the toll it imposed upon so many in John Vorster Square this also would be quite laughable.

The detainee wished to stand and stretch for he'd been sitting in the chair at least before sunrise. His behind was cramped and without feeling. He surmised that the young officer before him was uncomfortable, one who came and departed without leaving his mark one way or another on any of the prisoners. Unlike the others the African hadn't been physically struck by him. Well, he did not know if this officer struck any others. He was a cut different. He seemed to be on the outside of things looking inward. He was more like one of those jour-nalists who hang around to observe the scene in the street, who wear the local clothes, follow the lead of whoever seems to be in charge and never utter a word of protest or wince at what they witness but wait until they file their reports to suffer remarks.

This officer with his knees almost touching his own didn't enjoy his duties, pretended that he did but the pretense was a false front for the benefit of the one and the deception of the other. The prisoner evaluated all of them when he could. He managed this through the cover of his drowsiness, not difficult to play-act since he was denied enormous periods of sleep. With his head always down he'd move the way they willed him, "go with the tendencies," someone advised. When they snapped orders at him or false questions or demeaned him with an expletive or even struck him on the soles of his feet, he'd give a little, imagine that he was the upper half of a wild stalk. In that way he not only might cushion the blows but reduce the effect of the indignity, bifurcate it through mind control, apply a zen to it so that it was a religious experience to survive his time here. Not that some of them weren't clever and not that he didn't suffer, particularly from the veteran interrogators. But he had his ways and they had theirs in these games of trauma where the losers and the winners gained no reward. Thus he studied them as best he could, recorded all the subtleties and soft spots in their bellies. He knew their game and they were aware that he knew and so both adversaries seemingly checkmated. Rather than any loyalty to the memory of the good old Orange Free State or the Transvaal Republic or to Pieter Botha or Jan Smuts, these workers cared only to have their coffee breaks in the canteen or a swig of halfjacks in a back room while they compared scores and results from the tariff of black bodies and when tiring of the jibes and horseplay they'd count the minutes to the end of their shift so that they could scurry back to a waiting woman.

But now he wished to stand and so he calculated the risk. What would it be with this white man? He'd have to gamble. If his evaluation was accurate, those soft eyes, the almost pliant demeanor, then when the African stood the officer would stare at him in surprise, feign a shock, hesitate, then make a remark such as, "What in hell d'ya think you're doing there—sit down where you was!" And he would sit but not before his flesh stole a pinch of circulation.

So the African stood. His knees brushed the officer, they were that close, The African froze. To inadvertently touch one of them was an error he hadn't allowed for. His body was weak from inactivity and his muscles atrophic and so his knees touched the knees of the officer as he wobbled to his feet and froze in pain. The blood recirculating to his legs brought water to his cheeks and his eyes tightened. Then he placed his hands on his behind and while waiting his punishment he attempted to restore feeling there but his hands didn't work and he couldn't discern if he was actually massaging or not. In his confusion he continued to exercise. What was the officer doing? Why hadn't he reacted to this? The African's eyes were moist and all before him was in a blur. It was too much for him even to stand. The room tilted. How ironic, he thought. He bitterly recalled what whites believed— "Give them freedom and they won't know how to handle it anyway." Here he was, obviously being spared admonition and it was all too much for him to handle. His legs weakened and he tried to locate his chair but his chair didn't seem to be there and he missed it, missed the chair, missed it as if a prankster had pulled it away, and he toppled to the floor. But he took advantage of that also. He stretched his frame and sucked in the dead air and he wiggled his toes and fingers and jaw muscles in that manner called dynamic tension in exercise salons.

Now what would the white man do? Demand he rise from the floor and return to the chair? Maybe. But he couldn't move, not yet anyway. Then what? Call out his name in anger? Never that for to call a detainee by his name would be to give him status, Would he be kicked? A leather boot can be lethal. No, not this white man. He's much too soft. The floor was a delicious respite. He had succeeded beyond his wildest expectations.

John Breede stood not knowing what action to take. He studied the fallen man and debated whether to pull him back onto the chair. Had he soiled his pants again? Once before the detainee had defecated during Breede's shift and Breede had to bear the stench until his shift ended. What should he do? He stepped clear of the two chairs and paced the room with his hands behind him. Surely in this circumstance his fellow workers wouldn't be stymied. They'd treat the detainee appropriately. He knew that. They would pummel the fallen body as a punishment to it for having the audacity to have weakened from punishment. They would call in an aide if need be and between them entertain their imaginations. It was like anything else, one acted and reacted according to one's base instincts. That held true even under normal conditions despite orders and procedures on the daily behavior of torturors. (Of course Breede well knew that nothing in this building was under normal conditions.) If a worker had a rough day of it with his family or his vehicle overheated or a small bill from an unexpected source popped in from postal then the detainee would suffer the consequences. If an interrogator was bored or with a belly full of spirits he might spend his shift-time daydreaming while the detainee cowed before him not knowing what to expect. If there was a disturbance in the country, as say the matter at Uitenhage Stadium—and there it didn't matter that it was twenty-five blacks killed—the detainees paid for it. Their jailers exercised any of a choice of options not unlike those for a champion tennis player who probes his opponent's weakness and lobs deep, serves soft, plays back until he finds the flaw. Should one check out from supply a pair of plyers, a sharp metal prod or a rubber tourniquet? Should one employ scrutiny of the rectum or mindless queries? Stretch their ligaments or confuse them with obscure recitals of evidences? Use psychological torture or an old fashioned whipping? Some would sooner forget the responsibilities of the shift but rather read a newspaper on the toilet.

Little of this was for John Breede. He hadn't the constitution for physical abuse nor did he have it for reaching out to an African and offering assistance. After all the man was a revolutionary. That he fucked a white woman was incidental. Certainly Breede wasn't told what he actually did. Breede was only told to report to room one. Keep the detainee sitting in some form of attention. Don't speak.

Once he was ordered to kick a goose through the halls of the security building.

It was in the black of night and all the prisoners were asleep. The screeching goose crapped on the floor as Breede kicked it with the grinning faces of his fellow workers urging him on. When he herded the battered bird into the square he noticed that his shin was bruised under his trousers and blood came off in his palm. Since all the prisoners were awakened each interrogator on duty was shunted off to a room with special instructions. Breede's instructions were to ask three questions with no letup. "What is your address? How long have you been a member of the African National Congress? Who is your leader?" Breede intoned these questions for a steady two hours and the answers he received— "South West Township—I'm not—I have no leader" —tallied twelve words less in number than the questions did leaving Breede with the impression that he himself and not the African was a victim of harassment.

He looked down on the African and for the first time that he could remember he became curious about him. What was his name and why was he detained? Did he have a family and was he dangerous? What was it like to be born into black skin? Breede then wondered if he himself was now feeling empathy for the man and if so how could that be? Instead why wasn't he using his training on the detainee? Breede wasn't a skilled interrogator but he'd been instructed, drilled and disciplined over and over in the veld. How could he improve his skills if he never engaged in what he'd learned about the craft of torture? Isn't it true, as they say, that one trained in the intricacies of torture cannot easily exist without exercising his knowledge of it—if for no other reason than that of curiosity? A disciplined soldier who has extensive training cannot carry on indefinitely without combat. The powerful kukri knife can split a man's head open with a single chop if wielded properly, but of what value is a kukri knife without it ultimately splitting bone, of what value a night-scope without a night, an arrow in its quiver? It was very confusing to John Breede.

He studied the stark graffiti on the wall and thought it a dichotomy that it remained when it easily could have been painted over. It struck him that a few other rooms had anti-government slogans like the red room that had NO MO JO'BER NO NO MO or the one scratched in small letters of the name of the Law and Order Minister; LOUIS LE GRANGE WEARS DARK GLASSES. He thought it a ploy by the heads of security to remind the interrogators that these men and women were enemies of the state. In fact there was reason to believe that the security police themselves were the scriveners of the slogans.

He glanced at his watch and saw that his shift was close to ending. The African noticed Breede's action and interpreted its meaning. He sat up, stronger now, got to a knee and pulled himself back into the chair.

"You go home now?" He actually spoke to Breede. How well he knew him.

"Yes." Breede answered as if it was the only choice he had. Then he sat down again opposite and close to the African. "Why?" The African understood what Breede was searching for but instead he tilted his face indicating that the query wasn't clear. Breede said again, "Why? Why are all of you in our jails?"

The African said, "I don't choose to be here. Same as you."

Breede edged forward as if the black man had some hidden wisdom that might edify him, release him from his quandary, but the black gave nothing.

"So what will you do?" Breede continued.

"What?" The African seemed taken aback.

"Will you stay here?"

The African wasn't prepared for Breede's bewildering words.

"All of you—will all of you stay?" Breede made little sense. He looked off into the room as if it were his own private companion, his thoughts abandoning the black. The black quizzically studied him. He thought the white touched by the heat or the dead air in the room. Breede's eyes were half closed and his fingers clutched his knees and gathered the material in his trousers.

The door opened and in it stood a man. He wore a tunic. Breede seemed to come to life then. He straightened his back and immediately walked from the room leaving the prisoner alone again. When the door hushed shut the African felt life cut away from him. He quickly forced himself to review the events of the last few hours, evaluate them as well as he could before the next interruption by the next interrogator on the new shift with his own arsenal of instructions.

And so it went in John Vorster Square.

The Natural Father

Robert Lacy

H ER NAME WAS Laura Goldberg. She had thick black hair and a "bump" in her nose (as she put it), but she dressed well and she had a good figure. She worked as a typist in an abstract office in downtown San Diego, and when Butters first met her in the fall of 1958 they had both just turned nineteen.

They met through a boot camp buddy of his who had gone to high school with her up in San Francisco, where she lived before her parents were divorced. Within a week he was taking her out. Butters was still in radio school at the time and didn't have a car, but Laura did, and she began picking him up several afternoons a week in the parking lot across the highway from the Marine base.

They made love on their third date, on the couch in her mother's apartment out in El Cajon, with the late-afternoon sunlight casting shadow patterns on the walls. It was hurried and not very satisfactory and Butters was embarrassed by his performance. He felt he ought to apologize or something.

"It's okay," Laura said. "It's okay."

After that, though, they made love nearly every time they were alone together, often in the front seat of her car parked late at night on suburban sidestreets, with the fog rolling up off the bay to conceal them. One night they did it on her bed in the apartment, then had to spend frantic minutes picking white bedspread nap out of his trousers before her mother got home. Another time she met him at the front door, fresh from her shower, wearing nothing but a loose kimono, and they did it right there on the living room carpet, with the sound of the running shower in the background.

Butters was from a little town in eastern Oklahoma and hadn't known many Jewish girls before. In fact, he couldn't think of any. However, Laura's being Jewish didn't matter nearly as much to him as it seemed to matter to her. She was forever making jokes about it, and she liked to point out other Jews to him whenever they came across them, in restaurants or on TV. "Members of the tribe," she called them, or "M.O.T.'s." Butters pretended to share in the humor, but he was never quite sure what he was being let in on. Where he came from, tribes meant Indians.

Still, he was amazed at some of the people she identified as Jewish. Jack Benny, for example. And Frankie Laine. Every time they watched TV together in the apartment the list got longer. One night she even tried to convince him Eddie Fisher was a Jew.

"Bull," he said. "I don't believe it."

"He is, though," she insisted. "Ask mother when she gets here."

"He's Italian or something," Butters said. "I read it somewhere. Fisher's not his real name."

"Nope. He's a genuine M.O.T."

"Uh-uh."

"He is too, Donnie. Bet you a dollar."

"Make it five."

"You don't have five."

"I can get it."

"All right, Mister Sure-of-Yourself, five then. Shake."

They shook hands.

"How about Debbie Reynolds?" he said. "What's she?"

In March Butters was graduated from radio school and promoted to private first class. Then he was transferred to the naval base down at Imperial Beach to begin high-speed radio cryptography school. Imperial Beach was twelve miles due south of San Diego. The base sat out on a narrow point of land. At night you could see the lights of Tijuana across the way.

One night after he had been there about a month Laura picked him up, late, at the main gate, drove back up to a hamburger stand in National City, and told him she was pregnant.

Butters was astounded, of course. This was the sort of thing that happened to other people.

"How do you know?" he said.

"I've missed two periods."

"Jeez. Did you see a doctor?"

"Yes."

"What did he say?"

"He said I was pregnant."

"Yeah, but what did he *say?*"

"He said I was a big, strong, healthy girl, and I was going to have a baby sometime in October. He said I had a good pelvis."

"Is that all?"

"Yes. He gave me some pills."

"For what?"

"One for water retention and one for morning sickness."

"You been sick?"

"Not yet. He says I might be."

"Jeez."

They sat in silence for a while, not looking at each other. Finally he said, "Well, what do you think we should do?"

She spoke slowly and carefully, and he could tell she had given the matter some thought. "I think we ought to get engaged for a month," she said. "Then get married. I know where we can get a deal on a ring."

"What kind of deal?"

"Forty percent off, two years to pay."

"Where?"

"Nathan's. Downtown."

"You already been there?"

"I go by it every day at lunch."

"They give everybody forty percent off?"

"I know the manager. He's a cousin."

On the way back to the base Laura spoke of showers, wedding announcements, honeymoons in Ensenada. She said she thought they ought to sit down with her mother that very weekend, to get that part of it out of the way. Butters, who was hoping to get back on base without further discussion, said he thought he might have guard duty.

"You had guard duty last weekend," she reminded him.

"There's a bug going around," he said. "Lots of guys are in sickbay."

"Come Sunday night," she said. "I'll cook dinner. Elvis is on Ed Sullivan."

"I'll have to see," he said.

"Sunday night," she said.

Sunday was four days away, which gave him plenty of time to think. And the more he thought the more he knew he didn't want to marry Laura Goldberg. He didn't love her, for one thing, and he wasn't ready to get married anyway, even to someone he did love. He was only nineteen years old. He had his whole life in front of him. Besides, he couldn't imagine Laura back home in Oklahoma.

That Sunday evening he caught a ride into San Diego with one of the boys from the base, then took a city bus out to the apartment in El Cajon. Laura met him at the door wearing an apron and with a mixing spoon in her hand.

"Hi, hon," she said. "Dinner's almost ready."

Laura's mother, Mrs. Lippman, was seated on the living room sofa smoking a cigarette. She had her shoes off and her stockinged feet up on an ottoman. Mrs. Lippman was a short, heavyset woman with springy gray hair and sharp features. She always looked tired.

"Hello, Donald," she said. "What's with Betty Furness in there? Usually I can't get her to boil water."

"Hello, Mrs. Lippman," Butters said. "How's things at the paint store?"

Mrs. Lippman managed a Sherwin-Williams store down on lower Broadway and complained constantly about the help, most of whom were Mexican-Americans.

"Terrible," she said. "Don't ask. The chilis are stealing me blind."

Laura had fixed beef stroganoff, a favorite of Butters, and when it was ready they ate it off TV trays in the living room while watching Elvis—from the waist up—on the Ed Sullivan Show. The meal was well prepared. Laura had even made little individual salads for each of them, with chopped walnuts on top and her own special dressing. When they were through eating she put the coffee on, then she and Butters scraped and stacked the dishes in the kitchen while Mrs. Lippman watched the last of the Sullivan Show alone in the living room.

"You nervous?" Laura said to him in the kitchen. "You've been awfully quiet since you got here."

"I'm all right," Butters said, scraping a plate.

"Is something *wrong?*"

"No. I'm all right, I told you."

"Well, you certainly don't act like it. You haven't smiled once the whole evening."

Butters didn't say anything. He reached for another plate.

"Look at me," Laura said.

He looked at her.

"It's going to be *okay*," she said. "We'll just go in there and tell her. What can she say?"

"Nothing much, I guess."

"Do you want to do the talking, or do you want me to?"

"Either way. You decide."

"All right. You do it. That's more traditional anyway."

"What about the other?"

"What other?"

"You know."

"Oh. We don't mention that. Why upset her if we don't have to?"

When the coffee was ready Laura poured out three cups and she and Butters returned to the living room. The show was just ending. Ed Sullivan was onstage, thanking his guests and announcing next week's performers. Laura stood for a moment watching her mother watch the screen, then she set the coffee on her mother's tray.

"Mother," she said, "Don and I have— "

"Sh!" Mrs. Lippman said, shooing her out of her line of sight. "I want to hear this."

Onscreen, Ed Sullivan was saying that his guests next week would include a Spanish ventriloquist and a rising young comedian. Headlining the show, he said, would be Steve Lawrence and Edie Gorme.

"Oh, goodie," Mrs. Lippman said. "Laura, don't let me make plans."

"All right, mother." Laura had taken the wingback chair across the room and was sitting forward in it, her cup and saucer balanced on her knees. She was wearing her pleated wool skirt and a gray sweater, damp at the armpits.

When the Sullivan Show at last gave way to a commercial, she said, "Mother, Don and I have something to tell you—don't we, Don?"

Butters was seated on the sofa with Mrs. Lippman, the center cushion between them. "Yeah," he said.

Mrs. Lippman looked at Laura, then at Butters. She narrowed her eyes. "What is it?" she said.

"Don?" Laura said.

Butters was studying his coffee. At the sound of his name he looked up and took a deep breath. When he opened his mouth to speak he had no idea what he was going to say, but as soon as the words were out he knew they were the right ones.

"Mrs. Lippman," he said, "your daughter is pregnant."

There was a moment of silence, then Mrs. Lippman brought her hand down, very hard, on the armrest of the sofa. The sound was explosive in the small apartment.

"*I knew it!*" she said. "I knew it, I knew it, I knew it!"

She looked at Laura. "How long?" she said.

Laura was looking at Butters.

"*How long?*"

Laura looked at her mother. "Two months," she said softly.

"Who'd you see? Jack Segal?"

"Yes. Last week."

"I knew it. He won't be able to keep his mouth shut, you know. He'll tell Phyllis. God knows who *she*'ll tell. *Look at me.*"

"I didn't know what else to do," Laura said, her voice barely above a whisper.

"You've got a mother, you know."

"Oh, mother."

"Well, you've broken my heart. I want you to know that. You have absolutely broken your mother's heart. And *you*," she said turning on Butters, "you've really done it up brown, haven't you, hotshot? And to think, I took you into my home."

"God," Butters said, "I feel so rotten. I can't tell you how— "

"Oh, shut up," Mrs. Lippman said. "I don't care how rotten you feel. I want to know what you're going to do about it. Look at her. She's knocked up. You couldn't keep it in your pants, and now *she's* knocked up. So tell me: what are you going to do about it?"

Butters didn't say anything.

"Don?" Laura said. "Donnie? Aren't you going to tell her what we decided?"

He looked at Laura. His eyes were round with grief. "I'm sorry, hon," he said. "I really am."

Laura began to cry. Her shoulders shook, and then her whole body, causing her cup and saucer to clatter together in her lap.

"This is going to cost you money, hotshot," Mrs. Lippman said. "You know that, don't you?"

Their first thought was abortion. Mrs. Lippman knew a man there in San Diego who agreed to do it, but after examining Laura he decided it was too risky (something about "enlarged veins"). So Tijuana was suggested; somebody knew a man there. But this time Laura balked. She didn't want any Mexican quack messing around inside her. Then Mrs. Lippman got the idea of hiring a second cousin of Laura's to marry her ("just for the name, you understand"), and she went so far as to get in touch with him—he was a dental student at Stanford—but he turned her down, even at her top price of five hundred dollars. So eventually, as the days slipped away and it became more and more apparent that Laura was going to have to have the baby, they began scouting around for an inexpensive place to send her. What they found was a sort of girls' ranch for unwed mothers over in Arizona. It was church-supported and the lying-in fee was only a hundred dollars a month, meals included.

"What's it like?" Butters asked when Mrs. Lippman told him about it over the phone.

"How do *I* know?" she said. "It's clean. Jack Segal says it's clean."

"Well, that's good, isn't it?" Butters said. "That it's clean?"

"Listen," Mrs. Lippman said. "Spare me your tender solicitude. I don't have time for it. What I need from you is three hundred dollars—your half."

"*Three* hundred?"

"Three hundred. She'll be there six months, counting the post partum."

"What's that?"

"You don't even need to know. Just get me the three hundred, okay?"

That was in April. In the meantime Butters had washed out of high-speed school and had been sent back to San Diego to await assignment overseas. He was placed in a casual company, with too little to do and too much time on his hands, and it was there that he met, one afternoon in the supply room, a skinny little buck sergeant named Hawkins who rather easily convinced him that maybe he was being had. Happened all the time, Hawkins said. Dago was that kind of town.

Why, there were women there who knew a million ways to separate you from your money, and it sounded to him like Butters had fallen for one of the oldest ways of all. Then he asked Butters what his blood type was.

"O positive," Butters said. "Why?"

"Universal donor," Hawkins said. "They can't prove a thing."

The upshot was that two days later, following Hawkins' advice, Butters found himself sitting in the office of one of the two chaplains on base. This chaplain was a freckle-faced young Methodist with captain's bars on his collar and an extremely breezy manner. He tapped his front teeth with a letter opener the whole time Butters was telling his story, and when Butters was done said he thought Butters owed it to himself to ask around a bit, make some inquiries, find out what other boys Laura had been seeing.

"I mean, after all, fella," he said, "if she did it for you, why not someone else?"

And for a few days after that Butters actually considered getting in touch with the boot camp buddy who had introduced him to Laura. He knew where the boy was—up at El Toro, in the NavCad program—all he had to do was call him. In the end, though, he didn't do it. It was just too much trouble. What he did was to hole up on base instead. He quit going into town and he quit taking phone calls. He developed the idea that as long as he stayed on base they couldn't touch him. And it worked for a while. He was able to pass several furtive weeks that way, sticking to a tight little universe of barracks, PX, base theater and beer garden. But then one afternoon while he and Hawkins were folding mattress covers in the supply room a runner came in and said the chaplain wanted to see him, the other one. This chaplain's office was at the far end of the grinder, half a mile away, and as he made his way up there Butters tried to occupy his mind with pleasant thoughts. He didn't bother wondering why he was being summoned, and when he entered the office and saw who was sitting there he knew he had been right not to.

"Hello, Miz Lippman," he said. "I figured it might be you."

"You quit answering your phone," she said. "So I came calling. You owe me money."

This chaplain was Catholic. He wore tinted glasses and had a stern, no-nonsense air about him. He listened impatiently to Butters' side of the story, then he asked Butters how he, "as a Christian," viewed his responsibilities in the matter. He left little doubt how he himself viewed them.

"You *are* a Christian, aren't you, private?" he said.

"Uh, yes, sir," Butters said.

"Well, what's your obligation here then? Or don't you feel you have one?"

"I don't know, sir. I'm confused."

"Call me father. What do you mean you're 'confused'? Did you agree to pay this woman, or didn't you?"

"Yes, sir. But that was before I talked to the other chaplain."

"What's that got to do with it? Did you agree to pay her? Call me father."

"Yes, sir. Father."

"Did you have intercourse with her daughter?"

Butters blushed. "Yes, sir."

"More than once?"

"Yes, sir."

"Did her daughter get pregnant as a result?"

"Yes, sir. I guess."

"You guess?"

"I guess it was me. But it *could* have been someone else."

Mrs. Lippman bristled. "I resent that," she said. "Laura's not a tramp and you know it."

"Do you *think* it was someone else?" the chaplain asked.

"She's no tramp, father," Mrs. Lippman insisted.

"Do you, private?"

"No, sir," Butters said.

"That's what I thought," the chaplain said. "Now let's get down to business."

So once again it was agreed that Butters would pay half of Laura's lying-in expense, or fifty dollars a month for six months. But this time they drew up a little contract right there in the chaplain's office, which the chaplain's secretary typed and the three of them signed, the chaplain as witness. That night, lying in bed waiting for lights out, Butters thought back over the day's events and decided things had worked out about as well as he could expect. At least he could come out of hiding now.

Just before lights out the charge-of-quarters came in and said there was a phone call for him out in the orderly room. *Jeez*, Butters thought as he got up to follow the CQ, *what now?*

The phone was on the wall just inside the orderly room door. He picked up the dangling receiver and said, "Hello?"

"Hello—Donnie?"

"Laura? Where are you?"

"Arizona. Where do you think?"

"Well. How're you doing?"

"How'm I doing?"

"Yeah. You know: how're you doing?"

"Not too good, Donnie. Not too good."

"You crying?"

"Yeah."

He thought so. "What's the matter, hon?"

"Matter? Oh, nothing. I'm just pregnant, and unmarried, and three hundred miles from home, and scared and lonely. That's all. Nothing to get upset about, right?"

"Don't cry, Laura."

"I can't help it."

"Please?"

"I'm just so miserable, Donnie. You oughta see us. There's about thirty of us, and all we do is sit around all day in our maternity smocks *looking* at each other. Nobody hardly says a word. One of the girls is only fourteen. She sleeps with a big green rabbit."

Butters felt very bad for Laura. She sounded so blue. "Aren't there any horses?" he said.

"What?"

"Horses. Aren't there any horses?"

"*Horses!* God, Donnie, you're worse than a child sometimes. What do you think this is, a dude ranch? You think we sit around a campfire at night singing 'Home on the Range'?"

Butters fingered a place on the back of his neck. "Your mother says it's pretty clean," he ventured.

"Clean?"

"That's what she said."

"When did you talk to her?"

"About that? About a month ago, I guess."

"And she said it was clean?"

"Yeah."

"What else did she say?"

"Nothing. Just that it was clean."

"I see. Well, yes, it's very clean. Spic and span. And the food's good too. We had chicken a la king tonight—my favorite."

"We had meatloaf. It tasted like cardboard."

"Poor you."

"What?"

"I said, 'Poor you.'"

"Oh."

They fell silent, and the silence began to lengthen. Through the orderly room window Butters could see the movie letting out across the grinder. Guys were coming out stretching and lighting up cigarettes.

"Listen," Laura said finally, "I'll let you go. I can tell you don't want to talk to me anyway. I just called to tell you that I've decided to go ahead and have this stupid baby. For a while there I was thinking about killing myself, but I've changed my mind. I'm gonna go through with it, Donnie. I'm gonna do it. But my life will never, ever be the same again, and I just thought you ought to know that."

Then she hung up.

Two weeks later he was on a boat bound for Okinawa.

That was in mid-May. By the time he reached Okinawa, halfway around the world, it was early June. He had made his May payment to Mrs. Lippman the day after the meeting in the chaplain's office, and he mailed her his June payment as soon as he got off the boat. The July payment he mailed her too, but late in the month. The August payment he skipped altogether. And sure enough, not long afterwards, sometime in early September, the company clerk came looking for him one afternoon in the barracks there on Okinawa with word that the company commander wanted to see him.

"Did he say what it was about?" Butters asked.

"No," the clerk said. "He don't confide in me much. I think you better chop chop, though."

It was the same old story. The company commander, a major with a good tan, showed him a letter from Mrs. Lippman and asked him what was going on.

Butters told him.

"She claims you owe her money," the major said. "Do you?"

"Yes, sir," Butters said. He was standing at ease in front of the major's desk, looking at the letter in the major's hands. It was on blue stationery.

"How much?"

"A hundred and fifty dollars, sir."

"Well, what do you plan to do about it?"

"Pay her, sir. I guess."

"You guess?"

"Pay her, sir."

"Do you have it?"

"No, sir."

"Where do you plan to get it?"

"I don't know, sir."

"You don't *know*? You think you might dig it up out of the *ground*, private? Pick it off a *tree*? What do you mean you don't know?"

"I don't know, sir. I guess I'll have to think of something."

"You 'guess.' You 'don't know.' It strikes me, private, that you're just not very sure about anything—are you?"

Butters didn't say anything. A phone rang somewhere.

The major shook his head. "How old are you, son?" he said.

"Nineteen, sir. I'll be twenty next month."

"I see. Well, here's what I want you to do. There's a Navy Relief office over at Camp Hague. I want you to go over there tomorrow morning and take out a loan."

"A loan, sir?"

"A loan."

"They'd *lend* it to me?"

"That's what they're there for, private."

A loan! Now why hadn't he thought of that? Getting it turned out to be remarkably easy too. Oh, he had to answer a few embarrassing questions, and there was a final interview that had him squirming for a while, but when it was all over, in less than two hours, he had a cashier's check for the full amount in his hand, with a full year to repay it and an interest rate of only three percent. He was so elated at the sight of the check that it was all he could do to keep from dancing the woman who gave it to him around the room. Rather than risk temptation he sent the entire one-fifty off to San Diego that same day by registered mail. He considered sticking a little note in with it—something like, "Bet you thought you'd never see this, didn't you?"—but thought better of it at the last minute.

And it was funny, but in the days that followed he felt like a different person. He bounced around the company area with such energy and good humor that people hardly recognized him. One morning he was first in line for chow.

"Jeez, Butters," said the boy serving him his eggs, "what's got into you? You hardly ever even *eat* breakfast."

"Just feed the troops, lad," Butters said. "Feed the troops."

* * *

But then it was October, the month the baby was due. Throughout the spring and summer and into the early days of a rainy Okinawa autumn he had done a pretty good summer job of shutting it out of his mind. He had simply refused to contemplate the fact that what had happened back in February in foggy San Diego was destined, ever, to result in anything so real as a baby. But as October crept in it got harder. He found he couldn't help thinking about it some nights after lights out, couldn't help wondering, for example, whether it would be a boy or a girl. He hoped it was a boy. Being a boy was easier—girls had it rough. One night he found himself imagining it curled up in Laura's womb, its knees tucked up under its chin, its tiny fingers making tiny fists. And, lying there, he began trying to make out the baby's face. He wanted to know who it looked like, but, try as he might, he couldn't tell. Later that night he dreamed he was swimming underwater somewhere, deep down, and that floating in the water all around him were these large jellyfish, each of which, on closer inspection, appeared to have a baby inside. He couldn't make out these babies' faces either.

But October passed and nothing happened. At least not in his world. Nobody contacted him, by phone or mail or otherwise. Nobody got in touch. And as the days went by and still he heard nothing, slowly he began to believe that maybe it was all over with now, that what had happened was finally history and he could go about his daily business just like everyone else.

He had made friends by then with a boy named Tipton, from Kansas, and the two of them had begun spending their weekends in a tin-roofed shanty outside Chibana with a pair of sisters who worked in a Chibana bar.

One Saturday morning Butters was sitting out on the backsteps of the shanty, watching one of the sisters hang laundry in the yard, when Tipton arrived from the base by taxi, bearing beer and groceries and a letter for him.

Butters took the letter and looked at it. There were several cancellations on the envelope, indicating it had been rerouted more than once. He opened it up and took out a single folded sheet of paper. It read:

Dear Don,

The baby is due any day now, they tell me. You should see me. I'm huge. You probably wouldn't even recognize me. I think the baby is a "he." It sure kicks like one anyway. It even keeps me awake some nights with its kicking and rolling around a lot.

The nurses say I don't have to see it if I don't want to. They say it's entirely up to me. Sometimes I think I want to and sometimes I think I don't. Silly me, huh? Guess I had better make up my mind pretty soon, though, and quit all this procrastinating (sp?).

Don, since I know now that I am never going to see you again I guess this will have to be goodbye. I'm not bitter anymore. I was for a while, I admit, but I'm not now. And I'm still glad I knew you. I just wish things could have turned out better, that's all.

Best always,
Laura

P.S. You owe me $5. (See Clipping)

Butters looked inside the envelope again and saw a small folded piece of paper he had missed before. He took it out and unfolded it. It was a photograph clipped from a magazine—*Time* or *Newsweek*, it looked like—and it showed Elizabeth Taylor and Eddie Fisher during their recent wedding ceremony in Beverly Hills. They were standing before a robed man with a dark beard. Both Fisher and the robed man had small black caps perched on the backs of their heads. An arrow had been drawn, in red ink, pointing to the cap on Fisher's head, and along its shaft had been printed, in big block letters, also red, the initials "M.O.T."

Butters sat looking at the clipping for a while. Then he put it and the letter back in the envelope, folded the envelope in half, and stuffed it in his back pocket.

"Your mom?" Tipton asked.

"Huh?"

"The letter. Is it from your mom?"

"No. A girl I knew."

"Oh," Tipton said. "You want a beer?"

The legal papers didn't arrive until the first week in December. They were from the office of the county clerk of Maricopa County, Arizona, and they consisted of a form letter, a release document, and an enclosed envelope for which no postage was necessary.

They came on a Friday, as Butters and Tipton were preparing to leave town.

Butters read the form letter first, sitting on his bunk in his civvies. The letter was very short, just two paragraphs. The first paragraph said that a child had been born on such-and-such a date in the public maternity ward of such-and-such a hospital in Phoenix, Arizona, and that, according to the attending physician, it was free of physical and mental defects. The second paragraph merely asked him to read and then sign the accompanying release. The child was identified, the words typed into a blank space in the middle of the first paragraph, as "Baby Boy Butters, 7 lbs., 6 oz."

When he was finished with the letter Butters set it carefully beside him on the bunk and picked up the release. It was short, too, just a single legal-sized page. It asked him to understand what he was doing—waiving all rights and responsibilities in the care and upbringing of the child—and it cited the pertinent sections of Arizona law, which took up most of the rest of the page. Toward the bottom, however, there was a dotted line that caught Butters' eye. He skipped over much of the legal language, but he lingered at the dotted line. "Signature of the Natural Father," it was labeled. He looked at it. That was him. He was the natural father. He turned the page over to see if there was anything on the back. There wasn't. It was blank. He turned it back over and looked at the dotted line. Tipton was standing just a few feet away from him, waiting. They had already called their taxi. It was on the way.

He looked up at Tipton. "You got a pen?" he said.

The Outfielder

William Meissner

1

W HAT I LIKE MOST is the room to move, room to flow until I'm under the high flies, waiting for their whiteness to cover my palm. There's a beauty in the outfield, a grace. Out there, no one touches you. You throw long pegs to second or home, but these are the only lines of connection. No one seems to know what I mean, to love it as much as I do. The woman I love understands it, but not completely. I try to tell her about it, but there are times when, like the flag stiffening on the center field flag pole, she pulls away from me and doesn't want to listen.

2

The woman I love tells me look out into the world. Look beyond your self, your game. I love her for saying that. If she didn't say things like that, I would never love her. Still, she doesn't really know what I mean by the beauty of the soft cropped, green outfield.

We drive in cars a lot. Sometimes she talks to me, sometimes she doesn't. She never talks outfield. She purposely avoids talking outfield. She thinks I get enough of it during the games themselves. Sometimes she talks houses: kitchens, sunlight sliding through the slats in the blinds, homes. What we could have between us. She never talks outfield. How I love that game.

Sometimes we stand in kitchens and talk for hours. The floors are green and clean, and I brush my toe across the tiles. Sometimes we sit at a diamond-shaped table. Lifting my coffee to my lips, I look up at the walls. Just don't let it be everything to you, she says. I even love the *way* she says it: her strength, the way the words leap out at just the right moment.

3

She agrees with me when I say I'm lucky I'm not an infielder. Lucky I'm not a shortstop or third baseman, those guys who can take no more than three or four steps before they dive for the hard grounders. I can't stand the feeling of dirt beneath my cleats. Sometimes they look face to face with line drives that, if they hit you in the chest, would shatter your heart like a window. I'm glad I'm not a catcher, held stiff behind mask and shin guards, a crouched crustacean. Glad I'm not a pitcher, tearing my arm out of its roots while batters try to send each pitch flying to the moon.

Learn to be fast, I always told myself as a kid. Never be slow, or they'll stick you in the infield. I impressed them with the way my feet did not seem to touch the grass when I ran. Now, as a veteran, I must fight every day to keep my legs young.

4

Fans, she says, Fans are only superficial. They never love you the way I love you, she says. And I know it's true. She reminds me the fans don't know the real me, don't see me in the mornings, dropping my peanut butter toast to the kitchen floor. They have my photographs, touched up just right so they can't see the shadows, the time lines under my eyes. They don't see the chalky color of my face when I wake too early, my timing off, my timing off.

The fans love me, in their way. And I love them. Sometimes the sound of their cheers is like pure sunlight in my ears. But the fans only admire me in my white pinstriped uniform in center field under the floodlights; they don't see my shadow. I do, she says, and her timing is just right as she rounds her lips to say the words, just like a practiced umpire saying "Strike two." I stand up from my side of the table, brush her hair back with my glove hand, touch her cheek with my bare hand.

5

An outfielder has a certain liking for fences, walls. Walls seem to contain you better than open fields do. You might say I am a little in love with walls. They let you know your limitations, they speak strongly to your shoulders when you back into them. Sometimes they outline my life.

They stop those line drives between center and left that skip by too quickly for any human to reach. They send the ball careening off, skimming toward you, so you can barehand it and nail the runner trying to stretch it to third.

I love to play the wall. Sometimes the true test is holding on to the ball you've just caught, even though you've hit the wall hard and everything hurts. The fences make the game.

A high fly to deep center excites me more than a pop up which I only have to take a step or two to catch. I love the wait, back to the fence, as the ball approaches, high and flying and spinning with all its strength. I love it when the ball finally comes down out of orbit. Just out of reach, everyone says, just over the center field fence. Then the leap. The stretching of tendons. And I come down with a smile of white leather in my web, so bright it stings the batter's eyes.

6

The night she left me the outfield grass felt like crushed apples, crushed apples, crushed apples.

7

Timing. Timing is everything. Timing is knowing where you will catch the ball even before the batter hits it. Timing is knowing when to dive for the line drive that's falling fast, it's knowing which shoestring catches to go for, which are out of range.

If I drop a fly ball, I'm the only one to blame. Infielders can bobble a grounder, still throw their man out. With an outfielder, it's decisive: the fly ball cannot touch the grass or I die a little, right there in front of everyone.

Timing is everything when you're growing old. Timing is knowing the loss of a wasted moment, feeling its pain as you let it drop just beyond your fingertips.

Last night I dreamt of my first baseball glove. I used it for years as a grade school kid; it was a dark, leather glove with large, swollen fingers. I lost it somewhere in high school, but in my dream I slipped the glove on and the leather began to crack and flake. Then I tried to pull it from my hand but I couldn't. The crater-like pocket of the glove opened wide for me like a scream.

Timing is thinking about this long, high fly ball hit to center, this deep one that's backing me toward the wall. Timing is understanding this last deadly instant, with its correct spring of leg muscles, its reach, its squeeze. Thinking about it, ready for it. Yes.

8

A game isn't a game unless it's a close game.

Sometimes, when I'm standing out there, toeing the grass, watching man after man strike out or ground out, I think let them get another run or two. Let them start some small fires.

What good is playing if it's not hit for hit, run for run?

What does winning mean if you always win by half a dozen? What good is winning if you never lose? Closeness. Closeness is everything.

9

The score is tied after nine innings.

I turn around between pitches and see her in the center field bleachers, watching me. Though she's never come to a game before, she's here; I can feel her eyes, like two heavy weights on my shoulders. Now's my chance to prove to her that I've never dropped one in my career, never.

The grass glows green beneath my cleats on this night, this game that has lasted long into the night until fans can see their breaths in the moist August air. The beauty of it, I think, as I watch the next pitch, then turn to her, the beauty.

I can't see the stars this night, even though I know the sky is clear and endless. The bright floodlights build a wall between me and the stars. I know she understands the outfield, she wants to be out here with me. Her face is white and clean as a new baseball.

Another out, another run for our team and we can all go home. They'll turn off these huge rows of blindness and we'll see the heavens again, we'll see our faces clearly again, by touch.

I turn again and she's gone. An empty hole in the bleachers where she sat. I can feel the lines etching deeper into my face, like grooves in the dirt of the dugout floor.

The hit rises from his bat. It's high and long to deep center. I race back and back at full speed, watching the ball over my shoulder all the while.

The ball begins its descent like a circle of light from a tiny spotlight, and it appears the ball is just out of reach. I time my leap.

Up. Full extension, my left arm stretched upward until all muscles scream. The glove opens hungrily, lovingly for the ball, the ball, the ball. From this height I think I can see the stars again. The fans are screaming like sirens for me, her voice screaming for me, for the game, for the outfielder.

10

Back at home we are sitting at the table in the green kitchen. We ignore all walls. She takes a sip of her coffee, then stands up. I stand up, slide around the table and reach for her. With a pain that feels like flashbulbs popping behind my forehead I catch her in my arms and she embraces me and we hold on. We hold on. To everyone's amazement we hold on.

Taking Miss Kezee to the Polls

David Haynes

T HE RUBBER BAND "plinked" as I popped out the next three by five card. It said Miss Xenobia C. Kezee, who had voted faithfully in every election since 1925—local and national—was "in her 80's," a lifetime resident of St. Paul, and had lived at 887 Dayton for thirty-five years. She was a Democrat, although independent and opinionated. Her polling place: Hill Elementary on Selby. A college roommate, John—now Pastor John—who organized this "get out the vote drive" cautioned me that Miss Kezee would be ready to vote at 1:00 P.M. She expected promptness, courtesy, and cooperation. He would hear about it, and there would be consequences if she were in any way disappointed. Anything for the cause: I rang her doorbell with minutes to spare.

"Who is that and what you want? If it's you damn kids again I'm calling the police."

"Looking for a . . . Miss Kezee? I came to take her to vote."

"Stand over so as I can see you in my peephole. Who sent you?"

"Pastor Thomas from the church. You do remember that it's election day, Miss?"

"Hell, yes. Thomas didn't say nothin bout sendin no man. He usually send one of the sisters."

"Maybe you should call him."

"And maybe you should close your fresh mouth and stop givin orders." She opened the door. "You sit yourself down while I finish fixin up. I got me a gun back here. I'll blow your black ass to Mississippi if you tries anything, you understand me, boy?"

"Yes, ma'am."

This was not what I expected.

She scurried like a nervous squirrel around the visible areas of her house looking for valuables to hide from my pilfering hands. She was as thin as a willow branch and from the side curved like a question mark, her wrinkled face and hands the color of an old penny. Tied across her head were two silvery braids. She hustled back to her dressing area.

"What's your name, boy," she shouted from somewhere. I imagined her loading her gun.

"David Johnson, ma'am."

"You related to them Johnsons over on Iglehart?"

"No, ma'am. I don't know of them."

"Can't stand them fools, no how. Now, as I'm rememberin I ain't seen you up to the church neither. Let's see, you from around here? Seems like I know you."

"No. I originally come from St. Louis."

"St. Louis, huh." She popped her leathery-looking head around the corner like a turtle in order to get a better look at me. "I married me a man from down that way must be going on thirty years back. You familiar with some Huey's?" (Before I could say "no"), "Ornery nigger. Put his ornery butt out a here twenty-five years ago. A lazy dog. How you like my house, sugar? You don't see no dust, do you?"

"No, ma'am." But there was a dusty smell: like trunks of old books. The maple (or were they mahogany?) tables and chairs in the tiny sitting room and attached dining area were polished to a high luster. My fingers stroked velvety thistles and brambles that snaked upholstery on a comfortable couch and overstuffed chair. Heavy draperies drawn against the afternoon sun matched in a flowery blue. Doilies saddled the arms of the seating and strangled the tables like spider's webs, and the wide mantel of a little-used fireplace carried framed pictures—so many that, one face blended into another in nightmarish collage. "Everything is beautiful. You have a lovely home, ma'am."

"You don't see no dust, do you. You let me know if you do. I got me a girl comin in to help me out—this little yella gal what live next door. She as lazy as the day is long. You let me know if you see any dust and I'll take care of that heifer. And don't you be 'ma'amin' me You call me 'Miss Kezee' like other folks do. You got that, boy?"

"Yes . . ." It was getting late, and I had two yet to get to the polls. "Are you about ready, Miss Kezee?"

She emerged from the back of the house wearing a fire-red wig, pink knee socks and a faded dress with tiny roses on it. "You in a hurry, sugar? Miss Kezee don't need no rush. You like this wig? I got me two more, not countin my church wig." She was chewing; one rumpled cheek blown up like a rusty balloon.

"You look very nice."

"Let's go, then." I held the screen door while she locked a half dozen dead bolts. "Take Miss Kezee's arm while we walkin to the car, sugar."

"Afternoon, Miss Kezee," a round, dark woman fanning herself called from the porch next door. "How you feelin today?"

"Feelin just a little poorly today, May Ellen. Got a touch of this summer cold. You tell that Tonia she done a good job this week and I'll be payin her when my check come."

"Don't you worry bout that now. Looks like you got a new gentleman friend. Go on for yourself, girl."

She waved a hand at her. "I'm on my way to vote. Best be gettin your own self down there stead of messin in other folks business."

"All right, then, Miss Kezee. You all have a nice trip."

She sputtered to herself as I let her into the car. "Ignorant, big-ass, triflin gal. Bitch wouldn't vote if you paid her. All she got is baby on the brain. Done had a baby by every man in town—got five or six of em. Come in every color, they does."

"Now, you don't know that, Miss Ke . . . "

"She got one bout your color. Maybe that's where Miss Kezee seen you before, huh?" She laughed like a coughing fit. "What kind of car this be, sugar?"

"It's a Dodge Colt."

"Sure is uncomfortable. Make a left there."

"J. J. Hill is on Selby, Miss Kezee."

Her look said, "Is you crazy?" I made a left.

"Left again and go on down here a ways on Marshall towards Central." She hummed quietly to herself and did double-takes at everyone on the street. "Who that?" she'd mumble.

"Stop!" she hollered at the top of her antique lungs. "Pull it over right here, darling. How you roll this window down?"

I showed her. We were stopped in front of a ramshackle vegetable stand on a vacant lot. An old couple like crows guarded a table of halfhearted melons and pathetic tomatoes.

"Mattie! You got any kale today? Or spinach?"

"We bout out of everything today, Miss Kezee. Check back on Saturday."

"Uh huh." She waved and cranked the window arthritically. "Damn! Can't get nothing fresh. But, you like donuts, don't you, sugar? Make a right up here on Lexington."

"We should be gettin to the polls. We wouldn't want them to run out of ballots, would we?"

"Don't get an attitude, darlin. Miss Kezee don't vote without donuts. Another right up at University."

She hummed some more – noisy, tuneless songs – while I tried to figure out how to pay John back for this "little favor." She spit an oily wad into a napkin or rag she'd fished from my glove compartment.

"You keep your eyes open, sugar, and let me know if you see any hos out there on University so as Miss Kezee can give a little piece of her mind. Walkin the streets day and night like they owns it. And look up here. You see this dirty movie mess up here on the corner. That's the problem. They only put this here in the colored neighborhood. Can't even walk down here to the store no more."

"Don't get yourself too worked up now . . ."

"Lord, look who comin out of . . . Miss Henry's neph . . . Stop! . . . Roll this window down!"

"Miss Kezee, I'm driving!" She got it halfway down by herself as we cleared the intersection.

"Get your black ass away from that nasty stuff before I call your mama and . . ."

"Miss Kezee, please!"

"What you hollerin for? Donut place just up the next block." Miss Kezee's wig sat crooked on her head where she tried to force it out the car window. She bounced around like a sack of laundry as I turned into the steep and rutted parking lot.

"You come on in in case they try to get smart with Miss Kezee. You may have to knock some heads for her."

There were only three or four trays of donuts left from the morning rush. A pimply faced high school-aged white boy gave us a friendly can-I-help-you. She stared him down.

"What you got fresh back there?"

"All our donuts are made up fresh daily, ma'am."

She looked at me over her glasses with a see-what-I-mean look, pointing the fire-red wig in the clerk's direction.

"These here chocolate crullas fresh?"

"Yes, ma'am."

"Better be. Give me four. No ! Not that one. This one here with all the chocolate. How bout these long ones? They fresh?"

"Yes, ma'am. All our . . ."

"Better be. Give me four. Uh huh. You getting the idea now. Why ain't a child this age in school?"

"This is a work-study pro . . ."

"These chocolate cake fresh?"

"Yes, ma'am . . ."

"Better be. Give me four. That's an even dozen. You want anything, sugar? Pay up, then and let's get to votin. Miss Kezee don't have all day."

I was in shock; I glared at her.

"Go ahead! Pay him!"

Good thing I'd brought some extra cash. I paid and Miss Kezee snatched up her box of donuts, clutching them to her chest like her own newborn baby.

"Have a nice day," the clerk chirped.

"If these donuts is stale you go back in there and beat his ass, you hear." She whispered, I thought, loud enough for him to hear.

"Miss Kezee, I didn't expect to . . ."

"Used to be when you went in them places it was 'Auntie this' and 'What y'all want in here.' You know what I'm saying. I can't stand them."

I dropped it and drove toward the polling place.

"You want some of these donuts, sugar?" Miss Kezee stuffed herself with chocolate which smeared her face. She wiped her hands on my vinyl seats. "Bastard didn't put no napkins in this box. Have we got time to go back so you can rough him up?" She coughed her laugh again.

"No, ma . . ." I caught myself just in time, and laughed with her. "I think I will have one of those." They were already half gone.

"Who we voting for today, baby?"

"This is the primary election for the general elections in the fall."

"You must think I'm crazy or something. I asked: who are we voting for today? We!"

(Oh, that we.)

"Don't know that there's a recommended candidate as such. None of them seem like they're interested in our issues much."

"Haven't been a good one since Mr. Humphreys—H.H.H.! At least it seems that way to me. Voted for him for years. Is you married . . . how old is you, twenty-five, thirty?"

"Twenty-eight, and no."

"Why not? Can't find you one? I got a few little gals up to the church be interested in making a home with you." A damp, sincere hand gripped my arm.

"No, thank you anyway, Miss Kezee." (I'd met John's parade of future homemakers on more than one occasion.) Miss Kezee hummed to herself and looked at the neighborhood.

"Things be changing fast. New houses. New people. Seems like I don't hardly recognize it no more. Sad." She nodded off to sleep.

"Miss Kezee, time to go in and vote." I shook her arm. This time her wig had slipped forward on her head. A drizzle of drool interrupted the chocolate beard she'd smeared on her chin.

"Just a second, sugar." She wiped with a perfumy handkerchief. "Do I look okay, baby? Might be some eligible mens in here of a certain age, if you know what I mean."

"You look fine. I'm eligible, aren't I?"

"What I want with a man with a cheap ass car like this here? Open the door for Miss Kezee and help her in."

"Good afternoon and who have we here?"

We have an old black woman who will cuss your condescending white self out if you keep it up, I thought to myself. Miss Kezee was unusually quiet. Leaning weight like a sack of potatoes on my arm, she didn't answer.

"This is Miss Xenobia Kezee, here to vote," I said. Miss Kezee looked down from my arm to her shoes and back.

"Honey, is this your usual polling place?" The worker shouted as if to a small child. No answer from Miss Kezee. "Your granny's hard of hearing, huh? Is this where she votes normally, or is this her first time?"

"Miss Kezee has voted in every election for over fifty years."

"Oh yes, here we have her . . . on Dayton? Do you know . . . does she know how to use the booths?"

Since before you were born, I answered in my head. "She'll be fine," I said instead. I walked Miss Kezee to the booth.

"How we doin, sugar?" she whispered.

"You can't go in there with her." Miss Loud-Mouth masked her contempt with saccharine. I waved my hand at her in disgust. From within the booth I heard cursing and hurrumping: damn crooks—fools—cheats. Miss Kezee ambled out all weak and lost. I grabbed her arm and headed for the exit.

"See you in November, granny. You tell your granny I'll see her in November, okay?"

"Fuck you, too." I half-said over my shoulder.

Miss Kezee brightened up and lightened up considerably by the time I'd closed the car door.

"Sugar, Miss Kezee don't approve of no swearing. I'm a church going woman. Besides, ain't much good in saying what can't be heard, what with that meek whispering you does." Once again her dry hack.

"You were awfully quiet in there, Miss Kezee."

"Gotta give folks what they spect, baby."

"It's the nineteen-eighties, Miss Kezee. Nobody expects anything. Things have changed."

"Have they, sugar?" she snapped, and silently eyed me the two blocks back to her house where, in her parlour, she seemed remote—out of range.

"You sit a spell. I be right back." Moments later she returned wigless and wilted.

"You still here?" and then immediately, "I kindly thank you for all your trouble today, Mr. Johnson. I can't offer you no money."

"I wouldn't think of taking it. I enjoyed myself. Guess I should get my other two now."

"I won't be keeping you." She opened the door. "Thank you again." She gripped my arm.

I squeezed the wrinkled hand. "Goodbye, now, and take care."

"Sugar, I was one of the first, you know." And she closed and locked the door behind me.

I looked at my next address: two blocks away. Spying a chocolate stained seat, I wiped it off with a forgotten, perfumy handkerchief.

"Bus Is Coming!"

Nona Caspers

"Bus is coming! Bus is coming!" Philip warned from his watch at the far window. He took his jobs seriously even then.

I was in the first grade, responsible for dressing myself. So were Debra, Steven, and Julee. Except for Philip, the four younger children floated about the house, not yet equipped or required to deal with this September-to-May, Monday-through-Friday morning self-regimentation. Our mother, Mom was her name, slept in late, appearing only to point or grunt at misplaced shoes or books. We knew she was tired from her late-night reading about Anne Boleyn, Jane Seymour, or one of Henry's other trial and error wives. Being a devout German Catholic and productive of numerous heirs herself seemed to feed her fascination for these women's lives. Or perhaps she felt a metaphorical bond to their deaths? "Off with her head!" must have felt familiar.

She often told us how much she enjoyed school. (The thrill of learning, like drinking cherry Kool-Aid made with three cups of sugar, not two.) And how she pleaded with Grandpa to let her attend high school. But Grandma had just hemorrhaged to death birthing their tenth, and there was the farm to run. Still, Grandpa might have conceded if every man including the lumberman hadn't had to get in on it. He informed Grandpa that it would cost him at least a thousand dollars to send a girl to high school (and what would he get back?)— "You let a girl go on to school and you gotta buy them clothes!"

"Oh, I was so mad at that guy!" Mom would say. "Telling Dad that. It was none of his business. Sure, he had to spend all that on his girls, he had to have all the fancy clothes for his girls. I didn't care about the fashions. I didn't need all that. I could have sewed my own clothes . . . "

She has stayed up late reading ever since. This was okay with us, except for the underwear drawer.

"Bus at Messeriches!" Philip proclaimed.

All the t-shirts and panties that my sisters outgrew—frayed straps and bows, ripped elastic, yellowed crotches—got stuffed into the bottom drawer. My drawer. The only drawer I could pull out and push in by myself. The drawer Mom lined with orange-and-yellow contact paper. The drawer where I kept the magical agates Mary Jo and I found in our driveways. If we pressed an agate against our foreheads we would get a wish, as long as it didn't hurt anybody.

We wished for one of those harmless rock polishers from the J. C. Penney Christmas catalog. When this didn't work we both asked for one from Santa, along with a Barbie doll whose hair grew. The Barbies came, the harmless rock polishers didn't. (Off with their heads!)

This was also the drawer where I kept the black lace mantillas, earnestly folded into quarter circles, tucked under *My First Holy Communion* book. Signed by Sister Hyacinth.

The book had a shining white cover and the first picture was of a kind, pale Jesus walking with a pale boy at his right-hand side wearing blue trousers and a blue shirt. At his left side, looking up at him with dogged love, stood a pale girl wearing a pink dress and headband over her white hair. She looked like me, only cleaner and neater. No hair in her face.

My favorite prayer I had learned by heart was:

Prayer for Help

Holy Mary, my dearest Mother,
help me to be ready for
(here it read "communion," but I ad-libbed
according to the situation)
Give me some of Your great
faith,
hope,
and love.
Help me to be very, very
(very, very, very)
sorry for all my sins.
Good Saint Joseph

be with me
and help me
to make my heart beautiful
for Jesus, My King, I love you.
Come into my heart!
(Oh come, Sweet Jesus, come!)

"Bus at Spelderbergs!"

My older sisters had gotten to wear the black lace mantillas to church every Sunday. Mom said, "God wanted girls to cover their hair with a little something back then." She didn't know why HE changed HIS mind. Still, she let me wear them once in a while, special days, pinned to the top of my white head with her black bobby pins. Always a bit crooked as I genuflected with a straight back. Black lace I wore like angel's armor.

I could never open that drawer without slipping back to that "Bonanza" show where Little Joe almost fell in love with the Spanish woman who always wore black lace veils. I watched him kiss her cheek from under the yellow-cushioned coffee table. But before he could kiss her on the mouth, sealing their hearts forever, Pa and Hoss caught her father rustling cattle and she had to return to Spain in shame, or something.

As my tears dripped into my cup, salting the milk I had been sucking through licorice tubes, I asked the mantilla God why. If she had burnt up or been shot like the others, dying in Little Joe's arms, I could have accepted the pain like he did. His eyes glistened, he blinked a lot and his cheeks puffed like a frog; but he accepted the will of God, while I ran into the bathroom and knelt over the toilet, praying, "Help me to be ready for . . . "

"Bus at Olberdings!"

The bedroom door flew open. Julee glared at me, sitting in the middle of the floor circled by rocks with nothing on but a piece of black lace drooping halfway down my face. She reached in the closet, yanked out a yellow rectangle and a white square, threw them on the closest bed, and walked out.

At this point, or one like it, I would hurry my sturdy body into the always matching outfit, twisting my arms behind me to partially close the zipper or buttons or snaps. Then I would remind myself that if I didn't go to school, if I missed the bus, I would also miss Noon Recess! The swings.

"Bus is going to Meyers!"

Saint Mary's had the best swing set. Tall silver poles that never jumped. Wide flat wooden seats that never buckled. Thick silver chains that never bit into my palms. Every school day for three years I faced the door, five minutes to noon, ready to run. Sometimes Sister Madeliva would send me to the bathroom just before the bell rang. She and Mom were convinced I had a bladder problem.

I'd drip a little for them, but when that shrilling beat pealed up my spine I bolted up and out, forgetting to wash my hands. Tammy Remes and I made a pact one year: whoever got to the swings first would save the other their favorite. I got the middle, Tammy the left, and the right went to our newest girlfriend. We knew Eddy Blenker wanted to join us. But swinging was ours!

"BUS AT MEYERS BUS AT MEYERS BUS AT MEYERS . . . "

Standing on a swing rushing toward the sky I felt like one of those giant red-wood trees that people drove their cars through. Falling down and back I'd watch all the kids, nuns, and buildings swoosh into nothing but colors and shapes. I'd bring up sound from way inside, nonwords that bellowed out of my mouth as I gripped the chains, pumping higher and higher, my little-girl legs straining and heaving . . .

"Bus is here! Bus is here!" Philip screamed, running through the halls and down the stairs.

I was lying on my back across the bed, flying off my swing at the highest point, underwearless. Chest forward, arms straight at my side. Flying. Not like an angel but a bullet. Not toward the outdoor sky but the one painted on the dome ceiling of our church, with its cross-shaped stars and winged white babies. I'd burst through the dirty blue into another world. Not like heaven but a whole new place. Where kids who didn't want to go to school didn't have to, and where mothers who wanted to, could.

"BusiscomingBusiscomingBusiscomingBusiscomingBusiscomingBusiscoming!"

Horse Story

Cheryl Loesch

FOR HIS SEVENTH BIRTHDAY, Phillip asked for a horse. It was the same every Christmas and every birthday. He made a list of the three things he wanted most. Behind the number one was printed in large block letters: HORSE. Number two and three were always things he knew he would get, like cowboy boots or toy trucks. He knew he would never get the horse.

His mother and father shook their heads, wondering what to do with their horse-crazy son. Horse-crazy boys didn't worry about the details like where the horse was going to stay or what it would eat. Horse-crazy boys just dreamed about tall pintos that were better pals than dogs when the day's work was done. Not that Scruffy wasn't a good dog. She just wasn't a horse. Scruffy was number two on last year's Christmas list.

"Number One" charged through his dreams at night, sliding to a stop in a cloud of dust. Sometimes it was a black stallion, other times red or spotted. He always whinnied a welcome to Phillip, nodding at him to come and ride. Phillip would mount his bare smooth back and they would take off, faster than anything, through the mist. The horse would never let anyone but Phillip touch him; he bared his teeth and screamed if someone even looked his way. Phillip could talk to the horse and understand what the horse said back. The horse could follow any cow Phillip pointed out to him and cut that animal out of the herd. He was the best friend and cowpony a boy ever had. Not only that, but this horse, black, red, or spotted, was beautiful. He was big, long-legged and round-chested. His mane and tail were long and silky, as soft and silky, almost, as his shiny hide. He followed Phillip's voice with his small pointed ears. A little Arabian blood was plain in his face, which was as perfect as the horse in the magazine photo on his wall.

Pretending during the day was better than the dreams he had at night. Phillip would run sideways in a galloping motion around the fenced-in backyard, riding his horse. His hands gripped the reins as he flew along on his steed, one of a whole herd he kept back there. He saw the yard as a grassy plain; his mind magnified it to a hundred times the size of a small suburban plot. As he reached each fenced corner, he turned his stallion sharply. He could hear the hoofs plopping rhythmically, the slap and squeak of the leather saddle, the blowing sound his horse made. He could almost smell the pungent odor of horse sweat. He clicked his tongue to the horse and pulled him up short.

"REEEE-hee-hee-hee," he screamed and tossed back his hair, "REEE-hee-hee-hee." He lifted his leg over the imaginary horse's back, dismounting, and gave the beast a gentle pat on the rump.

"Nah-ha-ha. Her-her-her," he whinnied softly now. He walked the horse around to cool him off, his hand placed correctly under its chin. Scruffy thumped her tail on the ground each time he circled past her. Phillip sighed and turned the horse among his herd.

"Good horse," he mumbled.

In his room, he picked up his favorite book of horse stories. All he had to read were the titles. He knew the rest by heart. In the stories, girls tamed wild horses, horses were found by long lost owners, horses were saved from the dog-meat factory, and boys got horses for Christmas. Phillip put the book down and got out a piece of paper. He wrote the number one. HORSE, he spelled out in big block letters, and threw back his head.

"REEEE-hee-hee-hee!"

By the time he was thirteen, Phillip stopped expecting to be surprised like the boys in the stories with a horse for Christmas. He still made the list with HORSE at the top, just in case. He dreamed of a foal, a colt. It was sensuous, with a gleaming hide and long knobby-kneed legs. The colt's wide surprised eyes were full of mystery. His colt had a language all his own which Phillip vowed to learn as they grew together. He would train his colt slowly, gently, and when he finally rode on its back, it would seem as if the two were one. He walked around in his cowboy boots, and when no one was around, he would neigh softly. Phillip still rode his horses, but he never ran sideways or let his friends know that his hands were cupped around imaginary reins.

For his next birthday, Phillip listed a lasso as number two. "A real one," he told his baffled parents, "not just any rope." When he got the short slippery leather rope, he went out in the backyard with his friends to practice. They roped each other and they roped Scruffy until they decided that she really didn't like being hog-tied. Phillip took his turn with the rope. He lunged forward and snared his bull on the run. Stopping short, he backed up like a good cowpony would.

"Phillip!" His mother screamed from the kitchen window, "Get away from my peonies."

Phillip was so surprised that he jerked on the lasso and off popped the huge pink ball of a peony.

"Wal," he drawled to his friend, "Thar goes th' bull. Pulled 'is head clean off."

As he went through high school, Phillip didn't seem to dream as much about his own horse. His habit of wearing cowboy boots and chewing thoughtfully on a toothpick earned him the nickname of "Tex." The edges of his notebooks were filled with crude drawings of horses; horses galloping, horses trotting, horses eating, horses bucking. As a matter of tradition, he still put HORSE at the top of each birthday and Christmas list. Number two was always in the box he un-wrapped on those holidays, and he was always happy with that gift. He knew he would never get the colt.

By his senior year, Phillip had hung his lasso and spurs on his bedroom wall, but he still wore only cowboy boots. The only time he took them off was to lace on his football cleats. It pleased him to charge across the field cradling the ball. He would throw his head back and gallop wildly toward his goal. His eyes shone when he played, and if he was tackled, he came out from under the pile snorting, ready to run again. After games and practices, Phillip had a habit of cooling down by walking around the field. When his teammates teased his about it in the locker room, he just smiled good-naturedly and pulled on his boots.

In the last game of the year, Phillip ran joyfully with the ball. It was the last few seconds of play and this touchdown would count for the win. His legs stretched, nostrils flared, Phillip ran for all he was worth. He ran past the cheerleaders, suddenly checked his stride, then sped on. He didn't hear the screams of the crowd and of his teammates. His eyes were full of wonder as he felt himself float over the ground, far enough to score the winning points. He was swept away by his teammates, but he didn't hear their congratulations. His eyes were still full of the cheerleader who had almost stopped him from scoring the points. He saw her shining hair, her long sensuous legs. He had looked right into her wide surprised eyes so full of mystery. How could he talk to her? He had to talk to her.

Phillip went back to the field to have his cooling down walk There she was, in her short pleated skirt and cheerleader's sweater. He stopped. He didn't know what to say. She was real. She looked at him and smiled. Softly, hesitantly, he spoke to her, as if he were gentling a frightened horse. "Would you like to walk around the field with me?" She look startled, then nodded. Phillip felt his lungs swell; he tossed his hair and almost burst out with a neigh.

He made a list for his eighteenth birthday. HORSE, he wrote. Then he crossed it out.

The Lion. The Eagle. The Wolf.

George Rabasa

A T NIGHT, something comes between Claire and me. It's not Claire and it's not me. It is a third thing. It's not a thing you can see. I have never seen it. I have felt it. It always feels different. Claire has dreamt it. The dream of this thing is Claire's only awareness of it. She think that's all it is. This rift. A dream.

We've been married six years. In that time, some habits have become important to us. In summer we rise early and have coffee together. We share a cantaloupe and sit on the sun porch, enjoying the cool of the morning, the sunlight that comes streaming in through the tender new leaves of the poplar. The melon is almost too ripe, a musky fragrance fills the still air as Claire splits it in half.

"This is it," I declare, spooning out a morsel of its coral flesh. "The melon's apogee."

"Today was definitely its day." She agrees with me on many such things. "The peak of its melonness."

We know a thing or two, Claire and I, about melons and other matters. When we go to Lunds, people watch us go through the ritual of looking for the right melon. Claire searches through the bin, and lifts the most promising one in her small hands. She feels its heft, turns it every which way, caresses its texture, her fingers running lightly along the rind, stopping at a slight ridge here, an unexpected protuberance there, a telltale softening at the poles. Then she'll hand it to me to smell.

It can take several minutes to find a good melon, and all the time someone has been watching, following our selection process. People often ask us just what is it that we look for, to find the one perfect melon in the store. It's hard to tell, Claire says. It's many things. It's intuition.

They say thank you very much, and push on before we can tell them everything. As they go, they'll reach into the melon bin and grab the one closest at hand. That's one way to buy melons. But not the best. Nobody is lucky every time.

By eight-thirty we've had our breakfast—fruit, coffee from Chiapas that I grind myself in a dandy little mill made by the famous German armaments manufacturer, and sometimes cinnamon toast. We've listened to some Albinoni and skimmed the Trib. We've put on our blue suits with the white shirts and silk flourish of a tie. We look very much alike, Claire and I, dark blue and radiant on our way to work. She takes the Honda and I the Volvo. In the matter of automobiles, as in melons, we choose carefully.

"Wait." She stops me as I'm about to back down the driveway. "I had a strange dream last night."

I know I'm going to be late. "What was it?"

"All I remember is being lost in some ghettoish sort of place. And all the time I was being watched by people hidden behind broken windows, in doorways, inside parked cars with tinted glass."

"Interesting."

"It was frightening, actually."

Well, there's not much I can say in response to a dream, except that it is interesting, sometimes. "Anything else happen?"

"No."

"See you tonight." Our lips brush in a quick kiss. I back up into the street and head west, Claire follows down the drive and turns east.

That evening we meet after work and have dinner at Faegre's, a very nice place. The poached salmon for me, pasta for Claire. The service is good. The wine is good. Dessert is good. But we don't enjoy anything much. A day's labor leaves us both exhausted and smelling of other people's cigarettes.

After dinner, Claire takes the Volvo and I the Honda, and we race each other home. That part is fun. I go about forty-five, run every stop sign and one red light. I win. Claire takes a short cut but still comes in about a minute later. Winner gets to take the Volvo to work the next day.

It feels good to throw off my clothes and lie on the bed feeling the breeze from the fan travel gently up and down my skin. Claire sits on a chair. She shakes her hair loose and begins to brush it. We haven't said much to each other since dinner. I fall asleep long before she's through brushing. We're always closer in the mornings.

Around two I wake up thinking it's light out already. Nights have become turbulent times for me. I get up two or three times to piss, sit up and read, check the clock, turn the light back off. Claire beside me sleeps like a stone, her face in repose seems devoid of life and wit.

I kiss her dry, warm forehead and marvel at the unfamiliar touch of her skin. Do we become someone else when we sleep? Wide awake now, I lie on my back and stare up into the black starless void of the ceiling. I take a deep breath and marvel at how cold and thin the air feels. Beyond the ceiling, in all that vast region stretching about my house, I am the only living, thinking, breathing thing around. I float. Ah, how I float! Effortlessly rising from the bed, I'm lifted skyward, soaring up into the night, hurling into the chill heart of the universe, through the silent beats and rhythms of a language so abstract it is beyond song and meaning. Still, I know, somehow, that to a rare few this vacuum would make sense, its silence pregnant with revelation, every turn and every gust of dry wind a mathematical certainly. Ah, order! I know that even this arbitrary plunge from the comfort of bed and wife is steered with a sense of balance and purpose. There is nothing random about it—not in the sway and pitch of my body as it hurls into space, not in the unseen symmetry of the void or in the heady ether that I breathe. But even as I leap and soar and fall through space I feel I must eventually regain control. Surely an adjustment here and there to the tilt of my body, a correction to the angle of my arms, will allow me to manipulate the fates. Although I must admit that all the time a voice in my head says no, that all is flight, that there is no place to fall, that I must truly let go. Unfortunately, I'm just not the sort of person that pays attention to little voices.

I wake up a few minutes before the alarm goes off at six. Then, lying heavily on the rumpled bed, I open my eyes to the sight of so many good, familiar things. Ah, the lamp, the door, the window, the chair, the clock, the book, the plant, the shoe, the woman. I cry out with joy.

"What is the matter?" Clair wakes up suddenly.

"Nothing, I'm fine," I add after a moment. "Relieved, actually. For a while there I couldn't tell where I was."

"Yes," she agrees sleepily. "Like waking up in some Holiday Inn and not knowing where anything is."

It was not like that at all.

"When we first moved into this house," she continues, "I expected the bathroom to be on the right side, like in our first apartment."

"Actually," I began with something of an effort, "It was different from the feeling of waking up in a hotel room. I was lost."

Claire is quiet, feeling, I'm sure, somehow rebuffed. Yet I needed to set the record straight. Waking up in a Holiday Inn room is not in the same league as returning from a trip to the center of the universe.

"Was it a dream?" She tries again, seriously, to understand.

"No. Not a dream."

"I had a dream," she says.

I feign interest. "What about?"

"I was watching a bird. It was flying around in circles, making wide soaring turns, not going anywhere, just flying."

"What else?"

"Nothing else."

This morning we wear gray. Our shirts are pale blue, our ties liquid swirls of azure and silver. We eat kiwis, spooning out the tender green pulp right out of the shells; we drink Earl Grey; we nibble on toast. Today we both want to be quick and lean and hungry out there. It's a Big Day for both of us. I don't particularly like Big Days. The effort of dealing with a new face, of trying to accomplish Something Meaningful, of arguing one's case before a group are all disturbing breaks from the comfortable monotony of my average business day. Claire loves a Big Day now and then. Her week is not complete without at least one confrontation, a test of wills and intellect that fires her up like a handful of diet pills. But then she is climbing up the ladder, whereas I'm already pretty well ensconced on one of the upper rungs.

After work we meet at the health club. We are silent, determined. We move among high tech riddles of weights, sprockets, and cams, from one contrivance to the next, pushing ourselves at every turn, facing up to our frailties, thigh flab and stomach bulge, to humiliating muscle failure after a mere dozen repetitions. I feel drained. Claire looks radiant. A surge of blood flooding every vein and capillary brings a glow to her skin. I like the way she looks afterwards, clean wet hair hanging limp down the sides of her face, cosmetics washed off so that her eyes look out clearly, her lips plain like a child's. Lips that cannot lie. Eyes as clear as hers can only look upon that which is good.

Sometimes, when Claire thinks I'm asleep, she leans over and looks at me. I wonder what she thinks. But since she believes I'm asleep, I don't ask. I simply lie on my back, imagining the shape of Claire's face imprinted on the back of my eyelids.

The eyes that stare at me on this particular night are not Claire's. She is asleep on her stomach, her face turned away from me, her breathing long and rhythmical. There's no shaking this observer that from the far corner of the bedroom watches every move I make, every tremor, every breath. Nothing is lost on this unseen seer. I blink my eyes quickly. I stretch out my hand. I reach for the clock beside me to look at the time. Everything is observed, no detail is so insignificant that it goes unnoticed. I swallow, blink, reach, wriggle, breathe, shudder, itch, scratch, sleep.

The next morning, Claire and I go to the French Bakery for breakfast. We each have a croissant that is in itself, even before tasting, impossibly beautiful. Its golden crust is folded over just right; breaking it apart to smear butter and jam on it seems devastating.

"I'm just going to look at mine," she says, gazing down at the roll before her.

I nod my head, and continue devouring my now demolished croissant. It's very good. I glance up and see that Claire has finally surrendered and is peeling off each buttery flake at a time, placing them on her tongue like sacred wafers.

"Eat slowly," she admonishes.

I nod. I lick the jam off my fingers and feel like a barbarian.

"Did you have trouble sleeping last night?" she asks.

"I was awake for quite a while. But I wasn't particularly restless."

"Do you have a Big Day today?"

"Just medium."

"Me too." Then she adds slowly, as if feeling around her head for the right words. "I dreamt that you were awake all night long. That you just sat up on the bed and stared at me, and that I couldn't move or talk or forget that you were just sitting there watching me with this suspicious look on your face."

I don't know how to tell her that she has her lookers and lookees, her subjects and objects all mixed up. "Are you sure it was me in the dream?"

"Definitely."

All that day at work I'm constantly aware of who is looking at whom and who knows he or she is being looked at and who doesn't know they are looking at someone who knows they are being looked at or does not know for a while, then turns, suddenly aware of being looked at. We sit around a long rectangular table for a Big Meeting on budgets. There are a dozen of us in our blue and gray suits with one guy in brown at the end of the table. Most of us take a moment to look at the brown suit. It's not a hostile or censuring stare. It's just that, being the only brown suit in the room, it draws attention from the blue and gray suits. I don't suppose Brown Suit knew about this meeting beforehand. I mean, you don't ordinarily wander in wearing a brown suit when everyone else, including the top powers of the meeting, is in blue. If you do, you're going to get looked at. Until the novelty wears off.

In the afternoon Claire calls about weekend plans with friends, about a ping deep inside the Honda, about picking up wine on the way home, about donating money to the Orchestra, and about seeing a therapist.

There. The truth is out. Something has gone awry.

"I didn't realize anything was wrong," I say searchingly.

"I didn't say anything was wrong," she's quick to defend.

"Then why the shrink?"

"I guess I just felt I could be happier. And if I'm not absolutely, perfectly happy, considering I've got everything, you know, the good job, the house, money, friends, clothes, health and all that, then something must be missing."

I notice she does not mention me, the good husband.

"Your mother says you need a baby."

"Like hell."

Claire has dinner with a friend. Just like that. No other explanation. I bring home Chinese food and settle in for *What's Up, Doc* on cable. It's not all that great a movie—I've seen it three times—but it has one of my favorite sequences. It was done over and over in the old silent movie days, but it always works for me. Two men unload a pane of plate glass from a van and try to cross a busy street. To make things more difficult, there's a car chase going on. The guys with the glass pane seesaw from side to side trying to stay clear. It's all hopeless. It's wonderful.

I eat my way through six little cartons of Chinese Combo #7, and finally crack open the fortune cookie. I love their messsages. The one I get tonight says, "The unexamined life is not worth living." Sounds like Confucius all right.

I expect Claire to be home from her friend's before the movie ends. I've seen my favorite part; it's all downhill from here. At ten till eleven I call her friend. There's no answer. At eleven I go to bed. I tell myself I'm not worried or angry or hurt, and fall asleep right away. I wake up after an hour and feel the other side of the bed for Claire. I don't find her. I go back to sleep.

I wake up again some time later. This time I realize I'm not alone in the bed. But I'm unhappy about Claire having stayed out so late without calling, so I resist my first impulse to reach out for her. Instead I lie flat on my back, quite still, just like other nights when I've found myself thinking too much about unpleasant things, wishing I were somewhere else. I am not, however, an insomniac. When I'm awake I don't particularly wish I were alseep, or feel I should make some effort to pass out. Asleep is fine. Dreaming is fine. REM is fine. Theta is fine. Delta is fine. And awake is fine.

But tonight with every one of Claire's deep breaths, a pungent smell hangs in the room's still air. Relentlessly, it drives me to curl up and cling to the far edge of the bed, my face buried in the pillow. There's no escape. Gentle Claire exhales a storm of improbable smells. The cauldron of hell. The carnage of war. Hitler's flatulence.

Even after I think I've drifted off to sleep, the smells rise like plumes hovering faintly at the edges of my consciousness. Am I being to sensitive?

The next morning I find that Claire's side of the bed hasn't been slept on at all. I pad around the empty house. The Honda is gone from the garage. Coffee hasn't been made. There's no note by the phone. As I look for Claire, I realize I'm really searching for some remnant of the night's terrible smells. I point my nose all around the bedroom, inside the closet, down the stairs, in the guest bathroom with the bad plumbing, the disposal, the fridge, the garbage under the sink, in all the ghettos and mouse-corners of our more or less modernized, neo-Victorian home.

In my search I open one of Claire's dresser drawers. I bury my face in a bouquet of lace and silk and inhale deeply of her scent. Clearly, what happened in the night was a bad dream. And that I would dream this thing about Claire surprises me. Claire is good and clean and sweet. Her smells are lavender, spice, mint, myrrh, sandalwood, chocolate.

I have coffee alone. I stare at the phone. I leave for work in the Volvo. As I drive past her friend's house, I notice the Honda is nowhere in sight. When I get to my office, I dial Claire's work number.

"I'm not coming home for a while," she says, jumping right into the controversial part of the conversation. "I'll stay with Ellen for a few days. I've made an appointment with a therapist. I'll come by the house later for a change of clothes."

"Let's talk about this over lunch," I suggest calmly.

I suffer through the rest of the morning—a tightness in my chest like a clenched fist, a shortness of breath, a ringing in my ears. Marital strife is tearing hell with my blood pressure.

We meet at the Loring. A thin waiter with a terrible haircut shows us to a small table with three place settings. "Three for lunch today?"

"No, just two of us."

The waiter takes our order for paté, salad, Camembert and toast. But he leaves the third place setting, even after I motion for him to remove it. I can sense some third blind presence rising between Claire and me, making our conversation awkward and self-conscious.

She begins, "About last night . . ."

"No explanations necessary," I say magnanimously, "I did worry about you, but now that I see you're all right, well then everything's fine."

"It got late. I fell asleep on Ellen's couch."

"I understand."

"I had an awful dream," she continues hesitantly. "That you found me repulsive. And then I woke up and knew that is wasn't just a dream. That you actually hate me."

That evening when I get home, I find that Claire has been there and taken most of her clothes. There is a new sense of spaciousness everywhere. The bathroom is no longer cluttered with tubes and brushes and plastic bottles, gone are her combs and blowdryer, her diaphragm and contraceptive creams (the significance of this is not lost on me, though I give it no more than a moment's anguished thought), hair curlers, dental floss, tooth brushes, vitamins C, B complex, calcium and iron. They're all gone. As are more than half the clothes in the closet we share and several books from the headboard bookcase. I feel numb.

I dial Ellen's number. "This is so stupid," I say when Claire finally gets on the line. "You said you wanted to get away for a couple of days. You took enough clothes for a year."

"Are you angry?"

"No. Of course not."

"I'm doing what I have to do," she says. "You don't have to get angry about it." I slam the phone.

To tell the truth, I can't remember the last time I felt true, explosive, righteous anger. I never get angry at the office. I would be unprofessional. I don't get angry at waiters, or dumb drivers, at the weather, or the time of day. I don't get angry at the Volvo or the Honda, or at bicycles with flats or the toaster that burns my toast. I don't even get angry at Reagan or Khomeini.

But I am terribly angry at Claire. In fact, while I eat my dinner of Fish Florentine by Stouffer's Lean Cuisine and drink a bottle of a very ordinary white, I feel certain that I'm going to be angry at Claire for the rest of my life. If I live to be a hundred and eight, I will still be angry at her with the same unflagging outrage I feel tonight.

I revel in my anger. I find myself retreating to an earlier, simpler time when emotions were allowed to spill out unbridled. To a childhood filled with primitive hate and elementary justice. Hating Claire seems ennobling. A clean break from the convention that inhibits passion and rage and ecstasy. I feel that too long I've been in a world of emotional cripples. A place where lust, greed, vanity and ambition are all right. But where love, hate, anger, curiosity, awe, and joy are not.

By ten I've finished over half the bottle of wine. I put the cork back in and run out of the house to the Volvo. I back up with a squeal into the street, gun the engine down the familiar neighborhood to the house where my wife is sleeping. There are no lights in the windows, not a sound in the street. From the sidewalk I call out, "Claire! I know you're in there. Come out and fight like a woman."

There's no response. I tip the bottle to my mouth and drink the wine in big gulps.

"Claire! You coward, you deserter, you traitor."

I hear a door opening from a neighboring house, a couple of windows light up across the street. I step up onto the porch and try the door. It's locked. I ring the bell, wait for a moment, and then knock loudly with the flat of my hand. I pound again, and step back.

"Come on out, Claire, or I swear I'm coming in for you."

I feel wonderful. Threats and accusations emerge from my chest with all the power and drama of grand opera. As my shouts echo through the sleeping neighborhood, I have visions, in stark, primary hues, of me kicking down the door, marching into the house, and confronting Claire. With both hands I clasp the door handle and strain to shake it open.

I feel suddenly faint as wave upon wave of anger and nausea wash over me dragging an eerie flotsam of ancient, ancestral memories. I am early man. I am the ocean's first burst of life. I am lion. I am eagle. I am wolf. I pace the whole length of the porch, stopping every time I pass the door to give it a kick or strike it with my fist.

Suddenly, I stop and find myself standing silently in front of the door. I take a couple of steps back. Calmly I unzip my fly, take out my penis, and unleash a long, gleaming stream of urine at the closed door. The piss arches smoothly from my center, from the very depths of my being, across the width of the porch, landing smack in the middle of the door and trickling down in yellow rivulets.

Swinging from side to side I draw circles and figure eights and the letter G along the floors and walls.

My bladder empty at last, I zip up and retreat slowly to the street beside the house. Lights go on in the upper story, then downstairs, and Claire appears finally. She stands in the door frame, the light behind her outlining her like a halo, a wondrous vision in a flowing nightgown that shimmers with lace and silk, her lustrous brown hair loose to her shoulders, her small feet naked. She squints trying to make me out as I scurry in the dark, from tree to bush to fence, as stealthy as a cat.

"Go home," she calls out softly. "We can talk about all this tomorrow."

"First thing!" I say from behind the tree.

"Yes. But go home, please. One of the neighbors saw you and is calling the police."

She stands before the lighted entrance for a moment, as if to make sure I'm really going, then shutting the door softly, steps back inside the house. I hear the bolt turn and lock with a forbidding snap. But the image of her, glowing and pure, remains.

I stay behind the tree until morning.

Some time in the course of the night, my anger finally leaves me. It seeps out through my pores like some poison that has at last sweated out. I feel elated, purged, cleansed. I nearly drown in sweet waves of tenderness.

White-Out

Mary Kay Rummel

I N T H E D O R M I'm not supposed to talk; I already know that. The beds are separated by white curtains and we are separated by silence until I feel I will float away in white. I remember how we drove in silence, the back seat of the Chevrolet sagging beneath the black trunk I bought at the Goodwill for five dollars. I had lined it and painted it black. It was filled with neat piles of t-shirts and cotton underpants, black stockings and two pairs of black oxfords and long black slips made by my grandmother. My mother's fingers twisted in and out like my hair being braided. My father's face as he drove was locked beneath a frown. I had stayed home the night before to be with my family for the last time and they left me alone while they went grocery shopping. "Don't they realize I'm leaving tomorrow for life?" I thought as I walked to a friend's house. In the car they had to face it. I was leaving and they didn't like it. But I wanted it. Urgently. I walked in the wide convent door and my life changed. I was gone from home and I wanted that.

We were met by a skinny pale nun with large glasses who nervously whisked me off to a dorm to help me change clothes. I slipped out of the red cotton dress with a wide cummerbund. It was my favorite summer dress and I knew I would keep it in my trunk in case I went home again. I slipped out of the nylons which I had just begun to wear instead of bobby sox and left my black pumps on the floor. It was taking off my bra that bothered me the most. I was to wear an undershirt just like my brothers. I hadn't planned on that. I wanted to skip it but the supervising nun left me no choice. Over the undershirt went a black blouse, then a short cape fastened by a white collar. I put on a black skirt, long stockings, shoes and then over my hair a short black veil. This was the postulant's uniform. This I would wear for six months until I became a sister. And I wanted that. To be a sister. I had been thinking about this day for years. I knew I would be holy.

A stranger in black, I returned to my parents. They sat beneath an oak tree in the large yard behind the provincial house. When I walked up to them I was a sponge absorbing the dull pain in their faces. To escape I began looking for my high school friends.

Sara, whom I had just seen the night before looked the part even before she came with black eyes that often wandered upward and heavy black hair that had hung like a veil since second grade. Our long relationship began back then. Her mother knelt for long hours in front of the Virgin's statue, a black veil over her bobbing head. I could never understand why my mother gave me subtle messages about not playing with her when she had such a holy mother, but my mother only liked Irish and only certain kinds of Irish. Many of her own relatives were exempt from her approval. In second grade, Sara and I fought over the same boy. One day we were caught sending notes to Dennis signing each other's name. I wrote I HATE YOU and signed her name. She wrote I HATE YOU and signed mine. She was more intense than I, but I competed. In fifth grade it was for the holiest. She came back from the church that stood guard over our playground and said the Blessed Virgin's statue had smiled at her. I ran right over during recess and knelt for so long straining and begging for a smile. I squinted my eyes to possibly create one but that statue wouldn't crack. "Why her?" I thought.

When we had substitutes and passed notes, Sara stood up and lectured us. In eighth grade Sister Alma told the boys to vote for the girl most like the Blessed Virgin. She would be the one to crown the statue during the May procession. They had to support their votes. Sara won by a large vote because she had been standing up for principle against us all those years. I got only one vote from my boyfriend because he thought I'd make a good mother. I knew I couldn't compete any longer. In high school Sara and I went separate ways but now we were going to live together for five years of training. I assumed that she, the one most like the Blessed Virgin, would stick it out.

Sara, and all the other girls looked strange in black. The red slashes of lipstick they left on looked savage. We darted toward each other between clumps of tight-faced parents. The funniest looking was Katy. A curly rim of sunset red hair edged her black veil and her red freckles stood out in her pale face. I had met her at a journalism convention in Milwaukee in our senior year. I always thought we would be good friends. She told me then that she lived in Marshall but was coming to St. Louis in the fall to enter the convent. "So am I," I told her. We promised to write during the summer. After graduation I got a two-page letter from her written in tiny script in green ink. One Saturday night I started to answer her letter while I was babysitting. I wrote pages without stopping, telling her how scared I was to leave home even though I didn't like it much there anyway; about the boyfriend I met in the elevator at the telephone company where I worked. When I finished I looked at the missive, embarrassed. Katy had written two pages and I answered with a novel. I tore it up and wrote a two-page reply. "Now we'll be friends," I thought. It took a while to happen.

The first meeting that night was in a high-ceilinged classroom called the Novitiate. The floor, covered with brown linoleum and drab brown desks swallowed our thin bodies. The long windows blanketed us in darkness without a hint of starlight. We were silent and unsure as Sister Marguerite, our superior, gave us our schedule. "How will I ever get up at 5:30?" I thought. I decided to keep my eyelash curler although it was against the rules. It lasted long after the lipstick faded.

Now I lay on my narrow white bed and looked up at the curtains surrounding. They matched the long granny nightgown I wore. There were four beds in this dorm, one belonging to an older novice who was our dorm prefect. She was already asleep. So was the girl on my right. Suddenly, Laura, my other dorm mate whispered through the curtains, "Come with me, Jenny. We're having a party in the attic." I already loved Laura's bigness, her confident smile, her large arms. She seemed older to me. It was a quiet party. Five of us, including Sara and Katy sat on trunks under a waterfall of black stockings hanging from the lines over our heads. "How do they expect us to keep quiet all day?" Katy asked. "I'm not even going to try. It's impossible and it makes me mad." Her blue eyes blazed.

"It's the superior I hate already," Sara said. "She seems so nice but her eyes are mean."

I looked at Sara in surprise. I thought she would love everything.

Laura laughed at it all. "You can put up with it," she said. "Those small things aren't what it's all about."

I hoped she was right, but a small doubt started to grow. "She has to be right," I thought. A psychic told Laura that she was a reincarnated shaman. She felt something like that to me. Her voice boomed with confidence and drama. She had been to college the year before she entered the convent. "I was empty," she said. "That's why I came here."

I found I was different. Each day I felt emptier. For some reason, maybe because she had known me for so long, Sara was a monitor for my pain during the first few months. She could pick it up like a seismograph always knowing when I couldn't breathe because I was so unhappy.

"I always think," she told me, "there's Jenny in chapel. She must have that pain again."

"How do you know?" I asked.

"We don't have to talk. We know," she answered with a certainty that surprised me.

And she was right. Anger paralyzed my chest, made me hoarse, but I kept thinking it would get better and I had trouble talking about it. Sara was a dormant volcano most of the time, but she exploded each time a new secret about convent life was revealed to us.

Sister Marguerite, the superior, was a stone nun with eyes that burned like dry ice in an alabaster face frozen in a half moon smile or grimace. She seemed to be on a permanent fast, her belt always hung low from a missing waist. She never raised her voice or shoulders or eyes, as if she had forgotten the sky. Her words matched the way she looked. We sat in shock in our rows in the Novitiate when she passed our little leather cases with tiny chains on them for whipping our thighs and told us about Saturday night exercises.

"It's our custom on Saturday nights to pray to make up for the sins of the flesh which people are committing all over the world. It doesn't hurt much and it's a symbol of our chastity."

It was summer and we could cut across the yard to the chapel. I felt sick and ran toward it to pray and think. Sara was furious.

"How can you just go to pray about it?" she said. "I know it's the right thing to do but I can't." Her eyes blazed furiously. "How could they spring this on us?"

"Come on," I said. "Just laugh at it."

"It's really not funny," Katy joined in. "It's sick."

"I feel sick," Sara said. And she looked sick. Suddenly pale and tight like a twisted rope.

"We'll make it funny," I said thinking of Laura and how she would handle it. And we did the next Saturday night. We chanted "De Profundis" the song for funerals and in the dark hallway pulled up our skirts. The novice on my right took it very seriously; I could hear the chains hit her thighs. In my anger and embarrassment I laughed, giggled helplessly. Katy, on my left, joined in, especially when a late nun came down in the elevator and we could see each surprised face in its light. Sara, however, could never laugh.

"I don't understand it," I said to her. "Why are you so angry all the time? You were always so religious."

"I can't help it," she answered. "I feel so tense all the time. As if I'm going to be sick. I know I'm more religious than you are, but I hate Sister Marguerite. She thinks she's so holy."

We tried to encourage each other, but an old competition surfaced over Father Tim, the young priest from our church. We had known him since grade school and like all the other kids thought he was fun for a priest and probably not really a good priest. We couldn't have any visitors in the Novitiate except priests and Father Tim began to come to see me often. At first it seemed strange to talk as an equal to this man who had heard all my fumbling sexual confessions in high school. Then I started to look more closely at his reddish brown hair and freckles.

He had always played around like one of us but now he talked very seriously with me.

"I'm here because I want everything I do to have meaning," I told him. "I can't stand to spend my time on things I don't think are important."

"That's why I'm a priest," he told me. We stood at the window in the dark visitors' parlor and looked out at the greening parklike grounds. "I came here because I want to talk to you," he said. "I've never met anyone who is so much like me. It's like hearing myself talk."

I was eighteen and he was the only man I ever saw except for the old priest who said Mass every day and heard our confessions. I felt something hook my insides and pull me toward him. After he left, I felt confused. It was flattering to feel him falling in love with me, but I wasn't sure I wanted to be as much like him as he said I was. Sara said that he loved me and that I needed to be careful.

"He and I aren't alike at all," she laughed, but I knew it bothered her. All the months I had been in the convent I had been searching for someone to talk to, a friend, and here he was, but it didn't feel right. I never got a chance to solve the problem myself. Sara told Sister Marguerite about the reason behind Father Tim's frequent visits. The next time he came, she wouldn't let him in. He just disappeared from my life. I learned that it was loneliness that paralyzed my chest so I couldn't breathe. For the first six months I hardly slept at night, but walked the halls trying to ease the pain and anxiety of it. "It must be God's will," I thought, and Sara said it was.

Katy was depressed too. "This place is like the middle ages," she'd rage with a hysterical edge to her voice. "Why are they doing this to us?" At the four o'clock recreation time we stood outside in the autumn air, our moods matching our black clothes. Katy was always the center of the group, taller than the rest of us and the voice for everyone's depression. A round olive of a nun taught us theology and always asked us questions with predetermined answers. Katy could never answer them. She wanted to ask questions. "How can you just say what that nun wants to hear?" she asked me as we walked around and around the enclosed yard, our desperate feet wearing down a caged animal path. "She treats me like a heretic whenever I open my mouth," she said. I listened feeling grateful that we finally were becoming friends, grateful that she shared with me. When we studied *The Divine Comedy* and discussed the forbidden love of Francesca and Paolo, Katy asked the same teacher, "Sister, what is it really like?" An absolute silence greeted her question and the horrified look on the face of the olive nun. "I wouldn't know," she said. "I really wouldn't know."

"What *is* it like?" I wondered, Katy's question real in my mind. "Was it worth hell?" One night during the Great Silence as I dressed for bed I happened to glance through a slightly parted white curtain in the forty bed dormitory where we all slept and I saw Katy dressing. I averted my eyes but not before I saw pubic hair bright as the red hair that was now covered all the time. During the following days the image flashed continually into my mind. It felt sexual to me and somehow wrong. I knew I loved Katy. I thought about her as I scrubbed stairs and cleaned bathrooms, my long black robe pinned up and the sweat running through my covered up hair.

Each week I knelt before Sister Marguerite to ask for supplies like shampoo which she seldom gave me or to confess my infractions of the rules. She talked to me about Katy. "Stay away from her. Don't talk to her. The most serious fault you can have is to be too involved with other people. You belong to God. Sisters all love each other equally." I tried to avoid Katy after that, but it didn't matter. She had already started to change, growing quiet and no longer questioning. She looked tired and I heard her up at night. When I tried to approach her in the yard, she said, "Leave me alone. I just don't like you anymore."

"Did Marguerite talk to you, too?" I asked, but she never answered, just walked away. I never knew what had happened to my friend. The whole group was once controlled by her rebellion. We looked up to her, listened to her, agreed with her. We were now controlled by her silence, her distancing.

For a long time I fought the change in myself. Every week we knelt in the Novitiate with our veils pulled over our faces and told the whole group about some fault we had committed that week. For me, it was always breaking silence. One week I kept track of the number of times I talked when I wasn't supposed to and I counted two thousand little marks in my book. They were marked off by tens so they were easy to count. When I told this to the group, kneeling, with my veil over my face, everyone laughed and then I really was reprimanded. I had to lie with my face on the floor for a long time. "Jenny, calm down," people told me. "Don't be so emotional. Your feelings are all over the place." And they were. They were looking for some place to land. For a love that would sustain me. And I was drying up in the search. For a long time Laura kept me going. She had to clean bathrooms as I did, but she never got caught in the web of detail that circumscribed our days. She talked about theology, astrology, sacred numbers and special moons. She discussed all the theologians who were silenced by the pope. "We lived together in a former life, in a monastery in Greece," she told me and I believed her. Day after day we walked down to the southeast corner of the yard, across in front of the water tower to the squat brick laundry then up the other side where the caretakers' small stucco house signalled a real world which grew distant and disappeared in the haze of things we tried to forget, then back to the courtyard facing the side door of the chapel.

Laura helped me break the tension of trying to fit myself into a medieval mold. When it became unbearable we broke it by starting small rebellions like short sheeting the beds or getting cigarettes from the college girls. We moved on to producing plays.

Laura always directed. I played Piglet, then Romeo to a large-boned Juliet on the fire escape for the entertainment of all the superiors, including Sister Marguerite. With Laura I became dramatic, louder. We produced a book of poetry to tell ourselves we were still alive. I wrote poems that started like this:

> In the early morning light
> I will dress myself in white
> to give myself to you
> who gave yourself to me . . .

"You're trying to get votes," Sister Marguerite told me. I was. I was a plant without water.

One day she said as I knelt before her, "In this garden some of you girls are lilies, some are roses, but you, my child are a clover. You must stop trying to be anything else."

"Cows eat clover," I thought. I decided to be an iris instead, but I always wondered, "Is she right?"

"Is she right?" I asked Laura.

She hooted. "Don't you see they're trying to break you down? You're too strong, too smart."

"How can you keep believing in yourself?" I asked. "What keeps you going?"

"I told you I always felt empty," she said. "I want to be in a community that works. It'll be there after we get through this part. I know it will."

I had no certainty. Not any more.

"If I don't find it some day I'll leave, and you can come with me. We'll leap over the wall," Laura laughed.

Toward the end of the two and a half year novitiate I began to change. I read a book called *Achieving Peace of Heart* which taught me how to control my emotions. I practised deep breathing and removing myself from a situation when I started to feel something. I did this by losing myself in my senses so that I could keep from crying by feeling the wood of a pew beneath my fingers or by remembering the floor beneath my feet. So I started to walk slowly instead of running down the halls and I started to love silence. In fact, I preferred not to talk. When we read Elizabeth Bowen's *Death of the Heart* in literature class, I recognized myself in the young girl who learned to suppress her feelings. Still, I thought this was the best I could do with my life. This is what God wanted from me. "Jenny," people said, "you've changed so much. Gotten so mature." The nuns who used to stay away from me, the ones who I'd thought were better than I was, holier, started to come around. "Maybe," I thought, "I am finally deep."

After two and a half years my group was to make vows of poverty, chastity, and obedience as nuns. For two weeks before the ceremony we were on retreat and kept silence. I walked through the woods behind the college and sat in the spring orchard. "Why am I going to do this, commit myself to this loneliness?" I asked myself. But I knew it was because of this silence, this joy I had found in myself. I liked talking to myself. I was my own friend, my own love. I no longer hoped to find a person with whom I could share everything. "I'm not that interesting," I thought, finally, and wrote poems about empty weed pods and slim, ascetic poplar trees. These I showed to no one.

The day after the ceremony we moved to the Juniorate next door for two and a half more years of religious training and to finish our degrees at the college across the street. It was spring when we moved to the building next door and met Sister Honore, our new superior. She wore binoculars whenever she was outside in order to catch any quick movement in the slow budding film of green. Often she sat in the lawn chair and watched for birds. It was the watching and catching she liked, those slight shivers of color in the trees. Her eyes moved fast, birdlike. She sat tall surrounded by all of us young women who fawned over her. We were uncomfortable in heavy black robes that were too hot for the warm weather and uncomfortable with her. We wanted her approval but at the same time could feel the hard centers inside of us that wouldn't let her in.

During brief stolen moments between summer school classes Laura, Sara, Katy, and I often met at the pond on campus to talk. We dangled our legs over the twisted horizontal trunk of a silver maple and discussed Sister Honore's attempts to change us.

"She certainly takes her job seriously," Laura said one day. "She seems to think God gave it to her on her own private mountain. She is to lead us into the land of strong religious women."

"But why does she think she has to break us first?" Sara's eyes still blazed in restless anger. "She'll never break me."

"She won't break any of us," I told her. "We're different from the other groups that have come through."

"I'm hard inside," Katy said. But her eyes looked hurt. "She knows it too. Even though we're quiet she knows we hate her."

I didn't say it then, but I knew at that point that these three women had helped me hang onto myself. In many ways, however, Honore won. Our anger was fueled by what happened to Sara at the end of that summer. She became ill with rheumatoid arthritis. Her joints knotted up and her face became tight with pain. The flashing eyes grew dull. She often walked up stairs backward because she couldn't bend her legs. The elevator stood next to the stairs but Honore wouldn't let her take it. If she stayed in bed, none of us could bring her food. She wouldn't give her aspirin because she didn't believe in medication. "Women have to be strong," she told us. "Mountains."

*

Laura was strong too. She led our resistance. "Why has Sara been in the hospital so long? Why can't we write to her? It isn't Christian to leave her there alone." She spoke for all of us.

"I'll tell you what Christian means," Honore answered. "It means suffering alone. It means being silent. It means obeying one's superior. No, you aren't going to write to Sara. You can't visit her either. She's not coming back until she can hold her own. I'm going to make her a strong woman or drive her home to her parents."

I was silent. We all were silent, the hatred building within us. "Maybe," I thought, "I should talk to the superior above Sister Honore." She scared me and I thought she would send me home.

During the first few months in the Juniorate Katy withdrew more and more, faded from us and one day disappeared. Into the hospital, we heard, for psychiatric treatment. "They're giving her shock treatment," people said with the usual helpless concern. When I tried to talk to Honore about it she said it didn't concern me. In our morning class Laura asked about Katy day after day.

"Where is Katy? We want to see her." She was relentless.

"It's not your concern," Honore would always say. "You must learn to accept my guidance."

"I'm losing my confidence," Laura told me. "I feel as if I'm at war with her."

"You've survived so long; don't let her destroy you."

I encouraged her but I had my doubts. I knew that for Laura this time under Honore would be a test of survival.

In the Juniorate I finally began to break through the medieval walls that had buried my mind. Honore did her best to keep them intact. She held me to her with an ambiguous tie of love and hate. I hated her for Sara, for Katy, for many others and yet she was the first person in authority who was supportive to me in the convent. "You're mature, Jenny, and bright," she'd say. "Just follow my guidance and you'll be a wonderful nun. We need people like you." She almost convinced me except for the books. She was against literature. She told us how she stopped reading novels. In the middle of *Perelandra* she became aware of how absorbed she was and decided to stop reading right then. She never did learn the ending. We had to ask permission to read any books that weren't required in our classes and she always said no to me. Kneeling, I would hold up the books I wanted to read, *Kristin Lavransdatter*, *The Stranger*, *The Ugly American*, and always she took them from my hands and put them on her desk. "Just read whatever you want, forget about permission," Laura told me and finally, I did.

I ran to the college library, snowflakes flecking my black shawl, piling up on it. The English literature section was near the windows in the basement stacks. Through them I could see the slow rise of ground to the powerhouse tower and the ceiling of protective oaks in the woods around the building. At first I just peeked at books and then just decided to read. I copied quotes, planted them like seeds in my mind. "Our chief want in life is to find someone who will help us to find ourselves" (Emerson). "I celebrate myself and I sing of myself" (Whitman). "i carry your heart (i carry it in my heart)," (cummings). Each book, each quote was a step away from the life I was living. It took me four more years to read, copy and dream my way out. In one recurring dream I was trapped inside monastery walls, a maze of hallways and cloisters, each with a slightly different pattern, thick vaults over my head and doors impossible to move. Old nuns guarded them. In one dream I finally escaped, broke into wide fields and a starlit sky. I woke up with a great joy.

I shared this dream with Laura on my poetry hill in the apple orchard the day before we were to leave to go out to teach. "My dream goes like this," she told me. "I am standing before a group of old nuns trying to convince them that I don't belong as one of them. I want them to let me go. And I can't convince them. They keep telling me to stay. I wonder if in some dream I will talk my way out."

She did. But it took several more years. After five years of training we were separated. Many of the forty in our original group had already left the order. After a few more years only five out of the whole group would remain nuns. Laura, Sara, Katy and I were not among them.

Doña Baby

C.W. Truesdale

S HE WEARS spike heels into the jungle. It is necessary for her to lean on her husband's left arm. He is dressed in a burgundy velour leisure suit and is perhaps twenty years her senior. He is perhaps strong and rigid and rich enough to hold up her sinuous long curves, her lustrous black hair which spills out from under her sun hat and piles up in loose folds on her shoulders. No doubt he has paid dearly for her. The complex negotiations through the marriage-broker, the family pride, the honor.

She is like a puppet, but he is no ventriloquist. The last thing he dares do is to put pure Castilian Spanish into her mouth. He may be Argentinian.

He props her up in the clearing and moves gingerly away. He prepares his cameras, the tripod, a classy production number.

The Boras, a meager band who are among the last few remaining pure Indians in Peru, gather dancing around her. They offer her gifts. They ignore the rest of us. Crude berry necklaces, cloth dolls, reed flutes. They are wearing bark cloth skirts with curious hieroglyphic designs like the ones we bought yesterday in Iquitos. Except for the nursing mothers, they are all very old or very young. The teenagers, dressed in Levis, are tittering.

The Boras dance around her in a long line, like a serpent. The toothless old men beat bark drums in the background.

She has come all the way from Spain for this moment. And she knows how to smile like the Virgin. With long delicate white fingers, she reaches out for one of the babies and holds it, smiling, to her lips.

"Madonna, Madonna," they cry.

2.

Though I watch television a lot, I seldom take it seriously and am always dumb-founded when something really good shows up on it. Sometimes, I'm annoyed when this happens.

One night I was watching one of those pretentious arts anthology programs and not paying much attention, until it dawned on me that this guy was doing something very weird. I believe that his name was Fong, or Fang, though I'm probably wrong on both counts. For entirely personal reasons, I prefer "Fang."

I missed the beginning of his performance, though I could hear the familiar Satie piano music he was using, a strange choice, but, as it turned out, exactly the correct one.

His performance was — intensely — both an event and a voice-over explanation. I had the distinct intuition — perhaps from his carefully articulated and elegant movements, perhaps from the way he used the word "meditation" — that this "event" was something he had performed many, many times. Maybe it was the only real event in his life. As though each time he did it, he was preparing himself for a ritual sacrifice and at the same time doing a TV-type sports commentary, voice-over. It was very disconcerting. Like watching someone you love very much being made love to by a stranger.

3.

She was an older black lady, on the way home, she said, from a harrowing day at work. She seemed to fit very snugly into herself, like fingers into a glove.

It was the usual place, Phebe's, where I used to go when I was compulsively on the make, or just compulsive, as I was that night. It was full of actors and dramatists, as usual, out of work show people from the Off-Off-Broadway set. Even the waitresses. If I were still on my own, and in New York, no doubt I'd still be going there, to hone away at my story and polish it, until all the glittering depths of it shone like a ruby.

There are times when it feels wonderful to do that—once the rough edges have been ground away. To try it out on pure strangers. Just to see how it fits them.

She stayed a full hour by the barroom clock over the mirror, where I could watch myself talking to her and make slight adjustments of expression. At times she let herself cry and reached out her dark hand and brushed away the sweat from my brow. Other times she drew away. Her eyes grew hard and cold and I could tell she was struggling with the fear in herself. That I might try to involve her, or something even more basic, that I might hurt her brutally.

I needed to risk that. For that one hour I had to hold her, or give way wholly to the terror inside of me. Her trusting me was the warm line between ordinary humanness and Bellevue, between Art and Madness.

"I want very deeply," I said, "to send you my book."

She hesitated just a moment, then rummaged around in her bag. She gave me her neat white business card, and left.

4.

Fang is down on his knees, just in front of and a little to his left of the plain wooden desk chair. He is meticulously unwrapping the cloth roll that contains his props. The soothing Satie music is playing in the background. He draws two long satin strips about six inches wide from the roll and explains that he is about to perform the ancient Chinese ceremony of foot-binding. The Satie fades away, and we hear instead the voices of an older woman and a child. The child is sobbing. Fang explains that it is the voice of his mother. His little sister is sobbing from the pain.

At this very moment, he anoints his own left foot and ever so slowly begins to bind it. When he has finished with both feet, he rises into a cramped, semi-upright posture, then swiftly bends down onto his kneees again and removes two little pointed blood-red slippers from the cloth roll, which he places awkwardly on his feet.

I become aware of the Satie again as Fang sways over the cloth roll, like a cobra, and lifts up, firmly but gently, a plain cloth doll about a foot and a half long. He grasps her by the scruff of the neck, like a mother cat her young, and moves her across the platform in front of his chair, exactly as you have seen geishas move in Japanese films. Her movements, which are pure translations of what the mother is saying to her daughter about the lovely end and reason for such suffering, are tuned with such elegance and grace to the Satie you believe wholly in her reality. At that moment, Fang is his sister absorbed in her pain and dreaming of her lover, who is also Fang moving now, the male doll with its tiny penis in the same fashion, only more upright and vain, over the prone figure of the doll-woman. He places one hand on her calf and draws himself down until his mouth touches her feet.

You expect more. The Satie is now so erotic that nothing would surprise you.

Suddenly Fang moves. He covers them over almost roughly, as if he could not bear to watch them. As if they would do before my eyes what I wanted them to do.

Fang moves over the cloth roll again. He takes out two embroidered white satin garments and puts them on like a woman. Perhaps he is his sister, I thought, on her wedding day. I know that he is confusing me. I feel that he is doing this deliberately. He wants me to assume that these are wedding garments when in fact they are traditional Chinese mourning attire.

He bends way over now and rests his cheek on the floor. The music stops. The light fades away.

5.

Reynaldo, our guide, edges out into the clearing among the Boras. He looks beautifully up into the sun, like an eagle, and motions us to move on. We have exhausted their meager supply of trinkets and their repertoire. Tomorrow, there will be another group. And tomorrow.

Reynaldo is very quick. I am teaching him how to paddle the dugout canoes American-style. I am confident we will win the race tomorrow.

Reynaldo likes the American girls in Cuzco, where he goes on vacation. He especially likes the noisy blond ones from California, who come down to buy dope and study anthropology.

Reynaldo is half Indian. He has dark features, refined by a Portuguese mother. He has the same delicate dark luminosity you see in the children of Vietnamese women and American blacks. He moves with grace, like a Spaniard. But he smiles like an Indian. Or an angel, displaced and fallen.

Doppelganger

Bill Tinkham

A BOOK, YES, something to read.

Mark bent to his knees on the brown shag in his parents' hallway, his knees and the carpet having shared much long ago. Leaning back, sitting back on his heels, he stared at the bookshelves; old hardcovers, faded greens and browns, no titles as his mind drifted, thoughts wrapped noose-like around guilt. Reaching forward, absently testing the reality of the image, he snapped back; a book, right, yes . . . read, forget. He examined the titles: books on chemistry, engineering—outdated no doubt—how-to books, car manuals, *Birds of the Northwest;* nothing that had been touched for several years, nothing that would be touched again. What had his family read, anyway? The bookcase loomed like some high-rise graveyard, tattered books from another day, Mark stumbled into a couple of Max Shulman novels, chuckled to himself recalling the last Christmas he'd spent there, three years back, reading *Sleep Till Noon* and *The Many Loves of Dobie Gillis* at his father's suggestion. Good suggestion, but somehow rereading them—tonight—made no sense. Bottom shelf: old books of maps and points of interest used to plan a vacation years ago—so many highways rerouted, widened, shaded by the bridges of new highways—and a library book. The yellowing sticker taped to its spine: Mary Shelley, *Frankenstein.*

Mark slipped his legs out, shifted to sitting cross-legged, pulled *Frankenstein* from the shelf. "Women in Literature," that was the class, his first year at the university here, took it out while on a long weekend home, obviously never returned it. He'd calculate the overdue fine later, it'd be good for a laugh, later. Mark remembered looking forward to the horror the book purported, remembered how disappointed he'd been with the fright element, and how taken back he'd been by the monster's plight. A lonely book. He tucked it under his arm, scrambled to his feet. He considered the book he was about to read, a lonely book, considered swapping it for a Max Shulman. He decided it was a bit of a challenge, facing things; recalled an old math class, something about a double negative being positive. Flipping the hall light off, he trudged down the stairway.

Settling into what had been his favorite chair—old, high-backed and wooden, the cushions were his mother's work—Mark rustled the pages of the book. He scanned his parents' living room: cream-colored couch with blue and gold flowers—now gray and brown in the night's shadows—and the matching love seat; speaker cabinets in two corners and the long wooden coffee table—his father's creations. A jungle of plants in one corner, an old end table—never, despite plans, refinished—with a lamp and his parents' wedding picture on it. Snow rode the cold night outside the back window. The fires built in the fireplace to his right, the woodbox—again built by his father—and the cold Sunday mornings bringing in wood to fill it; memories. From every corner, every stain on the old blue carpet, memories converging like too many trains into a roundhouse, every track a ghost train, a past barreling in, whistles blaring, memories on a collision course, brought on by some apocalyptic error of time schedule.

Forcing himself to read, Mark started in on *Frankenstein*, "Letter 1" from Robert Walton to his sister, *You will rejoice to hear that no disaster* . . . He recalled the phone call from his sister's husband—she never handled disasters well—thought how technology had allowed him to receive the news so much more quickly, with immediacy enough to level so much more impact than a letter in Frankenstein's day. "Sorry to be the one to tell you this, Mark," Brad had said over the phone. "It's your folks, an ice storm in Nebraska on their way out to spend Christmas with you, um, a semi jackknifed, I guess . . ." Brad had gone on to explain the tentative funeral plans, handing the phone over to Gwen, she and Mark crying to each other for several minutes. *You will rejoice to hear that no disaster has accompanied the commencement of an enterprise which you have regarded with such evil forebodings.* No one appreciated his move to California, with claims of writing. What could he write there that he couldn't write in Minnesota? Claims and nothing more . . . Mark looked up, his parents in the wedding picture beaming back. Without being able to make out detail in their faces, he remembered the incredible likeness between him and his father, twenty-two in the photo, and Mark, now twenty-four, could've been his double.

I shall commit my thoughts to paper, it is true: Robert Walton continued in "Letter 2," *but that is a poor medium for the communication of feeling.* Mark felt he'd proved that in his own writing, but saw hope; his parents had always shown hope, urging him on—humoring him?—but they'd never see him a success . . . if he ever was. He glanced up, sighed at their celebrating faces; continued through the letters, Walton meeting the dying Victor Frankenstein and recording his incredible tale.

No human being could've passed a happier childhood than myself, Victor was setting the scene for his eventual demise and Mark thought of Little League games, the hoop on the garage, never even a threat of a spanking. He read on, worked at reading on, to put himself elsewhere. *Destiny was too potent, and her immutable laws had decreed my utter and terrible destruction.* Come on, let's not feel sorry for ourselves, Mark thought.

Frankenstein went on to explain his desire for education, his family's approval, his farewell to his family; to his best friend, Clerval; to his wife-to-be, Elizabeth — *I was now alone.* Mark looked up, again the wedding picture . . . at least Victor had everyone's approval. He walked over to the picture, picking it up, mirror image, he thought, from the same mold . . . He moved over to a small mirror in the hallway, rested the wedding picture on his shoulder. Twins, doubles; they couldn't have been more alike. . . . They'd had plans for him to be a doctor, wondered why he had no interest in science like his father, why he'd quit sports before high school — the son of a four-sport letterman. "Why do you suppose I left?" Mark's reflection asked the reflection of the picture. "How could I be you?" He looked around, felt there should be someone close by to wonder about his talking to himself. The wind rattled the front door and he wondered if there wasn't.

He returned the picture to the table, turned the picture away and settled into the couch. With a full view of the fireplace, he recalled the evening fires as a child, popping corn in a long-handled iron pot, the can of "magic" his father sprinkled on the fire creating deep greens and purples in the flames.

Mark read on through Frankenstein's travels to the university of Ingolstadt, his first meeting with a professor, his being reproached for his studies in the nonsense of alchemy, his early dreams crushed. *I was required to exchange chimeras of boundless grandeur for realities of little worth.*

Looking up, Mark imagined green and purple flames stretching in the fire, walked over to a dictionary resting on top of a speaker, laid it on the floor, stretched himself out next to the woodbox and looked up "chimera." *I was required to exchange chimeras of boundless grandeur for realities of little worth,* he read again, wondered why it took Victor Frankenstein to show him the truth.

Lying on the floor — the furnishings looked larger, he thought of his childhood, huge forts built from furniture — he continued to read. Frankenstein became determined to prove his professor wrong, to go beyond even his early dreams . . . to create a chimera, Mark thought. *I closed not my eyes that night,* Victor said of the evening he determined to try his hand at creation. Mark rolled over checking the clock — just before eleven.

Victor continued with his dream, obsession; remaining far from home. *Two years passed in this manner, during which I paid no visit to Geneva, but was engaged, heart and soul, in the pursuit of some discoveries which I hoped to make.* I had *hoped,* Mark thought, didn't do a damn thing but *hoped* enough. Writing, three years away from home. Writing, sending things out; eagerly, naively hoping for a positive reply. Three years tending bar, a little unemployment, a certain amount of fun, school was virtually free; telling the folks how much he'd written, hoping for a miracle.

Meanwhile Victor studied with a fervor, books and graves . . . *a churchyard was to me merely the receptacle of bodies deprived of life, which, from being the seat of beauty and strength, had become food for the worm.* The funeral that morning, his parents, *food for the worm.* Lying on the floor looking up, furniture somehow imposing from this angle, Mark crawled back to the couch.

Victor took a break from the recollection of his quest to offer a lesson: *How much happier that man is who believes his native town to be the world.* "Now you tell me," Mark muttered, "after I've gone out to see *the world.*" Then back to his obsession, gathering the tools to build a creature, fueled by *the first enthusiasm of success.* "I wouldn't know . . ."

And the same feelings which made me neglect the scenes around me caused me to forget those friends who were so many miles absent, and whom I had not seen for so long a time. I knew my silence disquieted them, and I well remembered the words of my father: "I know that while you are pleased with yourself you will think of us with affection, and we shall hear regularly from you. You must pardon me if I regard any interruption in your correspondence as a proof that your other duties are equally neglected." Mark wondered when he'd last written his parents, collect phone calls but when had he written? He stared at the gray, empty fireplace. They could've sat in front of a fire, reread his latest letter . . . or if he'd sent a story or two, they could've read to each other. Read his stories. Mark swung his legs up, laid back on the couch, a blank ceiling to view.

Victor stood above his creation, now showing its first signs of life, and its true ugliness and horror finally became apparent. *I had desired it with an ardour that far exceeded moderation; but now that I had finished, the beauty of the dream vanished.* If *I* had desired it with an ardour, anything beyond moderation, Mark thought, maybe I could've realized a dream . . . Tending bar, talking a good story, dreaming . . . Turning his head, he stared for some time at the brick fireplace wall, his father had told wonderful stories by the fire, Mark craning his neck to look up at his father, watch the story being told, the magic colors of the fire adding to the story, the dream . . . The dream, sending stories out, one break is all it takes, prolonging the dream, one break, call the folks, "Guess what . . ."

Mark set down the book, with elbows on knees he ran both hands through his hair, leaned his forehead against the palms of his hands for some time, glanced over at the clock—1:45. Without sleep occurring to him, he picked up the book, moved back to his old favorite chair, sat on the floor, his back against it. He found his place but now the wedding picture was able to look down on him. Mark crawled over to the love seat, turning the picture away.

The same night the monster came to life and ran off, Clerval came to visit, finding Victor in a terrible state. Soon Victor received a letter from Elizabeth begging him to come home. Every correspondence from Mark's parents included subtle and not-so-subtle hints that it was time to come back. But there was always school, a job he couldn't leave; all he wanted was some semblance of success, so the move would seem worthwhile. Success . . . dreamt of but not worked for. And so he'd been away the last two Christmas holidays, this year his parents deciding to come visit him, sunny California—getting as far as icy Nebraska.

"Merry Christmas," Mark muttered, remembering it'd just become Christmas Eve. Brad and Gwen wanted him to drive down to their place for Christmas Eve dinner and spend Christmas day. He said he'd think about it. It'd taken everything he had to be able to be alone tonight. He had to laugh, "Just me and Frankenstein."

Then another letter from Elizabeth: *William is dead.* William was his youngest brother and after Victor's return to Geneva, a friend of the family was condemned and executed for the murder. A murder Victor knew was committed by the monster he created. *Now all was blasted; instead of that serenity of conscience which allowed me to look back upon the past with self-satisfaction and from thence to gather promise of new hopes, I was seized by remorse and the sense of guilt.* Remorse, guilt . . . Mark read on. *Our house was the house of mourning.* He studied the empty furnishings, the gray fireplace, curtains shrouding the darkness pressed against cold windows. *I, not in deed, but in effect, was the true murderer.* Mark rose, walked about the living room, worked such thoughts from his mind.

He walked into the kitchen, wondering why he'd left. Obviously it was simply to do something different. To write, he'd said, it seemed easier, maybe inspirational, to write while doing something different. Travel, curiosity, and they said schools were all-but-free in California. Why had he stayed? He considered many things, standing out was the simple fact that he was having a good time. Mark checked the refrigerator, the clock above the stove said 2:40, though he hadn't so much as yawned. He poured himself a gin and tonic. But I did write, he thought, and went to school the whole time—part-time. Somehow time hadn't passed while he was gone, he never felt he'd been away for any length, certainly not years and always assumed he'd return with news of a certain amount of success preceding him. Assumed . . . dreamt.

Mark sipped from his drink as he walked back, stopped in the hallway before the living room, decided he'd had enough. He set the drink on the stairway, grabbed the book from the love seat, sat on the stairway with only a view of the inside of the front door and the dining room to his right. Outside the door's small window snow whirled past, Mark shivering without feeling cold. He grabbed one of his father's sweaters from the hall closet and returned to the stairs. Opening the book, he flipped through its pages—shadows blocking out, then burying each preceding page—until he found his place.

Victor Frankenstein sought to forget his sorrows with a journey into the serenity of nearby mountains, but instead met up with the monster, who had been following him for some time.

"Devil, do you dare approach me?" Victor began screaming vengeance on his own creation. Back and forth they went, Frankenstein raving about the demon he'd created, the monster wanting only a chance to explain. They created me, Mark thought, attempting to peer around the corner at the wedding picture but unable to see it, I didn't turn out as planned . . .

The monster finally talked Victor into listening to his story, his early days scrounging for food, being attacked by villagers, traveling the cold nights to avoid further attacks. *One day, when I was oppressed by cold, I found a fire which had been left by some wandering beggars, and was overcome with delight at the warmth I experienced from it. In my joy I thrust my hand into the live embers, but quickly drew it out again with a cry of pain. How strange, I thought, that the same cause should produce such opposite effects!*

Mark set the book down, went over and checked the woodbox. Nearly full. He went to the kitchen for newspaper, picked up the book and his drink on the way back. Building a fire he thought of warm and cold, being alone out of choice and being *alone;* sat cross-legged as close to the fire as safe, thought about reaching his hand in. The clock in the kitchen had claimed 3:30, but this was the monster's story.

Nuts and roots made more edible by fire, a constant search for shelter; the monster went out alone, learning. An early stoning left him leery of people, so he traveled alone, finally coming upon a small shelter, a hovel attached to a cottage and bordered by a pigsty. Through a small hole in the cottage wall he could view its inhabitants—a blind man, his son and daughter—the De Lacey family. He'd search for food by night and spy on the family by day, learning words, acquiring feelings; on the outside looking in, Mark thought, his relationship to his own family. The monster sought nothing more from life than to become part of the De Lacey family and watched them with a growing desire as they did their chores, cooked meals, read aloud to the old man; *but at that time I knew nothing of the science of words or letters.* "Who does?" Mark muttered, wondered how he saw himself in both Victor and the monster.

For a year he remained cramped and alone in the tiny hovel. During that time a foreign visitor arrived, who the family taught French, the monster using the oppportunity to learn the language himself. Being able to understand these people increased his feelings for them. Stumbling on a satchel of books, he read them, learning more; *they consisted of Paradise Lost, a volume of Plutarch's Lives, and the Sorrows of Werter.* It sickened Mark that the monster was better read than he.

Crossing the shadows of the living room, Mark moved to the dining room, tired of viewing the ghosts of his family as if through a small hole in the living room wall. The ice had melted in his gin and tonic, a sliced lime floating before the abandoned fire. Mark sat at what had been his place at the table, but found himself wanting to point out things he read to his parents, if only they were at their respective places. He moved around the table to his sister's spot, noticed for the first time two candles on the table.

The monster told of finally making contact with the De Laceys, waiting till the children were gone, and speaking with the blind man, who sympathized, swore to help in any way. But the children returned as he hugged De Lacey for his kindness, the daughter fainting, the son beating the creature with a stick until he fled. Returning the next day with the hope of again speaking with the blind man—blindness to his appearance being the only chance for friendship—he found that the family had gone, *broken the only link that held me to the world.*

Mark looked up, out of the dining room, through the hallway he could see his old favorite chair in the living room and the glow—faint pulse, he thought—of the remains of the fire. He crawled down on the floor, stretched out near the wall, the table looming above him. His old fort, the tabletop impenetrable by air, the four chairs protecting all sides. Now a shadow claimed that spot and from the floor a table could loom. Scrambling to his feet, he found himself climbing on top of the table, dismissing his own questions of why and settled, cross-legged, in the middle, facing where his mother had always sat. He had little worry of anyone seeing him and somehow relished the new perspective.

The tall, thin candles stood alone, seemingly waiting for some romantic dinner. Mark lit them both, climbed off the table, flipped off the light—the candles a pair of eyes in the darkness—and climbed back on the table, opening the book under the glow.

The monster went on to tell Victor of the killing of William, the framing of the family friend; demanding that Frankenstein create a mate for him or face the loss of more loved ones. Victor refused, but in time gave in, knowing the being he'd created; and again Frankenstein left his home, his friend, Clerval, insisting on going along.

Victor excused himself from Clerval for a period of time, found an island to do his work and set about creating another monster, aware that the first was always nearby. Nearly finished with his task, Victor was again struck by the horror of such a creation and destroyed the still lifeless form—saving the world from its terror and condemning the monster to a life alone. After leaving the island, he found Clerval murdered and later, on Victor's wedding night, the monster destroyed Elizabeth. *Why am I here to relate the destruction of the best hope and the purest creature on earth? She was there, lifeless and inanimate . . .* Mark slid easily on the polished tabletop, turning to face his father's place. He noticed a small, oval, stained glass flower hanging from the top of the window against the outdoors' black backdrop. Something new, he thought. He adjusted the candles for his reading, the small flames dancing on their wicks, melted wax like sweat sliding down their length, while the stained glass stole flickers of their light. He flipped the pages of the book, the movement sending the candles into a new dance.

And so Victor grieved the murder of his new bride, *so frightful an event is single in the history of man;* but it isn't, Mark thought, there are hundreds, thousands of traffic accidents daily, people die every minute and the survivors survive. I'm not alone . . .

The spirits of the departed seemed to flit around and to cast a shadow, which was felt but not seen, around the head of the mourner. Mark glanced at each candle, up to the stained glass flower. *They were dead and I lived . . .*

Finally Victor set out to revenge the series of murders, to destroy his creation. *I pursued him, and for many months this has been my task . . . I saw the fiend enter by night and hide himself in a vessel bound for the Black Sea . . . Amidst the wilds of Tartary and Russia, although he still evaded me, I have ever followed his track.* I've chased my dreams all over, Mark thought, but Victor's chasing the effect of his dreams. My dreams have had no effect.

My life, as it passed thus, was indeed hateful to me, and it was during sleep alone that I could taste joy. O blessed sleep! Sleep, twenty more pages, then sleep, Mark wondered what effect sleep would have on his own condition, *again I saw the benevolent countenance of my father . . .*

The monster, enjoying the sport of the chase, left Victor instructions in the snow to help and taunt him. *Follow me: I seek the everlasting ices of the north.* "Minnesota," Mark snickered.

And Victor followed north, finally—almost dead—rescued by Robert Walton's ship; Walton with his own ambitious dream of finding the North Pole. *"All my speculations and hopes are as nothing,"* Victor told Walton. *"From my infancy I was imbued with high hopes and a lofty ambition; but how I am sunk!"* High hopes and *claims* of a lofty ambition, Mark thought, shaking his head.

Victor soon died, another victim of his own creation. Walton, writing his sister of the death, heard noises from Victor's cabin, found the monster grieving over his creator's body, none-too-happy with his own triumph. He told Walton his side of the story, vowed to take his own life.

"But soon," he cried with sad and solemn enthusiasm, "I shall die, and what I now feel be no longer felt. Soon these burning miseries will be extinct. I shall ascend my funeral pile triumphantly and exult in the agony of the torturing flames. The light of that conflagration will fade away; my ashes will be swept into the sea by the winds. My spirit will sleep in peace, or if it thinks, it will surely not think thus. Farewell."

He sprang from the cabin window as he said this, upon the ice raft which lay close to the vessel. He was soon borne away by the waves and lost in darkness and distance.

Morning had snuck through the window, rays split by the stained glass flower, dust floating in sections of red and green sunlight cutting across his father's chair. Magic, Mark thought, closing the book, squinting into the brightness out the window, the wind drifting snow across the front yard. The candles still burned, wax built up on each holder like snow on a roof. He stared at the small flames, insignificant in the morning light, then looked about the dining room; couldn't believe he was sitting in the middle of the table, had spent the whole night reading *Frankenstein*, had attended his parents' funeral the day before. Staring again at the flames, he thought about Christmas Eve dinner, would they exchange gifts? Would they blame him? The colored sunlight rolled across his father's chair, the flames flickered in an unfelt draft; Mark licked the thumb and first finger of each hand and reaching into one flame, then the other, pinched them out, watching the gray smoke disappear.

The Camper

Madelon Sprengnether

H E C A M E in the fall when the leaves had just begun to turn, though I hardly noticed them I was so busy preparing classes and grading papers—a routine that I regarded as both pleasing and inevitable. I appreciated the regularity of teaching with its small necessities, its implicit acknowledgement of order. The seasons, on the other hand, disturbed me, their large rhythms too loose and undisciplined for me to grasp, the random rain of leaves a daily reminder of everything that threatened to slip through my hands.

He arrived one morning just as I was backing out of the driveway onto the long dirt road that led to the highway and the rural college campus a few miles away where I taught. I leaned across the front seat of my car, and struggled to roll down the window. "Who do you want?" I shouted. "If it's the Arnolds, they don't live here anymore, and we just rent."

He was driving a truck with a camper attached, not the kind that rides over the truck, but behind. This one was silver, with rounded edges, clearly a deluxe model. It reminded me a little of a blimp, but also of a mirror—it was so shiny. I was a little transfixed by it, and didn't really listen to what he said except to gather that he was looking for my husband Jim. "He's inside," I offered, waving him toward the house. "Just knock and then walk in. The door's unlocked."

I didn't think about him again until I was driving home in the late afternoon. My husband liked to have people visit, but he often forgot to tell me he had invited them. Our back-to-back working schedules meant that we had little leisure for talk. While I was gone during the day, he was usually away in the evening, either at his studio or teaching a photography workshop. We lived on the margins of academia, since I, as an Instructor, had a one-year contract, and Jim, who offered extracurricular classes, had no contract at all. I worried about this when I wasn't worrying about something more immediate, like how to make our small paychecks stretch to the end of the month. Jim, on the other hand, claimed not to be concerned. Of the two of us, he was, unquestionably, the more relaxed. And that was most likely what I fell in love with—his ease with people, his affability. He had, I believed then, what I lacked, an ability to take life as it comes.

Though the truck and camper were parked in the driveway, no one was home when I arrived. I poured myself a glass of wine and sat down to read. When I looked up an hour later, it was already dark, so that I could barely make out the shape of the camper with its dull sheen in the yard. It seemed to me suddenly like a presence, like a person who had come to take up residence. I also felt drawn to it, to its satiny surface, its air of self-containment. I wondered how many miles it had traveled, and where it had been. With such a vehicle, I caught myself thinking, I could go anywhere.

"Sorry I'm late."

The screen door slammed. "Honey, I want you to meet Michael. We got to talking, I guess, and I completely forgot about the time."

"That's okay," I said, "but where did you go?" I looked at Michael for the first time and took his outstretched hand. He was one of those people who don't really hold on when they shake hands, and whose fingers feel sort of boneless. "I was beginning to wonder if you'd be back for dinner."

"It's my fault," Michael said, evenly. "I wanted to show Jim my camper. With the curtains drawn, you can't really tell what time it is." After a pause, he added, "It's light tight."

So, another photographer. I was used to Jim's absences when he was working, either in the darkroom or out in the fields where he set up his heavy equipment, his absorption often causing him to lose all track of time. Gradually, I had learned how different we were in this regard. While I tended to be overly punctual, he thought of appointments and schedules as approximate. I found myself thinking sometimes, as I looked at him, that we did not really inhabit the same space. Yet I couldn't put my finger on anything odd about us as a couple. We seemed, or perhaps I should say he seemed, if anything, too normal. It was I who felt askew.

But then Michael also struck me as askew, though when I tried to define this to myself I found that I could not name it. I wanted to say that it was something about his appearance, yet he was neatly dressed, in khaki work shirt and pants, and his dark red hair and beard were carefully groomed. Maybe it was something about the pallor of his skin or the smoothness of his hands that made his work clothes seem incongruous. At any rate, I felt perturbed by him, awkward and off center.

Later, after Michael had retired to his camper for the night (having accepted our offer of dinner but refused the guestroom), I tried to find out more about him.

"Do you know why he's here?" I asked Jim. "Did you know he was coming?"

Jim said that he had talked with him several months ago when we were in New York and that Michael had mentioned then the possibility of a trip at this time of year to photograph. He didn't know how long he intended to stay—maybe a few days, maybe a week. Michael's mother had underwritten the cost of the camper, Jim added, with some envy. He talked admiringly about the facilities of the camper, with particular enthusiasm for the portable darkroom Michael had built.

"He has everything he needs," Jim said, at last. "And he has no responsibilities."

On weekdays I was usually too tired to think of sex, but that night I wanted comfort, so I turned to Jim in bed and started stroking his chest, gradually moving my hand towards his groin. He lay there with his eyes closed, too drowsy, I guessed, to respond. "That feels nice," he murmured once, but then rolled away from me to sleep. I lay awake for a while, in a state of mild arousal, then dropped off into a series of fitful dreams. In one of them I imagined that a large car, a 1950s cadillac, had run off the road and crashed into our front porch. I awoke with a start, and, remembering the camper in the yard, thought for a moment that Michael had rammed it into the house. I caught myself wondering if he expected his mother to pay for this too when I realized I had been dreaming. It occurred to me then that I was afraid of Michael and I decided I should think about this in the morning. Still later I had another dream in which the owners of the house were holding some kind of seance in the living room. Only everyone was naked, and the medium had put them all in a trance. Then they began to touch and arouse one another, moving in a kind of delicious slow motion. I was one of the members of this group at the same time that I was an observer. I wondered whether this is what they called a "spiritual encounter."

In the morning I felt ashamed of my distrust of Michael and resolved to be more hospitable, though my teaching schedule meant that I would see him only in the evenings. I even managed to forget about him that day until I returned home and caught sight of the camper in the driveway. It was sunset and the light reflected from the camper, as I approached the house, made it look unearthly. I was reminded of scenes from science fiction movies, in which some shining object descends from outer space into someone's cornfield. The house itself looked suddenly foolish, as though it were misplaced and temporary, as though the land belonged instead to the camper. "This is silly," I thought to myself. "He's just here to take pictures, and it's convenient to park in our driveway. Besides, he's only going to be here a couple of days."

This time, when I arrived, Michael and Jim were in the house looking at color transparencies on Jim's homemade light box. Nothing was out of the ordinary, and Michael himself, as if he had sensed my uneasiness, seemed particularly attentive to me all evening, talking softly about his work, about the special features of his 8x10 camera, and his passion for detail. I could see this in the transparencies themselves, which he placed ceremoniously, one after the other, over the opaque glass of the light box. They were stunning in their clarity and precision, the colors as vibrant as those of a stained glass window. I was entranced. I felt that my own world was drab in comparison to this, as though the transparencies contained their own reality, and once illumined, outshone anything I could remember having seen. At the same time, I felt a kind of perversity in them, each of them going dark when removed from the box, as though what they revealed were as inaccessible as the other side of a looking glass. I began to be aware also of the ritual nature of Michael's movements, his subtle orchestration of my viewing of his work. It was like theatre, I thought to myself later. I was a spectator at a performance so beautifully controlled that I had almost no awareness of it, of the way in which I was directed to play my part.

Everything about Michael was somehow meticulous, from the crease in his khaki pants to his carefully manicured fingernails. Next to him I felt sloppy, as though I had just spilled catsup on my blouse or gotten a piece of food caught between my front teeth. I began to look at his work more closely, as though I might find there some clue to his personality. In-between classes sometimes I even jotted notes to myself. "A nature photographer— likes close-ups—tree bark—matted leaves. Friendly enough, but doesn't like to be touched—wears white cotton gloves when he handles negatives. Won't stay in the house—why? The thing with the bees is weird—does he *like* nature or what?"

Jim was particularly fascinated by the bees. Michael had come into the house one afternoon with a large bumblebee crawling on his shirt collar. When Jim pointed to it, making a gesture to brush it away, Michael stepped back and laughed. "No, look," he said, with obvious satisfaction. "What do you see?" It had become a game—like one of those pictures in children's books where figures of animals are hidden in bushes and trees. The bee, in the meantime, inched towards Michael's pocket, then attempted to fly, only to stop in midair and drop back onto his shirt. A nearly invisible thread bound him to one of Michael's buttons, so that the bee became a kind of living ornament, small, wild, and for the moment, at least, captive. Jim was enthusiastic. He wanted to know how this was done. Michael, evidently pleased, invited him into the camper for a demonstration. Not long afterwards, Jim emerged with a bumblebee crawling on his shirt, which he wore up to campus, hoping to startle someone. Later, in the evening, like Michael, he released it.

Some days, we hardly saw Michael, who would be out in the field early to photograph. Other days he would transform his camper into a darkroom to develop his negatives, and on those days Jim would work with him. After two weeks, he still showed no signs of leaving, and I began to wonder how the camper, looking sleek and metallic, would weather the cold. I mentioned this finally to Jim.

"When's he leaving?" I asked, trying to make my voice sound casual.

"Oh, I don't know. Pretty soon, I guess." Jim paused, as if he were considering what to say next, then added slowly, "You know, I've been thinking I might like to go with him for a few days—to do some field work. I wouldn't be gone long, and I could make up my evening class when I get back."

"What about the car?" I said. "I'll need it myself. You can't leave me stuck here at the house." I knew as soon as I had spoken, however, that he had already thought this through.

"Oh, you can have the car," he assured me. "I'll just find a bus back to town when I'm ready to leave, and you can pick me up."

"And what about your students? Do you expect me to explain to them?"

"Of course not. I'll tell them."

"What you mean is that you've already decided. You really don't care what I think. You've already made your plans with Michael and you didn't think to discuss this with me at all."

"Look, what's the problem?" Jim said. "All I want to do is take a few days to photograph. You're making a big deal over nothing."

I made an effort to control my anger, realizing with a sudden detachment how baseless it seemed. "I'm really tired," I said finally, "and it's getting late. Can we talk about this again in the morning?" I turned away from him and started walking towards the stairs. To my relief, Jim said nothing.

We didn't in fact return to this subject the next day or even the day after. Instead we avoided one another, using our work schedules as an excuse. Jim spent more time with Michael during the day, accompanying him when he photographed, and came home late from campus in the evening. I purposely went to bed early, pretending to sleep when I heard him brush his teeth and undress. I had dreams that I tried to forget. In one of them, a colleague exposed himself to me, then showed me how he could make his penis curl back on itself, telling me this was a genetic trait, like the ability some people have to curl their tongue. I felt he was taunting me so I told him that I had double-jointed thumbs.

Then, just as I had resolved to confront Jim and speak to him, Michael invited both of us to have dinner with him in his camper. Being ushered into the camper, which I had come to think of as somehow impermeable—like a silver bullet—made me feel strangely apprehensive. But then Michael had a way of transforming the most ordinary activities into something teasing and mysterious. This evening was no different. He behaved like a master of ceremonies, as he demonstrated each of the elaborate fittings: the bench that opened up to form a bunk, the table that folded back to the wall, the small refrigerator tucked under our feet, even a portable toilet with its own sanitation box. Nearly everything in this compact living space was miniaturized and adapted to more than one use. Michael himself had designed it and his pleasure in describing its versatility was evident. He seemed suddenly childlike to me and vulnerable, like a boy who had just acquired a Swiss Army knife.

Dinner consisted of noodles and spaghetti sauce, freeze-dried and reconstituted with the addition of boiling water—another demonstration of efficiency. Michael had enough supplies of such foods to last at least six months. He had reduced his dependence on the outside world to a minimum, freeing him to pursue his obsession. I could almost read Jim's thoughts through the expression in his eyes, and I found my anger with him returning, along with a clear sense of resentment towards Michael with all his shiny gadgets. Gradually, as dinner progressed, I fell silent, unable to summon the kind of appreciation of his cleverness that Michael desired. I began to wish, instead, with all my heart that he would leave.

But Michael had another surprise planned. "Wait here," he said, after cleaning up. "I have something to show you." Jim looked up as if to speak, but Michael had already disappeared, carefully closing the door of the camper behind him. I felt uneasy, almost as though we were trapped. I had a fleeting impulse to try the door to see if it was locked.

"What do you think he's doing out there?" I said finally, my question hanging in the air in a way that sounded peculiar. "I mean . . ."

Just at this moment Michael stuck his head in the door, gesturing towards Jim to follow him. "One at a time," he said firmly as I started to rise. And then they were both gone. I sat down again mechanically, wondering at my own acquiescence. A few minutes passed in which I entertained lurid fantasies. Michael was some kind of psychopath, I thought, like that ritual murderer, who killed eight women, taking each victim into a separate room while the others waited their turn. Only one of them escaped by hiding under the bed. I made an effort to stop this train of thought. "If anybody's crazy," I reflected, "it's got to be me."

As if to confirm my self-indictment, Jim appeared at the door of the camper, saying, "Come on now. I think you'll like this." He led me across the lawn to where Michael was standing next to a tripod. Then he left us to return to the house. Mounted on the tripod was a long dark cylinder pointed upwards towards a bright round—one with the smooth curve and platinum sheen of the camper. After adjusting the focus, Michael motioned me towards the eyepiece. "There," he murmured, almost under his breath, as I gazed at the full naked moon, deep and brilliant in the country sky. I couldn't take my eyes from this light even as it edged slowly out of my field of vision, and when I stepped back finally from the empty glass I felt bereft.

"Who do you think you are?" I said, accusingly in the direction of Michael, whose figure I could hardly now distinguish in the darkness. I stood there for a moment, feeling both foolish and self-righteous. Then I turned away from him and walked resolutely towards the house.

That night I dreamed that the moon had burned to ash and fallen out of the sky, and that it lay at my feet like the heaps of withered leaves in the yard.

In the morning, I noticed that a few snowflakes were falling, the first of the season. And when I looked for the familiar shape of the camper, there was nothing but a whitish, frozen-looking patch of ground where it had stood.

Day Out

Dan Nicolai

after a song by Marty Zellar

A NOVA with giant rear tires and chrome hubcaps pulled up beside their little Chevette and raced its engine, in a crouch. The driver tossed his cigarette out the window and he pulled a Monsanto cap down low on his forehead.

"Oh man," one of the boys crammed into the back seat of the Chevette whispered excitedly, "JP, we have to, man, look at those two dirtballs!"

"Look, this is my parents' car, okay?"

The pair in the Nova stared over, old-looking and mean denim jackets and faint ragged mustaches. In the Chevette they passed a silver fire extinguisher across the back seat to the right side and poised its rubber hose at the window. "Look," JP began, "don't even— "

As the light turned green a jet of water sprayed into the Nova's open front window, soaking the driver and knocking off his cap as the windshield frothed and ran rivulets, how it looks in a car wash. JP steered a screeching left around the corner, ran a yellow light, sped down 4th Street past Hardees and the high school, the faster Nova looming behind. The Chevette was going as fast as he could push it when the Nova roared alongside, then pulled in front and skidded to a stop. With a quick U-turn JP darted down a familiar alley: mud from the spring thaw splashed the car's sides.

After driving a while JP turned to look at Tommy, who was still holding the fire extinguisher. "Thanks," he said, "way to go, asshole. Trying to wreck my dad's car?"

Tommy laughed. "Fucking A right I was. We could have taken them though, five to two. Why'd you take off?" He was the biggest of the five, a football guard who had made Honorable Mention All-Conference.

"I don't know," JP paused. "It's my dad's car, okay?"

"They were serious too, I mean," the boy in the passenger seat spoke quietly, half-turning, "I mean when they pulled that 'Dukes of Hazzard' move I just thought, you know, we're just screwing around but those guys were dead serious."

"Oh, okay, Trent." Tommy looked disgusted.

They drove around, down 1st Avenue and up Oakland past McDonalds, Dairy Queen, Hardees, then to 4th Street around the YMCA Oak Park Mall through downtown back down 4th again. All of them dressed pretty much alike, jeans and white basketball shoes, three wore blue letter jackets: except that two of them had dark hair and one wore glasses, they might have looked exactly alike to a traveler from another country, or even from outside this part of the state if such a person happened to somehow stumble into town. In the back seat they drank beer, ducking down below the windows and tipping up the bottles.

A group of girls in the Dairy Queen parking lot yelled to them but they were freshmen, the girls, a lot of blue eye-shadow and makeup, the kind that scratch boyfriends' initials into their arms with pencil erasers. JP drove out of town, on a country road through bean fields.

Across the fields a Conoco sign blinked orange-white-orange. Three bats circled a clump of trees beside the road, barely visible against the dark-blue sky. They leaned against the hood of the car drinking the warm beer, grimacing because the first two or three and cheap always taste bad.

"Who bought?"

"Nan."

"What?" They all laughed. "She's only sixteen."

JP shrugged. "I don't know, my sister buys all the time now at Viking. Since Nelly's not around I have to ask her all the time now."

"I heard his family's moving," Trent said. "It's so weird to think about him, just kind of going off. I mean, I just think of him as this regular stupid guy, fucking around working at Budget Oil."

"That Lisa Witkowski was in my government class and she hasn't been back since, that's like almost two months after the— "

"They never proved he did it," Tommy broke in.

"He raped her, man, you know how he used to talk about it," said Trent. "My uncle heard about it on his police scanner."

"God damn," they shook their heads, "what a strange guy."

Tommy had a joke: they lay back against the windshield. "Okay, so anyway there's this guy," he started, "and one night he's walking along the beach."

"And all of a sudden he sees this girl sitting there in a wheelchair. And he gets closer, okay, and he sees that she doesn't have any arms or legs, and she's crying.

So he's a nice guy, you know, a good guy so he goes up to her and says what's wrong, why are you crying?"

They had all heard it before but listened anyway, because Tommy was animated and good at telling a joke. The siren of a police car wailed far away in town.

"And the girl says, well, I'm nineteen years old and I've never been fucked. So he looks up and down the beach, there's no one there so he thinks, what the hell. He gets behind the wheelchair and pushes it down the beach toward this dock, out to the end of the dock and he pushes her off the end into the water. And he says there you go, now you're fucked."

How you laugh at an old joke, they laughed a little. A twelve of beer was left in the trunk. They sat on the car watching the freeway and didn't quite think, who is going to fuck us? and when and how, when we're not sitting drinking beer on this Chevette in the quiet night, the Conoco sign there.

*

The next morning JP's father looked over the top of his glasses. "The Chevette has mud all over it. What'd you do, go ditch riding?"

"Oh, yeah, I guess I went through some puddles."

His sister laughed. "Went through Seven Hills more like."

"Shut up, Nan." JP's head felt waterlogged and sick, and he put the Cheerios box in front of his face.

Their mother spoke from the kitchen, her voice muffled: "Please don't bring that kind of language into this house."

The family drove to church in silence, in the station wagon. As they passed Prescott Park, the athletic field named after the high school's great dead football coach, JP saw the man wrapped in a green blanket with long blond hair and a tangled beard, sitting on the grass near the water tower. Three small boys in baseball uniforms stood nearby, leaning on their bicycles.

"Who is that guy, I always see him around here."

"What? Oh him, that's, ah," JP's father pulled at his tight collar and tie, the old brown suit too small under the arms. "That's Pete Hanson's son, always seems to get somebody to listen to him."

"What does he do?"

"I don't know, as far as I know he doesn't do a damn thing. He ran for city council years ago."

Nan cracked her gum. "He comes into Walgreen's all the time when I'm working to buy the newspaper and stuff," she said. "He's always super polite but he has really long fingernails. I never want to give him his change. That would be so gross, those fingernails scratching my hand."

"He played baseball years ago, I think," their mother offered.

Church was the same as always. JP thought the familiar words along with the priest: father you are holy indeed the fountain of all holiness all creation rightly gives you praise, thank you for counting us worthy to stand in your presence . . . a dark-haired girl from the Catholic school was sitting two rows up to the left and he tried to catch her eye, maybe after Communion. The high school's hockey coach was reading something about the wrath of the Lord on the day of His burning anger, the pride of the ignorant and the insolence of tyrants. Out of his usual white golf shirt and red pants, he looked like a nice innocuous man up there—that is the hockey coach.

When they drove home after mass, the man was still talking to the kids at Prescott Park.

*

Nudging one another and snickering, the little boys stared at the man. He had a matted, straw-colored beard and his face was deeply creased: a faint musty smell hung around him, like a canvas tent rolled up and wet and left sitting in the garage.

"What d'you see, Birdman?" one of the boys asked while the others giggled and waited.

The man tipped his head back and studied the clouds drifting across, fat cumulus clusters in the western sky. "Turtle," he said, "another turtle, and West Virginia which was once a beautiful state . . . Lincoln. They teach you about Lincoln in school?"

"Yeah, sure, Birdman."

"Yeah, sure." Birdman sulked, rested chin on his knees and stared at the cars passing. "You guys play ball, or why the orange-and-blue get-up?"

"Yup, we're playing American Legion and we're gonna kick their ass!" the boy who had spoken first swore boldly.

"You heard of Moose Skowron of the New York Yankees, came through here with a Triple-A club years ago. He hit one over straight-away center." Birdman made the motion of swinging a bat while the boys talked about Legion, ignoring him. "Only two men ever to hit it over straight-away center, Skowron was the other."

A station wagon passed the field, Birdman saw and laughed, "Another fine upstanding local family on their way to praise the Lord!" He spoke like an evangelical preacher, squinting fiercely and raising the pitch in his voice. The boys moved uneasily astride their bikes.

"Alas, alas, great city that you are!" he burst out. "There's a bad time coming to you, in a single hour your doom has come!"

"Yeah, okay, see you later, Birdman." Birdman watched them ride over the practice field on their Sting-Rays. There was a kind of randomness in his posture as though he might be standing there or just as well anywhere else: some vacant-eyed person in a poorly fitting fur coat, slumped in the plastic chair of a large city's bus depot. He looked up but the turtles had dissipated. "The troubles of the world, Lord," he mumbled. "Lord, the bad time coming down at last on these happy-faced families in their brand-new cars . . . hmm."

On an adjacent field the high school baseball team was practicing, and Bird-man hooked his long fingers through the wire fence to watch the centerfielder shag fly balls. Nice arm, he mused, kid has a nice arm. Might have played some pro ball if you weren't going to be consumed by a rain of fire and sulfur. He laughed softly about the strangeness of that here.

*

A group of mentally retarded students walked slowly down the hall toward the art rooms. Teachers tried to keep them close to the side of the hall opposite a row of gray lockers, and other students gave them a wide berth. Trent and JP were leaning against their lockers talking when a huge, pear-shaped boy began to yell and flail his arms in a blank expression of panic. As the women instructors struggled to calm him the others stood shuffling their feet: quiet, slump-shouldered children wearing shirts buttoned to the top button, bright print dresses like the ones in consignment shops. A girl in a blue-and-white cheerleading uniform was coming out of the bathroom and stepped back, cowering in the doorway.

"He could do some damage, man," Trent said after the group moved on. "What do they think about. I wonder what's going on in their heads, you know?"

"They're probably geniuses," JP said. "They probably sit in that little room in the basement and laugh at us."

"You do the government questions?"

"Hell no. Going to practice?"

"I guess."

They stood there a while watching people walk. "Some guy got shot yesterday out by Beaver Creek, my uncle heard about on his police scanner," said Trent.

"What's your uncle do with his life, sit around and listen to his scanner all day?"

"Weekends he does. I guess they found the guy out in the middle of a cornfield, shot in the back of the head execution-style."

"Who was he?"

"My uncle says he saw the guy uptown all the time, they called him the snowman or something because he sold coke. They think he got shot by somebody in the drug business."

"No shit." JP shook his head.

"I guess, that's really weird, man."

They stood there. Watched girls. Very pretty, some of them, shoes clicking on the shiny floors and something gave an impression of blurring pastel colors. If you looked away for a moment, it was easy to forget which color it was, pink or yellow or sky blue or some other color used in dyeing Easter eggs. The overwhelming calmness walking by, JP's sister with the sweatshirt ripped at the shoulders and blue eye-shadow like the other freshman girls who two years ago wore pentagonal wire-rim glasses and plaid skirts, the sureness of it eased your mind.

And for JP stories of the gym teacher knifed in the parking lot last month, Nelly and the snowman and the old people slipping away in the Sacred Heart by the creek were stories on the news, with those kids in Africa. Anyway their deaths intruded only in that context, like an algebra problem: not much entertained and not talked about at track practice or on the way to class, by students hurrying with minds cleared as though by prayer.

The bell rang, startling JP. The halls were clear. Chemistry.

Later that night, JP was home trying to concentrate on some chemistry problems. His father, reading the paper on the couch, leaned back and groaned softly.

"Ohh, I don't know."

"What, dad?"

"Hmmm?"

"What don't you know?"

"Oh nothing. I was just," his father shook his head, "thinking."

JP tried chemistry for a while but he couldn't concentrate: the unbalanced equations danced in front of his eyes. Sometimes he would space out like this. It might be called daydreaming but this isn't so clear, in some indeterminate time, walking inviolate in a strange landscape and something about a guitar playing. After a while he got up and went to watch a ballgame on TV.

*

Sky in the west was turning to the riotous violets and reds of a storm front, now only a few flat clouds gathering on the horizon and Birdman sat vacant-eyed on a bench beside Oakland Avenue. Though he didn't generally keep up with the news, Birdman had heard somehow of Arlan Anderson's death, a good man. Was a good man.

He thought of their little marijuana business a long time ago: selling to high school kids and the occasional utility worker or policeman. Someone was always screwing up their careful plans, not that it had mattered. There was really no danger, as everything here it had seemed of little consequence.

Spit dripped out of his open mouth onto his beard. A paper boy with a sack of newspapers balanced on the handle bars of his bike whizzed by. "What's up, Birdman?" he called.

"Canada geese," Birdman pointed. "'The Scream.' Noah's ark."

*

JP.

He jumped awake in bed and looked up. The room was dark but there looked like dark figures in the doorway, leaning in toward him.

JP.

The figures swelled up and advanced across the floor, features indistinct in the weird gray light: there was no depth to them, like flat cardboard cutouts. He tried to shout but his throat was stuck.

Leave the town. Take your family and leave, we are angels of the Lord and we are going to destroy this place, the outcry reaching the Lord, we have been sent to. A gun was pressed to the back of his neck.

JP shook his head fiercely and sat up. He was sideways on the bed so his head had been lying across the wooden edge. The flat gray colors were gone, a streetlight shone through the window. Jesus Christ, he thought, I haven't had a dream like that in about ten years.

*

His parents ate fast mornings, cold cereal and rushing to make the 8:00 shift at the utility plant. By the time he came downstairs they were gone and he sat feeling sweaty at the table, because he hadn't slept well, and Nan was in the bathroom since 6:00 so he couldn't take a shower. She came bounding down the stairs as JP was desultorily poking at a bowl of Life: he noticed she was chewing gum.

"Nan."

"What?" She wore a huge gauze bow in her hair, like the rock star Madonna's.

"Nan, it's 7:30 in the morning and you're chewing gum already? Isn't that pretty gross?"

"So?" She glanced and repeated, "So?"

"I had a really weird nightmare last night," JP said. "I dreamed there were these kind of black ghosts in my room."

"Black, like Negroes, you mean?"

"No, not like that, I mean, I couldn't really see them, that's how you knew they were there because it was just nothing. It was like they were talking to me . . ." He looked up but Nan wasn't there, then heard her call, "Bye!" and the front door slam. JP decided not to go to first hour, anyway; it was review day in government class.

On his walk to school, late, JP saw Birdman coming out of Foodland with a bag of groceries. JP had gone a few steps past the store's door before he realized that Birdman was standing there, keeping the automatic door open and staring hard at him. The Foodland assistant manager looked up from a cash register: "Hey, buddy, you trying to heat the outside or what?"

"Smoke rising from the land, smoke like from a furnace!" Birman called, "You, you saw them!"

JP cut across a boarded-up gas station's corner lot and walked faster down the street towards school, his heart beating hard; he wasn't really sure why. He didn't ever, ever want to know anything about Birdman's life or have Birdman call to him.

"Don't play dumb, you were there, you saw them." Birdman took a few steps forward, off the black mat so the automatic door slid closed. "Wait!"

Looking back wildly, JP stumbled the last half-block, through the high school double doors and it was class time so no one was in the halls. He sat down against a locker. Jesus Christ, Jesus Christ, what was that about? And he thought of American Lit.; they were supposed to read *Walden* but he, JP, hadn't. When the bell rings, he should go up to 218.

In the library during third-hour study hall JP listened to Trent and Tommy: "That's all he talks about is his goddamn scanner," Trent was saying. "He comes over and eats and drinks beer and talks about the snowman, what he hears on the police band, what a fucking goon."

"Well, so?"

"I don't know, well, I guess I do know. It makes me think of when Nelly, you know, because my uncle did the same thing after that. And after anything else happens."

Trent shook his head. "That fucker was over at our house the same night talking about his scanner. All I could think was we rode in that same car all the time. You know, that same piece of shit green Duster he, that he drove off the bridge when they were chasing him."

"Well, you can't, I mean these things happen," said Tommy. "Nelly was a weird guy. It's not like one of us did it."

"No, I don't know. It 's just with all this shit I feel like something's going to happen or something."

JP started and looked up, almost blurted out the dream to them. The librarian came over then and told them to be quiet, this isn't a social area, so they sat there quiet until she went to the other end of the room. "What stuff, what happened?" JP said finally.

"Just this guy getting shot, right away after Nelly getting whatever you want to call it, and the stuff last month." Trent paused. There was a dull, thudding sound from a lower floor, like a hammer pounding on the walls. "Maybe this town is just getting to me, you know, maybe it's just boredom. This is kind of a weird place. We don't think it is but it is."

Out in the hall the mentally-retarded class shuffled by on their way to an early lunch. Staring out the door at them, JP whispered, "You know that guy they call Birdman?"

"Yeah."

"Why do they call him that?"

"I don't know; he just always has been. Maybe it's because of the clouds, that's what we always used to say to him—hey, Birdman, what do you see, or something like that. Why?"

"He knows me." Suddenly someone ran up the stairs outside and into the library: a junior girl they didn't know but recognized, and her face was pale. She opened her mouth and she shut it again.

"Mike shot Russ Jorgenson," she breathed out. "Mike shot Russ in the cafeteria,

Mike shot . . . " Teachers were running down the hall. The siren of a police car wailed, far away.

"That's Mike who, not Mike and Russ," Tommy demanded. "What Mike is it?"

"It might have been Kim," JP said. "Mike's Kim, and remember that part Friday what happened with Russ."

"Oh, fuck."

"They're best friends," Tommy said.

A loudspeaker crackled on the wall. The only time the intercom system had been used within their memory was once in a take-cover drill: the principal had come on and barked, "Take cover! Take cover!" twice before the speaker went dead and the classes were herded to the basement to assume the take-cover position, cross-legged with hands over your head, but it was only a drill. Now the principal seemed more tentative, scared almost.

"A student has been shot," he began. He cleared his throat. "In school. He is on the way to the hospital. Please don't interfere with the police by crowding around. There's nothing you can do down there. The rest of today's classes are canceled. Please use the north doors only and please go home. Use the north exits . . ."

The principal paused. "Go home, to your families."

*

JP went his usual route home, crossing the street automatically not looking both ways; there was no traffic this time of day anyway. As he turned the corner toward his house a red pickup truck pulled up to the curb, its horn blaring, and JP leapt back. It was Birdman: he had never seen Birdman inside any kind of motor vehicle before.

"Get in," cried Birdman. "Hurry up, let's go."

"Where are you going?"

"Come on! Don't you want to know? Don't you want to find out? Get the lead out!"

The principal hadn't said anything about practices being canceled. Was there track practice? JP didn't know. He thought of his parents and Nan and the news probably on the radio of Mike and Russ: all up the same sidewalk, same same same. JP stepped up into the passenger seat.

Birdman drove out around the water tower, past a cluster of gas stations at the edge of town. His long fingernails dug into his palms as he clutched the steering wheel.

"Is this your truck?" asked JP.

"Don't worry about anything in this town; it's as good as in the ground. You know it. It's been around once too often." He grasped the rear-view mirror and wrenched it off its mounting on the windshield, and he jerked the truck spraying gravel onto a bumpy country road.

"Okay, so, so where are we going?"

"Out. Now the time is come we're going out, what is amazing to me as one who has lived in this town his whole life is that's not a hundred cars coming out of there. The pile of sins there, piled up to heaven." He raised his voice as though singing. "The rotten evil sins at the heart of her."

By now JP was almost unconscious of the trees and barbed wire fence passing outside, bumping of the truck across ruts in the gravel road, and Birdman's waving hands song filled the small space inside the cab. He could remember feeling like this once before: in tenth-grade football practice the day before one game and the team had been laughing, clumsy and slow, when the coach dashed his cap to the ground and screamed, "I've never seen such a bunch of garbage! I've been coaching teams for twenty years and I've *never* seen anybody like you calling themselves football players. Get out of here! I can't stand to look at you!" As the shocked boys walked into the locker room JP had felt an almost reverential awe, and the next day the whole team played a great game for the coach who screamed, red-faced with his love for the game. Later a senior had told JP that the coach did the same thing last year and the year before; it was an act.

"If it's so bad, how come you lived here your whole life?" he asked Birdman.

"Well, I had to do what I could, been around the block a few times. Once it was not so bad here, before the bad things started and any place else wasn't just right." Birdman almost turned to look back but checked himself. "A guy has to do more than play ball and read poems. I would have stayed too, except when it's time," he stared almost pleadingly, "for the rain of fire and sulfur we had to leave."

They were about five miles out of town: on either side silos and leaning abandoned barns receded. JP looked over at Birdman. "How did you know, you know, about my dream?"

"Dream? Dream? " Birdman glared at him, crazy and bright. "You're not special. Don't think you were the only one."

This is too fucking weird, he thought. What am I doing talking here to this old guy. He's going to do like Nelly and drive off a bridge into two feet of water. "I have to go to the bathroom," JP said.

"Don't look back there!"

"I have to go to the bathroom, man, do you understand? I have to take a piss and if you don't stop, I'll piss inside the truck, inside your brand-new truck. Is that what you want?"

Birdman gave him a long look and pulled the truck over. "Don't look back; it's going to happen," he warned. "It's as good as in the ground."

JP got out and began walking backwards along the road, sweat breaking out as the sun heated his head and back of his neck and watching Birdman's face for a change in the pattern of dry wrinkles and crowfoot lines, for a sign.

He turned, and ran towards the town. Sprinting on his toes, pumping his arms, he concentrated on pulling the ground beneath his feet. The round top of the water tower glittered white in the distance.

"Don't!" Birdman cried. "Remember Lot's wife!" Birdman stood with his back to the town, listening.

For a while he gazed west across the fields as JP's footfalls receded into cricket's songs, and then he lay on the grass beside the road. Afternoon moved on and the sky gradually became a darker blue: as bats wheeled around above Birdman searching for gnats which hovered in swarms. In town lights were blinking on, the three vertical red lights of a radio tower flashed to warn low-flying aircraft away. Birdman waited, scanning the sky and noticed clouds gathered around the sunset, striking their irresolute poses of states, giant reaching animals and George Washington Crossing the Delaware.

What She Really Did

Ellen Lansky

"Darlin' face,'' Bud says to Darlene. "Can you make your Uncle Bud another cocktail?"

"Darlin' Face? You know she's not Darlin' Face." Gog says to Bud. Gog is Bud's sister; Darlene's grandmother. The three of them are sitting in lawn chairs set up in the front yard at Bud's farm—the traditional site for family reunions.

"Her name's Darlene, and she doesn't know about cocktails," Gog says, and pats her granddaughter's knee. "Except Martinis. This is my Martini girl."

"She ain't Martini, either," Cousin Tommy says as he drags up a chair next to Darlene. Tommy and Darlene are both twelve. Tommy is Bud's boy. He's big with a blond crew cut, blue eyes, and a red face. Darlene is going to be a small seventh grader. She has brown hair and eyes, and a dark tan for this time of year.

"It's Darlene," Gog says. "My own God-given middle name. Isn't that right, Girly Girl?"

"Gog's Girly Girl." Tommy laughs and gives Darlene an elbow. To Gog he says, "Why do they call you Gog anyway?"

"Bud did it," Gog says. "He couldn't say Gladys when he was a little boy. Gog was the best he could do, and it stuck."

"Thank your lucky stars, Doll Face," Bud says to Darlene, "that your name ain't Gladys."

"Gladys Darlene," Gog says. "That's me. And my girl is Darlene Louise."

"Darlene Marie," Darlene says.

"Darlene Marie Langsley," Gog pronounces. To Bud she says, "Did you know that her daddy's name used to be Lantzmann?" She pauses to drain her Martini, and passes the cup to Darlene who likes the green olives. "And he changed it to Langsley so he could get into medical school?"

"Is that true?" Tommy says to Darlene.

Darlene nods. "It had something to do with the number of Jews they'd accept to medical school back then," she says and picks up Gog's cup.

"Of course it's true," Gog says. "And it worked. He's a faculty physician now down there at the University Medical Center. Doctor Langsley."

"I like Lantzmann better," Darlene says. "I wish I had a Z in my name."

"Run make me another Martini, will you, Girly? And, Tommy, you fix your daddy a bourbon-and-soda. Go on."

"Martini Girl and Bourbon Boy," Tommy says and follows Darlene to the bar that's set up on a card table in the far corner of the garage.

*

What Darlene said she wanted for Christmas was a chemistry set, and she got it. She took it down to the basement, two flights below where everyone else lived. She set up her lab on her father's workbench. Spills wouldn't matter that way, and the workbench was tucked back in the concrete part of the basement they'd decided not to finish. Darlene liked the way the wrenches and screwdrivers hung from the hooks on the perforated wallboard. They were decorations because her father couldn't fix things at all. She read all the instructions and her father and then her mother and then her brother told her what's dangerous.

She knows about that. What she wants to do in her lab is not that volatile. Somebody gave her this little plastic box of shiny agates from Colorado as a Christmas present, and she's not about to glue them on a mirror. She mixes her chemicals, drops in a polished rock, and waits for it. She doesn't care if it turns to gold, and she doesn't want it to disintegrate. She wants to make it different.

*

Darlene and Tommy fix four drinks: two three-olive Martinis and two bourbon-and-sodas. They make a big production out of delivering two of the drinks to Bud and Gog, who are now playing penny-ante poker with their brother Al. Then they go giggling back to the garage, pick up the other two drinks, and step out the door to the back yard.

Darlene takes a big sip of the gin, and spits it on the ground. "Oh man," she says and shudders.

Tommy tries a man-sized slug of the bourbon, and spits it on the ginned ground. "Snake piss," he says.

"Here." Darlene pushes her cup at Tommy's left hand and takes his bourbon. "Let's switch."

"What?" Tommy says. He's red in the face.

Darlene with caution, tries the bourbon, tries it again. "Not bad," she pronounces. "Try that."

Tommy tries the Martini, swallows, makes a stewed tomato face. "Worse snake piss," he says. He moves to switch back.

"Nope," Darlene says and backs away. "I want this one."

"No way," Tommy says. He takes a step.

Darlene twists, holds her ground. "Cut it out, Tommy. I want this one. You have to be a gentleman."

Tommy's stopped cold. "A gentleman?"

"Yes. You have to be polite and let me have this one."

Tommy frowns, then tosses the gin. "Stay here," he says. He wheels back to the garage.

Darlene's about to protest the dumped gin and olives, especially the olives. She steps on them, one at a time. Tommy returns with a new cup and a smile on his blond-capped tomato face. "Down to the dairy barn," he says, as if trumpets were flourishing.

*

Darlene says it smells and she ain't staying, but she follows Tommy along the stalls. He turns into the last stall which has been swept clean of cow and now holds artifacts: an old milk can, some upturned buckets, a three-legged stool, a line of rakes, and a rusty old push lawnmower. Darlene rights the stool and sits on it as Tommy arranges the sturdiest bucket and a slatted crate into a little bovine cafe scene.

"Well," Tommy says and picks up his bourbon. "Cheers."

Darlene is impressed with this gallantry. "Cheers," she says. They touch cups and eye each other across the rims.

The bourbon burns a little, but Darlene likes it. She drinks with caution and keeps drinking because Tommy's not saying anything. He takes a big drink, hesitates, swallows, puts down his cup and says, "Ahhh." And blushes.

"You're going to be drunk," Darlene says.

Tommy stands up. "No, I ain't." He turns and bolts out of the stall. "Sit tight," Darlene hears him say.

She sits tight and sips her drink. The bourbon is hot inside, but she gives a shiver. A cow gives a tremendous moo, a sound like those that come out of the little toy tippy cans: this one amplified, as if it were a barrel. It's cool in the barn and it smells like the State Fair, though the air is thicker—crowded with cow smells and mouldering hay, old wood. And ghosts. Before this was Bud's dairy barn, it was Big John's—the man who came over from some grim German town. Big

John, with his granite cheekbones and knotty muscles and his wife Mary—big as a draft horse—they made this place. And Gog was here, with those old boys who are out there now playing poker. And Darlene's mother—every summer Gog would send her here to learn how to sew or cook or milk: to build character and a broad back.

"Darlene? You still here?" Tommy is back. He sets down four more cups, sits himself. He looks at Darlene, shrugs and says, "Well, cheers again."

"Cheers," Darlene says and drinks. She feels the bourbon like a current. "Are you getting drunk?"

Tommy takes a big drink, wipes his mouth, and grins, "Yeah." The cow a few doors down, her can tipped, gives another resonating moo. "Hush up down there," Tommy yells.

"Do you like cows?" Darlene wants to know. She sips tentatively for a smaller charge.

"Nope." Tommy drinks, smacks his lips. "Horses. My favorite animal. What's yours?"

Darlene considers this. "I don't know. We have a cat and a dog, but I don't really have a favorite animal." She stops, sips, and says, "I like bones."

"Bones!" Tommy splutters in his bourbon. "Like wishbones? Dog bones?"

"No. Real bones. Hands and feet especially. I like the way they look in those anatomy charts."

"That's weird."

"No, it's not. My dad lets me keep his anatomy books from medical school, and I have a chart of all the bones that I hung up in my, um, room." She says "room" because she figures it's none of his business about her lab.

"Does you dad bring you bones from the hospital?"

"Well, not exactly. He brings me plastic models, though. They're really cool. I have a knee joint that really bends and a shoulder blade. I'm trying to get him to get me a skull." She picks up her drink and decides not to tell him that what she really wants is a real-life skeleton that she can hang from a ceiling hook in her lab. Her dad gave her a small plastic one, mounted on a fake marble square like the knee and the shoulder blade. Darlene liked it okay, but she said she'd really rather have the real thing so she could hang it and bend it and make it rattle. Her dad said it would cost too much—even for a Christmas present.

"A skull? Yuck." Tommy drains his glass and picks up one of the fresh cups which have lemon slices and olives in them. "What's your favorite bone?"

"Hands and feet. I told you," Darlene says. After a moment's consideration and a sip of the bourbon, she says, "Hands, I guess. They're more useful."

"You know what mine is?" Tommy makes a grin that Darlene's seen on her brother's face.

"What? Your dick, right?"

Tommy laughs and turns redder than ever.

"That's not a bone, you know."

"Don't tell me that." His look says he knows it all.

Darlene feels she's way ahead of him. The bourbon's making her smart. "It ain't. It's just skin and junk."

"Spunk," Tommy says. He drinks about half his bourbon, spilling some down his shirt, laughing. "Skin and spunk." He eyes her. "You know what's spunk?"

"Yeah, I know what's spunk." She reaches for more smart bourbon.

"How do you know?"

Darlene takes another drink. "I've seen my brother do it."

Tommy's so surprised he knocks the cups off the crate. "What? You watched him?"

Darlene watches the ice cubes melting and the lemons and olives glowing on the barn floor. Then she looks at Tommy who looks as if his eyes are going to bug out of his head. She wonders how his skull would look skinned and mounted on a marble block. "Yeah," she says slowly. "In the basement one day."

"That's disgusting." Tommy's bucket upturns as he stands. He's impossibly red. "You can't do that." He turns and runs out of the barn.

"I did it," she calls after him. She sways on her three-legged stool, falls off with a whump that doesn't hurt. She wonders if this means she's drunk. "I did it," she mutters to the ghosts in the barn. She stands up, brushes herself off. "I did it," she tells the cows as she leaves the barn to join Gog and Bud and Al at penny-ante poker.

Spring Concert

Stephen Peters

"MICHAEL," MRS. HEINEMANN says to me. "Michael Tressler will please sing his alto part and stop showing off. There are no tenors in this group."

I was thirteen here, understand, and I had no nicknames in her presence. I yank my chin back and concentrate hard on singing alto, though when my voice has slipped a gear like this it is no use. This has been happening on and off for weeks, and Mrs. Heinemann's pleas have meant nothing to my willful vocal cords.

"Stay in alto just for tonight, Michael Tressler."

I wear a clean, short-sleeved shirt and a clip-on tie. Carla Rusinsky stands next to me in a strapless red sundress, and her golden hair is combed to one side and battened down with barrettes and left to fall on her bare shoulder. We are both frozen in place, afraid to acknowledge that the backs of our hands are touching. Mrs. Heinemann goes through the windup motion with her willowy arms, and forty seventh-graders lurch off into song again. She flaps her wings at us, mouths our lyrics with all her long face, and I breathe in Carla's lilac perfume until my voice careens back into alto.

"All right, people," Mrs. Heinemann tells us after we've slogged through another of her endless arrangements. "Listen now." She claps her hands and waits for us to settle into attention. "Be back here at ten minutes to eight and line up. That gives you five minutes to go comb your hair."

Billy Dreibelbis pushes through the back of the crowd and puts his hands on my shoulders. "Get me out of here, Mike," he says, and we muscle a path toward the door. "Is your voice really doing that, or are you faking it?" he wants to know. Billy sings soprano and, if anything, his voice is only getting higher.

"You can't *fake* that," I tell him.

I shake Billy off in the hallway and go find my father. He is at the usual spot in the lobby, leaning against a post, a paperback book stuffed into his sports jacket pocket, his belly turning the waistband of his trousers back in a neat, white fold. He has the trademark bushy black beard. I am circled and squeezed in his arms. "Where have you *been?*" He kisses the top of my head. "I've been out here *forever.*"

My father has driven sixty miles of Pennsylvania roads from where he lives to see my spring concert.

"The drive over was great," he says. "Everything's blooming its brains out. I kept the window down all the way to smell it."

He comes to all my concerts and to Parent-Teacher Nights, or he has in the past. Soon he and the bluegrass band he plays bass for will move to Louisville, Kentucky, and we won't see each other much until I am older. My father was the Original Hippie, the Last Great Beatnik. He and his friends had big plans to make it in the music world. I stand very straight, my shoulders back like a soldier's, thinking it would be better if he didn't hug me here. Since the Louisville announcement, I don't know what to say to him.

"Did you hear us warming up?" I ask.

His eyes look past me, focusing on nothing in particular. I know what he is going to say. "You sounded good." I get a light tap of his fist on my chest. "Really good."

"No, we didn't," I say. "We were practicing those songs because we can't learn them right. Everybody's really mad at her."

He is staring at his right cowboy boot as if something about it is terribly unpleasant. Then, in slow motion, he kicks an imaginary rock or can.

"Why doesn't she make you *smile* when you sing?" he asks for the 500th time. My father is a man given to enthusiasms, and I have very consciously pushed his Mrs. Heinemann-and-the-subject-of-singing button. "That would lift your voices toward some sort of *joy.*" Despite his girth and height, he is sometimes unbelievably graceful, almost dainty. He stands on tiptoe, gesturing with fine, long hands, his wrists white, thin, and hairless sticking out of his cuffs. People have turned to see who this raised voice so caught up in itself is. "And why—why, *why*—doesn't she choose simple music and just let you *sing?*" My face signals that his manner is becoming an embarrassment. "After all," he stage whispers, "the whole idea is to make music, to celebrate!"

I agree. We *all* agree. Even Mrs. Heinemann must agree, but I wish he would please shut up.

"My voice keeps cracking, " I tell him. "I don't think I can sing my part, but she won't listen to me."

All his considerable weight rests on one leg as he thinks about this. "It's because she's bored with her life, Mike," he sighs. "People need to grow, to move," he says.

I know he hopes I read his mind here. Without saying the exact words, he is trying to explain why he is leaving me again. I feel slightly ashamed of this man I am standing with in the crowded lobby. My friends have started drifting back toward the practice room.

"Are you giving me a ride afterwards?" I ask.

"Sure."

"I'll find you then," I say and leave him.

Everybody has the jitters. We line up on the bleachers, the closed curtain separating us from our audience of murmuring parents. The talk in the cafeteria and on the school bus all week has been that we are not ready for this concert, that we sound awful. Mrs. Heinemann decided five weeks ago we would do all new material. Now, with the stage lights bright and hot on our faces and with Carla's lilac mixing with another girl's rose, Mrs. Heinemann's right hand points in a karate-chop position and counts singers in tiny motions like a good knife dicing vegetables. Every few strokes she stops and waves us closer to one another, and our feet shuffle on the wooden planks. Carla and I try not to touch flesh to flesh. Mrs. Heinemann whispers instructions, holds her right palm up for our attention, points the left to Audrey Klinger, the accompanist, and to the stage hand who will open the curtain. Both hands come down, we swallow collectively, and Audrey begins playing "Consider Yourself" from *Oliver*.

As the curtain opens, I clasp my hands in front and watch Mrs. Heinemann's flapping wings for the signal to sing. Then Audrey misses a difficult run, gets lost, and we begin in disarray. But I am firmly in alto. We lug together, trying to find our way in the rounds and tempo changes of Mrs. Heinemann's fancy arrangement. Disaster. When it is over, the audience applauds politely, as it does no matter how good or bad we are, and a smiling, oblivious Mrs. Heinemann clicks her high heels to the microphone.

"Welcome to our" this, that, and the other, she is saying. I am looking out at the rows of faces for my mother and father, who will be sitting far away from each other. She goes on thanking people for their contributions, like a little child blessing everyone she knows in her bedtime prayers. I am struck by the sort of comment my father would make: "She is trying to spread the blame for this mess."

At the termination of this speech, Audrey starts the endless, over-moody introduction to "Moon River." The stage lights go down and pale blue ones come up. But not all the blue lights work correctly, and part of the chorus is left in darkness as the stage hands knock around in the back to fix the problem. Our parents chuckle nervously as the light finally comes up. Mrs. Heinemann, unfazed, waves her director's arms at us in a private dance. We are not yet singing.

Billy Dreibelbis once suggested that if that introduction were two bars longer she might actually start to fly. My father's beard and receding hairline somehow pop out of the crowd, and I know from how he stretches side to side and up and down that he is looking for me. Once, when I could tell he had found me on stage, he waved. And he kept waving until I acknowledged him by nodding my head yes. I complained about my embarrassment later, but he only shrugged and laughed. "That's the kind of person I am," was all he would say.

We are singing "Moon River" now, and we sound all right. No real enthusiasm, of course, but we manage to hit the right notes. We finish and move from song to song, but we have peaked on "Moon River," and everything else seems to only drag our spirits lower. The program is rigged against our ever soaring. Our parents shift in their seats, losing interest. And there on the stage, at thirteen, I was for some reason struck by the realization that my father was right to escape to something beyond the life of our little town. He was right to pay the heavy price in alienation and hostility I already knew I'd levy for this betrayal. I felt somehow unclean even thinking this at the time, as if *I* were the one walking off to suit myself. But then something happened:

Our program is almost over. The lights are up, and we have just butchered a complicated, disastrous medley. My father is scowling, boiling. I don't even have to look at him; I know how he reacts. Even Mrs. Heinemann seems to have come half-awake to how awful we sound. Her movements are heavier, her mouth has fallen, she closes her eyes as if praying just to get through this evening. She is looking down the barrel of forty angry seventh-graders.

Then Billy Dreibelbis whispers the name of a song we have done well all year, and many of us turn to look at him. He won't look directly at Mrs. Heinemann, but he smiles defiantly. Somebody repeats the title, and then somebody else. Mrs. Heinemann holds her hand up and stares at the floor to quiet us. But dresses rustle and heavy shoes clomp restlessly on the bleachers; more of us whisper the title.

She clicks over to the piano for a conference. Audrey's upturned face nods, and then Mrs. Heinemann comes back across the stage and says the title. Victory. We buck up, hug ourselves, and sing. It is strong, almost desperate singing. I have the sense that we are swaying. When Carla's arm touches mine, I glance into her face and, for one supercharged instant, we sing into each other's eyes. My father's neck almost cranes off his shoulders to get a better look at me. Carla and I edge closer. We are practically holding hands. Our hips are touching.

Then my voice suddenly shifts into a strong tenor, so strong it varooms past the other voices in the chorus and carries out into the auditorium. Somebody, a man, laughs, but I see, I feel, people take special note of me. Mrs. Heinemann's eyes panic, plead. But I can't stop myself. My father's voice climbs inside my head. "Smile, Mike! Smile!"

I smile, lifting both my voice and my face. I imagine the chorus bands together to push me forward. I am filled with a strange sadness and joy, an obedience to inevitability, an overwhelming awareness that the very lining of my soul is now irreparably torn and made visible. My father bounces in his seat; he is waving.

I was thirteen years old here. Changes were taking place in my life that I did not yet understand.

Was he waving me on, or was he only waving goodbye?

The Old Woman's Blessing

Donna Nitz Muller

T HE OLD WOMAN'S VOICE was unusually clear and even. For once she
wasn't whining. "Jeannie, bring me another pillow," she said. "I need to lay
taller."

The child stared at the harsh, wrinkled face some seconds before she grabbed
a pillow and lifted the bony head and shoulders. The old woman was silent through
this, which made Jeannie apprehensive. The child was accustomed to saying
nothing during her shift at the dying woman's bedside, but now felt obliged to
fill the void.

"All right now?" she asked while looking into the face of her grandmother. Her
own voice was tight and small.

The old woman's blue eyes were normally piercing, and Jeannie avoided any
direct contact. Today, in only the first few minutes of her two hours, she en-
countered those eyes. She felt that tiny jump like fingers snapping inside her.

The old woman's eyes were as lucid as her voice today, and Jeannie could see
that her grandmother was excited about something. She pointed a thin finger
toward the chair, and Jeannie sat. The fingers wiggled for her to move closer so
the child slid her chair across the cold tile until her knees touched the hard steel
bar beneath the bed.

"I knew less when I got married than you do already. Now days kids know
too much," she said and the mellow tones dipped away a bit to allow for a second
of the familiar frustration.

Jeannie took a deep breath and leaned back on the hard, wood chair.

"I know you're there, child. You can breathe. I was only thinking of when I married sixty-four years ago today." She stared straight up, her white hair pulled fiercely back from the high cheek bones.

"I thought I should die of fright," the woman continued, and Jeannie could think of no way to stop the old woman from saying anything more.

"Horrible, horrible thought, to be naked, to be touched," and a shudder from the woman rippled even the white bedspread across her breast.

"You were afraid of grandpa?" Jeannie's amazement at such a thought overcame her natural, deep reserve.

"Oh Lord, child, I was sure I would die. I pretended to have my period for three weeks, nearly half of the journey to this country." Her lips closed tight like a vise. And though Jeannie waited for the usual little laugh that accompanied memories from years before her time she understood that her grandmother would not even smile.

"When the boat was rocking in a screaming wind, the salt water splattering my sensitive skin so that even in our room my face burned, he decided it was time to set things right." There was no trace of softness in this memory. Jeannie looked toward the ceiling. She did not know what her grandmother saw there.

After a minute Jeannie asked her grandmother a question. She carefully concealed the importance of it because the old woman was contrary. Jeannie forced the question through her tight throat and between her tight lips. Her hands, folded on her lap, were so tight that her knuckles sent messages of pain. "Grandmother, wasn't he nice to you? Didn't grandfather love you? Didn't you know it was supposed to be nice, with your husband, I mean?" Jeannie blushed in the semi-darkness. It was as though addressing God Himself, or worse, questioning Him. The blush began to burn on her cheeks.

"No, no," the old woman said, her voice animated, higher pitched, but still too feeble to carry as far as the thick, heavy door. "Conceiving children was a darker secret than the devil himself. I was so stiff and scared that the pain nearly did do me in."

There were tears in the crevices of her cheek and neck. "And my husband cared not a whit about it. 'Don't cry now,' he told me. 'It has to be gotten done,' and he came near to striking me. Yes, in all our years together that was the one time he came near to striking me. Couldn't tolerate women's tears."

The old woman let her head sink deep into her pillows.

"Did you never know, Grandmother, how it could be?" Jeannie's voice was so soft and low that it might work as a lotion on the woman's wrinkled temples.

"Could it really be so horrible?" the child continued, barely aware that she spoke aloud.

"Horrible," the woman answered, and there was a long silence.

This time Jeannie knew that her grandmother was not asleep, so she waited.

She understood the old woman had a point in talking like this, so, she waited with a patience not natural to her.

"Your mother wasn't his. That's a secret I'll carry to my grave. I lay here trying to beg pardon for that sin, but I can't bring myself to do it. I can't bring myself to say I am sorry for this offense. It saved me from drying up inside. It gave me a short-lived glimpse of tenderness and love that I never forgot, never could forget. Of course, I ended it all when I was carrying your mother. But I can't ask for forgiveness and now I'll burn in hell."

"Grandma, you won't!" said Jeannie, and grabbed the limp, pallid hand, cold in her own and always, before, as concrete an object of fright as the child could name.

"Your real grandfather was a farmer, too. Had a family. It happened because we were both too innocent. Once I had my first taste of his slow, sweet lovemaking I couldn't do as I should have right away. Even when I did finally tell him we couldn't ever be together again he was kind. He was so kind, concerned about me. I cried till I thought I would break."

The old woman shook her head slightly, but never wavered her gaze from the white, shadowed ceiling. "Neither one of 'em knew about your mother's true origins. No need to make it all harder. I had children to raise."

Jeannie lay the white hand on the white, woven spread. She grabbed a kleenex and wiped the old woman's nose and cheeks. "Don't worry," she said to the woman's profile. "Don't worry about burning in hell, Grandmother," she sighed.

And so the woman at last had reached the core of the thing. She had been prepared to tell it. The child was surprised at not being frightened. Still, she glanced quickly at the lighted dial of her watch.

It was a long time before she could expect her mother. It was taking weeks for the old woman to die. Her grandmother was not to be left alone. This much, Jeannie's mother insisted, we can do for her. And so, Jeannie took her turn without futile complaint. And now it was still better than an hour before she would be rescued. She sighed aloud.

"You'll know better, child. You'll know to make it right the first time. Men are more decent now."

"Yes, Grandmother," she answered flatly and wondered about the truth of it.

"I wish I could be sorry. Then I could go ahead and die. It's such hard work to hash this out."

"Is my real grandfather still alive too?"

"No, I'm the last one."

"Well, he isn't burning in hell, is he?" she asked, and she fully intended it as a comfort to the old woman.

"No, no, child. It's not the man's sin," she said, and she raised her head to look at Jeannie but did not quite succeed before the fragile head fell back. Still the effort was such as to make Jeannie step back and bump the hard wood chair.

"Grandmother, should I call a priest? Please, Grandmother, let me call the priest," and she sat on the chair holding tight to the seat beneath her and twisting her feet about the legs.

"No, I can't die yet," she said, but she closed her eyes, exhausted.

Several minutes passed in silence and in the expanding darkness. "Jeannie," the old woman whispered, "there is a way."

Jeannie's stomach instantly knotted hard like a fist.

"Take my hand," the woman ordered her. She raised the long, white fingers from the bed.

"Wait for me to sleep and then say it for me. You do know the Act of Contrition, child?"

The old woman's fingers were suddenly so strong as to hurt Jeannie's hand. "Yes, Grandmother, I know it. But that won't work. Why would that work?" She was pleading with the old woman and knew the futility of it so well as to be reconciled before she finished her last word.

"Child, you know why. How come you're going to that expensive school if you're not taught anything important? If I'm unconscious you can say it for me. Just like baptizing. Only say, 'She is heartily sorry.' Always put her instead of I because you're speaking for me, understand?"

The old woman was very excited. Her eyes flashed and her fingers tightened.

"Oh, my God," Jeannie whispered.

"Not yet," said her grandmother, her voice scathing. "You have to wait until I'm asleep. The timing is most important."

"No, Grandma, I was," Jeannie started and then changed her mind. "Won't God know you're planning this?"

"Doesn't matter," the old woman answered, the excitement flashing from her eyes and being carried like an electric current through to her fingertips. "A rule is a rule. You have to save your old grandmother. Now promise me you'll do it right, just like I said. Don't you tiptoe out when I doze off. Promise me," she said, and the eyes looked at the child, and the hand squeezed even tighter.

"I will do it right, Grandmother."

"Good," the old woman whispered. "I trust you will. Remember your mother must never know. If you can save your grandmother from burning in hell and keep it a secret inside your own skin that's a sight more than I expected from you originally. You were always such a snip of a child." She had to rest.

"I'll bless you from the other side until your own dying day. I promise you that. You shut your eyes and ask me for help and whether you know it or not, I'll be with you." The old woman was so serious that her head moved up and down across her pillow and she moved the fix of her stare from the ceiling to Jeannie's ashen face.

Jeannie wondered how the woman, so awake, would be able to sleep. Jeannie had never known her grandmother to say more than two or three words in a row. The old woman never needed words to make her presence or her desires known. Now Jeannie watched her grandmother calm herself. The old woman closed her eyes and began to breathe evenly, trying to call up sleep.

The shadows across the room were nearly touching so that only a single line of dull light remained through the crack of the heavy curtains. Jeannie considered tiptoeing from the room and racing for home. Of course, she couldn't.

For one thing, she couldn't extricate herself from the grip of the old woman's fingers without waking her. For another, it really wasn't such a difficult thing to do. She could recite the prayer as the dying woman wanted.

She could do that easily enough. Easier than trying to explain to her mother why she left before her time was over.

She waited several more minutes, standing beside the high bed until the darkness covered them, and her grandmother's grip relaxed. She reached behind herself and grabbed her jacket, throwing it on the hard floor. She knelt and buried her face in the side of the bed.

Jeannie said the prayer aloud in her natural, soft accents. Her voice, even muffled in the spread, echoed mildly around them like a tent. "Oh, my God, she is heartily sorry," she said, and the words hovered in the room.

She recited the prayer through twice and then removed her hand from between the thin, hard fingers. She silently felt for the chair back and moved it back to its place and sat down.

"Thank you, child." The woman's hoarse whisper startled Jeannie.

"Grandmother!" Jeannie was so alarmed she felt a choking knot of tears in her throat. "Now we have to do it again, and mother will be here soon. You know she won't understand this predicament."

"No, we don't. It worked that time." The voice was no longer clear. The woman again shut her eyes.

Jeannie had just leaned against the chair back wondering why it had worked, when the shaded light came on. She rose to her feet and turned toward the door in a single, swift motion.

"Why are you sitting in the dark, Jeannie?" her mother asked without looking at her while throwing her huge canvas bag stuffed with folders onto the sink.

"Grandmother had a tough time getting to sleep. I didn't want to disturb her," the child answered, amazed at the calmness of her own voice.

The tall, slim woman crossed the room in two full, swinging strides. She checked the old woman with a gentleness that Jeannie had never noticed in her mother before. "Okay, sweetheart," she whispered while turning. She seemed to fill the entire room with her presence. "You can go on home."

Then, as Jeannie was leaving the room, her mother touched her elbow. "Today was her anniversary. She would have been married sixty-four years today. And I thought," she paused, apparently considering her words, and shrugging as she continued, "I thought perhaps today would be the day. You know the stories about how often people slip into the next life on a day like their anniversary."

Jeannie said nothing, but still she made no effort to leave. The two of them stood in the doorway, momentarily embarrassed by the unaccustomed frankness between them.

"I can only hope my marriage is as happy as the one she shared with my father. Right to this day she always had him somewhere in her thoughts. I don't know why I wanted to mention that to you." Her mother's voice was beautiful. Jeannie was often caught in the sound and didn't really hear the words.

"Yes," Jeannie answered, "she talked about him today before she slept."

At fourteen, Jeannie had a sophisticated look about her that seemed to say, "I am what I am, and I like it." She had an easy, graceful stride much like her mother's and appeared never to lose her calmness or her peace of mind.

Now both mother and daughter looked toward the bed where the sightly nasal sound of breathing had silenced.

The mother ran for an attendant. The child moved to stand against the bed. Jeannie stared at the quiet face of her grandmother. "Remember to bless me from the other side," she whispered.

As her mother entered she was telling the official nurse, "Sixty-four years ago today," and then she reached to wrap her long, shawled arms about her daughter. The child for some reason was sobbing violently.

Green Life

John Mihelic

EMMA JENSEN'S bony knees are pushing into the damp ground, but she doesn't care. She's too busy scraping dead leaves off the iris beds. She smiles at the loamy smell of the dirt, at the warmth of the April sun on her back. Under the gray-brown crust there's life in the dark soil: worms, tiny pale bugs, spiders dashing and waiting—all awakening as light and air flood in. She sighs from pleasure.

Mrs. Falk watches Emma from the kitchen window of the house next door. She sees Emma shifting her weight from side to side because her knees are getting wet. To Ruby Falk this is Emma's usual difficult way of doing things. Much easier to put down an old rug and kneel on that. Emma isn't wearing a scarf. Ruby watches her brush a wisp of hair from her face with the back of a muddy hand. She shakes her head and turns to Margaret, her daughter, who is feeding her baby at the kitchen table.

"Emma always has dirt under her nails," Ruby says.

Margaret doesn't answer.

"I can't get her to wear gloves when she's working in the garden," Ruby says. Still no answer from Margaret, who is humming as she spoons pablum.

Ruby turns back and slides her own rubber-gloved hands back into the dishpan. "I just don't think it looks good," she says to the dishwater.

Outside Emma stands up stiffly, her pleasure done. She rubs the grains of dirt from her bare knees, and right then between her legs she feels the spurt, warm and thick, the signal that yet another in her dwindling supply of eggs has died. She lugs her basket of wet leaves to the compost barrel. Then, without even a look back at the irises to admire her work, she goes inside to wash up and start her supper.

The two houses, Emma's and the Falks', were built by the same carpenter before the Great Depression. They look related, and the lush plant life surrounding both enhances the resemblance: bridal wreath, evergreens, peonies, rose trellises, irises, lily of the valley. But the personalities of the two houses remain distinct. It's a neighborhood of wide yards and picnic tables. The Falks' big two-story frame house looks mature and comfortable, intimately familiar with the comings and goings of children and husbands, almost smug. Next door Emma's one-story house looks ill at ease: a shy half-grown daughter peering out from behind her mother.

After supper Emma pulls her porch door shut after her, carefully locks it, and tucks the key in her purse. Clutching her unbuttoned coat against the chill, she crosses through the early evening light to the Falks'. Until recently she has moved with big strides and a bounce that made her seem younger than her age, still waiting, still willing to do just about anything, or try at least, if the right person came along. Now, as she walks she can feel the ache in her knees.

Mr. Falk comes to the door in his stocking feet, his vest open. He's been reading the newspaper.

"Howdy, Emma. Warm enough for you?"

But he is turning back to the living room before she can think of an answer. When she finally blurts out, "Sure is," the words seem to bounce off his back and fall to the floor.

"Ruby! Emma's here!"

"I'll be right down," Ruby calls down from upstairs. Emma is left standing in the hall with her coat on. She's polite. She waits.

"It's spring, Emma. Sap's starting to rise." The words come suddenly from behind the newspaper.

"Oh, is it?" Her voice cracks. She thinks for a minute he's serious, then, embarrassed, realizes he's not. It's Warren Falk's perennial spring joke. He mentions sap rising, he gets a laugh.

Warren is particularly fond of his own good humor with Emma. References to sex, he thinks, go a long way toward making her spinsterhood a lighter burden. He likes to see her cheeks redden.

Warren never makes his comments in the presence of his wife. No. They border the guarded terrain of his fantasies. More than once he has glimpsed a ripple of lean muscle in Emma's arms, or caught sight of the curling hair under her arms and been rushed by his imagination into musky sexual encounters. The two of them are always in less than tender surroundings: in a garage, say, or in the humid mustiness of a basement. Ruby would never understand.

Warren's relations with Emma in the presence of his wife, in the presence of anyone else, are sunny, distant, devoid of emotion. He's never touched Emma, never accidentally brushed her arm. Only his thoughts reach toward her, vapory tendrils that search briefly for an opening and then fade away. Behind his newspaper he is imagining her naked and bending.

Emma doesn't recognize any signals coming from Warren. She simply feels uncomfortable, pressured, when she's alone with him. When she thinks of Warren she automatically thinks of Ruby. He is a husband, Ruby's husband, and linked to Ruby as personally as a piece of Ruby's clothing would be. Any relationship with him that excluded Ruby would be as unthinkable as if an overcoat suddenly started to talk to her.

"Take off you coat, Emma. Sit down," he says from behind his paper.

Emma sits on a hassock near the door but she keeps her coat on.

"Any good times lately?"

Good times? Good times? Why does he always ask me that? She thinks of a salesman in a checkered suit blowing a party noisemaker. She thinks of men drinking from a hip flask behind the barn.

"No. You know me."

"You should go out more often. Kick up your heels."

Emma sees a woman in a long farm dress dancing a jig. She smiles.

Emma isn't unmarried because of a broken heart, or because she was homely. It's more a matter of poor timing, missed connections. She grew up on a farm. When she was still young and eligible she was extremely shy, and she suffered from the mindset that's typical of first-born women, particularly farm women: premature sobering and a preoccupation with all the matter-of-fact chores of running the family. She spent her time gardening, cooking, gathering eggs, caring for her younger brothers and sisters.

As a girl, Emma's fantasies were selfless and maternal, not romantic. She would lie on her bed with a hand mirror after a bath, spread her legs, examine her purple leaves, and try to imagine the sight and sensation of birth. She'd fold her arms as if cradling a head. But it was always the body of an infant she saw touching her own, never a man's. Tiny hands reached out and held. It was a tiny heart she felt beating against her own.

Of course, Emma had been willing to be courted. And she certainly would have made some bachelor farmer a good wife. But she was too tongue-tied to make the kind of easy conversation that would encourage a young man, too responsible to arouse much interest, especially prurient interest. On the whole: not much fun. So it was an old man who took her: Charles Borland, a retired and widowed cattle-buyer, a friend of her father. She was nineteen. At the supper table her father folded his napkin, scratched his neck, and squinted at her.

"Emma, old man Borland's wanting a housekeeper now that he's alone."

Emma felt her heart stop and then start again.

"He asked if you want the job. Pretty good pay. You ought to think about it."

Emma twisted a button on her dress. After a moment she started to cry and left the table. When her father had said she ought to think about it, he meant the matter was already decided. Emma had never fought anything as hard as she would've had to fight to keep from going to Borland's. It was a signal they'd given up on her marrying.

A month later on a cloudy Sunday afternoon her father drove his obedient daughter to town in the pickup. Her dowry as a housekeeper was a new dress and new shoes. Everything she brought with her to her new life was fit into a tied-up cardboard suitcase. As soon as she arrived she unpacked her things in the spare bedroom and went out to say goodbye.

"Now don't you come running home," her father told her. "You're a lucky girl." Then he shook hands with Borland and drove away, leaving her twisting her handkerchief into a hard knot.

"How about cooking some supper, Emma?"

Those were the first words Borland had ever spoken to her. She cried immediately, but a few minutes later, with her eyes dry, she followed him into the house. He was not an unkind man, simply a man of few words with no idea what to say to a girl of nineteen. That night she lay awake listening to him snore in the other bedroom. She heard him shuffle down the hall toward her room. Was this what her father planned for her? Why he'd told her not to run home? She was standing by the bed in the dark as he shuffled past to the bathroom. She waited, trembling, as he shuffled back down the hall to bed. Finally she fell asleep listening to the creaking of the house.

Eventually the lulling routine of living with Borland, the gardening, the housework that was easier than on the farm—all that made staying easier than leaving, and Emma gave up her weekly visits to the farm. After about a year, which meant she had missed a full growing season on the farm and had gone through a full season in town, Borland's house finally felt like her house. The yard felt like her yard. The flowers felt like her flowers. And Borland, in failing health, had become her family.

"Been out to your old stomping grounds lately, Emma?" Warren sticks his head out from behind the paper as he turns a page. He's talking about the farm. Although Emma's parents have retired, they still live there. One of her brothers runs the place.

"No," Emma says, "not since Christmas."

"Hmmmmm." Warren is reading again. "That family must be a pretty big herd by now." He sounds distracted, turns another page. "How many grandchildren?"

"Twenty-three altogether," Emma says, "and five great-grandchildren. They— "

"They all live pretty close?"

"Most of them do. Yes," she says.

Many years after coming to Borland's, when she was sitting in church at the baptism of her youngest sister's first child, Emma did feel a sear of regret and sorrow for the life she'd missed, but those thoughts were immediately pushed from her mind by a vision of Borland. "You're the only daughter I've got" – those were his words. They weren't literally true, but they made her feel good nevertheless. She had her life with him, and he was too old and too feeble for her to abandon.

Borland lived eight more years in still further declining health – gallstones, prostatitis, arthritis, finally kidney failure – while she cared for him like a nurse and mother: washing, massaging, feeding, comforting. He died in his bed holding her hand as he'd often said he hoped to die. She was thirty-five.

After the funeral Emma could see nothing but death around her: Death in the houseplants neglected during Borland's last months, in his possessions scattered through the house, in the withering blossoms in the garden, death even in a summer cloud covering the sun. If she saw a crushed bird lying in the street she'd have to choke back tears. And then Borland's children filed a lawsuit to break the will which had given her the house and a small savings account. So she was defending herself on the one hand against death marching toward her in all its various forms, and on the other against malignant life advancing on her with accusations of greed and manipulation.

Emma struck back with flowers. First she spaded up a 12' x 12' square in the yard for a new flower garden. Then she extended the flower beds that bordered the house an extra foot into the grass. Sick houseplants she pruned and repotted; the hopelessly withered she snipped and tossed in the compost barrel. For every plant she discarded she bought two new. It was as if she were a mad choir director urging the life around her to sing louder and then louder still.

Ruby and Emma had been neighbors for quite a while. Ruby watched Emma transform her yard and wondered what it meant, but she didn't ask. As a matter of politeness she would never probe for feelings that weren't on the surface and offered freely. But in addition to the question of good manners as she saw them, Emma's compulsive coaxing of the smells and colors of life from the ground was not something Ruby could discuss easily – the way she could talk about baby formula or brands of tea. The explosion of green life frightened her. She silenced her fear by concluding that Emma needed an outlet.

She went to Emma with a gift of a set of painted plaster figurines from Germany. By the time Ruby was Emma's age, she had collected at least four dozen of these small statues. Emma thanked her politely and placed the figurines prominently on the television set, but Ruby could see that her suggestion of the figurines as a new activity was not going to take root. Sitting in Emma's kitchen, her mission failed, Ruby impulsively invited Emma to help her with the Falks' yard, and Emma gladly agreed. The two of them then gardened both yards into profusion – Ruby directing, Emma spading, Ruby choosing, Emma planting, Ruby fretting, Emma weeding. Emma's grief was choked back into submission and the two houses began to look more and more like members of the same family.

Ruby comes down the stairs excited. "Emma, how are you, give me your coat!" She slips a hanger into it, picks a piece of lint off the collar before hanging it up. Emma makes sure her sweater is buttoned. Her hand drops to the back of her skirt, smoothing it. She follows Ruby to the stairs and up. Ruby is chattering. "We just fed him so he should go right to sleep. I'm so glad Margaret could come for the weekend."

The baby lies in an old-fashioned crib brought down from the attic. He's happy and alert, Emma can see that. When Ruby bends over him he gurgles. His pink hands reach for her dangling necklace.

"You shouldn't have to change him," Ruby says, slipping her fingers into the diaper to check for dampness. "We won't be gone that long."

"He looks real smart," Emma says. The room is close and warm. She loosens the top button of her sweater. She steps nearer the crib for a look and then steps back, deferent. Ruby is absorbed by the child. She bends over the crib, covering him with grandmotherly talk. Her fingers dart, squeezing a pink arm, pinching a cheek. They straighten a blanket, tuck in a vulnerable foot. Emma watches and envies Ruby. She can hold but not squeeze, touch but not pinch. She feels, almost as a pain, her place outside the veils of family, possession, and permanence.

"Hi, Emma! How's it going?" It's Margaret, combing her hair in the bathroom behind them. She's nonchalant, doesn't look away from the mirror. She puts on lipstick, blots her lips. She turns and smiles.

"He's a real little man," Emma says.

Margaret laughs. "You mean he's a real little devil!"

Emma feels a sudden blur of confusion. She has watched the Falk children grow up, feeling always like a secret older sister who was mistakenly considered an adult by the other adults in the neighborhood. Now here is Margaret wearing her lipstick and motherhood and confidence. Emma feels suddenly too old and too young at the same time, her long years of waiting with Borland now counting for nothing. A wave of humiliation passes over her.

Ruby is back on the stairs going down, still chattering. In the kitchen she shows Emma where the milk is, and the bottles, and how to heat them. "I always wash my hands before I handle any food for the baby," Ruby says as she washes her hands. Emma follows Ruby around the kitchen, nodding her head.

Ruby's in a frenzy of instruction-giving. She writes notes telling where they'll be going, when they'll be back, the telephone number of the poison center and the doctor. She turns on the stove several times so Emma can see exactly how to do it. She opens and closes the refrigerator. She offers last minute advice. She repeats herself.

"He'll probably cry a little after you give him the bottle but if you hold him with his head up he'll settle down."

"Mother, Emma knows all that!" Margaret tugs on Ruby's arm.

Warren waits by the door, holding his hat. "We're going to be late, ladies."

"I'm sure he won't be any trouble," Emma says as Margaret shuts the door on Ruby's anxiety.

Emma is alone. She turns on the television, turns it off, and sits in the quiet. She opens a magazine and turns the pages, tosses it aside and picks up another, drops it. She climbs the stairs to look in on the baby. He's sleeping, fragile, pale skin transparent like a sprouting plant. She touches his cheek. His mouth moves as he dreams of milk. His fingers curl and relax. She tiptoes out of the room. Stands in the hall.

She wanders the house. She stands in the center of the Falks' bedroom, touching nothing, hardly breathing, feeling suspended in the still air that surrounds her like water. She smells the sleep of years in the room, the scent of Ruby's perfume mingled with aftershave. The floral bedspread is museum neat. The hair brushes on the dresser are woven with Ruby's hair. A dress is flung across a chair. Shoes wait on the closet floor, pair next to pair, like ghost feet. Shirts and dresses wait together above.

In the bathroom: toothbrushes in the rack, touching, still damp. The clouded drinking glass with droplets on the rim. A wet washcloth on the sink. Margaret's make-up, a crumpled tampax wrapper in the wastebasket. Emma touches the back of her skirt. Ruby's plants in the window need trimming. She picks off a dead leaf.

Downstairs in the living room: a child care book with a bookmark lies on the table. Inside: photographs of Margaret and the baby, Margaret's husband and the baby, the baby alone smiling through new bewildered eyes. Tears of longing rise through Emma's cheeks.

She sits again in front of the television and watches, stares, watches again. She sees the baby upstairs, sees the Falks, Margaret, Borland dead eight years already. She sees Borland spitting and hacking, mounting the porch stairs one by one, clutching her arm with hands that are veined like leaves. She feels Borland touching her waist that one time, feels herself startled, spilling the coffee, stopping him. "You're the only daughter I've got." Borland had been her man, she thinks. There wouldn't be any others. "I was a widow from the start," she says out loud.

The baby cries. Emma goes to the kitchen to heat the milk. Upstairs she holds him close to her body to feel his moving warmth, squeezes him gently. He stops crying. She feels the heat between them. Slowly she slips off her sweater and blouse and drops them to the floor. She hesitates. He will see her. She thinks of Ruby, Warren, Margaret. What would they say? But she continues, unhooking her bra and then holding him tight against her naked breasts. He struggles, wanting the bottle. She reaches for it, intending to give it to him, but instead shakes several drops of warm milk onto her erect nipple and draws him toward it. He sucks, not gently as she expected, but harshly, almost violently, sending spasms of pain to her abdomen. He pulls the nipple in, greedy, filling his mouth, igniting more waves of contractions in her womb. She holds her breath in, frightened. Tears come to her eyes. Then he cries. The breast is dry. She breathes again, presses the warm bottle to his mouth and holds him against her bare breasts until he sleeps.

Emma is dozing when the Falks return, half dreaming about her mother and Ruby and Margaret in the garden talking quietly about plants and children.

"Emma?" It's Ruby's voice just inside the back door, but sounding far away. Then Ruby is standing over her.

"I must've been sleeping," Emma says. She smooths her blouse.

"Did everything go okay?" There is an edge of worry in Ruby's voice. "Did you have any problems?"

"Fine. He was just fine. No problems at all." Emma's voice is calm. She watches Ruby relax. "I gave him a bottle and he went right back to sleep."

"Let me get you some coffee. We had a good time too."

At the kitchen table they talk about the yard, about the work they'll do in the next few weeks of spring. Emma listens to Ruby's plans as she usually does, letting Ruby talk. Under her blouse she can feel her nipple, still tender from the baby's mouth. She gets up to leave.

On her way home in the dark, Emma kneels by her iris bed. She brushes the dry grains of soil with her fingertips. Then she works her fingers deep into the moist dirt beneath to savor the teeming life moving next to her skin. It will be enough. It will have to be.

Closed Mondays

Alvin Greenberg

TODAY IS MEMORIAL DAY, a Monday naturally, and I am sitting on the steps of the Museum in a t-shirt and jeans. A glorious spring day, the very edge of summer, the day that when I was a kid we always did take to be the real beginning of summer because it was the day when all over town, from country clubs to the municipal parks, the swimming pools opened. Across the street hundreds of people are frolicking in the park right now, with children, dogs, frisbees, balls, bottles, on the grass, in jeans, in shorts, without shirts. Lorna is sitting in the car.

Memorial Day: you would think that would jog your mind about history, wouldn't you? What I mean is, the Museum is closed on Monday. It's always closed on Monday. That's a fact, a historical fact, the kind you could look up: at the library, in the newspaper, in the Museum's own monthly schedule. Of course, it's also a fact that Memorial Day is May 30th, which is Wednesday, the day after tomorrow. A true fact. Just check the calendar. Only the government, of course, has long since decreed that all national holidays, regardless of the true date on which they fall, shall be observed on the nearest Monday. Except for Independence Day, which stays on the Fourth of July, no matter what the day.

Anyway, history being the sort of thing it is, it seemed to us more than likely that when a major holiday like Memorial Day fell on a Monday then it wouldn't be a Monday anymore, exactly. History changes things, right? And besides, don't these holidays always feel like Sundays? Just look at all those people in the park, sprawled out on the grass with their families and six-packs and picnic baskets and baseball caps pulled down over their eyes and not thinking about going anywhere or doing anything at all. So it's not really like a Monday, you see, so naturally, especially with people having all this holiday free time on their hands, the Museum should be open.

Which it isn't.

Lorna is wearing a white sundress, very pretty, sleeveless, just little straps over her shoulders, also very sexy in a sort of innocent-looking way, but not at all the thing for playing in the park, not even for sitting on the grass.

"Grass stains, William," she said when we were both still sitting in the car. "You think I want grass stains on my white dress? I'll never get them out. You go roll in the grass. Leave me alone."

We don't have a picnic basket, either, because we were going to have lunch in the Museum restaurant. No blanket to spread out on the grass, no bottle of wine, no frisbee, no dog. It goes without saying that they are not going to allow food and pets and fun games inside the Museum. We don't have a dog anyway. We used to have a dog but that's history now too. Sitting on the concrete steps of the Museum and trying to squint through the glare of the sun into the front seat of the Datsun to where I can barely make out the figure sitting behind the wheel, I begin to get the feeling that Lorna and I—that is, Lorna-and-I—are also about to become history.

There has got to be a certain amount of history, after all, simply in the matter of why Lorna is sitting over there looking very classy in a white sundress and white shoes and a white band around her blond hair while I am sitting here in jeans and a t-shirt. Perfectly fresh and nearly new jeans, however, and a t-shirt which I particularly like, because it's from the first and only marathon I ever got up enough nerve to run in, just last month. It wasn't always like this. In the beginning, if I showed up in jeans to pick her up, she'd be wearing jeans too, and if I'd arrive in a suit and tie, which was never all that often, she'd be wearing a dress and heels, and it always just happened like that without our ever saying a word to each other ahead of time about what we were planning to wear. That, like I say, was in the beginning, and it might be worth looking into. There are whole books now, I understand, on what happened in just the first six seconds of the universe, which seems like a bit of overkill to me but certainly shows you how important beginnings are. They are the very guts of history, you might say, whereas the present is all too often just a sort of blank face, like the way the Datsun is sitting over there staring at me with its lights and grill and polished hood, the sun glaring off the windshield so I can hardly see there's anyone behind it.

We congratulated ourselves, when we first pulled up here, on being lucky enough to find a parking place on this side of the street right in front of the Museum on a day like this. Just as we drove up a couple was throwing a pair of screaming kids into the back seat of an old Ford. We waited while they stood there on opposite sides of the car and glared at each other for a minute over the rusty roof; then finally they got in and slammed the doors and took off in a dark cloud of exhaust. May they have a long and happy history. Lorna pulled neatly into the spot they'd abandoned and turned off the key, and we sat there looking at the front of the Museum and realizing that no one was going in or out. To them, I suppose, it was just another Monday.

"Feeling pretty smug, aren't you?" she said.

I knew perfectly well that what she was talking about was how I was dressed, even though she didn't specifically say it—didn't have to: I saw the way she'd looked at me when we left the house. She threw me one first class look, what they call a "haughty look" in historical novels, which I think is the only place I have ever seen that word used. What I like about historical novels is how they take you into the guts of a period, I mean what people are really thinking and doing, what they wear and what they eat and drink and how they act with each other, while all that stuff that we were always taught was real history is just like a sort of shell around them, inside of which they are busy leading their lives. To me, that's the real history: the way people just go on leading their lives.

Well, she looked at my t-shirt with its purple logo and she looked at my jeans and she looked at my Sauconys, which looked nearly as good as new from the outside though the insides are so pounded down I can't use them for running any more, and then she looked at the ceiling. Then she went out the front door with me trailing right behind her. There was nothing there to criticize, really, and besides, we've always been good about not telling each other how to do things. If she'd wanted to go off to the clinic some morning in her green pajamas, I suppose I wouldn't have said a thing. She'd learn whatever it was she had to learn from how the other people reacted at work and she'd learn it much better than from anything I said. And vice versa the time I bought her mother a rod and reel for Christmas. What good is history if we don't learn from it; that's why I think it's mostly mistakes.

Maybe my getting out of the car was a mistake, too, which is what I'm sitting here trying to learn.

"Hey," I said, "let me go look inside and see if there's anything going on." The doors are glass and it wasn't quite noon yet, so I thought maybe it was just that they were opening late today; if I could see anybody moving around inside, there was hope yet.

"That's dumb," she said. My hand was on the door handle already, but I'm not one to walk away when someone is talking to me.

"Beg pardon?" I said. I have this habit of getting very formal whenever someone starts coming on hostile to me. It lets them know that you know what they're up to, and at the same time you don't have to get belligerent yourself. It also gives them a second chance. They can say, "Oh, nothing," or change the subject or apologize or just walk away or whatever. I credit it with keeping me out of a lot of fights. Lorna hates it.

"I said," she said, "that that's just the dumb sort of thing I'd expect from someone who'd go to the Museum in a t-shirt and jeans."

I knew she didn't say all that and she knew she didn't say all that, but at the same time we both knew that she did, because we both knew just what she had said—the simple, historical fact—and that what we were getting now was interpretation, which seems to be what peole always think they have to do with the simple facts. I didn't need it.

"I see," I said, though I wasn't a hundred percent sure that I did. That is, I didn't see why she was making an issue about what I was wearing, especially now that we were here, and more especially since it didn't look like we were going to get in anyway. Basically, I was just interested in the fact: was the Museum going to open today or wasn't it? If my clothes were an issue, it seemed to me that was really past history by now and should have been dealt with before we started out. She knows as well as anyone that I have to wear a uniform all week—she wears one herself, the same color as her sundress—and she knows that anyone who wears a uniform to work should have a right to be as casual as he wants on the weekend. That doesn't mean be a slob. I'm no slob. She would never have got hooked up with a slob. It just means comfortable. She looks comfortable in her sundress—or did till we got here—and I'm comfortable in my t-shirt and jeans.

By that time I had my door open and was halfway out of the car, mumbling something about just wanting to check but mostly just wanting a breath of fresh air. It was beginning to feel very stuffy in there. No sooner was I out then she leaned over and grabbed the handle and slammed the door shut behind me.

"You just take your time, William," she said.

It didn't take any time, of course—I could see right off that there wasn't a soul moving in there, and of course there's a sign on the door that lists all the museum hours, Tuesday through Sunday, and then at the bottom says "Closed Mondays"—but then I thought I'd better take a little time anyway. Just strolling right back and casually saying "Nope, nobody home" didn't seem like quite the right thing to do. It was an invitation to sarcasm, that was what it was. Going back with some sort of an apology would have been all right, if I could have figured out what I was supposed to apologize for. Going back and saying nothing was also a possibility, but it seemed to me that would leave us right where we were before. Like I said, it was probably getting out of the car in the first place that was a mistake.

So I'm sitting here on the Museum steps in this nice sunshine, watching shirtless young studs chasing soaring frisbees in the park across the way and girls in shorts and halters sitting on blankets sipping diet colas and little kids and big dogs chasing each other around in circles, and wondering what I've learned. Sometimes I think my real problem is that I know too much. I know that sounds like an odd sort of thing to be a problem, and that most people would probably like to know a lot more than they do, but one of the things I know is that knowing too much can get in the way of learning. Frankly, when Lorna and I first started going out, I did think of myself as pretty dumb. In a lot of ways I probably was. I mean, I had a good job, I was earning good money—assistant chief of security for a large corporation is not bad for someone my age, just ask around—and I'd put myself through school to get there, too, because they expect you to have some education for a responsible position like that. And with good reason, too, considering the kind of people you come into contact with. But there was a lot I didn't know, too, especially about people. Probably the fact that I had to work all the time, all the way through school and everything, and mostly in solitary jobs at odd hours—cleaning toilets in parochial schools, sweeping out factories between midnight and morning, locked in a plexiglass cage collecting money at an all-night self-serve gas station—has a lot to do with that, but I don't want to make excuses. When I met Lorna I was ready to learn. And she was ready to teach.

That was when we got the dog. Fido. I'm sorry, but that's the truth; that was its name when we got it, and even though it was still pretty young, neither of us could make the move to change it. We were still that new with each other, that neither one of us wanted to claim the right to rename it. Naming is a very important act. Like when you call someone "dumb," right? But I had to keep the dog because she was living in a new apartment that didn't allow pets, so I said she should at least get to name it. And she said no, since I had to be training it and calling it all the time, at least I should have the right to decide what to call it. So in the end we just left it Fido. It was an ugly little thing, anyway. Big head, short legs, thin white fur but black blotches in odd places, like over one eye. Poor little bastard.

It probably seems like a strange thing to do, to get a dog right at the beginning of a romance, but sometime along there in those first few weeks we were going together, it came out that each of us had always wanted a dog, but for one reason or another had never had one. For me, it had been school and work, the long hours that is; it wouldn't have been fair to get a dog and then just leave it alone all the time. And before that, my parents, who hated all pets, even goldfish or turtles, and made my sister give her lucky cricket away. For her it was always having lived in apartments that banned pets, even when she was a kid, which was probably why she'd moved into a place just like that on her own, even though she loved dogs. Pets are important: we agreed on a lot of things like that.

Besides, I think we both also felt that a dog would be one more thing to tie us together, I mean something really solid, not like the feelings, which were there, sure, but you can't get your hands on them like you can on a dog. Or maybe even a cat. At least I know I felt that way, which was why I was glad to have the job of taking care of Fido, in spite of his not being housebroken and all. He was there when Lorna wasn't around, and that was important to me. After a few weeks, when he'd learned to behave pretty well around the house, I signed us up for obedience school, being careful to schedule it on a night when Lorna was working—going to school herself, as a matter of fact—so it wouldn't interfere with our time together. She's a nurse and has to keep her training up to date, so every once in a while she takes an evening class at the University.

Needless to say, I wasn't prepared for what happened when I told her about the obedience course.

"You what?" she said. We were both in the car then, too. I'd picked her up at the clinic and we were going out to dinner as soon as she had a chance to change. It does seem to me that an awful lot of important things happen in cars. For good or for bad, they are certainly a part of our history, and I don't just mean mine and Lorna's. Fido's, too, for that matter. He was in the back seat.

Well, it turned out—in some people's opinion, at least—that what I was doing was not helping to make a better, happier, and more obedient pet, as the ads for the course promised, but engaging in an out-and-out power play. Namely, turning Fido into *my* dog.

"But I'm doing this for us," I protested. At least I honestly believed I was. All I'd been thinking when I signed up for the course was how we'd take him for walks together, and he'd heel and fetch and stay right with us and not run around picking fights with other dogs or pestering people the way some dogs I've seen do. But like I said, Lorna was a teacher—that's what she really wants to do, in fact: teach in a nursing program—and I was ready to learn. It was rush hour and the traffic was pretty heavy, both inside the car and out, but I felt that even in the midst of it all I was already learning something: namely, that things aren't always what they seem. A very important lesson, but, frankly, not always a very helpful one, as is often the case when we are told what things are not. I mean, does it help for me to say that that was not a Jaguar I was driving that afternoon?

Meanwhile I was trying to keep my attention both on the freeway traffic and on what Lorna was telling me, and I wasn't having an easy time with either. Friday afternoon brings all the crazies out on the freeway, hot to get to their end-of-the-week parties, and it doesn't look good for someone in security to have black marks on his driving record. And Lorna was coming on hot and heavy about manipulation which was not all getting through to me clearly both because she was rant-and-rave angry and because I was upset at seeing her angry like this. It was the first time that either of us had let go at the other like that. And I really was trying to understand—I mean, to explore my own motives, which she was so busy calling into quesiton—even though I couldn't see how sweet, ugly, little Fido, who I could see in the rear view mirror was sitting up in the back seat like a perfect gentleman, could be a symbol, as she said, of my attempt to take control of our relationship.

So, to get it over with, as soon as we pulled up across the street from her apartment building, and she hopped out of the car, not having cooled down one bit, while I was trying to ask her if we were still going out to dinner and what with one thing and another not paying as much attention to things as I should have done, Fido jumped out after her and on those short little legs of his was chugging across to her building, which he knew from having accompanied me to the door to pick her up so many times—well, the fact is, we often snuck him in for a few hours now and then—when the Caddy got him.

So, just like that, Fido was history. Ditto the lesson, argument, whatever it was. Something I should have learned, probably. Tears. Her fault. My fault. The driver of the Caddy was very insistent it was not his fault. Also very red-faced, like his car, and fat and drunk. Just go away and leave us alone, we asked, which suited him fine. In her apartment we both got a little drunk ourselves and never did go out to dinner. She hung on me and cried, "William, William" and "Fido, Fido" without much seeming to distinguish between the two, and I tried to figure out what exactly had happened, but the only thing I could come up with was that Fido was dead.

No, that's not really all, though in my humble opinion it was more than enough. No, if I learned anything else that evening, while I took turns drying Lorna's tears and my own, refilled our wine glasses, and eventually unbuttoned our clothes, what I learned was that there is a price to be paid for knowing too much and also that someone else usually pays it. Yes, I learned that there is no learning without loss.

Which, I decided some time later, was not a piece of knowledge worth paying for with Fido's life. When you think about learning from history, you don't usually think of history as being someone or something you care about.

Meanwhile I see from the Museum steps that there's this pretty young woman coming across the street toward me dragging a pretty little look-alike girl behind her by the hand, both of them looking very uncomfortable. They're both barefoot and dressed in identical green shorts and pink t-shirts with pictures of Mt. Rushmore on them, which reminds me again that it's a national holiday rapidly going to waste here. A Memorial Day to be remembered. Well, they're not too thrilled either with what they find out from me.

"Would you believe it," says the woman, "this whole goddamned park and not a single public john, not even a whichamacallit, satellite."

She was hoping, probably every bit as badly as I'd been, that the Museum was open, which of course I have to tell her it's not. The little girl is squirming around behind her mother, squeezing her legs together. I look around, trying to see if there are any other possibilities in the neighborhood, because obviously there isn't a lot of time left, and also wondering if Lorna is watching and, if so, what she's making of this. Across the street in the park I can see which guy these two belong to. He has a thick black beard and a terrific tan, and he's sitting on an old Army blanket watching them, shading his eyes with his hand from the sun, which is pretty much right overhead now. High noon. Also he's got the other hand on the collar of a young Airedale that's sitting beside him on the blanket, panting like crazy. Beyond the two of them there's that whole park full of people and, like she said, not a sign of a public toilet that I can see, even with the advantage of being up on the Museum steps where I can overlook the whole place. Across the park are a couple of churches, which are a good ways off—from the way the kid's squirming I have to doubt if they could make it in time—and not likely to be any help anyway, it not being Sunday. On the other side of the park is a row of stores along the highway there, but not the kind that's ever open on Sundays and holidays: the Firestone Tire Center and a dry cleaner and an office supply store and a few others like that. It looks pretty hopeless to me, and I look back to the park to where the guy's sitting, wondering isn't he going to be any help, he must be the father after all, but he's not there. He's about ten yards away picking up a stray frisbee and tossing it back to two long-haired blond teenagers in bikinis, standing there with their hands on their hips watching him.

And the dog, which of course he is no longer holding on to, is making a wild dash across the street to the woman and the little girl. And so help me, there is a red Caddy bearing down on it.

"Oh, shit!" I say. I jump to my feet although I know there's nothing I can do.

The woman looks around and screams. I look down at her from where I'm standing a couple of steps higher up and see that, behind her, the little girl has finally let go. There is a puddle already running down the concrete steps. Then I hear the thunk and the yelp.

By the time I get to the street Lorna is already there. She is kneeling in the middle of the street with the Airedale's head leaning against her. The dog is panting even harder now, probably in shock, and bleeding from a gash on its left shoulder, but it doesn't actually look all that serious. Possibly a broken leg and definitely in need of a vet, but the car wasn't moving all that fast, what with all the kids and picnickers around, and it was probably as much a case of dog hits car as vice versa. It'll live.

I look up over it at Lorna to tell her what I think, but what I find myself saying is, "Your dress!"

The skirt of her white sundress is covered with brown dirt stains and red blood stains. She doesn't even look at it herself. She gives me not exactly what they call in historical novels a "withering look," but something not all that far from it either.

"William, it's just a puppy," she says. For a moment there, I think that what I have heard her say is "William's just a puppy," but then I look down at the young Airedale again and realize I must have been hearing things.

Meanwhile, a considerable crowd has gathered around us. The woman with the little girl is standing right behind me, I see, crying, holding her daughter on her hip so that the wet stain is now spreading to her own shorts.

"It'll be okay," I tell her, "it just needs to be taken to the vet's right away."

The tall, gray-haired woman who was driving the Caddy is trying to lean in from behind the crowd to see what's happening. She catches my eye.

"I never saw it," she says.

"Lady," I tell her, "you never had a chance."

There's a sudden commotion in the crowd on the opposite side, and when I look I see that it's the black-bearded guy trying to push his way through.

"Jesus Christ!" I hear him saying, "Now what?"

Which is what I'm thinking myself as I look at Lorna. But that's always the question, isn't it: now what? And how much help is any of what you think you know, any of what you've been through before, really going to be when it comes to that? I'm not talking your practical stuff, of course—naturally all the first aid training I got when I started working security comes in handy at times like this—but all the rest, all the rest, where what it comes down to finally is that all you have got to rely on is yourself. On the best of days that can make you feel pretty dumb. But you have got to do what you can with what you've got—what you are—or else you risk falling back into . . . what? Stupidity, maybe. History, I suppose. And, I am thinking as I reach across the panting dog to brush some of the mess off Lorna's skirt, you do not want to close yourself down like that, now, do you? But I see I am just spreading the stain.

The Mai-Loan
and the Man Who Could Fly

Rick Christman

E ARLIER THAT NIGHT, the same night Sing met the man who could fly, one of the hotel waiters told about his wife who got killed by a gunship at the Cho-Lon Racetrack the week before. It seemed she was taking a shortcut on the way to the market when the gunner opened up. Sing imagined a leer on the gunner's face, like arousal, straddling his machine gun and pumping lead from between his legs like the seed of heavenly death. The fifty calibre cut her in half, and the waiter had to go to the Body Reclamation Center to identify her and claim her remains and only one half of her was there. The other half somehow got away from them en route and hadn't been found yet.

The whores playing cards at a corner table erupted into a violent argument, and Sing turned and watched them closely and deliberately. One slammed her cards onto the table and stood with hands on hips, ranting furiously at the others. It wasn't Kim but he kept watching anyway, as her long black hair bounced about against her cheeks, her head snapping from one to another. The others were cheats, she said, in league against her. They talked behind her back. They took customers from her. They hated her, she said. But soon she was cajoled into continuing the game that went on and on as always, from the time the bar opened in the morning until it closed at night.

The waiters always talked about dead wives or dead sons or daughters and Sing enjoyed listening to their stories, their voices, as he watched the flares float and the red tracers spit across the river. He was soothed by the familiar drone of their heartache, as he was soothed by the distant color of the war across the river. The waiter was crying by now, of course, and Sing noticed for the first time how the tears on the waiter's cheeks were like delicate chips of the finest handblown glass. He considered this, considered sitting forward and looking more closely, maybe even reaching out to touch, to see if they were genuine. But he knew without even beginning that he wasn't capable.

The eighth floor bar had been a classy place once; the round bar had twinkled with polished glass and suspended bottles; snappy, insistent, French-speaking waiters had rushed food and drinks, the room spinning and aswirl about the rich, the spies, and the journalists, at balcony tables among potted trees. But by the time Sing met the man who could fly, the war had dulled the polish and chipped the balcony pots, and the waiters lounged and ate openly before the customers. By that time it had become another half-baked restaurant and bar, another hangout for whores and pimps and the trafficking of drugs, though some of the waiters amused one another by still speaking French among themselves as if to act out just how far life had come.

The night Sing met the man who could fly, it was three years since he had arrived at the Mai-Loan, three years since he had been an interpreter and interrogator with the 1st Marines. He came down to Sai-Gon on a three-day R&R; his unit, what was left of the eighteen who had gone out—the medic, the radio operator, and himself—was awarded the rest along with the Bronze Star for salvaging themselves from an ambush that brought them so much more than they expected. The fifteen others dropped one after another in seconds, but the three of them were invincible. As the men they knew best on earth dropped dead, the three of them felt a power move within. They walked right out into the bush and scattered the others. They were actually close enough to see the eyes of the enemy, bulging in the face of such audacity and sacred power.

For the three days on R&R they couldn't look at each other, and they couldn't talk of anything else. They couldn't whore, they couldn't drink anything but Coke. The whores and the pimps kept their distance, and didn't even attempt to break the sacred ring the three men had established. Even the street kids and the beggars were driven away by their hollow, possessed looks, edging by to allow them plenty of room, crossing the street way up ahead when they saw the three of them coming.

They couldn't talk about anything but the dumb, dead motherfuckers, as they walked down the street, as they sat in bars, the expressions on the faces of the dead, their arms akimbo or stretched above their heads just so, their legs twisted, the color of their blood, their eyes round and wide and wet, like sliced cucumbers. And the three of them, the only three noncombatants in the whole marine corps probably, the only three who didn't carry rifles had finally picked up rifles for the first time. And there they were. And all the others, those trained, hardened killers, those dumb fuckers were dead. They shook their heads. They couldn't believe it. They talked day and night, in their enlisted men's quarters after curfew, in one of their rooms, on one of their beds. They talked because they couldn't sleep.

Then the night before they were to leave, they left each other at 10:30, giving each a few hours alone before the 7:00 a.m. flight back to Phu-Bai and the two hour mail truck ride back to the unit. Sing walked the streets until 11:00 curfew, ending up on the eighth floor bar at the Mai-Loan. He took a balcony seat and watched the lights of the war across the river, sipping a Ba-Muoi-Ba, the tracers, the flames, the bombs, so far away, so long gone in the night. He sat mesmerized and dreamy, his beer gone, his head resting back against the chair, until the bartender shut off the lights and a waiter tapped his shoulder. Sing bought a room down the hall for the night and didn't leave the eighth floor for three years.

*

Sing's father had been a marine, too. He'd been shot in the head in the Pacific and still carried a steel plate that on certain cloudy days, when something in the air was just right, rolled his eyes back in his head, lighting him up inside like a Christmas tree. And every Christmas Eve, once the tree had been purchased from Birch's Greenhosue, propped in Sing's wagon and dragged the eight blocks back to their house through snow-wet northern Wisconsin streets, and before the tree was on the stand and placed in the spot in front of the bay window for decorating, his father stood with arms extended, legs spread-eagled, a green Christmas tree bulb in each hand and a red one in his mouth. And as his only child looked on in delight, he asked out beyond the bulb like a 1920's gangster, "Hell, we don't need a tree, do we, Son?"

But his father's patriotism was so extreme and tinged with such terror and violence that it was nearly as if his father wished the bullet had killed him for his country, almost as if he was ashamed it hadn't. He lectured his only child on the corruption of the young and the loss of men with real balls in this crumbling world. A vein stuck out prominently in his forehead once he got started. He pointed at the television for illustration, ranting and raging for hours at the hippies, the pussies, and the sissies. He exhorted Sing constantly to keep his head high, to eat the good food his mother prepared, to keep his eyes open at all times and to never back down from a good fight. But always fight to kill, no matter who it was, no matter what. Grab the nearest rock if he needed to. People were out to get him, he said. Don't trust anyone. Always hold something back for reserve.

From the time Sing was eight, his father moved all the furniture out of the living room every evening and every Saturday afternoon and taught his son hand to hand combat on the living room rug. By the time Sing was twelve he could gouge, rip and choke his classmates at the least provocation. But he discovered as he grew older that he didn't want to rip his classmates' throats out. He worshipped his father as he thundered through the house like Goliath, and he tried his hardest to do anything his father wished him to do. But away from the house Sing found himself reading books, liking his teachers, and even secretly playing jump rope with girls. He grew straddling the world and enlisted in the Marines to please his father, but refused to carry a rifle to please himself. He didn't want to come home from the war as his father had, a hater of the world with buzzers in his head.

*

Sing's second night at the Mai-Loan one of the whores left her card table to come and sit next to him at his table. Her name was Kim, she said. She talked for two hours about her dead mother and father and two little brothers. She moved her long, mini-skirted legs back and forth from time to time as she talked. She had been working these three long years just to get them all out of there alive, away from the war, away from Viet-Nam forever. But now she spit on Viet-Nam forever, she said, because they were dead, killed that very week in their house on Truong-Ming-Ky. She could see how it had been for them, she said, splattered like mice in a barrel as they ran from wall to wall for refuge, scratching the dirt floor for the basement that wasn't there. As she talked, her angular, hollow-eyed face seemed drained, yet still longing for marrow and blood and human life. She finished by telling him that she would hire him as her protection if he wished. She didn't need it, but you never knew. She would supply his needs, she said. She could afford him now. She didn't care about money for herself anymore. Then she returned to her game and never spoke to him again.

So Kim took Sing on as her protection, though in his three years there he had to think about protecting her only once. An American civilian found his way up to the eighth floor bar, got drunk, and began punching Kim in the eyes and mouth with short, professional-boxer-like jabs and chopping right hands. There was no sound at all, other than the slap of skin and bone against skin and bone, and Kim was too amazed to even shout for him. So by the time Sing saw what was going on, the bartender broke the man's head with a chunk of lead pipe he kept behind the bar.

Sing slept late every morning and all afternoon read the Vietnamese newspapers, brought to him each day at noon along with his cigarettes by the twelve-year-old Mai-Loan doorguard, drugdealer and pimp in a turned up jungle hat with a Benson and Hedges 100 drooping from his chin to his shirt buttons. Then, from 2:00 in the afternoon on, Sing sat at his balcony table, drinking Canadian Club chased with Ba-Muoi-Ba. Before the bartender shut out the lights at midnight and went home, he left a bottle of whiskey and five bottles of warm beer lined up on Sing's table. After the bar was closed and dark and everyone was gone, Sing's glass clinked as he poured more whiskey and his cigarette hung down along the side of his chair until it burned his fingers and he put it out to light another. He drank and stared out the window until dawn, trying to remember if there ever was a time when there was anything but war across the river.

Kim supplied Sing's room, his newspapers, his food, his liquor, his cigarettes, and his one set of clothes. She could afford him; she was the best whore in the place. No one could compete with her lean dark beauty. They had few customers up on the eighth floor, but the best of those who came, came to Kim. And they paid what she demanded, no matter how outrageous her price of the moment was, pulling handfuls of piasters and black market M.P.C.'s from their pockets in green, red, blue, and tan profusion like Christmas. Even her most timid requests brought offers of cameras, refrigerators, radios, and cars.

Kim told the waiters to pay attention to Sing's needs. They knew when he wanted a drink and when he was happy. He ate what all the help ate, when they ate it. He shaved every third day but kept his blond hair long, like Custer, cutting it only every six months by chopping handfuls off with a razor-sharp, bone-handled kitchen knife. He wore a black pajama shirt and black pajama pants. He hadn't said twenty-five words in three years.

*

The waiter left and the man who could fly settled in at the seat across Sing's table. Sing was mildly disturbed, but the man who could fly began talking at once, as soon as he settled in. He talked on and on, his monologue weaving and bending and wrapping around Sing's head like an insistent, evil snake.

Sing couldn't see the man who could fly very well, though he was only five feet from him; he couldn't seem to make him out. Sing looked back across the river and listened, the flares bursting, the bombs falling, the war continuing.

The man who could fly said the war had seen its better days. It will end soon, he said. There was no doubt about it, now that the American pullout had begun, no doubt at all. Soon, very soon, the Viet-Cong will have things their way. They will make the country strong, they will make it Vietnamese again. And high time, too, he said, high time. They will ride into Sai-Gon like the heroes they are, like the French Resistance liberating Paris. The revolution will come, finally it will come. Viet-Nam will cleanse itself of American filth and degradation. The people will hold their heads high again. The whores and pimps and bartenders will be marched into the sea.

The man who could fly waved his hand dramatically over the table between them. Sing could barely make out a smile on his insubstantial face.

He had just come from Nha Trang and the collaborators were fleeing down Highway One in droves, their oxcarts clipclopping, banging out music to the revolutionary's ears. And the Americans were already gone from Nha Trang, their huge air base deserted. They were disappearing from bases everywhere, all over

Viet-Nam, as if someone had passed a magic wand over the country, as if someone had finally pulled the plug.

With great effort Sing turned toward the bar. He wished the man who could fly would disappear and let him be once again. He was uncomfortable now. For the first time in three years he was disturbed by a bee on glass, by a bee which refused to go away. But finally, when Sing looked back again, the man who could fly really had disappeared. Sing looked all around the room and out over the river and the street below. He seized his chair arms and wondered suddenly if he, too, might fly out the window.

*

For the first time in three years Sing returned to his room before the bar closed. He entered and went directly out onto the small, cement balcony without even bothering to turn on the light. He leaned out against the cement railing and ran his fingers along its roughness. The breeze in his hair made him feel lightheaded. He looked at the sky and the river and the street below. He saw a sampan filled with children and a withered old man. It bobbed and rolled and pitched forward on the end of the anchor rope, as the helpless old man pulled and pulled on the rope with all his skinny might, the children rocking from one end of the boat to the other. Down the street a tiny blue and white taxicab was parked, the driver and his fare—a black marine—both gesturing in the middle of the street, both oblivious to the traffic careening about them. On the curb in front of the hotel, an emaciated xich-lo driver talking with another marine suddenly threw both hands into the air and laughed all the way to heaven. Sing watched the doorguard below slip money into his shirt pocket with one hand and extend a pack of cigarettes with the other. And in the center of the street, in his tiny kiosk, a White Mouse directed traffic, his white-gloved hands moving in perfect coordination, orchestrating, pointing and directing each in turn.

Sing read of the American withdrawal in the Vietnamese newspapers, but he never believed them. They were fairyland: moviestars, gossip columns, husband advertisements, created sources and government control. He never took them seriously for a moment, especially the warnings of an imminent Sai-Gon surrender. But he saw the enemy come now, moving down the street, a great tangled blade of iron—tanks, jeeps, trucks, Freedom Fighters atop armoured personnel carriers, brandishing weapons and crying their maniacal love of Ho—heading down Le-Loi to the end and back again. And back again and again and again.

Sing looked out across the river, grabbed the balcony railing and gathered himself up on his toes like God. Huge balls of light from parachute flares popped and floated down the sky like eyes, and strings of red tracers wound round and round and up and down. He couldn't help himself. He began thinking of Christmas Eve in snow-wet city streets and of Christmas trees of red and green. He released the balcony railing and rocked back on his feet, letting his hands hang at his sides. He shivered and shook like bamboo as he felt the wind rush by his face, already picking up his long hair like fingers.

Conversation

Kathleen Norris

I.

THE RODEO CLOWN shouted: "Why is a woman like a candy bar? Full of sweetness and half-nuts!" Kids wearing oversized cowboy hats played at roping each other behind the stalls. "I thought it was a topless woman, but it was just two bald-headed men."

She was tired. She had noticed the cowboy looking at her in the bars for a few weeks now, but they hadn't been introduced. That shouldn't matter in a town this small. He could easily know anything he wanted to about her.

Today she was tired, an outsider, and the town was no place for an outsider on rodeo weekend. She had been looking forward to her first rodeo, but now didn't know how much more of it she could stand to watch. Slack-faced men and women drinking beer, eating, getting sunburned, waiting for someone to get hurt.

The bull riding shocked her. It seemed utterly senseless. When the rider fell, the figures of man and bull were indistinguishable, one from the other, in the dust. She had to look away.

She stood close to the fence at the rear of the arena, where horses came after they'd thrown a man. They were beautiful then. The men let three or four of them gather, and the horses would begin circling together. They were proud looking; their eyes were wild.

The kids were fighting now, calling each other names. They had tired quickly in this heat. The scoring confused her. Some men made no score, even after what looked like a good ride. Other, less spectacular riders got a good rating. She applauded everyone. The worst thing, apparently, was what they called being "gated," getting an animal that wouldn't buck. She watched the men closely as they walked out of the arena: slowly, most of them limping. All of them looked happy.

*

The bar was packed. The country band in the back room could barely be heard in here. She had seen just a little of the bull riding, she told him. She couldn't stand to watch it. "I don't see how anyone does it," she said. "It just looks too dangerous." He'd been sipping a beer, listening to her. He said deliberately, like a long, low whistle, "You're really different. You should hear those people. That's the one thing they come to see."

She asked if he still rode. "Nope," he said, "no future in it." She seemed to have touched something: memories, old wounds, because he continued, "Jesus, we had a time . . . we'd hit four, maybe five shows in a weekend, get drunk Saturday, then drive to beat hell Sunday." He was young. She didn't know: maybe four or five years younger than she. But he was reminiscing like an old man.

Then they were dancing, the fast three-step that always made her smile. She had told her husband that people here danced as if they had springs in the balls of their feet. Cowboys were serious about dancing. Even the young ones could dance like angels.

"My husband won't dance with me."

"What?" he teased. "A pretty young thing like you?"

"Oh," she smiled. "I'm old. He just doesn't like to dance."

He held her more tightly. When the music stopped he led her back to the bar.

Cowboys were so polite, she thought. They had an old-fashioned deference to women that surprised her. But they were earthy too. She thought of the outhouses at the arena, with "Bucks" and "Does" scrawled in black paint. She thought about the jokes and stories they told in here. Now someone was talking about a guy who'd stuck his pecker into a Foosball Table. "Raped that fuckin' table," a cowboy said, and all the men laughed. She finished her beer and said yes to another. "Watch him," someone said. "He's trying to put the make on you." "Not her," the cowboy said. "She's too sweet."

She was having a good time. She enjoyed being held lightly in the cowboy's arms. She enjoyed the music they were dancing to. She was still not sure she understood the way men had begun to look at her, with a frankly sexual interest. Had she changed somehow, or had it been there all along, and she'd just now seen it? She was nearly thirty and suddenly the whole world was in heat. It made her want to laugh. It had been a mystery; now it seemed so simple.

Listening to the cowboys, she suddenly felt very close to them. She imagined what it would be like to ride a horse. Maybe she'd learn. They were telling stories of staying down in the government pasture for weeks at a time. Just them, the horses, cattle and the land. It sounded good.

The cowboy touched her hair; she smiled. The room had become a fast current around them, and their conversation was adrift. It was easy, surprisingly easy. He said, "Let's get outside for some air."

She hesitated. Once outside, she'd be unsteady on her feet. She would want to kiss him slowly, make love to him slowly. But he'd just pull her close and say, "I want to screw the hell out of you." And she'd wonder if he knew how impersonal that sounded. It would be like that. He'd hurt her coming in and they'd fuck hard, too fast. The moon would be visible through his pickup window. She'd want to be as cold and distant as it was. He'd notice her shivering, maybe, and turn the heat on. But things keep better in the cold, she'd want to tell him, heat only rots them. She wouldn't remember if he came or not, or how it had felt, if she'd felt anything at all.

*

They were outside. The moon, unmoored, was a bright sail. He touched her breasts. "Don't, Cal." She took his hand away. He touched her there again, kissed her and said, "Oh, you're prime, real prime."

Look, she wanted to say: I'll sleep with you, you don't have to go through this. No lies. Nothing. Instead she said, looking into his eyes, trying to throw him off a little: "You want to fuck me, don't you?" He pulled away. "I don't usually get involved with married women. I did once, and . . . " He broke off, then continued: "It was just too much trouble."

Much later, when he had taken her clothes off and was telling her how soft and small she was, she thought about how you always said the same things to a lover. They weren't lies so much as charms to make it go all right, to keep evil spirits away.

"Jesus, you're soft," he repeated, laughing, nuzzling her. He seemed so happy, touching her breasts, her stomach, her thighs. Then he looked into her eyes and said, "You know, I never thought I'd have a chance at you."

*

He was a good lover. His slim hips fit easily over her broad ones. He was what she'd always imagined a centaur to be: strong and brown in the shoulders, impossibly pale in the haunches.

She didn't know where they were. She'd fallen asleep in the small camper; left over from his rodeo days, she imagined. A place to rest while someone else drove, a place to take women.

It was a field somewhere. She got out to pee and stepped into tall grass. He came around the truck to her, and she rested her head on his bare shoulder. The lights from farmhouses were as unreadable as stars. She shivered, and they went back inside.

They made love again. Then he sat with his back to her, smoking. He talked about himself: rodeo, the women he'd lived with off and on. He turned to her and stroked her hair and said, "Don't get upset now, but would you tell me your name? I only heard it once." So it's like this, she thought. Tasting a hard feeling in her throat, she said: "Christine." "Christine," he repeated, kissing her. And he began again, putting his hands between her legs.

As he moved inside her, she wanted to ask him how it was. She wondered if it weren't terrifying; if it ever felt as if he could disappear inside her. She told him he was nice to make love to, not like some men, who did it fast and then asked you if you came. "They actually ask you that?" he said. He seemed surprised. "Yes," she giggled. "It's not very polite."

They lay silent in the dark. It was strange to be with a man she didn't know. She remembered a night, years before, when she had taken a man home from a party. He had seemed in despair, an almost suicidal exhaustion. She had surprised herself by picking him up. She never had asked him what the trouble was. He had tried to make love, but couldn't. "That's all right," she had said, and he slept in her arms.

This was nothing like that. She and the cowboy were just having a good screw. But she didn't belong. It was dangerous to be in a place you didn't belong. It was getting colder. She moved closer to him, curling into his back. He stroked her side and said, sleepily, "Don't go gettin' me wrong. But you really are a great piece of ass." She suddenly felt very old. But he was being sincere: he meant it as a compliment. "Thank you," she said, closing her eyes.

*

Light flooded them. She saw him reach over her for a watch. "Quarter to six," he said, and looking back at her: "I bet you wish now this whole thing hadn't happened." He offered her a Pepsi. "No, thank you," she said, turning over on her stomach, feeling like a cat in the sunlight, feeling sick. "No, I don't regret it," she lied. What was she going to do? She said, "It will be hard, that's all."

Jesus, she thought. It'll be a fucking space walk, like starting out from the womb. But she said, coldly: "Look, we wanted to screw. We had a good time. There's no point in dumping on it now." "At least you're blunt," he said, lighting a cigarette. "It helps," she replied.

They made love again. He began to talk like a little boy, and she mothered him, kissing his head, his face, holding him. They stayed like that for a while. When they were getting dressed he asked her where she wanted to go.

"Home."

"What will you do?"

"I don't know."

She wanted to be home. Suddenly, feeling brave, she asked him: "What would you do if you were married to a woman like me?" He thought for a moment, then answered honestly: "I probably never would have married you in the first place." She started, as if his cigarette had burned her. "But I'd be pretty mad," he continued, putting the stub out. "First off, I guess I'd go look for the guy and beat the hell out of him."

By the time they had settled in the cab, it was over. She tried to think of something to say, and did try out a few words: to be friendly, to make herself feel better. He didn't respond. He's wondering why women always have to talk about it, she thought. But she went on anyway, feeling stupid, wishing it weren't like this. Sex was so good. Finally he said, "I sure got the top of the gate when I got you." Yes, she thought, it was a good ride. They parted quickly, without looking at each other.

II.

" . . . Like the land Zihm's farming. Sonofabitch'll blow away on him . . ."

" . . . The only way he'll come out on that . . ."

"Hell, they ain't got that kinda grass . . ."

"Well, now, figure how many bales he's hauling. That's big money."

Men were talking, shaking dice for drinks. A phrase drifted towards her now and then from around the bar. Money. Cattle. Wheat. The talk made her uncomfortable; it seemed like part of a survival instinct she didn't have.

She was thinking about words. Love you. Get inside you. Need a lover, or a piece. Piece of ass, piece of action; pieces. It's all right, she thought. You only have one language, that's the one you use.

An actress wearing a low-cut dress danced out past the curtains on "The Tonight Show." Conversation stopped. A man near her, very drunk, looked up with half-closed eyes and said, "I'd like to fuck her eyes out."

Three younger women were sitting across the bar. She'd seen them at the club with different men. Now they seemed to be talking about her. She watched them. They smiled, but in a hard way. Once in a while, one of them would look over at her. It's all right, she told herself drunkenly, suddenly feeling trapped. She smiled back, realizing how easy it was to sum up any life as a series of defeats. You saw that in a bar; in a small town. Little needs, little weaknesses. You didn't even have to be especially observant.

But it's all right. She almost said it aloud. Need is terrifying. It's better to talk about it, to laugh. Everyone needs some image to cling to. Hers was fuzzy to herself, but clear to them. The thought made her smile again. Some men here, if you took away their cowboy hats, would have trouble knowing who they were.

She couldn't help staring back, thinking how the women would watch her, and each other, tonight and for many nights, looking for clues. And they'd use each other: for comfort, it amounted to that. Of course gossip was cruel. But it was also magical. One did it religiously, for the forgiveness of sins, for the safe journey. Her secrets would be turned inside-out, and accepted in trade. She supposed a town like this could tolerate anything, as long as you understood the rules and let yourself be used.

"Jamie," she said, turning to her husband. She wanted to leave. But he was waving to some cowboy friends who'd just come in, motioning them over. It would be a long time now. She went to the bathroom and put some perfume on her wrists, in the hollow of her neck. Her make-up looked okay.

They were talking about horses when she got back. It was beautiful, Chris thought, beautiful to think about horses. Snorting, kicking, eating, fucking, pissing. Running alone, or in a group. She loved the way horses stood together in a field, rubbing their necks together, as if they were consoling each other, sharing long, complicated histories.

Kenny was in the middle of a story about a local man who broke horses for a living: how he'd once had such a tough one he ordered his wife not to come in the corral, no matter what happened. "Damn near got himself killed," Kenny said. "But he licked that horse."

Chris had seen men on horseback, working cattle. A man and cutting horse in action was one of the most graceful things she could imagine. Jamie asked something. He could always ask good questions. "Nah," Kenny replied. "They're pretty stupid animals. But, boy, that training takes, once you got 'em trained, they don't lose it."

Chris nodded, smiling vaguely. A circle had closed around the men, excluding her. Kenny and the other cowboy began talking about their weekend. It was always their main topic of conversation: how drunk they'd gotten, fights they'd been in or near, women they'd gone after. They were a little like a vaudeville team, playing off each other. "This one piece," the one said, "Kenny was goin' real good with a little heifer. Long blond hair, and . . . " he gestured with his hands. "But damn if she didn't gate me," Kenny said, shrugging.

So he wants to get laid, Christine thought; common human stuff. He was so young. She wondered if he'd ever been in love.

"Really had to talk my way out of one of 'em," Kenny was saying. "Husband showed up. And then I tried this other one. Usually when they see you try two in a row like that they won't have nothin' to do with you. But, hell, she didn't care."

Yes, Chris thought, that's true. She'd seen that in women; in herself. She wondered why it was. Shut up, she told herself. No one wants to know; you don't know yourself.

Kenny was still explaining to Jamie: "And goddamn if they don't go in heat on you about every three weeks. Some of 'em are even worse. My brother's mare . . ." he began, and Christine started: her face was burning, as if from a slap. She wished she had no face. His brother's mare.

"Christ, what a pain in the ass she is! Noisy as hell. She'll kick you too, when she's like that. One time Cal went to get her off the trailer and she hauled off and let him have it. He didn't touch ground until he was sittin' on it, five feet back. He just picked himself up and said, 'Guess I had that one comin'.'"

Don't, she wanted to say. Don't do this. Her husband was a shadow over her shoulder. The room was getting larger, more full of light. Didn't he know? But Kenny went on, full of the sound of himself, like a child in a fairy tale, going deeper and deeper into the magic wood.

"One time, we was down on roundup. And that mare, she was just wild. Wouldn't shut up. The girls had brought some food from town. And Cal, he just walked over and stuck three fingers in. Shoulda heard her. Like a pig. Right in front of them girls." Kenny laughed.

Chris slid off her barstool and walked to the bathroom. "What's on the beaver jukebox?" she heard Kenny's friend say. "Twenty-five days of rock 'n' roll, and six of ragtime!" When she came out, Jamie was ready to leave.

She woke in the middle of the night. She could feel something: steady, slow. She had grasped Jamie's wrist. His pulse was reassuring.

She got up later. She was a little hung over, and her throat was dry. That never used to happen. The bathroom light blinded her. She took off her make-up in front of the mirror. Her perfume was stale.

III.

How would she spend today? Only ten in the morning. She squinted at the clock, wishing she'd slept longer. What was on now? A talk show and "The Price is Right." She turned over, trying to bury the sunlight with her pillow. No good. She was hungry. She'd have to feed the dog first. And there were a few things to get. Eggs. Milk. All the good shows were off by three. She'd go then. Now she made herself some coffee. She liked the kitchen, its windows framed by cotton-woods. Today they were gesturing wildly. It surprised her how few branches broke off in the high winds they had here.

She went to the china cabinet. They had inherited the china, and Chris usually picked out a cup and saucer for her morning coffee. It made her feel civilized. Today she chose a rather plain one: small roses and marigolds. She turned it over: "Cerabel. Porcelaine de Badour. Belgium." She thought of the long journey it had made to South Dakota; how careful Jamie's grandmother had been to keep it from breaking.

She would knit. That way, she'd be doing something. She got out her pattern and read it carefully as she drank. She hated to unravel; to work for nothing and have to undo it all. Working very carefully, counting stitches after each row, she made it through the game shows into what the TV announcers called "daytime dramas," and into early afternoon.

She had begun to dream about the characters in the shows, mixing them up. It didn't matter. The shows were about all the same things: marriages, families, enemies, friends. The troubles were usually caused by such simple misunderstandings. Sometimes, though, there were real villains.

She marveled at how the people talked, how they never left anyone alone. They said to each other: "Tell me," or "You should talk about it." People didn't do that. They smiled and averted their eyes. They asked if you wanted more coffee, another roll. And maybe that was best; how you got by in a little town. Once a neighbor lady had knocked loudly at her kitchen door. She was carrying a bottle of wine. "Let's get drunk," she said, half in tears. She told Chris all about her husband, how he always came too soon and now wouldn't even try to make love to her.

Chris had said a few things. Maybe they should see a counselor, a minister. She felt pretty helpless. "Why don't you have kids? You shouldn't wait too long," the woman said sharply, eyeing Chris appraisingly. Chris never did know what happened. The woman avoided her after that.

Was it Wednesday or Thursday? She heard the garbage truck in the alley. Thursday. Good. Even though she wasn't working now, she felt better if the week had tilted towards the weekend.

There. She turned the TV off. She never watched the after-school cartoons. They made her sad. She'd sleep for a while. The eggs could wait. Jamie never ate them anyway.

*

The phone was ringing. Oh, goodness, the house is dark, she thought, stumbling to the phone. It was one of Jamie's friends. "Did I disturb you?" he asked. "Oh, no, I was downstairs doing laundry," she lied. "Can I take a message?" "No, I'll probably see him. You can tell him I called. It's about Sunday."

Sunday, she thought. They were probably going fishing. "Sure, Mel," she said, putting the receiver down. The cord was wrapped around her feet, and she had to step out carefully. Six-fifteen by the kitchen clock. She'd better hurry.

Mel went back to his seat at the bar. It was the time of day when angry women called up, wives tired with waiting, kids hungry and supper going cold.

"I pay for that food, dammit, and she'd better not tell me when to eat it!" one man said. He was drinking fast. Other men nursed their drinks. Many had an expectant look: when the phone rang, they poised like dancers. A name would be called, and a man would say, "Tell her I'm not here." Or he'd grin like a kid and make his way to the phone, accepting jokes from the other men: "Hey, it's the War Department!"

"But that Chrissie," Mel was saying. "She's not outspoken at all. Why, she's about the sweetest little thing you'd ever want to meet."

Chris didn't know that they were drinking to her virtue. She put some meat in the microwave to thaw. Jamie was usually home by 7:30. She liked to be ready. She measured out the instant potatoes.

*

He'd ask her how she spent her day, if she went for a drive. She did that sometimes, just to look at the country. "No," she'd say, "I worked on your sweater." And she'd show him what she'd done, how the left sleeve was growing. She knew it made him feel bad to see her depressed. They'd been getting along much better, so she didn't know what was wrong.

Tonight he asked: "Would you like to have a baby? Would that help?" "No," she replied. "I think that would make it worse." "Well, maybe you should see a doctor then. You've been this way a long time." Yes, she said. She would do that.

*

The doctor came, shuffling her file. She tried to remember what all was in it. A fall on ice. Sprained wrist. Nothing broken. Normal weight and blood pressure. Some yeast infections. A pregnancy test done after that rodeo cowboy. She'd been waiting about an hour. All the doctors were from a town thirty miles away. She'd never seen this one before.

"What can I do for you?" he asked, still looking at the file. "Well, I guess I'm depressed." It relieved her to say it, so she went on, talking too fast. "It's gone on quite a while. I thought I could take something, for maybe just a week or two that would help . . ."

"Do you have trouble getting to sleep?" he asked abruptly. "No, I want to sleep all the time." "How about your bowel movements? Are they normal?" "I guess. I don't know." She was getting uncomfortable. "You're not constipated?" "No." He wrote it down.

"Are you on any medication?" "Just birth control pills." "How long?" "About four years." Except for when I didn't give a damn, she thought. She'd been lucky. The doctor asked her more questions and finally said, "Well, you don't have the clinical signs of depression." He clicked his pen.

She almost laughed out loud. She shrunk in her chair. "Well, what should I do?" she asked. She was afraid she'd start to cry. "Well . . ." he looked at her doubtfully. "I can give you some tranquilizers, if you think that will help."

She smiled and said, "Something mild. I react pretty strongly to drugs."

He nodded, and wrote out a prescription.

IV.

She walked north on Main, into one of the first chilly winds of fall. She'd been buying things for the house: a new bathroom rug, a better reading lamp for the living room. The house had always seemed too dark to her, and finally she would change it. Today she'd picked out some new pillows for the sofa. She wanted to get home and see how they looked, but she had to pick up a few groceries first.

She was thinking about painting the kitchen. Anything would be better than the dull yellow it was, even a brighter yellow. She had looked at paint samples, and thought maybe she could do the job herself. She pulled absently at the stacked-up shopping carts.

"Well, hello, sweet things." A voice penetrated her fog. "Hi, Cal," she said, turning around: "How are you?" "Just getting off a drunk," he said, hoarsely, conspiratorially. He was buying donuts and tomato juice in small cans. She couldn't remember now what she'd come for.

Main Street was nearly deserted. The prairie waited at both ends. It had been over a year since she'd last seen him, and she was startled to realize she still thought of him as a lover. The way one is supposed to think of a lover, with a quick, involuntary grin.

There was a kind of conspiracy between them, she supposed. There would be. In a small town, things like that had a claim on you. She thought they might have been friends if she were a man. She could not imagine him as a woman.

He was being nice to her, nicer than she expected. He accepted her offer of a beer. They talked quietly in the bar, about how the year had been, if the winter would be a hard one.

"I should be gettin' on home," he said. "I got a deer to cut up for my ma before I hit the road again." "Yes," she said. "Get moving; I'm a bad influence on you." He laughed.

It was like being in a river: the currents separated them, and drew them together. They could warm her; they had almost drowned her. It would be so easy to touch him. He played the bartender for a six-pack to go. Horses. A dice game they played here, too complicated for her to follow. He won and she said, "I see your luck's still holding." "Take care," he said. She said.

*

She dreamed that night about a cowboy riding a night horse through a storm. It was dark, the wind blew in their faces. They could have tumbled to the stony ground. But the horse was sure-footed. It knew its work.

It was after a rodeo, Kenny had pushed her down in the dust. "I don't dance with whores," he said, spitting out the words. She thought she should ask him, but he had moved too far away: "What should I do then? I'll do anything you say." He was innocent, his hatred of her so innocent. He wanted her dead.

She and Jamie were lying together, a simple arrangement of skin and bone and hair. In the deserted arena, the wind played with pieces of paper, empty cups. From a distance, from across the prairie, it looked like a shipwreck. But they slept together in the ruins: easily touched, easily opened. The moon stood guard, protecting them.

She sat up in bed and watched the first snow falling. She could see, by moonight, that the back yard was blanketed. She slid back under the covers. Jamie's body was welcoming; large and warm. She kissed him lightly. He stirred sleepily and reached for her. They would make love. It would be a risk, but that was what she needed most.

Football

Don Gadow

HOP—SPREAD the feet wide—bring the arms up over the head and slap the hands together. Hop—knock the sides of the shoes together—arms slap the sides. As Al performed the jumping jack in unison with his teammates, the lightly frozen grass felt like little pillows beneath his aluminum cleats. He had to laugh to himself as he thought of his self-conscious, uncoordinated bumbling during calisthenics as a seventh grader trying to make the junior high team so many years ago.

Now the exercises were automatic to him, and he could devote his attention to more important things like looking along the sidelines for Karen, who suddenly waved to him, or at least waved in his direction. Al waved back, in love with her black and gold cheerleading outfit, her status as head cheerleader, the long red hair and freckles that made her an anomaly among the German and Bohemian girls at school. Maybe tonight his dad would say to him, "Allie, you played a good game. Take the car. Take a girl home."

The reddish cast of the harvest moon reminded Al of the Coleridge poem from senior English:

> "As idle as a painted ship
> Upon a painted ocean."

Only he didn't feel idle, just solitary, not really a part of the team, except for his friend Jerry Malek, but apart from it, like the Ancient Mariner, whose punishment was to forever confront the agony of being the lone survivor on the ship that was idled in a sea of red.

On calm nights like this the ball seemed to pause in the air, looking disproportionally large, like the barrage balloons that hovered over London in the old newsreel film Al had seen in history class; but benevolent, not like the "white monster," as the narrator referred to it. Then sometimes the ball was like a bomb, but falling crazily horizontally. After all, that's what the sports writers call a long pass, a bomb, and nobody could throw the bomb like Jerry.

By the sidelines Norbert stood pulling on his right ear lobe. Encased in that cheap cloth bib of gold with the number "22" carelessly scrawled in black paint, he felt like a temporary person. People said he was too moody. Maybe he was, he thought, but he had serious things to think about, not like his son Allie, or Al as the boy liked to call himself, who loved only to play football, and not like the men he drank coffee with, who weren't much different from kids themselves with all their talk about football, or baseball in the summer.

When he was fifteen, two years younger than Allie was now, Norbert graduated from eighth grade and went to work. His dad had told him, in German, "Every man in the boat must pull an oar." After working for a year, Norbert bought a brand new Model T on payments. He started chasing over to Yellow Medicine on weekends, money burning a hole in his pockets, drinking at Draeger's Blue Moon, where prohibition's light faded to dimness so far from the morality of the statehouse in St. Paul. His dad didn't say much about Norbert's running around except, "If you're old enough to work like a man, you're old enough to be a man in all things, even suffering."

"Angst" was the word he had used, denoting more than mere suffering.

Norbert shut his eyes and slowly shook his head back and forth as the spiders began crawling from the cobwebs they had started weaving twenty-five years ago. Is it new spiders, he asked himself, or do the same ones keep coming back, hibernating and then coming alive whenever the mind becomes hopefully spring-like?

Al hated Dad's Night. When he ran out on the field and stood by his dad at half time, his dad would stand there looking glum or bored, shabby in that Korean War Navy peacoat that he had been given by Al's cousin Benno. Maybe he thought wearing it made him seem more American. Goodness knows, Al thought, his dad had always seemed ashamed of his German background. Was it Emerson who said that every bad thing was balanced by a good one? In Al's case the good thing was that his dad's dislike for the old country heritage had led him to learn to speak English without an accent, unlike so many of the people around this town. He wondered how Jerry could stand hearing his own dad at the bank talking English with no knowledge of the letter "T," or worse yet, when he talked German or Bohemian with the retired farmers.

Al knew his dad was there only because the coffee crowd at Elmer's Cafe would be munching on the game along with their donuts tomorrow morning. In a small town like this people didn't have much to get excited about except high school sports. Whenever he thought about such boredom, Al couldn't wait to leave for college in Sioux Falls.

Norbert wondered if the other fathers were as embarrassed as he was to be here at the game, or if some of them really liked football. As he looked at Joe Malek, Norbert remembered how Joe couldn't speak one word of English when he started school but had risen through luck to become the town banker. Maybe that's how his boy got to be quarterback—it's all politics. The bile rose up into his mouth as it always did when he thought about other people's successes. "Whatever you do wrong, you will pay for," his dad had told him years before.

Twenty-five years ago, almost to the night, the three of them had sworn their pact of silence, an agreement that Arnie kept right up to 1942 when his ship was torpedoed in the South Pacific, a conspiracy that turned Cletus into an impotent drunk, a decision that had filled Norbert's conscience like hardened cement.

At Pavek's gas station Arnie went into the back room and ordered a pint for each of them and one to spare, "gopher poison" they had called it then. As they left town, headed for the Indian reservation, the corn shocks were stars in the harvest moon's magic lantern show. Three miles out of town, Wilbert Goresh, always trying to stay ahead of everybody else, was plowing by the full moon's light.

When they got to Yellow Medicine, Gloria, Phyllis, and Marilyn were in the usual spot underneath the cottonwoods by the mission church, where they were out of sight of other prowling white men. Gloria said, too, that she liked the rustling leaves that reminded her of the currents of water rushing over the rocks of the nearby Pipestone River. Her poetic nature was one of the things Norbert liked about Gloria—like Longfellow's "Song of Hiawatha," a poem he remembered from eighth grade, his last year of school. There were other things too: how she giggled after a few drinks, the way she let life's cares slide by, and, most of all, the risk—wrong race, wrong religion, wrong set of morals, her dissimilarity to the daughters of immigrants that choked Norbert's life the way fish traps closed off the paths of migrating northern pike in the spring-swollen creeks.

Warm-ups were just about over. Al felt loose tonight, in spite of the little nagging worries that were always there. He didn't worry much about contact, once he was reassured of survival after the first solid hit. Anyway, as a flanker he usually didn't get hammered, just bumped or pulled down gently. Tall defensive backs could cause problems, but Al generally outran anybody he played against in the conference, especially after a good fake. His shins were sore, though, from so many kicks by those metal cleats. His worst worry was losing the ball in the glare of the lights. But why worry? His dad always said, "Don't brood like the old country people. You're an American. Enjoy yourself." Al wondered why his dad never seemed to live by his own advice instead of sitting in his rocking chair, smoking cigarettes and staring at the black pipe that rose from the wood-burning kitchen cook stove.

As the Bruins ran to the sidelines for the final words from Coach Brunzell, Al looked again for Karen. He thought of how she looked in school when she wore that aqua skirt with the fine black rings that looked like honey comb and one of those sweaters that made a guy think. She seemed to like him, but did she like him more than any of the other guys? Without a car he couldn't ask her out. He decided to secretly dedicate a touchdown to her, like a Knight of the Round Table. Her red hair would be his talisman.

The first quarter was scoreless. Al saw right away that part of the other team's strategy was to contain him at the line of scrimmage. On their second possession he took a hard hit from the blind side that collapsed the wind out of him. That was one time when he wished he had worn the rib pads abandoned for the feelings of freedom and the illusion of extra speed.

The coach's pre-game pep talk hadn't affected Al. He didn't mind being called "chicken-shit," or even "gutless, chicken-shit bastards," the latest variation. Even if there was poison behind it, Al thought they had it coming with only one win in three games after being picked by the Willow County *Gazette* to win the conference. When push came to shove, Al had to admit, they weren't a hard-hitting team. When one parent tried to show off his big vocabulary by telling Brunzell uptown that the team played with more finesse than power, the coach growled, "Finesse is for card games. In football you got to knock the other guy's nuts off."

Most of the crowd chased the ball down the sidelines, but Norbert stayed in place. He had a moment's crawling sensation from his brain to his stomach when Allie was knocked down. What if he got hurt, like the player from Red Rock who got gangrene last year and almost lost his leg? How could he ever pay the medical bills, Norbert wondered. Sure Allie was good, like they said down at the cafe, but what good would that do if he got hurt, maybe crippled for life? How could he go to college?

Norbert had heard that people who work in factories can get hypnotized by the repetitive motion of the machines to the extent they feel a compulsion to stick their hands into the moving parts. Thoughts are like that. We know we shouldn't stick our present into the mind's buzz saw, but there is such a strong pull, a siren call that tells us this time maybe the past will make sense.

That long ago night had started so peacefully. The six of them parked in the usual spot up on the hill, where the granite monument erected in memory of the people killed in the 1862 Sioux Uprising spired against the horizon, looming larger than usual, reddish against the harvest moon. Now that the first frost had passed, the annoying mosquitoes were gone.

Alcohol primes the pump, they used to say. After a few drinks and a lot of laughs, they separated by pairs to their favorite hiding places. Norbert loved Gloria for her manner of touching his elbow when she wanted to tell him something, not like the German girls he had gone out with who seemed to hoard their affection for some time far away in the future. This night, as they looked up at the moon, she told him her grandfather's tale of the buffalo who had gone up to the moon, where they were protected by its spirit from the encroachment of the white man. He was distracted, though, by what her brother Bud had said last weekend in the darkness out behind the Blue Moon. As he walked past Norbert, he said in a voice like brakes worn down to the rivets, "Pelzel, the next time you see my sister, I'll cut off your balls with a rusty sardine can lid."

The score was 6-6 in the second quarter when Jerry called their favorite play. Al lined up flanked right, on the count took six quick steps out to the flat, and then cut straight upfield for the long pass. It was a great play, all speed and Jerry's strong arm, if the line held long enough to set it up. This time, though, the safety was playing deeper than usual and sped over to cover Al. As the ball came down, Al slowed up, turned while still running, and grabbed the ball over the left shoulder. Fortunately, it was not to his right. Once when Al had tangled his feet while turning right at full speed, he had actually fallen down, only to have Brunzell sarcastically comment, "Al, you must have a short in your wiring system."

Still running, Al turned, put his head down, and collided viciously with the safety, helmet against helmet. Al saw hundreds of red and white stars, almost like a huge American flag. As he fell, still clutching the ball, the taste in his mouth was like the smell he remembered from his childhood when he would turn the handle of the grindstone while his grandfather sharpened an axe.

Al felt like staying on the ground forever, but then he heard Jerry's friendly but concerned, "Get up, big shooter." As Al lay there, rotating his neck, he realized he had chipped several teeth. Although their helmets had face bars this year for the first time, Al dreaded getting a tooth knocked out or broken off. He knew Karen wouldn't like him with a silver tooth like some of the Bohemian farm kids had.

As Al jogged to the huddle, he saw the ball on the thirty yard line. They could score easily now and take a lead into halftime. He didn't even bother to look to see if Brunzell was sending in a sub for him. All the coach ever did when somebody got hit hard was rub his hands together like he had just bowled a perfect game. He never took a player out unless the guy made a mistake or had to leave feet first. Even then he would suspect the player of faking it, the way Delbert Pavek, the big tackle had tried to do in the last game in order to get a breather. "You can't get rid of beer except by sweating it out," Brunzell had wise-cracked.

*

Over the years Norbert had learned to pretend emotions that he suspected came naturally to people who had not been anesthetized by their pasts. As Allie got up, Norbert said, "Nice pass, Malek. That boy of yours can really throw the ball." As he faced back down the field, he was again conscious of the number "22" on the bib that symbolized the approaching halftime ceremony. He wondered why he had to go out on the field and stand by Allie, when everybody knew who everybody else was in such a small town with only thirty kids in a grade.

As the crowd again moved away from Norbert toward the goal line, the people were replaced by memories of Gloria and Bud Feather, people who were somehow more real to him even after twenty-five years.

Norbert had warned Cletus beforehand to keep his hot temper under control if they ran into Bud. "I don't want to take on the whole reservation," he had said.

Long after midnight they dropped the girls off by the church and headed north to go home. At the T road where they had to slow down to make a left turn, they saw someone ahead in the road, waving his arms for them to stop. "It's Bud," Arnie called out needlessly. In Norbert's mind was a vivid picture of Bud's threat, and possibly a little guilt too—he didn't want anybody fooling around with his sister either—liquor had intensified his fears and the innate sense of violence he had such little opportunity to exercise. As Cletus yelled, "Watch it!" Norbert swerved the Model T and barreled ahead, catching Bud with the right front fender and then running over him with a sound like stepping on a ripe cucumber. Norbert pulled ahead a few yards and stopped just before the turn. They got out and looked at Bud. His skull was crushed, his nose twisted almost off his face.

There wasn't much to do. Cletus got out of the car carrying the pint that they had planned to drink on the way home. Without saying a word, he poured the whiskey over Bud's shapeless face. What didn't flow into the open mouth dribbled past the distorted nose and skirted around his ear. "They'll think he got drunk, and somebody run him over. They'll never know who did it if we keep quiet. Nobody cares about Indians anyway." Then in a strangled voice, "Let's get out of here in a hurry." About a mile down the road they stopped to throw up their yellowish guilt. "It was an accident," Arnie said. "In a way, it's self defense."

Norbert waited all week, but the sheriff didn't show up. What bothered him the worst, he suspected Bud didn't even have a knife in his pocket, but he hadn't dared to look. He didn't go back to see Gloria either. Instead, he took his mother's advice and asked out Rosemary Ebnet, daughter of the depot agent. A year later they got married.

The Bruins had gone into what Brunzell called the "cattle drive." Line plunges and quarterback sneaks. A little pass over the middle to Al made it 12-6. As the reserve tackle ran in with the extra point play, Al looked to the sidelines for Karen's approval. Finished with the touchdown cheer, she had turned away to talk to someone as though football existed merely as a showcase for her social ambitions.

After the running play failed, Al left the field. He never played on kickoff teams. Maybe Brunzell did think he was a chicken-shit bastard. Besides that, now he had to worry about the halftime ceremony. He hoped his dad wouldn't call him "Allie," like he was still a kid. As Al looked down the field toward the receiving Cardinals, he saw his dad on the sidelines, in that awful Navy coat, pulling on his ear.

Just then Karen came over to him, smiling, gray eyes flecked with dots of colors like moist granite. "Way to go, Al. I'll wait for you after the game. We can walk uptown for a hamburger."

He was so surprised he almost forgot to grin. "Sure thing, Karen. It's a date."

"Hey, Al, there's a game on. Leave the girls alone for a minute."

Did Brunzell ever let up on the sarcasm, Al wondered. As he turned to the coach, Brunzell said, "Terrific catch, Al, on that long one. Lots of kids would drop the ball when they got nailed like that. You got a lot of guts for a little guy. I think you can make the team at Augustana if you work hard enough."

Norbert had accepted the congratulations of the crowd. In spite of the spiders, he returned the compliment. "Way to go, Malek! That boy of yours can really throw the ball!"

A Novel Theory of Extinction

Margi Preus

A L FIELDS HAD BEEN working on a theory of why and how the dinosaurs became extinct. The idea, in a nutshell, was that they suffocated. The atmosphere, acting like a kind of huge dry cleaner bag, came right down over their heads and they were just too dumb to do anything about it.

Al had lost his job and had gone to live in the country, retreating from the "now known world" as he put it. He lived in an old farm house where he spent most of his time in the bathtub. He shaved in the tub; he thumbed through natural history magazines; and, after years of showering, and though not sure he wanted to, he rediscovered his body. In the tinted water it appeared green; his soft belly like that of a Galapagos Sea Turtle's, exposed only at the moment of death; his toes hairy as early man's when he was still evolving from apedom.

Today he was supposed to go to see the doctor, but he had decided not to. He was on the way out. He didn't need a doctor to tell him that. It was his heart: it kept slipping. It did not stay neatly in place like most other people's; it just slid from one side of his chest to the other. He really feared for when it would find, and inevitably it must, the spaces between his other internal organs, and start slipping inevitably, irreversibly downwards.

So he didn't need to lose track of one more thing in his life—his job, his wife, his family—now his heart. The idea had come to him in the bathtub. Maybe it was the warm, slightly iron-tainted water that tinged the bath red, his pale forearms ribboned with blue-green veins, the razor in his hands. It would be easy, but it would be a nasty mess for the landlady. So he had conceived of another idea.

He got out of the bathtub, put on a suit and tie, and went out to the barn.

The barn was ancient and beginning to fall in on itself, leaning against the hillside. Some might have found it forbidding, others might never have noticed it; to Al it looked like a cool harbor of death. Leaning by the side of the barn was a ladder, overgrown with weeds. He dragged it away from the barn, anticipating but overcoming his horror of slugs and beetles scurrying for cover in the pale, flattened grass beneath.

He entered the barn. It was cooler and darker than outside. Shafts of light, single-purposed interrogators, filed in from missing planking. The straw on the floor was luminous as stained glass. The dust, white with age, seemed holy, as if it were brought in from a church.

He looked down and saw a cat, one floor beneath him. "A few missing floorboards," he pronounced. He slid the ladder over the hole in the floor, contemplated using it as a bridge, but abandoned that idea. Instead, he picked up one foot (he was too old for this, he thought), held his breath (I hope it doesn't take too long, he thought) and, flailing his arms, he jumped over the crack. When his foot hit the floor on the other side, a puff of dust arose and then there was a rush and flurry and white hurtling handkerchiefs—a flock of moths, a sendup of balloons, a visible beating of hearts, fifty of them, white and winged. His own heart lunged into his throat and he threw up his hands to stop it from going anywhere else. That movement startled the birds and they abruptly changed their courses or plunged anew from their perches so that the huge hall of the barn was filled with applause.

After a time the birds settled down and Al began to pick them out—swallows tucked in knot-holes and strung along the cross beams. Lining the rafters were rows of pigeons, most whitish, some gray, a black one, brown, a few spotted like appaloosas, head after head alike, shape after shape identical, rows of feathered bullets or tea cozies lined up left to right.

He leaned the ladder up against a rafter. That would do—there was an old milking stool in one corner of the barn—that might work. He tested the rungs of the ladder, climbing slowly. This must work out, he thought, I must do this one thing right. A bird flew by his shoulder, like a bolt of blue, like a flash of insight, Al thought. Something odd about this bird, like it didn't belong here—belonged somewhere else—in the jungle, in a Walt Disney movie. He swivelled on the ladder to look at it. It was a bird, larger than the others, with a slender neck and something odd about the eye—its eye was a perfect circle and a color—or just a deep, never-ending circle of darkness. The wings were slender as butter knives and though he didn't see a tail, he knew the bird had one—he could see it in his mind's eye, an extension of its slender body, and smooth as stone. There were a pair of them like that.

Al had an idea that he had seen these birds somewhere before, but he couldn't place them. He climbed down the ladder and sat on a hay bale, chin resting on his fist, tie hanging like a plumb line between his knees. He thought he should know what they were. "By God, I'm a paleontologist," he reminded himself. He pulled on his lip in a scholarly fashion. I just have to know what kind of birds these are, he thought, and then I'll get back to the business at hand.

So he paced, a skill—an art, really—he thought—a *sport* he had perfected when teaching freshman chemistry. The birds ruffled their feathers quietly above him, once in a while a bit of down drifted from the rafters, flickering in and out of the light. He could almost hear the birds sigh, shift on their perch, close their notebooks and check the clock . . . "What kind of bird is it?" he muttered to himself, the start of a quiz formulating in his mind.

He went back to the house and into the bathroom. Sitting on the edge of the tub, he stared out the window. He could see the landlady's laundry out on the line. She lived in a trailer house on the property. Though he seldom saw her, he saw her laundry, pillowcases fluttering on the line, sheets and towels flapping and flying. Something flipped over in his memory. He picked up one of the magazines and ran a thumb through the swollen pages, the colors of the photographs whirring by like a B movie. Then he began peeling the damp pages apart carefully.

There they were, those birds, in a glossy photograph of an Audubon painting, the lower bird stretching back his head, baring his flushed breast to receive food from the bird on a higher branch, the smaller, duller, obviously female bird who had her beak placed intimately inside his open mouth.

He rolled the cover back to expose the picture and went out to the barn. He leaped over the crack without thinking, his mind on other things. In the barn, he found a little stool to sit on, and a little splash of sun, so that he sat as if in bathwater. He sat very still and waited for the birds to calm down.

After the birds settled on their perches, he analyzed the two live birds against the drawing. They had the same small blue heads, the regal bearing. He noticed their long tails this time. They could have posed for the drawing, the pair of passenger pigeons. But, as he already knew, and now read in the accompanying article, the last passenger pigeon, Martha, died in the Cincinnati Zoo on September 2, 1914. The birds had been considered extinct for over seventy years.

Standing, with one hand holding the text, the other gesturing, he read aloud,

> "Let us take a column of one mile in breadth," a column of pigeons, he's talking about, "which is far below the average size, and suppose it is passing over us without interruption for three hours, at the rate mentioned above of one mile in a minute. This will give a parallelogram of one hundred and eighty square miles. Allowing two pigeons to the square yard, we have one billion, one hundred and fifty millions, one hundred and thirty-six thousand pigeons in one flock."

"I'm thinking small here," Al thought. "We're talking massive amounts of birds." He imagined crowds of people flocking like birds, men running, shirt tails flapping like wings, gathering masses of people nesting all together in parks, crouching twenty-five to a park bench, the hum of their voices like the din of bird calls, their footfall on the pavement like the thunderous flapping of wings, hundreds hanging from lamp posts, thousands perched on jungle gyms, all about to be struck down by heart failure in one fell swoop, savaged, decimated, annihilated.

He clutched at his own heart and staggered to his stool where he sat for a few moments, until he became conscious of what it was he was sitting on. Rising slowly and grasping the stool with one hand, he held it in front of him to examine it. Such a tool had been used to slaughter passenger pigeons. Yes, a stool just like this one—maybe this very one, held a pigeon fast, tied, pigeon leg to stool leg. As the bird struggled to fly, fluttering, straining, other pigeons were attracted—curious? Horrified? Trying to help out?

Then the merciless pigeon hunters threw a net over their innocent heads, and:

> ". . . Through its meshes were stretched the heads of the fluttering captives vainly struggling to escape. In the midst of them stood a stalwart pigeoner up to his knees in the mire and bespattered with mud and blood from head to foot. Passing from bird to bird, with a pair of blacksmith's pincers, he gave the neck of each a cruel grip with his remorseless weapon, causing the blood to burst from the eyes and trickle down the beak of the helpless captive, which slowly fluttered its life away, its beautiful plumage besmeared with filth and its bed dyed with its crimson blood."

Then the pigeons were dead. Just done for. All that bright blue dulled forever. Was there a bird heaven, where billions of passenger pigeons now roost, hundreds to a cloud, their glittering excrement the luster of the golden streets? Naw. They probably just rotted straight away. But think of the kind of heaven they created while they were alive, a great rushing of wings and the sparkling iridescence of their feathers—a sea of hurtling blue bodies.

Everyone had assumed these birds were extinct—just because nobody ever *saw* any. "Arrogance!" Al exclaimed. That could mean—it could mean . . . There could be dodo birds, snail darters, mastodons—dinosaurs! Still roaming somewhere . . . It was just as he'd suspected. There had been more to the world than they thought. There were things *they did not know*. We are so mind-bound, he thought.

He looked at his feet. Beneath them, through a crack in the floorboards, he saw the cat's face, looking up at him. Its eyes reminded him of his wife's eyes. We are so earth-bound, he thought.

Okay, back to business. He was not going to let himself get distracted. Al steadied the ladder, he put one foot on the lowest rung. Overhead, birds lifted off the

rafters. The movement made Al's heart lift—he felt it in his throat, almost choking him. He thought, I'd like to take one really good look at those birds.

Suddenly, it came to him: birdseed. There was birdseed in the shed. Just a quick
side-trip out to the shed and Al was back. He scattered the seed on the floor.
After a while and one by one, the birds fluttered down, picking like hens at the
seed. While he waited for the pasenger pigeons to gather courage, he read:

> "It was proverbial with our fathers that if the Great Spirit in His
> wisdom could have created a more elegant bird in plumage, form,
> and movement, He never did. I have seen them fly . . . in one un-
> broken column for hours across the sky, like some great river, ever
> varying in hue; and as the mighty stream, sweeping on at sixty miles
> an hour, reached some deep valley, it would pour its living mass
> headlong down hundreds of feet, sounding as though a whirlwind
> was abroad in the land. I have stood by the grandest waterfall of
> America and regarded the descending torrents in wonder and astonish-
> ment, yet never have my astonishment, wonder and admiration been
> so stirred as when I have witnessed these birds drop from their course
> like meteors from heaven."

Al glanced up from his reading to see if the pigeons had come down yet.
Something caught his eye—a tail and a taut rear end, sticking out from around
a corner. It was the cat, shifting its weight, one back leg to the other, quietly
writhing, tail twitching; its whole body a study of concentration. What was that
beast after, Al wondered. Then he realized—the birds! At the precise moment
the cat lunged out into the room, Al lunged out at the cat. It spurted from between his arms and Al fell face forward on the floor.

Al picked himself up and saw the cat again explode into movement, its back
legs tucked under as it leapt a distance across the room. And he saw the blue
plumage. Then it was fluttering, batting, feathers, the bird's wings all wrong, its
vulnerable, blushed belly exposed to claws, teeth, air, Al's vision. He wanted to
put his hands over his eyes—embarrassed for the bird, afraid for his eyes.

But he was frozen. He could not move, the drama playing itself out in front
of him, framed by a doorway. As if watching a film, Al was distant, the drama
intense—the cat all brawn, muscle and intelligence, all fascinatingly horrible beauty.

Two feathers, blue, hovered above the melee. (The cat had the bird in its mouth;
the bird beat with its wings; the cat set it down; the bird fluttered helplessly;
the cat batted at it playfully with a paw, now lying on its stomach watching it,
amused, now up and circling it, one paw out, tentatively touching it.)

The feathers were two small downy ones, probably from the bird's chest, which
had gotten caught in an updraft and now drifted unpretentiously down.

"Tetrapod vertebrates," Al said aloud. He'd been on the verge of a big break-
through—he just knew it. Then, the next thing he knew, he overheard his col-

leagues say his office smelled, "like old dinosaur shit." Shortly after that, he'd been asked to leave. His wife had asked him to leave, too. He suspected she didn't like him. He never did anything—go to movies, play sports—bowling did she mean? What did she expect from a man who studied dead things? Did she want him to play racquetball or something? With his heart always lunging about in his chest . . .

The cat lunged; it had had its kicks, it was time to dine. With one hard pounce on the stunned bird, it knocked her over. Her chest exposed, the cat tore into it with its teeth, ripping her flesh like a piece of fabric. The cat's head emerged, bloodied and triumphant, its jaws separated to accommodate some ripe and bloody organ Al could only assume was the bird's heart.

Now Al felt his own heart burst into his hands, which he swung, hot and wild, at the cat. The cat, hurt and startled, skulked into the shadows.

Al knelt by the bird's body. "Why didn't you fly?" he said, trying to close up the wound in her chest. It was, he knew, no use. "Why did you give up?" he said. It was, he also knew, too late.

He had let the bird die. He felt, somehow, that he had let the dinosaurs down . . . somehow he felt responsible for their extinction, too.

That was it—Al Fields himself had just assured the total extinction of the passenger pigeon. It was not the kind of notoriety he had hoped for.

It was dusk. Darkness sifted in through the cracks in the siding. He had a sudden sense of the horrifying passsage of time—as if it flew in on black wings—ichthyornis' maybe—brushing against his face like the darkness against the one glass window in the barn. He noticed the gray shadows made by his own hands; he noticed the wrinkles. With the swiftness of a kill, he felt himself aging, death as near as the approaching sky, the dark flank moving forward toward the thin slice of glass that made the window, against which it would press.

He lived a desperate existence, Al thought, never knowing where his heart might leap to next, nor whether it would be beating when it got there . . .

He might have changed his mind. For a moment, the discovery of the pair of passenger pigeons had revived him, made him want to live again—it was a find. Maybe it had been more than a find. But now . . .

It was time to do what he had set out to do. He had, he felt, the nerve. He had a necktie. He had a ladder. He felt good about this; it showed commitment—resolve—*action*.

He picked out the spot, the spot where the now deceased bird had roosted; it was conveniently vacant. Al rested the ladder against the beam. He removed his tie and holding it in one hand, began to climb. He climbed slowly, both feet getting a chance at each rung. The wooden rungs curled like tight waves under his arches. He curled his hands around each one. Something struck him as profound about how he would place his feet where his hands had just rested; and that his hands rested where a hundred feet had trod before him. He thought, for a moment, that if he looked up, he might see a line of men above him, farmers through the ages, climbing the ladder to heaven.

He looked up. The ladder was bereft of saints or angels but at the top, perched on the rafter overhead, was the one remaining passenger pigeon, watching Al with one elegant red eye. The bird shifted its weight, a breeze through the siding ruffled its feathers; its dark eyes flicked. Al believed he could see through it, see clouds behind it.

Al wanted to say something, but didn't know what. "Move over, buddy," he said, and the bird skittered sideways a few inches. With one more step he was nearly eye level with the beam. The bird's red legs looked surreal. Al felt for a moment that he was in an exhibition at a natural history museum, trapped behind glass with stuffed birds. The scene was so: A beautiful passenger pigeon—stately and dignified, the last of its species—was hidden in the midst of a barn full of feral pigeons and mourning doves and a man on a ladder, almost to the top rung, was preparing to hang himself from the very rafter on which the last remaining passenger pigeon balanced over a pair of silly red legs. The display would be in the extinct species section of the museum: Al and the pigeon, the last of their breed.

There was one other piece in this exhibition puzzle. Just as Al pulled himself up to the rafter, he had seen it: an untidy nest of twigs, and in its center one small, stone-smooth, perfectly white egg. But just as he had seen it, the ladder slid out from under him, and Al, scrambling for the slick, guano-encrusted rafter, felt his fingers slip. This was not how it was supposed to happen, Al thought, as he followed the ladder downward, "I have changed my mind."

He thought of Icharus on his downward flight, melted wax dripping into his armpits. He thought of Hermes' winged heels, of Pegasus. He thought of the rotten floorboards beneath. Portions of his life flashed (like the sun must have flashed in the eyes of Icharus) inevitably before his eyes. Odd things: raking leaves once; running home at dusk as a kid.

He floated downward as a speck of dust, as a nearly weightless bit of down off the feathery chest of a pigeon. It would take him forever to land at this rate.

He lit a match. He smoked a cigarette. (He had smoked when he was younger but gave it up when he started having heart problems. It was too much to keep track of—heart and lungs, body and soul.) In his mind he had a cigarette. He smoked leisurely, tilting his head back, pushing the smoke up from his bottom lip toward his eyebrows. He read a magazine, glancing at the pictures: reds, greens, blues whispering by in a blur.

Al mentally completed his dissertation on the extinction of the dinosaur.

He took his pants off and changed them for another pair. No, he thought, I must think deep thoughts. Then he thought of water—deep and gray, smooth stones cobbling the lake bottom. No, I must realize something; my life must have content, meaning, depth, before I die an ironic death. (He was falling now, Al realized, like a meteor from heaven.) But what if, he thought, I don't die, I fall through the floorboards, I break my collar bone. I have to go see the doctor anyway. The doctor stands over me. His stethoscope swings like a pendulum over my face. He says, "You have a bad heart. We'll have to operate." They cut me open, go after my heart, they dig and dig, they can't find it . . . This is how it goes, is it? This is really how things go extinct, not neatly and scientifically, perfectly encased in arctic ice, but crazily, falling off of ladders or ending up with heart surgery, or like passenger pigeons—so many in the flocks that they crashed into each other in flight and went extinct that way maybe. Netters, boys with rocks, cats. Or the few remaining birds left in the depleted flocks had no will to go on; they had so little choice in mates. Girlfriends, wives, uncles, brothers, cousins, mothers gone. They made themselves extinct out of sorrow.

Al held in his hands a live animal, a bird perhaps, a creature whose whole inner workings were in its heart. Each rapid pulse of its tiny heart pumped life around his body. He saw in his mind a clothesline of laundry, clothespins clicking in the air like grasshoppers, pillowcases shuddering in the wind and sheets like wings. He felt himself being lifted up, lighter than air, light as hollow bones and feathers.

Bingo

Davida Kilgore

I T W A S A L L a bad mistake. I shoulda knowed something was gonna go wrong cause the bingo game at the VFW Hall was ten minutes late starting and Harry Wade don't never be late in taking our money. But it was 1:40 in the afternoon when that little piece of man hunched up them stairs on the side of the 'lectric numbers board, perched on his bar stool, and pretended to smile at us, ying-yanging that spiel we all knows by heart. Old Harry's got a megaphone voice, but he always uses the mike anyways, trying to amplify hisself into something he ain't; looking down on us from that platform like Pharaoh gotta hold of Moses and made him promise to lead us to the land of bankruptcy. Not too many peoples like Harry, and he don't like too many peoples, either, but he loves our money and we love to play bingo, and when you play with the devil . . . Harry kept on flapping his jaws while we did our last minute card switching, ordered sandwiches and pop, and got our hands stamped.

"Good afternoon, all you nice ladies and gentlemen. Welcome to another Wednesday afternoon of bingo. As all you good people know, our Wednesday afternoon session is sponsored by the Sacred Order of the Purple Heart."

I like playing bingo, specially on Wednesdays, since even with my short legs, the VFW is stepping distance from my doctor's office . . . no matter what that man says about my blood pressure. That's all he ever says, "Jean Thompson, you have to take it easy. There's no need in taking the risk of getting yourself all worked up . . . " I tells him, "Hon, at sixty-five, getting up in the morning is risky. And don't nothing ever much happen at the bingo hall to get excited about; you either win or you don't." After all, I ain't no big time Al Capone gambler like my best friend, Marie Jenkins. But I do enjoy playing me a little bit on Wednesdays, Thursdays, and sometimes Sunday nights, even if it do mean putting up with the likes of Harry.

Harry went on with his speech. "Now all you fine people know that we play the big games here on Wednesday afternoons: $50 & $75, & $100 Progressives, Gambler's Choice, chance at a black-and-white TV or $50 cash, and, of course, the Fishbowl. Our first half-hour we'll be playing Free Card games. A single winner bingoing on the last number called will play however many sets he or she is playing free all afternoon, including the big games. All unplayed cards must be face down and there will be no switching of cards after the first number is called.

"Cards are 3 for a dime, 10 for 30, 14 for 40, 18 for 50 and so on, up to ten sets. For your dining pleasure, the girls will be serving hot and cold sandwiches, pop and the best quarter cup of coffee money can buy."

Marie and I checked our cards one last time while Harry finished up his speech. We always got to the hall by at least 12:45 to choose her cards; we had to. Marie had her own private system and you just don't know how hard it is to shift through umpteen cards, stacked fifty and sixty deep, trying to find her favorite combinations. See, I don't study up on bingo like Marie, to me a card is a card. I just pick em up and throw em down on the table. And couldn't care less what color they are. But not only did Marie have to play her favorite numbers, all the cards had to have red borders to boot. You just try finding a red 1/2 corner combination sometimes when you ain't got nothing better to do.

But Marie always said, "Jean, there are some cards you have to have or you may as well stay you ass at home. You have to have a 3/13, 65/75, and a 61/71 in the corners. You have to have at least one Straight-10, 20, 60, 70, and if you're going to play Ns, get yourself a 33/43, 31/41, and that damn 37 always goes with that damn 39."

Child, I know it sounds silly going through all these motions to pick some cards cause you could pick till your fingers fell off and Harry'd still call whatever number you didn't need. But I enjoyed Marie's company and quiet as it's kept, I was partial to a 62/72 combination myself. Besides, Marie had been playing bingo seven days a week, two sessions a day for the past ten years, and if she didn't know what she was doing, who would?

Harry clicked on the machine and the balls commenced to bouncing offa each other like kernels turning theyselves into popcorn in the big corn popper near the entrance door at Kmart. Marie knew the colors of those balls by heart; she would say, "If Harry would just shut-up for a minute, I could look my number out." Harry said, "Our first number out will be the Fishbowl number. Every time we call this number, we'll add five dollars to this little fishbowl on the counter, and some time after four o'clock we'll play a special game for all the money inside it.

"We're ready to start our Free Card games. Anything goes: Straights, Corners, Angles, Postage Stamps, Inside/Outside Diamonds, Inside/Outside Squares—they're all good. Good luck, now! Your first, and Fishbowl number is . . . O . . . 75."

Marie mugged her lucky grin cause she always played herself some O/75s. See, that number had been a winner for her . . . about . . . umm? . . . three years ago and she said, "You don't change a good thing. That number's hot and all I have to do is wait—it'll be hot again. You wait and see." And Lawd knows we'd been waiting . . . for months now. But that was Marie; she had more patience than a little bit, would put up with shit I wouldn't think about taking.

Everybody at the Wednesday afternoon—or any other afternoon or evening session for that matter—knew Marie Jenkins. Yes, Lawd, Marie was one good-lookin' woman for "sixty years young" as she used to tell it. You couldn't miss her: 200-some-odd-pounds squeezed into them old-fashioned red stretch pants with the seams down the front, a matching red imitation silk blouse, and red patent leather, open-toed pumps. We all knew that Wednesday was her lucky day and red her favorite color. We knew everything about Marie, or so we thought, including the fact that along with the red magnetic bingo chips with the matching magnetic wand to pick them up with, Marie had a .38 inside that big purse of hers.

Marie drove a five-year-old New Yorker that she kept in better shape than herself, or her house, which was the excuse her husband Fred, that old Poindexter-looking chippy, used to justify his affair with this here chick name of Thelma.

Thelma's one of those thirty-five-year-old heifers who didn't have the sense to realize she wasn't a teenager anymore. She wears those skin-tight shimmy britches and low-cut sweaters; bras so small they make her look like she's got three instead of two. The kind of woman, and I'm using the term loosely, that old men get off on. And since she always sat four rows across from us at the hall, Marie had to put up with Thelma's laughing and pointing at her all during the session.

Marie was just as sweet as she could be and that's why all of us, well, all of us 'cepting Harry and Thelma and her crowd, just loved her to death. Marie remembered birthdays when our own children didn't; she visited the sick and shut-ins listed in the church bulletin; if she had a dollar, you had fifty cents if you needed it; no one who knew her ever went hungry. And because we knew she'd do the same for us, we suffered right alongside her through her children's divorces, her colds, flus and recent operation. And Fred's death.

I'd almost forgotten Fred's been gone one year to the day till I looked at Marie and saw the way she was staring at Thelma: if looks could kill, Thelma'd be dead. I felt like maybe I should say something but Marie beat me to it: "Know why I was late getting here? I went out to the cemetery to put some fresh flowers on Fred's grave. It surprised me that I still miss him considering what he did to me. And to have to come up here and look at Thelma . . . I've already had one run-in with her today . . . Thank God we had those pre-paid burial plots."

I didn't find out till after the funeral that things had been bad for Marie for a long time. She always did so much for everybody else I figgered she was sitting high on the hog. Turns out Fred hadn't been paying the bills, or his insurance premiums, spending all his money on Thelma, instead, and Marie had been playing catch-up for months.

Why just this morning she'd shivered in a two-block-long government-handout line, waiting to get the cheese and butter Thelma and her friends volunteered to pass out every third Wednesday of the month. And Marie was so proud that I wouldn't've even known she'd been to the community center for help if that scandalous hussy, Thelma, hadn't blabbed it all over the hall.

I swear Thelma ain't nothing but an old refrigerator, can't keep nothing. You should have heard the things she was saying about Marie before she got to the hall today. Just couldn't wait to tell it: "You should have seen the old bingo queen. She was crying and begging us for some food, trying to con us into paying her NSP bill. I told her, 'If you'd stop playing so damn much bingo, you could keep your lights on.' I told her, 'We only help people with a real emergency and if you have enough money to play bingo, then you'd have enough money to pay your bills.' I told her . . ."

Nobody really gave a damn what else Thelma told Marie cause we all knowed it was Thelma, herself, who had spread the word about her and Fred in the first place. I knowed about that tramp and people's husbands from the git-go, but I would never have told Marie; some things better to find out for yourself. So it was bad enough Marie needed to win big today, but having to deal with Thelma sitting four rows away, gossiping to anyone who would listen, was a little much. I hoped Marie would win the Coverall and then tell Thelma to go kiss her own ass.

And Marie would tell her, too. She sang tenor in the church choir every Sunday morning, and yelled "Bingo" in bass every Sunday afternoon from the third chair from the right, third row from the right wall of the hall. She was a God-fearing woman but let's face it, bingo brings out the worst in a person.

Take Marie again, for example. Marie didn't like Harry, called him everything the rest of us felt about him but didn't quite have the nerve to say—in public, anyways. Her favorite line, the one she used when Harry didn't call her out was, "You old bald-headed, skinny-assed white bastard! Why don't you shake up your balls?"

Harry, he would cheese at her and say, "Why don't you come up here and shake them for me—heh, heh."

Marie would give him this po'-fool look and say, "Don't you wish?" and then the two of them would cut loose. They ignored the big "NO CURSING OR SWEARING ALLOWED" sign near the exit door and played them some dozens. But Harry ain't no complete fool; he wouldn't dare try and throw Marie outta the hall.

Well, like I was saying, Harry called out O/75 and Marie covered her numbers.

"B-10! I-19!"

Marie popped me on my arm and pointed at her cards. She had an out for a G.

"Jean," she said, "that old fart gave me my out. All he has to do is call any G: 46, 50, 60, any of the good ones, and I don't give a damn which one it is." Then she yelled up at Harry, "Be nice!" and I noticed her hand was shaking as Harry turned the purple ball in his hand. Purple balls are Gs.

"G-60!"

"Bingo!" Marie's voice bounced offa the walls—and out ear drums. Thelma and her crowd muttered, "Shit, that old broad always plays free." They knew that was a lie; it had been a long time since Marie had won the Free Card game. The rest of us yelled, "Go get him, Marie."

One of the collectors, name of Lucy, jogged over to our table and snatched Marie's card, knocking her chips across the table; some of them even rolled on the floor. Lucy called out, "Straight-10, 19, 60, 75."

Harry didn't like it worth shit. He hated it when Marie won to play free all day but he said, "One good bingo stopping on G-60. Are there any other bingos?"

He knew there weren't.

"Ten sets?"

Lucy nodded. Harry knew Marie always played ten sets.

"Ten sets free all afternoon to that lucky player."

Lucy brought over a five-by-seven, ten of spades playing card in a lucite picture frame that stood for Marie's ten free sets, slammed it on the table and I could just hear her thinking to herself, "I can't shortchange her today, but there's always that old biddy at the other end of my station, she never counts her change." One of these days someone is going to count their change and knock that cheap blonde wig off Lucy's head.

For the next twenty-eight minutes Marie made sure her cards had all the numbers Harry was calling. Her 61/71 combination was called. She changed a couple of other cards, between games like you're supposed to. I played a game for her while she went to the bathroom and by the time she came back to her seat, Harry was announcing the $100 Progressive.

"Okay, folks, it's time for our first big game of the afternoon. Cards in this game are ten cents apiece, no bonus cards. Straight bingo in five numbers or less for one hundred dollars! Just a reminder, folks: we know our Wednesday afternoon crowd is always honest . . ."

Someone in the back of the hall laughed. I can't prove it but I think that that part of Harry's speech is a signal to one of his house-players, and the collectors, that he didn't want any of the regular customers to win this game. Like I said, I can't prove it but it seems that one of the house-players wins every time Harry gives that speech.

"There will be no switching of cards after the first number is called. And remember, the last number called must be used in your bingo to have it honored.

All unplayed cards face down. Everybody ready?"

Somebody yelled, "Shake your balls."

Harry, he said, "I'm too old to be shaking my balls . . . heh, heh, hch."

"I know that's right," Marie yelled back. Harry rolled his eyes at her and called the first number.

"Your first number out is O . . . 75."

Everybody yelled, "Fishbowl!"

"We'll add five dollars to the Fishbowl. Next number out: N/39. B/13 . . . I/20 . . . B/8 . . . "

People started screaming at Harry:

"Slow down, fool."

"Where's the fire?"

"I'm still on B/13."

"Call the next number, will ya?"

Harry gave us a little time to catch up. "Okay, we'll slow it down. B/8 was your fifth number. Continuing on, we're looking for any bingo with the calling of N/37."

Marie covered her N/37s, realized she had an out, popped me on the arm again, and said, "G/51 will give me an inside diamond, and he hasn't called a G yet. Everybody's waiting on one, but a split is still money."

Marie didn't think bout an I being called would give somebody a Postage Stamp cause she didn't have an I out. Harry grabbed a green ball, called out, "I/23," and an elderly man, sitting way back yonder in the no smoking section yelled, "Bingo!"

"Bingo!" screamed the collector as she jogged over to the man's table and picked up his card. Harry shut down the machine. "Bingo has been called; hold your cards, please."

The collector called out, "Stamp-8, 13, 20, 23."

"That's a good bingo," Harry said, "using I/23. Pay that lucky winner $50."

Naturally, Marie thought it was unfair. She started bitching: "That old coot's only playing three cards and he wins $50. Harry could have called a G if he'd wanted to, damn his time. Always freaking with somebody's out."

"Come on, Marie, " I said, patting her hand. "It's just the first big game and you're playing free, so you ain't losing nothing. You still got all afternoon to win."

I'm usually pretty good at calming her down, so when Lucy came around to collect for the next game, I ordered two coffees; one with extra cream and sugar for Marie. She spilled coffee, chainsmoked Kools and started up, again.

"Why doesn't he play Crazy? Hell, I always win something with Crazy bingo. Why doesn't he play Three-Corners? Those are the only damn outs he's been giving me. Now you watch, he'll play Three-Corners and then he'll only give me two."

I didn't waste my breath arguing with her. Marie knowed Harry never played Crazy or Three-Cornered bingo on Wednesdays. She knowed that, usually, if you was playing free all day, you didn't win any money. Like the rich folks say, you got to spend money to make money. Some peoples lucked out and broke the free-playing jinx, and like somebody else say, rules were made to be broken. Well, if that was true, Marie needed to break one today cause NSP has rules, too, and the hardest one to get around is the due date on the fifteenth of the month, so rule on that.

That damn O/75 must have come up every other game. Seems like to me we was hollering "Fishbowl" so often there had to be at least $65 in the pot. Marie kept punching me on my arm.

"Just let me need that damn 75. Harry'll call 70, 71, 72, 3 or 4. I could smack his ass off of that stool."

"Shake up your balls," screamed a halter-topped redhead with saggy breasts.

Harry, he said, "Come shake them for me, cutie," and liked to slobber all over hisself about that girl. Then he jumped off his stool, turned off the machine, and pretended to mix up the balls. And let me tell you something; I bet if that broad gives Harry a little play, she'll be a house-player in no time flat.

Cause Harry's so trifling. Sometimes, not too often, mind you, but sometimes I felt kinda sorry for him. Those big bingo parlors on the Indian reservations were damn near driving him outta business. Them places had $10,000 and $100,000 pay-offs and those big money pull-tabs. Nickel-and-dime joints like Harry's weren't as packed as they used to be and he still had to pay rent and utilities. Lucy and her gang were ripping him off, and rumor had it the house-players wanted a bigger cut of the action to keep coming. But Harry was so scantchy I couldn't feel too sorry for him. He cheated us, his employees cheated him, and like Marie always said: "God don't like ugly."

At three o'clock we played another big game. The hall was getting crowded so Harry did his thing, again.

"Okay, folks, it's time for our second big game of the day . . . " He went blah, blah, blah, same old speech, and had the nerve to ask, "Everybody ready?"

"We've been ready for five minutes now. Just call, will ya. Jackass!"

"Shake up your balls!"

"Same winners all the time!"

Harry grinned. We all knew who the house-players were, and Harry knew we knew. That thug Frank, with his slicker than slick self, could walk into the hall just as a game was starting, throw down ten sets of cards, Helen would slither past him without collecting a dime, and Frank would win—just like that.

It's not like at them big bingo parlors where they held your card in front of another player's face so somebody could see the bingo was legit. At these small halls the collector just picked up your card and started reading it back in front of her face. Helen could make up any numbers she wanted to and from the catch in her voice and sneaky peeks at the board, I knew good and damn well that was exactly what she did. But how you gonna prove it?

Harry started calling. "N/31 is the first number out."

Marie covered her N/31s. I heard her pray: "Come on, Lord. You know I need this win. Pleasepleaseplease, just this one time and I swear I won't come here no more."

"N/41. N/35."

"Slow down please, Harry," said Thelma.

I don't know who Thelma thought she was fooling but I knew when she said that she was up to her old tricks again. What usually happens is one of her crew sits out a game and searches through the unplayed cards on her table, looking for a card with most of the numbers on it that Harry's calling. It don't have to have all the numbers, just close enough in case anyone happens to get a quick glance at it. Then she'll slip Thelma the card under the table, Thelma'll call "Bingo" and the two of them split the money, minus Harry's cut, of course. Marie popped me on my arm and nodded in Thelma's direction, cause she was as hip to that game as I was.

Peoples was still yelling at Harry. "Same numbers you called the last game." Frank, with his cheating ass, had to make it look good.

"G/52."

I could see Marie's shoulders tighten. Four numbers called, two to go, and all she needed was one more N. She smacked me, pointed at her cards, and yelled, "Come on, you old fool, call my N, damn it."

"O/75!"

"Fishbowl!"

Harry announced, "Seventy-five dollars in the fishbowl, folks."

"Damn the Fishbowl," Marie yelled. "Call my N. Been needing a N since the third number."

Marie started sweating and grinding her teeth. I knows how she felt. You'd get those three numbered outs and then you'd wait . . . and wait . . . and wait, and Harry never did call your number. I knew Harry wouldn't call another N. So did Marie.

The sixth number was B/2 and Marie looked like she wanted to cry. "Three damn chances and he calls a B. Well, at least let me win the fifty. Call my N right now."

Harry said, "B/2 was your sixth number. It's now an anything goes game with the calling of I/17."

I didn't need the $50 as much as Marie did, but I'd already lost $20 and $50 is $50. I never say what number I be waiting on cause that's bad luck, so Marie didn't know I need I/17. And much as I loved her, I enjoyed yelling, "Bingo."

Lucy grabbed my card, flashed her teeth at Marie, and called back my numbers.

Harry honored it: "One good bingo using I/17. Pay that lucky winner $50. Congratulations, Jean."

Marie and I watched as Lucy counted out three tens, two fives, ten ones and laid them on my table. Her wig shifted as she threw her head and switched back to the waitress station to record the pay-off. I started to ask Marie if she wanted to borrow a few dollars, and she looked like she wanted to ask for a loan, but didn't neither one of us say nothing. Harry started calling the next game.

"N/45."

That was the N Marie needed for the $50. Harry knew it, Lucy knew it, the regulars knew it. We all knew Marie played a red card with Ns/31, 41, 35, 45, and held our breaths expecting her to go off and call Harry everything but a child of God. But Marie didn't say a word. Not one damn word.

Harry wasn't even trying to stop hisself from laughing. I can't prove it, but I've always been under the impression that he wore those ugly, long-sleeved flannel shirts so he could slip a ball up his sleeve in case he didn't get a signal from one of the house-players. Harry hated to give up $100 till the last of the big games and he wasn't too happy about giving it up then, specially since the Wednesday Coverall was $500. And he really didn't want Marie to win the hundred after Thelma tipped him off about Marie's NSP bill. Harry hated Marie enough to make sure she didn't win a dime; if she did win anything big, there'd be a trick in it.

By now the hall was cigarette-smoke foggy; bingo halls about the only place left smokers got any say-so. Harry be bitching about how much it cost to run the air-conditioner on high, but he couldn't breathe no better than the rest of us so he turned it up. Once that air kicked in, it didn't take long to get chilly. Peoples draped sweaters across they shoulders but Marie was sweating across her forehead and down her neck; she had loosed the top of her blouse and her eyes looked glazed. Didn't look too good to me but Marie kept covering numbers as Harry said, "B/11 . . . B/3 . . . B/13."

That 3/13 combination was another one of Marie's favorites and I offered up a silent prayer, "Please, Lawd, let her win something." I asked Marie if she wanted a coke. She shook her head, "No."

"I/24 . . . G/56."

All Marie needed was O/72 and I knew she would perk up, so I left her alone. Harry had a red ball in his hand—an O.

"O-72!"

Sounded like everybody and they momma yelled, "Bingo." Marie never opened her mouth. She just sat there while Harry said each collector's name as she called back numbers.

"Marge?"

Marge read Thelma's card; Harry honored it. Dawn read Mattie Sampson's card; Harry honored it. There were too many winners to count; Harry kept on honoring. Marie still hadn't claimed her bingo so I called Lucy over to get the cards.

I knowed Marie had three winners cause she always took them cards home with her after the game. Then I took me an extra hard look at Marie cause it weren't like her to sleep a bingo.

"Got another bingo, Jean?"

"No, but Marie's got three."

"I didn't hear her yell anything."

Lucy and me was talking about Marie like she weren't sitting right there. I thought she would snap out of it when Lucy said, "Next time call your own bingo," cause Marie never let Lucy have the last say about nothing. But she just listened as Lucy called out:

"Harry, here's some more: 3, 24, 56, 72 . . . 13, 24, 56, 72—twice."

"That's good. Any more? Okay, folks, we've got a bunch of winners; pay each two bucks."

Lucy threw four crumpled and two Scotch-taped dollar bills down on the table. Marie never picked up the money, just flicked Lucy a look. And there was something else in her face, too. Something like death warming up. Thought it was maybe leftovers from her surgery. I told Marie she'd come out of the house too soon, told her she should have stayed home at least a month. Told her the same thing the summer she had that operation and had to play bingo sitting on one of those plastic donuts.

I figgered Marie was simply worn out. Bingo could play hell with your nerves, specially when you really needed to win. You'd get good outs, and like I said, after waiting and waiting and waiting for your ship to come in, it upped and did a Titanic on your ass, bes that way, sometimes. But there was only one game left before the Coverall and then Marie could go home and get righteous before the evening session: I'd never known her not to bounce back. And I knowed for a fact that Harry, Lucy, and Thelma—for all her big talk about Marie, Thelma played as much bingo as anybody—would catch hell at the evening session.

"Well, folks," said Harry, "following our Fishbowl game, we'll be playing the Coverall. The Coverall today is $500 in fifty-six numbers or less. After the fifty-sixth number the pay-out is $250.

"But first, we have $125 in the Fishbowl. Anything goes and we'll play it until we get a single winner. Cards are ten cents each. All unplayed cards face down. Your first number out is G . . . 48."

The Fishbowl game wasn't nothing but a money-maker for the hall. We replayed it five times before Tim, a collector who played on his days off, hit by hisself. Dawn called back his card and Harry said, "That's good! Pay that lucky winner $125." Hell, yes it was good—for Harry—cause we all know Tim had to kick-back fifty bucks.

"The Coverall is our last game of the Wednesday afternoon session. We'll give you a little time to change your cards, and we'll give these balls a big shake."

Harry hopped up and swiveled his hips like he thought he was some dead-and-gone Elvis Presley. Some of the new players laughed, but the rest of us just shook our heads knowing ain't no fool like an old fool. Harry was just killing time, waiting for the latecomers to get situated. At least they had enough sense to hold out till the last minute and only blow a dime a card rather than sitting there all afternoon going broke. After all, you only needed one card to win and just last week Cassandra Martin had walked in, spent the last thirty cents she had to her name—and I knowed it was her last cause her old man had just walked out on her and them four little babies—and hit the Coverall. So see there, God do answer prayer. I just hoped He was listening to Marie.

It had gotten awfully quiet in the hall. Couldn't quite put my finger on it at first, but then it dawned on me: Marie wasn't cussing anybody out. She usually cut up right before the Coverall, saying things like:

"Shake up those balls, Harry! Hey, Lucy, tell that chick to get off her lazy ass and bring me a coke with a lot of ice. You better not start calling yet, I haven't been to the john in two hours."

We'd crack up as Marie made a bee-line to the ladies' room. As soon as Harry heard the toilet flush, he'd call the first number. Marie'd sashay through the door, hitching in her get-along, still shaking her hands dry, ball up a fist at him and yell, "One of these days I'm going to catch you in the parking lot and then you better give your heart to God because your ass is going to belong to me."

Harry'd dare her, "You want to repeat that?" and Marie'd pat the side of her purse and say, "I didn't stutter! I can show you better than I can tell you." Harry suspected Marie was just sellling wolf tickets, but he weren't taking no chances on the price of admission just in case she wasn't. He knew what she carried in that big purse as well as the rest of us did and like I said, Harry wasn't no complete fool. He didn't call another number till Marie was in her seat.

Marie didn't say nothing today but, "I'm glad it's time for the Coverall; it's too damn hot in here. Why doesn't Harry turn up the air-conditioner . . . clear out all this smoke. After I win this $500 I'll run down to NSP, have those bastards turn my lights back on and then go home and slip out of this headache so I'll be ready to play tonight."

I looked at Marie . . . and Lawd have mercy, sweat was still sliding down her face. I hoped she wasn't too upset over that $50 I'd won but I didn't think she was. Marie wasn't like that, not with her friends, anyways. Now if Thelma had hit for more than those two dollars, well, that would have been a different story.

All of a sudden I started feeling guilty cause in a way, I weren't behaving no better than Thelma. Don't know what I'd been thinking about before but I decided right then and there if Marie didn't win the Coverall I would have her over for dinner and write out a check so she could get her lights back on. I couldn't just let her sit in the dark. Ain't loaded or anything like that but if I cut out bingo for a week—I could go that long with no problem, catch up on my housework—

it wouldn't be no skin off my nose to give her the money and I knowed Marie would do the same for me.

Marie finally picked her win up off the table and stuffed them raggedy little bills in her purse. Instead of putting the purse back on the floor, she left it in her lap and I could see the butt of her .38. I said, "Marie, it's against the law to carry a concealed weapon. I don't care if Fred did give it to you for protection. You're gonna get in boocoo trouble with that thing one of these days."

"Jean, Fred said if I'm going to walk around with a purse full of money from playing bingo, and everybody knew it, that I needed something in case of an emergency. That's why I let everybody know I have it. I'd blow their damn heads off, trying to rob me. You see I've never been robbed, don't you?"

She had a point, but I still didn't like her carrying a gun around, and a loaded one at that. You hear all the time about how somebody blowed their head off accidentally.

"Who are you going to scare with an unloaded gun?"

"This is true," I said, "but still . . . one of these days . . ." I let it drop as Harry started the Coverall.

"Everybody ready? The first number out is B/1."

By the sixteenth number, all you could hear were peoples shouting:

"Slow down, fool!"

"That number ain't been out all day. He must've let it slip outta his sleeve."

"I've got a board don't have no numbers on it yet."

Marie covered her numbers, smiling to herself. Five or six of her boards were filling up pretty good and I figgered she was remembering a story she told me a few months ago. I wasn't sure if it was true or not, but knowing Marie, it probably was. The story went like this:

"Jean, Harry slipped up and let me win the Coverall. And you know how they pay you off in those new, crisp hundred dollar bills? Well, Lucy was too lazy to snap them apart like she usually does and I got me an extra hundred. Did I give it back? Hell, no, I didn't give it back. Lucy's always shortchanging folks, and I would've loved to see her trying to explain to Harry why her station was $100 off. She didn't work here for a couple of months after that, remember?"

I laughed when Marie told me about it, although I was tempted to remind her that God don't like ugly. But it was good to see somebody getting that old buzzard back for a change—him and Lucy.

Harry kept on calling numbers:

"B/5 . . . N/32 . . . N/4 . . . G/60 . . . B/10 . . . O . . ."

"Oh, slow down," shouted somebody from the back of the hall.

"Oh, okay," said Harry. "O/70 is your next number."

The fiftieth number was G/48. Marie popped me on my arm; she had an out for the Fishbowl number: O/75. That number had been called all day but it hadn't showed up yet in the Coverall. The fifty-first number was N/39.

"I/18 . . . I/16 . . . G/57."

Word had spread around the hall that Marie needed O/75. I'd told her about letting peoples know what number you need. She didn't know it but most of us were paying more attention to her than we was to our own cards.

Harry grabbed a red ball, an O. Marie covered her 75s. A big smile dimpled her cheeks as she got ready to yell. Harry knowed we was excited, so he dragged it out.

"Are you ready for your $500 number?"

"Come on, Harry!" said Thelma. "Call my number."

Marie didn't pay no mind to Thelma. She was too busy inching down to the edge of her chair. I reached out and touched her arm, but she didn't even notice. Marie's eyes were glued to that red ball in Harry's hand.

"You old sorry sap-sucker, call my O!"

Thelma and Marie yelled, "Bingo!"

I grabbed Marie's arm and shook my head. "No." Marge jogged over to Thelma's table. Lucy switched over to our table, snatched Marie's card and called out, "Mistake! O/75 wasn't called."

Lucy laughed, threw Marie's card back on the table and strutted back to the waitress station. Marge started calling back Thelma's numbers. And then Marie stood up. Her purse fell, opened. I could see the gun. I tried to pull her back into the seat but she wouldn't budge.

The gun jumped into Marie's hand. Her first shot blasted the food counter; Lucy ducked under the table, knocking donuts ever which way. The next bullet nicked Thelma's ear and she just silently slid outta her chair and passed out. And I sat there watching the whole thing, too scared to move. I wet my pants.

Peoples was running like bats outta hell, screaming to wake the dead. Mattie Sampson was sitting closest to the exit door; she grabbed her coat and hit it. Mrs. Walker was sitting cross from me: she threw up Maalox. But didn't nobody try to stop Marie. Not even me.

And then Harry, he lost it, too. He was a pinball machine gone tilt, yelling into the mike, "Mistake! Please hold your cards . . . It's . . . . it's a mistake!"

Marie shot at the numbers board. The lights behind number B/1 through O/74 burned out, but for some one-in-a-million reason, O/75 stayed lit. Marie shot again. Balls rolled across the floor, cracking as peoples knocked into each other, getting the hell outta Dodge. Harry kept yelling:

"Mistake . . . it's a mistake . . . please hold your cards."

Bad a thought as it was, part of my brain said, "Don't forget to get Harry." But Marie messed up. She put the gun to her own head. I thought to myself, "Wait a minute, that ain't right." And then I grabbed out at her. I said, "Marie, Marie!"

I'll give you the money for your NSP bill. It ain't worth all this. Marie . . . "

I heard a blast. I couldn't move. I just couldn't. I was wet. Wet pee down my leg. Wet blood on my arm. Marie was red. No, her favorite color was red. Red clothes. Red shoes. Red blouse. Red trimmed cards. Red blood. Blood red running down her face.

Harry turned beet-red and screamed, "Mistake!" one more time before he flopped off his stool and fainted dead away. Weren't a mark on him. I swear I saw a red ball—an O—roll outta his sleeve as his head hit the floor. And then I yelled, "Aw, Lawd, Sweet Jesus, don't hold her to this cause it's all a mistake." And it was. Cause Marie forgot to shoot Harry.

The Shoes of Death

Jonathan Borden

R OGER AND VALERIAN were renting the bottom half of an old duplex in an Indian neighborhood near the Sensorium College of Artistic Growth, where Val taught a couple of classes of studio art. Their apartment was narrow, irregular, and outlined with dark woodwork. The rooms weren't big enough for Val to paint his canvases—like me, he needed the Cypress Grove, the studio we shared—but Roger had a drawing table in the living room. The walls of the apartment were covered with friends' art, including a construction I'd made from cookie cutters. The fireplace mantel was cluttered with hand puppets, lead soldiers, mounted knights, souvenir statuettes, and postcards from Mexico and out-of-the-way places like Lowry City, Missouri. The living room was full of Salvation Army easy chairs and sofas with overflowing ashtrays on the arms and empty beer bottles wedged between the cushions.

Most afternoons someone would drop by with a six-pack. New friends Roger had met while carousing would sit around his large drawing table while Roger carried on, setting off gales of laughter, replenishing their drinks, and giving them his drawings, which were destined to soak in the grease on the floors of pickup trucks or fade and curl on the rear ledges of junker cars.

I had been spending a lot of time at Roger and Val's apartment, especially after my days as a Visiting Poet with Roger. Roger worked for the Visiting Poets program at the elementary schools, and he asked me to help him out sometimes. We would visit four or five classes a day, reading poems and doing puppet shows.

We'd get up early and throw on some gaudy clothes like red vests and blue and white trousers—the students were always fanatically patriotic. We'd have a couple of snorts of blackberry brandy and drive in Roger's rattletrap to that day's school.

The kids loved Roger's fantastic jive. They weren't remotely interested in poetry, so we would try to find poems that told stories or included arguments for the hand puppets to act out. The all-time favorite poem was "Overheard on a Saltmarsh," by Harold Munro, which I performed with the help of two puppets. These greedy marsh creatures quarrel over a string of green glass beads allegedly stolen out of the moon. The puppets would tug back and forth on a string of beads, while the kids cheered them on.

At elementary schools you tend to miss lunch because you forget to bring anything. The student lunchroom is out of the question, and the teachers' lounge is all coffee. There's never time to drive to a restaurant. So we'd finish the brandy without lunch, with a class or two to go. We'd be half in the bag and half asleep by the last puppet show. On the way home once, Roger said he'd had problems with one of the teachers. She'd accused him of drinking on the job one morning when he hadn't even been in the school long enough to take a drink.

"I'd just walked in, and she said she could smell whiskey on my breath. I hadn't had a drop since I'd got out of bed."

"What time did you go to bed the night before?"

"Around one or two o'clock. Maybe four."

"You hadn't been drinking since you got out of bed, but it was too early to tell if you'd stopped yet."

"Damned if you do, damned if you don't. I've got something for you over at my place."

"What's that?" I asked.

"The shoes of death."

As we arrived at Roger's apartment, he was explaining something to me about the physical risks taken by morticians, who usually develop back problems from carrying overweight corpses. They can't lug them out in a sling or throw them on a dolly while the survivors are standing there. I didn't catch all Roger was saying because I was surprised to see Leatrice curled in an armchair.

"That's a charming frock," Roger said. She was wearing a blue brocaded dress with a voluminous skirt and an elaborate gray and brown open-knitted shawl.

"How autumnal," I said. It was November. She threw a semi-glare in my direction.

Roger opened a fifth of the whiskey he called Old Overcoat. We talked about the Grove, other artists, especially Val who wasn't home, and so on. Leatrice told us about a year she'd spent in Argentina, riding a horse across the pampas all year. When Roger punctuated some remark with his quick gesture to the side with both hands turned down, Leatrice said, "I'll have to use that in the dance."

"I didn't know you were a dancer," I said.

"Modern dance. I'm a dancer and choreographer in the Pierides Troupe. We're an amateur group in that we're only partially funded, but we aspire to excellence. I'm working on my part of our Thanksgiving festival. Everyone is presenting a dance based on poetry. I'm interpreting some of Roger's poems."

"Which ones?" I asked.

"I haven't completely decided yet," she said. "I'll include 'Sometime Soon' for sure. I'm mainly interested in distilling the essence, the ambiance of his work as a whole, rather than illustrating any one subject."

"You make me sound like a perfume," Roger said, "or a whiskey."

"What especially are you doing to distill his essence?" I said.

"Actually I'm incorporating his gestures, his movement, his style more than any poem or even his poetical style. I want to stretch our perceptions of the human body in motion, in space. I hope to raise questions such as How is seeing affected by habit and expectation? How does one's perception of what is real change? I still have lots of technical decisions to make. So far I've only blocked out the overall scope. This afternoon we're going into more basic movement."

I finished my drink and started for the door.

"Tom," Roger said. "No rush. Have another whiskey. I haven't given you the shoes of death." He went into his bedroom.

I got a beer from the refrigerator and sat on the sofa. Leatrice smiled and re-arranged her shawl. I was getting high again. I took off my shirt and put my red vest back on. I decided that for the rest of my life I would wear no shirts but only red vests.

Roger returned with a pair of white shoes. He kneeled at my feet and pulled off my shoes and slipped on the white shoes.

"They don't fit me," he said. "Maybe they'll fit you."

"Why are they the shoes of death?" Leatrice asked.

"A friend who works in a mortuary found them behind some stuff. They didn't fit him either."

"But what were they for?" she said. "In case a corpse shows up without his own shoes?"

The white shoes were light and airy. I soft-shoed around the living room, humming "Moulin Rouge." A few weeks before, Roger had given me a book on juggling. I danced into the kitchen, took three greenish oranges from the table, and returned, juggling.

Never had I juggled so nonchalantly. By concentrating fiercely on the oranges, I slowed their flight, making them pause at the top of each toss and giving me extra time to plan the catch. How the oranges clashed, like cymbals, with my red vest. "My new routine," I said, "the Astounding Ceiling Bounce." I began caroming them off the ceiling. They'd flatten slightly up there while pausing to contemplate their return route. Roger snorted, Leatrice applauded. The woman who lived upstairs came down and stood in the doorway. The oranges thudded softly at my feet.

Cindy, the woman from upstairs, owned the duplex, but I hadn't met her before. Her navy slacks and green shirt accentuated her slightness, but when Roger introduced us, she said, "Tom Purdue?—you must be mad," in a full, low-pitched voice.

Cindy hadn't expected to find Leatrice, I think. She frowned while Roger was telling her about his poetry-dance collaboration with Leatrice. Eventually Cindy flopped down on the sofa next to me. She told me she liked my beard, a comment women almost never make. I complimented some feature of hers, probably her thick brown hair, which fell past her shoulders. She stroked my hair.

"I love your eyebrows," I said. "They're so thick and straight."

"Let's go for a ride," she said.

She owned a dark green MG convertible in excellent condition. MGs in excellent condition were not common in that neighborhood, which was mostly inhabited by Indians sick of the reservations but caught in the ghetto. This edge of the neighborhood was slated for gentrification soon, and after a few repairs and cosmetic rehabilitation, the duplex would probably fetch a hefty profit. I gathered that Cindy's parents owned the building and let her live there and rent the first floor until she broke into some career. A suitable career would be driving in sports-car rallies. She handled the MG with a light concentration and no chat. I'm always attracted to women who drive well. I follow Roger's thinking in this matter. Roger says, "Trust the friend who treats machines like animals, animals like people, and people like angels."

It was already dusk as we swung through St. Paul and headed north on Highway 61. Cindy kept the top down although it was fairly cold. We pulled into Taylors Falls in the dark around six o'clock and walked down to the bridge over the St. Croix River. The tourist season was over, so we didn't have to deal with mobs waiting for boat rides. In the spring the full brown river rips through the gorges, but now, in early November, the river was sedate, still coursing steadily but patiently, dark in the channel of black rock cliffs with narrow ledges of red pines highlighted by leafless birches in dancing zigzags, as though Gainsborough had daubed them in at the last minute with his six-foot brushes.

We ate dinner in a restaurant that cleaned out all the cash I had. We walked up the ridge above the town. The moon's reflection in the river glinted more intensely than the stars or the lights of the town closing in on itself for the winter. We stayed at a white wooden Greek-revival hotel. Cindy turned out to have plenty of cash and charge cards.

For the next few days we roamed the nearby countryside, driving up and down the river. She didn't tell me much about herself except that she'd grown up in Minnesota in the town of Virginia, on the Iron Range. She'd never been married, had no children. She liked slow-paced movies like *Pretty Baby*. Her eyebrows gave her face a brooding air even when she laughed. Her slim-hipped walk was effortless, like the design of a canoe, as light and strong and purposeful and slightly asymmetrical as a feather.

One day almost at sunset, we boarded an excursion boat, powered by an engine but sporting a useless paddle wheel at the stern, and rode down the dark brown river—brown from shed tamarack needles, according to the paddleboat's pilot. In less than a mile of narrow gorge, the black cliffs suddenly gave way to sandstone and beaches where the river widened and sprawled. The white-haired pilot, slouched in his baseball cap, knocked back the last of his gin on the rocks and twirled the wheel for home. Now and then he would cut the engine and whisper into a crackling microphone while pointing at the assorted splendors of the jagged cliffs: the Cross opposite the Devil's Chair, the Lion's Head, the Elephant's Head with River-Drinking Trunk, the Old Man of the Dalles, the Turbaned Turk, the Hooded Witch. A murmur of recognition would ripple aft through the passengers as they hove briefly into the best angle to see the rock formations. The pilot seemed to shake these marvels out of his sleeve and then fold them gingerly like used handkerchiefs into his pocket, as though tomorrow he might produce entirely new phantasms.

On a clear cool afternoon as we drove out of a pine woods on a dirt road, we saw two hawks gliding very low at the edge of an unfarmed field. Cindy pulled over and lowered the convertible roof. The hawks together were systematically quartering the field. We stopped whispering when they reached us. Then the wind and the trees fell silent. Against the light gray sky, the hawks were solid black. The feathers at the tips of their almost motionless wings were delicately separated. The hawks ignored us and never dived for prey. After a complete survey of the field, without a pause or sound or apparent movement, they rose backward beyond the treetops.

As winter came on, I decided to wear more than a red vest. Cindy bought some clothes for both of us — jeans, shirts, sweaters. The nights were chilly, and we spent most of them in bed. I don't know if Cindy was treating me like an angel, but I couldn't ask for more than the rippling contractions that every night coursed through her—steadily, patiently, sedately. We drove home with a brisk rain drumming on the canvas roof and dripping chummily around our ears. The white shoes of death were hardly scuffed.

Another Savage Day in the Belly of the Whale

David Johnson

W INTER is a slack time in the Midwest. For the small-town journalist, the weather is the only news. Though the wire services suggest that life elsewhere is going on, it is hard to believe. Here, the snow falls and falls, and there are predictable consequences: school and factory closings, dead batteries and travelers.

The town's calm Scandinavian acceptance of hardship makes my job more difficult, for I have always tried to find the human angle in my story. But my readers have proved immune to the most sincere of my works.

But when the weather gets better, my work gets worse.

In fact, only yesterday I wrote something about the dog-turd-meteor shower that had pockmarked the snowbanks. The story set me laughing out loud, the laughter breaking into a hacking cough. That transition from the humorous to the pathetic was appropriate, for I had just clacked out what would amount to my letter of resignation—again. My editor, a man with the ravaged face of Boxcar Willie and the personal politics of Gordon Liddy, already had grave doubts about me. He didn't know that I wrote two versions of every assignment—one for me and one for him—but he was veteran enough to *sense* that the copy that crossed his desk had been edited in the way that personal letters are in war time, and those small, significant gaps suggested danger.

Maybe that's why I tore my copy up and filed a sick leave form. In truth, I wasn't feeling well.

And maybe that's why, after my third cup of coffee and Bacardi 151, I began checking my closets. Snowmobile suit, Sorrels, Bates winter motorcycle gloves, Green Bay Packer stocking hat, lawn chair, shotgun, rum—I had all the makings of a human interest story, everything except the straightman, someone who was willing and able to play the game of "good cop, bad cop." I got on the phone.

"Klaus, my man," I said, "it's time for some serious journalism."

"Your yard or mine?" Klaus the mad Italian replied.

"Mine. And bring your own lawnchair."

"Then pick me up. I lost my driver's license . . ."

I bet you did, you dangerous swine and it's about time. But I didn't say that. "Take the bus," I said. "They won't charge you for the chair. Volare."

I looked forward to seeing Klaus, whom I hadn't seen in months. I had last seen him just before his divorce—actually, his second divorce—when he was repeatedly coasting an engineless gyrocopter down the driveway of his duplex, trying to capture the sensation of flight, while his new wife and the child from his first marriage watched, incredulous.

We complemented each other, Klaus and I. He was change and I was stability, though neither of us was a decent husband, as the wives we have shared will attest.

Still, I was surprised to see the latest version of Klaus hobbling up the street toward me. He had a close-cropped military haircut and sideburns that swept forward like Elvis's. He looked like an Aryan Pillsbury Doughboy, like a plump hipster Marine. And the red moon boots made him walk like Karloff in *Frankenstein*.

Soon our two lawnchairs were placed side-by-side in the dirty snow of my front yard. I carefully stuck the bottle of 151 in the snow between our chairs. And we sat like two overstuffed totem poles—like Lars and Oly (Olly? Oily? Olé? Oleo?)— like two duffers rolled outside the Lutheran Home.

The name of the game was summer, and the rules were simple: Whatever we would do in summer, we would do now, in winter. So we sipped and talked, sipped and smoked, sipped and sipped. By the time we saw the mailman plodding our way through the slush, we were ready. At least, I was.

I had a serious drama in mind, a kind of literary high noon—T.S. Eliot at 500 paces. So I cupped my hands around my mouth and shouted at the postman in my best pirate voice, "I think we are in rats' alley where the dead men lost their bones." According to my script, the postman should have called back: "I remember those are pearls that were his eyes." But the postman was not quick to catch on. Perhaps he had stagefright or was culturally deprived, but he did not supply the appropriate response. I wanted very much to show the postman how sincere I was, so naturally I went for the shotgun, a purely symbolic gesture.

But Klaus, perhaps seeing the foam forming at the corners of my mouth, pushed me back in my chair. "Life is short," he said, "the day is long, and jail is a bummer."

You should know, I thought. I've lost enough money bailing you out. But I kept that to myself. Anyway, he was right—the day got longer, and warmer too. Even the snow seemed warm, and we saw no reason not to lie down on it, as we would on a sandy beach—but not before I stuck a Creedence Clearwater tape in my truck's tape player and threw open the doors and tailgate to maximize the sound.

The truck, a 1972 Ford Bronco, was the perfect vehicle for a working journalist in the Midwest. I had bought it about a year ago from a huge and horribly obese teenager who reeked of glue. I knew that smell, for I had sniffed my share of glue while assembling models of Nazi fighter planes in my youth. This lad had, apparently, laid away a good stock of the real thing before the feds mandated a glue that would stick plastic parts together without warping young minds. It may, in fact, have been a glue fancy that had led him to get out his Testors spray enamel and camouflage paint the truck—including its tires. I wasn't about to complain; the tank-like boxiness of the truck was right for such a scheme, and the lad seemed to understand when I asked him to paint a huge red cross on the roof of the truck. A war correspondent would, after all, need to travel behind the lines without fear of being strafed.

Mengele had been right about the cleansing value of music in the death camps. The Bronco's speakers, however, could not produce enough decibels to fully wash away the memory of the horrible conversation Klaus and I had while we sat in our lawn chairs. I did not record our words, thankfully, but they were sad. We spoke of the old men within us, of the skeleton each of us carried around that would someday demand its freedom, of the dust in us that longed to rejoin other dust. But before that day there would be terrors and boredoms and indignities that we could imagine all too well—the years of quacking and waddling and drooling. Finally I couldn't stand any more. "You bastard," I shouted, "I'm looking for a human interest story! The last thing I want to hear is the truth!"

In search of more sound, I stumbled into the house, because I knew I also had Creedence Clearwater on an album. I blocked the front door open with the speakers, then did my best to synchronize the record with the tape. But my timing was off, and the tape played fractionally ahead of the record, so that my old favorite came out sounding like this: "Doo-doo, doo-doo, doo-doo, looking—looking..." Which reminded me too much of both the dog-turd-meteor shower and the echoes one might hear while in the belly of the whale.

Later during our musical interlude, I heard "Crimson and Clover," and that strange vibrating song by Tommy James and the Shondells began to inflate a memory. First, I popped into shape, then a car sprang up around me, and finally a landscape unfolded and expanded—a smooth, Disney-like process.

The car, a Boss 302 Ford Mustang, was bright green with flat-black racing stripes. It was low and skittish as a go-kart, a high-strung screamer. The cold rumble of its engine and the lower rumble of its wide tires on the road somehow matched up with the vibrating of the song and lulled me into a stupor. Tranquilized in that protective bubble of raw sensation, I shot down the endless corn-bordered road, a green dream crossing a green oblivion. What strikes me now, though it didn't really register then, is the odd split perception I had; for although I was involved in the tiny world of the car's interior, I was also watching the car from some distance away, with an alien kind of awareness. I was like some science fiction crow perched on a telephone pole, and though I never left that pole, I was always beside the car. It was as if the road, rather than the car, moved. Or maybe it is better to say I followed the car like, to a child, the moon always seems to be following his parents' car. "Look, Mom," I said, "the moon is following us home."

I stopped at several country roadhouses that day, and at one I went on a crying jag, for no apparent reason. I'm tempted to say, now, that those tears were for the feeling of summer itself, the lazy sadness of that green green world. Or perhaps in some way I had realized my own awareness of myself followed me like the moon.

When that memory deflated, I was surprised to find myself standing up and Klaus facing me, as if we had been talking only a moment before. He took a long pull from the bottle of Bacardi, then fumbled in his pocket for a cigarette and matches. With terrible slowness he lit the Camel and then brought the match close to his mouth to blow it out, but then he belched . . . and a huge jet of flame roared out of his mouth—straight at me. There was no time to run and the sudden intense light blinded me just before the flame began to sear my flesh. Screaming, I leapt backward, falling over my chair, and burned to a crisp black husk, like a chicken wing dropped into a barbecue grill.

"So it's going to be one of those days, is it?" Klaus said. "Jesus," he said, reaching down to help me up, "you ought to see a doctor. This self-destructive behavior isn't good for you; it isn't *normal*."

Don't *you* talk to me about normal, I thought; none of my visions are any stranger than the sight of you playing aviator in your driveway. But what I said was this: "You sound like my first wife, and the judge committed her, not me." Which was true. She was a literal-minded person who took my visions too seriously, perhaps because of her Catholic upbringing. She fully believed I was possessed, and one night she decided to release me from the grip of the devil, by trying to pound a stake through my heart.

After thirty-five years at large in the modern world, I have to admit I've seen a lot of strange things, and some of them I may have only imagined, though I'm seldom sure. For children, reality is plastic, the imaginary as real as the "real," the invisible friend as real as a set of overstuffed parents. In America, where childhood and adulthood are so hard to separate—childhood being so prolonged and adult life being so childish—normality is almost impossible to define. At any rate, my flaming death would have made a fine story.

Colorful human interest stories are not so hard to come by, witness any cover of the *National Enquirer*. There's no shortage of celebrity spouse-beating, UFO sightings, singing skulls, parental cannibalism, or people sawing up cars and eating them piece by piece. Such stories may be twisted, but the journalist who reports them simply jots down the nonsense without question. That's what objective reporting is all about. And frankly the offbeat is a good beat. Too much straight stuff—obits, police reports, city council meetings, interviews with thoroughly ordinary local "personalities" or political candidates—will eventually harden the journalist, who will develop a distaste for facts and a taste for the bizarre. And one day an innocent Sunday section filler about a carp farmer turns into a savage story of mutant carp the size of killer whales prowling the Mississippi backwaters —complete with the hysterical accounts of several teenage water skiers. Eventually the leap from fact to fiction becomes not second nature but first. And the next step, as I know all too well, is the unemployment line.

The Jehovah's Witness must have snuck up on us while I was recovering from my vision of a flaming death. I didn't recognize him at first because he had the slouch and rumpled tweeds of a literature professor. But when I saw his long face, like the face of a cartoon bloodhound, I knew at once he was a seeker of truth— unlike my friend Klaus, who only told me the truth when he knew it would confuse or upset me—for only the burden of truth could so deform a face.

I wanted to let the Jehovah's Witness know I was a kindred spirit, a man who had felt the call—several, in fact—though other people had always misunderstood the source and the depth of my sincerity. Besides, the day was getting on, and I still hadn't found my story. I first tried the ancient language of the body: I winked and nodded and turned my eyes skyward and repeatedly gestured with my arms to indicate that I was spreading pearls before swine. But the harder I tried to make myself understood, the more puzzled and fearful his face became.

I recognized that expression. I had seen it some years ago when I was touring South Dakota by motorcycle. Sipping Everclear at Mount Rushmore, I had seen the great stone faces of the presidents begin crying; tears of molten rock ran down their cheeks. And the faces of the tourists, as you might imagine, showed a mix of emotions that only actors in horror movies have much experience with. The tourists were doomed, of course—the lava *would* catch up with them before they could make it to their overloaded Plymouth Volare station wagons and screech away. Naturally, they ran. But to their eternal credit, each and every one of them stopped and turned around for one last look—like Lot's wife—and one last click of the Instamatic.

The Jehovah's Witness, too, had been trying nonverbal communication, but I couldn't follow his frowns and shrugs. I was about to speak, but he beat me to it: "Do you know that the Bible offers you hope for the future?" he asked. The question threw me off momentarily, for I thought immediately of how my future would be if I couldn't come in Monday morning with a story. That pause gave Klaus all the time he needed.

"Listen, pal," he said, "we know all we need to about your pansy son of God. This is the '80s, and what we need is a deity who can kick ass. That's why we're

Satanists. Our man Lucifer is a go-getter, a self-starter—he gets the job done, he understands the bottom line."

"Ignore my associate," I said. "He just came from the dentist and he's half out of his mind from the nitrous oxide; lean close and you'll see he reeks of it."

I tried to draw the Jehovah's Witness out, but I kept being distracted by Klaus's pissing in the snow behind him. I couldn't help but admire such neat work—it looked as if he had used a stencil to produce the yellow 666.

My truck, I knew, would be a better place to discuss serious issues, and when I noticed that the Jehovah's Witness had a *Watchtower* clutched in one hand, I knew that I could use the universal language—money—to get him there. "Say," I said, "I'd like to buy that *Watchtower* from you. Come, there's money in the truck." And, of course, there was. Once a week I got a roll of quarters from the bank and a carton of cigarettes from the store, and scattered both about the truck's interior, just so I would always be prepared for emergencies such as this.

Of course I had him sit down so he could fish for as many quarters as seemed right—and I looked at the cover of the magazine. "Your Future" was printed in huge block letters, and above that was an open book. On the left page of the book a photo had been superimposed, and I couldn't fail to recognize that ominous mushroom shape. "Good god!" I said.

"Yes, praise the Lord!" he said.

But the other page apparently also had a photo, only I couldn't tell what it was. It was a swirl of black and white and gray; it looked like a marble cake.

"It's a peaceful landscape," he said. "You know, a smooth lake reflecting trees and mountains and the clouds in the sky."

"Is there any snow? Are the leaves still on the trees? Is the lake frozen?"

"No, I mean yes, well—there might be snow on top of the mountain, and I suppose the trees are mostly pines, but there isn't any snow around them, and the lake's not frozen, no."

I almost asked him whether there were any water skiers on the lake, but I was quite confident of my insight. Our choice was clear: Total destruction or the world of summer. "How do we *get* there?" I asked.

He opened the magazine on my lap and pointed to the title, "Can Your Future Be Changed?" But the inspired prose of the article swam before my eyes, so I asked him to read it aloud, then closed my eyes to listen.

His monotone delivery was soothing, so soothing that the after-image of the Big Fire, the atomic blast, gradually faded from my mind. But at one point his voice changed, gaining a terrible volume and authority, as he quoted from Isaiah. "*I am the one* that makes diviners themselves act crazily," he said. That snapped my eyes right open.

He was burning, melting, sagging and crumpling into himself, blackening and turning up at the edges. But I couldn't see any flames. And he was still reading, apparently, though I could no longer understand the words; it was all babbling and cooing, and the only thing it reminded me of was an old film clip of Helen Keller speaking at the London airport.

At first I tried to explain what I saw with logic. How could he burn without visible flames? Then it came to me. Some years before I had attended an Indycar race. Two cars had bumped at over 180 mph; then one slid into a retaining wall, spewing parts. It rebounded, spinning and screeching, off the track into the infield. The driver slithered out of the cockpit, seemingly unscathed, but he began prancing and beating himself like a victim of moon madness. Maybe, I thought, this is one of those colorful rituals drivers perform after surviving a crash—just as football players sometimes do a little jig in the endzone after a touchdown. But as several men with fire extinguishers converged on the driver, the announcer explained that these cars were fueled with alcohol which burns invisibly.

Had the Jehovah's Witness been into my Bacardi 151? Not that I could recall. Nor did he seem bothered by the burning. The fire did not consume him; rather he was preserved in a perpetual state of change within the fire.

No, no logical explanation. But there was something familiar in what I saw, some fine connection with a long ago memory, a strand as thin and delicate as spider web. I kept hearing "Sunday Sunday Sunday," like the echoing radio commercials for drag races in the summer. Then suddenly and horribly I *knew*.

I think I screamed, and I must have scrambled, trying to run while still sitting, and accidentally hit the gearshift lever on the steering column, moving it into neutral, so that the truck rolled backward down the driveway until it hit a snowbank and lurched to a stop. I heard a resounding boom, and I thought, "Well, that'll be the gas tank and that's it for me. A great story and I won't even get to write it."

I heard a voice, far away and fuzzy, as if it were traveling a length of string tied between two soup cans, calling my name—Klaus's voice. "Goodbye, Klaus," I said, speaking more to myself, for I knew he couldn't hear me now. "It's been a strange life, and I wouldn't have wished it on anyone else—except maybe you . . ."

"I already had the worst of your life," Klaus said. He stood just outside the truck, holding my door open. "I married your second ex-wife."

"I . . . I'm not dead," I said.

"Don't try to blame me for that."

"Where is *he*?" I asked, pointing to the passenger seat.

"Probably hiding in the basement of the Kingdom Hall. I gave him a taste of fire and brimstone," Klaus said, holding up my Remington and smiling.

"Noooooooooooooooo!" I howled.

"Well, what was I supposed to do? I mean, I heard this terrible screeching, like someone torturing a rabbit, and it looked like he was slapping you around pretty good—"

"You fool!" I snapped. "You just took a pot shot at the Burning Bush!"

And the minute I said that, I knew I'd never be able to tell the story clearly enough for Klaus to understand. Whenever I mention anything related to fire, he gets smug and tells me to see a doctor.

"Listen," I said, "God spoke to me through that man . . . like Dan Rather speaks to you through your TV. And he showed me why I seem to act crazily. It's all part of God's plan; you can look it up in Isaiah. And He knows the way to Summer!"

I could see Klaus backing away, shaking his head. "Your first wife was right," he said.

"All right," I said, lying, "I lied. That man is a run-of-the-mill evangelical, and I've got two days to write a human-interest story about him or I lose my job and can't make my alimony payments. You know what *that* means. Besides, you know I can't write a word until I get into the *spirit* of the thing."

My appeal was working, as I knew it would, but I hadn't given it much thought. The image of Summer, Eternal Summer, was too much in my mind—the crewcut green lawns in town, the darker green pools of shadow beneath the vast green elms, the endless green sea of corn in which our town and others floated, a Grabber Green Ford Mustang moving lazily as a wasp.

"Tears!" Klaus shouted. "There was tears in my eyes as I watched my daddy drive away in that old Ford."

"Tears, tears," I murmured. For it was true—I was crying. "Yes, there was *tears*— big, hard, hot, round tears—like a summer downburst fit to beat the corn flat, fit to blind the driver of a Ford rolling sad down the road."

It felt good to say that; it felt right. We had the proper spirit for this story. Our bodies shook with purpose. And so it was that we set off for the Kingdom Hall, bobbing and jerking like two glue-sniffing spastics, like God's own holy puppets, in the darkness of the whale's belly, two mad Jonahs ready to be spit up with a story to tell.

At D'Ambrosia's

Jeffrey A. Johnson

"ONCE UPON A TIME upon a lovely wooded shore there was a place that made it possible to live your deepest dreams. Come; explore; delight. Embrace the world of D'Ambrosia's. Opening so very soon, so very near, at the Shores West Mall, just minutes from the Twin Cities on Lake Minnetonka. D'Ambrosia's. Once upon a time, upon a time, a time, a time . . . "

Johnnie Hundelby did not need his mother to tell him that D'Ambrosia's was no dumb little five and dime. He was an employee; he knew. The commercials were his proof. On Johnnie's TV screen the landscapes shimmered—a city street with skyscrapers made of gigantic alphabet blocks, a jungle village steaming beneath a shroud of vines, a surface as bright and pocked as the moon's—and at the center of each was the lady, slender and tranquil, soft and sleek, forever on the verge of slipping out of some silk-and-lacy garment into a bath or bed or simply into pure thin air. D'Ambrosia's was wonderful. Yet his mother kept saying, "Johnnie, I can't quite believe it. I still have to pinch myself." She'd been saying it for three weeks now, ever since the man from Project Outreach had come to announce that he'd found Johnnie a job. "I can't believe that a certain young fellow I know could be so fortunate," his mother said. "Though I must tell you I'm the proudest I've ever been. Now just you remember, it's quite the elegant store. I trust you're acting accordingly."

Johnnie listened, and yessed when he was supposed to, but he saved his strict attention for the commercials, for the dazzling messages they brought him. On the eve of the Grand Opening, as he lay in his bedroom with the small comfortable weight of his TV resting on his stomach, he allowed himself to do what his mother said she couldn't: he believed. The job was his for good. He was the man for the job. And D'Ambrosia's would never be anything like the Worthmore store back home. Janitor work was janitor work, but at D'Ambrosia's there were no tattered SALE! signs taped up all over, no screeching chrome turnstiles, no smudged linoleum, no smelly hamster cages and turtle bowls, no grumpy head cashier always asking when, Johnnie, when are you going to dump the trash, scrape the gum, beat the rugs, sweep the walk, and when in the world are you going to get rid of that cricket in the stockroom, how many times do I have to tell you? No. D'Ambrosia's was large and fluorescent and peaceful, thickly carpeted, filled with gleaming racks and fixtures of glass and wood veneer, all stocked with fresh merchandise. At D'Ambrosia's he was on a crew. He had a title, Maintenance, and a foreman, Roscoe Taylor, who knew his business. Crickets had gotten into D'Ambrosia's, but Roscoe said that insect pests were no concern of Maintenance. Johnnie agreed. He had more important concerns. Paper towels. Liquid soap. Toilets. Trash mashing. His part in the overall job. There was no more being a lone sweeper, no more Johnnie the Worthmore gopher. And no more Dixie Frost either—especially not Dixie, with her blond eyelashes and her taut skirts, swiveling in a perfume haze through Cosmetics & Notions, sneaking into the stockroom to pout her glossy lips and croon Johnnie Johnnie Johnnie Johnnie hey Johnnie what's up? Whatcha doing back here handsome? When're you gonna ask me out? I said whyncha up and ask me for a date? Huh Johnnie?

"Stop it," Johnnie said, turning his head to look at the clock radio on his bedside table. 8:53. He stared at the crisp white numbers, watched them flip, quick as an eyeblink, to 8:54. He had to stop remembering Dixie Frost. He had to. On the other side of the TV he could already feel a distressing thrill in his flesh. He ground the heels of his hands into the bedspread. Why did this always have to happen? He agreed with everything his mother had ever said about Dixie. He knew that Dixie was unladylike and ill-brought-up and just about as unrefined as they come, and that the best thing to do with people like her was to go on about your business as if they didn't exist. But knowing was not the same as being able to obey. The clock blinked again, and Dixie's voice went right on in his memory, *Johnnie Johnnie,* each word like a brief hot touch. "Go away," he muttered. "Get out of here, shut up." The reply was a sharper memory—Dixie in the stockroom *Johnnie hey* her cupped hands brimming with caramel corn from the machine at the front of the store *kill it yet?* bright fingernails bright eyes long bright blond hair *let it alone then* one at a time picking up the kernels with the tip of her tongue *crickets sing pretty don't you think?* the sweet candy smell all around *Johnnie don't* her soft munching *don't don't* the slow lowering of her eyelids *if you don't kill it* the sly spread of her smile *if you don't Johnnie don't then I might just let you kiss me.*

His mother knocked once on her way into his room, calling, "Johnnie, lights out now, morning comes early."

Johnnie sat up fast, grabbing the TV before it could roll off his belly and onto the floor. He heard a long sigh from his mother.

"John Jerome Hundelby." He knew she was gently shaking her head. He felt her stepping closer, raising a hand to his shoulder, and he hunched as low as he could. "Relax and breathe deeply," she said.

"I am."

"I'm afraid I beg to differ." Her grip on his shoulder was so tight it hurt. He inhaled her smell of dry cloth and dish soap.

"I am so."

"Shh." She let go of his shoulder and began fussing with his hair. "Such knots," she said in the tone of voice she used for making him cheerful.

"Can't help it." Johnnie felt for the switch and turned off his TV. Dixie's presence was receding, slowly.

"Oh, I'll bet you could too, if you tried. When you lie in bed with your head propped up to watch your programs, you get so many cowlicks here in back."

"Ouch," Johnnie said, his eyes suddenly stung with tears.

"Sweetheart, I'm sorry, but this is quite some bird's nest. You'd only have a worse problem in the morning. Now, may I put your TV on the shelf for you?"

"No." He still needed it to hide under.

"You can suit yourself, Johnnie, but you don't have to be rude."

"No thank you."

She tugged at his hair in silence. Dixie was a distant whisper.

"No thank you."

"You're forgiven." She gave another sigh.

"Hey," Johnnie said, sitting up straight, remembering D'Ambrosia's. "Did you iron my tuxedo t-shirt?"

"Johnnie, please. Not to meet the owner of the whole store."

"It's better than a janitor shirt. I can wear it if I want."

"All right, honey. All right. Don't get upset."

"I'm not. I'm going to wear it."

"There," his mother said, combing her fingers one last time through his hair and sitting down on the edge of the bed. "I guess you'll be presentable, if you don't sleep funny and wake up looking like a ragamuffin."

"I won't sleep funny," Johnnie said. And no matter what his mother thought, he would be more than presentable in his tuxedo t-shirt. It was black and brand new and the design was correct right down to the bow tie. "You can take my TV now," he said.

"Good, Johnnie. That's very good." She took his chin in her hand and made him look at her eyes. "Do you need a towel?" she asked.

"No thank you."

"That's wonderful. That makes me so glad."

"Me too."

"Say," she said, rubbing her thumb across his cheek. "Somebody didn't shave today."

"I will tomorrow."

"I hope that's a promise. I want you to look your very best and most handsome when you meet—what was her name, Johnnie?"

"Christina."

"No, her last name."

"Roscoe just calls her Christina."

"Well, you make sure to find out her last name and call her *Mrs.* whatever it is." She stood and lifted the TV from his lap. "Oof," she groaned, carrying it toward his bookshelf. While her back was turned, he pulled at the crotch of his pajamas to make himself comfortable again, then crawled under the covers. "Do you know what I've been doing tonight?" his mother was saying. "I've been baking a lemon cake so that a hungry young man can take a slice to work with him tomorrow. But I might not have time to frost it if he doesn't get to sleep pronto." She was back at his bedside, leaning to kiss his forehead.

"Lemon frosting?" he asked.

"Lemon both, cake and frosting. You can dream about it all night long."

"Wait."

"Johnnie, sleep." She kissed him again. "Five o'clock will be here before you know it."

"Wait. You have to tell the story, okay?"

"Sweetheart . . . "

"You haven't for a long time."

"I just told it a few weeks ago."

"Please. You have to."

"Don't get panicky."

"I'm not." He closed his eyes and took some deep breaths to show her he was calm. "Start with the ages," he said.

"I know how it starts."

"Then hurry up, I need my sleep."

She laughed. "You" —she pointed her finger and zoomed in to pinch his nose—"are impossible sometimes, buster."

"But still," he said, prompting her, and warm shivers ran through him.

"True." She squeezed his elbow and held on tight. "Not for all the tea in China."

"Not for all the green cheese on the moon," Johnnie said.

"Never," said his mother. "Never ever."

"Tell it. Tell it now."

"What about you telling me something?" she said.

"Don't have anything to tell."

"You haven't said much about your job yet. You promised you would."

"I did. Told you about the other guys on the crew. Told you what the store's like."

"You haven't told me anything about your foreman. Roscoe. How he treats you. I like to know things like that."

"I don't know. He treats me fine." There was very little about Roscoe that Johnnie could tell his mother. He wanted to tell her everything, but she wouldn't approve. Roscoe smoked. He swore. He stole from D'Ambrosia's. He called himself a nigger and he called Johnnie and the rest of the crew reetards. Johnnie didn't mind. He'd been called dingbat, dope, dumbhead, and a lot of names that were just plain lies—drooler, spaz, mongy, frankenstein. Roscoe wasn't mean about it, but Johnnie knew his mother would cause an uproar with the Project Outreach people if she found out. Roscoe had only been mean once. Johnnie's partners were bragging during coffee break one day, saying they all had pretty girlfriends who would kiss and go further, so Johnnie had said me too, my girlfriend back home is Dixie Frost and she'll do plenty. The next morning Roscoe came to work singing I wish I was in Dixie, away away, I wish I was in Dixie's pants, away down south in Dixie . . . until Johnnie had yelled at him to shut up, shut up, shut up. So what could he tell his mother about Roscoe? That he steered a floor buffer with his hips, slow and close and steady, as if he was dancing with a lady? That he'd fixed up an "office" with pallets and empty boxes at the back of the loading dock so he could catch some sleep when things were slow? That he talked constantly about how much he hated the D'Ambrosia's company?

That at break time, when he wasn't planning what he'd say to Christina when he finally quit, he and the dock boss laughed about all the times they'd been drunk, all the times they'd been in fistfights and knife fights and gunfights, all the times they'd worn women out, made women howl, or sigh, or beg for more of the same?

"Tell the story," Johnnie said.

"Nothing?" his mother asked. "Nothing to tell me?"

Johnnie shook his head. He needed to hear the story. He knew it by heart—the events, the lessons, the goodnights at the end—but it took his mother's voice to make it true and useful. She had to tell it. Now was the time for D'Ambrosia's to become a part of it. He crooked his elbow to keep his mother's hand there and said, "I love you." He felt shaky, saying that.

But it worked. She smiled her proudest smile and turned out his reading lamp. "Listen," she said, and by the way she spoke Johnnie knew she had been planning to tell the story all along. "Tonight you are twenty-six-and-a-half years old, and I am fifty-nine. But once upon a time I was your age, and what do you suppose I was doing then?" Johnnie grinned and wriggled deeper under the covers as his mother began the list of events. The day of his parents' marriage. His own long-awaited and difficult entrance into the world. The time he broke one of his mother's beautiful china figurines and hid the pieces in the brooder house. The summer it didn't rain and didn't rain, and then when it did a tornado came and the barn collapsed like a house of cards, but down in the storm cellar they all lived to tell the tale. The day he rode his pony, Potbelly, clear into town and back without telling his mother beforehand. The night his father came home from the doctor and said *cancer*. The day Worthmore closed for good. His mother's deciding in the middle of an April blizzard to move to Minneapolis so that he would have more and better opportunities.

"And we couldn't hope for better than this, could we, Johnnie?"

"Uh-uhm," he murmured, yawning. His mother was telling the story perfectly, moving from the events to the lessons without changing the bedtime lilt in her voice, and Johnnie did not resist as he slid down toward the edge of sleep. D'Ambrosia's, she said, a fine fine chance for you, Johnnie, D'Ambrosia's, and he saw an endless spread of cool green turf, a herd of horses, and the lady, this time in profile, her face downturned, demure, a pale towel loosely wrapped around her body, a slim bent leg half lost in a frothy clawfoot tub, the horses pushing in on every side with their large oblong curious faces. D'Ambrosia's. So very soon, so very near. D'Ambrosia's. A sudden rise toward wakefulness made Johnnie aware of a new lesson—his mother going on and on about how some people had been the kindest she'd ever met, the most generous, the most dedicated, on and on saying they were practically angels in earthly garments, Johnnie, and they might very well have saved him if he hadn't been so stubborn about going in for checkups, and people talk about the good old days but as far as medicine goes they can do marvelous things now that they couldn't do years ago, so a person should never be afraid to see a doctor because they can cure almost anything if they catch it in time. Johnnie was about to open his eyes and ask if it was time for him to go for a checkup again when his mother went back to the familiar words, saying always remember Johnnie that the world presents us every morning with shiny clean slate to write on, and Johnnie be happy and thankful that you have a useful skill, and Johnnie pay attention when I tell you that a lady, and not only your mother but any lady you meet, a lady is a very special person and is to be treated at all times with the utmost respect and deference. Johnnie counted the lessons, waiting for the last one, the one about trials and disappointments making bonds stronger than ever, so strong that you wouldn't trade them for anything, so strong and rare and rewarding that one person couldn't get along without the other. After that came the goodnights, the last tiny kiss on the forehead and then sweetheart now sleep, listen to my voice, listen out the window to the night sounds, let them lull you off, I am just so full of pride in you John Jerome Hundelby because you try so very hard to be good, listen, listen, crickets and cars and breeze outside, pleasant dreams, happy dreams, sleep deeply now, deeply and well. Drowsing, numb, Johnnie did his best to obey, but at the last minute he remembered *if they catch it in time* and understood what his mother had meant. *She* was the one who had to go to the doctor. A tremor passed low in his stomach, and that made the voice he was hearing change—or had it changed earlier?—to Dixie Frost's, and she was whispering don't kill it Johnnie, sleep tight, sleep well, please don't kill it honey because you know they mean love, sleep hard sleep deep Johnnie crickets mean love.

Marvelous things, Johnnie told himself. In time. In time. Almost anything if they catch it in time.

D'Ambrosia's was filled with darkness and quiet. Roscoe was late. Johnnie and his crew partners stood waiting just inside the smoky-glass main entrance. Only Roscoe was allowed to go into the junction box room and flip the dozens of switches it took to light the store. Until he got there Security wouldn't let anyone beyond the ring of night-light at the entrance. Johnnie wished Roscoe would hurry. Work would take his mind off his mother.

Bleeding, she had said at breakfast.

Don't you dare panic, she'd said. Don't disappoint me, Johnnie. Think of other things and you'll be fine.

Once upon a time upon a lovely wooded shore there was a place that made it possible to live your deepest dreams. D'Ambrosia's. Dump trash. Check soap dispensers. Fill towels. Scrub porcelain and chrome fixtures. Do floors. Refill Kotex machine in ladies'. Replace mint deodorant blocks in men's. Double-check for cigarette butts. Rub fingerprints off door.

Now I've said all I want to say about it, she had insisted, stirring milk into his coffee. It's what's known as a female complaint, and it doesn't concern you.

D'Ambrosia's. D'Ambrosia's. There was a cricket, over by his partners. "Squeege," Johnnie called. He had never learned his partners' real names, so he used the names Roscoe had given them on the first day of work: Sucker, Wringer, and Squeege. Johnnie decided from the start that if they wanted to act cool just because they had new names and they all lived in a state agency group home, that was their privilege. He didn't want to take part in their secret conferences or their giggling anyway. He, at least, understood the importance of this job. Besides, he knew from his mother that those group places were not nearly so nice as a real home.

"Squeege," he called again, annoyed.

"What?"

"Look down."

"Watch out," Squeege yelled, stomping.

The cricket leapt into the shadows. "Missed," Johnnie said.

"No way." Squeege chased it into Juniors.

"Get back here," Security snapped.

Squeege shuffled back, hands in his pockets. "Would of got him," he said.

"They're fast," Johnnie said.

Security yawned and stretched, resting his feet on his guard desk. "Friday," he said. "Payday."

"Hey, yeah," Wringer said.

"Bar hopping," Sucker said. "All right!"

Security hooted. "You guys?"

"Counselors take us," Wringer said. "Wanna come?"

No, Johnnie said inwardly.

"That'll be the damn day," Security said. "Do you drink, you guys?"

"We dance," Wringer said.

"I can just imagine."

"With girls."

"The agency house next to ours," Squeege said, "they have girls in there. They have girls in there and they all have to be on the pill."

"Dream on," Security said.

"I'm not lying." He snickered, and Sucker and Wringer joined in.

Johnnie knew what was coming. They'd done the same joke on Roscoe. It hadn't been funny then, either.

It wasn't that Johnny didn't understand the joke. He knew about sex. A man and a woman loved each other, and they married, and that was why there was sex. Sometimes there was a lesson in the story about it. His mother's voice was always at its calmest and most reasonable when she told him that sex was one of the loveliest expressions of human respect and affection. Still, the lesson went on, there were other expressions, and there were certain people who weren't interested in sex. Those people knew who they were. They had other interests. In any case, sex was never to be made a subject for crudeness and jokes.

"Some *really* pretty girls, " Squeege was saying, " and every one is on the pill. The counselors stick the pill in their orange juice."

"Don't you want to know why?" Sucker asked.

"Not especially," Security said.

"Don't you?"

"Nope."

All three partners shouted at once. "Because we're irresistible!"

"Yeah," Security said, "to barnyard animals, maybe."

"Barnyard animals and your mama." Roscoe was suddenly there, standing behind Johnnie, lean and a little swaybacked and smoking the first cigarette of the day. One of the big glass doors was slowly settling shut. "Matter of fact," he said, "I understand this boy Squeege had her in a steamy state of mind just last night."

"Sign in," Security said.

"They tell me she was hollerin like a stuck hog. Won't be long we'll have a new litter of Security runts underfoot."

Wringer and Sucker started punching Squeege in the ribs.

"Hey, Roscoe," Johnnie said.

"Hey, John. Say, what is this here? Let me go get the lights so I can check out this new wardrobe item."

"Tuxedo t-shirt," Johnnie said.

"Real nice."

"Sign in and show me your I.D., Roscoe," Security said.

"Man, you sign in for me," Roscoe said, heading for the loading dock. "You know anybody else works here looks like me?"

"I can't do that."

"Always used to," Roscoe said. "What else you got to do? Sign me in on time, too, show some initiative." And then, laughing, he was out of sight in the dark store.

Johnnie watched Security. He didn't unclip his pen. He looked pleased about something, and very proud, sitting there behind his Security desk in his private Security alcove.

"God*damn*." Roscoe's voice carried all the way from the back of the sales floor. "Gonna have more manikins than customers around here."

In the silence that followed, Johnnie remembered the doctor appointment.

For the last time, his mother had said, it's a little abnormal bleeding. They're going to do what they call a D and C to find out what's causing it, and that's a very routine thing for them to do. It's nothing to get so worked up about. I'm sure I've mentioned it several times in the past few weeks.

Well—I forgot. But you didn't say bleeding, you said test.

Amost every woman has this test sooner or later. They consider it minor surgery, but that's really an exaggeration.

You're not explaining everything. What if you're not all right?

I wish you wouldn't be such a baby about this. I'll be feeling fine by morning.

Aren't supposed to keep secrets.

Johnnie. It's not as if I'm bursting with secrets I refuse to tell you. Now why won't you do as I've asked? Say—tomorrow's Saturday. We'll both sleep in and then we'll have French toast. How does that sound?

I don't know.

I know you. You're a French toast eater. There's the van, now. Here's your lunch. Give me a kiss and do a good job at work, and I'll be very happy if I find you've handled this in a level-headed way.

Bleeding. Surgery. D and C.

"Hey," Squeege said, pointing, "Dummies."

Catch it in time, if they catch it in time.

On the high ceiling the fluorescent panels were flickering to life in groups of four. As the light spread, Johnnie looked into the store and saw that overnight it had become filled with figurines as large as ladies. Everywhere he looked he saw them, alone or in groups of two or three, breathtaking in their elegant clothes and graceful poses. And then one of them moved, coming toward the entrance from a shadowy aisle, stopping once to rub the fabric of a blouse between her fingers. Her dress was filmy and it rippled with mother-of-pearl reflections. Johnnie recognized her.

"You're on TV," he said.

"You noticed!" She struck a familiar pose, one hand outstretched, the other held tightly to her chest. In the commercials her hair was in a bun, or in ringlets, or pulled to one side, but now it was down—long, straight, and shiny-blonde. She smelled sharply of perfume, and of mint, like chewing gum. "Which ad do you like best?" she asked.

Johnnie thought first of the cool green pasture, the antique bathtub, the friendly horses—then of the jungle, the desert, the city, the mountaintop, the shore. "I don't know," he said. "All of them."

She lowered her slim eyebrows at him. "You're not bucking for a raise already, are you?"

Johnnie's partners snickered. He blushed, and his face smarted in three places, where his electric shaver had mown off the heads of pimples.

"Personally," the lady said, "I like the one where I'm standing like this" —she struck another pose— "in a silk wrap among the dead volcanoes of the moon. In fact, we're using the same backdrop for the fashion showcase upstairs. But anyway, guys, I'm Christina, Christina Ambrose, and I'm glad to have you working for me." The store was fully lit now, and she turned to survey it. Johnnie paid attention. She worked her gum nonstop, mostly with her front teeth. Her hair kept falling over her face. Three times she reached up to catch a thin lock of it with a maroon fingernail and drape it behind her shoulder. "Or rather," she said, spinning quickly on her high heels, "the D'Ambrosia's organization is proud to welcome you."

"Thank you," Johnnie said.

"Tell me," she said, stepping toward Johnnie and his partners. "How do you like working with Mr. Taylor? You know, Roscoe?"

They all said, "Fine." Johnnie wanted to say more, to tell her how things were so much better at D'Ambrosia's than they could ever have been at Worthmore, but she was standing awfully close. He couldn't keep from imagining what her hair would feel like if she bunched it into a ponytail and brushed it across the back of his neck, as Dixie Frost had done once in the musty Worthmore stockroom. Stop it, he told himself. She's a lady.

"I see," she said. "Well."

"Well, hey," Roscoe said from the doorway behind Security's desk, where, as Johnnie knew from repeated warnings, no one but Security was ever supposed to be. "How do you do, Christina? I see you met my reetards."

"Get the hell out of there," Security said. "Now."

"Ain't we high and mighty," Roscoe said, "long as Christina's around."

"And I want to know how you got in there in the first place."

Johnnie expected Roscoe to say he'd huffed and he'd puffed and he'd blown the door down, or to make some other smart remark, but he said nothing. He was smoking harder than he usually did, drawing the smoke in quickly and sending it out a long way. His neck was sweaty, the ropy muscles gleaming through his open collar.

"I asked you a question," Security said.

"Leave it be," Christina told him.

"Yeah," Johnnie said, startling himself—he hadn't known he was going to speak.

"Hey, Johnnie," Roscoe said. "You and me, John."

"So, Roscoe," Christina said. "Good to see you again. How've you been?"

"I'm all right." Roscoe slouched his way around Security's desk, his cigarette flapping as he talked. "I been tendin thcse reetards you sent over."

"Roscoe, please don't use that word."

Roscoe shrugged. "I must say you're lookin fine today," he said. "How do you manage it, so bright and early?"

"I have a Grand Opening to set up," Christina said. "I've been here for over an hour. I see you still can't seem to get to work on time."

"Aaah," he said, "you know you love me." Christina gave a giggle, and Johnnie heard clearly what his mother would have said: He's awfully breezy with her if you ask me. "And I absolutely guarantee," Roscoe went on, "that you'll love these reetards when you come to see how beautiful they are on the inside."

Christina's smile vanished. "There was a time," she said, "when these boys would not have been considered employable. Now D'Ambrosia's is . . . "

"Once upon a time," Roscoe said, "people knew better than to mix their business and their social charity work."

"I said that's enough, Roscoe."

"Might of asked me if I minded."

Christina looked at Johnnie. "I don't believe this guy," she said, trying to smile again. "I make him my foreman at my newest, most important store, and he docsn't appreciate it."

"No, I don't," Roscoe said. "I sure do not appreciate such a fine place where they spy on the employees. Never had that in the other stores."

Johnnie saw now that Roscoe wasn't feeling breezy at all. Roscoe was scared.

"Nobody *spies*, Roscoe," Christina said.

"Hell they don't." He pointed to the doorway behind Security's desk. "It's a damn peepshow down that hallway in there. But you don't tell nobody about these things."

"Times change," Christina said.

"Yeah, right." Roscoe stubbed out his cigarette against his thumbnail. Johnnie saw sweat-beads on his forehead and veins standing out on his arms. "Like to get me a seat at one of the ladies' dressin rooms sometime. Be better than lookin in on the employee locker room."

For an instant Johnnie pictured a lady in a cubicle, putting on silky things just for him. Then he remembered the night before, his mother's single knock as she came into his room, her cheerful voice saying *Johnnie lights out now*, the sigh she gave when she saw him hunched around his TV.

"I'll talk to you about it later," Christina told Roscoe. "Come see me before you pick up your paycheck." She turned to Johnnie. "I certainly like that shirt," she said.

Johnnie heard his partners start to whisper among themselves. He knew it was impolite not to return Christina's smile, but he wanted her to know he was on Roscoe's side.

"Your name is Johnnie, right?" Christina said. He nodded. "Well, it's a wonderful shirt, Johnnie. Very chic. Now, Roscoe, why don't you introduce me to the rest of your crew."

Johnnie's partners stopped whispering and began to sing, "We don't have tux-eedoes, we don't have tux*ee*does."

"Oughta have straitjackets," Roscoe said.

"Relax, Roscoe," Christina said. The partners were still singing.

"Shut your damn dumb mouths," Roscoe ordered. "Okay, Christina. The fat one there is Squeege. Windows. One with the glasses is Wringer. Moppin'. Leftover one is Sucker. Runs a vackum cleaner."

"And Johnnie?"

"I figure you can guess. Or don't you have unmentionable functions?"

Christina rolled her eyes. "Okay, I get it," she said. Her giggle ended with a sigh. "That's always been your saving grace, Roscoe."

"What's that?"

"You're so entertaining."

"Ain't I, though?"

"Puts on a helluva show," Security said.

"You watch your *mouth*," Roscoe said, whirling on him.

"You watch you step," Security said.

"Guys," Christina said sharply.

"You *die*," Squeege said, slapping his foot down hard. Johnnie saw the cricket sail to safety.

"I don't believe it," Christina said, her voice high and angry. "I just do not believe it. We've had the exterminators out here twice."

"Relax, Christina," Roscoe said. "You always got bugs in a new building. Crickets make it sound like a summer night in here."

"I'll have to call them again. I cannot open a store with those things hopping around." Johnnie watched her as she walked away. Halfway across the sales floor she stopped and called, "Roscoe, I'll be upstairs by the fashion showcase. Get your guys started now." She waved, turned, and with one last shimmer of her dress she was lost in the merchandise.

"Hey, Roscoe," Security said. "Tell me how you got in that hallway."

"Hell," Roscoe said. "I'd of found it sooner if I didn't have these goofs to look after. Ain't nobody can get around this store better than me."

"Sure," Security said, quiet and smug.

Let's work, Johnnie pleaded silently. Roscoe's stories of fists and knives and guns seemed ready to happen.

"That Christina," Roscoe said, lighting another cigarette. "Don't she just love her charity work. It makes her day to come jaw with the help."

Let's work, let's work.

"You know what she needs?" Roscoe went on, leading the crew across the store toward the loading dock. "She needs somebody to give it to her till she's shiverin and snarlin and beggin for him to quit. And then he has to keep on givin it to her and givin it to her and givin it to her."

Roscoe stopped, so abruptly that Johnnie bumped into him. "Jesus," he said, stepping over to a figurine and rubbing the sweater it was wearing, rubbing its chest with his thumbs. "They got nipples."

Johnnie's partners sputtered with laughter.

"What a whorehouse," Roscoe said. "Come on now, get your stuff and get to work."

Johnnie saw a cricket and stomped. He got it. It was dead for good.

Johnnie was on his last bathroom, the upstairs north men's. He had worked straight through his lunch hour. Stopping would have meant having nothing to do but think about the doctor appointment—especially now, since he'd learned from Roscoe during coffee break that surgery meant *cuttin* and female complaint meant *cuttin down there*. But don't you worry, Roscoe said. You get your ass back to work. Sounds like your mama's just shy.

The disinfectant fizzed in the toilet bowls and the glass cleaner misted on the mirrors, and Johnnie felt better. He killed two more crickets and made sure their corpses got into the trash masher on the dock. As long as he kept working his mother's voice stayed with him—her bedtime voice, the voice of the story, saying you are my very good Johnnie and you always do your best. Every so often a spurt of worry rushed through and left him trembling. Work, he told himself. Work and think of pleasant voices. He filled the paper towel dispensers *come explore delight* poured the emerald soap into the jars above the sinks *not for all the tea in China would I ever give you up* shined the mirrors until they were deep and streakless *hey John you and me* rubbed the chrome and porcelain to an utter gloss *I am just so full of pride in you* recalled the beauty of the commercials and knew he was helping to make them true *D'Ambrosia's once upon a time embrace your deepest dreams* and everything was fine until he finished the upstairs north men's—until, as he was backing his cart of supplies out the door, he saw that the sleek low out-thrust urinals looked like caved-in horses' skulls.

He was already starting to panic when Christina called, "I could use your help for a minute." He left his cart in Fine Leathers and went to where she was standing, in a doorway at the edge of what had always seemed to be a wall of mirrors.

"No," she told him, "it's a lighting trick. It looks like mirrors until some special lights go on inside here. Then it becomes the fashion showcase." Inside, on the back wall, was the landscape from Christina's favorite commercial, rough and bright beneath the starry black sky. "We're showcasing this dress I have on," Christina said.

Johnnie nodded.

"Hold her," Christina said, pointing.

Johnnie had been trying not to look at the naked figurines—a lady and a man.

"Hurry up, now."

He knelt and touched the cool plastic skin. A cricket chirped.

Don't kill it Johnnie.

"Those damn little monsters," Christina hissed.

"What's a D and C?" Johnnie said, staring at the floor.

"Hmm?"

"D and C. Surgery." Christina would know about female complaints.

"Oh. Well—why do you ask, Johnnie?"

Johnnie shrugged.

"It's a type of minor surgery, I suppose."

"Roscoe said cutting."

"You shouldn't necessarily believe everything Roscoe says."

"Oh." Johnnie wanted to say *Oh yeah?*

"It's more of a scraping than anything to do with cutting."

Scraping sounded worse.

"Hold her steady, Johnnie."

Johnnie looked up. The figurine had hair like Christina's. Christina was lowering a dress just like the one she had on over the head of the figurine.

They got nipples.

"You can do better than that. I need her steady."

You could cut her, Johnnie thought. You could cut this figurine and she wouldn't bleed. You could cut her and get a slice of flesh as pure and rich as pound cake or Velveeta.

It was a mean thought and he tried to be sorry for it. He looked away from the figurine, but he couldn't ignore Christina at his side—the smoothness of her legs, the rustle of her dress, the tang of her perfume.

Shiverin and snarlin and beggin they got nipples.

"I have to go," Johnnie said.

"I'm not finished yet. And we still have the man to dress and pose."

"I have to go." But he couldn't go, couldn't get up and walk now. Christina would see what he was thinking.

"Johnnie," she said, kneeling and touching his arm, "what is it?"

"No thank you." He yanked his arm away and curled up on the floor, hugging his knees. He needed his mother. She could touch his arm, straighten his hair, tell him the story. "Come on," he said, "please." Christina said his name, and he squeezed his eyes shut and shook his head. He felt her get up and move away. "Please," he said. Dixie answered. *Kiss me Johnnie kiss me.* "Cut it out," he begged, but she wouldn't, and she was joined by others, ladies from TV, ladies from magazines, ladies he'd never heard speak. His mother's voice wouldn't come to him. She was bleeding, he was sure now, bleeding away at the hopsital, and there was nothing he could do to stop it. And nothing she could do to stop the ladies' voices. They were pitched higher now, hot and breathy and demanding. Johnnie clutched his knees and pressed his face to them, forcing them against his eye sockets. The voices kept rising, led by Dixie's *please Johnnie don't* and Johnnie saw their secret places *you know they mean love* breasts and thighs and deep between thighs *please Johnnie don't kill it don't Johnnie don't* scented and smooth and soft. He imagined his touch in those places, and he knew an instant too late that he was going to need a towel. He sobbed, and that felt good, letting the sobs wrack his body—that felt good, at last something felt good, and he cried until Roscoe got here.

"Hey, John," Roscoe said. Johnnie wouldn't look at him. He stayed in a tight curl on the floor of the fashion showcase. "Come on, John, stretch out now, take it easy."

"No."

"Don't you be that way," Roscoe said, making him straighten his legs and back. "Now what in the . . . "

"I'm sorry," Johnnie said.

From the showcase doorway, Christina said, "I'm glad you're here, Roscoe. I didn't know what to do."

"What the hell, Christina?" Roscoe said, as mean as Johnnie had ever heard him. "What the hell kind of a charity project is this? Why don't you just shove him up against some real pussy?"

There was a silence. Then Christina said, "I know you're angry. But I will not tolerate being spoken to that way. Is that understood?"

"Get away from here," Roscoe said.

"Is that understood?"

"Listen, when I find a pink slip in with my paycheck I say whatever I want to."

"I thought I told you to see me before you picked up your check."

Roscoe didn't say anything. Johnnie took a long wet quivery breath.

"Do you understand the reason for your dismissal?"

"Eight years I been workin for this company. I saw that peepshow, I figured I had trouble, but I didn't expect to see no pink slip."

"Roscoe, we had no choice—you left us no choice. I'd like to keep you on . . . "

"Sure you would."

Christina cleared her throat. "Johnnie," she said.

"You leave him be," Roscoe said.

"Let me know when I can come back and finish my work," she said, and then she was gone.

Roscoe patted Johnnie's shoulder. "Take your time, John."

Johnnie rubbed his eyes dry. "My pants," he said. They felt clammy.

"Shirt, too, I bet," Roscoe said. "Sit tight, we'll fix you up."

Roscoe took care of everything. He went to Men's Casuals and got Johnnie a pair of blue jeans and a sport shirt. "But I refuse to be known as a man who steals underwear," he said. "You can go without till you get home." On the loading dock he showed Johnnie an unused clothing rack where he could hang his wet things. "Now," he said, "you get your lunch and go on back to my office. And just stay there till quittin time. I'm gonna go back out to Leathers and pick up your cart."

Johnnie gratefully obeyed, crawling back among the pallets and boxes to the cigarette-burned piece of cardboard that Roscoe called his office rug. As he ate his sandwiches, his apple, and his cake, his mother's voice returned to him. John Jerome Hundelby, he heard her say, full of disappointment and shame. He was tired from crying, too tired to apologize. He stretched out on the cardboard and closed his eyes. The dock was quiet. Everyone else was out on the floor, upstairs or down. He thought of nothing but the lemon taste of cake in his mouth.

He half-woke once to the smell of cigarette smoke, opening his eyes to see Roscoe beside him. "Go on and rest," Roscoe said. "You got time." His voice went on as Johnnie tried to doze. "Always been your saving grace," he said, laughing. "Well, I got the upper hand now, you see if I don't. And so do you, John. After what she did. Don't you dare go feelin bad about it. Next time you see her, you stare her right down." Johnnie wanted to say *Okay Roscoe you and me* but he couldn't pull himself out of his drowse, and Roscoe didn't seem to be waiting for an answer. He was talking about how he was gonna show Christina some entertainment all right, and Johnnie listened until the words mingled with the sound of the crickets and the soft mutter of his own heartbeat in his ears. Before it was too late he thought of all the words for goodbye he knew—so long, farewell, take care, be good, good night. He wished them all for Roscoe, and he slept.

"I know you guys should be on your way home by now," Christina said. "But these crickets. The exterminators couldn't make it. Now of course I'm paying you overtime. I have a Grand Opening reception right here in twenty minutes. I thought—well, I thought you could try to vacuum up any stray crickets."

"Vackum," Johnnie said. He and his partners had been stopped by Security as they were getting into the Project Outreach van to go home. Christina had called down to say she had one last job for them.

"You don't have to talk like him," Squeege said.

"Can if I want," Johnnie said.

"Let's go, guys," Christina said. "Hurry." She motioned for Johnnie to come closer and whispered, "No hard feelings, okay?"

Johnnie stared.

"Where's your tuxedo?" Squeege said as they went to plug in their vackums.

Johnnie didn't know. When he'd awakened, alone in Roscoe's office, his shirt had been missing from the rack where he'd left it.

"Did Roscoe steal it?" Squeege asked.

"No." Anyone could have stolen it—his partners, the stockboys, anyone. Anyone would be thrilled to have a shirt like that.

"He got canned," Squeege said.

"I know."

"He begged Christina for his job back."

"You're lying."

"Security told me. First he got mad and then he begged for it back. Security saw him put that watch in his locker. Yesterday."

"Shut up, you're lying," Johnnie said, jabbing his vackum plug into an outlet and turning on the noisy machine.

It was a furious, joyful slaughter. The crickets were easy to spot on the orange carpet of Fine Leathers, and the roar of the vackums seemed to flush more and more of them out of hiding. Johnnie saw some drop right out of the glossy leather coats. Their leaps were in vain. The long wand of Johnnie's vackum picked up so many of them that he lost count. Each crisp body made a satisfying plink when it hit the inside of the wand's snout. This event deserved a place in the story, Johnnie decided. The day Johnnie Hundelby killed every last cricket and made D'Ambrosia's silent and lovely just in time for the Grand Opening. He could almost hear the way his mother would tell it. Almost. The vackums were too loud. He began to hear Dixie, though. She pleaded *don't* as he killed, and he laughed. He laughed all the harder when she recited her whole little poem: *Don't kill it Johnnie because crickets mean love, hear them singing in the weeds, look at all the stars above.* She could say it a hundred times. He had a vackum bag full of trophies to put up against the one escaped Worthmore cricket. Her rhyme was like a funeral song for all the murdered crickets. Johnnie pushed his vackum wand faster, going into every corner of Fine Leathers, breathing in the thick salty smell of the merchandise, believing, as he had the night before, that he was the man for the job. The trials of the day had only made him stronger. He would make Christina see that D'Ambrosia's could only be marvelous with Roscoe as foreman of the Maintenance crew. She would beg Roscoe to come back. And Johnnie's mother would be all right. Johnnie would insist that the doctor fix the complaint, whatever it was. Everything would be wonderful. Everyone would be fine.

The lights began to go out, four at a time, in sequence across the ceiling. Johnnie knew instantly that Roscoe was in the junction box room, flipping the long columns of switches. He saw Christina at a sales counter, shouting into a telephone. His partners had shut off their vackums and were standing together near the mall entrance to the store, peering at the ceiling. Behind them, shoppers were staring through the plate glass. Salesladies carrying cash trays were looking up, too. Johnnie grinned and reached to turn off his vackum—but there was one more cricket. It escaped the first pass of his wand, and the next, springing to avoid the nozzle. Johnnie chased it around the racks of leather coats, making a final lunge as the store went black.

He heard a plink, and felt a tiny impact in the hand that held the wand. Then, behind him, a light went on. He turned. The fashion showcase was lit from within.

The two figurines, the lady and the man, were there among the dead volcanoes of the moon. The lady had Christina's hair and dress. The man was wearing Johnnie's tuxedo T-shirt and nothing else. The man had his arms around the lady. The lady had her legs around the man. Her head was tipped way back. Her blonde hair hung down straight, unmoving.

For a moment Johnnie felt nothing. His vackum was still running, but he could hear his mother's voice now. It was sweet and reasonable, and she was saying, Johnnie, Johnnie, pay strict attention now. Some people simply have other interests. And those people know who they are. Don't they?

When the panic came it was nothing that could be soothed by deep breaths or cake or the story or the kind of secret tantrum that brought his mother to him with a heavy sigh and an old bath towel. He imagined his mother dead. He pictured her pale and sealed away from him in a coffin, emptied of her blood and her voice and her pride in him; and the panic was not that he could imgine it, but that he could wish it.

He did wish it.

In the next instant he repented, *if they catch it in time, if they catch it in time*, but he knew it would do no good.

They got nipples.

Sleep hard sleep deep Johnnie hard Johnnie deep.

Givin it to her and givin it to her and givin it to her.

Once upon a time.

D'Ambrosia's.

He did wish it.

He turned off his vackum, finally, and stood in the darkness before the bright fashion showcase, listening to all the crickets he had failed to kill.

The Broken Dam

Stephen Barth

R ANDY MCENDERS flew search and rescue for the guards when he came
back. He did this very well. There was no mountain pass, avalanche, jumbled
freeway pileup, or raging forest fire he couldn't set his bird down in, make pick
up, and lift before the slightest harm ever actually came to him or his charges.
He never in his entire career missed a pick up.

It got close. He lost a gunner to rocket exhaust before he came home. They
were making pick up in the zone. A squad of Cong came out of nowhere and
opened up. The rocket went straight through both doors of the Huey and took
out a gunship on the other side. His gunner lost an eye and most of his hair when
it went past.

McEnders found out then that the only difference between being alive and being dead was the dying in between.

He died for a long time.

They finally declared his flying career at an end during his annual two week
guards training camp. His c/o was called out at three in the morning to talk him
out of a jeep he was attempting to run through pre-flight warm-up.

McEnders was taken to a quiet place. He learned to dress and feed himself, and
eventually to sweep a floor, wash his own clothes and all of the other necessaries
of daily living. He took his discharge papers, moved to Minnesota, and bought
a swamp.

The swamp he bought had an island in the middle. It boasted a pair of connected ponds on one side, along with beaver, loons, a pair of heron and enough mosquitoes to ensure privacy. A fire trail ran through the swamp, connecting his island to a country road. He bought a chain saw, ax, grill and a '63 Chevy pick-up, and moved in.

McEnders spent his first summer building a cabin out of the thicket of full grown aspen on the lot. He half-hewed them according to the directions he found in a library book, and laid them on a hand-poured concrete footing. As his disability checks arrived, he added a sand point for water, shingles on his tar paper and, eventually, electricity. He waited until he had someone to call before putting in a telephone.

He met her at the end of his second week in the finished cabin. She worked in the small bar he had picked for his weekly contact with civilization. She caught his eye immediately. It wasn't just the fact that she was the only waitress in the small bar. She wore tags. He thought he recognized the steel chain, and was certain when he heard the "clink" under her shirt as she cleared his table and spun on to another customer.

After checking his own to see what the chain looked like, McEnders remembered to ask her about it two weeks later. He held her eye after he tapped his empty glass to order a beer, looking at her neck and pointing to his throat.

"Surgical nurse," she responded shortly and turned away.

The next week, he wore his own. He thought she noticed right away, but she didn't meet his eyes until almost closing time. She passed in front of him, waited until he raised his head to look at her, and raised an eyebrow.

"Chopper pilot," he said.

She nodded and moved on down the bar, wiping silently.

When he got up to leave, she met his eyes again. He looked over the shabby little bar, back at her, and raised an eyebrow.

"Blood," she answered. He waited; she looked at his sweat-stained t-shirt and faded fatigues, then met his eyes.

"Rockets," he answered. She nodded again, and he left. McEnders had made conversation.

It resumed two weeks later. McEnders was closing the bar. There were no customers. She poured two beers, and came around the counter. Sitting down beside him, she said, "Childress."

He stuck out his hand, "McEnders."

She shook it gravely and asked, "Be around long?"

"Built a cabin," he answered.

They finished their beers silently, then McEnders got up to leave. She raised her glass to him and said, "Next week?"

"Next week," he said.

She smiled.

In the weeks that made up that fall, he learned she, too, had tried it.

"Every place I moved, they needed E-R nurses." McEnders nodded, sipped.

"Come a day, I'm walking down the sidewalk, and I see this gorgeous dude." She pauses, lifts her glass, "All I could think was 'he's been working out, probably lose a lot of blood fast. Need five pints to start, at least.'"

She listened to the parts of his story, broken into weekly installments, and nodded at the end.

"Had to make pick up, huh?" she said softly.

"Never missed," he said.

She nodded.

It snowed that winter, in great screaming blizzards vomiting out of the Northeast to dump a foot of snow at a time. He bought snowshoes for his weekly trip. In spring, before the last snow had released its choking grasp on the willows, he started the next room of his cabin.

The water was high in the ponds. Away and across to the other side of the far pond, he could see only the top of the posts on the dock. When the owner came for the first of his four trips of the summer, McEnders saw him take the dock out.

He looked up one afternoon while smoothing logs to see Childress watching him. He put the ax in a stump, pulled his t-shirt on, and went into the house. She followed him, and they sat on his wobbly, straight-backed chairs drinking iced tea.

When they finished, he showed her his home. They walked around the island, then he took her down the road toward the woods. In the narrows between pond and swamp, he showed her the small diameter culvert he cleaned every morning, and the beaver filled every night. He went a few yards further up the road—something he hadn't done yet that spring—to find the water from the pond washing in a smooth, flat stream across the road. He stared silently for a moment, then turned back, shaking his head.

They sat in the yard, silently watching the loons and drinking iced tea until she had to go to work.

She brought her own ax the next Sunday. The work went faster as he used a jig to mark the line on the log, cut down to the line with the chain saw, and she knocked the chips off to flatten it.

They worked together through the month to get the logs ready. When one was complete, they hoisted it onto the cross-stacked pile to cure. Their work was broken frequently by downpours, as the weather worked to make up for the melted snow. McEnders made no progress on the water level. The culvert was plugged half the time, as the beaver filled it up each dusk.

He was joined at his table on the Friday night after they finished the last of the logs. The man from the other pond pulled up his chair and heavily sat down. McEnders stared at him silently.

"I'm Donald Johnson," he introduced himself, holding out his hand.

"McEnders," McEnders responded shortly, sipping his beer.

Johnson held his hand out for a moment more, then picked up his beer with it, coloring slightly. He sipped, then asked, "You doing anything about those beaver?"

"Clean the culvert every morning."

"My dock is ruined, and the water's up to the floorboards on my cabin," Johnson said angrily.

McEnders sat silently, looking at him.

Seeing he wasn't going to get a response, Johnson continued, "If the water gets any higher, it's going to ruin my cabin." He glanced out the door at the pouring rain.

McEnders nodded.

"Why don't you just wait for them some night when they come to fill it up, and shoot them?" Johnson asked.

"Don't shoot," McEnders replied.

"What do you mean, you don't shoot? You've got to have a gun around here— everybody up here does." Johnson looked confused.

"I—don't—shoot," McEnders replied slowly and distinctly.

Johnson said, "Christ, a loony. What are you, some kind of ecology freak or something?"

McEnders stared at him calmly.

"Well, if you're not going to do anything about them, I will. I'll be up here next weekend—you stay away from that culvert then."

McEnders asked, "What you going to do?"

Johnson answered with relish, apparently having rehearsed the idea in his head for some time. "I'm going to rig a trip wire to a couple of shotgun shells and set it in the end of the culvert. Beaver comes along to fill it in—BOOM!" He threw his hands in the air to show boom.

"You stay away from that culvert, now, you hear?" McEnders nodded. Johnson got up and left.

Childress brought him another beer. He looked at her and shrugged at her glance.

It rained heavily all week. Childress showed up as usual on Sunday afternoon, but they got only one log notched before it started raining. Standing under the eaves on the pond side, they heard Johnson's car go by.

Childress had just started to get her ax when they heard a muffled thump and a scream.

McEnders took off running in the downpour. He came to the culvert and saw Johnson slumped over the edge of the road with his feet in the water. The current was running streams of red from his leg into the mouth of the culvert. Looking at Johnson, he saw a length of wire in his hand, and guessed he'd set the mine before setting the wire. Childress came running up.

She gasped at the sight of Johnson lying on the ground, staring transfixed at the blood in the water. They were both frozen. McEnders stood, reflexively grasping a stick that wasn't there in his right hand. Childress wiped her hands on the front of her wet shirt repeatedly.

Johnson moved and groaned.

Childress jumped, shook her head, and forced her feet to move in broken, jerky steps to where he lay. Kneeling beside him, she saw bone and ragged flesh in his right calf. She took her belt off and wrapped it around his thigh just above the knee.

She turned around to see McEnders staring off across the pond, hand grasping the stick, rain running down his face and into his sightless eyes.

"McEnders—get that truck," she yelled.

He didn't hear.

She yelled at him to get the truck again, and he shook his head darkly. Twisting a beaver-chewed stick from the mess of fill piled by the culvert into the tourniquet, she got up and faced him.

Putting her face by his ear, she yelled at the top of her lungs, "McEnders— PICK UP!" He seemed to come back from somewhere far away as his gaze focused on her.

She yelled again in the rain, "Go get the truck!"

He nodded and ran back down the trail. They loaded Johnson into the back. McEnders drove while Childress rode with Johnson to loosen the tourniquet. When they had him safely tucked away in the hospital, and had given enough answers to the deputy who came to the waiting room, he drove her home.

McEnders pulled in front of her house, and took the truck out of gear. Childress sat on the seat beside him, blood spattered on her jeans and shirt, hair in rags behind her ears. He turned to look at her, and saw her silently staring at him.

Rain drummed on the roof of the truck. McEnders finally glanced at her clothes, then nodded in the direction of her house. She was back out of the house with clean clothes and a packed bag in five minutes. Throwing the bag in the back, she climbed into the truck.

McEnders drove home.

New Day Coming

Jacquelin Hillmer

T HE WORDS "born of the Spirit" flew down from the pulpit, and Helen winced as though she had been stung. The increased fervor in Eric's voice made her rigid. Helen looked up at her husband, dressed in his clerical robe of beige linen and a green stole. He was dark and slim, and his thin face grew intense as he gazed directly into each face below him. His eyes hit hers and glanced away quickly. Gradually his voice modulated, and the sermon ended almost with a sigh.

After the service Helen stood outside with the children in the shade of a tall maple and waited while Eric shook hands with people at the door of the white clapboard church. David kicked up some dirt with the toe of his brown oxford, but she said nothing. Nathan threw himself forward from her arms and reached out toward David, but Helen just shifted the baby to her other hip and said, "Not now, Nathan. Daddy will be coming soon."

"Here. Let me take that load for a while."

Helen turned at the sound of this deep friendly voice and smiled at the sight of Alice Smaby. Helen handed the baby over and reached down to smooth her dress. "Thanks, Alice. He does get heavy."

Alice was a member of the congregation and a friend, a big, strong-looking woman. She wore a black straw hat with one yellow silk rose attached to the brim, and her face crinkled with smile lines. She handed her large black leather purse to David, and after receiving a nod from his mother, he opened it and dug down to get a hard peppermint candy from the supply he knew Alice kept there. Alice swung Nathan up in the air and made him laugh at the breeze she created.

"It's sure a hot one today, ain't it?" Alice said to Helen. "I thought for a while that we were in for a hot and heavy sermon, too. Guess some of us felt lucky to get out with none of that Holy Roller stuff."

Helen laughed at her older friend's bluntness. "Holy Rollers isn't what the people call themselves, Alice. They say they're filled with the Spirit."

The church in this small Minnesota town was part of a two-point parish assignment for Eric, his first after graduating from seminary. They had moved here two years ago, and the years had passed with nothing special to show for all the time Eric spent preparing sermons, visiting the sick, baptizing, confirming, marrying, and burying. But within the past five months a growing number of parishioners had been "touched by the Lord" and had begun worshipping at midweek prayer meetings. Eric had just recently joined them, having had his own conversion experience two months before at a friend's church. At Eric's insistence, Helen had attended one of his first meetings and her skin still prickled with discomfort when she thought of the unreserved piety she had seen there, so different from the more formal prayer and worship with which she and Eric had been raised.

The meeting began with a Bible reading and a Sweet Jesus song. The people sang softly, and some joined hands and swayed back and forth in their seats in a slow rhythmical movement. A very short man began talking about prayer concerns and a need for healing. Eric seemed to be a participant more than a pastor; many others spoke with authority. Gradually the atmosphere changed. An almost sensual feeling tugged at Helen, and she watched uncertainly as people stood and raised their hands high in prayer. One woman shouted out a prophecy. A man spoke some words that sounded like a foreign language and though it became quiet, no one seemed alarmed. As Helen looked around, she was surprised to see such peaceful expressions on so many faces.

Later Eric asked her what she thought of the meeting, and Helen answered that it seemed strange. He assured her she would like it as the new ways became more familiar, and he invited her to come again. But she found excuses not to go, and he stopped asking.

Helen turned to ask Alice a question when David tugged at the diaper bag draped over Helen's left shoulder and whined, "When can we go home? I'm hungry." Helen looked down and brushed his dark hair back from his forehead. At four years David was a small replica of his father. Before she could form an answer, Eric's voice broke in.

"Alice, I'm glad you're here. Can Jennifer still babysit for us tonight? The dinner Helen and I are invited to is for six-thirty, and I want to leave at six o'clock sharp."

"Don't worry, Pastor," Alice answered. "Jenny says she'll be home from the movie by five. I can drive her over if that will help."

"That would be great." Looking around at his family, he continued, "Let's go. I'm ready." And he strode ahead of them to the car.

Sunday lunch had been simple, a salad and sandwiches. Helen was just finishing the few dishes when the phone rang. Eric took it, and Helen heard him greet his spiritual mentor with a loud, "Hello, John!" Eric sat down at the kitchen table, and Helen listened absently to Eric's side of the conversation as she put the dishes into the cupboard. She heard his voice drop several notches in volume. "Is she making progress? Yes. I think so."

Helen stiffened and slammed the cupboard doors shut. As soon as Eric hung up the phone, she turned to him and demanded, "Am I the one who is 'making progress'? Do you have to talk about me right in front of me?"

Eric slumped in the chair, but he answered in a calm way. "John is concerned about the spiritual welfare of our whole family. It's important that newcomers to the movement put their homes in order."

"And I'm out of order, I suppose! Eric, I'm trying to be open about this. I'm trying to understand. But I need time—and some room—"

Eric interrupted her, "You're not giving it a real chance though, Helen. If you'd come to the prayer meetings more often, then you'd see. Then you'd understand the peace they give me." He paused before continuing. "When I see some of the wives who are so full of joy at the love and miracles in their lives and in the renewed life in the church, it's hard for me to come home and accept the way you are. You're so—down-to-earth."

Helen sat down in the chair opposite her husband. Her voice sounded sullen. "Maybe you should marry one of them."

"Don't be foolish." Eric rose from his chair and reached for his car keys. "I'm going to the study at church. You can call me there if you need anything."

Helen remained seated after the door closed behind him. She remembered their first year here, how excited they both had been about Eric's call and their new home. In the beginning Helen had gone with Eric to visit members until she felt she knew them almost as well as he did. And she had done other things. She taught Sunday school and helped with the children's choir until Nathan was born. Eric had seemed glad to let her do the things she was comfortable doing. He had been so busy. So tense at times—wanting badly to do well.

Engrossed in her thoughts, Helen didn't look up until David walked over from the family room and asked, "What can I do, Mommy?"

Helen got up. "Give me a minute, David," she answered. "I'll think of something."

Helen scooped Nathan up from the floor and nuzzled her face against his baby softness. She filled the bathtub with lukewarm water for the boys to splash in for a while. When they were cool, she got the Play-Doh out for David and put Nathan down for a nap. Helen picked up a new novel but put it down after a short time and leafed through some magazines. Then she put them aside and, after checking on the boys and telling David her plan, she got ready to take a cooling bath herself.

The bath helped. While toweling herself dry, Helen examined her reflection carefully in the bathroom mirror. She was in good shape for a woman in her thirties. When she washed and brushed her short brown curls as she did now and took time to apply make-up to highlight her green eyes, she looked very attractive. Helen dressed in her underthings and a robe and laid out a dark blue dress that she knew Eric liked. "I feel like I'm trying to win my husband back from another woman."

Louise and Carl Smythe were the hosts of the evening dinner party, new friends of Eric's he had met at a prayer meeting. Located in Fergus Falls, their home was a large red brick house with a big picture window in front. As Helen entered, she looked into the living room and saw plush blue carpeting, chairs and loveseats upholstered in matching blue velvet, and a stone fireplace.

After welcoming Eric and Helen at the front door, Carl seated them in the living room and explained that Louise was still getting ready. Carl was a small middle-aged man with dark, receding hair and a slightly caved-in chest. Within a few moments Helen learned that he was a successful insurance salesman and that he and Louise had one son, Jerry, who was a junior in high school and spending the evening with a friend. All three of the Smythes were actively involved in the big Lutheran church just up the hill, Holy Trinity.

Then Louise swept into the room, and Eric and Helen and Carl all rose from their seats to greet her. Louise was a small woman with a pink round face and blond curls piled high on her head. She wore a long silk gown that flowed loosely from a peasant-style neckline. The floral design of the dress material was done in shades of pink and orange and white, and it was surprisingly attractive. Though the flabbiness of her upper arms gave Louise's age away, she presented a very appealing picture. Standing next to her, Helen felt out of place.

Louise took charge of the conversation immediately. She loved new things, she said, and one of her current interests was creative cooking. Tonight she was going to serve them a Japanese dinner, and she was wearing this long dress to carry out the theme. They would eat soon, but first they could sip a little sake from these adorable little goblets she had found at Coast to Coast.

Carl made an effort to be ceremonious as he distributed the sake, and as they resettled themselves, the conversation turned to religion and the church. Louise was a new and enthusiastic member of the Holy Spirit movement, and she told of driving many miles to get to prayer meetings. Carl supported his wife's new commitment but didn't attend meetings with her regularly. "At least I'm not entirely alone," Helen thought.

They moved to the dining room where the table was set with a white cloth, white dinner plates, and orange napkins; orange tiger lilies were artistically arranged in a shallow oblong dish in the center. Louise prepared chopped vegetables and beef cubes in a wok at the table, and there was tea to drink.

The food tasted rather ordinary. Louise and Carl talked about their son Jerry of whom they felt very proud. He wasn't like other young people who got mixed up with drugs and everything that led to. Jerry was involved in a religious group for athletes, and he sometimes led Bible studies himself. He attended prayer meetings when he could; he was a fine young man.

Helen sipped her tea and slowly began to relax. Then Louise turned to her and asked, "Why aren't you a member of the movement, Helen? You know, there's a new day coming in the church, and I'm sure you'll want to be a part of it along with your husband."

Caught by surprise, Helen couldn't think of an answer. Louise didn't wait and continued asking questions. "Have you ever dreamed of Jesus, Helen? . . . Have you ever had a vision? . . . Do you believe in the presence of Jesus?"

Helen faltered as she formed affirmative answers. At one point she blurted out, "I do believe in God!" but Louise, and Carl, too, kept on talking. And then they all bowed their heads in prayer, and Helen heard someone pray that she, Helen, would feel the real presence of God. More words and then another petition—that Helen would receive the Holy Spirit. More words—words spoken in a tongue that Helen could not understand. And then there was silence. After a very short time, all rose from the table and Helen and Eric were ushered to the door where the usual polite thank you's and good-bye's were said.

In the car Helen huddled near the door, and Eric sat up straight behind the wheel. He laid his right hand on the seat between them for a moment but then lifted it up again and resumed his former position. He spoke quietly, "I told you what kind of people they were beforehand, Helen. They're my friends."

"I'm your *wife*, Eric." Helen's words ended in a loud whisper. She knew she could not continue speaking without crying, and she'd be damned if she'd cry.

Eric gripped the wheel and looked straight ahead. They rode home in silence.

The next day was still close and warm, and Helen rose early from her edge of their double bed. She took some aspirin for her headache, showered and dressed, and went downstairs to prepare breakfast. She and the boys were already eating when Eric joined them. He ate little, and they spoke even less. The noise of the children, the sounds of dishes passed around the table, and the intermittent radio forecasts of severe afternoon weather filled the emptiness between them. Eric said he would be gone all day. He planned to study in the morning and make hospital calls in the afternoon; he would eat lunch at the hospital cafeteria or downtown. Then he was gone.

The long day stretched out in front of Helen. The two churches Eric served were located in adjacent communities, and their parsonage was an old farmhouse between the two towns. Helen's closest friend was Alice Smaby, and she lived three miles away. On long lonely days like this, Helen sometimes found herself talking out loud to no one in particular. Now she said, "If worse comes to worse, I'll get out the Plymouth and drive over to see Alice."

Alice lived on the family farm where she had grown up and where she was now raising two teen-aged daughters by herself. Her husband had drunk himself to death ten years before, and since that time Alice had rented out her land. She supplemented her income from the land rental and her social security checks with a part-time bookkeeping job in town. But she was always home afternoons and had made herself available to Helen from the very beginning. Helen felt very lucky to have a friend like Alice and a place to go where she could talk openly. Helen corresponded with several pastors' wives who had no one to whom they could turn for a private talk. Just last Christmas a pastor's wife in the neighboring district had had a nervous collapse, and Eric had talked about the pastor's career being jeopardized.

Helen spent the morning doing the laundry; there was always a lot of wash on Mondays. She put the round plastic wading pool out in the backyard for the boys to play in while she hung the clothes out to dry. It took some time to pin the boys' small-sized play clothes to the lines, and it was a relief to begin hanging the large pieces that belonged to Eric. She ran her hand down the sleeve of one of his shirts as she turned to pick up another from the wash basket and thought about the previous evening.

Now she wished she had gotten up and left the table in the middle of the prayers. But she had not expected to be prayed over; even the memory of it made her shake her head in chagrin. The religious words used by spirit-filled Christians sounded right, but they made her feel so judged. So alone.

Helen sat down at a picnic table near the boys and began folding diapers. Her gaze wandered over her garden at the lawn's edge, packed with tomatoes and zucchini waiting to be picked. She guessed she was a garden variety kind of Christian, just as down-to-earth as Eric said. "But can't a person be practical and spiritual at the same time? Can't a person praise God in quiet ways? I believe and I have feelings; I have religious feelings. Do I have to be giddy and effervescent for Eric to know that?"

Looking up from her work, Helen saw dark clouds forming above the trees to the south and wondered what time the storm would hit. Perhaps it would be the last storm this summer. If only the breakfast-time silence between her and Eric could be the last for this year! Since Eric's conversion, it seemed that they always talked to each other across a canyon of unspoken thoughts. She would do anything to return to some kind of companionship. Almost anything.

After lunch Helen decided to make a special evening meal and pulled a large steak from the freezer; perhaps a good dinner would help improve the atmosphere for her and Eric. While Nathan napped, she hurried to get the clothes off the line. The sky was growing dark around them, and the rising wind began pulling at the trees. Inside again Helen asked David to help her close the windows, and they finished just before the rain hit. They stood together at the front door and watched the downpour until the noise of the water pounding against the roof and walls of the old house woke the baby, and he cried. Helen hurried to get him from his crib.

At four o'clock the three of them gathered in the kitchen, and although the storm outside continued to rage, everything was under control within. Helen had turned off the radio that crackled with static and put on a Samuel Barber record. The potatoes were baking in the oven, and David was showing Nathan how to build tall towers with wooden blocks on the floor nearby. Helen started to prepare a fresh batch of a favorite salad dressing when the phone rang.

Eric's voice spoke into her ear. "Helen, I ran into John at the hospital, and he's invited me to a meeting tonight. So I'll eat here with him. Don't hold supper for me."

"But, Eric. I've already started it— "

"Well, you can put what's left in the refrigerator. It can keep, can't it?"

Helen bit her lip. "No. It can't keep," she answered.

"Good. And how is it out there? Do you have electricity and everything? Are the boys okay?"

"We're all right." Helen forced the words out from a dry mouth.

"Good. Well, I just wanted to let you know my plans. I don't know when I'll be home so don't wait up for me. I'll see you in the morning."

Helen dropped the receiver into its cradle, turned quickly toward the sink and stared out the window at the dark sky. David came over and pulled on her arm. "What's wrong, Mommy?"

Helen continued watching the storm while she answered, "Daddy's not coming home for supper. He won't be home until late." She paused and her shoulders slumped forward as she spoke to herself. "Maybe—maybe I should give in and go to the prayer meetings."

A streak of lightning flashed in the sky and a great crack of thunder shook the house. The baby whimpered, and David squeezed Helen's arm. "I'm scared," he said.

Helen looked at her frightened sons and the half-made dinner and fought down a flutter of panic that began to crawl up her throat. In a voice that cracked only a little, Helen said, "I think we've been alone enough for one day." She reached over to turn off the oven and moved toward the baby. "Grab the toy bags for the car, David. We're going to Alice's."

The storm hadn't diminished at all, and the road was in worse condition than Helen had expected. The strong wind pushed at the car, and though the windshield wipers were going full speed, it was very hard to see. Helen opened the window next to her a little to keep the windshield from steaming up, and a cool wind fanned her forehead. The knuckles of her hands grew white as she grasped the wheel. David sat next to her, searching through his bag for a special toy car, and Nathan sat in his car seat near the door and drank juice from a plastic bottle. They seemed unaware of the tension Helen felt, and she was grateful for that.

Helen heard the blaring of a horn as a semi loomed up in front of her. She turned the steering wheel with a jerk, and the car hit the soft shoulder, making them spin around on the wet pavement. When the car stopped, they were sitting half off the road, facing sideways. The truck was gone.

They were all still buckled into their seats, and although Nathan cried for the bottle he had dropped, no one was hurt. David looked up at her and asked, "Can you fix it, Mommy? Should we wait for Daddy?"

Helen took a deep breath. "I think I can back us out of here. And I think we're very near to Alice's house. David, I want you to help me by taking care of Nathan and keeping him quiet. Will you do that for me?"

"Sure, Mommy."

Helen looked around. They weren't in any danger yet. There would be trouble only if another truck drove up the road in their lane and didn't see them in time to stop. Helen started the engine; the wipers and lights worked okay. She put the car in reverse and prayed silently, "Please-God-please-help-me-help-me." The car moved a little—and then the motor died. Helen braked, swallowed hard, and repeated the whole process. This time the sedan moved steadily backward, and the front wheels pulled out of the soft dirt on the shoulder. Helen backed the car up all the way, put the gears into forward and slowly moved back into the right lane.

The turn-off to Alice's house was on the right, and there would be no need to cross over in front of ongoing traffic. Helen strove to hug the white center line and avoid the shoulder, and within five minutes she saw the red reflecting lights that marked the end of Alice's long driveway. Helen turned in; now they would be okay.

Humming a little, Helen turned up the semi-circle at the end of the drive that passed right in front of Alice's front porch, but she became silent when she noticed a large piece of white paper posted on the door. She stopped the car and spoke to her sons, her words giving form to her fear. "Wait here. I'll see if Alice is home."

Alice's scrawled note said her girls were on an overnight and she was staying in town at her sister Jean's and would be back Tuesday afternoon. Helen stared at the paper as if she could dissolve it with her eyes. The wind and rain blew across the porch rail, hitting against her bare legs, and the storm became a roaring noise in her head. She turned to stare at the smooth gray landscape, and she saw the car in the distance and the two children entombed within. Slowly she walked down the porch steps, down the path to the car, muttering to herself as she went, "Stupid, stupid, stupid rain."

Inside the car Helen sat unmoving for a moment, her wet clothes plastered to her skin and her dripping hair stuck on her head like a heavy cap. In answer to a question from the boy beside her, she heaved out an answer. "Nobody's home. Nobody in the whole world is home."

The boy complained of being cold and hungry. She looked at the two children dressed in thin summer shorts and shirts, with goose bumps on their skin that grew larger and larger, turning into leathery alligator hide as she watched. Her own skin was just like theirs, and she supposed she was the mother alligator. She should take care of them; she should do something.

Helen turned the key in the car ignition and moved a lever on the dashboard to "heat." As the car moved forward, her head cleared and she saw Nathan leaning sideways in his car seat, his eyes half shut, and David, watching her with an uneasy expression on his white face. She smiled crookedly at them as remorse swept through her. Poor kids; they looked so tired and cold.

After stopping the car in the middle of the driveway, Helen pulled a blanket forward from the back seat and tucked it around both boys, keeping a corner for herself. It looked like Nathan would be asleep soon. She spoke to David, "I know you're hungry, but I need to rest before I tackle the highway again. Can you wait a little longer, David? Then we'll go home, and I'll fix you a hamburger."

The worried look left David's face, and he smiled at her. "Okay," he said. He leaned his head on her shoulder and snuggled down into the seat next to her.

Helen put her hand on David's bony knee and turned to look out over the boys' heads. A large black patch loomed outside; Alice's shed must be open. She could pull in there and get out of the rain, but they were safe enough in the driveway. And the car was warm now. She turned off the motor. Both boys slept.

Weariness overcame her, and Helen leaned her head back against the window. To fight off the loneliness that crept about her feet, she sang a song to herself. The black patch ahead of her grew smaller and smaller, receding until at last the vast space in which they rested filled with a brilliant light. In the distance she could see many people walking with arms linked together. They were singing the same song she was singing but with strong metallic voices. A tall man walked in their midst; he towered over the crowd, and as they approached Helen recognized Eric. She ran toward him, and he smiled and stretched his arms out to her. But then his arms and the arms of all the people separated from their bodies and reached toward the sky. She watched the smile fall off Eric's face.

Helen breathed quickly, gasping for air and expanding her lungs until she felt herself rising like a balloon. The floating arms came closer and closer. She turned her head back and forth and looked for a place to escape, but she could find none and finally closed her eyes in desperation. When she opened them again, the storm was over.

Already awake, David pointed it out to her. "Look, Mommy. See that big tomato in Alice's garden? It's just like the sun now. The sun is all red."

Helen rubbed her hands over her eyes and looked for a long tme. The world was wet and quiet now. Gazing from the tomato to the sun, she recited, "Red in the morning, sailor take warning. Red sky at night, sailor's delight."

David giggled. "Can we go home now?" he asked.

Before she could answer, Nathan woke with a cry and Helen reached over to right him and reassure him with her touch. Then she righted herself and started the car.

"Red night. Dee-light," David sang. As they drove toward the highway, he reached for his toy bag and pulled it onto his lap. "Can I tell Daddy about the big truck?" he asked.

Helen looked down at her son and smiled. "Mmm," she said. "Tomorrow."

The Deerhide

Stephen Rosen

God gave each deer just enough brains to tan his own hide.

—Indian saying

"CHRIST, how can they live in them things?" the man driving the car said. He took his right hand from the steering wheel and tilted the bottle of blackberry brandy almost to the vertical. He held the liquor in his mouth until he felt it sting his nose, then he swallowed like a loon, his Adam's apple moving the entire length of his long neck.

The big man in the passenger side of the car made no reply. He stared out the car window at the Indian shacks along the road. Their red-shingled roofs looked gray in the rain. Smoke did not rise from the cement-block chimneys but lay like ground fog over the yards and road. The Indians' dogs ran up to the ends of the driveways and barked at the car.

It was October. Wet black tree trunks in the woods; yellow leaves falling. From the "ditchbanks" came the smells of wet leaves and rotting logs.

"I think I'm a little drunk," the driver said. He wore a cowboy hat with a long feather in it.

The big man kept staring out the window. He wore a leather visor over bluish black hair that fell over his shoulders. He had one toothpick in his mouth and one behind his ear.

"Hey, Moon, do you think the squaw will tan the deerhide for me?" the driver asked.

The big man said nothing.

"Moon, they say that when a squaw does a hide it's so porous that you can blow out a candle through it."

Moon nodded, not looking at the driver.

The driver tipped the bottle again. Moon turned and watched him. The driver lowered the bottle, looking at Moon. They looked at each other in silence.

They passed a sawmill. They drove through the part of the reservation where the new housing project was going up.

The man in the cowboy hat had turned to Moon. "You ain't said much." He offered him the bottle, grinning.

"You're runnin' your mouth too damn much, John."

"What are you saying, Moon?" The man with the cowboy hat was still trying to smile.

"You know what I'm saying, John."

"You're wrong, Moon." Now he was not smiling.

Moon did not answer.

"Sometimes you're really stupid, Moon."

"Sure, John. Whatever you say, John." Now Moon was smiling.

In a few minutes they turned onto a long gravel driveway. An Indian shack was set far back from the road; back there you could see the fog in the spruce trees.

In the yard a little Indian boy was playing with a big Husky. The Husky was white, but more than white because everything else was dark and muddy. The boy and the dog were having a tug-of-war over a leather glove.

The shack was one of those in which three generations of family sleep in one room. At the side of the shack was an old black Cadillac with its hood missing. Next to it lay a rusty box spring. Behind the shack the top half of a satellite dish was visible.

The big man got out of the car first, carrying the deerhide in a big plastic sack. The man with the cowboy hat got out and staggered a little. He called coaxingly to the dog and slapped his pants to get it to come to him. The dog came up and barked at him. The man started to talk to the dog in that overly familiar tone that people often use when they are afraid of a dog.

Moon asked the boy where his father was. The boy pointed to the shack, and he and the dog rushed off toward it. The two men followed. They grew serious as they approached the door.

Inside the shack it was dark and smoky and smelled of fried fish. An old Indian man with a shaved head was trying to get a fire going in a barrel stove. He went on with his work, seeming not to notice the visitors.

A large Indian woman stood at the gas stove frying fish. She was dressed in a man's shirt and pants, and she was barefoot. She was middle-aged, but the early white in her hair, her bent figure, the worn-out look on her face, made her look like a very old woman. From time to time she held a steaming cup to her cheeks to warm them. She glanced at Moon and went on frying the fish.

The boy tugged at the old man's pants, and the Indian looked up and saw the visitors. Neither his face nor his movements showed surprise.

The young man with the cowboy hat took the sack from his friend and held out the deerhide.

The old Indian got up from the stove and studied the visitors.

The man with the cowboy hat grinned foolishly. Moon took off his leather visor and kept turning it round and round in his hands.

The Indian put down the piece of firewood and started toward the visitors. He crossed the small room in a few quick strides, but to the two men this felt like a long time.

The Indian's expression was neither friendly nor unfriendly. Without a word of greeting he took the deerhide. He felt it, rubbed it, smelled it, all the time watching the man called John. The old Indian looked him up and down. He looked at his clean hands, at his leather coat, at his boyish face.

Moon was looking at the floor. The other man rubbed his boot against the mud and yellow leaves that were stuck on his other boot.

The huge dog had fallen asleep on the floor with his head on the boy's lap. The boy never took his eyes off the dog. He smoothed the dog's closed blonde eyelashes. He whispered something in the dog's ear and then kissed his pink nose.

The Indian took the hide to the woman. Though the stove had started to give off heat, she still huddled within herself. She took in the condition of the hide in one glance. She did not touch it. She looked up at the old man with a grunt.

The Indian, admiring the hide in his hands, returned to the two visitors who stood very close together near the door.

"Did you keep the deer's brains?" he asked. His whispered voice startled the two men more than if he had shouted at them.

Both shook their heads though he had addressed only the one with the cowboy hat.

The Indian's face became grave. He repeated, "Did you keep the deer's brains?"

"No," they said together.

The old Indian was looking at his feet, thinking about something. He walked over to the stove and tried to fit two logs into it. He stood close to the stove absorbed in thought. For a moment you could smell singed hair.

The Indian walked up and down in front of the stove with a worried look. Presently he returned to the two visitors.

"Do you have the brains of another animal?" he asked.

The man with the cowboy hat looked puzzled by his question, and Moon was looking away.

"Do you have the brains of another animal?" he asked again.

The two men looked at each other as though one of them had asked the other the question. The man called John turned to the Indian and said "no" with his face.

The Indian looked at the beautiful hide in his hands and grew thoughtful. After meditating over something for a few moments, he went over to the woman. He held out the hide to her, nodded toward the boy and the dog, and spoke to her very rapidly in Ojibwa.

She went on frying the fish and did not look at him.

He took the fork from her hand and spoke to her in a pleading tone, in Ojibwa. She shook her head in refusal.

He grabbed her arm and yelled one, short Ojibwa word at her.

She tore herself loose and went to the window. She stood motionless in front of the window, her back to the others in the room.

It grew very quiet in the shack. No one moved. Now and then the pitch from the pine logs in the fire popped. An old clock ticked. Outside the window the rain fell on the leaves like fine sand.

After a few minutes the woman went back to frying the fish.

The visitor in the cowboy hat was drawing a figure 8 with his boot on the floor. His big friend pretended not to have seen what had happened and stood looking out the window.

The old Indian, who had gone over to the stove, got up and started walking up and down in front of it. Again he aproached the woman, this time very cautiously. He touched her arm and whispered to her.

She did not answer him.

The old Indian turned from the woman and went to the visitors. He stood before them in silence a few moments and then said, "You do not have the animal's brains. It cannot be done." He made no move to give the hide back to them.

The man with the cowboy hat spoke up. "I will pay." He took out his wallet and pointed to it. "You will get money. Very much," he said in that loud voice and childlike speech often used with foreigners.

The Indian listened without replying.

The man with the cowboy hat grew more desperate. Very slowly and very loudly he said, "Do you understand? I will pay. Understand?" He held out his wallet and pointed to it.

Without answering, the Indian walked over to the stove. He ran his thumbs under his suspenders, thinking. He looked over at the boy. The boy looked up at him, and when the boy saw the old man's face, he stopped petting the dog.

The Indian cracked his knuckles. He looked at the boy and he looked at the woman, and he looked at the boy again.

The old Indian motioned to the boy to go with him to a doorway leading to another room. The boy gave his dog a big hug and got up and followed the man.

The woman for the first time looked up from her frying. She looked right at Moon. She narrowed her eyes on him, like a cat. She did not say anything.

From another room came the sound of doors opening and closing, a man's voice, silence; then a boy crying, then screaming. There were rapid footsteps, furniture was knocked over, a door slammed. Then all was quiet.

A minute or so passed. The old Indian came back into the room, but not the same man who had gone out a few minutes earlier. He stopped at the stove. His right hand, searching for the back of the chair, found nothing. It was as though he were a blind man in unfamiliar surroundings. Then he saw the two strangers by the door. His whole expression was concentrated in his eyes. He looked first at the man with the cowboy hat, and longer at Moon. It was the sort of look that judged not the two men standing before him but both their peoples.

The Husky, missing his master, jumped up on the couch and looked out the window. His nose was pressed against the window and the window started to fog up. His ears stood up. His tail, curled back in the shape of a comma, never ceased moving. He began to whimper, jumped over to the front door and pawed at it, then looked back at the Indian for an explanation.

The Indian went up to the visitors and said "ten dollars" as if he had said "get out."

The man with the cowboy hat took out his wallet and gave him the bills. The Indian took them without looking at the man. Then he took the rifle from the top of the refrigerator, grabbed the dog by the collar, and went out the door without a word or look to anyone.

With the man and the dog out of the room a different silence settled in. The two men felt the Indian woman closer to them, yet she had not taken a step. She stared at Moon. The two men did not know how to leave.

Outside there was a rifle shot. The two men exchanged glances. The woman turned her back to the visitors. They saw how the sides of her face made strange, jerky movements. They knew enough to leave.

Outside the rain had stopped. It was cold. The two men walked quick toward the car. Near the pumphouse the Indian was bending over the dog. Moon looked away so he would not see what the old man was doing to the dog.

The boy was nowhere in sight.

Back in the car the man with the cowboy hat began to chatter, as if suddenly a spell had been lifted from him. "It's gonna freeze hard tonight, Moon."

The big fellow said nothing.

The car turned out of the driveway. "Ten dollars," the man with the cowboy hat said, and shook his head laughing.

Moon just looked at him.

The man with the cowboy hat took the bottle of brandy from the glove compartment. "That squaw bitch . . ."

Moon knocked the bottle out of his hand. "Shut your goddamned face before I bust it in!"

They drove back to town without another word.

Two: A Story of Numbers

John Solensten

H UNKERING UNDER the wind and snow as he sits in his duck boat, Dr. Liv wonders why he is there. He is one of two dentists in Odin—the one with the funny name. In Norwegian it means life, but only a few people—older, wiser ones—know that. Dr. Liv is at the business of killing ducks and the irony of it tickles him a little under the numbing cold. The gray-lap water beats through the buzz and hum of the bending reeds and rocks him slowly. Twenty yards out on the open water his decoys, wooden on the waves, bob up and down and tug at their anchor strings. Farther out on the snow-veiled, sullen expanses of Heron Lake long traceries of migrating scaup vortex down to rest on the water and then to fly again. They know. In the morning the wind will be still, the land snow burdened and the lake an eye of blue ice—except in the very middle where a few birds will linger—hurt or crazy or whatever they are.

Wet snow drips from Liv's enormous ruddy nose. To keep warm he hugs himself, looking down occasionally at the thin gunwale that separates him from the rages of water. Under the surface there are fields of silt four or five feet deep—silt oozed from the farm fields through creek and tile. He shudders and thinks of going home. Men have been found standing up in the lake, the silt up to their necks—one with his gun still across his arms. Hunting still. Still.

The white bellies of the mallards flash in the corner of his eye and pass behind him. Turning is a stiff and clumsy thing for Liv, so he lets them circle. The two of them hang on the wind above him, their wings moving slowly. A pair of curly tails they are—a drake and hen—from Hudson's Bay or God-only-knows where—a far north anyway. And wheat fat they are too . . .

Liv is amazed. They swing and drop into the shallow water closer to the shore. They begin to feed, paddling and then tilting their bottoms up like sails of distant sailboats. He cries out to flush them and they rise nearly straight up, their wings flailing. Liv aims at the drake's head. The shot punches them and they both fall, one plummeting; the other flapping down sideways to splash in the weeds.

"Damn it!" Liv cries. The limit is one mallard and one of them is wounded. He rows madly toward them. A wounded mallard is crazy—a cunning diver—like shooting a submarine.

He sees that the drake is dead and bobbing around and around in a savage, convulsive circle. The hen swims away, only her periscoped head showing.

And Liv paddles, hurtling toward her, pausing to shoot, paddling, pausing to shoot. Until, finally, she is flapping wildly on the surface, then lying still on one side, her gleaming eye accusing him through the gray-green froth. Liv picks her up and slides her over the gunwale.

It is necessary to make an extra trip to town to get rid of the second bird. He cannot take a chance on getting caught with two birds. Yes, the possession limit is two, but one must be cold. They insert a little thermometer into them to see if they are warm or cold. The drake is caught in the weeds. He floats on his belly so his form is long and dark. The hen he has in hand—dun, long and graceful she is—and delicate her orange feet and steady her brown-glass eye.

When Liv pulls his boat on shore he sees the sheet of ice forming all along the shore, broken only where an ancient derelict wooden boat points its crude square prow toward the open reaches of the lake.

His old Buick sits looking out on the lake with glaucous eyes. The snow doesn't stick to the waxed black surface except at the back window. Liv opens the door and thrusts the hen on the floor mat in the back seat.

He drives as fast as he dares toward Odin and worries about the dark, the early dark. Through the horizontal veils of snow trailing across the gravel road he sees an old Chevrolet dragging its muddy bottom toward him. What? Two old men sitting together like that? Both live in the Roosevelt Hotel in town. The hotel is a monastery of sorts. The hotel is full of moss-backed old men who play cards and sleep and look out of the lobby window at the street and come down to eat beef commercials at the Square Deal Cafe. Celibate old patriarchs, each in his room. But not those two. Something else.

The old Chevrolet passes without greeting. Those two—Oren and Olson. They are not like the others. They are companions, lovers. O and O—orifices of difference.

But Oren is dying of cancer. Said so matter of factly. Came in to get a toothache fixed. His head was stained red purple—like a huge blear of a birthmark—on one side and the incision was stitched up like a wide, thin, upside-down grimace. "Just pull the tooth so it don't hurt so much," Oren said. "You could take the gold and give it to somebody, I suppose," he said. "I won't have much use for it after a bit," he said.

Olson waited for Liv to finish with Oren that morning—Olson with the curly white hair and big pink face and pouted mouth and wide, sad, gray eyes. Oren was quick and dark—not a farmer, but a jeweler with hands delicate for watch repair—hands that fluttered like the wings of a pinned bird when he was excited. Together, they had played basketball and such things in high school. Their pictures were there in a glass case in a hall. They stood arms over each other's shoulder—Oren and Olson at the forwards.

As Oren sat in the dental chair that day, waiting for the novocain to take effect while Liv stood silently aside, Olson came over to the chair and began to weep and Oren's jeweler's hands sought the tears like jewels to hold them a while and Liv stepped away into another room to hunch his shoulders with the weight of another mystery before pulling the tooth (inlaid deeply with gold) and putting it into an envelope they left behind with him.

In town Liv takes the mallard into his garage and puts it behind the woodpile and hunches his shoulders on his secret. Savage and illicit it is.

As he drives back toward the lake, the snow is steadily doing its frolic architecture on the fenceposts and strawsheds and hammocked hills. At the public landing, when Liv drives in to park, the two of them are sitting close together in the Chevrolet. Liv hurries into boots and shell belts and feels like a frog in all his mottled green when he is dressed to go and retrieve the other bird.

He cannot resist a final look at them when he stands at the prow of his boat ready to launch it. Their heads are together, a hand curled at one face. He waves. The hand removes, but doesn't wave back.

When he pushes the boat out, the ice cracks and shatters and screeches as its sharp edges cut at the sides of it. As he moves beyond the ice, the waves crash over the prow and Liv turns the boat north, rowing hard for the weeds and the dull bobbing of his dozen and a half decoys. He stops and tries to disentangle two of them because they are making a loud cluk-cluk noise as they hit together. The decoys are plastic perfect, their anchor cords gold-and-weed tangled where they ray into depth.

Drake. Where is the drake? He rows and rows. Above him, swinging off the gray wind towers, the migrating birds set their wings and sail down to rest far, far out on the lake in black rafts from which restless multitudes rise and drop, rise and drop.

The drake rests in quiet water. His head is velvet green, his legs orange. Liv fears him—even dead. Remembers his rage at being shot, his circling convulsive rage like a clockwork duck, around, around, around. Indignity and now dignity. I will not hunt again, Liv announces to himself. I have killed the swans at Coole, the two. This is not love; this is death.

He pulls the drake from the water. Blood seeps the eyes, the bill. Purple there too—at the neck and deep white plumage for the north, the ice. What is the secret of the North? Who guides them far down the pathless sky? He covers it with a gunny sack.

Darkness flows steadily down the hills to the west of the lake as Liv hurries to take in the decoys, rowing up to each, pulling it into the boat, winding the anchor cord in.

Snow geese yelp above him and slide sideways down the wind, their wings barely moving except in little rippling tremors as they sail over and slant down.

Liv sees the farmhouse lights begin to come on there on the brow of the pine hills. God is not asleep, he muses. He will find me a pillow for my head and wake me through the tall window of his morning. But this is that kind of night, that kind of night. Liv rows for the shore and aches in his soul for human companionship. The wind is relentless and has tired him out. And he dare not drift too much. Submerged heads of cedar trees are there somewhere past the place he must turn to the landing.

He sees his car, beetle-browed on the little hump of the landing. He turns the boat and the edge of ice screeches at the aluminum sides of the boat. The ice resists. He stands up, pitching the prow up on the ice. Again, again, again. Rocks it and rocks it to break a path through the shell.

It occurs to Liv, because he has not thought to see it that there is another path parallel to his through the ice—a path of shattered and floating ice fragments already freezing into solidity.

On the shore the old Chevrolet—theirs—sulks behind his Buick under a low willow, its dark headlights aimed blindly toward the water, its high-humped brown body downing with the snowfall and settling in, settling in.

Where is it?

The old boat, tarred and nailed, is gone down the other path through the ice. It is a soggy thing, stern and square in its prow—an old farmer's boat, water-eaten and ponderous with moss and mortality.

Liv stands up to see and then he is his own sail. The wind catches him, his hunting coat balloons up under his arms. He scuds backward and lets it happen. There is something to see. The water is shallow. His flashlight beams through the swirl of snow. The water is not deep. It is the silt that is deep—the silk soft fields of fine soil etched by water that is deep.

And, of course, they are there under the wash and wave, green and gray as fish, rocking in one seat of the old boat. They sit together as in an aqueous pew, their legs in the silt. Surely they have stood up and broken the boards and sat down, hand in hand, to bubbly doom. Eros and Omega.

And he leaves them there. He rows numbly back to shore to drag his own boat, squealing on stone and gravel, over to his car. He leaves it there too because he has to call someone to retrieve the two of them, to tug and float them back on shore. In the morning the ice will prevail. You cannot leave them out there in their Arctic.

He hurtles the car through torrents of snow, bucking the new little wedge drifts, the car huff-huffing as it breaks through them.

It takes a long time to call, to explain. The sheriff. Dense man of law. It is like driving toothpicks into ice.

"Where are they again, exactly?" Sheriff Meyer asks, testing Liv, his voice cool and metallic on the phone.

"I have not been drinking, sir," Liv replies. Ah, reputation is no bubble, he muses.

"You couldn't get at them?"

"Should I pull them up like carrots?" Liv asks.

"What time was it when you saw them?"

"When it was very late. Now it's damn near too late forever and you will have to chop them out of the ice," Liv says.

"Well . . ."

"Well, hell! I'll get some farmers with block and tackle and lanterns," Liv says.

"Now don't get carried away," Meyer says. "I've had enough rope tricks with that Unitarian preacher, damn it. I know where it is."

"It's the path through the ice nearest the point," Liv says. "You can't miss them. They are there where the . . . you'll see where they stopped breaking the ice."

"You be there too," Meyer says.

Liv hangs up and takes two shots of Jack Daniels, blended and aged.

In his garage he turns on the light and picks up the hen mallard and holds it up with the drake. He cannot, for the life of him, figure out what to do with them. "What am I going to do with you?" he asks them. Nothing. Their long bodies dangle at the necks; the orange legs make little flames of cold fire under each. All but one of their fires gone out. He cannot, for the life of him, figure out what to do with them.

He lays them on the still-warm hood of the Buick. Soft is their repose on the liquid wax black surface.

He goes into his bedroom and removes all of his hunting clothes and all of his other clothes. God, to be in the sheets of Molly Lee, to hear her heart under a big warm breast beating, to tangle in her summer weeds and mosses, to hear the quacking of her laughter while the wind whistles everywhere around their bed. He could tell her about the two of them—the both two of them—and she would cry for him, for him. Cry. Cry.

But he knows the sheriff will want to know many things. He talks to his bottle of Jack Daniels. "What do you think about all this, Jack?" he asks. "To hell with the sheriff!" Jack says and Liv hurries into his dental office where the phone is. Dials. Thank God, the old central, the telephone operator is gone. Had ears like an elephant.

Ring.

Hoarse hello.

"Molly, this is Liv. I wish to discuss various and sun-dry subjects with you and I wish to not tell the truth with you—that is, in your bed . . ."

"Then, do come over, Dr. Liv," the voice says. "And if you wish, bring Jack with you."

"Yes, I will," Liv says, standing there numb and naked and red-fuzzed and lank-peckered and shivering. Until he sees the packet with the gold tooth in it—Oren's tooth—and then he hurries to get dressed and to walk through the snow on the solid walks through the pine-bearded darkness to her white arms, which are there.

The Anobiid

Ian Graham Leask

A WARENESS RISES from an abyss and you're stimulated by pink light piercing your eyelids. As yet there's no inner sight: no self. Slowly, you cross the boundary between inside and outside.

Then there is the sound of bells.

Then there is the sound of birds.

A fading dream flickers, its severed tail vanishing; but without halting it, fixing it with memory, you let it unthread itself and hurtle into darkness and deformity.

You feel and see.

Your parents' bedroom. There is a slight shock because you're on the floor in the corner, opposite their double bed, in a makeshift nest of eiderdowns and musty smelling winter curtains. You're sweating. You want to shut out all sound. You're sorry that you can't sink back into oblivion and escape the gruesome pink light cast by the red curtains in the window facing due east.

It's around nine o'clock on a bright morning in early autumn.

This is like selecting the peripheral pieces of a jig-saw puzzle—this haphazard registering of details with straight edges. You're learning to be selective, to not choose terrible pieces from the center of the picture. But the room is full of smells and impressions which cause a prickling sensation to creep along the layers of your skin. You know what you've done but you hold the hardness of it behind the vision of your mind's eye.

These pealing bells of St. Clement's mean it's Sunday.

Sunday.

You used to sing in the choir. For a second you smell thick incense, and a small part of you is soothed by the ringing bells. And the sparrows—it sounds like a mighty flock of them—are squabbling in the gutter which overhangs the window. You're not sure what woke you from such a deep sleep, bells or birds.

Downstairs and along the passage in the kitchen, you hear the kettle begin to wail, low at first, then louder like a train coming out of the night. Your mother is there, clattering things. Soon you must face her.

The number twenty-five grinds by in the Broadway, its weight shuddering up the building to the floorboards under you. You put your hands over your ears and shut your eyes so that colored patterns swirl around in the red blackness. You can feel your own heartbeat through the palms of your hands: nine beats every ten seconds; "fighting fit" your father would say. You want to shut out all sound of him but your memory booms with night movements, crashes and shouts. You sit up so quickly that your back muscles hurt. Inside your head you plead: Be quiet, be quiet, be quiet.

Somehow Mother made the double bed without waking you, but she left clothing strewn over the furniture in the room. The pink light coming through the blood red curtains is similar to what comes through eyelids, only back where the brain should be is a dried up shrunken pith in a hollow skull. It's painful to be so condensed. Coming from the void, like the afterbirth of your waking, you experience the sudden knowledge of death. It is there in front of you, a familiar but uncontrollable pall dropping across your vision, invisible yet black. When you die you leave the world and enter oblivion and the world carries on without you for ever and ever amen. You try to stave this off:

All things bright and beautiful,
All creatures great and small;
All things wise and wonderful,
The Lord God made them all . . .

but the sweet song doesn't soften the stiff knowledge of nonbeing. Your face sweats. You're committing some big sin.

You suffer in this state until the bells stop. When the sparrows fly away, it sounds like the single flap of a giant prehistoric wing. And now you can hear your mother again, down at the far end of the maisonette, clanking kitchen utensils. Your dog, who always sleeps beside you, is gone. You touch your face and feel the swollen cheekbone; your jaw is stiff and painful to open, and you're sweating, sweating.

Memories out of the walls, out of the snowy ceiling which absorbs shadows, out of the mirror, the wardrobe, the drawers, the smells of bedding, attack you. The last crisis, a year before perhaps. Your mother flew across the room like a rag doll and landed in your long tin toy box, her legs in the air, one slipper flying off. Her nightie went up around her waist and you saw her deep slit open like a toothless grimace. You stood in the doorway, shouting. He came toward you, his face expressionless, lips tight; his left fist hit your stomach and the right went bang in your mouth, splitting the upper left side of your lip. You spun away, stepped into your little room without windows and fell gasping on the bed, acting a little. He returned to her . . . she screamed your name . . . you heard punching and kicking . . . "Woody! Woody!" Tremblilng, you went and stood on the landing by the stairs and yelled: "Leave her alone, you fucking bastard!" The house shuddered as he left her and ran across the room in a fury. He pulled the door aside and flew at you, but you ducked and with all your weight, barged him under the left ribs, so that he tumbled down the stairs.

He lay half way down, puffing, trying to rally the muscles around his war-injured vertebrae. "You've hurt me," he said. "You'd better come and help." He didn't feel beaten because you'd cheated, fouled him like the hooligan you'll always be. You helped him up the stairs; he was suddenly an ancient man with fragile bones. "You're bleeding like a pig," he wheezed. "It isn't manly to bleed like that. Stop it." And when you helped him into bed, your blood dripping on his tea-stained singlet which is all he ever sleeps in, he tried to hit you again from his prostrate position. You can still feel the wind of it—it could've knocked you senseless. You went to your room and slept until noon the next day, missing school again.

From that night on he got sicker and sicker. Doctor Lenox said it was alcoholic poisoning, but you knew that pushing him down the stairs had set it all off. There is something beyond what a doctor can know.

Your father was dying. You carried the television upstairs and put it on the chest of drawers close to him. You and your mother would sit in the double bed with the dying man and watch "News at Ten," "Danger Man," "The Saint," "The Avengers." One night there was a news flash: President Kennedy had been shot. You thought the world would soon be at war. The room smelled sickly sweet, a smell you couldn't get used to: it clung to you, you took it to school with you, you could smell it on your fingers.

Watching television late at night reminds you of death.

You came home one night from a dance and found the place filled with a queer atmosphere. All the lights were dark yellow and your mother sat by the coal fire wrapped in an eiderdown. She told you things that made you shiver and keep an eye out over your shoulder.

Your father was in his crisis. His soul was trying to pull away from his body like a fly from glue paper, but it was stuck fast in him, corroded into place by a half a century of abominations. He was trapped between life and death, locked in the temporal, the corporeal, like a vampire, a zombie, an artificial human. When she'd gone to check on him, she'd seen a black cloud hovering over the bed. The room, as always, was lit by one heavily shaded lamp. The cloud, she said, had tried to descend onto him, but kept bouncing back up, sometimes as far as the ceiling. In his delirium he repeatedly said there was a Highlander waiting for him in the corner. Mother was afraid and came downstairs, shut all the doors except the one to the living room so that she would hear him if he cried out, and sat by the fire with the dog, hoping you would come home early, but you didn't. At midnight, she heard someone walking around in the bedroom. She said the dog began to whimper and moan. Everything was quiet for a while until a heavy man came clumping down the stairs in hard walking shoes, a giant man with red hair and a kilt. He walked down the hall into the kitchen, and she knew that the crisis was over and that your father had cheated death.

"And all this happened tonight while I was at a dance?" you asked.

"Just now," she said. "It all happened just now."

Terrified, you went up to see for yourself. He was lying comfortably, with the eiderdown pulled up to his chin, looking around the room with his wild blue eyes.

"You all right, Dad?"

"Yes, Woody, my lad. How was the dance? Were there lots of pretty girls?"

"There were, but they're all taken. And the ones left are giggly and stupid and plastered in make-up."

"Och, well, you're all bairns yet. There's plenty of time to grow up, isn't there?"

"I suppose."

"Will you do me a wee favor and get me a glass of milk and a chunk of white bread?"

"Okay."

"Thank you. And ask your mother to come up."

"Dad?"

"Yes, lad."

You sat beside him on the bed and put your arm across his chest:

"Why can't you always be like this?"

So that he couldn't see your eyes, you laid your head on the quilt. He put his fingers through your hair. His heart was beating rapidly under your ear. He said, "You need a haircut, Mister Woodentop. You look like a yobo. Go on, bugger off, and get me some supper." He ruffled your hair and gave your head a gentle push.

Keeping your face turned from him, you went to the door.

"Dad?"

"Yes, boy?"

"Was there a man up here earlier? Mum said there was a man, a Scotsman."

"Hell's bells," he laughs. "What on earth . . . "

"I don't know. She said she saw him come down the stairs and then she knew you'd be okay."

He laughed:

"That's my Guardian Ancestor yarn by the sounds of it. I'm afraid Mum's always been quite bonkers over that sort of nonsense. It's that touch of blarney running through her, I'm afraid. Now, what about my milk?"

Once, much later, you dreamed that the Highlander was leaning over your bed, looking into your face. You screamed and Mother came into your room and sat beside you. It was three A.M. You shouldn't be frightened of him, she told you, he's here to protect you. He protects your destiny against the forces that would, if they could, break up the pattern of life. He'll always be there to back you up.

Another time, you were frightened in the night and cried out. There was something invisible in the room. Mother came in and said there was no such thing as ghosts, that a great big thirteen stone prop forward like you had no need to be afraid of shadows. What you wanted was to crawl into bed between your parents and sleep safely one last time, but you were bigger than both of them by then and it would've looked ridiculous.

This room terrifies you. Vaguely you know that your mother has dislodged something in your mind with her Celtic propensity for spinning the supernatural into daily existence. You're sick of lies, they always end in battles; you're sick of battles, you want peace. There's no future for you—what will you be when you're thirty, fifty, seventy? A failure with an absurdly pompous name: Woodruff. And then Woodruff will die and be oblivious as the world goes on without him for millions of years until the whole thing has clustered into a system of cold pebbles circling a chunk of coke.

You hear your mother come to the bottom of the stairs and listen. She will want you to rest, she won't give you a wake-up call. She walks quietly back to the kitchen.

Last night was a culmination. Your analytical powers are too primitive to identify what it was, but there's something you can never go back to, something which must remain forever inchoate; you've got the smell of your father's blood in your nostrils.

You leap, naked, from the floor and look for your dressing gown. It is in a blue pile on the gray carpet next to your father's side of the bed.

Behind the door is your father's old brown dressing gown. You pull it on, ramming your arms down the sleeves. You stamp into your slippers, trying to control the hairs which are beginning to stand up on the back of your neck.

Attempting composure you begin to descend, counting each step, resisting a look back up in case you catch a glimpse of the kilted legs on the landing behind the bannisters. It's a predominantly white stairwell, with a skylight in the sloping ceiling which floods the stairs with light from the western side of the roof. The walls are white, the bannisters and wainscoting are cream, but the struts have been punched out, and pale splintered wood shows where the square heads have broken away from under the cream railing. Above this the railing is smeared with dried snot and blood.

Half way down you stand still: look, there's nothing there. It's all a lie, a dream. No dream, your mother has said, I've seen him. He's your ancestor. He's always there.

Last night your father drank two bottles of Teacher's, and around one o'clock, he wanted to kill everyone: your mother, you, the dog. He put a carving knife down his sock for protection against the ancestor he saw staring at him wherever he looked. "It's my dirk," he said. "Get out from under my roof, you traitors. You've brought this mercenary into the house, this devil. It wants my blood . . . blood will have blood. Get it out of my sight!"

You look up and the emptiness of the landing scares you. You bound down into the hall.

The hall is different. You associate it with anger, and anger is safer than fear. The long walls of the hall are painted with pink distemper, but it's very dark because there's no light coming from the lounge, and so the pink is distorted into yellows and grays. Mother hasn't opened the curtains or started the fire in the lounge. You feel cold.

The kitchen is thirty yards away at the end of the hall but there are three closed doors to pass before you get there. With your left hand you touch the railing of the stairway that descends to the street beside the shop window of the chemist. You could go down the stairs, open the front door and look into the street; it might be full of sunlight, or it might be a white blur—there might be nothing beyond the conspiracy of the door, just a sanitary white void the opposite of sleep.

Underfoot are sharp particles from the grandfather clock. You switch on a light to inspect it. The clock is stopped at one-thirty-five. Quick, avoid being sucked back into the electricity of last night: switch off the light.

The clock's silence is weird; its first silence. It has internal damage. You heard its parts falling through it when you helped Mother lift it upright after the police and ambulance men left. The carpet is covered in spilled faeces from the serried flight holes of wood-boring beetles that have infested the clock for generations: "Xestobium refuvillosum," your father would call them. Once he told you that they're impossible to eradicate and that their tapping in the old oak clock had accompanied many a solemn family death. The yellow powder is like dried blood leaking from a pharaoh's sarcophagus. You bend and touch it with your fingers, sniff it into your nose, finding no smell. The old antique will soon snap in half from its own weight.

You're standing between the two bedroom doors. The first door, which you managed to pass without thought, leads into a room where the deaths of Mr. Lloyd, Mrs. Turk, and Mr. Robinson occurred. The bedroom door that you have yet to pass used to be called the lucky room because no one had died in it. But the Reverend K. C. Jones changed that.

The rooms are empty because Father has driven away Mother's convalescence business. The old people won't come now because it's known that your father sits steaming in his lounge chair all day drinking whisky and smoking pack after pack of Players. There have been no referrals since Reverend Jones passed away six weeks ago. If his family hadn't all been so old there would've been a law suit.

You stand in front of the stopped clock, listening to your mother finishing yesterday's washing up. When she seems to be done, you walk to the half-decorated kitchen and look in as she picks up a cup of tea and sips, staring out of the window.

Paint cans are stacked in the corner by the back door and two brushes have gone hard in a large Maxwell House jar of evaporated turpentine. For over a year the woodwork has been sanded down, ready for priming. The kitchen smells of turps and earthy potatoes. Mother blows on her tea, sips it, staring ahead fixedly. You want to shake her, wake her up; but her light red hair tumbles over her shoulders, the hem of her white nightie is showing beneath her green dressing gown and her sleeves are rolled half way up her forearms.

Outside, indirect sunlight reflects off the whitewashed brick wall of the building across the alley. It's not going to be a sunny day, but overcast and gray as usual. You stay in the doorway and murmur: "Mum."

Your mother spills some tea in her saucer as she turns around. Her right eye bulges like two ripe compressed plums. The deep purple mass threatens to burst off her face. The cheekbone back as far as her ear is blue and puffy. Sensing your suffering, she quickly turns her face away from you.

"Oh, darling, you scared me. I thought you were Dad in that old dressing gown."

"Sorry."

"It's all right, my darling. Funny you should be wearing that. I bought it for him at the bazaar in Bombay the year before you were born. I was just dreaming about India . . . how I loved it. I expect you'd like a nice cup of tea."

"All right."

You feel as though you fill the doorway. For the first time there is a scent of your father—his shaving cream on the collar of your dressing gown. You go and squeeze into the chair between the table and the refrigerator, the dressing gown pulling tightly across your shoulders.

Visible through the window, perched on an orange chimney pot above the gray slates of next door's roof, is an almost motionless seagull. It puffs out its chest, the yellow bill thick and hooked at the end, made for digging deep in the guts of dead fish.

"I wonder what time it is."

"God knows. He buggered the clock good and proper, you know." Facing the window again, she picks up a pint of milk, shakes it above the draining board and selects a mug from the rack of drying china.

"Not that one," you say. "Any but that."

She reselects, pours in milk, then a teaspoon of sugar, and holding the pot above the mug with both hands, pours the tea. Its steam smells like hot flowers. She lowers the pot, snaps off the flow and plonks it back on the hob. Stirring the tea with a spoon in the mug, she turns and brings it to you at the table.

Watching her monstrous eye, you absently stir your tea. She goes back over to her place by the sink and picks up her own cup.

"How's the tea?"

"The best."

"You've not tasted it yet, boy."

"Good smell."

"Are you hungry? Want an omelette?"

"Don't mind."

She puts her tea down, comes over and holds your face in her cold hands and asks, "Did he hurt you, love? I saw him catch you one before he staggered upstairs to try and find his bottle."

"Hurt me? Christ, Mum, it doesn't matter if he hurt me. What about you— look at you. And look at him. What about him?"

"But are you hurt?"

"Nothing worse than I get from rugby."

Touching your swollen jaw, she says, "If he's harmed those lovely teeth of yours, I'll kill him." She places her forehead on yours so that the tips of both noses touch and you can see window light penetrating deep into her hazel iris; it makes you think of the sea. She has made up her good eye with fresh mascara and her skin smells of Ponds Cold Cream. Her smashed eye is demonic: If the lid should open, you might shriek in terror.

"You mustn't think about it, darling. Keep it outside you, separate."

"But I keep playing it back."

"What?"

"That last hit."

"It's a bad dream. Let it go out of your head, my son."

"But I did it. I can feel every second of it. The impact is still in my knuckles, all up my arm and into my neck."

"Some things are fated to happen."

"Rubbish! That's bloody rubbish, Mum, like all the family stories, all the ghosts and weirdos from the past. It's all bullshit. I'm absolutely sick of it."

"Well." She turns her back to you, probably thinking you're hysterical. And, of course, you are.

The dog whines and scratches to come in at the back door. Another gull lands on the roof opposite, and a flock of sparrows flashes across the window. Mother turns and gets a carton of eggs out of the larder—a peppery smell of spices, cheese, earth, damp plaster, comes into the kitchen.

She says:

"Have you got rugger today, son?"

"It's Sunday. I played yesterday."

"Oh yes. Who did you play? Did you win? Did you score a try?"

"Mum. Will he be all right?"

She opens a drawer, hunts noisily for something among the cutlery. "I expect so."

The dog scratches louder at the back door.

At the other end of the table, at Father's place, there's a folded copy of last night's *Evening News* with the crossword half done in your father's immaculate lettering. Its incompleteness is infuriating. You would finish it yourself but you know you're stupid and won't be able to get the clues: Good for nothing but rugby and being a dustman when you leave school. You are a brainstem, laddie, perfect cannon fodder for the Americans to use in their next war. It is hard for me to believe that I have brought a being into the world with the form of a god and the content of a reptile.

Mother says:

"It was like having Titans in the house with you two going at it. The whole place shook. He's had it his own way long enough; he'll think twice before throwing his weight around in future." Then she starts her ubiquitous routine:

"The booze has done it to him, of course. Rots the brain, rivets the soul to the rib cage. And he's drunk up any heritage you might've expected. The bills from the off license still aren't paid and probably won't be—you never recover from liquor debt—if they make me bankrupt too, we're finished. But he'll be okay: that bugger's tougher than old boots."

Mother opens the back door, letting in the dog who parades around the kitchen, grinning and fanning his tail. Your eyes are on the matte red hues that spoil the gloss of his coat. You ask:

"What'll they do with him?"

"Stitch him up, dry him out and send him home, most likely. He'll charm them, just like he's charmed everyone who ever confronted him over his behavior. They'll be thinking it's all my fault by now. He'll have them eating out of his hand with those big blue eyes of his. You can't help admiring it: there's something irresistible about him, you see. I'd swear he's a reincarnation of that Rasputin chap."

"But all the blood . . ."

She interrupts you:

"I'll deal with that. Don't think about it."

"It's in the gray carpet. Last night it was as black as tar. I threw my dressing gown over it."

"He's got black blood. Black blood from a black heart."

You shake your head:

"No. It was red. I could smell whisky in it. It pumped out of his eye and onto the carpet. I tried to stop it but it kept coming, pint after pint, and he just sat on the edge of the bed insulting me, letting blood flow onto the carpet and turn black."

"Oh, for heaven's sake, stop being so morbid, it's unmanly. Enough about blood."

"No, Mum, no. It made a black pool in the carpet. It'll be in there forever, it'll be in the floorboards forever, it'll come through and stain the living room ceiling."

"You're getting on my nerves, Woody."

You slug back your tea and push the mug across the table. You both watch the dog lap water from his bowl. After a minute, Mother says:

"I always call you and I shouldn't. I shouldn't involve you . . . the things you've seen in your young life."

"I'm not a child anymore."

"No. You're a big strong lad, but it is wicked of me to call you when he starts."

"He'd have killed you."

"I doubt it. I can handle him."

"If you can handle him, why do you always whip him into a rage? He's all right until you start needling him."

"I see: I'm to blame then."

"No, of course not. But you do egg him on. You twist the knife in him and you both start saying terrible things. You think I don't understand it all but I do."

"What an imagination. What have you heard? Nothing! And what about the things he's said to me? Christ almighty!"

"I know."

"You don't know. You think you do, but you see you don't. I've spent my last penny on that bastard. He's wasted everything since we came back from India. I buy him his booze and fags and he sits on his arse all day, complaining of his bad back, his so-called war injury."

"His back was hurt in the war."

"Is that so? Why can't I get a pension out of the Admiralty for him then? They're very hush-hush and frightfully polite, oh God yes, but there'll never be a pension. I bet he ruined his career with some heinous outrage; he was an incorrigible piss artist even back then."

"Well, Mum, it's you that buys the booze. Then you hide it when he's had a few too many. Buy it for him, and then take it away? That's brilliant, that is. It turns him into a human cyclone."

"You're a stinker to blame me. How can you suddenly take his side when you've seen all that's happened over the years?"

"Nothing's changed. I'm just trying to think more clearly."

Her face is pale; she's gritting her teeth. "Humph, it'll be a miracle the day you get a clear thought. You'll never have the mind of your father, you know, and . . . "

In a low calm voice, you interrupt:

"I don't believe him, but he told me once that you manipulate me against him. You don't, do you?"

She stares at you. Her swollen eye seems to throb: you're more frightened of her than anything alive. She turns around and pours another tea, her nostrils flaring as if what you said brought a filthy smell into the room. She mutters:

"He's jealous. He hates us to confide. But believe what you like."

"I'm sorry, Mum. I'm just confused. Stuff isn't the way I've been told anymore. I used to believe everything but now it's all such bullshit. All of it. Do you know wht I mean?"

"I know damn well what you mean, my lad. Life's not easy, as you'll learn all too soon."

"Wouldn't you say I am learning?"

"You'll learn. I've tried to protect you from the worst of it, but soon you'll find what a lonely thing life is. It's time for you to grow up . . ."

You roll your eyes. There's a throbbing in your ears again. You can't communicate now; she's talking from deep inside herself where the actual meaning of words doesn't matter, only the emotion that sends forth the sound. She's disconnecting from you, sounding instead of speaking, and the only things you can rely on are hard, real things like chairs and table tops and animals who can't think deeply enough to create mysteries.

Your mother has her ugly eye pointed at you. She says:

"Anyway. Why did you hit your father so hard?"

She cracks eggs into a blue bowl as you stare at her.

"I was protecting you."

"You followed him upstairs and you punched him. I was down here . . ."

"You were in the bathroom with a cold flannel on your eye . . ."

"I was beyond help. You followed him upstairs and beat him up."

"Mum, I won't let you do this, you know it wasn't like that. You should argue fairly. Why are people unfair in arguments? Why do they say what they and the other person know to be wrong? Why is it like a game?"

"Life is not a game of rugby. There are no rules for arguments. You've got to just get on with it." And she raps on the top of your head with her knuckle, speaking through clenched teeth: "Why" rap "don't" rap "you" rap "wake" rap "up?" rap.

"That hurt."

She begins vigorously beating the eggs in the blue bowl.

"Go and tidy the bedrooms and light the fire. I'll call you when the omelette's ready. Go." Her red hair has come down across her cheek and the taut muscles of her forearm stand out as do the distinct veins in her large sculptured hands.

You go into the hall. The grandfather clock is leaking dry yellow faeces. You go past it, stand at the top of the stairs that lead down to the white street. The rooms of the dead have their doors closed, and upstairs, a ghost that you know doesn't exist awaits you. If you can get rid of him, disperse him in the sleep void, you will know there is no such thing as a soul, and if there's no such thing as a soul, you are lost, doomed to the black eternity that yawns below the thin net of dreams that your life swings in.

Behind, you hear your mother mutter something. It takes a while to understand the words, for them to become English. She'd said:

"Bloody vicious little swine."

Her words make you hollow and silent as you stand still in the dark hall. You wish, oh how you wish, that circumstances were such that you could be new again, and that it would be possible to love such a thing as a father.

Tomorrow You'll Forget

Marianne Luban

NEAR WHAT USED TO be the Five and Dime is a little cafeteria where I used to eat my lunch every day. I'm writing copy for a living now, but I'm also trying to write stories in my spare time. My name is Bob Samuels. This is not one of my stories; it belongs to me in no way.

As I really didn't spend much time there, it didn't matter to me that the cafeteria was hot in summer and, during the winter, that the big window facing the street was always clouded over from the steam. It was perfectly homely and typical in every respect. Squares of jello quiver on shreds of lettuce and nobody ever asks for a breakdown of the content of the hot dishes.

When you have only a half-hour for lunch, you eat quickly and there is not much time for socializing with your fellow diners. The patrons are mostly regulars and you come to accept them as part of the atmosphere, the daily routine. I liked to sit near the window in summer in order to watch the world go by, but sometimes I was forced to squeeze into a corner where the Woman always sat.

She is the most reliable of regulars and never takes a place near the window, caring perhaps neither to watch nor be observed. She is an elderly woman, thin and used up, who looks as if she has an exhausting and thankless job somewhere. Not an office job, surely; her clothes are too tacky and worn for that. In all seasons she wears the same stretched-out cardigan over her other garments. Since I had never seen the Woman wearing a coat, I assumed that she, too, works nearby.

It seems she cares about her hair. Oddly enough, she keeps it dyed a delicate shade of blond and it is always neatly arranged. Sometimes I stared at the Woman and briefly glimpsed the idea of a long-lost beauty. Yet, in the next moment, I was convinced that it was a silly notion. She was ugly and always had been. Those burnt-out eyes of hers were fixed on some point in the cafeteria with the zombie gaze of someone who just doesn't give a damn anymore. If I tend to write about the Woman in the present tense, it is because she still frequents the cafeteria. Of that I am positive. It is only I who cannot go back.

Once in a while there were disturbances in the cafeteria. People would laugh too loudly at some joke or the cook would burn something in the back, releasing a mighty oath. Small but jarring things like that happened about once every lunchtime, but the Woman never paid any attention. If someone threw a bomb through the window, I believe the Woman would simply refuse to give up her place, ignoring a shower of glass and catsup.

Somehow I had always managed to avoid sitting next to her. To tell the truth, I was afraid. I guess I thought she wasn't playing with a full deck. I possess that fear of the unbalanced that I know is within us all. It is a dread of latent, unexpected violence. Most of us keep our hostilities in check and are wary of those who might not have the same inhibitions. It is unfair to say that the Woman appeared violent, however. It's just that I had the odd idea that someday, sometime soon, she would break into a scream. When that happened, I didn't want to be too near.

But it was inevitable. There were simply no other vacant seats. The Woman never even glanced at me as I lowered my tray. She merely kept on eating in that deliberate manner I confess I hate. It bothers me when a person's fork takes an age to reach his lips and each mouthful is chewed a hundred times at least.

Naturally, I noticed it right away. Things like that just catch the eye. What is it about a tattoo that makes it so startling? Most of them are plain silly: hearts, girls in grass skirts. Yet they all suggest mutilation and so we stare. The Woman's tattoo was the worst kind.

Being a Jew, myself, I like to believe, as does every Jew, that I can spot one of my own. But my neighbor struck me as being absolutely un-Jewish in every way. Not so much her face; faces can fool you. It's just that she was so damn unanimated, so bland. Nevertheless, she had those blue numbers right there on her forearm.

Wouldn't you know, at the moment of my discovery I paid too little attention to what I was doing and upset my coke. The ice cubes flew across the table like dice out of a tumbler and some of the liquid sloshed over onto the Woman's tray. I mumbled something and went to the counter to get a rag. When I had cleaned up the mess, I resumed my seat and began to eat. The Woman, for her part, had never interrupted her own meal and acted oblivious to the embarrassing incident of the coke. Since my wariness of her had disappeared, curiosity had taken its place.

"I'm sorry," I said. I meant that I was sorry about having spilled on her tray, but, as my eyes were on those numbers, I think she understood that I was offering my belated condolences. I suppose it surprised her that anyone could say such a dumb thing. Anyway, she noticed me for the first time in two years.

The Woman looked down at her arm and then at me.

"What can you do?" she shrugged.

I couldn't help smiling. With one gesture, a Jew materialized before your eyes. "I would guess that you're from Poland," I ventured. "Am I right?"

A line formed between the Woman's eyebrows and she looked at me with either suspicion or amusement.

"You're a smart young man," she drawled. "I am from there. I was born in Warsaw. This," she said, tapping her tattoo, "is my diploma. It means I am a graduate of Auschwitz, summa cum lucky, you might say. I was in another camp, too, after that. You are Jewish?"

"Yes," I replied, "of course."

"Of course? So what do you know about Warszawa—Warsaw?"

"Nothing, actually. Except that it was heavily bombed during the war."

Her blue eyes were fastened on me now. Yes, I was certain of it. She had been attractive once. Perhaps even a beauty. How could I ever have thought otherwise? Her English was very good, also. There was even a hint of something British there—or so I imagined.

"The old Warsaw no longer exists," said the Woman, "but, in my dreams, nothing has changed. When I wake up all I want is to be there again in spite of all that happened."

"Have you ever thought of actually going back?"

The Woman sipped her coffee, holding it carefully with both hands. "Go back to what? It's over now. The beautiful times are gone. A young man like you would have liked being there. Oh, yes, it was not dull. It was wonderful to be young and to look good. It was unthinkable not to be able to dance. When the music stopped, we scarcely knew what to do." She chuckled, but it came out more like a gasp. "Well, of course, we soon learned to dance to a different tune."

"But you survived," I said. "That implies a great deal. I mean, it must have taken a lot of— "

"Courage?" she supplied, eyebrows lifted.

"Well, yes, naturally."

"Those with courage were killed off almost immediately. Brave people are not survivors. Don't forget it."

"But surely . . ."

"No," she interrupted. "The ones with courage went to the ovens with their babies. The ones still living left them on street corners in rucksacks."

I was appalled. "It's really impossible to judge people under those conditions, isn't it? A madness took over. Even good people weren't themselves. At least that's how I would understand it."

"You weren't there, young man. I was, and even I don't try to understand. But

I know one thing. People don't really change no matter what happens to them. Do you want to know how I came to survive?"

"Well, sure, but something tells me you weren't capable of giving up your babies to save your own life."

She stared at me as though she wasn't sure I was for real.

"I had no babies. I was a *kurveh* . . . a whore."

Stuck for a response, I noticed that I had automatically polished off my food. I glanced down at my watch. My half hour was up and then some.

"I have to go back," I nearly moaned. "It's been nice meeting you, but I really have to go to work. I'm already late."

Idiotically, I showed her the time. She acknowledged it with a nod. I was horribly embarrassed to be leaving her just like that after what she had told me. But she showed no sign of sharing my discomfort, nor of taking pity on me. She continued eating, apparently in no hurry to return to work, herself.

On the following day I fell all over myself in order to get a place near the Polish woman. She was there before me, as usual, wearing that awful sweater that had been washed to the consistency of limp cotton. It occurred to me that perhaps she had been saving that vacant seat, knowing that I would return to hear the rest of her story.

"Do you mind?" I asked her. "May I sit?"

"Why not?"

I was resolved there would be no mishaps that day and placed down my lunch as if I were dining on live grenades.

"By the way, my name is Bob Samuels."

"Halina," she answered simply.

"Look, Halina," I began, but she had no patience with my fumbling diplomacy.

"Concerning," she broke in, "concerning what I revealed to you about myself yesterday, I want you to know that I was not doing that before the war. I was innocent in those days, really, too stupid for words. I exist today only because in nature's lottery I drew a pretty face. I know it's difficult to believe now. But I swear to God it's the truth. I'm not a survivor in any real sense. Even my face did not survive." Halina smiled at me in a wry fashion. "I was very young when the war began, younger even than you. My father had a shop and I worked for him. I helped customers try on gloves and hats. I was barely out of the gymnasium. I was seventeen.

"One day, a man came into the shop and asked for assistance in selecting a tie. He was old, perhaps even forty, but as magnificent as a prince. While I showed him the ties, he asked me a lot of questions about myself: what I did for amusement, what was my favorite perfume. I replied with the name of the most expensive fragrance I knew of but, in truth, I seldom wore perfume. But he did, my customer, a wonderful scent that, together with his presence, addled my senses and I could hardly speak. Finally he said, 'I can't decide. These silks look pale next to you. You are the most beautiful girl I have ever seen.'

"I don't remember what he bought that day, if anything. He was so charming and genteel. I forgave him his advanced years as he seemed handsomer than anyone I knew. He could have been a film star."

"No doubt he thought the same of you," I said.

Halina twisted her mouth. "Very likely he was already laughing at me. A foolish girl, I must have seemed to him, a little sacrifice with neck exposed for the knife. Immediately, after I met him, I received in the post a bottle of the perfume I had mentioned. Tied to the flask was a little card asking me to meet the sender at such and such a place at a given time. There was no signature, of course."

"So you went, right? If you hadn't, there would be no story."

"Yes, but the story would have been another one," said Halina. "His name was Adam Feder. I suppose he was a well-to-do man. Anyway, money flowed from him. He was in business of some kind, but he never wanted to discuss it with me. I don't know why. Perhaps he was protecting himself from the day an irate Halina would storm into his place looking for him. When I asked him to tell me what he did for a living, Feder would say that it was demeaning for lovers to speak of crass matters. I could not reply because it occurred to me that all I knew about were dull and commonplace things. One could scarcely speak to a man like Feder about one's schoolgirl adventures. But I got by with listening and making admiring remarks. It seemed to satisfy Feder and he constantly expressed his delight and good fortune in having found me. He took me to fancy places in parts of the city where he was not likely to be recognized. Sometimes, though, I imagined that this did not actually worry him, he appeared so free of anxiety. He was witty, affectionate and a complete gentleman. I loved him to distraction. One day I could contain myself no longer and so I asked Feder if he loved me as well. His answer was, 'A silly question. How could I fail to love you? Next to you I am nothing more than a poor old fellow.'

"When I began to sleep with him, we made love in a little flat he was keeping especially for that purpose. Nowadays, I might have moved myself into that flat but, in 1939, unmarried girls lived with their parents until they stood under the wedding canopy. And, needless to say, they did not sleep with married men. I was under constant pressure to invent new and convincing alibis to explain my absences to my mother and father. It hurt me to deceive them, but my love for Adam Feder overruled everything. It seems to me I would have committed murder for him I adored him so. I cannot tell you how deeply I cared; such things are beyond words. My only happiness was to be with my Adam who, in reality, was the Adam of another woman. When we were together, the world, Warsaw, the troubles brewing for Poland didn't exist for me. I had no patience to actually sit down and read a newspaper. I did listen to the radio, but the news flashes had nothing more than a fleeting effect on me. When one is young and silly and in love, one doesn't contemplate catastrophes. A major upheaval is when one's lover is late for a rendezvous and, should he not come at all, only then does the world come to an end.

"If I was oblivious to the events of 1939, you can imagine Mrs. Sarah Feder didn't give me any sleepless nights, either. I was not even curious about her. Feder had told me that they were of an age and that made her old, not to be taken seriously as a rival. I had never seen her and I did not wish to see her. True, I did begrudge her the time Adam 'had' to spend with her, but I was basically a very proper girl at that stage and believed that a wife had priority over a mistress. You see how it is? The minute one finds oneself in a socially unacceptable role, one feels at a moral disadvantage and stops fighting for one's basic needs. Somewhat, perhaps, but never too much. One becomes undeserving in one's own eyes. It is really too unnecessary, too sad." Halina patted my arm. "I must stop or nothing will stop me. Eat, eat. Your lunchtime will be over soon."

"No, don't stop now," I told her. "I plan to stay here until you're finished. The office can run very well without me. I'll make up some excuse."

Halina smiled. She and I were close friends now. We had known each other forever.

"I'll be here tomorrow. You know that."

I said, "I don't care about tomorrow. I am in the year 1939 and a beautiful girl named Halina is eating her heart out over a man with a wife who both exists and doesn't exist. Tomorrow doesn't count for me any more than it does for her. Please go on with your story—oh, how selfish of me—you have to go back yourself."

"I have gone back," said Halina. It was true. The years had fallen from her. Her eyes were luminous and her skin flushed. Her lovely hair-color was now in harmony with the rest of her appearance. She was charming; how could I have ever thought otherwise? Even the sweater seemed a piquant affectation. For the past two years I had been observing another woman.

Halina stirred some more sugar into her coffee, too much sugar, as if to counteract the bitterness of what she was about to say.

"Don't worry about me," she told me with a kind of sigh. "I am in no hurry at all. Can you say of your own life that those you loved the most gave the least of themselves in return? Of course you can. It's an endless and universal lament. A perverse law of nature. As you've already guessed, my affair with Feder came to an abrupt end. Perhaps the inconvenience of it had become too much for him. For me, it had become simple to get away. My parents were caught up in the worsening situation in Europe and the rumors of impending war. They hardly noticed my comings and goings anymore. If they suspected I might have a secret boyfriend, they figured the war was likely to take him away in any case. I don't believe it occurred to them I might not be seeing a fellow my own age.

"In August of 1939, Adam Feder took me to a restaurant where they had this terrific orchestra. Naturally, I wanted to dance. The tango was very popular and nearly every hit song, happy or sad, was set to the tango rhythm. But Feder didn't feel up to dancing. I suggested we order something to eat, but Adam stared at me in a strange way. 'Have a drink, Halina,' he said. 'Have one yourself,' I laughed. 'Maybe it will put you in a better mood.'

"Feder placed his hand on mine. 'Halina, this is the last time we shall see one another like this. My wife knows about us. Don't ask me how she found out. She may have her own spies, for all I know. You understand there is nothing I can do, Halina?'

"In the background, the singer was performing a tune called 'Wanda,' which is about a man who would have done anything for the girl he adored. It was one of my favorites. I would never hear that song again, would never want to hear it.

" 'No,' I told Feder, 'I don't understand. I love you and I know you love me in spite of what you are saying. I'll never let you go.'

" 'I beg of you not to make this difficult, Halina.'

"Although I was fully aware that what Feder was saying to me was a lie and an evasion—did he truly think I believed he had no choice?—he had never looked more beautiful to me than in that sickening moment. I saw him as a fallen angel and not the devil that he was to so ruthlessly tear the heart out of a young girl. He had not many gray hairs yet, but somehow the sight of them held a tremendous poignancy for me and each one was dearer to me than my own hand. I should have hit him over the head with the wine bottle, but I only wanted to throw myself into his arms and plead with him to take back his rejection of me.

" 'Halina, you're not going to cry, are you? You must go outside if you're going to cry. You'll be so ashamed if you make a spectacle of yourself.'

"Cry. I was too stunned to cry. I could scarcely breathe. I felt as though my heart were being squeezed like a sponge and that I would momentarily suffocate.

"Feder added, 'Halina, my darling, you knew I wasn't a free man.' He pressed my hand reassuringly as though *he* were forgiving *me* for something I had done. I snatched my hand away as though it had been burned. I left that restaurant with all those dancing people and the baritone singing a Krukowski hit entitled 'Tomorrow You'll Forget.' But I never forgot. I might have, I suppose, if life had continued normally. I might have met another man and gotten Feder out of my system. But, as it turned out, my heartbreak of that evening was only the beginning of a long nightmare for me. As you know, Germany invaded Poland, and Poland fell. Then came the black night that lasted for what seemed a century."

The cafeteria had nearly emptied. There were only a few persons left who watched us furtively, wondering, no doubt, what a middle-aged woman could be saying so earnestly and at such length to a man of my years.

"How long was it before you were taken away?" I asked, but my voice sounded odd to me, too American, like an interviewer.

"Oh, years passed. Not that time meant anything to me, particularly. I was physically ill most of the months after Adam left me. I ate haphazardly and seldom went out. I heard talk about the campaign against the Jews but, as I was considering suicide, anyway, I was unmoved by the danger. I no longer worked in my father's shop because I couldn't concentrate and made too many mistakes. Soon there was no more shop. Who could afford my father's expensive hats and ties any longer? My father was crushed and I suppose we were bankrupt. How we ate didn't concern me. I was one hundred percent self-centered in my grief.

"By 1940 all Jews had to move into the Warsaw Ghetto while all the Gentiles who had lived there had to get out. Our family, too, went there from our nice apartment in an upper-class part of town and was installed in a crowded, squalid building. Our neighbors were desperate people wearing white armbands with blue stars of David, all of them were hungry and foraging for food. But food was scarce and the staving died literally in their tracks. A corpse in the street was no more unexpected in the Warsaw Ghetto than a crumpled cigarette package is here. Typhus raged and this illness became more feared than the Nazis. By 1942, 100,000 Jews had perished in the ghetto.

"In that same year the Germans began to intensify their terrorizing *aktions*, which consisted of dragging Jews out of their homes and murdering them in view of everybody. But it was rumored that if able-bodied men and women voluntarily reported to an area called 'Umschlagplatz,' they would be deported to 'the East' to work. Well, anything seemed more tolerable than the ghetto, so my parents decided that we ought to go there and take our chances. We had heard all kinds of stories about this 'selection place.' Sometimes everyone who showed up was immediately taken away by train and at other times, the SS was fussy. They formed two groups, a right and a left. The only ones that were chosen for the right side on those occasions were persons who looked strong and capable or those who might prove useful for some purpose or another. Very pretty girls were always motioned to the right. Pretty boys, too, sometimes. When this method of selection became common knowledge, people took pains to make themselves appear younger or older if they were not quite adult.

"My parents, however, did nothing to themselves. They were both over fifty and knew they weren't fooling anyone. But my mother, thinking I would have a good chance, made me put on my best clothes and do a full makeup. And I obeyed like an automaton. I felt exhausted and thin and personally without hope. It seemed incredible to me that anyone, much less a German, would find justification for my continued existence. How could it be, when even someone I loved more than my own life had no use for me?

"Have you ever seen an Hieronymus Bosch painting? What he would have made of that selection place! It was something from the netherworld, total chaos, the wailing and pleading rising as from out of hell itself. The SS tried to keep things moving in an orderly fashion, but how can there be order when families are torn apart, loved ones shoved to the left, that dreaded left, marked for extermination. Of course, we all denied the possibility of the latter, while at the same time our very bones ached with the certainty of it.

"When I heard the sentence 'links' pronounced on first my father and then my mother, my legs turned to water. I now realized the odds were good that I might be sent to the right group, myself, and I grew frightened of being separated from my parents. I only wanted to be near them, come what may. I kept my eyes glued on my mother, desperately trying not to lose sight of her as she and my father were being pushed back into the crowd.

"Suddenly I felt my head being jerked around and found myself looking into the face of a German. I remember that it was not a face to inspire terror. His were ordinary features, even kindly ones if one can go that far.

" 'You don't look Jewish at all, Fraulein,' I heard him say to me. 'Are you sure you belong here?'

"I replied that it was my parents he had just sent to the left.

" 'Perhaps they are not your true parents. If you are adopted, you don't have to be here. Could you have been adopted?'

"Before I could answer, his superior officer came over to see what was holding up the process.

" '*Was ist los hier?*' he demanded of the other German.

" 'Sir, is it not amazing? Here is a perfect Aryan type. I thought she might have been adopted by the Jews.'

"The officer scrutinized me from beneath his black visor. I could not see his eyes, only the death's head on his cap leered at me.

" 'A beautiful girl. But we can't be sure, can we? Anyone can claim she is adopted. We haven't the time to investigate these things. Send all the Aryan-looking young women to the right, whether they have children or not. Understand?'

"As he motioned me to the right, the lower ranking SS man actually said, 'Mach's gut,' which is German for 'take it easy.' "

Halina paused. I wanted to ask her if there was a chance she actually might have been adopted, her parents having been so much older than herself, but instead I said, "Did you ever see your parents again?"

"Never. I can't even say whether we were sent away on the same transport."

"So you found yourself completely alone in the world. How old were you then?"

"Twenty. But I wasn't alone for long. The fact is, I was actually adopted by another person. This is what happened: When the train stopped and the box cars were opened, those of us trapped inside more or less fell out onto a large platform where other Jews were already waiting. For what, even the best-informed of us could only guess at. The stench was unbelievable on that train and the ones who could still breathe simply stood gasping for air when we were let out. I stretched myself out on the platform. I had not been able, due to being tightly packed in with other bodies, to lie down for what seemed an eternity. My legs were in excruciating pain and I smelled from vomit and shit, excuse the expression.

"Confusion was still the order of the day. People were frantic to know where they were and what was to become of them. Some, of course, didn't care and were already like sleepwalkers, their mental balance having collapsed beneath the enormity of the cruelty and suffering.

"When my legs ached less I got up. It was then that I received another shock. Not more than a few feet away from where I stood were Adam Feder and his wife. She was clinging to his arm and shaking her head to and fro in a way that said she simply couldn't go on. He was patting her shoulder in a detached manner, not looking at her at all. It seemed a hundred years ago that I had accidentally run into them in a store after our split-up. Adam had looked through me as though I had been transparent. And I had said nothing. There had been nothing to say. On the platform though I burst into tears and rushed over to Feder, throwing my arms about his neck. I don't believe I actually expected him to comfort me, but I did think he would acknowledge me, perhaps even keep an eye on me for old times sake. The games that were played in Warsaw seemed too stupid and of no avail whatsoever in view of our predicament.

"But Feder had played those games too long. He pulled off my arms. 'You've made a mistake, young woman.'

"'Adam, for God's sake!' I shrieked.

"'Young lady, this is no way to behave. You're upsetting my wife.'

"In Yiddish they say 'It went dark before my eyes.' Well, that is what happened. I went berserk. I clawed at my former lover's face and called him names that had never passed my lips before. 'I'll show you how to behave,' I sobbed over and over. 'I'll kill you, you lying bastard!'

"A German finally dragged me away. He was laughing and I saw he found me a great joke. So did some of the Jews. They were laughing as well. I had created a diversion, something to take their minds off their own suffering. A couple of kind women took charge of me and calmed me down.

"'Listen, doll-face,' one of them said to me, 'if he's got anything coming to him, he'll get it all too soon, anyway.'

"Then bedlam broke out in earnest. Men and women were being divided into two groups by gender, couples literally being torn apart. I didn't much care about that in my own case as I had no one, but I couldn't bear the shrieks and tears of the women. I say I couldn't bear it, but the truth is I took it pretty well—much better than the old Halina would have. A year before such misery would have moved me to tearful sympathy, but I, the new Halina, had cried myself out over the months. There was simply nothing left. My sobbing over Feder's coldness moments before had been the last of it. My heart turned to stone that day on the platform. I felt the actual weight of it in my chest.

"As I was being herded away with the rest of the women, I felt a hand on my arm and heard my name spoken. Sarah Feder was trying to get my attention. I took it for granted she wanted to dress me down and so I made an effort to avoid her. But I couldn't shake her off. There were too many women crushing against us. How did she know my name? Had Feder let it slip out when he was fighting me off or had she known it all along?

"'Please,' she begged, 'I must talk to you. You're only a child. He had no right to treat you like that.'

"'You have a rotten husband, Mrs. Feder,' I told her savagely.

"'I know. Wait for me, Halina. If we stick together, we'll do better.'

"To make a long story short, I let her attach herself to me and, do you know, that woman never left my side again until the day she died."

"It's incredible!" I cried out. "The wife becomes like a mother to the mistress. That's what happens when the world goes mad."

"True enough," agreed Halina, "but you have it backwards. It was I who was like a mother to her. This was the pampered wife of a wealthy man, don't forget. She was virtually helpless and a nervous wreck besides. I had to watch that people didn't snatch the bread out of her mouth. She plugged herself into my current, confident that I was strong and spirited from the way I had attacked Feder. Maybe her faith gave me confidence, too. She seemed older than most of the women in the camp where we finally wound up, and at that time it was a mystery to me how she had managed to survive the selection. Now I believe she might not even have seen her fortieth year. She looked like an old lady to me but she had a pair of huge Jewish eyes like candles. Maybe it was the eyes that had pulled her through. She talked too much and I thought sometimes she would drive me crazy. She wanted to know all about my romance with her husband down to the smallest detail. Then she would start in cursing Feder and all his 'whores,' as though she had completely forgotten that I had been one of them. Sometimes she would tell me about the days when she and Feder were young and in the first bloom of their relationship. Then she would weep and kiss me as though I was the cherished offspring of that union. Most everyone thought that I was actually Mrs. Feder's daughter. The Feders never had any children, only poodles. I don't know whose fault it was, but I suspect that Feder would never give that much of himself to any woman, not even his wife.

"The truth is, Sarah Feder was a pain in the neck to me, but she was old enough to be my mother and to have her near me caused me to miss my own mother less.

"One day I asked her, 'Sarah, did you know about Adam and me before the Germans came?'

"Her answer was, 'What did I know? I didn't want to know anything. I was like those three apes, deaf, dumb, and blind.'

"After a while Sarah stopped talking about her husband so much. When she did refer to him it was as though he were someone long dead. She perked up somewhat and started doing some of the work that I had been doing for her. It was our job to cut the valuable metal buttons off of the clothing of murdered Jews. For that we were entrusted with pairs of fairly sharp barber scissors with small holes. These 'weapons' had to be turned over to the guard every night. But first we faced the ordeal of removing them from our swollen fingers. I swear to you that we cut off a mountain of buttons from the coats of little children alone.

"But just as Feder's wife was beginning to pull her own weight, she came down with a fever. It was unthinkable for her to lie down and rest during the day for then she would not survive the daily selection. I knew they wouldn't send her to the sick hut. She was simply too old to be bothered with. It was either keep on working in spite of the illness or be sent to the gas chamber. I worked twice as hard to cover up for Sarah and hoped the female guard wouldn't notice how awful she looked. She could hardly sit up. I forced her to eat and keep going but she grew half delirious and even leaning against the wall couldn't keep her upright. I grew panicky and even promised her that, if she would hold out a couple of days more, I would find out where Adam was and take her there with me. I invented the story that I had found a few real gold buttons and would use them to bribe our way.

"Her eyes opened wide. The fever made them glow with an eerie intensity. 'You're lying, Halina. You don't want to bring me to Adam. You want to see him yourself!'

"I couldn't believe my ears. 'How can you say such things, Sarah? I'm not interested in Adam anymore. You've been more of a friend to me than he ever was. It's you I care about.'

"Sarah Feder gripped my arm with surprising strength. 'Stay away from him, Halina,' she croaked.

" 'Stop it!' I said fiercely, trying to pry off her hand.

" 'You don't understand, my angel. He destroyed my beauty and gave me a life of bitterness and suspicion. He runs after beauty but he spits on it, pulls it through the mud. Never go near him again!'

"At that moment the guard came over and shoved me away from Sarah. Sarah had already collapsed on the floor. The guard was furious with me, as though I were responsible for everything.

" 'Your mother has got typhus!' she raged. 'You've been covering up for her, you little shit! Now her lice will be all over the rest of us!'

" 'She hasn't got lice!' I snapped. 'She's got influenza. She'll be over it in a day or two. The buttons are being cut. Use your eyes and look at them all.'

"She looked at them all right. She grabbed two handfuls and threw them in my face. Then she began to beat me with her club. I only threw up my arms to shield my head, even though those scissors were stuck to my hand. I thought if she took it out on me she would maybe forget about Sarah and let her live another day. But I failed to reckon with Adam Feder's wife. Maybe it was the fever, the delirium that made her do it, but she jumped up like a tigress and stabbed that guard in the throat with her scissors. This was the act of a woman who had once been too fine a lady to put her hand in cold water.

"The guard didn't die, but that was the end of my so-called adopted mother and nearly of me, too. I was a pretty well hardened specimen at that point, but fate had it in store for me that I would grieve first for the husband and then for the wife.

"On the other hand, fate arranged matters and snatched me out of the fire. I knew as soon as that Brunhilde felt better she would make life miserable for me or even send me to my death. When it came time to eat what was laughingly called our evening meal, I went outside into the yard as I had still not been able to pull off the scissors, which had raised a painful blister on my hand. I was hoping to find a woman with whom Sarah and I had been friendly and ask her to help me remove them. But I didn't see her and, if I didn't get back quickly, someone else would finish off my soup. I was resigned to eating with my left hand when I saw a man, an SS officer, staring at me on the other side of the barbed wire.

"'*Grosse Probleme, schones Fraulein?*' he asked in a pleasant tone.

"I placed the voice right away. It was the top official from the selection place in Warsaw. He still thought me beautiful, as he had on that day, even after what I'd been through. True, my hair had grown back and I no longer had a bald, shaved skull, but I felt that I had finally grown ugly beyond recognition. There were no mirrors in the women's barracks, but I was later to see that I had still not changed much, that I was one of those freakish people who simply continue to bloom no matter how severe the drought.

"From that moment I became a whore for the Nazis or, I should say, the private whore of one whom I shall call Martin Lentz. His true name has been eradicated from the earth and is not for me to pronounce. Oh yes, I was also once again the mistress of a married man.

"It was actually against the laws of the Third Reich for Aryans to screw members of inferior races, especially Jews. But quite a bit of it went on and the Germans just pretended it wasn't happening. A great many things were taking place at that time that the entire world simply refused to acknowledge, so you can imagine a little thing like a Jewish concubine-cum-housekeeper was easy to sweep under the carpet. Especially if she happened to look more German than the German himself. I'm sure that no one in the camp where Lentz was in command suspected what my background was and Lentz passed me off as a real Pole. As soon as I began to feel safe I regretted everything, knowing I had become a despicable creature. But there was no going back.

"I lived well from then on and lacked for nothing. Lentz wanted me to call him Martin, but I avoided calling him by any name as much as possible. I didn't object when he made me have my tubes tied against pregnancy. I never expected to live to be thirty, much less have children. I didn't hate Lentz at all, for that matter, and even making love with him ceased to be a trauma after a while. That is not to imply that I cared for him in any sense of the word. I cared for no one. Not for the Jews, not even for myself. Psychologically, I had removed myself from the camp and spent hours just daydreaming about my life in Warsaw before evil had come into its own in the world.

"It remains only for me to say about this bizarre situation that Martin Lentz truly loved me. What had been denied me by Adam Feder, this member of the Master Race, Lentz, lavished upon me without reservation. His greatest fear was that the Nazis would win the war soon and he would be forced to go home to his wife. I think he missed the children, though, this man who was untroubled by the idea of millions of children going up in smoke.

"Yes, Lentz often thought of his children. He loved to play with my hair, braid it, comb it, as he spoke to me of them. Only I and his little Hansi at home had hair of that color, like real gold, he said. To this day it refuses to turn gray, as if by Lentz's everlasting order. I looked more like little Hansi's mother than Lentz's own wife, he claimed. What a laugh that was. But I had lost my sense of humor.

"Were you wondering what had become of Adam Feder or have you forgotten him? I still thought of him quite often, but I never dreamed he was still alive. How that fastidious, dandified character made it through the Holocaust, I'll never understand, but there he was one day in the yard with the others. Feder was the merest ghost of himself, but I would have recognized that face anywhere, no matter what. Of course I made sure he saw me right away, but this time there were rows of electrified wire between us. Do you think that it didn't pass through my mind that he would once again refuse to know me? But by now times and fortunes had altered themselves beyond a hint of what had formerly been. Feder looked as though he'd been struck by a bolt of lightening. When he assembled his wits, he rushed over to the fence, coming as close as he dared.

" 'My God, it's Halina! Halina, don't you remember me? My beautiful darling, you don't know how happy I am to see you!'

"Then it must have dawned on him that I looked too well, that my dress was too fine, for he backed off a little.

" 'But, Halina, what are you doing here?'

" 'Working, Adam,' I said, 'working hard.'

"He didn't pursue it. 'Well, at least you're alive and well. Will we see each other, Halina?'

"I assured him that we would. 'Adam, aren't you going to ask me what became of your wife, Sarah? She was with me at Auschwitz.'

" 'She's dead.'

" 'How did you find out?' I wanted to know.

" 'I never thought she'd make it. She wasn't the type to survive, poor Sarah.'

" 'Maybe not, ' I replied, "but one thing is for sure.'

" 'What is that, Halina?' Feder asked, coming nearer again. He was smiling at me in the way that used to make me melt. I believe he thought I was going to tell him that I still loved him. It seemed he wanted to reach out and touch me.

" 'Watch out. You'll electrocute yourself,' I cautioned. 'The fact is now, Adam, that you are a free man. How does it feel to be a free man at last?' With those words I turned away.

"From that day forward I lived only to torment Adam Feder. No, you mustn't imagine I did him any physical harm. On the contrary, I protected him. I told Lentz he was a relative of mine and that I would be grateful to have him unmolested. Lentz was anxious that Feder might spill the beans about my being a Jewess, but I told him that one warning from me would seal Feder's lips on the subject. This, you may be certain, put Feder in a most uncomfortable position. He could never be sure when I might decide to be rid of him. After all, he had the goods on me, especially if the Allies were victorious. There might be plenty of persons who would take the position that I should have died rather than sleep for three years with a murderer of my own people. If and when we were liberated, the inmates of the camp might decide to strangle me themselves. Not a day went by that I didn't pass casually by Feder and murmur, 'Don't make things difficult, Adam. You've got to go on pretending you don't know me or I don't know what I'll do with you.' It got so he was afraid to speak to anyone for fear that I'd think he was informing on me.

"So now what do you think of me, young man—Bob Samuels? Are you sorry that you spent this time listening to me? Do I disgust you now?"

I toyed with my fork. The noonday light had long ago left the cafeteria. Halina and I were the only patrons in the place.

"I think," I said, making sure to look her in the eye, "that you saved a man's life and tried to save the life of a woman. You may have spared people misery whom you never mentioned. The great harm was to yourself. You'll pardon my bluntness, I hope, when I tell you that is plain for anyone to see who has eyes in his head."

"Thank you," whispered Halina. "You are a very kind young man. If I had met someone like you in Warsaw before the war, I know everything would have been different. I would never have done what I did. I could have hidden myself from Lentz before he had a chance to take me away from Auschwitz. I might have tried to keep alive from day to day like the others did because I would have had something to look forward to. But I met Adam Feder instead."

"What about Feder?" I asked. "Did he make it?"

Halina shrugged. "I took care of this egotistical bastard until the last. When the Allies were approaching, Lentz fled and took me with him. I ditched him as soon as I was able. After that, I managed as best as I could. If I saved Feder, it wasn't out of compassion. I hated him, only him. That's why I didn't feel more revulsion for Lentz. I didn't even have a crumb of hate to spare for that one. Believe me, I would have been glad to spend the rest of my life persecuting Feder. He was a murderer, too, in his way."

I shook my head, no longer knowing what to say. I felt tired and confused. The cafeteria now seemed as gloomy as a cave and Halina appeared haggard, even witch-like. Her thin hands looked like claws. I imagined them tearing the flesh of Adam Feder. Halina venting her hatred on him one last time as the Allies marched into the camp. I had been prepared, no eager, to feel sympathy for Halina, but now I realized she had never solicited my pity. She had told me her story matter-of-factly and, had I pronounced her a monster, I don't believe she would have been upset. I envisioned her recounting the same tale to everyone who would listen, smiling inwardly as she waited for the listener to pass judgment on her, laughing silently at his inept attempt to explain her behavior, the lack of feeling that enabled her to endure the caresses of a slaughterer of her own kind, wanting her to be the heroine instead of the bitter opportunist.

I gazed at the people walking by the window and was momentarily unsettled by how sinister they appeared, how singularly incapable of doing good.

Perhaps Halina had read my thoughts. "Why are you so sad? All of it happened long ago. It was a bad dream, but it passed."

"I'm not upset," I lied. "I'm just thinking."

"I know what you're thinking—how can this old lady go around telling such things about herself so calmly? Doesn't she care what people think of her? Actually, I don't care. I only know what I think, how I feel about myself. Do you want to know what that is?"

"What?" I said, rather nastily, I'm afraid.

"I was wrong," said Halina. "I thought because I was young and pretty and a victim that I had the right to preserve my life. But that was false. Many persons younger and prettier and certainly more gifted were reduced to ashes. What I had was a great opportunity and I refused to make use of it. I had fallen into Lentz's hands, certainly, but, in a way, he had also fallen into mine. Every night I could have taken his pistol and put a bullet into his head. I could have killed him more easily than Yael did Sisera in the tents of ancient Israel. Yes, that is exactly what I should have done."

"What good would that have done? You would have been killed yourself and somebody just as bad would have come to take Lentz's place."

"That's true. There's a never-ending supply of evil in this world, but so what? It's up to every decent person to strike a blow where he can, not simply survive and let others do the striking." Halina gave a little moan. "Well, I was complacent, but I received my punishment. That part I didn't leave to others."

"I don't get it," I told her. "You mean that, out of guilt, you did something to hurt yourself?"

Halina smiled in an odd and terrible way. "I guarantee it." She patted my hand. "You'd better go now, Bob Samuels. I've exhausted myself and probably gotten you into trouble. Go, nice young man. You've been as patient as a saint."

I left Halina. I never went back to the cafeteria again. I didn't have the courage. I didn't want to hear any more details. But for a long time I felt burdened with the thought of what I would have done had I been Halina in her awful circumstances. Ultimately, I had to give up wondering. I realized the futility of trying to put oneself in the place of another.

That same day I went back to work just as the office was about to close. I made up a story for my boss about having been detained by the police after witnessing a car accident He looked at me rather quizzically but only said, "You look like you've been in an accident, yourself."

On the way to the bus stop going home, a funny notion came to me. On a hunch, I slowed down in front of a little store that had a display of hats in the window, flamboyant hats like those black men are given to wearing. There were ties, too, wide crazy ones with palm trees and setting suns. Through the dirty glass I caught sight of Halina hunched over the counter, conversing with an old man. At first I thought he was a customer, but then I saw he was wearing a classy, well-cut suit and that his accessories would never come from a shop such as this one. I knew for sure he wasn't a customer when Halina seemed to speak sharply to him and give him a dirty look before she went into the back room, not to reappear.

But the old fellow wasn't leaving. He got behind the counter, himself, and turned a mirror-stand around so that it faced him. Carefully adjusting his own tie, he looked at his reflection with one eyebrow cocked, as if he were a sharp-looking thirty-year-old getting ready to impress a date. The old man was so busy preening, he never noticed me.

There was no question in my mind that I was observing none other than Adam Feder, Halina's husband, a survivor in every sense of the word.

The Privacy of Storm

James C. Schaap

T HAT JANUARY blizzard was one of those storms people talk about two days before it hits, but one of those that comes in anyway—despite all the hoopla. Glenda thought most of the highly touted storms swooped north to dump themselves on the Twin Cities. Others, heavy-bellied, never made it up the prairie to Siouxland; they lumbered along through Missouri instead, taking slow but sure aim on Chicago. The ones people talked a lot about rarely came—it could have been a rule, like February's groundhog.

But the weatherman said this one was all geared up to get them, and this time, after two long gray days, he was right. Glenda wished Nicky was still young enough to forecast storms. When he'd been a toddler, she swore she could tell when the storms were coming by the way he'd crowd her, upstairs and downstairs, even in the basement—never begging attention really, just a bit squeamish about leaving her side. But he was older now. Every night his father had him out in the barn for chores, even though he was still too young to help much.

That baby Nicky should be able to feel storms coming wasn't such an odd notion either. Hank Lemmons bought buffalo one summer when he got sick of beef prices, and he kept them on his place, a mile north and a half west. Lemmons became a true believer in buffalo, singing their praises whenever he could, as if he was sure the whole world would be better off going back to the days of the Yankton Sioux. It was Lemmons who told her that a buffalo could smell blizzards—how they bunched up around whatever shelter they could find maybe a whole day before a storm. "Better even than arthritis," Lemmons told her one winter morning. "I don't need a radio."

When Mark and Nicky came in for supper, she heard the rustle of their jackets in the back hall, the zing of their zippers, and Nicky's heels banging against the basement step. "Careful there," Mark told him. "You'll ram a hole in those boots sure thing, and your mom won't let you hear the end of it."

She disliked the way Mark cast her as the villain.

The two of them came up the steps into the kitchen. "See how dark it is out there," he said. "She's starting to roll now. It's going to be a big one." He bit on a raw carrot from the relish tray, then pulled out a chair and sat.

Glenda dried her hands and looked out beneath the shade she had drawn earlier in the afternoon to cut out the draft. The barn seemed less than a shadow in the mist of snow. "Doesn't seem so bad really," she told him.

She broke a stick of margarine in half and dropped it in a dessert dish, knowing full well Mark wouldn't like it so hard and cold, just out of the fridge. He picked up a roll and split it with his fingers. His cheeks burned from the lines of his chin to his temples, where the imprint of his cap pressed his straight hair up around his forehead.

Winter storms excited him, even though he knew they were dangerous. She could feel it in his quick movements, the way he buttered the roll up near his eyes.

"You can plan on storms whenever things are happening in the barn," he said. "If I've got sows farrowing, we get dumped on. It'll be late tonight probably."

When she put down the bowl of pea soup, Nicky's nose scrunched up, just as she knew it would. "You think you're not going to like it, don't you?" she asked him.

He crossed his arms over his chest.

"I can't help thinking about Rachel up there in that trailer," Mark said. "Can you imagine what it must be like to hear that wind howl if you lived your whole life in Florida?" He jerked Nicky's chair up close to the table and pointed at the soup. "That stuff'll put hair on your chest," he said. "Just eat it."

She had known the moment she reached for the split peas that Nicky would hate the soup. Mark didn't care for it much himself. But her mother always said that in life you didn't necessarily have to like some things that, plain and simple, had to be done. It wasn't until you got older that you really started to understand how much life was like cod liver oil or something.

"Come on, Nicky—no dessert otherwise," she said.

"Feels so icky in your mouth," he said.

That angelic blond look was long gone. Second grade already and his dad had bought him a BB gun to shoot sparrows in the barn.

"You going to check on Rachel?" Mark said. "Give her a ring."

"She's just a kid," Glenda said. "She doesn't worry yet." She cradled a spoonful of soup and blew on it gently, while behind them the radio voice ran down the hog prices and talked about open gilts. With the wind outside, she thought it was the right kind of night for pea soup.

"You got everything ready just in case we got to stay put for a while?" he said.

She knew Mark didn't mean it to sound like he was her supervisor. It was only his way of checking. For eight years she had heard him say things that way, and there were times she disliked the voice of his authority, the purity that shone from his eyes like a Sunday school badge.

*

When she had finished the dishes, she turned off the radio and picked up the phone because Mark was right about calling Rachel. They were newlyweds, little Rachel and her husband, Hilbert—a nice kid, a serious kid that everybody on the ridge called Hibby. "Hibby and Rachel" it had said on the napkins they had printed up for their wedding reception in Siouxland. They had been married in Florida, of course, where Rachel's father was a preacher. Her maiden name was Bleyenberg, and most people knew her father because he was a preacher who had been born and reared not too far south of town.

Now his daughter, a surgary blond, perfectly tan, had come back to make a home where her own father had once lived. She and Hibby had met at the preacher's alma mater. They got married and bought a trailer on an acreage. The place had an old barn, a machine shed in pretty good shape, and a couple of run-down buildings not much use to anybody. Hibby worked in town on the kill floor of a packing plant, but he raised some hogs in the barn. Mark helped him nail up a pen outside the east wall to get him started, because Hibby wanted to farm. He was like Mark that way. They both wanted to farm in the worst way.

"Rachel?" she said, "this is Glenda. You're in for your first big storm, you know that?"

Rachel winced, as if she were already scared.

"What's the matter?" Glenda said.

"Hibby's in town on second shift," Rachel said. "I was thinking how nice it would be, locked up for a couple days together—you know?—and he's in town. It's like a bad joke— "

Glenda remembered the way a northwest wind made the windows of their own trailer sing when she and Mark were first married. She tried not to remember the trailer anymore, that honeymoon time, because it seemed so far behind them.

"It would be funnier if I wasn't all alone," she said, her voice coming up through the receiver in twists of emotion—humor like frosting over everything else.

"Maybe you ought to walk over here if you think— "

"Then Hibby comes in and I'm gone?"

"I mean, if you're going to be sick about being alone— "

"He's coming yet, I'm sure of that. You know how men are."

She and Mark had them over to play cards when they first moved in down the road. Ten years difference there was between them, and Mark claimed at first he didn't know how to talk to them—whether Hibby should be a little brother or a friend. Glenda knew what she thought of Rachel. There was still so much she had to know about.

"If you get lonely or something, come on over— "

"Maybe I'll just call."

The silence between them stretched uncomfortably. She and Mark used to hang on like that before they were married, when Mark was away at Tech. It was expensive, but sometimes they would just stand there and breath into the silence, as if there were some part of each other reaching all the way through the wire. "Just give me a ring then, Rachel—anytime," Glenda said.

"How long do these things last anyway?"

"Maybe just overnight." She knew better.

"What happens if he doesn't get home anymore?"

"He'll stay in town. He'll be all right."

Rachel took one long breath into the mouthpiece.

"You got power, and you got food," Glenda said. "It's going to be — "

"What happens if my furnace goes out?"

"Burn down the trailer," Glenda said.

Rachel's laugh stumbled out slowly.

"Just keep in touch. Call me every half hour if it gets bad—you promise?"

"You think I'm helpless up here?" she said.

"You've never been through one of these things, Rachel— "

"Back in the dorm— "

"Look around—you're not in the dorm anymore."

Glenda remembered how it was when they were in the trailer. She and Mark would sit across from the wall where the gusts hit, even change the position of the television just to stay away from the wind sneaking through the thin walls. Once Mark lit a candle just to show her the draft.

She didn't even like to have coffee at Rachel's—that's how much she disliked trailers.

*

Whenever they played Rook, Mark always insisted it should be the men against the women, like some silly playground game, "Boys Catch Girls." Glenda guessed Hibby didn't like the pairings, because he'd always sit there and bid against his wife, his cards fanned out in one hand, his other hand down on his Rachel's thigh. It wasn't principle or anything with Mark, only habit—as if teaming with his wife would be silly when two women and two men made such natural rivals.

One night in late fall Hibby and Rachel came over for pizza.

"Thirty-five," Mark bid, his cards in one neat stack on the table.

She had no patience for his bidding so ridiculously low, even though she'd heard him say a hundred times how low bids are the only way partners have of communicating. She didn't have a bad hand, but there wasn't enough for a real trump suit

"Pass," she said, even though she knew Mark would have hiked up the bid if he held her hand. He always gambled on the blind.

"Oh, Glenda," Rachel said, "I can't take anything."

Hibby bid fifty, and Mark took the first-hand bid cheap at 125 when Rachel pulled up her nose and quit. Mark was merciless; he had this way of slapping down cards with a flick of the wrist, and smacking the table with the heel of his hand, as if the two or three really important tricks were stunning blows.

"Been over at Senard's yet?" Hibby asked him in the middle of the third hand.

Glenda didn't like anyone talking when she was trying to choose which card to play. She tried to concentrate on the trick out in front of her.

"I'm not going to do it anymore this year," Mark said. "It's a shame too. I got this big, absolutely useless barn out there. Senard could build me a pretty decent set-up for the money, but I guess it's not going to happen yet."

She knew very well what Mark was saying.

"You going to hatch those cards or what?" He looked at her and rapped the edge of a card against the table.

Glenda tried to remember what had been laid.

"Hog prices aren't hurting anybody right now," Hibby said. "Some people say they're still going up."

"I know," Mark said. "It's not money that's holding me back either—" and he stopped right there, leaving the truth standing naked before them. It was perfectly clear that she was the one holding him back. He left this gaping hole—big enough for Hibby to know who was at fault for there being no new steel building this year.

She dropped down a big counter, and Mark swept it up with a low trump, just as if he knew exactly what she would lay.

*

"You wouldn't believe what happened," Rachel said when she called a little before nine. "He took off work early in order to get home, because they were going to close up anyway—because of the storm, you know?—but he slid in the ditch between here and town, so he's walking. I love it. It's so romantic. He called from the Hermanson place."

Laughing came easier to Rachel now. "He was alone in the car?" Glenda asked.

"I guess so."

She knew she could slay Rachel with worry if she wanted to. She tried to figure out what she could say.

"So what's the big deal?" Rachel said.

"I just hope he doesn't try to be a hero about it— "

"He said it's pretty bad out there, so he's going to stop at every farm place and call me—just to tell me how he's doing."

Glenda had the telephone company put in a long cord so that she could look out in the yard while she talked on the phone. She raised the shade and stared at the vapor light above the machine shed, its blur cut and stretched by the wave of snow running almost horizontally through the bright blue of its glow.

"Don't worry about it, Rachel— " she said.

"I'm not worried," she said. "He said he was coming."

*

Mark sat with his holey gray socks up in front of the TV. He wore two pairs, so at least his toes weren't sticking out. Nicky was already asleep because most of the day he'd been outside. Mark had put him up to bed without a fuss.

The sound of the wind was like a train of railroad cars so long it never quite made it past you, its low rumbling moan so constant that you heard it only when you remembered that there was a time when it wasn't there.

Mark wasn't really watching the television. His wrist bounced slightly off the arm of the chair as if he was listening to music that Glenda didn't hear.

"You think she knows what it's like for him to walk home on a night like this?" he said.

Glenda looked up from the catalog as if his question had awakened her. "I don't know. I don't think so."

He brought his hands up in front of him and took little careful bites around the ends of his fingers. "Must be a lonely thing for a girl like that, being up there alone most of the time." He pulled his hands away from his face and curled his fingers up to check his nails.

"You sure are worried about her— "

He turned to her. "I mean, the waiting. That girl's just waiting to get pregnant, isn't she? Have herself a little kid."

Mark was right. In December Rachel had Glenda over to help make Christmas candy, and she told her as much in no uncertain terms. "We're trying to have a baby," she said, while both of them stood there with sticky fingrs. "It's something I've always wanted, I think," she said. "Not many of my college friends understand it, but you know what I mean, don't you?"

With a smile and a nod, Glenda tried to say that she knew.

"That's a full-time job in my book," Rachel had said. "I want to get just royally pregnant."

Glenda put a fold in the catalog page and put it down next to her. "How is it you think you know something that personal about those two kids?" she said.

He yawned and rubbed the heels of his hands through his eyes. "You're not going to believe this, but I got sows that got the same look in their eyes."

"How can you say such a thing, Mark?" she asked.

"Didn't think you'd like it," he said.

She kept her eyes down on the catalog. Someday, she thought she'd have courage enough to tell him how much she hated his hogs. "How many other women you see in those sows?" she asked.

"Never did a census." He lifted his feet from the hassock and slid himself forward in the leather chair, arms braced up, his back leaning forward.

"What an awful thing to say," she said.

He twisted his head as if to say that she could take it or leave it, then he got to his feet and stretched, his arms rising in an arch up toward the ceiling.

"Where are you going?" she said.

"Don't ask," he said, his back toward her, both arms extended straight out to the side. He turned his upper body at the waist like an athlete loosening up. "I don't want you telling me that I'm getting old." Then he turned and faced her, his hands on his waist.

"Some things don't need to be said, Mark," she told him, picking up the catalog again.

"I'm going outside to put up ropes," he said. "I know you're thinking that too much worry is a sign of old age."

"Sometimes I like the thought of you being old," she said.

He stood there above her and put his holey sock on her knee, then gave her leg a little shove and walked away.

It was already close to ten. She guessed it would take him an hour or more to string the ropes between the house and the barn, to give himself some direction if the storm grew as bad as the howling made it sound. In a couple of minutes she could watch the TV weather, alone.

*

"He just called me from De Beys'," Rachel told her when she called again, just after ten. "Two miles to go."

"Could he see all right?"

"He said it was the cold that was getting to him more than the snow. Arnie gave him another sweater."

"Why don't you call your dad?" Glenda said.

"What on earth for?"

"Just to talk— "

"You think I want to hear how nice it is in Florida?"

"Maybe it's a dumb idea."

"He'd get a kick of it, all right—"

"I mean—maybe, if you get bored."

"It's kind of exciting right now, to think of Hibby out there bucking snowbanks just to get home to—"

She wanted to tell Rachel about the danger—make her grow up a little. "You got heat and everything yet?" she said.

"Really, Glenda, what happens if my furnace goes?"

"Put on the oven."

Rachel's laugh came in a blur over the wire. "Sounds like Hansel and Gretel or something—having your oven open."

Glenda twirled the cord through her fingers, something she never allowed Nicky to do.

"How we going to get the bedroom warm if the furnace goes out?" she said. "It's all the way on the other side of the trailer—"

"You been married six months—do I have to draw pictures?"

"It was a dumb question—"

"You just be waiting at the door and give him a squeeze for me too," Glenda said.

*

It had become all the rage for Siouxland young couples to have wedding receptions in restaurants or taverns. For years, they had been held in churches, but the old ways were gradually falling, like the old barns people used to rely on. But Rachel was a preacher's daughter, and Hibby's folks weren't the type to spend big money on a splash, so their Siouxland reception had been in the Fellowship Hall of the church. Glenda thought that was nice.

Hibby and Rachel were already married for a month, and that made the reception a little different, maybe a bit more quiet. All evening, it seemed, the newlyweds held hands, and when they looked at each other, somehow there was less of that embarrassed teenage passion other couples have when they cut the cake right after the ceremony. Not that they weren't in love. But even a month of marriage had aged them, made them exchange glances in a way that seemed less sly than the normal newlywed peeking.

For lunch the people marched up in rows toward three tables set with fruit, cheese, and salads. Maybe it was a Florida touch in the middle of Siouxland, a refreshing change from ham buns, potato chips, and dixie cups full of freshly cut cole slaw. Of course there was no liquor.

Mark himself started rapping his glass with his fork, the old way of telling the young-and-in-love that it was time for a full-fledged, married kiss. Hibby honored the request with great passion. But later, maybe the fourth or fifth time the glasses started tinkling, Hibby directed the request back at their neighbors, pointing directly at Mark with nothing less than the knife for the wedding cake. Suddenly, a church full of eyes turned on them. Glenda didn't know what to do with her hands when Mark picked her up by the shoulders, kissed her firmly on the lips and held it for what seemed forever, while all around them folks were oohing and aahing as if some perfect bronze foal had just been paraded before half the town at the 4-H fair.

"You know, you haven't kissed me like that for maybe five years," she told him before bed that night.

"That's a record that needs to be broken," he told her.

He didn't need to ask her—not that night.

One afternoon on their honeymoon, Mark had told her how before they were married he used to have such great fantasies about her in church. That was what she felt on the night of Hibby and Rachel's reception. The way they stood there together, the way they played with all the jokes, the way the two of them kissed in the chorus of ringing glasses—the two of them in that kind of love that people struggle not to outgrow—all of it affected her that night of the old kisses.

*

Mark was still outside when Rachel called again at 11:30 to say that Hibby had just been at Hank Lemmons's and was on his last leg. Rachel said she was so excited after Hibby said goodbye that she had forgotten to call them for a while. When she finally remembered, she worried that she'd wake them, because after all it was so late she figured they would be snuggled up in bed.

"No one's sleeping here yet, except Nicky," Glenda told her. She didn't tell her that Mark was out stringing ropes.

"I'm so excited," Rachel said. "This is so great. Nothing like this ever happens in Florida."

Years ago, Mark's roommate at Tech had tried to make it home one Friday night with a carload of kids when he should have stayed put in the middle of a storm. They went in the ditch, and with little gas in the tank, they decided to try to foot it to the nearest farm house. In the driving snow they could see no lights, but they walked, arm in arm, down what they thought was the road, changing directions whenever their steps fell off into ditches on either side. Blinded, they walked too close to death, and some went crazy in snowbound panic. Some had to be carried, half-laughing, half-wailing, almost against their will. Finally, they spotted a light in an old barn just off the road, on a deserted farm place. It was a horror story that everyone talked about back then, but Glenda didn't tell Rachel any of that.

"Maybe a half hour yet, you guess?" she asked.

"I expect him any minute," Rachel said. "He's anxious to get here. I can feel it in my bones."

"Try to remember to call when he gets home," Glenda said. "I mean, just to let me know that everything's all right— "

"Once he gets in the door, I'll probably forget," she told her, with a growly laugh. "You know what I mean, don't you?"

"I wasn't born yesterday," Glenda said.

When she put down the receiver, she wondered whether it wouldn't be better if people never grew up, never lost Rachel's enthusiasm.

She pulled a kitchen chair up next to the refrigerator and took down all the candles she could find from the cupboard where she kept stuff she rarely used. She laid them on the counter between the kitchen and the dining room, along with matches, then picked up a little around them, so that if she had to grope in the dark they would be there.

It was more than an hour since Mark left to put up the ropes.

Tomorrow it would be calm and cold, she told herself. Tomorrow drifts would run like waves between the buildings, curl around the corners of the house and stand there between barn and house as if they'd been there since the beginning of time. Tomorrow the temperature in the stillness would drop below zero, and the snow would crack beneath Mark's boots when he stepped in the back hall.

Out in the grove a kingly ringneck pheasant paraded around on some winter mornings, as if it were a pet. Sometimes she would see him out back, his feathers rich with gaudy coloring, from the green of his neck through the rich brown that lay beneath the march of chevrons down his tail. Against the blinding white, he seemed almost painted, like a cartoon drawing strutting over the crust of frozen snow. She wondered how he would suffer the storm.

Once Mark caught Nicky shooting at the pheasant with his little air rifle, and he scolded his son for what seemed to her less naughty than horrifying.

When she raised the curtain, she saw only a blur of light from the shed in the shredding lines of blowing snow. She wondered how much longer it should take him to string the ropes.

*

She realized once upstairs that she had no reason to check up on Nicky. There was no reason to think he shouldn't be fast asleep, and he was, his body only half-covered with blankets, one foot, warmly covered with a boot from his favorite football pajamas, hanging over the edge of the bed as if it were mid-summer.

Nicky would sleep in nothing but his briefs all summer, and most of the time he would need no covers, not even a sheet. Nicky was like his father that way. Always hot, even in winter.

She closed the door to the closet he had left open on the northeast side of the room where the brunt of the storm was punishing the outside walls. A closed closet door would take the edge off the cold. In the dim light from the bathroom, she could just see the innocence on his face. She picked up his foot and edged it back beneath the blankets, then smoothed back the hair from his forehead, as if she were preparing him for church.

She stood there and let the silence of the house surround her, the blizzard's slow siren rising and falling. The snow was too light to sound against the window; the temperature had fallen already. Beneath the closet door, cold air inched out from the outside wall and swept across the wood floor, sneaking through the worn edges of her houseslippers.

In winter she loved to put her cold feet up against Mark's calves when they lay, their backs together, in bed. He never seemed to mind.

It was nearly twelve when she came down from Nicky's bedroom, and Rachel still hadn't called. Lemmons probably told Hibby to take a lesson from his buffalos and stay overnight. But Hibby wouldn't have listened, not with Rachel waiting for him.

Glenda picked up her carpetbag from the bottom drawer of the bureau in the dining room, and pulled out some of Mark's gray socks, but before she started mending, she went around the house, putting on lights as if she were expecting visitors after church. She sat in the kitchen in a padded chair with the socks out in front of her, then rose and pulled up the shade so Mark could see the kitchen lights through the storm.

She wondered if he had worn enough clothing when he went out to string up the ropes.

Farm socks were gray because there was no reason for them to be pretty. They wore like iron, kept his feet warm, and ran up above his ankles high enough to cover the bottoms of his long johns, but they looked forever dirty, even on Monday afternoon after a wash, when she lined his upstairs drawer with clean pairs. It took years to wear them through, but when they did they usually gave out right at the point of his toes. She told him he bought them too tight, but it was one of those things that he never seemed to hear. Every piece of dress clothing he owned she had bought for him at some time, but coveralls and socks were two things he bought for himself in town.

There was a time when she enjoyed mending them. That first year in the trailer, when everything was new to her, when watching him shave and strut around in his underwear seemed naughty and sweet, back then she loved sitting there with him in front of the TV, her fingers twirling needles for him. Everything was different then—making him lunch as if she would be getting a grade, buying him ties, feeling him next to her, asleep, with his hand over her breast, feeling desire run through her so spontaneously, any hour of the day.

One summer afternoon he had come in from walking beans. It wasn't hot, and he wasn't sweaty. But maybe he was. Maybe she didn't think of it then. More than a month already they had been married. She had made turkey sandwiches, because her own mother said turkey was a good thing to cook—cheap and usually good for a lot of different meals. He came in without his shirt, his neck and back and chest bronzed, and they had dessert in the bedroom.

They heard the doorbell but had never heard any car come on the yard, and there they lay as if caught in the act. It rang again and again.

"Let it go," Mark said.

"You left the TV on out there," she whispered.

"Who cares?"

It rang again.

"Mark—" she said. "They'll know we're here—"

He put his finger up to her lips.

Some guy on the TV was trying to sell used cars.

Four times it rang, then twice in succession. All the windows were open, and she'd left the salad on the table, right there in front of the door.

In the very middle of it he reached over and kissed her, and she was powerless to move, afraid of making a sound. With her chin she pushed him away, fighting back giggles.

It rang again, then there was a blast of fists on the screen door.

"We've got to answer—"

"Sshhhhh—besides, what's it going to look like now? He's been there for five minutes." He grabbed at her ribs, and she turned her face into the pillow to stop from laughing aloud.

When they heard the car pull away, Mark stood there naked, looking out through the window. "It's the preacher," he said.

"You got to be kidding—"

"At least he knows we got a good marriage," Mark had said.

She sat there remembering, her hands full of gray socks. It was after twelve already. Through the kitchen window she could see the snow swirl as if in clouds. Mark had been gone for two hours. Sometimes pheasants died in blizzards when their eyes froze shut.

She thought of calling Rachel herself. The walk from Lemmonses' couldn't have taken so very long; by now Hibby must have made it. She could call and find out. She wanted to know for sure that everything was all right with them. She stuck the socks back in the carpetbag and sat at the desk near the phone, running her finger around the circle in the middle where they'd printed their number.

Mark should have been in by now, and Rachel should have called. Maybe Hibby was home. She could call, but then she'd disturb them—catch them in bed, like the preacher. It shouldn't be hard to know what was happening, just from the number of rings—if Rachel was sitting there waiting, the phone wouldn't ring more than twice. If she wasn't waiting, it would go on and on—five rings and she'd know what was happening.

She picked up the receiver and listened for the buzz. The phone wasn't dead. She dialed six digits then waited to be sure she was doing the right thing. Even four rings and she would know what was happening. This time she would be the preacher. "At least he knows we've got a good marriage," Mark had said.

Mark was still outside, of course, She put down the phone because she wasn't ready to talk yet, wasn't ready to hear Rachel's voice puffing from the run through the trailer from the bedroom.

And she wasn't ready to tell her that she was worried sick about Mark right now. Hibby would think he'd have to come over, and Rachel would be alone again. She couldn't be responsible for that. Maybe Rachel would insist on coming along. That would be worse.

For the first time, it dawned on her that it wasn't Rachel who needed her, it was she who needed Rachel.

Just then the chirping of the back door hinge came up through the hall and kitchen behind her. She heard him pound his boots on the rug at the door, and she listened to the sound of his coat slipping from his shoulders, the creaking wood beneath the back steps. Joy and relief ran through her arms and hands and fingers.

She twisted out of the chair and went to the top of the steps, where she saw him, his back to her, unlacing his boots.

"I swear I'll never understand those sows. Something in a storm that makes them want to farrow—I'm sure of it," he said without looking up. "You weren't worried, were you? I figured I'd better stay out and supervise."

His coat hung from its hood on the hook.

"Maybe I should have come in to tell you, but I figured after this long together you wouldn't worry anymore." He turned his face up to her at the top of the stairs. His cheeks were proud red, and his hair was tinged with sweat that ran in a band around his head. Frost and snow turned his mustache into silver brush beneath his nose. "Tell me you weren't worried, Glenda— "

She hid her smile purposely. "You don't have to know everything— "

"Glenda," he said, "you're kidding— " He slapped his gloves together over the rug on the floor and laid them, one beside the other, on the shelf along the wall.

"Rachel's fine," she said. "Hibby's home."

He stood up and smiled, then came up the stairs in his socks and stood beside her. "I'm getting so dumb old," he said. She took him and held him, his arms around her like a blessing.

"I started to worry about losing power, so I got the heaters going now. Things are popping out there, just like I told you. I went upstairs and got down some extra straw—just in case I'd need it later." He patted her shoulders his way, almost too hard. "That old barn comes in handy sometimes, I guess, Glenda."

In her fingers, the flannel shirt felt warm and moist.

"Maybe a little brandy would chase out the chill," she told him. "A nightcap."

He took her shoulders in his hands and narrowed his eyes. "What're you offering anyway?" he said.

*

She was still awake when the phone at the side of the bed rang. She watched it ring—three, four times—in the glaze of light from the digital clock Mark had given her for Christmas. It was two o'clock.

Finally, it woke him. "You just going to let it ring?" he said.

"You just go back to sleep," she said. "It's none of your business— " She put her arm over his chest and reached for the phone with the other hand.

"Glenda? I'm so sorry," Rachel said. "I just thought of it now— "

Mark's breath lengthened softly. He was already asleep.

"It's all right," Glenda said. "Everything's all right."

Flowers in January

Judith K. Healey

W HY DID I DO IT? You might as well ask, my family did, every one of them, my mother with shock fading all across her face and dad, well, he turned his face totally away, but then he'd done that before and he'd always come around. Although this time mom said he was still furious when they got home; he sat in the kitchen for a long time, staring, and when she sat down and tried to talk to him his face reddened and he pounded his fist on the table and then she said he cried, I'd never seen him do that in all the years I've known him . . .

Oh, well, even if I can't explain to them maybe you will understand. It was in the spring that I met Zae. I still remember the flowers were out and Gordie called one Saturday; he was my second cousin and we wound up taking one of our classes together. I never knew him real well before we did an evaluation project, you know, one of those graduate School of Social Work projects that neither of you is interested in but you think you might use some of the data in your major paper and we got to be good friends so when he called on Saturday and said some people were coming over, I felt like seeing him. And sure enough his place looked just like he did, sort of messed up, records all over the place and lots of books; sometimes at parties if the conversation did not suit me I could look at people's books and these were, oh, my kind, not just social work books but Fanon and Cleaver and Friere. Books around change questions, about the way things are for some people, maybe for all of us and maybe I smoked a little too much because I didn't know anyone there. I do remember moving out the back door to the little yard where there was a table loaded with beer and wine and someone was cooking sausage on a grill but there was another sweet scent. All I could smell was these flowers, alyssum, that's what it was, all around when I met him, that's what I remember and he was just sweet, there was no other word for him. I saw him as soon as he came, it was late and he just walked over to me and sat down and spoke softly as if we'd known each other for ages, he said, "I wondered where you were," and, oh man, I was gone, and then we both started to giggle. I was a little high already and we just sat there and smoked for a while then he put his hand on my arm and we just left. I mean there was none of this small talk like in high school or college; where do you live? what is your major? what does your dad do? It was just us and all the rest didn't matter, oh, I can't explain it any other way, if you haven't been there you won't understand and if you have I don't need to say anymore. It was sweet in bed too. I was really high by that time but it didn't matter, he was everything to me and if I had been sober it would have been no different. We left the lights on I remember and his skin was so soft and brown and he was tender and he made the room swing around and there was a haze around the light on the ceiling, I remember that too. And oh, God, there was never a man as gentle as he was, I thought, he couldn't have been very high. And when I woke up in the morning he was gone, there was a space in the bed where he'd been and it almost felt warm. I remember I had a terrific head and I decided to stop drinking wine, stick to pot, no afterhead and it was all like a dream to me but I could smell those damn flowers that had gotten into my clothes my hair my hands my mouth.

I didn't see him again until Christmas or almost Christmas, I lost track of the days but snow was falling one Saturday morning and I remember I had some old Dylan on and was trying to get myself together to work on my paper. Gordie called. I can still hear his voice and he said Zae's in prison and I said who? Because I didn't even know the name and he said Zae, you remember, and oh, yes, did I ever. Then it all came back. So? I said, remembering too that after that one night of touch and swimming light, I hadn't seen Zae again and part of me said, What kind of a name is that anyway? But Gordie kept right on going and said he was on his way up to see Zae and Zae was asking for me and would I come and Jesus, I didn't know what for. Why do you go see someone in prison when all he ever was to you was a terrific fuck? That can't happen there and besides, we'll both be sober; on the other hand those damn flowers were everywhere and how can I explain that I was still on the phone and pulling on my jeans because there wasn't much time?

Another thing you won't understand unless you have been there is the prison, the slammer, the Big Mama, Jesus there's something about it! When I walked in I shrank up next to Gordie and he looked a little schizy himself, just a flicker in his eyes. Of course he'd never been there he was such a nice middle-class kid, so straight, his father was a doctor in Edina but I knew he'd been dealing and

I knew why he looked so hunted. That goddam middle-class conscience, he grew up Catholic. It's like you're always scared. You're driving and you see a cop, you remember all the stop signs you've run, how you always speed on the open road, there's something called guilt all right.

Now Zae, on the other hand, indeed that was or is his name and when I asked about it he said it was the name of an African king, sure I said, but he looked terrific when they brought him in to see us, he looked like his name belonged. No guilt for him, I could almost hear him thinking how only honkies have middle-class Lutheran neighborhoods where you learn guilt with your alphabet. And he seemed real glad to see me, said he thought I'd never come, and his words were as soft and brown as his body and oh his eyes and I remembered his gentleness and felt warm.

And when he got out two weeks later I was his sponsor and he moved in with me right away without even asking, I mean there was no conversation between us much but we got along together just fine. I took the quarter off from school, told myself I'd work on my paper but I really just wanted to be with him. We would sleep late like kids and wake up and make love and then sometimes go outside and play in the snow and then make coffee and sit. Sometimes he would talk about how it was growing up in Alabama, the hot summer nights when kids ran in packs 'cause there was nothing much to do, and how they were always in trouble but then what are kids for, right? And any time I would get close to a serious question like what had he done lately, what had put him away for six months, he'd just tease me, make me laugh, and sometimes we would wind up right there on the floor and who could argue with that?

All through the month of January it was a delight, like one great snowball of fun, the trouble is I can't really get the feeling back much when I sit down to think about it because February came so fast and you know how bitter the winter gets in Minnesota. Those are the feelings I get when I remember that year.

It changed slowly at the time although it seems abrupt when I look back on it; after Zae had been out four, maybe five, long lovely weeks things began to fall apart beginning with him staying out late one Friday night. After we had us a terrific dinner, I had gone out shopping and when I got home and called for him the house was empty: a strange kind of emptiness like the echo of my own voice coming back in someone else's tone. You have to understand it seemed like we'd been together forever and that we were together almost every minute but still when that old echo rolled back at me, I got this sinking feeling. I knew I really didn't know him very well at all, and there was a quick catch in my stomach. Oh, of course he did come in that night a few hours after midnight and he was a little high; I could tell right away as he slid into bed, warm with cold breath. Without turning around, I said where were you? And he said out and there was silence and I knew things were going to be different. I wanted to turn to him but I knew, I just knew, I couldn't do that and we both fell asleep quick.

The next day there was a strain between us. It was like we'd been traveling down this road together walking in perfect rhythm and suddenly we hit a construction zone and it broke us all up, there was no rhythm; he slept late that morning and I got up early and went for a walk in the snow. I wanted to bring us back to before but how? It wasn't even that I wondered where he'd been, if he'd seen some other woman or if he had friends he didn't want me to meet, none of that mattered. It was the unexpected, it was like some giant foghorn was sounding and I was heading for the rocks.

I had some coffee when I got home and got in my car and drove to see my friend Sal. We hadn't spent any time together since Zae had gotten out of prison and come to live with me but she knew how I felt; of all my friends Sal knew the most. She was a black woman but she didn't hold it against me that I was white and living with one of her men. She could have, you know, some do but she and I had been classmates for two years now and I could tell her about anything; she was just getting up, boiling water for instant coffee, and the windows on her small apartment were starting to steam up. What will I do, Sal? I felt like some whiney broad—how had I gotten this way so fast? Sal gave me a tough look. I could have told you, she said, but of course you never asked, you were hell-bent on havin' him and you didn't ask anyone; oh well, I wouldn't ask either. But what should I do, Sal? I wanted her to look into her half-drained coffee cup and spin out the next six months for me, just six months that's all, then I'll be ready to let go. But it was so beautiful bound up with someone in all that snow. Sal looked real serious at me. Honey, she said, what was he in for when you first met him? Dealing, I guess, Gordie never said a lot about it. Well, she said, dry and kind, you got yourself a peck of trouble; my advice to you is to get back to work, finish your paper and get your degree 'cause you sure got precious little goin' for you with that man and it's gonna get worse. I knew it was, I knew it was.

He didn't do that again for two more weeks and then he disappeared on a weekend, but this time it was less unexpected. I did indeed get my paper out, though it was hard to work on it with him around. Mostly he continued to sleep late in the mornings and I began to go to the library on the weekdays and when I would come home he would get up. Things were mostly good natured.

The morning the Sears bill came he was home but sleeping, so the mail was there and sticking out of the box and it was the first thing I saw as I came up the sidewalk. I thumbed through it while I pulled my snow boots off and saw a letter from my parents. Oh, Christ, I'd been able to put all thoughts of them out of my mind for six weeks, here we go, I bet they're coming to town and what will I do with Zae; could I put him in the closet? And the image flashed across my mind and I knew, when I could think of hiding him in fun, we were on our way down hill on a fast scooter. Then I tore open the other mail quickly and glanced at each piece, a few advertisements dressed up in color to relieve the February blahs, but no, I couldn't afford anything right now, my stipend from the university was meagre and Christmas had dented my savings and then I saw the Sears bill. Jesus Christ, they made a mistake was my first thought, the damn computer. Catholic guilt again, every time the billing computer at some store made a mistake I felt it was my mistake, I always felt like I owed the goddam bill anyway whether I did or not, just because they said I did. But I knew I hadn't bought anything since Christmas so I couldn't possibly owe them seven hundred fifty dollars for items charged since the January cutoff date, and I threw it on the counter and began to make some coffee and then I went back and looked at the bill again and a little shiver of light started to push its way across my brain, even though I resisted.

By the time Zae came down I was experiencing strong nausea, I think I made the coffee too black and also I was terrified of my anger, but most of all I believe I was beginning to be terrified of him and he put his arms around me and rubbed his cheek against mine, as if he could read my thoughts, uncanny. Let's go do something special today, he said. Like what? I asked. He said oh, I don't know, how about if I take you out for lunch? I don't think we can afford it, I said icily. That was a joke, Zae had no money to speak of and every time we had gone out to eat in the past six weeks I had taken us, counting out my pennies like every other graduate student, in or out of love, across the country. Oh, I've got some money, he said cavalierly and then I knew he had because, after all, I knew *we* did not have a new stereo, a two hundred dollar camera and a cuisinart and I got real scared and my head got this light feeling like I'd just had a joint. My knees were giving out and I knew I had to think, I went into the bathroom and locked the door.

The next afternoon I called Gordie. Zae is gone again, I said, come and talk to me, I need you. Uh, maybe we'd better meet somewhere else, how about the Mill? He said. See you there in half an hour. Did I hear him drag his answer? Maybe he knew too much, oh yeah, I could see when he walked into the Mill he knew too much. Hi, Gordie, I remember I said it very casually. Hi, he said, and then I said, Gordie, I got trouble. I put my hand on his arm so he would have to look at me because he was kind of looking around like he didn't want to meet my eyes or even worse, was maybe afraid. He did look at me as I touched him, and oh, his eyes; Is Zae dealing again? I asked and Gordie laughed a little tight sound. Why would you say that? He was very nervous, rubbing his right hand over his left, comforting himself. Why the fuck would I say that? I almost screamed, I could see Gordie was uncomfortable but I didn't care. You know what's going on, Gordie. I can only see an edge, I only know the pieces are missing, that man is slipping away, like he's melting right out from my arms, what is it? He's using again, isn't he? He's dealing, too. I felt like a teacher and student both, answering my own quiz, for one awful minute I stood right outside myself and saw the whole scene and I saw Gordie's face go pale. And he's in business with you, isn't he, Gordie, he's got my goddam credit cards, two of them anyway, he's charging on my accounts all over town, he's out all night and I can tell he's using again. He's shooting sometimes too, and then I just have to leave the house. Gordie put his hand on my arm, finally moved. By then I didn't care but I did notice, why don't you go to the police, he asked, and I said no, no. All through the month of February, all through this strangeness, I did think of the cops at least once a day. I can't do that, I said. Why he asked, probably more for himself than for me. I just can't yet, no, not yet, but can't you do something with him? You're his friend, make him stop. I started to cry, the goddam tears coming and I couldn't help myself. Gordie just sat there looking at me and he was slipping away too, slipping away folding right down underneath the table in his brown jacket, into the brown floor and I just got up and left him.

That afternoon my parents appeared, I just can't tell you how I felt when I came in from the supermarket and they were just driving up in the blue Chevrolet my dad kept insisting he couldn't afford to trade in. They drove up at the same time I was coming from Lake Street and we met right in front of the house. Hi, I said, real casual. I felt like I'd eaten a jar of cold peanut butter in a gulp and they each gave me a hug; we went inside but I was quaking.

Zae wasn't home, I was so glad. I guess for just one minute I thought my parents might save me, Ed in his argyle socks and his bowler, the same kind of hat he'd worn for twenty years, well, why not they were coming back now. If you keep a thing long enough it's bound to come back he's always said, and Stella in her green-olive coat and she wore a hat too. I'd never noticed it before, but she always wore a hat, just as she did when I was young and no one wore hats then either, and for one brief moment I thought it might really work, they might save me. How are things going? Ed asked as they settled in the living room. I'd made tuna fish sandwiches and turned the heat up. Well, just fine, I smiled. He nodded and of course we both knew they knew me well enough to see. Where's your fella? That was Ed's way of being nonchalant. Well, he's uh, gone right now, he's not here all the time, you know . . .

Where did you say he works? Stella chimed in, you really didn't write us much about him you know. I didn't know whether I wanted Zae to walk through the door and blow us away or if I wanted my father to call the police. Listen I finally said, after a silence so long my whole childhood fit into it, I think I want to tell you some things. Yes, said my father, sitting back and crossing his legs. Zae has been living here for two months. Yes, said my father, you already told us that; then there was another balloon of silence. I think I want him to move out but I don't know how to get him to do that. Why ever would you want him to go, I thought you liked him? Stella's eyes grew round with her struggle to understand. It's a long story, just believe me he should go, but things are never that easy. Well, in my day, Ed began but something in Stella's face stopped him and he leaned forward, like a miracle, and patted my knee. What can we do to help you, Honey? There are some problems, Dad, I just have to work them out myself but I think I've made a mistake here . . . you see, we had a ceremony so I can't just put him out on the street . . .

What are you saying, what are you saying? My mother had a face like a saucer. In her life there were quiet village streets with no traffic and in June the churches coughed out stiff figures in white and crinoline and young hairless men in dress suits like paper dolls with clothes tacked on. Wearing white and tuxedos for a few hours tells the rest of town that things would be different between them and there were the flowers, of course, the sweet smell of alyssum and the trees were in blossom; it was all on her face as she struggled with my words.

We had a civil ceremony, we're legally married, yes that's right it does complicate things, Gordie was there and Jeanette, she came high, I should have come high but that was later; there was snow, not flowers, and city hall doesn't look like a church in my town, so maybe it all didn't count. So you see, I was saying to them, I can't just throw him out, it 's going to be more difficult than that. Where did this happen, where did you get married as you call it? Ed leaned forward right to the end of his chair and I said city hall, early in January and Stella said oh, well, if you're not married in the Church, why that's a different thing, that's different, isn't it, Ed? So if you did this thing, Ed was saying, not paying any attention to Stella, why do you want to get out of it now? Because it's not working out, Dad, because there are problems. I got up and paced the tiny living room. Look, can't you just believe in me, take my word for it? I need help, not some lectures. Young lady, he said, don't talk to me that way, I'm still your father even though you are twenty-three years old and by the way, I wish you would act your age. He lit up a cigarette with a careful motion, something he always did when he was nervous and didn't know what to do with his hands; Stella started to clean up the dishes, that's what she did when life became too complicated. And just then, lucky for them because the conversation was bumping down a nowhere path, Zae walked in.

Ed carried it off well, but I must say Stella was only saved from the floor by the fact that when her knees gave way she happened to have a couch under her. Zae, oh hi, I said super casual and he smiled his charming smile and if looks could win he would have carried it off but the conversation was very stiff, words moving heavily back and forth, hanging in mid-air like clothes frozen on the line and pretty soon Ed and Stella put on their coats and their forty-year-old hats and began to leave. And I walked outside with them and how could I tell them I was glad to see them and it was okay that they couldn't fix my new problem like they had been able to fix things when I was little and had a stomachache or an earache or a teacher who didn't like me and for one minute Ed put his hand on my shoulder and squeezed it and then his face scrunched up and he turned and Stella hugged me and whispered why didn't you tell us? And then, as if she regretted saying it, she jerked away and dove into the open car.

Well, I worked it out myself of course, as the snow melted or almost melted, all cruddy brown and laying in desolate humps around, sort of in between time, not winter and not spring, there was no beautiful snow that we had played in and tossed in in January and no flowers yet poking up like when we first met and it's surprising how the good stuff only lasts for a little while and the pain seems to go on forever before you can do anything about it. I finally went to the police, I couldn't afford the bills and he just kept saying that it wasn't him, oh, he never got mean, never hit me or anything but I came home and told him I'd gone to the police; I was real scared and I told him to leave and never come back and he went, just like that. I guess he never thought I'd go to the police. He was gone an hour and I stayed in the kitchen when I heard him come down the stairs, just stayed there, sitting at the table smoking one cigarette after another thinking, when he's gone I'll get my paper finished, maybe I can wallpaper the bedroom, go to a play once in a while, there are lots of things I can do. I watched the snow melting, grudgingly falling in gobs from the neighbor's dirty roof. He just melted away; I think he went to stay with his cousin in Kansas City . . . I don't think he'll ever come back.

Fireworks

Mark Vinz

A WEEK BEFORE the Fourth and they're popping all over the neighborhood —the little ones are all that are legal now, the ones we used to call ladyfingers, the ones we wouldn't be caught dead with.

You'll put an eye out, my grandmother said every day. She was certain of it. I hated to disappoint her, but that's what I did best—blowing her jar lids thirty feet in the air, blowing up my model planes, vegetables from the garden, dolls and toy cars, grasshoppers and garter snakes. Your cousin lost his finger, Grandma said, but I knew that was from a blasting cap, not a firecracker. My cousin told me he couldn't figure out what it was so he thought he'd take it apart and then it went off and he was sitting there staring at the place his finger used to be.

I used to dream about missing eyes and fingers, that legion of wounded boys who didn't listen to their grandmothers. Even now, I have that dream sometimes— there must be a lot of us who do. Tell me, Grandma says, what are you going to do when you've spent all your money on fireworks? What are you going to do when you've blown everything up?

Pianola

Kristi Wheeler

L AST NIGHT, when I made love, I thought of this. But she beside me did
not know. I thought there is no music in the flesh without a death rattle,
that Widow Skillin's pianola had broken bellows, that it wheezed and I wheezed
pumping it. Is it those parts of the past we leave out of ourselves that separate lovers?

When I was ten, the Skillins lived in town, but I had no reason to see them
except these—that Mama'd told me not to mess and meddle with them—that I'd
seen the old man walking to the post office in a canvas coat with pockets bulging,
talking to leaves, "love, love," while four boys and me the fifth followed him with
"Bottles, oh Bottles Skillin" —and mostly that I'd once kissed the girl Mari Heather
Cagwell Skillin three times on the mouth and she'd counted one for the Father
and two for the Son and three for the Holy Ghost. Which was blaspheming,
so I'd given her a bone awl from the Indian graves, which I said would kill her
because she'd called it by its wrong name. "Bone owl," she'd laughed, "bone owl"
because she was only seven. These were my reasons which I kept to myself, for
I could keep all secrets except that one about my cousin's birthday horse. And
he was only my second cousin.

When Bottles Skillin had died and Mari Heather had asked . . . does it have
anything to do with bone owls . . . and I had said . . . no of course not it was
cancer . . . and she had asked . . . what is cancer . . . and I had said . . . well,
I heard it, well I don't know, well he was your grandfather . . . they moved out
of town, taking Mari Heather with them.

It was two years between then and the time when the furrows of Skillins' southwest forty were wet and I ran . . . when it was March because the ridges on either side of my feet were still hard with what Mother called a hairnet of frost. Mud cracked where I smashed along with my boots. Maples were spiked for sap. I passed the bedsprings lying beside Skillins' drive. Jump on the springs. That would make the curtains move. It was so quiet. A white tetherball hung limp on a pole. Slap and slap, I slowly tossed the ball, once so high it twisted down and hung itself. Then I coughed once and three times louder, stayed and waited for someone to come out so I could say I'd been to Skillins' —and had swung Skillins' tetherball—and had been seen.

But when Mari Heather opened the door and walked down the path, I still did not leave. Her breath came onto the air like milkpods bursting. So I untwisted the ball and swung it at her. She let it bounce off her shoulder and said nothing. I shrugged. "My God, won't you talk now?" I could see she had forgotten my name and the bone owl.

But then she pushed the ball back. It hit me. "You swore, Nils William."

"I did not. I said Gawl."

"So, Gawl is swearing."

"No, it ain't."

"Yes."

"God, you don't know anything about swearing." I snorted and backed away from her.

She pointed at me. "Nils William Carter, Grandmother says you will come in."

I tossed my head, but my wool cap slid off, which made her laugh, which I didn't want. So I said, "No, I will not. What makes you think I want to anyway?" I twisted my toe down into the garden. "I'm going back."

She turned toward her house. Hair was in her mouth. "Go then. Who cares?"

Since she left me to choose, I came with her all right but far enough behind so she would not know. I took time to pet one cat that had no tail. And one that did.

Skillins' kitchen was dim and heavy with the sweet reek of last fall's canning. Dozens of hairy potato cuts were lined along the windowsills for planting. One corner of the room ran out to a root cellar. A spider scutted out from the stove woodbox and up a wicker chair where Mari said I should sit. She called up the stairs, "Grandma, that boy is here now." Then she went outside. I was alone.

The old woman, the widow Skillin, came down slowly, heavily, as if her legs were wood blocks. Fat fell down her arms and when she pulled the light chain, they were spotted blue with loose veins. I did not put my feet on the crossbar under me. I did not ask her about her son and daughter-in-law, the parents of Mari Heather, because it was guessed—and thought—and some said known that those two did not really "work" in the Moose County lunatic asylum, that they did not even "visit" there, that they "lived" there all the time, all year round. So

I tried to talk like company. I said, "It is a fine day Mrs. Skillin yes it is it is late though thank you I must go."

She laughed with no teeth, so that she sprayed the table once and once my face. "No, you will not go. You will stay. You will play the pianola." When she asked if I had ever taken piano, I turned away.

I had for five years taken piano as I had once taken liver oil in a spoon that was old-spittle-brown-silver. And I did not like one any more than the other. "Yes," I said.

So she told me we would go upstairs. We had to walk up arm in arm like Mother and Father in church because of her heart which caused her ankles, which hung over her shoes like rolled socks. She could not take two stairs at once. Tacked to the end of each step were strips of potato sack so she would not slip, I found I had as much time to look around as I did in school to look up river between one lesson and another, between spelling and reading. There was a cuckoo clock in the stairwell that was broken, so the bird hung out all the time. And there were ten oval, death's-hair wreaths along the wall, each a little higher than the last.

After eight steps I asked, "What is cancer?" because I could not wait any longer. She clutched my arm till it hurt. "Cancer is a sickness."

"Can you catch it?"

"No. It just comes. It comes very slowly till you can't eat."

I nodded. "I know about that. Like peas. I can't eat peas. They give me cancer. Like Vick's Vapo Rub. Vick's Vapo Rub on my chest gives me a fever."

She was silent. I asked on the eleventh step, "What is a pianola?"

"It is what your husband gives you when you have arthritis in your hands." She looked at me. We were the same height. "And when he has been unfaithful."

"Yes, unfaithful is when you don't pray before you go to bed."

She touched my lips. "Unfaithful is what you will be many times." When we were on the landing, I could look through the round window and see Mari Heather, stooped, carrying wood buckets of maple sap back and forth to the barn. Widow Skillin said, "Move on," and we did.

Behind the curved bubble-glass of the corner cupboard, behind stoneware as blue veined as the old widow's arm, was a snow scene in a ball sent by her husband when he went to Chicago, and left her home, and heard an opera, and had a woman. I had never seen it snow in a city and wanted to and asked, "Can I shake it?"

She said, "No." Then she coughed, which I guessed was cancer. We went into the living room. A piano stood on the east wall so that light could hit the sheet music from the west. It was an upright. People were always trying to buy it from her. But her price went up and up because, in the first place, her husband had sold his father's gold watch and a fine team mare for that piano. The varnish was dark, was one coat on another, was dull, cracked like the frozen furrow mud I'd smashed through down the field. It felt rough where dust had been covered over with finish again and again.

I asked, "Is this a pianola? It looks like a regular piano."

Then pointing past the couch I could not sit on, to a wooden chest which took up half the wall, she whispered, "If you can push this into the piano all the way so they join, so these hammers lie on those keys, you will have a pianola. And it will play itself, if you pump, if you take off your boots." Sliding it in front of me sometimes, leaning into it with my back, shoving it with my legs, going backwards and butting it with my rump, I pushed the pianola around the braided rug and onto the piano. My eyes were wet and my face was wet and my whole body was wet. My hair steamed like after a bath. She said, "That is fine. Now take off your boots." As if I were ready and didn't need a rest.

After I climbed onto the wind-up stool, she turned me round and round higher and higher till I was tall enough. I was still puffing. She went to a small cabinet. I cannot remember all the names of the rolls she took out. But they were in long narrow cardboard boxes that were wine-red with a tag on each end. She would hold them up to the west window one by one, turn them around as if the names might change on her and then say, "Damn," like a man, and then slam them back into their wooden slots in the cabinet. "Damn," and slam till my head ached, and all for maybe fifteen minutes till she had found five rolls she wanted me to play.

There was one "Nocturne" and one called "King Stephen Overture" which she dedicated special to Bottles Skillin, whom she called Beloved Stephen and who was in that tin picture above me with her on her wedding day. I said, "She was pretty," though I knew the widow that stood beside me was the woman that stood in the frame, but I couldn't say, "You," because they didn't look the same.

She said, "Pump." I pressed the pedals one at a time, slowly because I had to stretch. Nothing came but a low, whirring sound. Then she put her hand on my shoulder and squeezed. "Pump." When I slammed one foot and then the other over and over, music came at last, jerking along, hardly like any music I'd ever heard. It rocked my whole body or maybe I rocked my whole body playing it, but I coughed and all the time she was telling me how she had played piano for the silents down in the city called Saint Paul which was once called Pig's Eye—that her husband had turned pages and had watched the chorus girls kicking while she played—that he met them afterward to kiss the hand of "the lovely lady of the lovely legs." She said, "Pump." The longer I pumped the more she coughed. And I coughed. She said the bellows were broken and that was just the hell of it. It roared and sometimes sighed but all the time the music went heaving on, jiggling the picture over my head. So I looked up because I was dizzy watching my feet and dizzy with her talking. I saw she looked like Mari Heather and I saw too, when Widow Skillin bent down, a thin moustache hung over her lip and did it come from kissing Bottles Skillin who had a moustache up there in the picture and would Mari Heather have one? But I couldn't ask her because the widow was saying louder how he had taken one girl to Chicago to the opera and had bought the pianola all on the same trip and couldn't I play louder? She said, "Pump." While I kept rocking and kicking at the pedals and coughing and the sweat breaking out, she told how he had got a new roll for the pianola each time he had got a new girl and "Pump." And he had spat blood and she had put cold rags on his fever and finally I couldn't breathe. The tears came into my eyes and I cried because I didn't know what she was saying, because I was numb from my legs down and my side ached as if I'd run. Then when I kicked once with both feet together, the room was rolling backwards fast-but-slow, and the chair tipping, almost falling, into her arms, till she was crying, till she whispered, "I'm sorry. I'm sorry." And then she set me up again.

When I stood, she asked, "Do you want to play 'Gavotte Stephen' —if I sit on the couch—if I don't say anything?"

"No."

"Do you want to make it snow in Chicago?"

"No."

"Well, will you come again—to see Mari Heather?"

Then with "Yes," and "Yes," and no in my mind, I went down the stairs past those ten wreaths and the clock whose bird stayed out all the time, and never never came back in.

Boundary Waters

Mary Logue

S EARCHING the clear lake, Edna sent a bit of herself tumbling to its depths. As the sky turned dark blue, the lake turned black. Both she and Tory, without looking at each other, had quit paddling. In the dusk, the color leaked from the sky. It was a good start, Edna thought, to the canoe trip she had planned for herself and her sister.

"I still don't see it. Are you sure we're going the right way?" Tory called from the back of the canoe. The map was spread out over her knees.

"Paddle harder."

They turned the canoe to the left but still aimed at the shore. Edna didn't know what they were looking for: a clearing, a beach, the remnants of charred wood. She watched for a break in the tree tops or a channel through the weeds that crowded the shore line.

"I can't read the map anymore," Tory said.

"Don't look at the map, look at the shore. It's nearby, I'm sure."

They moved closer to the shore and paddled slowly. A mosquito sung in Edna's ear and she swatted it away. Behind her she heard Tory swear and slap her arm.

"I thought you said there'd be no mosquitoes."

"A few stragglers, maybe. This late in the season they're rare."

"So do we consider ourselves lucky to run into the few remaining?"

"I guess," Edna said calmly. Maybe Tory had picked up that rhetorical humor in New York; it had the sound of people pushed too close together.

As Edna turned to look at Tory, she saw the receding shoreline at a new angle, one that revealed the slip in the weeds the canoe could glide through to reach the campsite.

Edna stared at the tent roof above them, swaying in the wind. She was still surprised that Tory had accepted her invitation to come on this trip. Edna had called her in New York and suggested it. Tory's birthday was in late August and Edna had offered her the birthday present of a plane ticket to Minnesota and a week trip into the Boundary Waters, a national park with over a thousand depthless lakes that spotted the border of Minnesota and Canada. She had thought the trip was for Tory, but came to realize as she packed her bags that she herself needed to escape.

She and Guy had installed air conditioning in their suburban Minneapolis home and tall elm trees shaded it, but in the last few months something had been crackling between the two of them; it sparked like static electricity when they got too close, and it made them avoid each other.

She heard Tory's gentle breathing and thought of Guy's body floating alone in their king-sized bed. They had been married for twelve years. Guy had been a fullback on the football team, a minor hero. One crisp fall night they had made love in the breezeway of her parents' home and afterward he had asked her to marry him.

For a moment, before she fell asleep, she wished she could reach out and touch Guy's shoulder.

In the morning they came to their first portage, a dirt path cut through the woods of about ten canoe lengths. Edna carried the canoe and Tory struggled along with the backpack slung across her front and the Superior pack, a huge canvas Voyageur-style pack, slung across her back. They both groaned from the soreness of newly discovered muscles.

The next lake was small and oval shaped, skirted with rushes. They heard whispering in the air. Halfway across the lake, Tory stretched her arms above her head and said, "Remember those cabins Mom and Dad took us to and called it camping? We'd wait until they were playing bridge and were a little drunk and then we'd sneak off and meet our friends at the recreation hall."

Edna laughed. She had been popular at the recreation hall. They'd play the jukebox and dance to Sonny and Cher and the Beach Boys. She had hair down to her waist and wore bell bottoms.

"Didn't you and Guy go camping once?" Tory asked.

"Yeah, we backpacked into Glacier. Rained the first three days we were out. Everything was wet and Timmy cried every day for one reason or another. I cried too so Guy wouldn't pick on him. The last day, the day we were hiking out, it cleared up. It made the trip come out right. I think we'd even try something like that again."

Tory stripped down to her white undershirt. She had never had big enough breasts to need a bra. The lake was stirred by a slight wind, and it was near eighty degrees. "You want to just drift for a while?" she asked Edna.

"We have a long portage to make this afternoon."

"But we're not really going anyplace, are we?"

"Not exactly, but I thought it'd be good to try to make Lake Crystal our turn-around point."

Tory set down her paddle and leaned her head on the crossbar. Edna kept paddling in even, steady strokes.

Edna walked into the woods to gather branches for their evening fire. It had been the chore she and Timmy shared; he would find the kindling and she would search for logs the size around of her arm. She remembered the worried look on his face when he asked her why she was going on this trip without him and Dad. "Sisters need to be together too," she explained.

When Edna got back to the camp, she heated up a can of tomato soup and wondered how her two boys were doing. Guy cooked breakfast Saturday mornings when he didn't go golfing, but that was the extent of his cooking. Since she was gone, she knew they would start in the kitchen with all good intentions but then would slowly drift into the living room and sit in front of the TV with spoons and jars of peanut butter and marshmallow goo. They would be happy together and Timmy would go to bed late because Guy would let him stay up and finish the movie.

Edna set the pan of soup on a stone near the fire where it would stay warm and watched Tory try to put up the tent.

Through Tory she had come to know New York City. Tory explained to her the difference between the East and West Villages, "like banks of a river they are divided by Fifth Avenue and the Bohemians have congregated on the side toward Europe where there are clusters of Ukrainians and Puerto Ricans." Edna wanted to visit her, but couldn't see Guy letting her go to that wilderness alone and she didn't want to stay in a hotel many blocks away from her sister. It wasn't the Met she wanted to see or even a Broadway play. Rather the small Ukrainian bar where Tory had met her boyfriend, and the theater where Tory practiced the lines to some off-off-Broadway play.

Sometimes she was so afraid for Tory she would wake up in the night and think of her walking alone down a street of solid buildings except for one alleyway where a man could pull her to the ground, ask her for money, and run his hands over her body. She was afraid of the discouragement Tory must feel from auditions that go all day and lead to nothing.

Tory fought with everything. She was fighting now with the tent and Edna bit her lip to keep from telling her how easy it was if you put up the tent poles at the same time, not one and then the other as Tory was trying to do.

It rained in the night. Edna woke feeling like she had wet the bed but discovered water had leaked in through one of the tent windows and pooled around her feet. When she peeked out of the tent she saw that Tory was already up and making coffee.

"We had a visitor last night," Tory said.

"You mean the rain?"

"Another one. A bear." At night before going to sleep, they had carefully strung up the Superior bag over the strongest limb on the tallest tree they could find. They would hang the bag so it would dangle below the branch, out of the reach of the bears.

"Did he get anything?"

"Yeah, that's what's so funny. I think he was frustrated about the food so look what he did to the toilet paper." Tory held up a roll that looked as if someone had been preparing confetti for New Year's Eve.

"I'm glad that wasn't me."

"Do you realize we haven't seen anyone since we left?" Tory asked.

Edna ignored Tory's question and asked her, "Do you think what's his name is missing you?"

"You mean Cal?"

"Is that short for Calvin?"

"Yeah, but I'd never dare call him that. We've only gone out for a couple months. He's one of the cool New York type of guys. He'll call me on Thursday to see what I'm doing on the weekend. But that doesn't mean he'll ask me out. He just wants to be sure I'm free."

"He sounds like a jerk," Edna said.

"He can be, but he's also a good actor and handsome in the way I like . . . thin, dark, a little twisted. To answer your question, no, I don't think he's missing me. But he might be thinking about me once in a while. No question about Guy and Timmy missing you, is there?"

"No, for better or for worse, I'm sure they are. A day or two they like but when I'm gone for too long one of them has to do the dishes and the laundry. They argue about that and are glad to see me when I come home." Edna poured the remaining coffee over the coals and wondered how her boys would get along if she never came back home.

Lake Crystal was a leftover from the ice age. In sixth grade Minnesota history they had been taught that a moving mountain of snow had scarred and pitted the face of their home state like a scouring pad. There was no soft sand beach on this lake. Their campsite perched on a rock finger that pointed northward into the lake. The water fell dramatically away on both sides. Before setting up camp they stripped off their clothes and dove off the rock into the lugubrious water. It was not dark because it was dirty or clouded with algae. It was dark because there was nothing for sunlight to reflect off of in its depths. The stone was slate and jutted out from the water like an extrusion from another time on earth.

"Let's play that game we played as kids. You know, where you have to do the dive that the person before you did. Kind of follow the leader." Tory's hair was almost straight under the weight of the water and her bangs fell into her eyes. She slicked her hair back and waited for Edna to respond.

"Okay. But let's trade off. First you do a dive and I follow, then I get to do one."

"Okay. I start." Tory did an old favorite of theirs, a dive with the arms tight at the sides. They called it the Popeye dive because it had a cartoon quality about it. Edna did it, but bent her head as she hit the water. When she surfaced, Tory nodded approval.

"I didn't do it right," Edna confessed.

"It doesn't matter. Now, your turn."

Without thinking, Edna did the one dive that had always given Tory trouble, the one she used to disqualify her if she wanted to win the game. It was a cartwheel dive. She arched her back, her hands hit the cold stone, her feet curved above her and the water gulped her down. She surfaced to hear Tory shouting, "No fair. You're playing dirty."

"You don't have to do that one. Do another. I forgot you had trouble with that one."

"Oh, no. I'll give it a try."

Edna clambered up the slippery stone and watched as Tory rocked back and forth, gaining the momentum and the courage to turn upside down before slicing the water. Edna wanted to stop her from doing it. Ever since she had had a child, she had learned a new kind of fear. She understood why their mother had yelled and slapped them when they had fallen off their bikes, how mad she had been that they had taken such risks with the lives she was trying to give them. Edna had now learned to hold herself back and not let her fear stop Timmy from learning how to skateboard. When Tory had asked her if she should move to New York, Edna had said yes to their parents' no and lent her the money to get started. Edna stepped back from Tory as she bent to start the cartwheel. Tory's legs splayed wide apart but her hands were steady against the wet rock. She shrieked and her body slapped the water like a clap of thunder, then she came up gurgling.

Spitting out water she gasped, "I think that's the best I ever did that."

The night fell slowly. A mist bloomed on the lake. After setting up camp, the two sisters returned to the edge of the water which was the color of molten iron, gray with streaks of the setting sun. A loon cried across the lake and it started the two of them giggling, its plaintive half-laugh, half-cry so human in its intensity that it made them nervous.

Edna wrapped her arms around her legs and wondered if this was the time to talk to Tory about her problems.

Tory opened her arms and stretched. "I wish we'd see a moose. I've never seen one."

"Guy saw a moose in Canada when he went hunting with his father. Thank God they didn't have a license to kill it. I don't even like venison much." Edna remembered the deer strung over the top of the station wagon. Guy had been so proud of it she couldn't let him know that seeing it dead, flies lighting on its eyes, had made her wince as if she had been hit in the ribs. She had walked back into the house on the pretense of making coffee while they had hung it in the garage. The next morning Guy brought it to the butcher's and after that would occasionally ask her to pan fry him a slab of it with onions for Saturday lunch. She did not want to hurt Guy or let him see how much she was being hurt. She held up the canoe paddle and hit the ground with it. Edna wondered what Tory knew of her life, if she saw how ordinary it had become.

"Tory, if someone asked you, how would you describe Guy and me?"

"A cozy couple."

"Why?"

"You two grew up together."

"You and I grew up together."

"You know what I mean. You're so close. You've been together so long. You've built a life."

"Well, we're not that close."

Tory nodded and turned to look at the opposite shoreline as if it would be easier for Edna to talk if she were not being watched.

"We're having problems. We married so early, neither of us knew what to expect. All we knew was how our parents were together. His parents sleep in separate bedrooms. They take separate vacations. They play bridge and fight. His father drinks so his mother burns the steak. He thinks that's normal or at least acceptable. I see our marriage drifting away."

Tory looked at her and her eyes were the murky color of the lake. "Have you talked to Guy about this?"

"I can't."

"Why not?"

"If I admit anything is wrong, the whole thing will fall apart."

"What whole thing?"

"My whole life. Everything I've done." Edna searched for the right words to explain so Tory would understand and stop asking her all these questions. "I've accepted what he does for so long that I don't think I have the right to complain."

"What does he do?"

"Nothing. I don't think he's touched the back of my neck in a year. I always liked that. He'd rub the back of my neck when he knew I was tired or sad. I don't even know when he quit. When I noticed, it became real important. I'd wait thinking maybe he'd do it. God, if he'd do it now, I wouldn't even care about making love."

"Is he seeing another woman?"

"I wish. Then I'd have something to tell you about. When he's not working, he's at home. He takes Timmy to shoot a bucket of golf balls, he puts up the shelves I need for storage, he works in the garden, he fiddles with the cars. He loves his home, he loves Timmy, and I'm so tied into it all that I'm sure he thinks he loves me."

"What happens when you go to bed?"

"Sometimes he'll pull out work to do at ten o'clock and I'll fall asleep. Or I'll go out with the girls and he'll be asleep when I get back. But when we're both there in bed together, the TV is always on. He got cable and there is never not a good movie on. A couple months ago I thought maybe it was my fault, that I wasn't forward enough. I took a long bath and crawled into bed next to him. I pulled his head back and gave him a long kiss. He turned away and said, 'Don't. I haven't brushed my teeth yet.' I curled up on my side and waited for him to brush his teeth. He never did."

"What're you going to do?"

Edna touched the back of her neck, comforting herself. "I don't know. One of the reasons I asked you to go on this trip was so that I had an excuse to get away. I think Guy, in the last month or so, has finally noticed something. He yelled at me the other day about how I parked the car in the garage. I kept thinking it was just a phase we were going through and it would disappear. Now I'm afraid."

"You're going to have to talk to him."

"God, I get sick just thinking about it. How can you talk nonchalantly about not having had sex for four months?"

"Remember Tony? When we hadn't had sex for two months I decided to find out why. Turned out there was another man."

"That couldn't be the case with Guy. He used to play football."

Tory laughed. "I don't think that makes a big difference, but, no, I don't think Guy is gay."

Edna stared at the lake. She had talked about it. Talking about it again wouldn't be so hard. She wouldn't be able to do it right away. She knew it would take her at least a few days to settle back into the house. It would be messy and dirty. She would make some phone calls and buy groceries, but when everything was straightened up, then she would see her loneliness again. She would miss a breeze across her shoulders, a whisper in her ear, and she would begin to grow brave. The water's surface looked like dull metal, solid, but she knew that her paddle could cut through it.

"I'll take it."

"No, you won't. It's my turn." Tory leaned over the canoe, tilting it up to set it on her shoulders. She winced as the canoe bore down on her shoulders, shredding the skin.

Edna led the way. She remembered this portage. It was a long walk with puddles of dank water that would force them to go through the weeds.

At the halfway mark there was a canoe rest. Edna stopped there and waited for Tory. The canoe rocked precariously on Tory's shoulders and then seemed to tilt forward more than usual. The path was slippery and it was important to watch out for tree roots that curled out of the ground like giant earthworms. A trickle of sweat rolled down Edna's forehead and into her eye. It stung with salt. She blew upward and her hair lifted off her forehead. The canoe rest was only a piece of weathered pine nailed up high between two trees. Tory was almost there. She heard Tory's hoarse breathing and watched the canoe float down the path like a submarine about to come up for air.

The canoe rest was just off the trail. When Tory stepped toward it her toes locked under a root and the canoe lurched forward. Heaving the canoe off her shoulders, Tory turned to get out of its way as it came crashing down. Tory fell and the canoe clanged against wood.

"Tory, are you all right?" Edna screamed.

Tory lay still on the ground. Her eyes were pinched tight shut as if she were still waiting for the accident to be over. Edna shed the packs and bent down to examine Tory's ankle. The shoe had stayed under the root but her foot had come forward. It seemed to be all right.

"Tory, try to sit up."

"I'm scared."

"Okay, let me feel you." Edna ran her hands over Tory's legs and then over her arms. "You seem to be all right. How's your back? Your neck?"

Tory raised herself up to one elbow. Edna gave her a hand and she stood up carefully.

"You all right?"

"I guess."

"You should have said something."

"I didn't see that damn root."

Feeling her face tighten up, Edna turned away so Tory wouldn't see. The canoe was lying on its side. A tree branch had broken off from its fall. Edna stuck her head in the canoe and examined the seam at the bottom. "Shit. This really does it." She pulled her head out and flared her nostrils. "The canoe is broken."

"What?"

"There is a hole in the canoe. You've cracked it right along the seam."

"Can we fix it?" Tory asked.

"Are you kidding? Probably no one could. We're going to have to leave it here and walk to the portage and wait for someone to come."

"Edna, we haven't seen anyone in over three days," Tory reminded her. "It's off season. We can't just sit around and wait."

"So what the hell do you suggest?"

"Walk out."

Edna gathered up the packs, talking to Tory but not facing her. "Listen, don't talk to me for a while."

Tory took the smaller pack fron Edna as she attempted to swing it onto her back. "Give that to me. I don't mind silence, but I'm not going to take you playing the martyr." Edna started to walk away as Tory added, "And I'm not going to say I'm sorry. It just fucking happened and I'm glad it's the canoe that's broken and not me."

"I am too," Edna said.

They left the canoe turned upside down next to the canoe rest. When they reached the lake, Edna looked across to the distant shore, wishing they could skim above the water's surface. There was no path around the lake as it was not meant to be skirted. Edna appraised the density of the woods in both directions. The trees rose high above the pine, oak, and a few maple. Stuffed in below their branches were shrubs and bushes, blueberry, raspberry and wild rose, woven into a tangled underbrush. She checked the maps and, as the next portage looked closer to the south, she pointed that way.

Moving ahead of her, Tory held the brambles back so they didn't snap in her face. Tory's head was bowed as if doing penance. They had three lakes to walk around before they got to Sawmill. It would take them days to walk out, especially if the underbrush continued to be as thick as it was around them.

They walked for an hour staying near the shore. Edna knew even though Tory had had the accident with the canoe that in fact what was happening to them now was her fault. She had been the one to call Tory and bring her back to Minnesota. The dimming light from the clouds told her the sun was setting. Her ankles were pricked by briars and were beginning to itch. She could no longer stand to look at Tory's back.

"Tory," she called out and Tory stopped. "I'm sorry about this."

Tory turned around. "Why are you sorry? I thought everything was my fault."

"I'm sorry because I wanted it to be so good. This," as she paused and raised her hands a few rain drops started to fall, "is a disaster."

"Don't say that. You don't know. You always think you know. See the difference is I didn't expect it to be perfect. You did. You plan the dinners that I burn, you rent the canoe that I break. I don't plan anything. With no plans, nothing can get ruined."

"Oh."

"I'm having a good time," Tory said.

"You are?"

"This will make a great story to tell my friends in New York."

"I wanted it to be peaceful."

"Why? Just like your life, so peaceful nothing's going on?"

Edna was stunned. "No, I just thought you might need some peace and quiet after New York."

"Listen, I like action. That's why I'm here. I like to take risks. But you're not interested, are you?"

Edna set down her backpack and plunged through the scraggly blueberry bushes to get to the lake. She took off her shoes and walked up past her burning ankles into the water. Tory was behind her on the shore. Edna turned around and said, "You don't know either. Maybe my problem is that I worry too much about you and too much about Guy and not enough about myself. When we get out of here, I'm coming to New York to visit you."

When Edna woke in the morning, she could feel her heart beat in her swollen ankles. It was the slow throb, throb of a sluggish heart. Troy was still sleeping and Edna slipped out of the tent so as not to wake her. Looking at the lake through a mesh of twisted tree branches, Edna caught sight of a canoe moving across the water like a dolphin surfacing. In her t-shirt and underpants, she ran to the water and dove in, swimming after them and yelling.

They paddled over and pulled her into the canoe. "How come you're out in the middle of the lake drowning?" a man in his mid-thirties asked. His hair was dark brown and long, his beard dark red and trimmed close. A boy of seven or eight offered her a towel.

"Our canoe has a hole in it."

"It sunk?"

"No. But we're stranded. We're trying to walk through the woods. My sister's over there. Could you help us out? We're headed back to Sawmill."

The boy groaned. "Dad, you said we'd be to Lake Crystal today."

"Johnny, this here's a damsel in distress. We'll get to Lake Crystal soon enough to catch more walleye than you can eat."

Tory and Edna took turns canoeing in the front while the father paddled steadily in the rear. His forearm was as thick around as a fence post. He laughed at their camping stories and told Edna he had thought she was a mermaid. "I was hoping you wouldn't have nothing on."

"Dad." Johnny was mad at being relegated to the bottom of the canoe.

"Sonny, your mom isn't the only beautiful woman around."

He told them he was divorced and Edna laughed when he explained that he was still faithful to his ex-wife in spirit if not in body. "Even when I'm with another woman I think of her. She's a hell of a woman. Johnny, how many boyfriends has she got now?"

"Three. Two musicians and a lawyer."

"You mean the guy that handled the divorce?"

"Yeah. He's trying to teach her to play chess."

"Why that little bitch. Excuse me, ladies, but she can still get me riled up." He hummed a song under his breath, then asked, "So where are you two from?"

Tory answered, "She's from Minneapolis and I'm from New York."

"Christ, New York's the greatest city in the world to visit and Minnesota is the only place to live. Don't I always say that, Johnny?"

"No."

Edna sensed how disappointed Johnny was, not so much from having to turn around and head back, but from having to share his father with two women.

"Is this your first time up here, Johnny?" she asked him.

"No way. Dad and I come here every year."

"How long are you staying?"

"Only two days then I have to start school."

"My kid already started."

"You have a kid too?" He squinted up at her.

"Yes, and he's just about your age, but doesn't have near as many freckles as you."

After the next portage, Edna told the father he didn't need to take them across Sawmill. "We were planning on another day camping so it won't hurt us to walk around Sawmill."

As they climbed back in the canoe she handed the paddle to Johnny and said, "I think it's your turn to canoe for a while."

"I liked him," Tory said as they waved goodbye to the father and the son.

"Yeah, it was nice of him to help out."

"Were you attracted to him?" Tory asked.

"He had an interesting face."

"Would you go to bed with him?" Tory persisted.

"Stop it. I don't think of things like that." For a moment she pictured him standing naked in front of her in the forest. He reminded her of a tree, hair dark as bark covered his body. "Maybe."

When they got to Sawmill they decided to stick close to the water's edge. The clear shoreline appeared only intermittently but at least the weeds were thinner there. They lowered their backpacks to the ground to take a breather before they started their hike around the lake. Tory stepped out onto a rock that jutted up from the water. She turned to smile at Edna and, slipping on the algae, fell into the lake. It was surprisingly deep and she was up to her waist in water.

Edna stepped out carefully to the rock and leaned over to help her out of the water. "You just didn't think."

Tory took Edna's proffered hand and tugged. Edna's foot slipped on the same treacherous green slime. With a startled scream, she bellyflopped alongside Tory. "You bitch. You pulled me in."

"It's not so bad, once you get used to it." Tory sprayed her with water.

Edna sprayed her back. "Fuck you."

Tory dove for Edna's head and tried to dunk her underwater. Edna braced herself and grabbed the back of Tory's hair, pulled her head to within an inch of the water's surface. Tory squirmed out of her grasp and wrapped her legs around Edna's waist. They fought hard and felt each other's differences. Tory offered little to grab onto and could squirm out of anything; Edna was hard to move and had great gripping strength in her hands.

Placing her knee in the middle of Edna's back, Tory flipped her down into the water. Edna tried to scratch her while Tory locked an arm around her neck. "I'm going to dunk you under," Tory threatened.

Edna started to laugh. "Don't, Tory."

In Tory's arms, Edna went weak with laughter. It was infectious, but Tory kept a grip on Edna. "Say I'm the best sister in the world."

Edna was unable to pronounce a word, only hoots and howls coming out of her mouth.

Tory shook her. "Say it."

Edna managed to scream out, "You're the best," at which point Tory let her go and they both fell back into the water, laughing. They convulsed with laughter as they had as children, sitting under their parents' baleful eyes at the dinner table. They rolled in the water, hugging their sides. When one started to calm down all it took was a look at the other to start her off again. Finally they both tapered off and eased back into the water and floated in silence.

Edna felt Tory's hand grab her wrist. She thought how, from a plane flying overhead, they would look like lily pads growing in a lake, or they would look like what they were, two sisters holding hands.

Rufus at the Door

Jon Hassler

E ACH YEAR the ninth and eleventh grades of Plum High School were loaded on a bus and driven to Rochester for a tour of what was then called the insane asylum. The boys' health teacher, Mr. Lance, and the girls', Miss Sylvestri, led us single file through a series of gloomy wards and hallways where we were smiled at, scowled at, lunged at and jeered by all manner of the mentally deficient. I recall much more about my ninth-grade trip than I do about my eleventh. I recall, for example, how the faces of the retarded absorbed the elderly Mr. Lance, how he gazed at them the way we freshmen did, as though he were seeing them for the first time, and yet how he displayed none of our pity or shock or revulsion; his gaze, like a good many of those it met, was intense but neutral. I remember the middle-aged Miss Sylvestri bouncing along at the head of our column and—as though reading labels at the zoo—calling out the categories: "These are morons, class, and over there you have the imbeciles. In the next room they're all insane." I remember my relief when the tour ended, for the place had given me a severe stomachache. As we boarded the bus, Miss Sylvestri turned back for a last look and waved cheerily at a balloonlike face peering out the window of the broad front door and said, "That's a waterhead, class, and now we'll go downtown for lunch."

Mr. Lance drove the bus and Miss Sylvestri stood at his shoulder and delivered an unnecessary lecture about how lucky we were to have been spared from craziness and retardation. She wore a long coat of glistening black fur, and the shape of her tall hat fit the definition, in our geometry text, of a truncated cone. She asked if any of us realized that we had a moron living in Plum.

Pearl Peterson's hand shot up. Pearl was the ninth grade's foremost sychophant. "Henry Ahman," she said. "Henry Ahman is a moron."

"No, I'm sorry, Pearl. Henry Ahman is an epileptic, there's no comparison. Come now, class, I'm asking for a moron."

I knew the right answer, but I kept my mouth shut for fear of losing face with my friends. This was the year a lot of us boys were passing through our anti-achievement phase. We had taken an oath never to raise our hands.

"Please, Miss Sylvestri," said Pearl, "would you tell us again what a moron is?"

Swaying with the traffic, Miss Sylvestri said that morons were a little smarter than idiots and a lot smarter than imbeciles. She said that morons could do things like run errands for their mothers while idiots and imbeciles couldn't leave the house. Sometimes imbeciles couldn't even get out of bed.

The impassive Mr. Lance found his way downtown and parked in front of the Green Parrot Cafe. He looked into the mirror that showed him his whole load, even those of us way in back, and he said, "Chow time." But Miss Sylvestri begged to differ. She said nobody was having lunch until somebody came up with a moron.

My friends and I groaned anonymously.

Pearl suggested the Clifford girl.

"No, I'm sorry, the Clifford girl is an out-and-out imbecile."

Somebody else, a junior, said, "Gilly Stone."

"No, Gilly Stone's problem is polio."

Finally out of hunger—the jolting bus had settled my stomach—I shouted, "Rufus Alexander."

"That's correct—Rufus Alexander. He's very low on the scale but he's still higher than an idiot. He's what you call a low-grade moron."

We were permitted to eat.

At the west edge of Plum, Rufus Alexander lived with his mother in a little house near the stockyards. Rufus was about thirty-five and his mother was very old, yet his hair was turning gray at the same rate as hers. On Saturday afternoons they walked together to the center of the village to shop—the tall, bony-faced Mrs. Alexander striding along with her shoulders hunched and her skirts flowing around her shoetops; her tall, grinning son stepping along at her side, his back so straight that he seemed about to tip over backwards. Though he walked fast to keep pace, there was in each of his footsteps an almost imperceptible hesitation, a tentativeness that lent a jerky aspect to his progress down the street and reminded me of old films of the Keystone Kops. Whenever he came to a stop, he always clasped his hands behind his back and stood as though at attention; from a distance, in his long gray coat and white scarf, he might have been mistaken for a diplomat or a funeral director. At home Rufus sat in a deep chair by the front window and listened all day to the radio. Passing the house on my bike, I used to see him there, looking out and grinning. Mrs. Alexander had raised three older sons, but it was Rufus she loved best. He was hard of hearing and mute, though on rare occasions he made guttural noises which his mother took to be words.

In order to go about her Saturday shopping unencumbered by Rufus, who couldn't turn a corner without being steered, Mrs. Alexander would deposit him either in the pool hall or in my father's grocery store. She would look in at the pool hall first, because there Rufus could sit on one of the chairs around the card table, but if she saw that her card-playing son—her oldest son, Lester—hadn't come to town, she would lead Rufus down the street to our store and place him in my father's care.

Not that he needed care. He was content to stand at the full-length window of the front door, looking out. For as long as two hours he would remain there as though enchanted, his hands clasped behind him, his eyes directed at a point slightly above the passing people, his face locked in its customary grin. When someone entered or left the store—Rufus would shuffle backward and allow himself to be pressed for a moment between the plate glass in front of him and the glassine doors of the cookie display behind him, and then as the door went shut he would shuffle forward, keeping his nose about six inches from the glass.

Although our customers were greeted week after week by this moronic face, and although he obscured the cookie display, I don't think Rufus had an adverse effect on our business. Everybody was used to him. In a village as small as Plum the ordinary population didn't outnumber the odd by enough to make the latter seem all that rare. We became, as villagers, so accustomed to each other's presence, so familiar with each other's peculiarities, that even the most eccentric among us—Henry Ahman, who had fits in public; the Clifford girl, who was an out-and-out imbecile—were considered institutions rather than curiosities. I noticed that most of our customers ignored Rufus as they came through the door, while a few, like me, gave him a fleeting smile in return for his incessant grin.

He had an odd face. His round, prominent cheekbones were rosy, healthy-looking, but his eyes were skeletal—deep-set eyes under brows like ledges, blue eyes perfectly round and (I thought at first) perfectly empty. I never saw him—except once—that he wasn't grinning. Though I told myself that this was an un-conscious grin, that he probably grinned all night in his sleep, I couldn't help responding to it. Returning time and again to the store after carrying out groceries, I smiled. As an exercise in will power, I would sometimes try to control this reflex. Facing Rufus as I opened the door, I would tell myself that his grin was not a sign of good will but an accident of nature, and I would attempt a neutral stare, like Mr. Lance's, but it was no use. (I could never resist smiling at clowns either, even though I knew their joy was paint.) I asked my father one time if he thought

Rufus ever had anything on his mind, if he understood what he was staring at—or staring slightly above. My father said he wondered the same thing himself and had concluded that Rufus was only two-dimensional; there was no depth to him at all. And this, for a time, I believed.

Then one Monday morning—it was around the time of my first trip to the insane asylum—word spread through town that Rufus had another dimension after all. It was said that during a Sunday picnic in Lester Alexander's farmyard, Rufus had flown into a rage. The picnic was attended by scads of Alexanders from far and near, and three or four of his little cousins began to taunt Rufus. They made up a song about his ignorance and sang it to him again and again. He rolled his great round eyes, it was said, and he made a mysterious noise like a groan or a belch (it was not reported whether he lost his grin) and he set out after the cousins, brandishing the long knife his mother had brought along for slicing open her homemade biscuits. Hearing about it, I couldn't believe that anyone had actually been in danger. I pictured Rufus tipping backward as he ran, too slow to catch his quick little cousins; I pictured the knife—a bread-slicer, dull at the tip; I pictured the many Alexander men—strapping farmers all—who could easily have restrained him. But on the other hand, I could also imagine the alarm. I had attended a few of these farmyard picnics, invited by friends, and I imagined how it must have looked to a bystander; the afternoon hazy and hot; dozens of relatives deployed across the sloping, shady lawn; the children shirtless under their bib overalls; the women at the outdoor table, uncovering their tepid hot-dishes and their runny gelatins; the men smoking under the trees; then suddenly this heightened racket among the children and everyone turning and seeing, to their terror, the youngsters scattering and shrieking (half in fright, half in glee) and Rufus hopping jerkily over the grass, the bread-knife in his hand, the blade glinting in the sun as he thrust it stiffly ahead of him, stabbing the air. As it was told the next day, Rufus's wild mood quickly passed and a half hour later he and the smaller children, full of food, lay down together for a nap in the shade. But he had given his brothers and their wives a terrible fright. Rufus would have to be put away, his brothers told their mother. He would have to be taken to the insane asylum.

Never. As long as she lived, said Mrs. Alexander, Rufus would never leave her side. Not once in his life had he disobeyed her; never had he been anything but gentle. How would any of *them* like it, she wanted to know, if they were teased and attacked by a bunch of impudent snips? No, if anyone was coming to take Rufus away, they were coming over her dead body.

And there the matter rested. The three sons refrained from saying what they foresaw. They foresaw the day when their mother would die and Rufus would be whisked off to Rochester.

After the upheaval of that Sunday afternoon, Mrs. Alexander no longer left Rufus at the pool hall, for it was card-playing Lester who had been the first to speak about putting him away. In my father's keeping, then, Rufus was placed each week without fail. Now and then I would glance up from my work and see him there and wonder how it would end. Morons, according to Miss Sylvestri, sometimes died young. Maybe his mother would survive him, and wouldn't that be a blessing? His brothers' secret intention—like all secrets in Plum—had become public knowledge, and I didn't see how Rufus, after all these years of fixed habits and mother love, could adapt himself to the gruesome life of the asylum, particularly now that he had exhibited strong emotion. Hearing of his anger at the picnic, I now suspected that Rufus was capable of perceptions and emotions beyond what my father and I (and probably most of the village) had formerly believed. Now, though his eyes were consistently shallow and his grin steady, I had a hard time thinking of him in only two dimensions. This was a man who knew things, who felt things, I told myself, and therefore if he outlived his mother he was bound to come to grief. I didn't ask my father what he thought about this. I was afraid he would agree.

In the autumn of my junior year, Mrs. Alexander died. Rufus apparently didn't recognize death when he looked it in the face, for although the coroner said she had been dead since midnight it wasn't until the following noon that Rufus went next door and by his moaning and wild look alerted Mrs. Underdahl. No one could say for certain how Rufus, waiting for his mother to wake up, had spent the forenoon, but judging later by the evidence and what we knew of his habits, the village imagined this:

Rufus got out of bed on his own and went into his mother's room to see why she hadn't awakened him, why she hadn't started breakfast. The depth of her sleep puzzled him. He was capable of a number of things; he could dry dishes and dress himself, but he couldn't figure out why his mother lay so late in bed. He put on his clothes and breakfasted on biscuits and milk (or rather cream, for he opened a full bottle and swigged off the top) and he evidently passed the rest of the time listening to the radio. In my mind's eye I see him sitting in his favorite chair by the window, soothed by the voice of Arthur Godfrey. I see him grinning when the audience laughs and grinning when it doesn't. At noon he went back into his mother's bedroom and pulled her by the arm, and when she didn't respond, he tugged harder. He pulled her out of bed and onto the floor. Then, seeing her there at his feet, twisted among the sheets, he perceived something new. A door in his dense thinking opened on an emotion he had never felt before. Not anger this time, but fear. He went straight to Mrs. Underdahl's house and called up the same belching groan he had uttered at the picnic. His great blue eyes were rolling, Mrs. Underdahl later told my father in the store, as though he sensed that this day marked the end of his childhood and now, in his late thirties, he would have to face the world alone—far off from his mother's house, which had been arranged to fit so well his simple needs, far off from his mother's love.

I was one of the altar boys at Mrs. Alexander's funeral. I looked for Rufus among the mourners, but he wasn't there. I supposed, correctly, as it turned out, that he had already been taken to Rochester. At the cemetery it rained. There were dozens of Alexanders standing three-deep around the grave. The little cousins, wearing short pants and neckties, were as antic as ever. While the priest blessed the grave and read aloud the prayers of burial, the cousins shrieked and played tag among the tombstones. Impudent snips, their grandmother had called them.

Six months later my classmates and I were bussed to Rochester for our second look at the unfortunates. Over the years I have tried to figure out why everyone who went through school in Plum during the Lance-Sylvestri era was twice required to pass through this gauntlet of retarded and insane humanity. Surely all of us had been sufficiently impressed the first time by the smells and vacant faces of this dismal congregation, sufficiently impressed by our own good luck at having been spared. One thing we did learn on this second trip—and this may have been the lesson our teachers had in mind (particularly Mr. Lance, who taught it by example)—was how to look impassive in the face of chaos. I had the same pain in my stomach that I had had two years earlier, and one of the inmates leaped at me and tried to pull off my jacket, but, like most of my classmates, I played the stoic from the time I entered the broad front door until I departed. I acted this way because I was sixteen, the age when nothing seems quite so crucial— especially if freshmen are watching you—as appearing to be above it all; nothing seems quite so clever—if joking would be out of place—as disdain. I discovered that I could be really quite good at looking neutral. The trick was simply to tell myself that none of these crouching, drooling, gawking people were experiencing the misery that visitors pitied them for. They had no knowledge—no memory—of life as it was lived among the normal—life, say, in Plum. Unaware of any better form of existence, they were content. Brainless, they possessed the peace that passes understanding.

But then I saw Rufus. We were boarding the bus when Miss Sylvestri suddenly pointed behind us at the broad front door and said, "Why, that's Rufus Alexander." I turned and saw two men on the doorstep with their backs to us. One was an orderly, the other a tall, white-haired man with a straight spine and his hands clasped behind his back. It was Rufus, all right, and I was surprised—not only because his hair had turned white, but because he had slipped my mind over the winter; I had forgotten that he lived here now. Where had he been during our tour? Outside, strolling the grounds? Or had he been present in one of the crowded wards we passed through, and had a familiar face told him that we were the Plum delegation? Had he tried to follow us out to the bus? The orderly had him tightly by the elbow and was steering him in through the door we had just come out of, but he seemed reluctant to go. Though he didn't struggle, there was a hint of unwillingness in his movements, a hesitation in his step.

This time Miss Sylvestri did not lecture us as Mr. Lance started the bus, but she sat visiting with Pearl Peterson in the front seat on the driver's side. I sat in the back, next to a window, and looked straight at Rufus. The broad front door was now locked and he was standing behind the glass. Our two windows were scarcely thirty feet apart. He didn't look as healthy as he used to. The color was gone from his face and his ledgelike brows were sharper, deeper. While the whiteness of his hair was alarming (in six months it had grown much whiter than his mother's had been), the astonishing thing was the look on his face. He wasn't grinning. His face, without the grin, was that of a much older man, the jaw hanging slack, the cheeks hollow. In his round blue eyes, without the grin, there was something obviously very deep, like yearning. Obvious to me, at least, because his eyes were aimed directly at mine—not slightly above me, the way he used to look at things—and they told me that he had indeed tried to follow us out to the bus; moreover, they told me that mine was the face that reminded him of Plum. I looked away. Mr. Lance shifted gears, and I never saw Rufus again.

Stiller's Pond

Jonis Agee

LOOK, I just want to tell you what it's like out there, what the wind and the water do. How still. How I am walking by the pond in Stiller's cow pasture. It was January, and twenty below zero. Before the light comes up, I can't sleep. I want to be somewhere. The pond is frozen into these little waves the wind puts there, starched on top of it. The kids won't be skating there anyway, not since a long time ago. The pond didn't have to freeze sheet clean, because none of us would ever be skating there again. And as if it knew, the pond always froze in peculiar shapes. As if someone was still under there trying to get out. If you stood over those places where the water bobbed dark, speckled with stuff churning up from the bottom, you'd think you could see a face, pressed and distorted against that little skim of ice, like something from dinner your mom put plastic over and plopped in the fridge, until later when you looked and it was unfamiliar again through the moisture-beaded wrap. At one end the cattails stood at attention, stiff as boys in ROTC, backs swayed in a pose you knew they'd never be able to walk out of, and little tatters of dried leaves waved like flags from the stalks. Around them lay the litter of last summer.

It was in those left, standing the way they are now, that they found her, hair tangled around. They had to chop part of it off to get her out. That's what the adults told us, and if that quick thaw hadn't come up, it would've been April before she was noticed. He was a different matter, bobbing like a cork in the hole that stayed warm over the spring. Still, it was hard to tell the difference between him and the water at that distance. You couldn't get very close, but the thaw sent him skimming over the edge so his tuber-white face rose up like a signal at sea and someone finally saw it. I suppose it was lucky the thaw came—and the kids. Though they knew they wouldn't be skating with the ice that way, they came down to the pond as always, just to fool around. Throw rocks. Build a fire. They weren't permitted to build fires anywhere else. But somehow it was okay if you had a legitimate winter excuse like skating. Sledding was marginal, but skating was okay for fire building. Being kids, they figured the permission was for location rather than activity, so they went to Stiller's pond whenever the arson rose up in their hearts.

To this day I can't look at those cattails without thinking of the way they told the little ones to pull the dried leaves and stalks for kindling—and the confusion they must have felt when the lady's hair wouldn't let go of them. She was face up too, as though sleeping in bed at home, watching the stars through her little attic window before she nodded off. She'd seen a lot more than that since then, every night anchored there like a boat, her arms treading water gently like oars holding her steady. And the hard part was that when they finally dragged her in, men in hip boots with hay hooks and ropes so they could get a grip on her, her eyes had been plucked out by the turtles, removed with the skill of surgeons. So the lids fell gracefully sunken over the holes.

Surprised they had left the rest of her, the men said, knowing the winter hunger of turtles drifting sleepily to the surface for oxygen before they dropped back like stones to the bottom mud. And strange, how the water had filled in the scars on her face, softened the bones until she became sweet and round and beautiful to the men, who recognized her only from the long blond hair, the dirt rinsed from it by the month in the water, and from the broken front teeth. And I think that was what bothered them the most, that she came out of the water better than she went in, that they were able to see her firsthand the way he must have, in his heart, when he would meet her at Stiller's pond after her parents were long asleep, and after her sisters and brothers were long asleep, and after the cows were long settled, and the pigs and the horses heavy in sleep from their day's work, even the poultry, sleeping on one leg in the roosts, as passive as camels in the dark stench of the hen house.

And old man Stiller, refusing to help pull her out, refusing the use of his team, his wagon, his ropes, refusing the use of his blankets to wrap her in, and finally refusing her body in his house, even his barn, where she might have lain like an animal in a stall until the fires softened the ground enough to dig even a shallow hole for her. And the mother, as hard as the father, and the children staring out the windows like portholes at the distant ocean of events they couldn't begin to understand. Incurious as the buildings that held them, they never asked, even later, for the grave of their sister. And only the fact that the children weren't allowed to come again to the pond to skate or build their fires ever served notice to them that their sister had floated like a log for a month in their cow pond, had been dragged out like a burlap bag of drowned cats behind Rofer's buggy horse, and been wrapped in his wife's quilt, never to be used again, and stayed wrapped like that until put in a homemade box with the dull nickel nails winking out of the mismatched corners, and been dropped with a clattering bang into the shallow hole of frozen dirt, and covered once more into darkness, only to resurface in May when the ground heaved her up again, like the pond before it, as if something in her must have the light of day, the light of night, and been buried once more, a final time, with huge stones placed on the coffin to hold it down the nine feet they had dug to be certain that this time the body, holding its quilt around it like a cape, would not wiggle its way back into their lives.

Grandmother told the children she was coming back for her eyes. Parents told the children to ignore what Granny said, she was just trying to scare them. But they told the children never to skate on Stiller's pond again, never. And the one time they tried—and each of them did—they got whipped, hard enough to make an impression. So when they became our parents, they told us never to go to Stiller's pond, as it was still called, and we got whipped hard enough to make the same impression. At least we never skated there. That was as specific as they had made it, and we were specific in our obedience. What we did was spend summer afternoons there, hooking turtles and dragging them up on shore, turning them over with sticks, because some of these were snappers and we couldn't tell which, so they all got treated to our punishment, beaten and prodded with sticks the big ones could snap in two. We would watch, thrilled at the sight of the pointed beak, which we knew had plucked an eyeball out of a socket with the ease of pulling a grape from the arbor vines. Though some insisted their parents had told them to look on the bellies of the old turtles to find which ones had taken her eyes because we'd find their image there still, we never found such a thing and soon enough stopped believing we would discover a transparent hole where she could look out, still trying to see things she shouldn't. But for a while it had worked and I remember our fear when we turned each turtle over on its back, the claws waving helplessly in the paddling feet as we took turns checking the underside. The younger children, overcome, would go screaming and crashing through the cattails and weeds up the banks, until we told them it was all right.

The Stiller children moved away, died, fought in wars, and came home. Always, someone survived to work the farm, though in the community heart they were stained with this memory forever. That followed a pattern too, the old ones would hint, only to be shushed by the parents. The darker gleam of interest would lead us aside one time finally when we were old enough, and the rest of the story would follow. How when they dragged the man out, unlike the Stiller girl, he had been eaten at, like a piece of suet hung in a tree for the birds. There were peck marks all over the front of his face and body, the clothes ripped to threads on the front, intact on the back. This was what they discovered when they rolled him over. The whiteness that had revealed him was the remaining uneaten chunk of cheek and the milk-white bone, polished by the silky bodies of small fish swimming in and out of the face. The men in particular couldn't stand this story because *everything* was chewed on. And when they were finished with that, the turtles turned him over and gnawed the rest.

That was bad enough, but the worst part was that no one could identify him. Stiller wouldn't come near him, and rumors had it that both the hired man and the oldest boy had disappeared that night. Mrs. Stiller never spoke a word about it. She might have identified the rags left on the body at least, but no—so he was buried in another shallow grave next to the girl's, only he didn't come up in the spring. In fact, by the time they began digging the hole to proper depth in May, the box had sunk another two feet and filled with water. When they tried to move it, the seams burst and the thing fell apart in their hands. Inside there was even less of the man than before. Almost a skeleton, the men told people. As if he couldn't wait. That was handy, though, because when they made a new box, they could make it half the regular size, just dump the bones in and save a lot of work digging the deeper hole too.

As I'm walking out here by Stiller's pond, I remember the old mystery and fear that always mingle in the air around this place. Now, of course, I understand that it was the not knowing—the obscenity of the two missing men that made it impossible for our parents and grandparents to tell us the truth and, therefore, to let us continue skating at Stiller's pond. The other man was never heard from again, whichever he was. Maybe he was at the bottom of Stiller's pond, weighted with the heavy sleeping bodies of turtles. During the summer, the cows still walk in their ritual paths to the pond, still muddy the edges, plowing the ground with their hoofs, leaving pocks that freeze in uneven holes to trip small feet in the winter. The cattails still grow at that one end, waving in the summer as graceful and lithe as women. Sometimes I almost imagine I see the hair they chopped off so many years ago to pull her out, still woven like a basket to trap the silvery fish that lurk in the cool dark shallows we can't quite reach when we hunt here as children. And out in the middle there's the tree limb that broke off long ago, and then the tree itself dropped to the ground and was sawed up and hauled away, leaving only the limb humped up like a sea serpent, dark and sinewy, along whose length ride the turtles that rise like ancient people from ancient sleep every spring and crawl up the back of the limb to sun, their necks stretching the tenderness where the skin is paper thin and throbbing with a heart that once fed on the eyes of a woman who tried to cross the pond one winter.

As I start across the pond under the sliver of moon that lies like a knife in the night sky, I remember the last thing our grandmothers told us, the last whispered secret that leaked out of those lips withered by year after year of disappointment and concealment: They weren't wearing skates. "And that's why," they always declare with malicious joy, "you can't go there—ever—you hear—ever." Thus sealing forever in our hearts the desire for the place, a desire that can never be satisfied, a desire we give our children for Stiller's pond.

Rubbish Day

Edis Flowerday

W ILKIE WATCHED the point of intense, white light flare in front of his right eye. For two months now, whether his eyes were open or shut, the light came at odd hours. He knew the light wasn't real. His doctor took great pains to make that clear. "It's merely a neurological phenomenon, like the aura of a migraine headache. There is no light. It's truly all in your head."

"The other day upon the stair, I saw a light that wasn't there." Wilkie lay in bed, his eyes tight shut. "I saw it there again today. I wish that it would go away."

The point of light finally faded, and Wilkie opened his eyes. The cement wall by his bed looked damp, but then it always looked damp this time of year. There was too much moisture in the ground from the spring thaw, and it seeped into the basement walls. Wilkie knew that it was time to move his music boxes back into the middle of the floor, away from the creeping mold. Perhaps he could pile them on his *National Geographic*s. As for the pile of old wall clocks, there were too many of them—stacked like cordwood behind the furnace—to bother with moving them. Most of them were beyond repair anyway, their wooden cases succumbing to creeping patches of strange, phosphorescent mold.

The kitchen door opened, its felt sweep dragging, and light shot down the stairs and stopped just short of the floor drain.

"Rubbish day," Betty said. She pulled the door shut. It clicked.

Excitement grew on Wilkie's face. "Bring out your dead!" he shouted. He threw back the tatty quilt and drew his bony legs up to his chest. With a vigorous, although stiff, kangaroo kick, he shot himself out of bed, and stood on the fraying rag rug, swaying for a moment before he settled into his usual hunched stance, his angular head thrust forward six feet above the ground.

"Garbage day, trash day, diamond-in-the-rough day," Wilkie chanted, marching barefoot in place. He pulled a pair of orange socks from the top drawer of his battered, blond bureau and smiled at them. They were ugly and had a strangely viscous feel. He had bought them twenty-five years ago. They came with a lifetime guarantee. Wilkie sat on his old, straight-backed, wooden chair and pulled them on. Then he fetched his wrestlers' shoes from beneath the seat. The shoes were new, bought just last week at the Rag Company. He loved the support the high tops gave his ankles, and he loved the way the white circles on each side came just at his anklebones.

"Waste and swill and offal." Wilkie opened his pasteboard clothes press and pulled out the pants to his old tuxedo. From the middle of three open boxes of jumbled shirts, he chose a turquoise, black, and white Hawaiian print with pewter buttons shaped like palm trees. He shook the shirt out and smelled it. It was only slightly musty.

"Garbage, trash, and rubble. Rubble, toil, and trouble."

Another swish of the door's felt sweep, another flash of light, and "Breakfast," Betty said. She pulled the door shut again.

That door. Wilkie squinted up through the gloom, screwing his concentration to a fine tune. How long ago was it, he wondered, when Betty came to the door that night and stood there waiting for him to look up from a disarticulated wall clock—a Seth Thomas long-drop. When she realized he intended to ignore her, she closed the door with slow significance, giving it a definite jerk-slam at the very end. "That's fine with me, Lady Jane," he remembered saying; and he hadn't come upstairs until morning.

It was that morning when he caught her standing naked in front of her dresser mirror, staring at the skin of her belly. It hung in finely wrinkled folds, like the skin on the neck of a turkey, only not so purply. The baby had stretched her beyond her limits—beyond the limits of her belly and her breasts, too. In the last of the pregnancy, angry red striations had crawled up from under the bulge and threatened to ride as high as her navel. Then, when the child was born dead, her breasts, not knowing, filled with milk anyway and swelled enormously until they stretched over bluish welts that didn't go away when the milk did.

Wilkie was moved by the sight of her. He breathed out a low whistle that was meant to be sympathetic. "This is your body, broken for me," he said. Betty snatched up her chenille bathrobe and clutched it in front of her while she backed against the wall. She never let him see her naked again.

It was thirty-five years ago, then. That was the year of the baby that looked so healthy in its little coffin—plump and rosy, large for a newborn. He always wondered what they did to make it look so sweet and touchable. He always meant to ask the undertaker.

Wilkie smoothed the quilt over his cot and started up the stairs. He paused for a moment's speculation before opening the kitchen door. Would it be the red one? The blue? Or the off-white? Blue, he bet. He opened the door. It was red.

Betty stood in the haze and the bacon smell of the kitchen, wearing her red polyester pants with the matching shirt jacket. She had identical outfits in navy and off-white. There was a time when she mixed and matched the components, but not anymore.

"Don't let them do anything to me," Wilkie told her. "I want to look good and dead. I want to look all green and buggy-eyed when they shovel me under. I want people to look at me and say how ghastly old Wilkie looks. How horrible. How awful in death."

Betty turned away from the stove, holding two plates of bacon and eggs. Wilkie reached for one, and she jerked it back.

"That's mine," she said. "This is yours."

Wilkie stared at the two plates, searching for fine distinctions, before accepting his on faith. He carried it to the table while Betty turned her back and very privately pulled off her apron.

How dry and papery she's become, Wilkie thought. Her long, thin braid of rat-gray hair, wound into a bun at the base of her head, reminded him of a steel wool scouring pad. An unused, grade 3, steel wool scouring pad. How devoid of fat, or juice, or flavor she was now. How stringy. And shorter. Or was that just illusion? Maybe the matching tops and pants made her look shorter.

Back in those dear, dead days when he first knew her, Betty wore silky dresses with hip-skimming dropped waists and flouncey skirts cut just a tad longer than anyone else's. Those dresses made her look tall and slim—taller and slimmer than she actually was. She dressed well for a country girl. Every Monday she came into town, riding in a Model T with her brother driving. She stayed all week with Eugenia Rasmussen, who also taught girls to paint pansies in watercolor.

Now Wilkie watched Betty eat her breakfast, and he was fascinated. She minced her food like a rabbit, trying to keep her face motionless and composed. She was afraid of wrinkles. She had been for years. That was why she seldom smiled.

"Eat, before it goes cold," she said.

Betty used to smile, Wilkie thought. She used to wait in front of the school until he came riding up—the third man on a horse, sitting behind his two older brothers, holding on for dear life so as not to fall off over the back. She'd smile, all right. Well, that was probably a pretty amusing sight. But it attracted her and amused her so that she even let him deliver her now and then, riding two on a horse, to Miss Rasmussen's house.

One day she seemed to descend from the horse in dreamy slow motion and float weightless to the ground, her skirt billowing out around her. She turned up her face, framed in a sleek bob of brown hair, and said, "I have secret ambitions."

"What was it you wanted to do?" asked Wilkie, a fork of eggs halfway to his mouth.

"Today?"

"No. Years ago. When you had ambitions. What was it you wanted to be? After we finished high school?"

Betty stared at him until a sour little smile of irony began to pull at the corners of her mouth.

"No! Tell me!" he demanded, suddenly boyish and angry. "I want to know."

"An undertaker," she said.

That was it! Wilkie remembered now. They were out in her father's car, and Wilkie was driving. His brother Tom and his girl were in the back seat. Just outside the gate to her father's farm, Betty hopped out of the car and pulled a jug of hootch from a hole hidden under a patch of turf by one of the fence posts. They decided not to go into town to the movies, after all, and went down by the river instead.

"I think I'll go down to Lincoln and work in a bank," Tom said, after a shot or two. His girl giggled.

"I think I'll own the bank you work in," Wilkie said, stupidly, embarrassed. He grabbed Tom, and they started to wrestle. Tom's girl giggled.

"I'm going to be an undertaker," Betty said.

The boys stopped rolling on the grass and stared at her.

"Oh, man. Remind me not to die in your town," Tom said. "I don't want no woman looking at my dead body."

"Why not?" Wilkie asked.

"They strip you nekkid, dumby."

Tom's girl screamed.

Betty went to sit in the car, and, after a little while, Wilkie followed her. She was like a magnet to him in those days.

"Hah! Poor old Tom." Wilkie said it aloud.

Betty glanced up for a split second.

"Tom's dead now four years," she said.

"That long?"

Wilkie started to wipe up the egg yolk and bacon grease with a scrap of bread when the point of light came back. It danced around the plate as Wilkie followed the motion of his hand with his eyes.

"You are my sunshine, my only sunshine," he croaked in sync with his hand.

Betty grabbed his hand and made him stop. They stared at one another until she dropped his hand and looked away.

"You *have* got more decent clothes," she said.

Wilkie couldn't remember what he was wearing. He looked down to check.

"This shirt, when alive, graced the back of the venerable Mr. Conover from over on Buchanan Street." He fingered the fancy buttons. "Actually, I'm surprised the Missus didn't cut the buttons off. She's as tight as a tick. Never throws out anything worth keeping." He stopped to think about that. "Hey! Get it? Never throws out anything worth keeping?"

"You deliberately try to humiliate me," Betty said.

"Naw. You've done that to yourself."

Wilkie stood and went to get his faded denim jacket from the hook by the back door. Behind him, he heard the angry scrape of her chair against the floor and was surprised to feel her hand close on his arm.

"What about yesterday?"

Wilkie tried to remember. "It was warm yesterday. I washed the car."

"And then what? What happened after that?"

"I stretched myself out on the hood and got a little sun." Wilkie shrugged. "A guy my age can use a little sun on his battered, old bones. It felt darn good, too."

"Do you think I didn't hear you talking to the Jensen boy?"

"Sure, we talked. He's a nice kid. We always shoot the breeze."

"He asked if you were up for air."

What was she getting at? Wilkie wondered.

"You said you were, that you'd crawled up out of your hole to see what was going on in the world."

He still didn't get it.

"Why don't you just announce to the whole world that you live in the basement?"

She left in a huff, and, presently, Wilkie heard the door to her bedroom close. She had retreated to her inner sanctum and was no doubt sitting in her fancy boudoir chair, gazing at the big old doll she placed in the center of her bed every morning. The doll was dressed like a bride, and Betty always arranged the skirt of its gown in a full circle around it. God! Wilkie hated that doll!

He went outside and crossed to the garage. His old Mercury, nice and clean, was parked outside on the cement slab. Wilkie jerked up the garage door so hard it fairly shot along its tracks and clanged to a stop overhead. From his collection of balloon-tire bicycles, Wilkie chose an old, blue Schwinn and hooked it up to a battered, red Radio Flyer wagon. Without glancing up, he wheeled the contraption to the kitchen door and loaded the wagon with the cardbord boxes and plastic bags Betty had set out before breakfast.

Trying hard not to wobble, he mounted up and pedaled down the drive. His legs were too long to fit easily under the handlebars, and it took an effort to get up speed, pedaling, as he must, on the sides of his feet with his knees well out to each side. At the front curb, he stopped and unloaded the rubbish.

He knew Betty thought he was becoming physically unbalanced. She told him as much when she suggested he ought to stabilize his two or three favorite bikes with outrigger wheels and turn them into glorified trikes. All they really needed, he maintained, was the handlebars raised, which he'd get around to one of these days. Maybe he'd even raise the seats and put sheepskin pads on them so they wouldn't be such a pain to his bony seat. If he ever got to the point where he really needed stability and, perhaps, a little horsepower, Wilkie had the plans already drawn up for a dandy three-wheeler that was a cross between an Easy Rider motorcycle and a geriatric trike.

He'd seen one once, made out of no better parts than he already had stored in his garage. The rig came putt-putting right down the main street of one of those little towns out west where Wilkie used to have accounts. It was pushing its miniature front wheel along at the end of a swooping curve of pipe that must have gone on for six or seven feet.

"It was so absolutely perfect, it was downright embarrassing," he told Betty. "There was a box on the back, for carrying things. And there was a big extra seat behind the driver. This guy in jeans and a sleeveless t-shirt and mirror sunglasses was driving it, and he had his wife on behind—at least, I guess it was the wife. And she was wearing mirror sunglasses, too. She was straddling the shaft, with her feet on the running boards, and she didn't even have to hold on. Somebody ought to patent a rig like that and market it. Maybe I'll just do that, myself, one of these days."

"Don't bother with the extra seat on my account," Betty told him.

Wilkie set off, pedaling like a bear in a circus, down the street of wooden bungalows that had all been new and identical in 1946, when he and Betty first moved in. Every single one was different now, irretrievably individualized with breezeways and decks and family rooms off the backs. Maybe Wilkie would build himself a room off the back of their house. It would sure beat the basement. He sniffed spring in the air and felt inspired. His neighbors would be cleaning out their houses. The pickings would be good.

By the end of the block Wilkie had his speed up, and he started to cruise the scene with his own brand of cool professionalism. He could assess the potential of any trash heap while moving by at a steady five miles per. He hadn't gone three blocks before something caught his eye. He slammed on the brakes, stayed on the bike just a tad too long, and had to catch himself as it started a slow fall to one side.

Over on the curb there was a glass and metal object, about ten inches tall and five inches square. It had brassy innards, which were visible through a moveable plate of beveled, lead glass. The glass, miraculously, was intact, with not a chip on its surface. Wilkie scrutinized the gears inside and noticed that one set of wheels, mounted side by side on a rod, had numbers and letters embossed all around the facing edges. A dry, cracking, fabric typewriter ribbon was strung beneath.

Wilkie felt all around the thing and found that someone had wired a big, old key to a protruding screw head. The key was about three inches long with large, wing-shaped flanges at its top. He unwired it and poked it into all the openings he could find. At last he hit pay dirt and wound the device up. Nothing happened.

Deliberately, Wilkie peeled off his denim jacket and spread it neatly on the pavement. He slid the beveled glass from its grooves, laid it carefully on the jacket, and began rotating the numbered and lettered cogs with his thumb. It wasn't long before he heard a click, a whirring sound, and the staccato beat of a bell that was fifty times louder than a cheap alarm clock and ten times as annoying.

Wilkie tried to turn the thing off by moving the cogs along, but they were frozen in place. He snatched up his jacket—flipping the glass onto the pavement where it shattered—and dropped it over the alarm. He stepped back several paces, wary of anything with a mainspring wound tight. Once, years ago, he had tangled with a marble mantel clock, having taken a screwdriver to it while it was wound. The explosion left bits of metal embedded in the ceiling and walls and broke the window over the kitchen sink. As the mainspring lept uncoiling across the room, it took a piece of flesh out of his right cheek.

Betty had rushed into the room to see him standing there, all bloody. She started to cry. Then she grabbed a tea towel and pressed it against his face. "I can't turn my back on you for a minute, can I?" she scolded. "You're just like a little kid." As she drove him to the doctor, she mused that a scar might improve his looks. While he was being stitched up, she vomited in the next room. She was just preg-nant. "It was going to be a present for her," Wilkie confessed to the doctor. "I was going to fix it up."

The alarm bell finally ran down, and Wilkie noticed that a woman was watch-ing him from the side door of the house. "You old fool!" he said straight at her. She disappeared.

Wilkie touched his cheek and rubbed the old scar before hunkering down in front of the alarm box again. With both arms outstretched, he tried to get a grip on the treasure. It was heavier than he expected, however. On the second try, he tilted the thing to one side so he could get a hand underneath. Using his legs for leverage, he lifted in the recommended way; but it still wouldn't budge. A multiplication of gravity was fighting him, as if the thing were sitting on top of an electromagnet. Again he eased up to take two or three deep breaths, and then gave it his all—legs, arms, and stomach muscles tensed, breathing stopped. A whole explosion of tiny points of light dazzled his eyes before he relaxed his grip and gave up.

Squatting there, he watched past the points of light to the spot where he knew the alarm box was. It came back into view as the light faded. "Now, don't you go away," he told it. "You're the kind of trash a body would kill for."

He clapped both hands on his thighs and straightened up too fast for the kinks that had settled into his knees. He was bent forward, gripping the nearest garbage can, trying to ease the weight off his legs, when a pain knifed up through the back of his head and out through the inside corner of his right eyebrow. He fell and brought the garbage can down with him, rolling alongside its clatter out into the middle of the street.

Bright sheets of neon-green water flowed over Wilkie's eyes in a direction that was totally illogical, considering his present condition. The water had a smell—like the sweet, rusty smell of his mother's coffee grinder when it was just opened on a dry winter's day—and because the water was filling his whole head, the smell became stronger, unbearable, suffocating. With the increased pressure, his ears began to ring, and then a buzzing sound invaded his face with an intensity that made his nose tingle.

Wilkie inhaled as much air as he could manage and pushed out a long wail for help on the exhalation. The woman came back to her side door, but Wilkie didn't see her, not with the glowing water still cascading over his eyes. It was spectacular, almost as good as Niagara Falls by night, he thought. He might as well try to enjoy it.

At length the curtain of rippling water became static, split into a million amorphous jellies, and fell away from Wilkie's eyes. He lay on his side, his cheek on the cement, and blinked, trying to focus on the surface line of the street. Presently he saw motion half a block away. It was Betty. He recognized her red outfit. Her slacks and matching top came halfway along from the corner of the street before her head and hands joined up. Wilkie lifted his head, intending to call out to her. Before he could make a sound, however, Betty and the street began to revolve. It looked like she was running through the fun barrel at an amusement park. He laughed.

"You're doing okay, kiddo. Just look at you, never missing a step. I didn't know you had it in you."

Betty knelt by Wilkie, but she kept on riding the fun barrel around and around. Wilkie was amazed.

"How do you do that?" he asked. He lay back flat and studied her. "Why don't you fall off?"

Betty's face floated away from her shoulders and hung close to his. She looked fuzzy and soft, as if she were being photographed through a gauze. All that whirling around had fleshed her out again. Now she reminded him of the exquisite creature she had been when she was young and always had a matte finish like a bisque doll.

Wilkie propped himself on his elbow. "It's this thing I found," he whispered to her. "All I have to do is figure out how it works." He glanced around to make sure no one else could hear. "I think it's some kind of time machine. I want you to have it."

Wilkie rolled over and hiked himself up on all fours. He could hear Betty cry-ing and wondered if she were trying to say something. He began crawling toward the curb. If he could just keep his eyes glued to that machine, he was certain he could get to it. He didn't blink when the sunlight began dancing off the metal in all directions. He persevered when the whole thing became haloed in a glow that grew until the contraption seemed to burn. It was the flash of the explosion and the shock wave that caught him unprepared. It seemed to happen inside him, it was that close.

Then there was the jolt of hitting the street and the effort to focus on the fading light. And then darkness.

You Ain't Dead Yet

Barton Sutter

MARK FLUNG a final shovelful of cement into the mixer and stuck the spade in a pile of sand. "She'll be done soon!" he hollered at Elmer, who was knocking the forms off a fresh burial vault. Elmer nodded and coughed. Like Mark, he wore a red bandana across his face. The air inside the Sunwall Brothers' Vault Company was heavy with fine gray dust. By the end of the day his lungs felt so thick that more than once as he sank into sleep Mark had imagined his lungs were hardening, slowly turning to concrete. Still, it was the best summer job he'd ever had. The pay was decent, Elmer was good if quiet company, and the nearness of death made him feel serious, adult, and curiously alive.

Elmer helped him maneuver the mixer over a new set of forms, and they worked hard and fast to fill them before the cement could stiffen. Then they cleared their throats with a shot of cold water from the hose and stepped out into the bright sunlight. They sat with their backs to the wall of the cinder-block building, and the breeze cooled their skin and dried their damp clothes. Elmer's gray shirt was stained with white patches of salt. The man smelled, Mark thought, like somebody's basement. Elmer was a bachelor and so taciturn that, though they had worked side by side all summer long, he still seldom spoke unless Mark put a question to him directly. At first Mark had thought it was the melancholy nature of his work that made Elmer so quiet, but Eddie disproved that idea. Elmer's partner and older brother, Eddie was a glad-hander who spent half his time driving around the county, drinking coffee, smooth-talking the undertakers. Mark preferred the honesty of Elmer's silence. Elmer had gotten his breath back now and broke out his pipe. His tobacco smelled like apples and smoldering leaves. Because there was so much time to pass on the job—waiting for cement to dry, driving to and from the cemeteries, waiting for funerals to finish—Mark had taken up smoking, too. He lit a Lucky Strike. Elmer called them coffin nails.

"Well, that's done," Mark said. "How else you plan to entertain me today?"

"Delivery up to Deep River. We got twins this time. Old man whose wife passed on several years back. He buried her in a wooden vault, and I guess the family decided as long as we were going in there anyway we might as well put her in concrete, too. Eddie hauled her vault up there this morning."

"Wait a minute. You mean we're going into the grave, take her casket out of the vault, and transfer it to a new one?"

"That's it. Sort of a transplant. We'll do that every once in a while. Not much to it, really. The Crusher will have her all dug out by the time we get there."

This was a new one, and Mark wasn't sure he liked the idea. He had taken a lot of kidding about this job, but, aside from a few bad dreams, it hadn't troubled him much. Building vaults was just construction work, and setting one in a grave was hardly any different from installing a septic tank. The only funny part was lowering the coffin and placing the lid on the vault. Otherwise the job was surprisingly ordinary. This transplant business sounded spooky, though. Too much like one of his father's jokes.

"Time we got going," said Elmer. "Funeral's at four."

Mark was hoping that Elmer would offer him the wheel, but once he had checked to make sure that the vault was locked in place on the truck bed Elmer got in on the driver's side. Sometimes Mark wondered if the man even knew he was there.

They headed north out of town. Although it had been a warm September, the leaves had already begun to yellow and brown, and the power lines were strung with migrating swallows. Mark mopped his face with the red handkerchief. His father had razzed him about that bandana all sumer. He said Mark looked like an outlaw. He told the neighbors that his son was riding with the Sunwall Boys. Mark would drag in from work, and his father, fixing supper, would turn from the stove and say, "Well, how did the grave robbers do today? Come on, I won't squeal. What did you find? Jewelry? Some nice gold fillings?" Mark was pleased and surprised to hear his father talk like that. They had buried his mother the year he entered high school, and his father had grieved for two years. Mostly at the sink, for some reason. How many times had he wandered into the kitchen to find his father up to his elbows in soap suds, weeping over a stack of dirty plates? Either the old man had cried himself out, or the teasing was a way to ease the pain. In any case the bandana had become a standing joke, and Mark had worn it around the house all summer long, pulling it over his face whenever he had a favor to ask. "All right, old man," he would threaten, aiming a finger at his father's belly, "your car keys or your life."

They were on gravel now and dropping into the Deep River valley, raising a wake of dust. Elmer stopped on the bridge and turned off the motor. He was an odd man, Mark thought. He always took time to appreciate things.

The river was slowed here by a series of small dams and backed into marshes and mudflats to form the Deep River Wildlife Refuge. The water was low this time of year, and the breeze blew the rank stink of the exposed bottom through the cab of the truck. Mark noticed a raft of big white birds floating far out. Shorebirds skittered over the sandspits, crying. Near the bridge a great blue heron stood like a prehistoric relic, a patient fisherman with all the time in the world. A flock of blue-winged teal dropped over the ridge, their wing-patches flashing in the sun, and skimmed the water below the bridge, peeling the surface as they landed.

"Pretty," said Elmer.

"I'll say," said Mark. "You do much hunting, Elmer?"

"Not anymore. Used to. When I was a kid. Not for a long time now. Sold my guns here a few years back. Fun went out of it somehow. I still like to look, though."

Elmer turned the key, and the teal, startled, took off. The truck ground uphill, and the steeple of Deep River Lutheran rose like the mast of a schooner against the sky.

Elmer pulled in past the parsonage, around behind the church, and eased the truck down the grassy lane between graves. He parked beside the vault that Eddie had delivered, and they got out, the cab doors slamming like gunshots in the quiet countryside.

The Crusher grinned at them from the grave and wiped the sweat from his face. "About time you boys got here," he said. "And here I was thinking you might like a little extra exercise. Too late now. I'm damn near done."

"Sorry," said Elmer. "We had some forms to fill."

"Yeah, sure. Shame on you both. Leaving a poor old man to break his back in this heat. Could of died of the sunstroke today. Hi, kid. Hand me that water jug, would you?"

"Well," Elmer said, "you couldn't pick a more convenient spot to keel over."

"Ain't that the truth? This wouldn't be such a bad place to be planted, either. It's a nice view. I seen ducks flying up and down the valley all day."

"Prettiest graveyard in the county, I'd say."

"Except for the slant of the hill here gives me a hell of a time. Reach me that level, Elmer. Close enough. You boys relax, now. I won't be a minute."

Mark and Elmer squatted beside the grave and watched the old man work. Of all the people he'd met on the job, Karl "The Crusher" Lundquist was Mark's favorite by far. Built like a bear, The Crusher had wrestled all over the Upper Midwest in his younger days. He said he had beaten Bronko Nagurski in his prime, and Mark believed him. Eddie said The Crusher had retired from the ring after he broke an opponent's neck, but Mark hadn't been brave enough to ask the old man if the story were true. Way up in his sixties now, The Crusher had his Social Security and only dug graves in the summer. The hard labor, he argued, preserved his health. Mark loved to watch him work. His tools were always sharp and bright, and he moved with casual efficiency. He was down to the bottom of the grave now, shaving and slicing, scraping and squaring off. As he worked, he talked.

"Can't bury this one deep enough, if you ask me. Milowski," he spat. "I ought to go down an extra three feet for that bastard. I knew the bum. You seen his place? Silos all over, tractor as big as a house. Made out of money, they say, but the bugger couldn't buy his way into heaven if I was in charge. I never seen the like for luck. If it hails, it hails on his neighbor's place. Milowski picks up the pieces. Born with a horseshoe up his ass. Took every farm on that section. Him and the bank. I seen what he done to his woman, too. They got married, she was the prettiest piece you hope to see. Stop your heart just to look at that woman. High-toned, too, but nice, you know? I can't understand it. Here she is, the prettiest thing in the county, and she marries the most mean-hearted son of a bitch I ever met. And he busted her, too. Just broke that woman down. Worked her like a horse, and she was nothing but a nag by the time she kicked off. They say it was natural, but to my way of thinking it was murder pure and simple, murder over the years. The day she died I told Vera, Vera, that man should get the chair. She knew what I meant. I hear he died of a heart attack, but you could have fooled me. I don't believe the bastard had one. I'd like to see them cut him up. I'd like to see an autopsy. Know what I think they'd find? Liver. A big, fat, black liver right where the heart should be. Wasn't nothing but bile in that man's veins. I swear. The stingy bastard buried his woman in a wooden vault, and, from what I hear, the family felt so bad about it, they figured they put a puke like him in concrete, it's the least they can do for her. They knew. They knew what he done to that woman. Anna Marie, that was her name. Anna Marie, and she was a lady, too."

Mark looked over at Anna Marie. The Crusher had lifted the heavy load of earth off her vault, and the wooden box, reddish and stained at the corners by some sort of rot, lay exposed. The Crusher had scarred the lid with his shovel.

"That does it," The Crusher said. "How you want to go about this, Elmer? You think we need the belts?"

"Naw, let's try it by hand."

"Okay by me. You boys think you can hold up your end against an old man?"

"Hope your Medicare covers rupture," said Elmer, and he and Mark jumped into the grave. Mark stumbled over a spade and brushed against the wall, creating a small landslide.

"Careful," The Crusher warned, "or you'll bury us all."

They forced a pick and shovel underneath the vault, pried it loose, and dragged the wooden box to the middle of the double grave. Then they knelt beside the vault and clawed at the earth until they could work their hands beneath it. "Lift with your legs now," The Crusher said, "not with your backs. Ready? Heave!"

Mark pressed his face against the damp wood and strained. Groaning as if in pain, they hoisted the vault waist-high, paused for breath and a better grip, then lifted on up, slipping and swearing, and then they had her over their heads. Mark looked up at the moldy bottom. He and Elmer lunged and propped their end on the edge of the grave. They hustled back to help the old man. The Crusher counted to three, and they slid the vault like a heavy toboggan out of the grave and onto the grass.

They hauled themselves out of the hole. Mark was trembling.

"Heavier than I expected," Elmer said.

"Yeah, I guess she's a little waterlogged."

Mark looked at the wooden box with dread. "What now?" he said.

"Better sink those vaults," Elmer said. "They'll be here in under an hour."

They put their shoulders to the carriage, in which the heavy concrete vault hung suspended from pulleys and lightweight cable, and rolled it into position over Anna Marie's empty grave. Mark and The Crusher steadied the vault, Elmer turned the crank, and they slowly lowered the concrete box into the hole. Mark jumped down and unsnapped the cables. Sweating in the sun, they wheeled the second vault off the truck and sank it beside its mate. Then they hooked the heavy lids to the carriages and hid one behind the church. Elmer called for a break.

They sat beside The Crusher's pickup and drank from his thermos of ice-water. "Hot," the old man said. He poured some water over his head. "One thing about my job, at least you get cooler the further down you dig."

"This heat won't last," Elmer said.

"Nope. Nights are cool already. We'll get the deep frost before you know it, and I can retire again. Used to be, I'd dig right through the winter. Had to burn tires to thaw the ground. What a mess. Cemetery looked like a junkyard. And cold? Christ. Work up a sweat with the shovel, freeze your ass if you stopped to rest. I'm glad them days are over. Summers I don't mind, but come December I'll take the TV and a hot buttered rum. What about you, kid? You must be just about done with this monkey business."

"I leave for the U on Monday. I guess I won't see you again."

"Well, that won't kill you. What you plan to take up up there? The teacher's time?"

"That's it," Mark smiled. "No, I thought I'd try pre-med. I thought I might like to be a doctor."

"Oh, sure, and put me and Elmer right out of work. What do you want to do that for? Christ, there's already too many old buzzards hanging around. Just this morning Eddie was telling me if we don't get a flu epidemic pretty soon we'll all be on welfare. That's the trouble with people today. They all want to live forever. Not me. I was up to the nursing home last Sunday, to see my old pal Swenson?

Had himself a stroke last year, and the poor son of a bitch can't hardly talk. About all he can do is sit there and moo like a goddamn cow. And he was the strongest son of a buck! I could of almost cried. So I'm sitting there with Swenson drooling all over this nightie they've got him in, when who comes rolling by but Alma Berg? Hell, I went to school to that old heifer! She's about four hundred years old, and there she is, still hanging around. And for what? She's flat on her back, and they roll her up to the window, and I can hear her mumbling around. Crazy as a goose. 'Sky,' she says. 'Blue sky.' Way to go, Alma. She's about four years old. And then you know what she says? This really got me. There's this maple tree outside, and the leaves are starting to turn, real pretty, you know, and she looks at that, and she says, 'Look at the flowers. Look at the lovely flowers.' Then she turns my way—she's damn near bald—she turns my way, and she says, 'I just love spring. Don't you love the spring?' 'Sure,' I go. 'Spring. Love the spring. Real nice, Alma.' I had to get out of there. Christ Almighty, give me a shovel. I'll dig myself a hole and pull the dirt in after me. That got me, though. 'Look at the flowers,' she says."

"I'll give you a shovel," said Elmer. "We've got about forty minutes to get this place in shape."

Elmer got a crowbar from the truck, and they stood before the wooden vault. "Here goes," Elmer said, and he drove the crowbar under the lid. The nails complained, and water oozed from the wood like sap where he forced the iron in. He worked his way around the vault, gradually raising the lid, an inch here, a half inch there. Mark and The Crusher pushed, Elmer pried with the bar, the wet wood squealed, squawked, and the lid popped free. It lay on its back in the grass like a door into the earth, a ragged row of rusty nails, twisted and bent, staggered around the rim.

Bruised by green and purple mold, the gray coffin looked diseased. Mark imagined it new, shining and smooth. His mother's coffin had looked like a treasure chest. At the funeral he had hardly mourned his mother at all, but the thought of that rich, copper-colored casket sunk out of sight had troubled him for days.

Nobody spoke. They had made such a racket raising the lid that the silence now seemed huge. Mark wondered what was left of the woman inside. He thought, very quickly, of Egyptian mummies, of Lazarus and Jesus. He stared at the coffin, thinking it looked as flimsy as cardboard, thinking how thin was the membrane of metal between himself and the corpse, and he knew when they lifted the casket it would break in their hands like rotten fruit.

The silence grew, and he heard, at its heart, a dull bass beat, and, above the bass beat, the quiet seemed to whisper and twang, to crackle and sing. He might have been standing inside a power station. He knew this feeling. This was death. This was what happened. A quiet so deep it disturbed the molecules of the air. He could hear them vibrate and hum. He could feel them. He had felt this before, at his mother's funeral, as he stood staring down at the lifeless body that seemed to be made of translucent wax. He wanted to run, but his legs wouldn't work, and then, as if the air had turned into water, he heard the distant sound of Elmer's voice. "Let's go," it said, and he found he could move after all but slowly, as if underwater, as if he'd been shocked, as if his limbs had been shot full of novocaine.

Slowly he moved to one end of the coffin. Elmer nodded, and he watched his own hand reach inside the wooden box and grasp the corroded metal handle. The Crusher hugged the other end of the casket and grunted, "Ready? Heave!" Mark strained at the handle, and then they had her up and out of the box and were shuffling sideways. It was lighter than he had expected. Maybe she's nothing but dust, Mark thought, and the handle broke off in his hand. The casket dropped, Elmer said, "Shit," and Mark slipped, fell, and skidded against the casket.

He sat up. He was all right. Then he looked at his hand. It was green, and his arm was coated with mucus, and the side of his shirt was wet. And then, as if he had fallen on a hornet's nest, he was up on his feet and turning in circles, tearing at his shirt and screaming again and again: "Get it off me!"

The Crusher grabbed Mark from behind and held him, ripped the soiled shirt down the front, and, using it like a rag, he scrubbed the fungus off Mark's arm. The old man released him and stepped away. "There," he said. "You're okay."

"I'm all right!" Mark shouted. "I'm okay."

"It's only mold, Mark," Elmer said.

"I know it. I'm sorry." He was hot now not with fear but with shame.

The Crusher kicked the casket. "At least we didn't bust the son of a bitch."

"Thank God for small favors," Elmer said. "Why don't you take a break, Mark? We can handle this."

"I'm okay."

"I know. But go have a smoke, anyway."

Flushed with embarrassment, Mark carried his dirty shirt to the truck, plucked the pack of Luckies and the matchbook from the pocket, and threw the shirt on the floor of the cab. He lit up, inhaled, and was suddenly sick. He hurried behind a row of shrubbery, paused as if trying to remember something, then sank to his knees and threw up.

A song sparrow sang from a fence post. The silence was normal now. He could hear a tractor throbbing in a distant field. So that was the bass beat he'd thought was death itself. That was a good one, he thought, confusing death with a John Deere. He picked a few dusky blue berries off a juniper bush, chewed them, and the foul taste in his mouth was replaced by the tart, clean tang of wintergreen. He wiped his face with the red bandana, walked to the grave, and took a long slug of water from The Crusher's thermos. They had already lowered the coffin and dropped the lid on the vault.

"You okay?" Elmer asked

"I'm fine. Sorry to make such a fuss. Here, let me do that."

He took the shovel from Elmer and began flinging dirt on the vault. The clods of earth burst on the concrete lid with a hollow sound. Elmer knelt beside the grave and started assembling the brass frame on which the coffin would rest during the graveside service. Trying to atone for his hysteria, Mark worked furiously while The Crusher shoveled slowly but steadily, pacing himself. The grave was quickly filled, and they leaned on their shovels, panting and wet with sweat.

Elmer looked at his watch. "Twenty minutes," he warned. "Go get the grass, Mark."

Mark ran to the truck and hauled out the artificial turf. He draped the heavy carpets over his shoulders, struggled to the grave, dumped the rugs, and ran back for the other set. By the time he returned The Crusher and Elmer had carpeted the grave of Anna Marie and gathered the grass like green bunting about the base of the brass frame. They spread the second set over the mound of raw earth beside Milowski's grave.

"Now the tent," Elmer said.

They had it down to a system. Elmer raised the canvas on the poles while Mark drove the stakes and drew the guy-lines taut. The Crusher collected his tools and tidied up the gravesite. Then they all stood back to admire their work. The brass frame gleamed in the sunlight, and the artificial grass disguised the dirt. The pale green awning, that protected the mourners from precipitation on gloomy days, would shield them from the sun today. The tent was sometimes rented out for carnivals and church bazaars and, consequently, made the gravesite almost gay.

"Good," said Elmer. "Let's clear out."

For the next half hour their job was to make themselves invisible. Mark and The Crusher wheeled the second carriage out of sight. Elmer drove to the rear of the cemetery and parked behind a screen of evergreens. The Crusher pulled his battered pickup alongside, got out, and squeezed into the cab beside Mark. He poured coffee from a thermos and passed the cup.

"Here they come," said Mark, and they watched the funeral procession turn into the churchyard. The headlights of the cars burned dimly in the daylight, and the little flags on the fenders fluttered in the breeze. The heavy hearse eased up to the grave, and the doors flashed open. He could see Severson, the mortician, giving directions. The pall-bearers crowded close.

"Hope they got some he-men to carry him," The Crusher said. "He ate like a pig."

The pall-bearers rested the shining casket on the brass frame and stepped away. A parade of mourners filed up and huddled beneath the awning as if the sunshine were rain. Severson nodded. The minister stepped forward and began to read from a little black book.

"Wake me up when it's over," Elmer said.

The pleasant murmur of the minister's voice mingled with bird songs and the rustling of the nearby cornfield. Mark looked at the faint green stain on his arm. He spit on his fingers and rubbed, but it wouldn't come off. It would have to wait until he could shower. The sun warmed his bare chest, and his eyelids grew heavy. He bowed his head.

He was afraid he was going to dream. He had moved all his things to the basement in June, and, though sleeping was easy and cool down there, the dark was deep, and the first time he dreamed he was buried alive he was unable to find the light. He'd left the lamp burning from then on. Not all his dreams had been nightmares, though. His mother had visited him several times. They had laughed and reminisced warmly, and he had wakened from those dreams so gently he had felt as if he were floating on his back. Recently, though, she had scared him. He was following a dark, hooded figure down a spiral staircase, and, knowing who it was, he called to her again and again, trying to get her to stop and acknowledge him. Finally, she turned, and her face was a cold, flat mirror. Transfixed, he stared at his own image, and as he stared his features melted as if his face were wax and bared the skull, and his eyes clouded over until they were pale as milk, as mild and bland as the blind eyes of a statue, and he felt himself turning to stone. He woke from that nightmare screaming so loudly his father had come pounding down the steps to see what was wrong. "Go away," Mark had told him, still crazy with sleep. "Everyone I want to talk to is dead."

He was half asleep now, but he could hear singing or was it the wind? It was singing. They were singing about the river. The beautiful, the beautiful river. Shall we gather at the river that flows by the throne of God? And then he came wide awake as The Crusher said, "Mark? Elmer? Come on, you goldbricks, they're leaving. Time to get back to work."

The last few cars were pulling out. Mark and The Crusher lowered the coffin, disassembled the frame, and rolled up the grass while Elmer conferred with Severson. They struck the tent and were stowing it in the truck when Elmer walked over.

"Think you can finish up alone, Mark? Severson wants to talk business with me and Eddie, so I've got to go back to the shop. I can ride in with him, but that means you'll have to take the truck."

"Sure. No problem."

"Good. We'll come back for the other carriage tomorrow. Karl, maybe you can help him here, and then come on in for your check if you want."

"Don't worry about us. You just get your pencil out and practice up your penmanship."

"Greedy old bugger, isn't he?" Elmer said. "Okay, see you later, then."

They waved him off and wheeled out the carriage they had hidden behind the church. They lowered the lid on Milowski's vault, and, as they swung the hooks free, The Crusher spat in the grave and said, "Bye-bye." They rolled the carriage onto the truck bed and locked it in place.

The air was growing cooler now, and they shoveled at a leisurely pace, working just fast enough to keep warm, the day's work all but over. The late afternoon light slanted across the cemetery, and all the stones threw shadows on the graves.

"Good riddance," The Crusher said, loading his spade with loam, "to bad rubbish." The dirt hit the vault with a solid thump.

"I don't think," Mark said, "I've ever seen anyone take more satisfaction in his work."

The Crusher laughed. "Well, this one was special. Couldn't have happened to a nicer guy. Normally, you know, you don't take much pleasure in putting people under, and sometimes you feel pretty bad if it's a young one, say, or someone you grew up with." He sighed. " 'Let the dead bury the dead,' The Good Book says, and sometimes I feel half dead myself. Hell, who knows? Maybe you'll be dropping the lid on me this time next year."

"Baloney," Mark said. "You're stronger than most guys my age."

"That may be, but I'm running out of pep, anyway. What's the point? Half my friends are gone, and the rest of them can't even go to the can without a nurse to show them how."

"But you've got a lot of younger friends."

"Yeah, but it's not the same. And then I miss the old lady, too. The winters get awful long without her."

"How long ago did you lose her?"

"Five years next month. We used to get snowed in, you know, and we'd play a lot of gin, and, I don't know, it was fun. I never cared much for solitaire, myself, and it seems like the bed never really gets warm anymore. I used to call her my hot water bottle." He laughed. "She hated that."

Mark watched a nightcrawler ooze from a clod at his feet. "Well, even if you do kick off," Mark said, "I won't be here to bury you. I've had enough of this. I think I'll try to get a job as an orderly next year. I'd rather be helping people stay alive, even if I'm only giving enemas to old men. This just gets too depressing."

"I know what you mean. It's a lonesome kind of a job. But then somebody's got to do it."

They smoothed the dirt over the double grave and set the sod back in place. Then they arranged the flowers that would melt back into the earth with the first rainfall. As they walked to The Crusher's pickup Mark clanged the blade of one spade against the other. They rang like a small bell. "Well, anyway, it's been fun, sort of. I liked the hard work, and Elmer's a good guy. And I sure have enjoyed working with you."

"The same to you, kid." They laid the tools in the bed of the pickup. "The first funeral we worked together, I told Elmer, you got a good one there. A hard worker and a smart kid who don't act it." They shook hands, and The Crusher got in. "Best of luck with the books, now. And you come see me whenever you're back in town."

"Thanks," Mark said. "I will."

They nodded good-bye, the pickup coughed and roared, and Mark stood watching until the old man disappeared.

Proud that Elmer had trusted him with the truck, Mark drove the gravel road carefully, gearing down and descending slowly into the valley. When he reached the bridge, he turned off the dike, drove out to the dam, and parked. The marsh was wild with waterfowl, and as soon as he cut the motor his ears were filled with their gabbling. He could hear swallows twittering, too, and the creak of insects and frogs. Excited, he picked his dirty shirt off the floor and got out. He slammed the door, and a pair of wood ducks shot out of the channel. The wind off the water chilled his bare chest. He sucked in his breath.

The shoreline was mostly muck and reeked with a sour odor, but the water ran more swiftly through the channel. Mark knelt on a wash of gravel there, soaked his shirt, and scrubbed his forearms clean. He wrung out his shirt and wiped his face. Then he sat back on a piece of driftwood and smoked, watching the water turn to wine, watching the sun go down.

He was about to leave when he felt them, heard the rush of their wings, and there they were, ghostly and strange as angels in the half-light but nonetheless real, row after row of snow geese skimming the cattails and flooding above him, close enough to touch. Paralyzed with excitement at first, as the final row passed over him, he reached up, felt feathers. The startled goose honked, veered off, and there was a thunderous beating of wings as the whole flock ascended, then coasted down on the dark water, far out.

No one was going to believe this, he thought, but he hurried toward the truck. He wanted to get back to the shop in time to tell Elmer. Coming up the path, he felt something crunch beneath his boot. He looked down. Skin and bones. What was it? He turned it over with his toe. Carrion beetles scurried away. A muskrat, most likely. He ran to the truck.

When he turned the key the motor groaned and quit. "What now?" Mark moaned. "What is it now?" He flicked on the lights; the battery was good. He kicked the accelerator and tried again. Then he read the gas gauge. "Damn it," he said. "God damn it!" he shouted. "God damn it all to hell anyhow!"

Now he was going to be late. Now his father would worry, and Elmer would think he was dumb. First that rotten casket. Now this. He would have to walk to the nearest farm and hope that someone was home, and even if he could beg some gas and a ride he was going to be late.

He got out of the cab, slammed the door, and then, instead of walking away, he sat down on the running board. The wind off the marsh was cold, and he crossed his arms and rocked a little. He wasn't going anywhere. He was beat. Defeated and ashamed, he sat in the dark and listened to the small birds and animals disturb the dry weeds. He thought of Milowski and Anna Marie, the carcass he had stepped on, his mother and Jesus, and he knew he was going to die.

Because that's life, he thought. Either you were somebody decent or you were a bastard and then you died. You had a heart attack and went down like a cow in a slaughterhouse or you got cancer and they cut you to pieces. Then what? Nothing. Worms and beetles and mold.

His mother had taken two years to die, and the morning his father had called him downstairs to tell him she was dead, he was glad. First there was a lump, and the doctors removed it. Then she went back, and they took her insides out. And then there was the morning she had called Mark and his brother into her bedroom and said she wanted to show them something. She had thrown back the blanket and said, "I wanted to show you this because people will talk, and I'd rather tell you myself." She had gone on talking, but her voice was only a murmur because Mark had never seen a woman's breasts before, and it was so different from what he'd imagined, so strange and nice-looking, and the air in the room began to vibrate and buzz, and he knew that his mother was going to die because she only had one. Where her other breast had been, her chest was flat, the skin pinched by a lumpy, purple scar.

Later there were radiation treatments, prayers, and other operations. She had lost her hair and gone blind. The two of them had spoken little then, communicating more and more by hand. He rubbed her back. She read his face with her fingers, as if his features were braille. She wanted kisses, but he was horrified by her breath. Every afternoon that final autumn he had walked home from school repeating, "She's dead. You know she's dead." He prepared himself so well that when she finally did die he couldn't even cry. He and his brother had come downstairs, his father had put an arm around each of them and told them and wept, and Mark had been absolutely calm and wide-eyed. What he remembered most clearly of that moment were the Indians on his brother's pajamas.

Rotten with disease, his mother had screamed a lot that last year but slipped away peacefully in the end, dreamy with drugs and free of pain. On the final night she had smiled at the nurse and said, "I believe that Jesus is my savior," then turned her face to the wall.

Mark did not believe in Jesus or in medicine or prayer. He didn't believe in anything. Or did he? Those geese, maybe. And dirt. He believed in dirt.

As an experiment he had dug a compost pit in the garden in June, and he had been amazed by his results. He had dumped some garbage into the hole—coffeegrounds, egg shells, bad bananas—and seasoned the whole mess with dead leaves and grass clippings. He'd covered this refuse with a layer of loam. Two weeks ago he had returned and sunk a spade in the compost pit. Instead of the sour slime he expected to find, he discovered nothing but earth—good, clean dirt. It was the only miracle he had ever witnessed, and he had talked about it for days.

That was the only afterlife he believed in, and what had he and The Crusher and Elmer been doing all summer? Sealing embalmed bodies behind cement walls, they were ruining the only form of resurrection there was. Unless you counted dreams, and how could you? What were they but chemicals gone crazy, a mishmash of wishes and buried memories. You might as well believe in UFO's.

People said death was like sleep, but the dead didn't dream. Did they? If he dreamed his mother was living, did she dream he was dead? No. It was just a blank. A black blank.

He was never going to sleep again. He would lie on his bed and look at the light bulb until his brain burned out. For now he would keep his eye on that low star. Star light, star bright, first star I see tonight. So bright, he thought, it must be a planet.

As he stared the star seemed to move and grow, and he knew, then, it was coming for him. Then the star divided into the twin headlights of a truck, and The Crusher's pickup came grumbling down the dike, stopped, and the lights died.

The Crusher got out and walked over. "What happened, kid? We waited over an hour."

"I ran. Out of gas."

"Well, that's nothing to cry about, for Christ's sake."

"Who's crying?"

"You are."

Mark wiped his cheeks. "Oh, no," he moaned. "I didn't mean it. Mean to. I mean. I just ran out of gas, but first that lousy casket, and then the truck wouldn't go, and I was so tired I felt so stupid I just sat down, and I started to think."

"Well, it wasn't your fault you ran out of gas. What the hell? It's Elmer's damn truck. He should have checked it before you left. Look," the old man said, "you got goose bumps. You must be freezing. Here. Put this on." He held out his jacket, and Mark pulled it on. It was smelly and warm, and the wool scratched his bare back. "What were you thinking about that made you feel so bad?"

"I don't know. That casket. And all those people we buried this summer. My mother."

"Oh, yeah. That would do it. I remember your mother. She was a good woman."

"I've been dreaming about her all summer. I've had a hard time sleeping."

"Yeah? You never said anything."

"It seemed too stupid."

"That can happen, though. You ask Elmer sometime. And Vera. After she died she kept coming to me in the night and crying. She kept me awake for a year. Oh, boy. One night I remember I dreamt I was buried beside her, and I kept trying to lift the lid off the vault all night long. I had whiskey for breakfast that morning, I'll tell you."

"Really? Really bad, huh?"

"I'm telling you. They stopped after a while, though. Oh, she'll still visit me now and then, but now it's kind of nice. We're younger, most often, and maybe it's after a match, and we're out on the town, and she seems just as real. I like it."

"Do they mean anything?"

"What?"

"Those dreams. Do they mean anything?"

"Oh, I wouldn't know about that. I never put too much stock in them. Just kind of take them as they come, you know."

They listened to the waves run against the shore. The wind off the water was cold.

"Crusher?"

"Yeah?"

"Do you believe in life after death?"

"Like in the Bible, you mean? I don't think so. Nope. I believe in life before death. Come on, kid. You're too young to be brooding about this stuff. You got your whole life ahead of you—school, a good job, women and drinking, a family. You ought to leave this kind of thing to old farts like me. Tell you what. Let's drive into town, and I'll treat you to supper. Then we'll fill my five-gallon can and come back here and try to bring this old pig back to life. What do you say?"

"Okay," Mark said and got to his feet. He was going to be all right.

"Good," The Crusher said, clapping him on the back. "Let's go. You ain't dead yet. Not by a long shot."

And Say Good-bye to Yourself

Susan Williams

"It's a poor sort of memory that only works backwards."

The White Queen,
Alice in Wonderland

M OST PEOPLE my age remember where they were when Kennedy was shot. I remember where I was when I found out about Judith Campbell Exner. It was in a bait shop outside White Bear Lake. A Saturday. I was coming from my friend Mary Kaye's place on the lake, trying to get back on the freeway to Minneapolis and lost, as usual, and I stopped at this bait shop for directions and there was the *St. Paul Pioneer Press* on a crate of tackle with the headline and her picture – Liz Taylor as Vegas showgirl.

How Sinatra or Peter Lawford or someone had introduced them. How she'd phoned him hundreds of times in the Oval Office and met him at the Carlyle Hotel in New York. How they'd made love, she said, in every major bedroom in the White House – in spite of Jack's bad back – when Jackie was out of town, or in town. How she was Sam Giancana's girlfriend at the same time (and maybe Sinatra's) and how that somehow implicated the Mafia in the assassination. Or meant the President was being blackmailed by the Mob. Or by J. Edgar Hoover, who had bugs in every second bedroom in Washington. Or Jack was leaking Justice Department secrets in the sack. Or she was spilling Giancana's nasty business. Or the President tried to use the Mafia to get Castro but they finally got him instead because Bobby was closing in on them. Or something. And the other girlfriends. Students and starlets and heiresses and hairdressers. Out of the woodwork. More than he'd have had time for if he'd been a stockbroker or mountainclimber. Or a movie star.

I don't remember driving home. I found my way without directions.

Some things you know are true because of how much you don't want them to be true, so I made up arguments against it and argued with people about it. It wasn't true, or it didn't matter. But I knew it was, and it did.

The thing that really bothered me about the story was Jack telling a friend—I don't remember who—how beautiful she was and how she could have sold it but here she was giving it away. Okay, so he was no romantic. A little fucked up about women. That old he-goat of a father of his—it was him. Bringing women to the house. Hitting on his sons' dates. ("Try me when you get tired of him. I'm twice the man he is.") Gloria Swanson showing up on family vacations. All that screwing around under Rose's holy Roman nose. But I didn't know about all that when I heard about Judith Campbell Exner.

I was on a bus to New York when I heard about Marilyn—August 5, 1962. On my way to take a ship to Rotterdam to be an American Field Service exchange student to Belgium. Sixteen. Thirty-six seemed almost old enough to die.

My Belgian family lived in a pretty river village in the French-speaking south between Liege and Namur and we didn't like each other very much. The father was a dentist with bad breath and his wife rarely spoke to me. The children were shy and so was I. And homesick. When the mother got sick they used it as an excuse to pack me off to Brussels to another family, which was okay with me except I was in love with a boy in the town who looked just like James Dean— Etienne. But that's another story.

But before I could go to my new family in Brussels (they were on vacation somewhere) I had an interim family. A rich family. Aristocrats with a country estate about half the size of Belgium near a town named after their family, with stables and tennis courts and peach orchards and a wine cellar and private art gallery and a mile-wide library.

The first morning, after a four- or five-course second breakfast, I went for a walk with Ione, the oldest daughter. She had been an exchange student in New Jersey the year before and lived with a CBS cameraman and his family and fallen in love with a boy who looked like Marlon Brando in *The Wild One*. She had three albums of snapshots of him and said she was going back to America to marry him but I knew she wouldn't because his father was a longshoreman and the Cordonnets were stone snobs.

Ione's father, Jean, was in Brussels but from his picture he looked a lot like her mother, Jeanne: tall, thin, chilly people with chiseled noses and lobeless ears and pointy little teeth and tan, leathery skin and clothes in rich fabrics and subtle colors that all matched and all matched their hair and skin and upholstery. And generations of money behind them. There was no one like them in Blooming Prairie. Or Hollywood.

I loved the country house. I felt like Jane Eyre turned loose in Mr. Rochester's library. Acres of Morocco-bound classics in dark oak bookcases with sliding glass doors and a ladder that ran around the room to a deep cream windowseat that turned gold in the sun. I wanted to stay in that room forever.

But we left for Brussels the next day. Saturday. To join Monsieur. The women went to mass first and I stayed home—they were careful about not inflicting their religion on me—and started *Portrait of a Lady*. After mass we arranged ourselves in the long tan Mercedes that matched their matching luggage and Madame's cashmere sweater and swirley skirt and ran so quiet it made you want to whisper and drove through the matching woods to Brussels to the Avenue des Americains, where they owned most of a handsome old red brick building.

Inside everything matched, all white this time and cream and peach and shell pink and pale yellow and colors I didn't even know the names of. My hair, which everyone had always said was beautiful, was about seven shades too red for this setting.

It was Saturday but everybody had appointments anyway—Madame to have her legs waxed, Ione for a haircut, and Vincienne, the younger daughter, who I loved for her knotty knees and elbows, to be fitted for a first communion dress. Monsieur would be home for dinner, for which we would, of course, dress. I scrunched up in the softest chair I could find, overlooking the Avenue, with a copy of *Catcher in the Rye*. The maid brought me a cream soda. I felt like I was in a movie. If only, somehow, they would each meet with a separate, painless (I didn't hate them), but fatal accident and I could stay here alone forever. Or the women would die and Monsieur would come home and fall in love with me and marry me and come home once a month or so to bring money to keep all this going and leave me to read and look out on the Avenue forever. And then after awhile he'd die (painlessly), leaving me plenty of money and I'd send for Etienne, whom I truly loved.

But he came home before I'd even finished my cream soda. He looked like his pictures. He was in a snit about something. He asked where Martine, the maid, was. He didn't appear to be in love with me. The women talked to me in English for practice but he steamed away in French without moving his lips or giving me time to translate, much less answer. He was so taut and tan, his skin stretched so close across his cheekbones, his nose so impossibly thin (how did he breathe?), ankles so slender under his skinny socks, he made me feel thick and pasty and mid-western. He got bored with my stumbling French in about a minute and went to find a drink.

Next time I saw him, after Madame and the daughters had come home, he was, as my father would say, "three sheets to the wind." He seemed to be in better humor at least, teasing Ione about her gamin haircut, making her pirouette so he could see it from all sides, teasing me about drinking milk instead of wine. "And I suppose you eat corn in Minnesota also," he said in precise English. "In this country we save that stuff for the pigs."

We sat down to dinner. Cold clear soup and a fragile fruit salad and three colors of rice and bite-size potatoes and thin strips of carrots and another vegetable I didn't recognize and little twists of tan bread and trout with the heads on. I wasn't used to eating so much at a sitting (how did they stay so thin?). Or so late. At home we ate supper at six, not dinner at eight. Vincienne's chatter danced too fast for me to follow. I was nodding off into my fish when Monsieur Cordonnet's voice jerked me awake. "Et Kennedy? Your President Kennedy? This species of rich boy you have chosen? What about *him?*"

What *about* him? I loved Kennedy more than I loved Montgomery Clift! Monsieur was slashing away in French again, stabbing the air with his fork, his face suddenly red and clenched. Had I fallen asleep and missed something? His eyes shot around the table, daring anyone to speak, then locked on me. *"Cet mauvais espece de . . ."* I couldn't follow. Vincienne was quiet, twisting her napkin in her lap. Madame was trying to swallow her lips.

"Qu'est-ce que vous dites?" I squeaked, finding my French and nearly spilling out of my chair at the same moment.

"This rich kid doesn't know how to be President!" he snapped, slapping the table. The trout jumped off his plate. "He will run us all into disaster—he and his companions."

"You object to his *money?*" My voice startled me. His eyes tightened on me. My stomach bunched up.

"And you? What do you know? An infant from an baby country. What does your father do in that country?"

I looked around. Madame's mouth was twitching. Martine appeared and hustled Vincienne out of the room. Ione studied her trout. Mine was rising up in my throat. Cold came off Monsieur Cordonnet's face at me. He was three chairs away but I could feel it. I wondered about the etiquette for throwing up.

"Mon pere est un . . . salesman," I choked. "He sells water softeners. He voted for Kennedy." He hadn't. "I rang doorbells for him." I didn't. "Everybody works for their man in America. Everybody votes." I was panting. I'd told my first family, when they asked how fast Americans drove and seemed disappointed when I said seventy miles an hour, that this was the *slowest* speed the law allowed. Monsieur was playing with his knife. The weather had changed around his mouth. Was he smiling? Martine had slipped back and was refilling his wine glass. Without looking at her he closed his hand around her wrist. "What do you think?" he said to the far end of the table. "Do you think our young lady from America is ready for a drop of Beaujolais now?" No one answered. His fingers ticked on the table. "Ione will pour," he said. "Come Ione."

"It's really time Ione turned in also," her mother said with a little twisty smile. "She must study tomorrow for her mathematics exam."

"Ione will pour," her father said. "Come, my dear." Ione had been piling up the fingers of her left hand—1-2-3-4-3-2-1. She looked at her mother with no expression, then at her father, then slowly backed her chair away from the table, still looking at him, and walked around the table. He handed the bottle to her, neck first. His other hand spidered over the small of her back. She didn't move until he took his hand away, then she walked to the end of the table with an empty face but with her long vanilla throat thrown back and poured me a glass of wine.

At first I couldn't sleep that night and when I did I dreamt about his voice. Talking to Ione. Just loud enough so I could hear. Telling her not to cry. One of them was crying.

She looked fine at breakfast—beautiful in a lemon dress with yellow lace braided into the pockets and her new short haircut. She looked a little like Audrey Hepburn in *Green Mansions*. Audrey with breasts. The two of us ate breakfast alone. After breakfast she asked if I would take a walk with her. She had to borrow a book from a friend who lived beyond the park. As we walked, she talked about Jimmy, her American boyfriend. She showed me the last letter she got from him, half English and half high school French. She wanted to be a writer and live in New Jersey with Jimmy. I told her about Etienne, embroidering a little. She thought I should run away with him. She was sure my second family would be even worse than the first, who never even *tutoied* me in seven weeks. We didn't talk about the night before or her father except when we stopped to watch a man throwing a stick for his dog. She said her father was a champion dog trainer. She liked to watch him put his prize collie through her paces—heel, three steps, turn, sit, wait. One day he made the dog wait, frozen in her show pose, eyes on him, for twenty minutes. "And I watched," she whispered. "I couldn't move. It was like a dream." The pulse jerked in her neck.

I didn't see her father that day and the next day he left for Zurich on business and I never saw him again. The next month, when the Cuban missile crisis happened, I wanted to phone him and ask him what he thought of Kennedy now but I didn't.

By then I was living with the Joufflus at 22 Rue Van Campenhout. They were comfortable as overstuffed chairs. They braided my hair and counted my freckles and giggled at my French and took me to tons of American movies. They *tutoied* me immediately. They thought I was skinny and tried to fatten me up with peanut butter and banana sandwiches which their daughter, an AFS student in Seattle, had written them about. They would have got me bushels of corn on the cob if I'd asked for it. We partied for three days around my birthday in November and three weeks later, when I had to leave to go home, we all cried and hung on each other and we wrote once a week for about a year and then sent Christmas cards.

Last month, just before Christmas, I went to a hypnotist to try to get over this married man I thought I was in love with. He had me hypnotized, I guess, finishing sentences to reveal my "psychic history," and the last sentence was "I'll never get over _____" and I said, "Kennedy's murder." I wonder.

We lived all over south Minneapolis, my son and I, and one time we lived next door to this black guy who was a decent guy—he took Josh fishing—and a good neighbor except he drank too much and carried a gun. One Saturday night he got thrown in jail in Eden Valley for carrying a gun and being drunk and black in the suburbs. He phoned me the next morning and I went out and bailed him out and on the way home he told me about this white guy he ran into in the drunk tank who was bragging about screwing his baby daughter—four years old. Said there was nothing like it except he couldn't do it too often because it took about two weeks for her to heal every time. Fred, my friend, said this with a straight face but I figured either he was making it up—he was always coming up with stories about kinky honkies who did things black folks would never even think of—pissing on hookers or poisoning their kids for the insurance money or something—or the white guy had lied to him.

I dreamt about it a few nights and then a few months later we moved away and I forgot it. A few years later they started arresting people in Eden Valley for having sex with their kids. Unemployed pump jockeys who lived in trailer parks first and then shoe clerks and shopkeepers and schoolteachers and cops and doctors. Even grandparents with their grandchildren. It made the CBS evening news about a week in a row. A whole freaking sex ring. I'd never heard of such a thing. Then I remembered Fred.

They say Marilyn was molested as a little girl, for years, by half a dozen foster brothers and fathers. Now they're saying she was in love with the Kennedys—Jack first and then Bobby. Somebody puts out another book about it every other month or so. Somebody wrote that she called Peter Lawford after she took those pills that August afternoon and told him to say good-bye to Jack. "And say good-bye to yourself," she said, "because you're a good guy too."

When somebody told me, in front of the freshwater fish tank on the fourth floor of the old zoology building after psych. 101 that Friday afternoon that the President was shot I knew he was dead, no matter what they said. Some things you know are true.

An Apprentice

Carol Bly

I CROSS MOST OF St. Paul to take my violin lessons. Then I drive slowly around Georgia's half-block, along Hemlock Avenue, and through the north/south alley. I locate the regulars. They are of two kinds—the same four men who generally are on their foot, laughing, shouting, dealing, waiting for the Hemlock Bar to open at six—and the three men who sprawl, elbows propped, right on the four low steps leading from the sidewalk up the low slant of Georgia's lawn. These are more languid than the crack pushers: they lie at ease and blow their smoke straight up, pursing their lips at the sky.

For my first two lessons, I gave those men the stairs: I climbed up the grass slant, keeping a good ten yards between them and me. But by the time I was learning the Third Position and could do "Go Down, Moses," with harmonics on the G string, I thought: if Georgia Persons doesn't give way to these guys, neither will I.

So I make myself pick a way between them up the concrete stairs. They never move an inch, but they always stop talking and their eyes creep over my black-plastic Hefty bag. Inside it my mother's old violin case does not bulge the way garbage would. I have my music-stand top since someone, when breaking into all of the apartments in Georgia's building, went off with one of hers. I have my chin support, the Friml and Kuechler and Handel sheet music, and *A Tune-A-Day*, my violin lessons text. I am nervous that the smokers think, why *not* knock over that sturdy, timid-faced woman of forty-one? Why *not*? She might have a ten or a twenty in the chipped shoulder bag, even though she wears her grubbies. And they must think, whatever's in the Hefty isn't garbage. Who'd bring garbage to 4303 Hemlock where there are generally several sacks of it on the front porch floorboards, not to mention the sacks left in the downstairs hallway for weeks at a time. I step through these men prissily, lifting my bag over their pot-fragrant skulls, and I imagine their brains as indeterminate magma. Whatever thinking they do, the thoughts haven't cooled enough to be distinct the way the central metals of our planet aren't quiet, reliable rock yet.

Georgia has opened the screen-and-torn-plastic door a couple of inches as soon as she had seen my car so I will know she is there to let me in. She and the other tenants of 4303 – the Born-Again on the ground floor and two men a flight above Georgia – have decided that the usual mechanical voice-check and relay lock aren't safe enough: they arrange for their guests' arrivals by phone. Then they crouch on the unlighted staircase until their guests' heads show through the scrim of door curtain.

Now Georgia opens the door wide for me. I bound in, taking the Hefty sack safely past her. She gives the street and yard a last wide scanning, like a bridge officer just leaving the conn. "I see the Boy Scouts have their troop meeting on my steps today," she says in her friendly, sardonic tone. "Good fellows that they are," she adds. "They invited a goodly number of policemen to their meeting in the alley yesterday, yes they did, and finally the policemen invited a number of them to a picnic somewhere – at least, they all climbed into two vans together! Very nice! Very nice indeed!"

Her ironic style restores my humor. It seems right that a disciplined artist should use archaic phrases and should nurture indignation against slobs. I follow Georgia's huge behind up the stairs. She always wears print dresses with dark backgrounds and large flower patterns: in the unlighted stairway, the white peonies and hydrangeas on her skirt lead the way.

Georgia is only ten or fifteen years older than I am, but her face is full and soft from her having taken prednisone for a year and a half. She has arterial enteritis, and the drug saved her eyesight in the first weeks. Now the doctors keep lessening her dose: they consider her much improved. Georgia wears hearty makeup – eye shadow bright as poster paint, paste rouge on each huge, viscous cheek. I try to draw her out since I am interested in serious illness, but she explained the symptoms, the diagnosis, and the regimen to me once and refuses to go into it further. On what I have to guess are her bad days, all her makeup – shadow, rouge, and lipstick – looks lightly positioned, temporary, like an airplane parked. It might lift away.

She won't complain, even when I deliberately, hopefully, model complaining for her. I think of myself as someone coming to her only to learn the violin. I ought to glad of having this discrete task as an escape from the rest of my life, but I have the slack-focused habit of dropping personal anecdote into our talk.

I talk about the first, even the second, laser vaporization I have had, a procedure for treating pre-cancer and cancer of the cervix. Georgia waits through my talk. I try to intrigue her with bits of lifestyle at the In and Out Surgi-Center at St. Alban's. When I stop talking she says, "If you will hand me that Strad of yours I'll tune it for you."

She turns sideways to me and whines my violin strings with her thumb while striking for her piano's E, A, D, and G keys with her free hand. At one of our sessions I told her I had not practiced very much because my ex-husband had asked the eldest of our children to tell me to have the younger children clean and well-dressed for his wedding that week. Old friends of mine were going to the wedding without a qualm. When I was through talking, Georgia said, "It is impossible to have a good lesson if you do not practice." She added, "Impossible." Then, after a little pause, she added, "Men are repulsive. As always."

She is a martinet of a violin teacher—the only kind, I decide. At first I thought she wore her makeup and her rayon, floriate dresses for her one other adult student—a dentist. But it turns out she despises him because he wants to learn the Handel immediately and will not do any of the exercises in A Tune-A-Day, which Georgia assures me is the definitive violin study-book, better even than the precise exercises of Wohlfahrt. During my first weeks of lessons, she told me how little the dentist practiced. By the time I was in the Third Position, and starting the Third Position and learning the languid, swooping vibrato of beginners, I heard no more of the dentist. I expect she has dropped him. Now she has only me and several dozen Hmong and Laotian children many of whom do not speak English. I imagine her extending her arms like fat bridges to them, pressing their half- and three-quarters sized fiddles to their necks, and poring all her theory of bowing and fingering, in English, into those full, black eyes. Once—only once—I exclaimed, "How good you are to them! What wonderful patience you have!" Georgia promptly jammed her violin into her throat. "They do not have trouble with atonal music. They are not hobbled by preconceived ideas about where do should be," she said.

I vow to be her best student. Sometimes, when I have mastered something difficult, like sliding thirds cleanly across two strings, Georgia says, "That's very good. Very good. Also, it is pleasant that you do not tell me that your mother forgot to put your A Tune-A-Day into your bag. And that your mother forgot the rosin so you could not practice." At long intervals I get only hints about the rest of her teaching life. "Ah! You've practiced very well!" she says, looking at me from the center of her serious, drug-changed face. "Why have you practiced so much? Have you only just now arrived from The Boat and therefore haven't learned yet that there's Welfare and you needn't do a lick of work, ever?"

It sounds like such a friendly opening I pick it up quickly. "Then are the earnest Asian people learning to rot in America?"

But Georgia is back to my bowing. "Wrists! Wrists! Wrists leading lightly," she says. "You needn't get revenge on the violin. Play it gently. Especially—be easy on that tiny, slender E string."

At other times she notices that I am doing something right when I least expect it. Several times, when I have thought she wasn't listening, but was putting her feathery handwriting under my country-day-school manuscript printing in the assignment book, I find she has been listening. "Ah! Lovely! Very nice sound, that! Very!" she murmurs, still writing. "You must always do good work. If it sounds bad, go back and get it right. You must play at concert level all the time." Then she gives her small laugh, drops the assignment notebook onto the piano bench, turns to accompany me with her own violin. "It is just a question of time now! Before Memorial Day, I would say!"

She lets her soft fat pour on the chin support; the spidery fingers, so thinly hung to the flesh of hand and wrist, make their hummingbird-speed vibrato. One good violinist can make another violinist sound better: in fact, you can have three or four indifferent players playing, provided at least one of them can do the uncompromised bowing and vibrato which thin a string's sound to its lyric bone.

But I am too curious to continue. I stop and ask, "Before Memorial Day, what?"

"Oh," she says, "The St. Paul Chamber Orchestra, of course. They will call, probably at midnight, wanting you for concert master, and of course, like Cinderella, you will have to go. Naturally you will mention to them that I am your teacher."

Georgia wanted to charge me four dollars a lesson. I told her that was absurd. "But I don't need more," she said. "I have my salary from the school (where she teaches the Hmong and Laotian children), and I have another private student. I have Minnesota state employees' health coverage."

I tell her that the violin teachers I called up told me that a teacher of musical integrity must charge starting at $12. Each month I hand her a check for $48.

"This will pay for your lessons through the 1990s," she says each time, dropping my check into the little velvet lining of her violin case. I envy that velvet lining, with its blood-colored fur, and its neat little zipper. I would buy one with part of a child-support check, but I am loyal to the ugly case I inherited from my mother.

"Now the Handel," Georgia says briskly.

It is in E major, but the first movement is *adagio* so I have a little chance. From somewhere under the cry and grind of my efforts, I begin to hear Handel's lilt. It isn't pathos which makes Handel so tuneful: it is character. Under my fingers and crimped bowing, his beauty is only beginning to show. Even so, I can hardly believe I don't live in a state of gratitude all the time.

Georgia refuses to play it all through once so I can hear the full beauty. Fat arms go up—but drop. "No, no," she says, "You make it beautiful yourself. The first time you hear it all through and it sounds beautiful will be when you yourself do it. And now," she says, "That is enough for today."

She looks ill. I put everything away as fast as I can.

"I will let myself out," I tell her.

"No, no!" she says in her singsong ironic tone, "I will see you safe into your car," and she follows me down the stairs.

Of course it is a relief to get away from one's teacher. No matter how good a teacher she is, it is a relief to escape. Once I am in the car I daydream of going back to smoking. I daydream of stopping for some greasy fast food. I sing a descant, which like Girl Scout camp descants, rides its resolute third above the melody without break, ruining any music it attaches to. I want to feel the *easy* emotions: I drive along in my car, leaving behind slatternly Selby Avenue and Hemlock Avenue and Dale Street, and I sing "You Want to Pass It On," a tune from twenty years ago when I was a Born-Again Christian. My thoughts get silvery and loose like fish. I think of my mother, who died when I was a kid. I was not allowed to have violin lessons. She said it was ridiculous: I had no gift. Why give lessons to someone with no gift? Right, I think, without rancor, and I start humming "Abide With Me," imagining the fingering for the key of D, key of G, key of E. I do an upside-down vibrato on the left side of the steering wheel.

I have been home two hours when a man calls and asks who I am. Then he asks, "Are you a relation of Georgia Persons?"

"She is my violin teacher. Why?"

"I am a policeman, at 4303 Hemlock Street," he says. "Is Georgia Persons a close friend? Just your teacher or what?"

Right now my children are my close friends but I am trying to ease them more and more away, into their father's care, just in case. I make it a point to think of them only a few quarter-hours a day. Old college friends are close friends, but right now they avoid me because divorce might be catching. And whatever makes people have surgery once and then surgery again and even again might be catching too. Sometimes on the Hardangar plateau, in the endless landscape of scraped stones and freezing creeks high above the treeline, you see a walker in the distance walking another path which won't cross yours. The other walker may stay within view for as much as two hours. You feel an affinity for him or her, because you are engaged in the same energetic project. The people who feel like friends to me at the moment are Georgia and the nurse-anesthetist at St. Alban's.

"We will send someone around to pick you up," the man says. It is clear that Georgia Persons is dead.

I always wore the shabbiest jeans and tees to take my lessons from her. I meant to give the impression of someone without a nickel so the alley and sidewalk folk would leave me alone. Now I put on a silk orange shirt, a silk jacket, and a flowered skirt: it is full and has the huge roseate flowers of spring 1990 styles. I put on stockings and a new pair of yellow high-heeled pumps. "Well, Georgia," I say as I dress, "It's for you, since you won't get to hear me play for the Chamber Orchestra after all. Don't feel bad," I say, trying for her exact ironical note: Everyone in the St. Paul Chamber Orchestra may not have musical integrity after all, although we have to admit they sound as if they do."

The policewoman's car is astir with air conditioning. We ride in great comfort to Hemlock and Dale. "It was assault and she died," the policewoman tells me. At Georgia's house, not only are all the regulars there, on their feet for once, collected into a little group with two policemen watching them, but all the alley types are standing around on the grass. Three police cars are parked askew in the street, with blinkers going. All around and in the neighboring bits of yard, people hover in groups, not a single person smoking anything.

"We're using his apartment for now," my cop says, jerking her head towards a man standing beside a policeman on the porch. I realize this is the Born-Again Christian.

In his apartment, three people approach me and stand close around. Was I there two hours ago? Yes. My lessons started the better part of an year ago. Was anyone else ever in Georgia Person's apartment when I was there? Whoever stole her music-stand top, I think. I decide I had better mention that. They listen, as they do to everything I say, taking no notes. I mention the dentist. Yes, they have his name already, but he refused to come. He said he was not a friend and had quit taking lessons from Georgia because she did not "address his needs." All the while we are talking in the middle of the room, I must have seen that there is a slightly raised stretcher on the floor, but I avoid the idea, thinking of ways I will insult the dentist if I live so long. I will find time to insult the Born-Again Christian, too. It turns out that a first-rate violinist was assaulted and killed and her body left drooping over his pile-up of garbage bags in the staircase landing. I tell myself how much the author of Ecclesiastes would disdain the Born-Again Christian. Of course none of that does any good: the policewoman takes me gently over and I am shown a three-cornered opening to Georgia's face. The fine craft of her brain, whatever of her that can fly, clearly has got away.

The following week, I am to have two laser vaporizations and one small ordinary surgery done at the same time. All three procedures can be taken care of in the In and Out Surgi-Center, as before, but I feel like a girl at the Scout meeting who is a little too old and really should join the serious organizations of adulthood. I know that any future surgery they have to do will be in the main, serious part of the hospital, where patients survive or they don't.

As before, they hand me my papers, a folder called "Welcome to In and Out Surgi-Center," and a zipper bag long enough for my clothes. I undress in a cubicle and emerge to claim a comfortable lounge chair in the waiting area. There are several of us, in our chairs spaced informally about. We all have our angel robes and light blue dressing gowns over them. We are mostly graying or white-haired or bald. We look so much alike it is a reminder that our insides, cervixes, kidneys, veins, are more alike than not.

I note how kindly each of us is treated: white-dressed people lean over to drop a word; someone brings a magazine. It crosses my mind that if the St. Alban's In and Out Surgi-Center were part of a gigantic lab experiment in human outcomes, we were probably the "control group" —the ones you handle kindly but don't give any of the hopeful treatment to. None of us has eaten in twelve hours, so we give one another shy, starving smiles. We doze in the marvelous chairs. From time to time, a nurse wakes one or another of us to go to a curtained area, where we get anesthesia on a gurney.

In my curtained area, I find the same nurse-anesthetist I had last time.

"Oh!" she says with a laugh, entering the IV, "I'd know you all right! You're the one who is learning the violin! It isn't everyone you meet that studies a tough instrument like that, I can tell you!"

"I remember you, too!" I crow back.

Now she tells me in a triumphant tone, as she disappears behind the dripstand, "I remember that you're fussy about what we do for you! You told me to give you something which leaves your brain in good condition, that would kill pain but leave you conscious because you wanted to experience the procedure—and you didn't want sodium pentothal, which we don't have anyway, because you were afraid you would use foul language. You thought I'd *forget* all that?"

I tell her, "I also remember that you told me the ordinary dose of fentanyl is 1 cc and I told you I wanted half, and you said, Oh just relax; you had already entered the full dose into the intravenous. Tricky, I thought."

"I know," she says in her gentle nurse's tone, "And I have done it again."

She has come back to my side. "How are the violin lessons going?"

"Very well," I tell her. "I have one of the best teachers in the city, it turns out. It is important to study with the best, especially if you yourself are not particularly gifted."

"Gifted schmifted," the nurse says. "What's gift?"

Now the tremendous boost of the fentanyl, not to mention the sugar hit of the glucose drip, comes into my elbow. After its overnight fast, the body is pathetically grateful. "I feel my I.Q. not only not *dropping* but actually going up," I tell the nurse.

"Could it go up?" she says with a laugh. "I didn't know they got any higher than what you came sashaying in here with."

It is precisely the tone in which Georgia Persons had told me that the Chamber Orchestra would need me by Memorial Day of 1992 if not 1991, no question.

The drug makes me every second more airy. I like to keep everything in a kind of bullety focus, so I monitor the drug working in me as sensibly as I can: yes, you are getting smart-ass with the drug, I think, but also *intraveno veritas* I think, too, and I notice I am dissolving into smart-ass peacefulness. The world looks unrealistically softened, but the scrim over everything looks like wise scrim, and I raise myself up to lead my bow hand gently with my wrist, not sawing, not vindictive, gently taking the right wrist forward and back down right, upward and left again. I keep the left elbow bent in the required, absolutely unnatural position under a violin, with the wrist bent the other way so the fingers can work.

"What's going on?" cries a cordial-enough male voice.

I hear the nurse explaining that I am demonstrating how much more difficult it is to hold a violin than any other instrument—than a cello, for instance. Anyone can hold a cello without tiring. You are working at it against your knees. One can nearly droop above a cello.

But now I am a little lost and notice only that other people in white or green go drifting by outside the furry edge of my cubicle. One of them is my surgeon. It crosses my mind (though now I am wafting a good deal) that if he loses me in the end, it might hurt his career. No, I reply to myself, coming to sense by main force of will now, nothing hurts anyone's career. People continue to do whatever they do now. The Hemlock Street Boy Scouts, as Georgia called them, will continue to smoke mild dope and sell serious drugs. The Born-Again Christian will go on explaining to new tenants at 4303 that the last thing in the world he would do is take credit for God having chose him, rather than someone else, to work through with his gifts. The Born-Again Christian will continue leaving his garbage in the tiny hallway and on the front porch. And at St. Alban's, the nurse anesthetist will go on letting patients ask for .5 cc while she administers 1 cc.

And I will go on being afraid of death all the months which lie ahead of me even though I have had Georgia Persons as a teacher of courage. Now I imagine her as hard as I can, because the nurse is wheeling my gurney into the actual icy surgery itself, where a crew of people dressed up in green-insect costumes are engaged in bee-tasks here and there. And now I remember what it is that lifts us above the flower-patch of our fears: it is our good teachers, of course, but behind them it is the artists themselves—Handel or Friml or Kuechler, doing their work. Georgia was right: men are repulsive. And women are repulsive, as well. But there are always a few artists ghosting around who invite us to do the work of beauty, and who give us back our humor when we are terrified.

The Amazing Human Torch

Judith Katz

I N THE BEGINNING was the fire, *ha esh*. It burned in my sister Nadine Pagan's eyes, then lit up like the burning bush around her head and took with it most of her hair. It spoke to us like God spoke unto Moses. In a high thin voice it sputtered, "Your sister is a lunatic, your middle child has gone mad." For who else but a crazy person would steal the *Shabbos* candles from off the kitchen table and with them light her own head on fire? Who else would run as she ran through the house, shrieking until my mother caught her by the arm. "You *dybbuk!*" she screamed, shaking my sister as if she could put her out like some match.

Around in circles my father spun, first in one direction then another, pulling at his chin as if he had a beard. "What to do what to do what to do," he muttered, and still Nadine burned from the hair down until I myself came running and screaming, and poured water on her head, dumped it out of a wastebasket until she was quiet and the fire in her head went out.

We all stopped and stared. The house smelled like someone had burned at the stake. Nadine's eyes were huge and hot. She did not cry, neither did she shout. We stared at her and she stared back. For the first time since I could remember, the house was absolutely quiet.

Suddenly my mother took matters into her own hands. She slapped Nadine first on one cheek then the other. "You want something to cry about, how's this?" she shouted. "It's not enough to set yourself on fire like a Buddhist nun, you had to do it with my grandmother's candlesticks, and on *Shabbos!*"

My father looked deep into Nadine's hot face. "See how you've upset your mother!"

I could stand it no longer. "Nadine just tried to burn herself up! Call a doctor! Get an ambulance!" The words stuck in my throat like mud.

My father spun toward the telephone.

"Sure, call a doctor," my mother spat, "call the hospital and a million psychiatrists. While you're at it, call the fire department too. This is your older sister Nadine, Jane. Take a good look at her. She's a real beaut."

It wasn't the first time Nadine exploded. Ever since Grandma Minnie gave her that violin, Nadine and my mother rubbed against each other and made dangerous sparks.

Our Grandmother Minnie had this violin. It belonged to her father, our great-grandfather, *Zayde* Yitzkach, who carried it with him on his lap to America all the way from Poland. He treated that violin better than he treated his own kids, that's what Minnie told us.

When he got to Ellis Island the customs officers made our great-grandpa take his violin out of the case to make sure it was really a violin. This was, after all, a time of American gangsters with Jewish last names. Our great-grandpa obliged, but then the customs men wanted to break the violin open to see if he was smuggling anything inside.

Before they could snatch it out of his hands, *Zayde* Yitzkach put the violin up to his chin and played. In the middle of our tired, our poor, our huddled masses yearning to breathe free, our great-grandpa played a Yiddish lullaby. For a fleeting moment, perhaps the only moment in its history, all of Ellis Island was quiet except for the sweet, sad music he made.

My great-grandfather was declared a musical genius by his brother-in-law Tutsik and two customs guards. He collected his wife and five children. Tutsik found my great-aunt and their children, and together they boarded a train for New England.

In their new home, my *zayde* played violin for weddings, bar mitzvahs, and funerals. He also taught his oldest daughter, my Grandma Minnie, to play. She was a good student and when she learned enough, she gave lessons to the neighbor children and earned extra money for the family. She met her husband, Grandpa Irving, when he brought his little brother to learn from her. He brought her a piece of fruit from the family store at each visit, and over the weeks, months, then years, Irving courted Minnie with apples, bananas, oranges from Florida, until they finally wed.

By then Irving had his own store and he and Minnie lived above it with their children, in chronological order, my aunt Miriam, my uncles Davey and Mike, and my mother, Fay. Irving ran the store and Minnie gave lessons and between them they made a decent living and their children did well in the world.

But Fay, my mother, was unhappy. She saw my grandmother teaching all the neighborhood children to play the violin. She admired the cases they carried and the delicate instruments within, and she longed to play as they did, as her mother did, on *Zayde* Yitzkach's violin.

Grandma Minnie, however, refused to teach her.

"I didn't refuse. I wanted to save her from grief. Simply put, your mother had no talent. I knew this from the day she was born. Her hands were all wrong. Why frustrate her? I only told her I didn't have time to teach her."

Every time a neighbor child came for Minnie's lessons, my mother fumed inside. She was a good girl and never said a word. Instead she bore her rage silently. It grew and spread like a fungus. From time to time it leaked out my mother's eyes.

Time passed.

My mother Fay met my father Mel. She was buying shoes at his family's store. He was impressed with the turn of her ankle and the fact that she spoke intelligently on several subjects. She was enamored of his soft-spokenness and the gentility with which he slipped her foot, with the aid of a shoehorn, into his latest styles.

Mel knew Fay and they begat Electa and then Nadine and then me, the youngest sister, Jane. Electa and I had moderately happy childhoods. Nadine was silent and far away from the day she was born. Even though her face wasn't scarred until she set herself on fire, it seems to me that purple ring had always been around her face. Electa and I played with the neighbor children, we read, jumped rope, went to the movies. Nadine sat and stared, with that wild look in her eye, out the window, into the woods behind our house, up at the moon and stars.

All of us visited Grandma Minnie but it was only Nadine who was allowed to play her violin. "Of course I let her play. She had a gift. I knew it the minute I touched her tiny hands. That girl will win prizes, I said, and I knew what I was talking about."

So while Electa and I ferreted through Minnie's closets for fancy dresses and costume jewelry from another time, Nadine sat in the living room, plucking and pulling at the strings on *Zayde* Yitzkach's violin.

One year for my mother's birthday, Minnie made a big party. When the gifts were all passed around and the wrapping paper was folded up or thrown away, my grandmother cleared her throat and clapped her hands. "Now Nadine and I have a special gift for you, Fay. I taught her the tune, but it is her own ability which gives the magic I know you will all perceive.

"And now," said Minnie, "a birthday *freylach*." She waved her hand and Nadine began to play.

And what music! For three generations and four families time stood still. Though a *freylach* is a happy tune, by the time my sister Nadine was done there was not a dry eye in the house. When first she finished there was complete and stunned silence. Then my uncles and aunts hooted and clapped. They stamped their feet, they pinched Nadine's cheeks. "A prodigy!" Uncle Dave declared. "Ought to be on Ed Sullivan," said my aunt Miriam, "What do you say, Fay, aren't you proud of your daughter?"

All eyes, including Nadine's which smoldered, were on my mother, who sat with her arms crossed in front of her and tapped one foot. Her lips were pursed, her eyes narrow.

"Who taught you how to do that?"

"I taught her," my grandmother said.

"You taught her but you wouldn't teach me."

"That was years ago."

"But you wouldn't teach me."

"The girl has a gift!"

"And me, I have nothing, isn't that true, *mameh*?"

"I wouldn't go so far as that– "

"Happy birthday," my mother muttered as she walked out of the room, "happy birthday to me!"

After that there was no peace between my mother and my sister Nadine. Minnie gave Nadine the violin to bring home. The secret was out now, Nadine had a talent, she needed to practice. But the fact of the matter is, when the violin came home with Nadine that day, my mother went mad.

Whenever Nadine practiced my mother found a reason she should stop. Either she must clean the bathroom or wash the dishes or vacuum the carpets first, even after Electa or I had done that work ourselves. Or sometimes when she began to play my mother developed sudden migraine headaches and Nadine must stop, she must, the music made her pain too great.

Eventually Nadine stopped practicing altogether and then her life became pure hell. My mother shifted her displeasure from the way Nadine did chores to the way she looked. Her clothes needed mending or else ironing or else were out of date. Even when Nadine managed to get her clothes looking just the way she thought my mother liked them a new shoe dropped: no matter what Nadine did, no matter how she combed it, tied it, or tucked it behind her ears, my mother always hated my sister's hair.

I cannot name the exact day it started, but one autumn morning when Nadine was fourteen, she began to rebel. "Your hair looks like a rat's nest," my mother told her, "go comb it."

Instead of leaping from the kitchen table as she usually did, Nadine stuck a piece of bread in the toaster and waited for it to pop. "I said go comb your hair." Electa and I looked at each other across the jam and butter. My father poked his head out from behind his newspaper. The toast came up cheerlessly. "Did you hear your mother?" my father asked.

Nadine picked the toast out and began to butter it.

"You heard your mother, now what are you going to do about it!"

Nadine smiled at my father and began to chew. For a few minutes there was no sound around the kitchen table except for the crunching of toast and the nervous clatter of Electa's and my silverware on our breakfast plates.

"She smiles!" my mother finally boomed. "If you think I'm going to let you out of the house looking like that you've got another thing coming!"

Into the bedroom they went, my mother wielding a comb. She pulled it through my sister's hair as if she were raking the lawn. When she was done, my mother came back to the kitchen rubbing her hands, triumphant. "Nadine!" she shouted over her shoulder, "Hurry up, you'll be late for school."

Nadine crept in with her coat on. Her shoulders were up around her ears. The edges of her hair were smoothed down, but her eyes were red from crying. "There, doesn't she look much better?"

Neither Electa nor I said a word. From that day on, I'm not sure Nadine spoke either. Still my mother kept on about her hair, which Nadine took to wearing in a tight ponytail behind her head. The more my mother picked, the darker Nadine's eyes grew, the more silent she became. She stooped when she walked and spent hours in the basement, doing what only God knew. Electa thought maybe she was developing mass murder plans. "You watch, Jane, she's going to explode one day and kill us all, wait and see."

And it came to pass that my sister Nadine spent many days and many nights in the hospital psychiatric ward. She had the best help for disturbed adolescents that money could buy. She had a private room and that room had a window which looked out onto some woods below.

My sister Electa went away to college and my mother was asked by doctors not to visit Nadine at first, so the only company she had besides her psychiatrists and the nurses was my father and me.

I came to her by bus. Always I found her, head in hands, staring out into the woods. I brought her tapes of music by famous violinists. We listened to them together and fat slow tears slid down Nadine's cheeks. They slipped into the gully of her purple scar and down her gritty neck. For the longest time, Nadine did not speak, but only glared and grunted. I wrote her notes and handed her paper and pencils to write back but she ripped the papers up and broke the pencils in two. Even though she scared me, I went to see her.

My mother sent presents with me or my father. Cookies she baked herself, a new nightgown, a box of candy. My father, when he went, always brought flowers. He appeared in her doorway like a reluctant suitor and pretended to knock. Then he pulled up a plastic chair close to the bed and the two of them stared at each other sadly.

One day the psychiatrist and my father came to see Nadine together. "The word is," my father said, "you might be ready for a visit from your mother. What do you say?"

Nadine looked at my father with her animal eyes but did not answer.

"It will be a short visit, Nadine. Your mother is very eager to see you."

Nadine's eyes traveled from psychiatrist to father then back to psychiatrist.

"She'll come with your father the day after tomorrow."

When my mother arrived she was laden with gifts. Nadine sat on her bed and looked at the packages. Then she looked up at my mother. "Don't you want to open them? I brought them for you."

Nadine turned her head towards the woods in the window. My mother, taking this simply as a sign of catatonia, reached out to touch Nadine's new curls. "Your hair is coming in nicely," was all she said.

"I'm surprised you're happy to see me with any hair at all!" The ragged edge of my sister's monster voice confused my mother. She jumped back as if stung.

"I only wanted to tell you how pretty you look."

"I have an ugly mark all the way around my face! I look like I have been in a train wreck. My voice sounds like a human cement mixer. How can you of all people tell me I'm pretty!"

"Nadine, please, you're upsetting your mother."

"Look, Nadine, at all I have brought you."

"Sweet things and frilly nightgowns! Who cares! Look at me! Both of you! Hear my voice!"

My mother became livid. "You ingrate!" She slapped Nadine.

Nadine's nostrils flared. "You can do that at home but you can't do it to me here. I'm a sick person in a mental hospital, so don't try any of that here."

"Is this my daughter? How can it be? Listen to her voice, Mel! My daughter doesn't sound like that! There's a *dybbuk* inside her! Just listen!"

"There's no *dybbuk*, Fay. This is America in the twentieth century. That is really your daughter who said those things. She is mentally ill."

"That's right. I'm nuts, look at me!"

"You can't talk to me like that!"

"I can," Nadine growled, "I'm a patient here. I'm under doctor's care and I can do whatever I want. I can tell you anything I want. Right now I want you to *get out of my room!*"

Now there was silence. My mother stepped back from her daughter, my father pulled his invisible beard.

"Your room?" my mother hissed, "Who do you think is paying for this room? Who hired the doctors, who wants to find you a good plastic surgeon so that some day, if all is well, you can look normal?"

"*Normal? Look at me! I will never look normal! Get out of my room!*"

"You *vildachaya!* Wild animal! This is some gratitude for everything we've done!"

Then without another word my mother descended upon Nadine and began to hit her with both fists.

My father rushed out of the room and came back with an orderly who gathered up my mother and escorted her out. "You don't understand," my mother told the young man as he helped her with her coat. "She's my own daughter but she has no respect for me."

"It's a shame," said my father, who followed closely behind.

In time Nadine was released from the hospital and my parents had to figure out what to do with her. At first she lived in our house, but she wouldn't look at anyone but me, no matter what we did. Nadine sat like a cat in the living-room window and stared out all day long, or she looked down at the floor in front of her or at her plate on the kitchen table. She was falling deeper and deeper inside herself, to where, no one knew.

Finally my Grandma Minnie offered to take her in. So we packed her a bag and took Nadine to live with my grandmother. There she thrived, although she still hardly spoke. For it was not only the scar around Nadine's face that was destined to stay forever, but also her strange, strangled voice. This was further proof of my mother's theory that a *dybbuk* was lodged inside Nadine. I, her new-world daughter, assumed with my sister Electa that fifteen years of silent screaming finally let loose in Nadine's throat and tore her vocal cords to shreds.

From the time she woke up in the morning until she went to sleep at night, my sister Nadine played her violin. My grandmother coached her, but in a year Nadine outdistanced her teacher. "There's not another thing I can do for you," Minnie told her, hands in the he air. There was talk of Julliard conservatory, music scholarships, awards for emerging artists, but Nadine would have none of it. She wanted to play for her own pleasure and no other.

My grandmother heard Nadine's arguments, shrugged her shoulders, and tapped her foot. "If that's what you want out of life, go in health, *zei gezunt!*"

Not many weeks later, that is exactly what Nadine Pagan did. She gathered up her precious violin, put on her favorite shoes, and walked out the door of my grandmother's house toward the tiny town of New Chelm.

The First Indian Pilot

Diane Glancy

T HE SECOND WORLD was a black wool blanket. Black as the iron skillet. Greased. Corn popping from the skillet like white stars pinned to the air over the black wool earth.

"Put the lid on, NOW!" Grandmother said. The old grandmother, not the young one. The old women lived so long, a house could have two grandmothers easy. Louis watched her dress that hung longer in front. The apron tied to her rubbery waist.

In their house the nephews were old as the uncles. Barefoot & cruel. Poking one another into trouble.

The black wool earth seemed to move in the distance. The sameness of the night was easy for Louis. He was colorblind. He also had poor eyesight & his eyes would not stand still. Even after eye-surgery they jumped like corn in the skillet he thought.

The far lights of Oklahoma City were not connected with the earth. Maybe that was the way the earth looked from a plane at night. Louis watched the earth, soft & moving from the bodies under it. He wanted to fly the planes he heard from Tinker Air Force base. But no Indian was a pilot. His brothers told him that. No Indian was anything but in the way. A left-over walking in two worlds.

What else could they do? They could live in the second world Louis saw from the window. But he didn't want that. They could live in the first world, the old one, distant & alien to him. He'd really only heard stories which lived sometimes in his head when his grandmothers talked. Or they could walk in that floorless space between two worlds. One foot in each world with those violent eruptions he heard sometimes between his mother & grandmothers, his mother & brothers.

The popcorn had a sound of a jet in the distance. Louis straddled the windowsill & lifted his arms. "Arrrrmmmmmmmm." He mimicked the sound he heard during the day when he sat in the dirt yard & watched the planes rise from the flat earth.

He couldn't fly anyway. Ye ho. His eyes rattled back & forth. His brothers looked at one another & laughed. Then the girls laughed. They were grasshoppers. Something to chase when they got older. Their faded jeans & shirts pale as popcorn under the lid of the skillet.

Monochromatic.

Louis remembered the word he'd heard at the hospital. Why didn't they just staple his eyelids closed like the screen to the opening in the window? But even it ripped out. Because he sat on the windowsill all the time his old grandmother nagged.

"You know that screen needs to be nailed closed again," she said to Louis, shaking the skillet & swatting at a fly.

No it didn't. How else would the cat get in? The flies like burnt kernels from the bottom of the skillet?

They were all packed into that small frame house between Oklahoma City & Okemah. Even though it was dark, the heat of the day stayed in the house. He had to have the openness of the window. The flat Oklahoma sky ruffed its blackness over him at night. The popcorn still pecked like hard rain during spring storms.

Louis sat in the window & pretended he was a pilot. All the while his old grandmother made popcorn for his nephews & the brothers that were still around. Louis had scratch marks on his legs from the torn edge of the screen. "Tsoo. Tsoo." He shot at the little birds that must be asleep in the bush. He shot at the waterdish his grandmother left in the dirt yard. He could see it shining in the light from the window.

He looked up at the stars. The Coma Berenices. The constellation he learned about. Didn't pilots navigate from the stars? The constellation was also called Berenice's Hair. He looked for the white fuzz in the sky, but the stars were jerking around in their orbits & he couldn't tell. Just like his dizziness. They said it came from his eyes.

Louis read the constellation book after school while his teacher graded papers. When his eyes jumped & he couldn't read any longer, she read the words for him. Then there were tutors & the other people who came to school. He liked the ones who played the banjo & guitar.

The voice of his nephews & brothers popped in the kitchen & he looked at them. They were fighting over the bowl of popcorn, pulling it back & forth.

"AYYYYheyy," he lifted the bowl from the table until they kept their arms out of the way & took the kernels with their hands. The bowl was almost empty. The old grandmother went to the wood-stove. Louis held the bowl on the table while the nephews & brothers finished.

All of them could see what he couldn't. He had memorized the colorwheel. Blue. Yellow. Red.

What were they? He had asked. But no one knew what to say.

The colorwheel made things look the way they did, & he didn't understand. Light or dark but he knew that. Maybe it was the way the banjo was different from the guitar. Or something like the difference in the scale. Maybe the spectrum of color had a similarity to the music he heard at school.

Blue. Yellow. Red.

Were they like the different notes? Not well played sometimes.

What was color like? It came through the eyes. He knew that.

The new corn popped in the skillet. He lifted the lid when the old grandmother wasn't looking. It was pure as a spirit leaping from its body. Sometimes he could forget his eyes & fly. But then the night felt black again when his eyes got to jerking. A blackbody. Something that absorbed all light falling on it without giving back any reflection. His oldest brother had a curtain of it at his window so he could sleep in the day. Once he had a night job as a janitor, but now he just drank into the dawn. No Indian was anything.

"Here, get that lid on the skillet!" His old grandmother harped. Some of the corn shot from the black skillet like parachutes over the edge of the stove. The nephews jumped down from the table & picked the corn off the floor. It was puffy as the old grandmother's feet in their dirty houseshoes. She clucked her tongue at them. But he saw her eat the fallen pieces too.

The corn in the large skillet seemed to lose its popping & the old grandmother got a twig from the kindling he had piled in the corner of the room. None of the older brothers would help. They were lost in the second world. He memorized the colors they all saw but him.

Blue. Blue-green. Green.

Yellow. Yellow-red. Red.

He held the colorwheel in his hand. An orbit the earth followed in its way past the Coma Berenices?

If he were a girl he would get off easier. Girls were never colorblind. They just carried it for their sons.

He wanted to be anything but the youngest of the uncles. All the evils of the olders rolled onto him. The buffalo wallows that caught the runoff. Only he did not want the rain he felt sometimes behind his eyes. The grandfathers were all dead. The fathers gone to New Mexico or Los Angeles. They'd be in the dirt yard one afternoon & gone the next. Sometimes he could hardly remember them. Maybe they got tired of having nothing to do & fled to barrooms & the rows of beds in missions. The boyfriends of the nieces still came around, but they too would disappear like the colors he didn't know.

Now the corn had a sound of a low backfiring. One of the older brothers when he went off to drink in Oklahoma City or Okemah. The eruption of the neighbor's dog when the cat wandered into his yard. The growl of heat-thunder that woke him sometimes.

"What color is the kitchen?" Louis asked.

"I can't remember what it used to be," the old grandmother said. She had grease on her fingers from oiling the skillet for more corn. Little salt-beads on her fingers. The colors got harder. He had read them.

Vermilion. Manganese. Sienna.

What were they? Parts of other colors? The sound of guitar & banjo playing different songs. Maybe an Indian flute.

He asked about the pile of kindling in the corner of the kitchen. He had gathered it for her. She said it was brown but that wasn't on the colorwheel. Was there also a first & second world with color?

He knew it was a brightness he didn't see. Little sparks that came from cans & jars & the torn shirts of his nephews when they got in fights at school & the tube his mother put on her mouth when she went out.

A sort of light that things carried.

He knew it was a combination of things. The sound of the cat when the old grandmother stepped on its paw. The buzz of flies. The nephews fighting over the new popcorn in the bowl. The grandmother clucking.

But not separate. Not one at a time. But all had their own way of sounding together. All had their way of sounding out their own kind of light.

The land was greased. It was enough to pop them like corn. Mid-August, they couldn't walk on the pavement without jumping. Even after dark, Louis could feel the heat rise from the yard as he sat in the window. Wasn't his race popped off the earth? Weren't they unwanted? Where could they go? Follow the grandfathers into the black & white sky at night? The first world was gone & the second world had come to take its place.

But he couldn't see it like it was. The second world looked black to him with flat, white stars nailed to the air. He wanted to call back the old earth. The first one.

Yo!

For a moment something flashed in his eye. A falling star. A gist of what could be color. A slash of something other than what was?

Louis rubbed his sore eye like the bubble a pilot pulled over the cockpit.

Something flashed & Louis reached for it again. It was like the sound of a story or the moving tribe. It was something he couldn't quite understand.

He reached from the window & stepped from the second world up.

Fire Sermon

Lyn Miller

I STOOP BESIDE Lakshmi's grave on the windswept hill, and use a small stick to dig a hole. I want to bury a coin beside the headstone. Before me in the distance I see the downtown skyline, the mirrored panels of the new, modern buildings reflecting back with glaring brightness the trees and the sky of this hill. The world around me is on fire. It is October in Minnesota, and the maples have gone up, carmine, vermilion, lemon, plum, ochre. The lobes of the leaves like fangs lick thirstily at the sky. The trees splash themselves in the depth of it and are not quenched, not satisfied. I stand among them like Daniel in the lions' den, only I am burning, as he did not. But still I am not afraid. I believe in fire the way I once believed in God.

Fire first came into my life on Memorial Day when I was eight years old. Daddy was up on the roof patching the spot that leaked into my attic bedroom, his toolbox hanging somehow from the fold of the roof. He stood on the slant, but his feet looked secure as a fly's on a wall. He was a fixer, fixing was his life, and I believed there was nothing he couldn't make right.

He was hammering, and the hammer banged like firecrackers on the shingles. Mother was in the kitchen baking brownies, and the thick, sweet smell drifted out the windows and doors, made the newly-returned robins in the hedge lift and swivel their heads. To celebrate Memorial Day, we were going on a picnic. Amy was with Mother in the kitchen, smacking a spoon on her wooden highchair, while in the backyard Teddy stood by himself under the old apple tree, pushing a yellow plastic airplane through the air and making a buzzing noise; Joe and Mitch poked in the dank, leafy window wells for salamanders. Or worms. If they found worms they were going to fish next to Caesar's cesspool, under the willows, with string attached to long twigs.

I was sitting in the soft dirt next to Mother's trellis of blue morning glories. Our yard was a stretch of cool, fine dirt on which light rains fell and ran like tiny clear marbles. Spring had come early. It was a warm day, the sky almost violet. Neighbors up and down the street raked and swept, called across their fences to one another, laughing. The air was thick with the scent of Schelinskys' honeysuckle. The morning glories were delicate gramaphones, their petals soft as skin, blue as the veins in Mother's legs; bees floated in them with a quiet, steady hum.

Then from the clear sky came the whine of airplanes. We all glanced up. There were two propeller planes with small American flags on their sides, flying in formations together for the holiday. As I sifted the fine dirt between my fingers, I watched them soar and drop, light as paper. They dipped so low they seemed to graze the top of Schelinskys' giant elm, then darted upward again with a moan and streaked toward each other.

Suddenly, a boom, like a cherry bomb. My hands sprang over my ears. Dark scraps shot into the blue. A ball of fire like a small sun sank fast behind the house, leaving a long, straight trail of smoke behind it that twisted and billowed and soon filled the air with a choking stench that drowned out the aroma of brownies and honeysuckle.

Just before the fireball dropped into the trees, a dark dot popped out of it, and out of the dark dot, a flare of white.

Daddy stood watching with his hand as a visor. "Holy smokes! Holy smokes!" he cried. Mother flew out of the back door, Amy on her arm, and let the screen door slam. "Oh, God," she breathed, looking up. Daddy scrambled down the ladder. "Round Lowry and Central. Went down around Lowry and Central." He could tell such things; he had shot down planes in the Navy. Maybe it was as a sailor he dashed automatically to the blue Dodge. We all followed him, climbed in, and fled as if our own house had been hit. The neighbors stood looking at each other and at the smoke and at us racing down the street.

Other people were running for their cars, too. We followed the smoke. Sirens screeched. The air grew thicker and thicker and it was hard to breathe. Open the window, Daddy. No, roll it up. The glass went up and down, up and down, like an eye with a tic. He didn't complain. He just kept pressing the button, the knuckles of his other hand white on the steering wheel, eyes reading the sky.

People crowded the streets, some standing and staring up, others running, dodging, up the sidewalks. Cars moved in slow herds. The blue sky was a grainy black, and getting blacker, because now other things were burning. Flames bared themselves like bloody teeth here and there among the roofs and branches in the distance.

Daddy pulled out of the stream of cars and gunned up an alley. He had grown up in this neighborhood and knew its paths. When we were almost to the heart of the fire, Mother put her hand over her mouth. "Oh, what if it's Aunt Ella's?" I thought of Aunty Ella in her pink housedress with the lapels, a cameo brooch on the left point, her hair in a net fastened with bobby pins. I could see her in her rocker with the needlepointed headrest, gazing through her thick glasses at the geraniums in her flowerbox, when suddenly an airplane burst through her front window. "My heavens," she would say, and duck. The plane would glide out the back door.

We parked the car in an overgrown lot teeming with dandelions and purple clover. Daddy strode ahead between houses, and the boys gamboled after him. I stayed close to mother and Amy. Then we saw it. A row of white houses with green lawns and gardens of tulips. But the white houses were turning black and crumbling. Their windows were red, flickering eyes. The tulips were drowning and melting. They lay on the ground like big drops of blood. The street was packed with fire engines and police cars. "Stay back!" the policemen cried. Firehoses slithered and snapped like pythons. I jumped away from them. A piece of the plane, like the tubular husk of a dead monarch butterfly, lay on the lawn next to the blackest house, which was missing most of the roof and one side. It was not Aunty Ella's. The boys ran around yelling and making the sound of machine guns. A-a-a-a. I stared at an old lady, just like Aunty, who stood in front of her disintegrating house screeching and holding up the empty pouches of her arms to the tendrils of smoke.

I followed the smoke up and saw the flare of white, now just a streaming tatter, in the top of a tall, budding tree. There was something dangling, high up, something blackened and upside down, flopping in the wind, with pieces like arms. It was like it was walking on its hands in mid-air. Men were trying to reach it with the cupped hand of a crane, but the crane was too short. Someone had put on a treetrimmer's belt and was climbing. Maybe the wind would shake it loose. I was sweating, my eyes stung. "Daddy!" I cried, and grabbed at his hand, but he jerked it away, staring with his mouth open at the tree top. Amy's eyes were wide. I thrust my hand over them. "Daddy, let's go!" I begged, but mother batted at me to shush.

Finally all the fire was gone. There were just seven sagging black houses with empty eyes, and water flowing away. Someone had brought the old lady a sweater and was hugging her. Men lowered the thing in the tree on ropes.

We sauntered back to the car. Teddy had brought his yellow plane and was tossing it up and watching it fall to the ground. "Did you see him, Dad, did you see him up in the tree?" Joe demanded, as if asking for some explanation. Joe hardly ever talked; he was the strong silent type everyone adored. "I saw him, son," Daddy answered gravely. Mother sighed and tossed Amy to him. "I don't know why we have to go chasing every time a spark flies. You're as bad as any kid." I thought this, too. We went home. We didn't go on a picnic. Mother dished out the brownies but I didn't want one.

After that, I hated the morning glories. I thought any flower that stayed open only a day was stupid. I hated the dirt, because it was like ashes, nothing green would ever come of it. And I hated Memorial Day.

I couldn't sleep. When the house was dark, it looked gutted. I could smell smoke. I got up at all hours and tiptoed around, sniffing sockets, ashtrays, the stove. The night itself was like a big empty burning-barrel and our house no more than an old box tossed into it. Any minute God could strike the match.

When Daddy came to talk to me about not sleeping, I hid my face in my pillow. He petted my hair and asked softly, "Are you still Daddy's little girl?"

"No!" I bellowed. It was all his fault. He made me look. But I burrowed with a shudder into the crook of his skinny elbow.

Twenty years later, Daddy, who wanted to fix everything, was dead of all the things he couldn't fix. The boy with the yellow airplane died at twenty in the explosion of his Army helicopter, which plunged into the Sea of Japan, yielding up only a broken rotor blade in the net of a fisherman. On Memorial Day after his death, Joe and I went to the national cemetery to see his marker in the section for bodiless graves. Joe got drunk afterwards, and, losing his temper for the first time in his life, punched a policeman and spent the night in jail.

The fall after the plane crash, Joe and I struck back. We were on our way to *Guns of Navarone* at the Heights Theater. It was a chilly Saturday afternoon, the clouds a dirty gray like lowing sheep. We were wearing our jackets with the plaid flannel lining, and strode with heads and shoulders hunched against the wind. We often walked together that way.

We passed Jackson Pond, where we skated all winter, and came up to Kriesels' field. The field was not really Kriesels', even the abandoned and condemned house that stood on the northwest corner of the square block of scrub was no longer Kriesels'. But they had lived there, seven ragged and stupid kids. We never saw their parents. We called the Kriesels names at school, pushed them down. Nan Kriesel was in my grade. She was even more of a beanpole than I was, and her skin was like cellophane. Her forehead and arms and legs were a roadmap of red and blue veins. She always had a sore in the corner of her mouth, and her hair crawled. She flicked at it, scratched, shook it out, which made us refuse to sit by her in class, and run from her on the playground. The ties at the back of her dress dragged, and she wiped her nose on them. She never wore socks. She always breathed with her mouth hanging open, giving out the smell of a sewer hole, and her eyes were empty and hard as a doll's. I couldn't decide whether to knock her down or give her an orange.

After Kriesels abandoned their house, we used to think we saw a light in it. It was haunted, we were sure. A sign on the door read CONDEMNED, KEEP OUT, DANGER, but that only encouraged us. We sneaked in and investigated. There were jagged holes in the walls, the ceilings, even the stairways. It was as if the house was eating itself up. There was a torn couch in the living room, a dresser with a few clothes in the drawers, a yellow metal table in the kitchen, all waiting, as if they didn't notice no one came, and that the walls were disappearing. "This is where they ate," we whispered with awe, pointing, "this is where they slept."

We never stayed in Kriesels' house for long. The smell was terrible, as if cats, or boys, had been spraying the walls.

"Remember them?" Joe said, as we came near, that day of the field fire.

"Yeah. Remember Nan?"

We paused to look, in case there was a light in the window somewhere. The street beside us was dug up, the hazard marked with a row of little black cannon balls, each with a flame at the top. There was a throat-sticking smell of soft tar. Joe glanced at the burning balls, and at the field. "I wonder what would happen if we rolled that ball into those weeds." I was startled. Joe was the perfect son, the one who never stepped out of line. I followed his narrow gaze toward Kriesels'.

"What if it spread?" What if it went as far as the shopping center? What if it burned up the whole city?

"It won't burn nothin' but the field," he replied scornfully. "There's a street all around it."

"It could blow."

"It won't."

I trusted him. "What if they catch us?"

"We'll be in the movie before anyone sees it. You won't tell, will you?"

"No."

The ball was heavy. I helped him get a hand under it, and we gave it a heave. It plunked into a patch of weeds, and they crinkled to nothing. We ran.

As we dropped into our seats in the almost deserted theater, we heard sirens. I looked at Joe. "Don't be a chicken," he snapped. We sank down so our heads were not visible from behind.

We stayed through the movie twice. When we came out, night was falling. We made our way up to Kriesels' field, and saw the house. It was the same as always, only the front door was flapping. Our faces fell. But the field was black. The milkweed pods, the goldenrod, the weeds we called wheat, the wild violets and sprigs of sumac, the straw grasses, all were a uniform, brittle, warm-smelling black.

We waited nervously for a few days to be found out, but after that I started sleeping again, and Joe went back to behaving.

It was not until we we had moved into the new rambler that fire took its revenge. The rambler was a house no one else had ever lived in. No more dirt yard or dirt cellar. No more mice. No leaky roof. Before we moved, Joe and I took walks to peer through the big, glinting windows. It was empty, but not like Kriesels'. It was empty with the new, the not-yet. We could rollerskate in the cement basement. Daddy was going to put in a jukebox for dancing.

Across the street sprawled acres of undeveloped railroad property: a woods full of thorn trees, a broad, hilly field where pheasants nested, a sandstone quarry, and a dump. We lived over there, dodging the railroad dekes, who tried to catch us shinnying under the fences that bore NO TRESPASSING signs, on our way to the expanse of the white and gold quarry.

One summer my brothers and I and the neighborhood boys built a village called Hoboland just down the embankment from where the field met the road. We hauled branches from the woods, wearing gloves against the thorns. No taking live limbs, we ruled. From the dump we dragged slabs of cardboard from refrigerator boxes, boards, tires, wire, tubeless TVs, and whatever else we saw some use for. Each of us built a fort. We appointed a mayor, a policeman, a fireman, a carpenter, a newspaper boy. Joe, of course, was the mayor. Mitch was the cop. I was the decorator, whose main job was to plait grass for curtains. Teddy was banished for throwing his hammer at Joe. We planned to live in a society without crime or want.

Weeks went into building and refining the village. My own shanty was built against the embankment. It was constructed like a teepee, with branches and boards trussed together; but rather than pointed, it was a long rectangle. I used old flowered sheets for wallpaper and a mildewed rag rug for my floor. My textured ceiling was made of a holey white chenille bedspread from Grandma Stronsky's attic. The grass curtains over my door were laced with red sumac.

We begged our parents to let us sleep in the village. Finally one night they gave in. Joe, who was a Boy Scout, built a fire in a dirt pit, and we cooked hobo soup for dinner and told stories about grizzly bears, wolves, and ghosts. But as darkness came, the sky grew threatening, and Daddy and Mother called us home.

When we woke up the next morning, and hurried back to Hoboland, we found it burned to the ground. The whole field, from the asphalt street to the dump's muddy road, was charred and bare. Mr. Orlicky reported that around midnight he saw a motorcyclist stop above my shanty and toss something into the dark.

The parents, enraged, discussed the fire endlessly. We kids were silent.

By the time Cravens' house burned, I had started college. We had lost the rambler to debts and had moved into a cramped, sunless house where bats hung in clusters on the attic door. Sometimes they strayed. Mother found one on the wall above her bed. Teddy found one on his pillow. Once when Mother slid a foot into her Kickarino, it stubbed a dead mouse. The only yard was an overgrown driveway.

Daddy was gone. After nearly putting a knife into himself, he was living like a bum in the old Anthony Hotel downtown, penniless and in love with a woman fond of whiskey and bowling, who could throw frying pans as fervently as he did. Joe was resisting the draft and reading Sartre and Nietzsche. Mitch had become an expert on the Civil War. I was still trying to keep my hands over Amy's eyes, unable as I was to keep them over mine. But she was thirteen and vivacious, and now that my hands were slipping, pot and boys took their place. I had loved for the first time, and lost.

The Cravens' fire happened in January, the day after New Year's. It was fifteen degrees below zero. A month before, we had received a telegram from the army saying that Teddy was missing. At 8:12 A.M. I heard the sirens, at first far off, then nearer and nearer. In front of our house their shrieking faded like a missile and died. The enormous engines shuddered and snorted like beasts, rattling the house. I threw on my clothes and dashed downstairs. I could hear the familiar popping and crackling, smell the familiar smoke.

Across the street, flames lashed out of Cravens' upstairs apartment like a wind-blown mass of red hair. Without putting on a coat, I skipped between the trucks and moved close to the house. Little Tommy, who was two, was wrapped in bath towels and clutched against the formidable bosom of Ida the storekeeper, whose wrinkled brown potato face was turned intently toward the door of the burning duplex. Tommy's feet were red and puffy. In a car behind Ida, leaning in the open door, I discovered Tommy's dad and another man, clad only in undershorts, holding forth arms turned to raw meat. Their hair and eyebrows were singed off. There was a smell of cooked flesh nothing like steak on a grill. Mr. Craven was rocking. "My baby, my baby's in there. I couldn't get at her." Laura was only five months old.

We all stared at the door, scarcely clothed and oblivious to the cold. We could see the black shapes of firemen shifting across the hazy windows. Finally two of them emerged, carrying something. It was a small stretcher, its canvas sling white as a cotton diaper. In the center of the white lay a small black stick, a lump of coal. They carried it slowly, reverently. It passed before me. Laura Craven.

By the time of the trainyard fire on Stinson Boulevard, I had lived in thirty-five places, including a convent and a psychiatric ward. Daddy was dead, keeled over of a heart attack at forty-nine. Mother owned a house in the suburbs with a lawn big and green as a meadow. She had married a man who did not chase fires, a man she had loved before Daddy, back home on the Iron Range, when she was still pretty and vivacious. Mitch ran a large-scale cleaning operation, and Joe was a hermit, writing stories in a basement crowded with furnace ducts. Amy was on her third husband.

I no longer hated morning glories. I grew them in the backyard and marveled at them because they died every day. Dust I admired because it was final. Lakshmi, the woman I lay with the night of the fire, was all the beauty my eyes could bear. Thick, black, flossy hair. Wet, deepset eyes that gleamed like rubies. A voice rich as oil. Proud, full breasts oozing milk.

We were sleeping, entwined, when the explosion quaked the house. It woke me up and I thought, drowsily, it must be a gust of wind slamming into the window. A storm was blowing up. I dozed again, and in an instant there was another blast. My eyes snapped open. Another. The window gave the sound of a sheet catching wind on a clothesline. I was close to it and rolled back, thinking it would shatter. Then I looked out and saw the whole sky ablaze. The window was red from edge to edge. This is it, I thought. The end of the world.

I shook Lakshmi. "We have to get out of here! The world's on fire." She laughed at me. "Look!" I cried. She looked. We dressed quickly. I was wild. She was amused. She picked up her box of jewels, I grabbed my journals, and we hurried out. The fire was not on our side of the block, after all, but across the street. Still, a few feet of tar made a shaky firewall. People all down the block were herding their children out the door, clutching bags. Did they, too, think when they woke that this was it, the long-expected bomb, the holocaust? Some of my neighbors got in their cars and drove off. The rest of us inched toward the opposite boulevard, which yielded abruptly to a ravine gashed with railroad tracks. The heat coming up was intense. It was not a bomb exploding, but the gas tanks of semi-trucks parked along the tracks, which kept exploding, one after another. Just behind them stood a train; in the wind boxcar after boxcar flared and spit flames from its dark maw. Our whole line of sight was a parapet of fire.

The fire trucks had a hard time getting close, because of the ravine and the tracks. Meanwhile, we gathered on the bank until there were a couple hundred of us, stretched along and above the tracks, holding out our hands to the heat. It was 2 A.M. People brought beer. Somebody set up a hibachi. Another turned on a boombox and played rock and roll. We passed around Ripple chips and cookies. Every time another tank exploded in a whirling purple ball, we cheered and hoisted our beers into the air. The fire marshall ordered us back, but we strained forward. The exploding trucks were at a greater distance now, and we were fearless. The roundhouse went up, and the truck office, and every weed and scrap of litter between the straps of iron.

Somebody tapped me on the shoulder. "Didn't you go to Edison High?"

"Yeah."

"You're one of the Reeds. You lived across that muddy field from us when we were little."

"Yeah. You're Chuck Stone."

"Hey, remember that plane crash?"

"Yeah, I remember."

"That was cool, wasn't it?" His face was unnaturally bright. He had on a t-shirt with a picture of the Grateful Dead. "Here, have a beer." He grinned as he yanked one off the plastic holder fastened to his belt. I took it. "Cheers!" he yelled, and thrust his can toward the blaze.

A hose finally reached the roundhouse. It sizzled in the water and sent up a shimmering blue sheet of vapor, like a mirage on the highway, then the flames died down. "Boo!" the people cried. But a heap of sparks leapt to another boxcar. The straw shot up into a red dance like something raised from the dead, and everyone shouted and clapped. We stayed, feasting and dancing until there was nothing left but black flatbeds and a pink strip of dawn.

Eight years later, Lakshmi herself caught fire. Cancer began in the breast with the ever-milky nipple and spread to her brain, her liver. I watched the pale yellow sear though her brown-bread skin, the ruby glow of her eyes fade into cinders. She stuffed herself with fistfuls of rice and threw up blackness. Her mind raged and then began to snuff itself out thought by thought. I held the basin, wiped her bloody urine, lay down beside her and held her in the too-shallow cup of my body, stroking her scabrous, spongy scalp. We walked together, as long as there was walking, on the burning coals. At the cemetery after her funeral, I watched, stone-still in the grass, as the ribbons reading "Sister," "Wife," "Friend," were torn loose by the wind from their wilting bouquets and scattered down the hill.

Now, her daughter with the same lustrous and stormy eyes has turned four, and likes to play with matches. Here at the grave, the wind blows over the yellow chrysanthemums I have brought, and they sway in the breeze without bending their heads. In my car await twelve crimson-tipped candia roses. Because I am in love again, and all, all is burning.

Songs of Innocence

John King Kai Ming McKenzie

T HE WHOLE CREW showed up at my doorstep, it was at six, expecting me
to feed them. They wanted to be fed *right then*. Donny, who'd only been
in the program for about two weeks, was especially high on himself, and he wanted
me to know it. He banged open the screen door, bringing in flies, and yelled,
"Hey Ollie, come on out, we're hungry!" I was upstairs looking at some books,
never mind what books, and he sure scared the heck out of me.

Not right then, but after I'd squared some things away, I went down to see who was
making the fuss. And I saw not just Donny, but Marge and Truman and I saw you, too,
at the back. Shepherding them. You had that sack of muffins. What kind were they?

My brother and his ugly, terrible wife were out at Burger King just then, so
I was all alone. Donny wanted me to make him some soup.

"Make me some Hambeen soup, Ollie! I came out here to have some!"

"What's Hambeen soup?" I asked him.

"The kind in bags. Just add water."

I didn't know what was going on. I didn't know how to make any soup. Then
you came up and said that since I hadn't come to the meeting at the clinic, you
all invited yourselves over to my house to see what was wrong.

I got mad. If I can't make it to a meeting now and then is none of your business.
I still have to count when I think about it. My brother Roger says I have the
right to be mad. He's mad too; he said he might go over your head about it. I'm
not sure how he'd do that.

Then Marge opened the fridge up, peering into that greasy light like it could save her. She found the leftover chicken, and I knew it was a goner. "All I can say is, I'm not cleanin' up after you," I said. She kept dropping skin on the tiles. Some flies landed to investigate. Later, the mice would come and run off under the stove with it. I didn't mind the mice as much as the flies. You can even tell mice apart. All flies are identical. There was only one fly in the house until you dropped by.

You tried to get me to *verbalize*, but by then it was all I could do to keep Donny from going up in my room. He wanted to see where I slept at night. You said, "Pay attention to what I say, Oliver," but I didn't. I had to physically touch him, which is against the rules.

In my dream you were showing us pictures like you always do, but they were much worse than normal. There was one of a white dog on a leash. You could see the legs of his master behind him. The dog was cowering, because all this blood was being sprayed at it, a big gush of red blood that was showing up real well on his white fur. You couldn't see where the blood was coming from; it was just somewhere off on the right. The dog was very scared, but then in the next picture he wasn't scared anymore, actually he was licking up the blood from the pool where it had collected. And still his master just stood there in his leather shoes. I think I know who the master was. I think he was you.

Anyway, you got us all to sit down at the card table in the living room. Marge brought her chicken wings to keep her happy, and you had the muffins in one of Roger's good serving dishes, so everyone ate for a while. "Aren't you going to have a muffin with us, Oliver?" you asked. Flies had followed us in from the kitchen. I declined to eat a muffin, and then you called us to order.

You say you never record our meetings, but then how come you always put that ashtray out from your bag when you start? None of us smoke. None of us are going to start smoking just because you got us a place to ash. I caught on to that ashtray trick right away. You may have noticed that I don't talk so much about why actually I have to be at these meetings anymore. That's because I know what's inside the ashtray.

So we were all talking about absenteeism, because of me. I told you the only reason I missed is because Roger's wife, whose name is Nikki, didn't want to drive me. I can't drive myself. You know that I don't have a license anymore. Marge said it was hard to make it every day, but weren't the benefits worth it? Donny, you might not have noticed, grumbled at that remark quite a bit.

Then Truman began to get upset at how long it was taking for the program to effect a change in his behavior. I suppose, if I'd been trying to get cleaned up for as long as he has, without much sign of progress, I'd get discouraged too. Truman must be thirty, isn't he?

"I'm coming to the conclusion that we can't help me just by talking about stuff. Talk never changed anything. I need something drastic, I'm afraid."

"Now, Truman," you said, in your smoothest voice, "We're not going to be able to fix things up with anybody if we don't know where the problem's at, right?" Truman gulped his breath and nodded, shaking now. "And I'll tell you this: My job is only to show you where the problem lies, and then to coach you as you go inside and tackle it yourself."

Truman changed his tack. "I can't do anything about it. It's not up to me. I need some surgery; I need a cure." He was talking into his shirt collar; he was holding it up to his mouth and getting the edges wet with spit.

"It is up to you. It's only up to you. I wish . . ." here your voice got quiet, ". . . I wish that there was some way I could get in there with you and help you. But I can't."

"I can't stop it by myself."

"Yes, it's easy, it's all in your head."

"I'm paralyzed."

"If you say you are."

"Stop it."

"In some respects, Truman, I'd have to say that you're doing this to yourself. You are prolonging your own recovery."

Truman flushed, and tugged his shirt back down.

"And, what's more, I think you know this yourself. At some level, yes, I'd say this is a conscious decision." You leaned back in your folding chair and it squeaked. Truman wouldn't meet your eyes.

Another one of the photographs you showed me in that dream was of an infant, a baby girl I think. She was biting happily at the neck of the dog from the previous picture. Of this you said, "She hasn't learned anything yet." I don't know just what you meant by that, but I think it's a clue.

"I'm tired of you," Donny said, "you wimps." He got up noisily and went into the kitchen.

Marge laid her big, greasy hand on Truman's. "Don't listen to him. Chins up, Truman."

"Okay," he said softly.

I know that Truman really doesn't want to fall back to his old behavior. He told me he dreams that someday they'll trust him enough to put him back out there, where he can have his own place and get a family together. I'd don't know from where he'd get all this, but that's what he wants. He said he'd keep the place up real well, with some flowerboxes out front. Every square foot of his family's home is planned out in a 3-D model in his head. He can go up and walk around in it, he told me, and get things ready. I can't stand that. I can't stand that stuff myself, but he apparently is still in love with the world. I told him it looks good because the rough spots are being hidden from us, that if it weren't for the program it would be one day gone by, one day without pills, and then we'd probably jump off the couch screaming at what we saw. Or at what we felt.

That's what got us in this program anyway. You wouldn't have gotten our names off any list unless we'd *screamed for help.*

"Hey Ollie!" Donny said. From the echo, I could tell he was at the top of the stairs. I hadn't heard him go up. "What is this weird shit? You sure have funny magazines."

I jumped up and ran through the kitchen to get upstairs; I was running so fast, I almost hit my head on the wall when I turned the corner. Donny was beaming down at me, one of my copies of *Hustler* in his hands. I pulled myself up the banister to get to him faster.

"Put those away Donny, I mean it!" I was breathing hard already, and I was practically standing on top of him.

"But these are funny, I like looking at them." He had the November one out. It was one of my oldest. It was wide open to Amber Lynn.

"Don't you have respect? Jeez!" I just snatched it from him and went to my room to put it away. I heard his cowboy boots behind me.

"Is this your room?"

"Donny, I think they're calling for you downstairs." I was beginning to wonder when my brother and his wife were going to show up. They'd never seen my magazines.

"No. This is more interesting," he said, stretching the last word out. He made it sound dirty. His eyeballs were wet and bright; he was staring, and his hair stood up stiffly on top of his head. "I wish we were better friends."

I put the magazine back under the bed. He came and sat down on it. I was really disturbed, and I tried counting it out, but I was still disturbed. A fly came through the field of dust in front of the window and landed on Donny's black t-shirt. It bumbled around on his chest for a while, and then flew up to his face. He kept watching me from the bed, not moving. The fly sat at the corner of his mouth, rotating, cleaning each foot in turn. I never noticed how long Donny's eyelashes were, but now that he was turned sideways to the window the sun made them sharp silhouettes like spiders.

When he spoke, the fly moved off. "I don't want you to be a wimp like Truman. It's not too late." He held out his hand, gesturing for me to approach.

My hand also went out, a reflex. Across that great airy canyon between us. His fingers were cold and dry. It wasn't a bad feeling, like I'd thought it would be.

I ran down the stairs, almost falling. You were right there at the bottom, arms crossed. I told you so, you seemed to be saying. Did you know what I was thinking? It seemed like you were up in my room with Donny and me. It seemed like you were telling me to leave.

"I'm glad you decided to rejoin us, Oliver," you said. I could hear Truman sobbing in the other room. A chair squeaked. "We can get on with the meeting now."

"What about Donny," I said. "I want him to get out of my room; he went in my room without permission."

"Donny?" you called up to him.

"I'm busy," he said.

"Come on down, we've still got some muffins."

"Have you ever seen any of these magazines?"

I was watching you while you talked to him. I tried to signal you, but you wouldn't look. My heart was beating fast. You were playing it cool. You were going to bring him down out of there with will power. I could tell.

"I don't have time to look at silly magazines, Donny. I've got important work to get done down here with the rest of the group."

"Are you going to teach them how to be wimps?"

"None of them are wimps. They're a very brave bunch. I wish you could be so brave."

There was a short silence. Then Donny screamed. "I think they're *wimps*. I hate this dumb program. And I hate you!"

He came down deliberately, one step at a time, stomping with his boots. His eyes were watering; he wouldn't look at me. I backed up and let him pass. You tried to keep from showing how satisfied you were.

The last photograph was the little girl, and the white dog, but now their positions were reversed. The dog had reached back with his long snout and nipped the girl's ear. Blood ran down from it. The teeth of the dog. What did the dog feel? *Tenderness*. You whispered something in my ear, and I tried to slap you away. You were a fly. You were flies. Your green bodies glistened as the summer sun shone through them. You caressed my body at every point, surrounding me as in a womb. Flies are your manifestation. What you are really I don't know.

When Roger and his nasty wife got home, at dusk, they looked surprised. They don't like any of the other patients in the program. Nikki curled her lip; she looked disgusted to see them. You said the meeting was just over, "But it's nice to meet you folks, I'm glad to see that Oliver is in good hands."

Donny was on the porch by himself, sulking. No one had noticed him go there.

You went up and said something to him, and then he went to the van with the rest. Truman turned to wave at me. "You better show up tomorrow," he said. He looked so vulnerable, right next to the road. Cars raced by so fast, I thought one just might jump the curb and knock him over.

"I will."

You won't let Donny get me. No matter that you look down on me, I know you want to keep me safe. And you always know what we're thinking. You are dedicated to us. You keep tabs. I heard that they make robots small enough to to travel inside our bodies, with cameras to relay information. These robots would be smaller than insects. The fly that circles my room, not landing, might be one of your agents. Each compound eye might be a battery of camera lenses. Once a fly sat on my lamp and watched me all night as I paged through my books.

I'm sure that real flies don't sit so still. I've been trying to catch them, but they can read my mind and evade me every time. They must be very sophisticated mechanisms. I wish I could take one apart, but I don't want to destroy something that's not mine. And these flies are your agents. Am I right? You don't have to reply to that. That would be a breach of security. I only trust that you have good intentions. You won't let the outside in. Donny is definitely from the outside, as you are well aware. You know everything. You.

The Habit of Despair

Gary Eller

T HE M.P.S WERE clean and quick, and the fine Southern accents they carried for the fragments of communication required in the course of their work must have added a sting to Vernal's outlook. But they had their papers right. They came through the green and white storm door of the double-wide with its plywood add-on, and there in front of those pee-smelling and puffy-faced kids, announced that he, Private Vernal Gene Frew, also known as Vernal Eugene Olson, was under arrest for desertion from the United States Army.

Vernal lay flat on the couch by the wall where he'd tacked his seal skin, and across the room from the new TV he'd bought with the bonus money I gave him. He was strained from finger-wording his way through the Coho story in *Field and Stream*, but to accommodate the M.P.s he raised his arms while they put cuffs on his wrists and lifted his feet while they slipped irons around his ankles. Then they stood him up, and one on each side, walked him out to the car, commandeered from the island police department just for the occasion.

I knew Vernal well enough. I gave him a job after my friend Sid gave me a job running the Anagak Island Hardware. I guess since Sid was acquainted with me from the old days, he expected that I'd be drunk half the time and less able to think up ways to steal from him like his other managers had. He was partly right.

Sid insisted his life was headed for grander purposes than stove bolts and hollow point shells, and he wanted time to concentrate on finding those purposes. The store was the only hardware on the island. The first thing I did was figure out what items we sold that we had monopolies on, then I had the clerks mark them all up twenty percent. Sid thought I was a genius.

I'd been there maybe four weeks and was still swollen with authority and good feelings when I met Vernal Frew. I was in the back when he came in. I watched him as he approached, walking straight-spined the way a shorter person will, but halting and careful, like he expected someone might leap out from the Thermos display and give him a good scare.

"Y'all har-rin?" he asked.

Vernal had a bad eye—it wandered, curious and solitary—making it harder to pay enough attention to understand him. "What's that?" I said.

"Help," he said. "Y'all need help? Um lookin' for work."

By then the commotion of his wife and kids caught up to him. There were four children, all with black mop-head hair, though only one or two of them were Vernal's. The baby, lighter-skinned than the others, was in its mother's arms. Vernal introduced them all, including the baby, playing a finger under its fat chin. But I only caught his wife's name, Wanda. She was an Eskimo from St. Lawrence Island, and had the straight black hair and perfect skin common to Indians and Eskimos. She looked at the floor when Vernal pronounced her name.

As it turned out my sporting goods man had just given his notice. I asked Vernal if he knew anything about guns.

"Bin farn 'em all my life," he said.

I took a hunch, figuring he was pressed hard for a job, and I hired him cheap. It was a good choice. Vernal moved a lot of merchandise for us. Eskimos in from the villages liked him, and trusted him. They called him Bernal.

"Where's Bernal?" they'd ask, leaning over the handgun case, palms flat on the glass. Vernal would hear them and come out of the back room, happy to get away from the puzzle of invoices and stock cards.

"If it ain't Joe Tommy," he'd say. "Didn't know y'all was in town. Did you get you a moose? I heard tell the salmon are runnin' in Shishmaref."

They knew Vernal had married an Eskimo, and even if she wasn't highly thought of, they realized that marriage and a lack of education would hold him to the country. They liked that he said he was from Tea Hook, West Virginia because it sounded so far away and because the place seemed like it might have something to do with the Civil War. He'd also gathered some local fame from a time he'd been a hero when his seal hunting party became stranded. But mostly they liked the benefit of his expertise with guns and the easy way he handled them.

"Now that would make you a quality piece," Vernal would say, if he noticed a customer eyeing a particular hunting rifle, such as an average-priced Mossberg. "But first let me show you this one here, just in case you had in mind to go after seal." Then he'd reach for a Wetherby or even a Sako, knowing full well that seal was exactly what the customer had in mind.

Vernal would never hand the gun over directly. Instead he'd hold it just out of reach, delicately, sighting down the barrel, polishing the stock with his handkerchief, all the time talking up the virtues of that rifle—its accuracy, its range, its power. Only when his customer was primed would Vernal place the gun in the person's hands, holding it so it had to be received just above the trigger guard where the balance felt best.

Things worked. Sales went up, Sid stayed away. I felt enough in control that I started spending late afternoons at the Board of Trade bar. I noticed Wanda come in now and then with two or three girlfriends. They'd take a table near the jukebox and listen to Ferlin Huskey tunes. They talked a little, danced gently, smoked Kool cigarettes from one another's packs, and in an hour sipped maybe a third of a beer each. It was all harmless. They dropped their kids off at one of their many relatives just to be with other adults in an adult world for a while. It was less than the equivalent of a tea party in other places.

I might smile and wave to Wanda, keeping it proper and polite. She was Eskimo, I was white, and her husband was hired help. But one afternoon I was a little juiced, and though I knew it was stupid, I asked her if she wanted to dance. She looked at me like I'd called her a name.

"Me? I can't," she said. And she stared at the floor while I stood there with one arm stuck out, feeling foolish.

I should have let it go then, but there's always that mystery between men and women. It doesn't have to do with race or age or married, or rich or poor. They don't have to speak the same language. It doesn't even have to do with lust. There is curiosity involved, and it includes both people, and the tiniest thing—just a glance is all—gets it going. And like many a habit, once the thing starts, it carries itself.

Not that there was any denying my interest. There was something, a composed spirit and smoky attractiveness about Wanda. Her friends had the appearance of Eskimos, short and middle-thickened, like they were getting ready for winter. But Wanda was pinch-waisted and light. In her blue jeans she looked fit and ready, like a Montana cowgirl at a rodeo. And she had a way of tossing that tress of dark hair back over her shoulder as if it were a handful of troubles.

My luck started slipping when Sid got into one of his spells of interest in the store and found my microwave oven order—a mistake, I admit, since most of the outlying villages didn't yet have electricity. A couple days later the store mail included a memo Sid sent from home, advising that purchase orders for high ticket appliances must henceforth be authorized by him. He signed his full name to the memo, middle initial included.

Vernal lived with Wanda and all those kids in a double-wide back of the gravel pit. I could see the place when I drove by on twelfth street. A propane tank leaned against the far end, with the copper line coiling in through the corner of a window. Strips of loose plastic flapped in the wind against the plywood add-on. Vernal was drawing a hundred and forty a week before deductions. They were probably getting food stamps, and with Wanda being Eskimo they likely qualified for a little aid of this and that kind. Getting by, if you can call it that.

I let Gertie in the office know to bump Vernal up ten dollars a week, and when Sid learned of that I got another memo in the mail. When it came I made a draw slip for a hundred dollars which I covered by under-ringing the Evinrude that Jack Kanalak paid me cash for. I tucked the hundred in Vernal's shirt pocket behind his pack of Lucky Strikes. Tears came to the man's eyes. He took my hand in both of his. "I'm mighty grateful," he said.

By then I knew that I wasn't about to be retired from Sid's hardware with a pension and a party, so I figured I better help myself to some moving money. The department with the highest volume was sporting goods, and the department head with the least amount of business sense was Vernal. A good combination from my point of view. I started to skim from his register, ten or twenty at a time, just to see what would happen. I figured to up it to a hundred a day come hunting season.

After a few days—time enough for word of my generosity to pass from Vernal to his wife—I spotted Wanda at the B.O.T. and sent a round of Michelob to her table. I waited a few minutes before I walked over.

"Wanda, that's a pretty sweater you got on," I said. "New, ain't it?" Then I reached for her elbow. "Feel a little more like dancing today?"

I've never like dancing. But when I pulled Wanda against my chest and tucked her arm under my own to begin the slow two-step, which was all I knew, I felt some of what people must dance for. I shuffled to the left, one step, then another, then a step back. Wanda followed. This was a woman who'd given birth four times in not many more years, but she was as light as a broom. She danced with me, stepping with me, giving me my way, yielding, across and back the little wooden dance floor, while through the window the afternoon sun, weak and thinned so far north, trickled in to mingle with the smoke and the stink of the beer.

I found myself wondering about those four kids and their fathers, how many fathers were involved, and how many times it took to conceive the babies, and if they'd been goals of lovemaking or just some kind of accident. Wanda didn't talk. She would never let me know what she was thinking—love or hate. That was her way of defending herself, but I was working against it, drawing that resistance out of her and plugging it with curiosity. The song ended and Wanda stopped moving. I held on to her.

"Can I come see you sometime?" I said. She looked at the floor. I think she saw me in a new arrangement, like a principal at a graduation party—or maybe it was the big color TV that I knew Vernal had put the hundred bucks down on.

"When?"

"On an afternoon, maybe when the kids are down for their naps."

She moved her foot back and forth on the floor as if to grind out a cigarette. Then she gave the toe of my boot a little tap, than another. "Vernal, he likes you," she said.

"Vernal's a good man."

"He's glad you hired him on. Working at the hardware."

"Can I come see you tomorrow then?"

"No, not tomorrow," she said, and she walked away.

I waited several days. I left the Blazer parked out on the road, though anyone that came along could spot it and make the connection if they had the bent to look for those things. The four-year-old, sleepy looking in a raggedy Seattle Mariners t-shirt answered my knock. I smiled. Wanda appeared behind him.

"Charlie, get back to bed," she said. I stepped inside. As Wanda steered Charlie to the back room I took my coat off. The color TV already had a gob of purple jam or jelly smeared along one corner of the screen. The arm to a doll and a couple fishing magazines were on the floor by the couch. Above it on the wall was a seal skin, stiff-haired and mottled.

Wanda came down the hall, tossing her hair over her shoulder. She stopped at the corner where the hallway turns to the kitchen, listening for the kids' voices and the thumps they made jumping from the bed to the floor. Finally there was silence.

When I kissed her, her mouth was wide and ready. I put a hand on her breast and worked it until my fingers felt the nipple respond through the fabric of her blouse. I undressed her from the top down. In the unsure way of a first-time lover she seemed not to know if I wanted her to help. I twisted her bra off and she was naked and beautiful. I pulled her to the floor, not wanting to move from that corner and risk breaking the mood. Only when I was in her, braced for leverage against Vernal's new jam-stained color TV, did Wanda emerge from her shyness enough to make a sound.

The next time I came by we made love in front of the baby. Wanda ignored her, and that aroused me more. Afterward, I asked Wanda about the seal skin.

Vernal had shot it, she said. He was real proud because he got it at the end of a hunting trip he'd taken with Wanda's two brothers and her father. They were in the long boat, had engine trouble, and drifted away from shore. They made a landing after two days, but it was foggy and they dared not move. They ran out of food the second day ashore, and were down to four rounds of ammunition. The three Eskimos had a conference and decided that Vernal should be the one to take the gun with the four bullets and look for game. It was an honor on top of the great responsibility, and it was with one of those bullets that he got the seal.

We'd been lying on the floor, and I heard a stirring from the back bedroom. One of the older kids was waking up.

"That's a thing to take pride in," I said. "Where'd he learn to shoot so good?"

"In the army, I guess." Wanda's hands were behind her back as she concentrated on fastening her bra.

"I didn't know he was in the army," I said. I'd been in the service myself, and I was sure I'd have noticed if Vernal had listed it on his job application.

"Could be I'm wrong and it was somewhere else," Wanda said. "Men don't tell me all that's on their mind."

I pulled Vernal's application. There was a space with several lines for military service in which Vernal had written a single word: None.

That afternoon I pinned Wanda between my hips and the kitchen floor of the double-wide, and she wrapped her dark legs around me while the baby spit and squawked in the high chair three feet away. Then she told me about Vernal. He'd even changed his last name. He hoped they'd never find him so far from West Virginia. It had been several years now, and he was just beginning to think that maybe they didn't care anymore, and that it might be forgotten after all. He'd never done anything wrong except walk away. He even left his combat boots behind, in place beneath his cot, all spit-polished for inspection.

Wanda begged me not to let on to Vernal that I knew. "Don't worry," I said. "If you can't trust me you're in real trouble." And I kissed her on the lips.

Three days later she told me not to come back for a while.

"You feel guilty?" I asked.

She laughed. "You whites, you're so stupid. This with you and me is nothing. The Eskimo way, the old ways, they got no—what do you call it—monogamy. That's your idea."

"Then why?"

"You can't see it." And she looked away, as always, avoiding my face. "I like dancing. You'll never take me where we could dance."

"Sure I will," I said.

Wanda put a fresh cigarette between her lips, and struck a match, but stared at its flame without lighting the cigarette. "I got four babies. By the time they're gone I'll be like my mother. Always cold. Coughing all the time in the night. The things I got right now is those kids, the new TV, and to dance with Vernal."

I stayed away a long time. Now, I watched her in the B.O.T., and knowing she'd been available made it all the worse. It was unfair—I'd gone the uneasy miles of conquest, making pretending unnecessary. The only obligation we had left that was attached to any truth was to please each other. I wanted her available again. I watched and listened while Ferlin Huskey sang and Wanda danced.

Vernal asked to talk to me away from the store, and I spent a fidgety two hours at the B.O.T. waiting for him. I decided if he confronted me about Wanda I'd deny it, now that it seemed to be over.

Vernal ordered a can of beer, any brand, no glass. I ordered an Old Style for myself and paid for both.

"It's about my gun sales," Vernal said, his bad eye scanning my face. "I figure somethin's off. Last weekend there wasn't but twenty-one hundred in the cash register. I sold more than that in deer rifles."

Deer rifles, I thought. I wanted to cry with joy. Still. "Are you sure?" I said. "As I'm settin' here."

I listened, watching that nervous eye, trying to read everything. But the rest of his face showed nothing. Trying to find meaning in it was like plumbing the expressions of a goat. I thanked him for coming forward, and asked him to please not say much while I looked into the situation on my own.

The next day I made the call to Fort Richardson. They pushed me along a command chain of five different people, and I kept telling the same story. In between they called me back, asking for more details. In a few days, a man in a suit came to the store, looked around, and was gone on the evening flight. He was there just long enough for me to know.

The Aleutian fog blew in the day they arrested Vernal. The plane couldn't get out directly so they took him to the city jail to wait.

I'd been a little out of sorts so I started drinking around eleven, nipping from a bottle I kept in a file drawer. By the middle of the afternoon I was bleary and mixed-up from what daylight and alcohol do to the system, and I got a notion that I wanted to see Vernal before they flew him away for good.

The M.P.s at first would hear none of it. But the store had helped out with the police department fund raising, and the chief told them I was all right. They said I could have five minutes, and I had to stand six feet away.

Vernal was in a cell alone, down the corridor from where they housed the drunks, the pot heads, and the wife beaters. They let all of them have radios, and the radios blared with the same tunes you had to pay for in the B.O.T. Vernal shook his head when he saw me, as if he'd just had a piece of bad luck.

"I'm sorry about this, Vernal," I said. "But don't worry. They'll soon get it cleared up in your favor." I knew there was zero chance of that, but I had to say something.

"No, no," he said. "Wasn't none of your doin'."

I'd sobered up a little, and was starting to feel uncomfortable. The other prisoners turned their radios down, and I felt like everyone was listening to me. I asked Vernal if he needed anything. He shook his head.

I told him the job would still be his when this was all over. He smiled at that and shook his head again, as if it was a shame I couldn't seem to understand the serious nature of what had happened. It was warm in there, and I started to sweat, and I was tired. Vernal stood there, a hand on each of two thick bars, staring at me with that one direct eye while the other looked up, down, here and there. I was unsatisfied with the visit, and with myself. I could think of no more to say, and I wanted nothing but to leave. I reached to shake hands, but remembered the six foot rule, and I changed the shake into a little wave.

"Eddie?" he said.

"Yeah Vernal?"

"I just wanted to let you know I liked working for y'all."

"Don't mention it," I said.

"I'll tell you, Eddie," he said. "I never had a job I liked 'til you gimme that one. I love to think of the way them old boys looked at me when I'd hand them a firearm, all bright and smelling of oil and gun bluing. They figured I really knew what I was talking about, didn't they Eddie?"

"And you did, too," I said

"Eddie?"

"Yeah?"

Vernal licked his lips, searching for more words, more ways to express his laid-open feelings—but he'd exceeded his limits. "I'm just tickled to know ya'," he said.

The weather broke that evening and the plane took off. I drove over to the double-wide, and Wanda let me in. Vernal's magazine was still on the floor, open to a photo of an Oklahoma Chevy dealer straining to hold his salmon to the camera. It was probably the picture Vernal was looking at when the M.P.s crashed in. Now he was 27,000 feet in the air and on his way to fifteen years of hard labor.

The tension of everything brewed a sexual hunger in me that wasn't to be put off. I nudged Wanda toward the hallway, past those black-haired kids watching TV. But Wanda wouldn't be nudged. The more I pushed, the more she stood her ground.

"What's wrong?" I said. I knew it wasn't the kids, and I was pretty sure she wasn't all that choked up about Vernal.

"I was just thinking I'd like to dance," she said. "Dance me back to the bedroom."

The kids were watching a show with background rock music that jangled the whole place. I did my best, bumping my hip into Wanda's crotch, following the beat, sliding along the ridges of the paneling to the bedroom.

"Vernal, he could dance," Wanda said. "Even at the Legion Hall with that concrete floor—he made it feel like the carpet at the Captain Cook Hotel."

We made love on her bed, on Vernal's bed. Then I stood up to put my clothes on. Wanda just lay there, with her legs parted a little, stroking the top curve of one breast where she said it stung a little, from my teeth.

"You turned him in, didn't you?" she said.

I pretended to fiddle with my clothes, shaking them out. "What was that?"

"You told on Vernal." Her chin was angled down, like she was searching for something on her breast.

"Goddamn," I said. "How could you even think that— for one thing he was the best gun salesman I ever saw. And for another, I like him. A whole hell of a lot more than you do, probably."

I was pleased with the last thought, and I let it hang in the air so it would be there and ready to bump into her own arguments. She stopped rubbing her breast and looked at me.

"You know something, Eddie," she said. "You're an asshole and I wouldn't give you a bullet if I had a bucketful of them."

She lay there and I felt her dark eyes burn into my back as I pulled on my shirt and pants, then my socks and boots. And while I dressed I thought about Vernal.

There was something in him that I'd been reaching to when I saw him in jail. It was in his face, and in his eyes. His expression had things to say, ideas too complicated for his words. His face offered a recognition, a granting that he did know who he was, and where he was going, even if it was nowhere. It was a taking up of the habit again, the habit of despair. It wasn't just acceptance, it was that he was glad to have that acceptance. He was already serving those fifteen years, and Wanda and the babies and his job and the TV were just stops along the way. Vernal was a guy who had to grab his happiness fifteen minutes at a time, and even then he lived knowing that his pitiful bit of joy could be gone, just like that.

That's all he'd get in his life, but then I realized—why the hell should I care—it could have been me, and no one told either of us we deserved any better.

The kids were still watching their show when I came out of the bedroom. For a minute I stood there in front of Vernal's seal skin, watching the kids and the TV, but I was anxious to leave—I didn't care to be there when Wanda came out.

But before I left I went to the kitchen and found an old dishrag that I doused in warm water. I came back to the TV and worked on that purple jam stain until the screen looked as bright and clean as when Vernal first saw it. Then I tossed the rag back toward the kitchen sink, picked up Vernal's magazine from the floor, and closed the storm door behind me.

Drinking

Mary LaChapelle

A MAN AND A woman have their lines in the river called the St. Croix. They're sitting under a tree. Their poles lie listless next to them, and little by little their lines have been pulling out with the current. But now her red and white bobber was hesitant, as if unsure any longer of its direction, and his bobber, which was all white, stalled too. Then they both drifted in the direction of the shore.

"It's a crosscurrent that's got them," Tim said. "They're bound to get snagged by the banks."

"Let them," Mary said, pulling him gently by the pocket of his shorts when he moved to get up. "Tell me about this first time you were here, about this woman."

"Well, it wasn't exactly the first. I'd been canoeing here with a friend before. But after that, I had it in my mind that I wanted to bring someone special."

"Was she special?" Mary asked, and for a moment she wasn't sure of her intentions or of her tone in asking. She might have made it seem she was jealous.

"I thought so at the time . . ." Tim put his arms behind his head and crossed his feet at the ankles. This pushed against the backs of his old tennis shoes, which made them splay at the sides and exposed the fairer skin on the sides of his feet. " . . . In that way you just don't think many people can be. You know, she wasn't going to turn around and tell me something I already knew." Tim was surprised to hear himself put it this way, since this was an expression he hadn't used in a long time.

"Was she pretty?" Mary asked.

"Very, but fine, not necessarily sexy."

"Like me," Mary said.

"Yes." Tim smiled and looked out over the river.

"Except for the fact that I'm also somewhat sexy."

"Yes." Tim looked at the orange water and remembered how he'd waded into it ahead of the woman. He'd been quiet about how it felt, knowing she would step into the sand herself, and it would feel to her a little more like a magical thing if he said nothing. The sun was just right. He hadn't gone in until he was sure the light would be even with their shoulders, slowly pressing down into the water around their waists.

"But you were drunk?" Mary said.

"Right, but trying to do it well."

"Of course," Mary said. "If you can't do it well. . . " She turned on her side listening to him. He was looking out at his story as if it were on the other side of the river. And she looked over to the far bank, at the birches and poplars and pine. There was a scrap of someone's bright yellow tent peeking through the trees. It was the kind of yellow they always used in cartoons for the sun.

"I had the proverbial Volkswagen van."

"Let me guess. Blue," she said.

He laughed. "Red, I'm afraid. I would have liked blue, though.

"Anyway, I'd met her at a festival, funky, very surreal, like Mardi Gras. And a friend of mine had just been talking about her. He'd just been telling me about this woman, someone he'd gone to school with, you know. She played the flute, orchestra employed. He went on and on—like she was this veritable paragon— about her impeccable character."

"And you met her just a few minutes later."

"Yeah, she'd been holding up one of these wonderful puppets, holding it up for someone in the parade. And when she gave it back, my friend, Ben, recognized her, but it was like I already knew who she was."

"I wish you'd tell me what she looked like."

"She was beautiful, good bones, good skin, good teeth. Ben said, 'I can't believe it,' you know, and so on, but it didn't matter. I was looking at her. I'd tipped some tequila just prior and, you know, there was charisma. I could feel it in my eyes."

"Right, Tim."

"Yes!" Tim turned to Mary and put his hand on her arm. "That does happen."

And Mary felt reprimanded. "I know," she said. And she did know, especially with tequila, she knew that brief peak, when you feel enlightened, more like marijuana, the illusion that light could be brimming over and coming out of your eyes.

"And you know," Tim said, "there was that element of destiny present. Ben had just sung her praises, and there she was. Her face was so peaceful, and it was like she could feel my look, but she wasn't going to take it any other way but within her own stride. She was with other people. We talked for maybe only a minute."

"But how did you finally get together?"

They were interrupted by a motorboat clipping past, its wake behind it. It wasn't long before it had rounded the bend, and they could only hear it. But the wake pushed the water up on the banks, almost covering their feet, and their bobbers were tossed on the reckless crest.

Mary pulled her legs away from the water.

It seemed to Tim that boats shouldn't be allowed to travel so fast in this part of the river. He put his head back against the tree, waited for the roar of the motor to die away.

He pictured the sign, ST. CROIX STATE PARK, posted at the entrance. He passed it every time he drove Highway 8, and he wondered if there was a time he passed it that he didn't think to himself, If I could only. . . . What? That was always unclear. But the last time, he had decided he would bring Mary here. It was an almost half-hearted decision. Just a decision that had quietly culminated from all the times he had passed the sign and all the times he had begun to think, If I could only. . . .

"Bird-watching." Once the motor's noise had died, he was able to answer Mary's question.

"What?" Mary was incredulous.

"It's true," he said. "The very next weekend. I'd crashed at a friend's house. It was getting late, but we'd been on a toot. He'd been telling me that he had to knock it off, that he had to get up to go bird-watching with a friend, but I didn't want to leave, you know, didn't want to be alone."

"What was his name?"

"I don't know. I had such a multitude of friends back then. I was persuasive, as usual, and convinced him to stay up with me a little longer. I said I'd get up with him in the morning and go along."

"And you sat up the rest of the night talking about birds?"

"I think we did, as a matter of fact."

"I'm sure you were both quite expansive on the subject."

"I'm sure," Tim said. "But of course at that point I was blacked out. The next day my friend was horribly hung over, and he held me responsible. I had to wake him up. We both took showers. It was only 6 A.M. It was drizzling, and he'd thought maybe his bird-watching date wouldn't want to go after all. So he called her, used her name, but I never made the connection."

"Poor guy," Mary said. "Obviously she was set on going."

"Yeah. I drove his car. She was waiting outside her house wearing rain gear. I didn't recognize her until she pushed her head in the car. She looked a little sleepy."

"But more alive than the two of you, I'd expect."

Tim smiled, remembering. "I reminded her of our meeting, and she just settled into the backseat, smiled, and said, 'Yes'."

"Yes, she already recognized you? Yes, she remembered now that you mentioned it?"

"I don't know," Tim said, but in fact he had always believed that she remembered him. They had driven to a kind of reserve. He would never remember the directions. The windshield wipers were going, an awkward squeaking against their silence in the car. His arms were heavy and his mind in a fog. But a special song had come on the radio, one that had been the theme song with a past lover, and that he still held very dear. The speakers were in the back seat just behind her head, so he'd felt that they were sharing a past, even if they didn't speak, and he was comforted by the remote certainty that they would become intimate.

"The land we hiked on was by a river, because I remember seeing trout fishermen when our path crossed it."

"And you saw birds?"

"Absolutely. But only the two of them had binoculars. I wasn't used to listening to them or seeing them. She, on the other hand, had a lot of experience, had been all over the country with her father as a little girl. She would just stop on the path, point without saying a word. My friend would raise his binoculars. I'd stand next to her, and she'd pass her binoculars with the strap still around her neck. She'd tell me the name and things about the bird. We had to whisper."

"Ooooh!" Mary said.

"Ooooh, yourself," he said.

"No, really," Mary said. "I love it: 'suspended passion,' the tension. Did your hand brush against hers when you were sharing the binoculars?"

"No," Tim said. "I didn't want to put her off in any way. And passion?" Tim said. "What if there was—would that have been so bad?"

He remembered how very quiet it had been on that path except for the light drizzle, the rustle of her rain jacket when she raised the glasses. He'd been wearing a trench coat, not the sort of thing one wears hiking. But he had the collar up, and with the mist still rising from the ground, there was something right about that. He had felt that while she was showing him a world, he'd brought a slightly mysterious world of his own with him.

Mary thought back to their own courtship. How good-naturedly he had stood out in her new circle of friends, how unquestionably handsome he was. She'd always been glad that she hadn't met him in an AA meeting—that he hadn't been put in the context of metal folding chairs and Styrofoam coffee cups and the wash of rhetoric in some church basement.

The meetings had been necessary, but there was also a loss of feeling, a numbness that began at that time and even now lingered like an overdose of novocaine. She would listen to the others' stories, like the mother who drank steadily from a bottle she kept hidden behind the clothes dryer. "People at parties were always surprised at how low my tolerance was to alcohol," the woman would laugh. "Two drinks and I would be such an intense and passionate person. Sometimes it would only take one. One to upset the normal level in my blood. My husband always told them it was because I was so petite." She'd laugh. "My son once drove me home early from a family reunion." Her eyes would always fill with tears at this point. "He said I had kissed him on the mouth. He was nineteen." She always said this with complete horror, as if she hadn't already told them the story many times before. "And he never told me until years later when he was finished with school."

"You have to forgive yourself," people would tell the mother. Mary hoped no one in the group felt contempt for her, the way she sometimes felt toward this woman.

They all seemed to have their one special story. There was the insurance man who wore plastic gloves the whole first year they were in group together. He had disappeared for a week-long binge, telling his wife he had a convention. Then he came home on Monday night, lit the grill for dinner, and when the coals were white, picked them up in his hands and held them until he lost consciousness.

Mary often gazed at those gloves, which were transparent green and always seemed to have some oozing substance bubbling under the surface of them. As grotesque as his story was, it didn't seem to bother her as much as some of the others. It was cruel, but also clean—a clean break. Whenever he looked at his hands, they would be both then and now. He didn't have to go deep back into his regrets to remind anyone what he was afraid of. His hands were always in front of him, horrible and simple.

Tim had been part of something clean and new the summer they first knew each other—picnics with a social group and bicycle trips. Like a teenager again, he seemed to throw himself into everything that was physical. He bought a sailboard and took it out every weekend, waving to them from the lake. He must have realized he was like an emblem for their whole experience, the sun glinting off his sail as it did, taking them back to a kind of adolescence where their possibilities were pure again.

Even their coming together had seemed unpremeditated and easy. He'd encouraged her to try the board, and she'd spent the afternoon out on the water, being dumped and swallowing lake water, bruising her legs against the board. But there was an elation, even in pain, to be struggling with something so clean.

She finally had it sailing and took it for a distance, leaving him behind, laughing and treading water. But she couldn't bring it about and fell again. He had swum after her. Her suit had come down when she started to hoist herself on the board again. He brought her back into the water. As she'd tried to cover her breasts, he'd taken her hand away. He pressed carefully against her in the water, fitting his chest against hers and wrapping her legs around his hips.

They had been careful as lovers, as if neither of them could bear to show how experienced they really were, as if they were starting over. There seemed a silent agreement that drinking and love had been an all-too-integrated passion. So they were afraid, sometimes a little stiff and, Mary had to admit, sometimes a little bored.

The whole sailing incident had rushed back to her mind one day when she'd broken an apple open. The first of the season, so white—she was startled, even humiliated, to remember how equally white her breasts had been that afternoon. And she often wondered if Tim would ever have thought of her as a lover, if he hadn't seen them that one accidental moment. Maybe he had been as numb as she and had to be surprised into wanting someone again.

"Are you with me?" Tim laid his hand on hers. The sun had changed; it was shining right on the water closest to shore. The water was so clear in the shallows that she could see particles of light glinting from the sandy bottom. She could see where the river got deep farther out because it was a dark swath in comparison.

"Yes," she said. "Now tell me how you went from bird-watching to being lovers?"

"Well, we weren't ever lovers, not like you mean . . . "

This Mary had assumed and somehow, now the story seemed more dangerous. It made her feel that it wasn't finished for him. That he still wanted the other woman.

"You haven't told me about the drinking. I thought this was a drinking story?"

"Just wait," he said. He poured her some tea from the thermos next to him. She could tell just from looking at it that it was merely warm. Cinnamon tea—she couldn't help associating it with their early romance. He had brought a package of it over on their second date. "Just smell this," he said. "Isn't it wonderful?" He'd brought candles, too, and put a tape on her stereo. Even then, so early on, it seemed he couldn't begin to be with her until he had created a certain atmosphere. And today she felt his usual insistence in making their time a certain way. Their lines were in the river not as much to catch fish, she felt, but because there was something ideal in the posture of two people with fishing poles beside them.

He didn't pour a cup for himself from the thermos, and she decided there was no point telling him it was tepid. It didn't matter; there was nothing he could do about it.

"So we went to breakfast after the hike," he continued, "at a restaurant on the highway. We both sat across from her in the booth. My friend was feeling a little better by then, and it hadn't occurred to me that he might be actually interested in her himself."

"Good, Tim."

"Right. But while he was feeling a little better, I was feeling a little worse. I was cooking off some of the alcohol, and I felt really hot. He was keeping the coffee cups filled, like he intended to stay. But I was so hot, I could feel the flush, and I was sweating. I finally told her."

"Just her?"

"Well, them." Tim felt a pressure in his bladder and was surprised, since they had already used the facilities at the ranger station on the way in, but he ignored it and continued the story.

"She found a spigot outside, and even though it was still drizzling, she turned it on and let it run cold."

He didn't know how to tell Mary about his shirt, even if it was the part he always remembered most about that day. Because he was sweating, he was sure she could smell the alcohol he was burning off. Yet she seemed to look at him so kindly. "Just rinse off," she had said. "You'd feel better." It made sense that he should take his shirt off. It wasn't that he was embarrassed about his body; he had a good body. In fact he had wanted to. He remembered this overwhelming belief that if he just removed his shirt, she would look at him and know him. It could be that simple. Sometimes he fantasized about the first time he would remove his shirt with a certain woman. It became, in his mind, such a momentous thing to do.

"I couldn't take off my shirt," Tim said.

"What?" Mary asked.

"You know, to wash up."

"Well, why not?"

"I couldn't be sure of anything."

"Sure of what?" Mary put her fingers around his thumb. She couldn't picture what he was saying.

"It seemed I could lose her right there if it wasn't the right time. It always seems like I have to wait for the right time to do something like that."

"What do you mean?"

He looked blankly at her, when she had expected this was a meaningful question.

"No, it had to be another time. I knew that much." Tim's bladder situation felt suddenly more insistent. "So I got my shirt all wet rinsing under the spigot, and my friend came out, all pissed off, and asked me for my share of the bill right away. He wasn't very attractive about the whole thing."

"Well, you can be grateful for that, because eventually you were the one that took her out."

"Yeah. I called her, and we went out to dinner a couple of times. There was something almost prim about our conversations that I enjoyed. Only because I looked forward to breaking it down—to getting through to her."

"The river, Tim, can we please get to the river?"

But Tim was looking distracted. He got to his feet. "I have to find a bush or something."

He left so abruptly. Not that she doubted his reason, really, But for someone who valued outings like this so much, it was strange how suddenly he needed to eject himself from the middle of them, as though he couldn't stand living through what he had earlier so much looked forward to. He did this sometimes in restaurants, before they had even finished their meal. He'd say, "Let's go out for ice cream now or catch the 7:30 show."

She watched him walk over the park grass, which was mottled by splotches of shade from the many trees. He walked in and out of the pieces of shade until he eventually disappeared into a stand of bushes.

The river had taken on the flat glare of afternoon light. There was a long black log floating down the middle. It had found the main current, and she imagined it could have been riding that current for some time. It looked oblivious to time or change or the damage it had suffered. It made its slow progress through a patch of lily pads, their delicate edges ruffling against the coarseness of its bark, and then on it drifted into the distance, beneath the orange clay bluffs hunching over the river like great shoulders.

She thought of the log as a *she*. Automatically. Just the way one attaches gender to all sorts of things: dogs are he's; cats are she's; trees can be both. But this one was a she. She'll go on, Mary thought, out into the Mississippi, and then on some more, not feeling a thing.

Tim had found a a small cove where the grass was growing tall around it. It was a place where no one on the shore or on the river could see him. He walked into the grass. It tickled his bare arms and legs. I'm sober, he thought—a statement he had made to himself in many other situations this past year. This time it was because he could feel the grass so sharply against his calves. And because it seemed very odd to be peeing out here when he wasn't drinking. It was strange because this was often the time that he would have been telling himself, I'm drunk. There had always been that benign first trip to the bushes, when he'd be standing there, listening to himself, trickling down on the leaves or the stones, or whatever was beneath him. And he'd realize that he was both inside and outside his body. The man outside his body would be sober and almost fatherly in his concern, his affection, his disappointment, standing just to the side with his hands on hips, saying, Here you are again, you son of a bitch. And the inside part of himself would just be there, wherever he was. If it was a field, he'd be buzzing a little like the bee and be sticky like the pollen and fuzzy like the grass. The first trip to the bushes was invariably happy. Then there would be a small period of orientation: yes, he was peeing; yes, he was doing it properly. Some accounting: yes, he'd had three beers and part of the bottle of whiskey; who was it that was waiting for him to finish; how much had they drunk; and were they waiting in anticipation for him to come back?

But now it was different. Now he was in possession of himself. Strictly one person. And he and the grass were separate things. This was the St. Croix, a cool breeze was coming from somewhere. And he was impatient. Telling Mary this story, he wanted to get to the end of it. Sometimes you started a story, and then, hardly into it, you lost confidence. He was only continuing out of sheer willpower. He was already so very disappointed with the day. Why, he didn't know.

"Geez!" he murmured to himself. His shirttail was caught in the zipper of his fly. He'd heard a large fish plopping in the water nearby. "That figures." He thought of Mary looking into her fishless part of the river.

They'd been together over a year. He didn't know if they would ever be in love, the way people were supposed to be. He walked through the rough grass. And yet, there were these almost accidental times with her when she would make some awkward gesture, or laugh abruptly at him or herself, when he believed that she, more than anyone he had ever been with, knew the unspeakable things that get into people's hearts, that were in his heart.

Once he had answered the phone at her apartment. It was a man, a voice slightly tinny through a long-distance connection, but underneath that his voice was svelte, assured. "What do you want?" she had said before anything else. "No," she had said. "No." And then she had hung up. She was sitting on the carpet with the phone in her lap. She looked immovable, like a stone. Then he saw that her hand was clenched so hard around the receiver that it had turned white. He knelt down and pried it away, letting her grip his own hand. She began to lose the stony look and continued to squeeze his hand.

"That's okay," he said, meaning she could squeeze even harder if she needed.

And then she looked up and said, "I'm never going to be the way I used to be."

"How?" he wanted to know.

"Hot and desirous and stupid and ugly." She'd turned away from him and spat the words into the room.

"Let's talk about it," he said.

And she'd snorted at him as if to say the suggestion was banal. She made him feel foolish. "What sense do we make of the dramatic details?" she said. "I'm tired of them," she said. "We both have our own groups. We can go on ad nauseam there. Can't we just be good to each other, without swamping ourselves in the details?"

"The river." Tim gazed over the water and remembered. "It couldn't have been more beautiful."

Mary looked around, thinking most anyone would find this place perfectly lovely now.

"It was a different kind of day from today," Tim said, "not just sunny. It was already late in afternoon when we arrived. The clouds were moving, so the sun would come and go."

Tim had been rubbing Mary's hand absentmindedly with his thumb. It became irritating to her, she slipped it out and rested it on his knee instead.

"I'd brought a picnic: good wine, bread, artichokes, tomatoes, . . . "

"All your favorite things," she said, "except the Wild Turkey."

"That comes later," Tim said. "But I have to tell you, the day was very different—it was like the river would look completely golden, and then it wouldn't and then it would because of the clouds. For a while the sun was below the clouds. Have you ever seen that?"

"No." But, almost immediately, she remembered that she did in fact see it like that once after a thunderstorm. She'd left a lot of people back at a party. It had gone into the morning. Those that were left had passed out. If it hadn't been for the thunderstorm, she would have continued sleeping. But she found herself in her Dodge Dart, hating her life, driving down the road. The farmers called it a "spent" thunderstorm—when the big, gray clouds are left without the rain. The sun rose underneath the clouds that morning so that all the houses she drove past were a deep orange and the sky above them a deep gray. She had almost made a U-turn back to the house so she could tell someone. But she decided that the phenomena would change before she even reached them, or whoever came to see wouldn't see what she saw.

"It's like the clouds are pushing the light down. That's when we went into the water. Mary" —Tim put his hand around her waist— "the water was so soft!"

"What did you do?" She let herself settle ever so lightly against his arm. And she realized there was a longing within her—she wanted to be in that water; but at the same time she felt repulsed, afraid that this was just the kind of wanting that tricked you.

"Water ballet," he laughed. "It was one of the things her mother had gotten her involved with in high school. She looked silly doing these pointy-toed things upside down in the water. It was as if she was sharing the more absurd side of being a princess. And I liked her even better for it.

"Afterward, we changed into dry clothes under a blanket. We were sitting on the top of a picnic table. She was already dressed, and I was leaning over, futzing with my shoes. The blanket fell off my shoulders, and my shirt was off. She put her hand very gently on my back and held it there like she was trying to sense something.

"That's when I pulled out the Wild Turkey. It wasn't like it bothered her. She took a little in her glass. And for the next few hours, we watched the trees get dark against the sky, and we drank. We talked about everything, about my dad, and the time I was hit by a car running after my brother's school bus, and the time that Hank fell out of the chestnut tree in our backyard."

"I didn't know that," Mary said.

"Yes, nothing happened to him. He bounced. You know what she said? I remember, she said, 'You have a very physical family.' She told me things I hadn't thought of before. She told me about herself, too. As we got into it, the air was getting cool, like September, but we just wrapped in the blanket, and everything was changing as it should. The moon came out. We were trading secrets, back and forth. I wanted to make love with her and I almost . . . "

"What, Tim?" Mary had been stroking his hand.

"Well, you know how it is when you're getting drunk. But you keep drinking, and you keep watching to see if it makes a difference to them?"

"Yeah, I know," Mary said.

Tim uncrossed his ankles and brought his knees up to his chest. "Well, it made a difference. I could see it, like a cloud passing in front of her face."

Mary looked down at his gray sneakers, and the thought crossed her mind that he might have still had them as long ago as that day with the other woman. She looked at him. "You can't forever be ashamed about that, Tim," she said. And as soon as the words were out, she knew they were too simple, a phrase she would have given to any member of her AA group, something easy, and which she felt nothing about.

His face flooded with anger. "That's not the only thing!" he shouted. And instantaneously he imagined the park sign at the entrance to the road vibrating from the sound of the shout. And it became clear to him why he always had the impulse to return here: he was still looking for that perfect day. If only he could make a perfect day and still drink and drink perfectly with someone else, and they could drink too and drink perfectly. And if there wasn't that, what could he do? What could he want instead?

We're both still so sick, she thought. She didn't know what to do. She got up and waded over to where their bobbers had floated into the shore and began to untangle them, pulling her hair behind her ear as it fell forward and got in her eyes. It was all awkward. She hated anything as frustrating as these tangles almost as much as he did. That's why he had tried to prevent them from drifting in the first place. Still, he had let them, just like she had. And now the line was wet, and there were pieces of weeds clinging to the mess.

He was bending over her on the shore, his hands on his knees. He was sorry he had shouted. He wanted to explain. "Mary," he said gently. "Don't you ever miss it?"

"What?" she said, coldly, not looking at him while she pretended to be working the little knots apart. But she knew he meant drinking. She still didn't know if she could talk about that. If she could say yes to that and still survive.

"Mary?" he said.

And when she looked up, behind the strands of hair that had stuck to her mouth, she was sobbing. He looked at her small shoulders, so bare and quaking they were like the two parts of a heart. And he knew even before he had done it that the next moment he would be in the water with her. That it would be cold: a cold shock and then a starting over again.

The Halfway House

Wanda Kolling

"I DREAMED ABOUT my old boy friend last night," Flo said. "It wore me out."
Flo's gold bracelets clanged; her highly arched thin eyebrows arched still
higher. Her raucous laughter filled the kitchen, where five of the boarders crowded
around a table covered with garish maroon oilcloth spotted with orange flowers.

Allison knew without looking at him that Dominick was grinning, his slack
mouth half-open. Part of Allison was aware, too, of the rips in the oilcloth table
covering, of the cockroach scuttling out from underneath the refrigerator, of the
wing missing from the gaudy maroon plastic butterfly next to the refrigerator
handle.

But for the most part, she was conscious only of the warm sweet syrup-covered
bit of French toast in her mouth. She was hungry—so hungry after six months
of cold cereal, juice and coffee in this house, after six months of watery porridge
and an orange and coffee at Melrose State Hospital. The French toast was good,
so good.

The back door opened. Boots thumped across the brown linoleum floor to
the yellowing stove on which sat a big black empty skillet and a huge iron-gray
coffee pot.

"You ate all the French toast!" Joe bellowed, his face flushing red. "Jan made
at least eighteen slices!"

Allison looked up, startled, looked away from Joe quickly. Her hand holding
the fork trembled. She saw Louise staring out the window at the littered back

yard. It was hard to tell whether Louise ever saw anything; her face was as usual expressionless. Her face, under dark hair squeezed into a bun, looked squeezed, too—all seamed and wrinkled. Dominick stared sullenly down at his plate—if he wasn't snickering, he was sullen. Flo looked boldly at Joe, her eyes bright with expectation.

"Now there's none for me!" Joe's face grew so darkly red it looked purple in the morning light. "Whatdya expect?" He turned to leave the kitchen. "Of all the cruddy deals..."

Milt, a large flabby man of about thirty, who worked around the house doing dishes and dusting and sometimes cooking, spoke up. "I'll make you some French toast, Joe."

"You think I don't know how to make French toast?" Joe snarled. "Nobody knows how much I shell out to feed you people!"

The five walked out of the kitchen with guilty looks on their faces. They threaded their way through the dining room and into the living room, a windowless narrow room not much bigger than a hall, so narrow two people could not walk abreast into it. In it were a plastic-covered chair and three overstuffed lumpy armchairs with end tables of imitation walnut with thin stick-like legs. On a table at one end of the room was a black-and-white twelve-inch television set.

Dominick turned on the television to a game show. Dominick and Louise and Allison sat down, lit up cigarettes.

Boots thumped on the linoleum floor of the dining room. Joe entered, his face once again contorting in rage. "Get some newspapers under those ashtrays! You want to burn holes in the end tables? They're brand new. You want to dish out forty bucks apiece?"

The three obediently put newspapers, the old *National Enquirer*s stacked on one table, under their ashtrays. Louise's eyes never left the contestants on the screen as she placed a newspaper under her ashtray. Joe walked on outside, whistling.

"What a guy!" Dominick said. "One minute he's yellin' at you, the next minute he's laughin'."

Flo had already climbed the stairs, her bottom and hips swinging. Now Allison walked up the stairs to her room. Allison could hear Victoria in the room next to hers reading her Bible aloud. Victoria said she didn't need breakfast; the Lord was her sustenance. She didn't need coffee to wake her up; God awakened her.

Allison held one of her good dresses in front of her body and looked into the discolored mirror over the dresser. It was one of the dresses she wore when out applying for jobs at business places one after another. She had lost fifteen pounds in the past year. Her brownish-blonde hair looked limp and thin, a result of the medication she'd been taking for the past twelve months. Her brown eyes were beseeching, wounded under heavy lids.

"Damn the medication," she said.

Not quite the picture one presents to a personnel person—the personnel persons who, anyway, only had to learn of her hospitalization to say that Allison was "not quite suitable." Perhaps she should lie about her institutionalization, as her psychiatrist at Melrose had recommended, but Allison was by nature truthful. Anyway, she was sure that there was about her now something indefinable that suggested Melrose State Hospital.

Yet her lawyer—that tall, trim man who reminded one of good restaurants and expensive tailors—had told her that only if she got a job and held it could she expect to get back Sue and Jimmy.

Sue and Jimmy. She stood trembling looking at the faces of Sue and Jimmy in the silver frames on the dresser. Sue had Allison's brownish-blonde hair and the perfect oval of her mother's face, but there was a pixie quality about her that didn't come from her mother or her father. Jimmy, too, had brownish-blonde hair and Allison's fine straight nose, but his brown eyes sparkled with mischief, suggesting pranks and outrageousness. These pictures had been taken two years ago, before their home was disrupted. Both Sue and Jimmy had a wistful, edgy look about them now—a puckering about the eyes and a drooping of the mouth— that was alien to their ages and haunted Allison.

Allison dropped on the bed covered by a frazzled chenille bedspread that wouldn't stay smooth, the color of tarnished gold. She looked up at the one lamp, on it a cheap tipsy shade that she couldn't straighten, with a mottled Parisian scene.

Her eyes strayed back to the pictures of Sue and Jimmy. She would see them next Saturday at the drugstore, have lunch with them in that atmosphere of noise and hurry with an impatient waitress tapping her foot and people waiting to get their booth. She would long to ask them what they had had for breakfast, did they still take their stuffed animals to bed with them, did they say their night-time prayers.

But she knew by the still, closed masks that would come over their faces that all she dared ask were some awkward questions about school, questions any stranger might ask. Allison sighed deeply, put one hand to her face, then let it drop despairingly.

She got up and went to Victoria's door. At her knock Victoria swung open the door. She was tall, an angular woman with a lean face holding deepset, wintry eyes.

"Do you want to go for a walk, Victoria?" Allison asked.

"I guess so. There's nothing else to do. Where shall we walk to?"

"Just anywhere," Allison said. Then she added with vehemence, "Anywhere to get away from this place!"

Victoria looked at her with surprise. Allison's usual tone of voice was quiet, listless.

Allison and Victoria passed through the living room, where Dominick turned his eyes from the television set to them. "Say, Allison, don'tcha wanta come up to Tom's Tavern with me this afternoon? A few beers'd do ya more good than all those pills you take."

Allison smiled at him. "No, thanks."

Dominick said, "Where ya off to?"

"Victoria and I are going for a walk."

"In this neighborhood? What's there to see?"

"Nothing."

Once outside, Victoria said, "Why on earth do you talk to that man? Joe takes in scum."

They stopped when they reached the long city sidewalk. Allison said, "Should we go to the right or the left?" She added with what was almost enthusiasm, "I know. Let's go to the bakery. I want to get a chocolate eclair."

"How can you be hungry? You just had breakfast," Victoria reminded her.

"I know, but I just love chocolate eclairs. Down at Melrose, I had a chocolate eclair and can of orange juice every day at the Canteen. I never thought we got enough Vitamin C."

"The food at Melrose was good," Victoria said definitively.

Allison retreated to a subject on which they might have some agreement. "I wonder how Jan manges to get along with Joe."

"He beats her in their bedroom," Victoria confided. "They talk about me, and then he beats her."

Allison knew without looking at Victoria that Victoria's hands had flown to her lips, as if she were sniffing her fingers. Victoria's eyes would have grown secretive, cunning.

The huge old houses they passed were not even reminiscent of their former splendor. This had once been a fashionable neighborhood. Now the houses, dilapidated, were rooming-houses or cut up into efficiency apartments. The October wind caught up dead leaves from unraked lawns and scattered them among squashed cigarette packages, wrinkled candy wrappers, and cartons from the nearby White Castle hamburger shop. The wind nipped at Allison's and Vicotria's noses, ears, and bare hands.

They passed a playground. "There must be more dogs in this neighborhood than there are kids," said Allison.

Allison and Victoria entered the bakery, where a woman wearing a threadbare coat and thin scarf was haggling with the clerk over the price of day-old bread. The woman at the counter limped over to get the eclair for Allison.

Once outside again, Allison said, "Let's go somewhere and have a cup of coffee. I never get enough coffee at the place."

"Coffee's one of the reasons you're so nervous," Victoria said.

"Maybe, but I want to have a cup of coffee and a cigarette with our coffee," Allison said in a small discouraged tone. "Joe never lets us have a cigarette with our coffee."

"Cigarettes make you nervous, too. Besides, they're bad for your health."

Oh, for God's sake, shut up! Allison screamed inside. She said nothing; she showed no sign of her anger. No matter what anyone said or did—her ex-husband, her lawyer, Joe or Jan or one of the boarders—she showed no emotion.

At Melrose State Hospital, if you gave vent to anger or any other emotion you were thought to be sicker and given more tranquilizers and put in the Quiet Room. There you could not watch television, you could not read, you could not talk to anyone; you sat silently in a bare, locked room.

They passed the playground again. Allison stared hungrily at a small boy with sandy hair, playing third base. Something about his small sturdiness reminded her of Jimmy. The only time she felt like a person now was occasionally on a Saturday when for a split second the kids' faces might light up the instant they saw her.

They walked many blocks slowly back to the boarding house, where nothing would have changed unless Jan was on one of her cleaning crusades when everyone would be banished to their rooms.

Oh, yes, one thing would be different. By this time, Joe and Jan would have finished with the morning paper and Dominick would have it. He would be reading the crime news aloud in his stumbling, faltering way. Most of the crime centered in this neighborhood, and hearing it frightened Allison.

When they arrived, she plopped down into one of the easy chairs in the living room, taking out a cigarette, making sure a newspaper was under the ashtray.

Dominick's voice droned, competing with a soap opera on television.

Allison interrupted him, surprising herself. "Can't you read anything other than crime news?"

" ' . . .woman stabbed in her apartment at 501 Slater.' I like to read about places I know. Politics and that stuff is too much for me."

"Lunch!" Jan's voice rang out around the house.

The boarders filed into the dining-room with its scrawny plants on the two window sills, nothing on the dingy mauve walls. Plates with bits of beef swimming in gravy on slabs of toast were at the seven places on the table.

"Ooh. . .I can't eat chipped beef on toast," Allison said in a small voice.

Milt silently went into the kitchen, came back with two slices of dry toast on a plate, placed it beside Allison's plate.

"Whatsa matter. . .you a fussy eater? We serve the best food of any of the boarding houses in town. Across the street they get soup and sandwiches twice a day. Nothing wrong with chipped beef on toast!" Joe's voice was loud, angry.

Jan interrupted with a rushed, blurred table prayer.

"Everybody eat!" roared Joe.

Milt was sitting next to Allison. "Any luck job hunting today, Allison?"

"I didn't go. I went for a walk with Victoria instead."

"Might as well. Nobody'll take you once they learn you've been at Melrose.

I walked off fifteen pounds of shoe leather when I got out of there looking for an opening, and I've got computer training." Milt's tone spoke of quiet desperation become resignation.

Joe broke in. "Whatdya think this is? This is eating time, not talking time. Everybody eat!" His voice cracked like a whip.

Milt and Allison bowed their heads over their plates. Across from Allison, Louise stared unseeingly. In the hush Flo's gold bracelets clanged; Dominick's feet scuffled under the table. Allison munched listlessly on her dry toast.

"Dry toast, eh?" Dominick said. "Dint your ma ever teach you to eat everythin' on your plate? Why dontcha come up to the tavern with Flo and me this afternoon and have some brew?"

Joe roared, "I said enough talk! Everybody eat!"

Allison was shaking when she reached her room. The roar of Joe's voice echoed in her ears. She knew she should go looking for a job, but she just couldn't. She sat down at the card table next to her bed, inserted typing paper into her old Smith-Corona, opened the library book she used for typing practice. Her fingers wouldn't go where she wanted them to.

She grabbed the bakery bag. She gluttonously devoured the chocolate eclair. It soothed her for a delicious moment. It gave her a feeling of peace. She heard Joe's boots thumping in the hall. Guiltily she squashed the paper bag and hurled it into the wastebasket. Joe forbade eating of anything, even fruit, in the rooms. Food brought more cockroaches.

Joe's square, heavy bulk appeared in the doorway. "You sick?" he accused. He glowered at Allison, his face purplish, his eyes bulging, his neck swelling with rage.

"No...no," Allison mumbled, looking at the wastebasket. The white paper bag was obviously from a bakery.

"There's...shit...all over the back stairs," Joe said.

From the room opposite came Louise's voice, weak, a whine. "It was me. I'm sick. I've got the flu."

"God damn it. Get up and clean it up. This ain't a nursing home."

"I can't. I'm sick. I will later."

"God damn it!" Joe's fist pounded the air. "Do it now!"

Allison got up from the bed where she was sitting while trying to type. "Where's the mop and pail?"

Allison washed her hands. She looked down at her wrinkled, dirty dress. She smiled. She walked to the doorway of Louise's room. "It's taken care of," she said. "You can sleep as late as you want to."

Louise's eyes met hers; there was a spark of recognition between the women. "Bless you," Louise said and closed her eyes.

Allison sat down at the card table again.

"Huh!" Joe's frame filled the doorway. "I thought all you was good for was to sit around and type—Miss Ladyfingers—as though you was too good for the rest of us."

Allison poised her fingers on the typewriter keys. She lifted her head. She stared into Joe's eyes.

"You can go to hell!" she said.

She felt a sense of self, a sense of direction, strength rushing into her. She began to type. Her fingers obeyed her.

I WILL GET SUE AND JIMMY BACK, she typed without error.

The Plant Lady

Sara L. Spurgeon

W HAT SHE HATED most was looking in the bathroom mirror before she
left for work each night. The mirror itself was bad enough — small, cracked
and stained. It seemed to have a permanent, greasy film over it that caused it to
reflect everything back slightly darker and dirtier than in real life. Standing before
it each night, she had to force herself to raise her eyes. This is what people saw
when they looked at her. A fat, lumpy face, liver colored circles under her eyes,
bad skin and stringy hair. She couldn't see anything below her shoulder, but she
knew what it looked like, just more of the same badly disguised in her baggy
work overalls. She was only twenty-six, but she knew people thought she was
ten years older.

The rides to and from work had become particularly disturbing of late. I-94
eastbound into downtown St. Paul was under construction. She never actually
saw any workmen, but each night the on-ramps and traffic lanes were subtly
altered, though nothing really *looked* any different. She wondered, not for the
first time, if any of it was real. If she were to mention the construction to, say,
a clerk at the 7-11, or someone at work, would they agree that it was a terrible
inconvenience, or would they give her a strange look and ask *what construction?*
She was afraid to try.

They called her the Plant Lady at work. The maintenance crew, that is. She
was not really a part of them. They worked for a janitorial service and cleaned
the lobbies and restrooms and lounges of several downtown buildings each night.

She worked for a wholesale florist company which provided plants for the various offices. Her job was to water them, clip the dead leaves, check for bugs, and once a month, shoot them full of fertilizer.

She loved working with the plants, the cool smooth touch of their leaves, their exquisite silence, and the pale, tender green of each new shoot. She guessed she talked to them, though she was never aware of it. The maintenance crew, mostly lanky young black men, awkward and graceful as storks, never seemed to know quite how to treat her. They greeted her each night in their gruff, sing-song voices, but then watched her warily from the corners of their eyes whenever their paths chanced to cross in the empty lobbies or fluorescent-lit corridors. It seemed they could only speak to her as a group. For herself, she merely mumbled to them, head down, blushing, she was sure, as she felt their eyes on her.

She dreaded the drive home every morning. She still lived in the same apartment she'd shared with her grandfather. It was in a dark, run-down tenement near the river. Yawning smokestacks from the nearby factories kept the place constantly in shadow. Day and night, the clanking of the rail cars and the hollow boom of barges being loaded and unloaded pierced the gloom. While images of her parents, who had abandoned her when she was four, refused to come, visions of her grandfather seemed to linger everywhere. The scent of his sweat was in the nicotine-stained curtains and his voice seemed ready to lash out at her from darkened corners. She sometimes found her heart was pounding if she opened a door too quickly, half thinking she had seen him standing, waiting for her.

Her favorite part of work was cleaning the plants. Each leaf had to be carefully wiped with a damp cloth to remove the dust. As she learned from her instruction manual, indoor plants, removed from the cleansing effects of wind and rain, could become so coated with dust that their leaves would no longer admit light or air. So she became their wind and rain. She quieted her breathing to a slow, deep rhythm as she gently stroked each leaf, their cool greenness slipping smoothly under her fingertips. Their wet, green scent curled into her nostrils as she stood close to them, surrounded by their quiet, almost secretive rustling. Sometimes she opened her mouth to breath it in, as though she could taste it on her tongue.

She had no plants in the apartment. Her grandfather would never have allowed them, and even though he was gone now, she hesitated to bring any in. She was afraid they would wither and die in the poisonous yellow air. She did not own a television or radio, either. Somehow, the atmosphere of the apartment served to choke off extraneous sound. Though she had been living there alone for nearly ten years, she still crept silently through the cramped rooms, sidling unobtrusively along the walls and taking only shallow, cautious breaths. She was in agony whenever the phone rang, which thankfully wasn't often, because it required her to speak out loud, and the sickly brown light of the place seemed to wrap itself around her chest and throat.

Moving through the empty offices, dragging her squeaking little cart full of clippers and rags and fertilizers behind her, she often stopped to marvel at the things people chose to put on their desks or hang on their walls. Miniatures of their homes, transplanted, *recreated*, who knew how many miles away. Why? This was what she was unsure of. Many of them had plants. These she always checked, though it was not part of her job. Whenever the maintenance crew caught her ministering to one, they would nod and grin and call out *Yo, Plant Lady*. Sometimes, one of them would wink at her. When this happened, she always jerked her hands away, embarrassed and blushing furiously.

It was the pictures, though, that drew her most. Sprouting amongst the coffee mugs, needlepoint, and curling pieces of construction paper childishly decorated with crayons or watercolors, they seemed menacingly alive and immediate, as though they were always awake and watching over the scattered piles of paper clips and pens and invoices. The people who worked in the cubicles had lots of pictures, many more than the people who had offices with walls and doors. In the cubicles there were pictures of children, husbands, wives, parents, even pets. Almost always, these people smiled with their mouths open or laughed with their heads thrown back and their throats trustingly exposed. Standing in the quiet of the empty cubicles, staring at the pictures, she sometimes mimicked them, throwing her own head back, mouth open wonderingly.

Work had been relatively uneventful Tuesday night. One of the young men on the maintenance crew had brought in a small plastic baggie full of marijuana, and the rest of the crew had cheerfully followed him down to the boiler room to smoke it. As they trooped past her, the one with the baggie had paused and looked at her questioningly, as though he might offer her some, too, but she turned her head quickly, pretending not to see, and hurried away. They had shrugged and continued down the back stairs. She could hear their sharp laughter echoing and fading down the stairwell for a long time. After that, she had the whole building to herself.

A little before 4:00 A.M., she finished up and let herself out the service entrance next to the loading dock in the back of the building. The single, flickering light above the dock threw the alley into harsh angles, all blue planes and black corners. She had reached the bottom of the clanking metal staircase and was making her way around the dumpster when she saw him. He was curled in the shadow of the building she had just left, and he was dying. She saw this in an instant. His matted gray hair was resting in a pool of vomit, and skeletally thin legs in frayed, filthy trousers were drawn convulsively to his chest. Without thinking, she started to move closer, to crouch down next to him, but the smell of the vomit and the stale urine drove her back. She saw he was watching her from sunken, yellow eyes.

I'll call an ambulance, she whispered, but he shook his head. She hunched down against the wall, staring at him. She couldn't take her eyes away from his. Vaguely, she felt the rough concrete digging into her arm. She noticed the ends of his fingers were missing on his left hand, the stumps blackened from frostbite. His breath ground out of his lungs like gravel, but his eyes never left hers. After an endless moment, she realized what she had to do. *I'll be right back*, she told him, her own voice gasping and strange in her ears.

She hurried back up the stairway, gripping the cold metal handrail until her fingers ached. She knew exactly what she needed, but it was on the eighth floor. She rode the elevator with her heart jumping in her chest, her finger poking again and again at the "8" button. As the doors finally slid open, smooth and silent, she caught a faint reflection of herself in the glass wall of an office. Her own figure was blurry and indistinct, framed by the precise blackness of the doorway. She stepped out quickly. For a moment, she thought she had seen the reflection of her grandfather behind her.

He died when she was seventeen. She had stood and watched him, and it took exactly twenty-three minutes. As he lay gasping and writhing on their kitchen floor, she thought of every time his fist had slammed into her face. She reviewed in meticulous detail each instance he had forced her to pull down her pants and bend over his bed, ticking off mentally every belt, hairbrush, and board he had beaten her with. When the heart attack had finally left him blue and contorted, halfway under their kitchen table, she had checked her watch, then waited another twenty-three minutes. This time she counted off each time she had been sprayed by his spittle as he screamed at her, his enraged, purple face and saliva-flecked lips only inches from her own. She imagined she could feel each drop burning into her face like acid. When she finally called the paramedics, she told them she'd just arrived.

The dieffenbachia was in the central reception area on the eighth floor. It was large and healthy, but starting to look a little shaggy. She was planning on trimming it soon anyway. It was a variegated dieffenbachia, and the huge glossy leaves were striped and spotted with creamy white. She pulled a pair of clippers from the back pocket of her overalls and stepped forward into the cool embrace of the plant. She ran her hands lightly over the leaves, tracing their stems and looking for any that were damaged or broken, gently snipping off over-sized ones that could drag the plant down or ruin its balance, pruning back a single new leaf just at the joint so that two new ones would sprout from the stub of the old. She hadn't meant to do the whole plant, but once she started, she had gotten lost in the intimate rustle of the leaves, seemingly the only sound or movement in the building.

Blinking suddenly, she remembered herself and why she was back on the eighth floor. She got a black plastic garbage bag from the supply closet down the hall and began stuffing the dozen or so leaves she had clipped inside. She wondered how many she would need, but guessed this would be more than enough. She carried the bag back down to the elevator, pausing a moment, her stomach fluttering, before she stepped inside. While she rode it down, she stood in the corner with her back pressed firmly against the wall.

As she let herself out the service entrance for the second time that night, she had a sudden sinking feeling that she had imagined it all. When she walked around the dumpster, she would be alone. She squeezed the bag of leaves to her chest and took a long, shaky breath. No, he was there. She walked slowly to him and knelt down. His yellow eyes followed her but it was impossible to read any expression in them. Somehow the stench around him was even worse. Very faintly, she could hear the sparse traffic on the interstate, but the alley and surrounding streets were silent, only his labored breathing moved between the buildings.

She opened the bag and chose three or four of the pale new leaves. These, she had read, were more potent than the older leaves. She placed them quickly and fearfully in his blackened, twisted hands. *Eat them*, she mouthed soundlessly. Her voice seemed to have fled. He understood though, and immediately stuffed one of the leaves in his mouth. She watched in fascination as the big glossy foliage disappeared. As he ripped and chewed them, he seemed to gain strength. His yellow eyes glittered and his harsh, heaving breaths came faster and faster. He began choking after only the second leaf, but he grabbed a third and forced it into his mouth, his jaws working frantically. The book had said that dieffenbachea leaves caused extreme irritation and swelling of the tissues of the throat and mouth. Normally, they would only be fatal to young children, but she had known immediately they would work for him.

His sunken yellow face was turning red now, and frothy saliva flecked with green covered his lips. His choked breathing had almost stopped, the air unable to get past his swollen throat. His bulging eyes were locked on hers and he jerkily reached out a vomit-stained hand towards her, the stumps of his fingers twitching. She had to force herself not to pull away, but his hand fell short. Steeling herself, she reached out and patted it gently, and he looked at her with the most intense gratitude she had ever seen before the convulsions took him. When he finally lay still, she stayed on her knees beside him for a long time.

When she stood up, she left him as he was, with the open bag of leaves beside him. It would look like he had gotten them out of the dumpster. She walked back to her car feeling curiously light, as though only the weight of the heavy ring of keys she carried was keeping her on the ground. As she drove back through the empty, brightly lit streets, she wondered if she could take a cutting from one of the plants to start at home.

Trap Lines

Thomas King

for Christian

W HEN I WAS twelve, thirteen at the most, and we were still living on the reserve, I asked my grandmother and she told me my father sat in the bathroom in the dark because it was the only place he could go to get away from us kids. What does he do in the bathroom, I wanted to know. Sits, said my grandmother. That's it? Thinks, she said, he thinks. I asked her if he went to the bathroom, too, and she said that was adult conversation, and I would have to ask him. It seemed strange at the time, my father sitting in the dark, thinking, but rather than run the risk of asking him, I was willing to believe my grandmother's explanation.

I am sure it was true, though I have had some trouble convincing my son that sitting in the bathroom with the lights out is normal. He has, at eighteen, come upon language, much as a puppy comes upon a slipper. Unlike other teenagers his age who slouch in closets and basements, mute and desolate, Christopher likes to chew on conversation, toss it in the air, bang it off the walls. I was always shy around language. Christopher is fearless.

"Why do you sit in the bathroom, Dad?"

"My father used to sit in the bathroom."

"How many bathrooms did you have in the olden days?"

"We lived on the reserve then. We only had the one."

"I thought you guys lived in a teepee or something. Where was the bathroom?"

"That was your great-grandfather. We lived in a house."

"It's a good thing we got two bathrooms," he told me.

The house on the reserve had been a government house, small and poorly made. When we left and came to the city, my father took a picture of it with me and my sisters standing in front. I have the picture in a box somewhere. I want to show it to Christopher, so he can see just how small the house was.

"You're always bragging about that shack."

"It wasn't a shack."

"The one with all the broken windows?"

"Some of them had cracks."

"And it was cold, right?"

"In the winter it was cold."

"And you didn't have television."

"That's right."

"Jerry says that every house built has cable built in. It's a law or something."

"We didn't have cable or television."

"Is that why you left?"

"My father got a job here. I've got a picture of the house. You want to see it?"

"No big deal."

"I can probably find it."

"No big deal."

Some of these conversations were easy. Others were hard. My conversations with my father were generally about the weather or trapping or about fishing. That was it.

"Jerry says his father has to sit in the bathroom, too."

"Shower curtain was bundled up again. You have to spread it out so it can dry."

"You want to know why?"

"Be nice if you cleaned up the water you leave on the floor."

"Jerry says it's because his father's constipated."

"Lawn has to be mowed. It's getting high."

"He says it's because his father eats too much junk food."

"Be nice if you cleaned the bottom of the mower this time. It's packed with grass."

"But that doesn't make any sense, does it? Jerry and I eat junk food all the time, and we're not constipated."

"Your mother wants me to fix the railing on the porch. I'm going to need your help with that."

"Are you constipated?"

Alberta wasn't much help. I could see her smiling to herself whenever Christopher started chewing. "It's because we're in the city," she said. "If we had stayed on the reserve, Christopher would be out on a trapline with his mouth shut and you wouldn't be constipated."

"Nobody runs a trapline anymore."

"My grandfather said the outdoors was good for you."

"We could have lived on the reserve, but you didn't want to."

"And he was never constipated."

"My father ran a trapline. We didn't leave the reserve until I was sixteen. Your folks have always lived in the city."

"Your father was a mechanic."

"He ran a trapline, just like his father."

"Your grandfather was a mechanic."

"Not in the winter."

My father never remarried. After my mother died, he just looked after the four of us. He seldom talked about himself, and, slowly, as my sisters and I got older, he became a mystery. He remained a mystery until his death.

"You hardly ever knew my father," I said. "He died two years after we were married."

Alberta nodded her head and stroked her hair behind her ears. "Your grandmother told me."

"She died before he did."

"My mother told me. She knew your grandmother."

"So, what did your mother tell you?"

"She told me not to marry you."

"She told me I was a damn good catch. Those were exact words, 'damn good.'"

"She said that just to please you. She said you had a smart mouth. She wanted me to marry Sid."

"So, why didn't you marry Sid?"

"I didn't love Sid."

"What else did she say?"

"She said that constipation ran in your family."

After Christopher graduated from high school, he pulled up in front of the television and sat there for almost a month.

"You planning on going to university?" I asked him.

"I guess."

"You going to do it right away or are you going to get a job?"

"I'm going to rest first."

"Seems to me, you got to make some decisions."

"Maybe I'll go in the bathroom later on and think about it."

"You can't just watch television."

"I know."

"You're an adult now."

"I know."

Alberta called these conversations father and son talks, and you could tell the way she sharpened her tongue on "father and son" that she didn't think much of them.

"You ever talk to him about important things?"

"Like what?"

"You know."

"Sure."

"Okay, what do you tell him?"

"I tell him what he needs to know."

"My mother talked to my sisters and me all the time. About everything."

"We have good conversations."

"Did he tell you he isn't going to college?"

"He just wants some time to think."

"Not what he told me."

I was in a bookstore looking for the new Audrey Thomas novel. The Ts were on the third shelf down and I had to bend over and cock my head to one side in order to read the titles. As I stood there, bent over and twisted, I felt my face start to slide. It was a strange sensation. Everything that wasn't anchored to bone just slipped off the top half of my head and hung there like a bag of jello. When I arrived home, I got myself into the same position in front of the bathroom mirror. That evening, I went downstairs and sat on the couch with Christopher and waited for a commercial.

"How about turning off the sound?"

"We going to have another talk?"

"I thought we could talk about the things that you're good at doing."

"I'm not good at anything."

"That's not true. You're good at computers."

"I like the games."

"You're good at talking to people. You could be a teacher."

"Teaching looks boring. Most of my teachers were boring."

"Times are tougher now," I said. "When your grandfather was a boy, he worked a trapline up north. It was hard work, but you didn't need a university degree. Now you have to have one. Times are tougher."

"Mr. Johnson was the boringest of all."

"University is the key. Lots of kids go there not knowing what they want to do, and, after two or three years, they figure it out. Have you applied to any universities yet?"

"Commercial's over."

"No money in watching television."

"Commercial's over."

Alberta caught me bent over in front of the mirror. "You lose something?"

"Mirror's got a defect in it. You can see it just there."

"At least you're not going bald."

"I talked to Christopher about university."

"My father never looked a day over forty." Alberta grinned at herself in the mirror so she could see her teeth. "You know," she said, "when you stand like that, your face hangs funny."

I don't remember my father growing old. He was fifty-six when he died. We never had long talks about life or careers. When I was a kid—I forget how old—we drove into Medicine River to watch the astronauts land on the moon. We sat in the American Hotel and watched it on the old black and white that Morris Rough Dog kept in the lobby. Morris told my father that they were checking the moon to see if it had any timber, water, valuable minerals, or game, and, if it didn't, they planned to turn it into a reserve and move all the Cree up there. Hey, he said to my father, what's that boy of yours going to be when he grows up? Beats me, said my father. Well, said Morris, there's damn little money in the hotel business and sure as hell nothing but scratch and splinters in being an Indian.

For weeks after, my father told Morris's story about the moon and the astronauts. My father laughed when he told the story. Morris had told it straight-faced.

"What do you really do in the bathroom, dad?"

"I think."

"That all?"

"Just thinking."

"Didn't know thinking smelled so bad."

My father liked the idea of fishing. There were always fishing magazines around the house, and he would call me or my sisters over to show us a picture of a rainbow trout breaking water, or a northern pike rolled on its side or a tarpon sailing out of the blue sea like a silver missile. At the back of the magazines were advertisements for fishing tackle that my father would cut out and stick on the refrigerator door. When they got yellow and curled up, he would take them down and put up fresh ones.

I was in the downstairs bathroom. Christopher and Jerry were in Christopher's room. I could hear them playing video games and talking.

"My father wants me to go into business with him," said Jerry.

"Yeah."

"Can you see it? Me, selling cars the rest of my life?"

"Good money?"

"Sure, but what a toady job. I'd rather go to university and see what comes up."

"I'm thinking about that, too."

"What's your dad want you to do," said Jerry.

It was dark in the bathroom and cool, and I sat there trying not to breathe.

"Take a guess."

"Doctor?" said Jerry. "Lawyer?"

"Nope."

"An accountant? My dad almost became an accountant."

"You'll never guess. You could live to be a million years old and you'd never guess."
"Sounds stupid."
"A trapper. He wants me to work a trapline."
"You got to be kidding."
"God's truth. Just like my grandfather."
"Your dad is really weird."
"You ought to live with him."

We only went fishing once. It was just before my mother died. We all got in the car and drove up to a lake just off the reserve. My dad rented a boat and took us kids out in pairs. My mother stayed on the docks and lay in the sun.

Towards the end of the day, my sisters stayed on the dock with my mother, and my father and I went out in the boat alone. He had a new green tackle box he had bought at the hardware store on Saturday. Inside was an assortment of hooks and spinners and lures and a couple of red things with long trailing red and white skirts. He snorted and showed me a clipping that had come with the box for a lure that could actually call the fish.

Used to be beaver all around here, he told me, but they've been trapped out. Do you know why the beavers were so easy to catch, he asked me. It's because they always do the same thing. You can count on beavers to be regular. They're not stupid. They're just predictable, so you always set the trap in the same place and you always use the same bait, and pretty soon, they're gone.

Trapping was good money when your grandfather was here, but not now. No money in being a mechanic either. Better think of something else to do. Maybe I'll be an astronaut, I said. Have more luck trying to get pregnant, he said. Maybe I'll be a fisherman. No sir, he said. All the money's in making junk like this, and he squeezed the advertisement into a ball and set it afloat on the lake.

Christopher was in front of the television when I got home from work on Friday. There was a dirty plate under the coffee table and a box of crackers sitting on the cushions.
"What do you say we get out of the house this weekend and do something?"
"Like what?"
"I don't know. What would you like to do?"
"We could go to that new movie."
"I meant outdoors."
"What's to do outdoors besides work?"
"We could go fishing."
"Fishing?"
"Sure, I used to go fishing with my father all the time."
"This one of those father, son things?"

"We could go to the lake and rent a boat."

"I may have a job."

"Great. Where?"

"Let you know later."

"What's the secret?"

"No secret. I'll just tell you later."

"What about the fishing trip?"

"Better stick around the house in case someone calls."

Christopher slumped back into the cushions and turned up the sound on the television.

"What about the dirty plate?"

"It's not going anywhere."

"That box is going to spill if you leave it like that."

"It's empty."

My father caught four fish that day. I caught two. He sat in the stern with the motor. I sat in the bow with the anchor. When the sun dropped into the trees, he closed his tackle box and gave the starter rope a pull. The motor sputtered and died. He pulled it again. Nothing. He moved his tackle box out of the way, stood up, and put one foot on the motor and gave the rope a hard yank. It broke in his hand and he tumbled over backwards, the boat tipping and slopping back and forth. Damn, he said, and he pulled himself back up on the seat. Well, son, he said, I've got a job for you, and he set the oars in the locks and leaned against the motor. He looked around the lake at the trees and the mountains and the sky. And he looked at me. Try not to get me wet, he said.

Alberta was in the kitchen peeling a piece of pizza away from the box. "Christopher got a job at that new fast food place. Did he tell you?"

"No. He doesn't tell me those things."

"You should talk with him more."

"I talk with him all the time."

"He needs to know you love him."

"He knows that."

"He just wants to be like you."

Once my sister and I were fighting, my father broke us up and sent us out in the woods to get four sticks apiece about as round as a finger. So we did. And when we brought them back, he took each one and broke it over his knee. Then he sent us out to get some more.

"Why don't you take him fishing?"

"I tried. He didn't want to go."

"What did you and your father do?"

"We didn't do much of anything."

"Okay, start there."

When we came home with the sticks, my father wrapped them all together with some cord. Try to break these, he said. We jumped on the sticks and we kicked them. We put the bundle between two rocks and we hit it with a board. But the sticks didn't break. Finally, my father took the sticks and tried to break them across his knee. You kids get the idea, he said. After my father went back into the house, my youngest sister kicked the sticks around the yard some more and said it was okay but she'd rather have a ball.

Christopher's job at the fast food place lasted three weeks. After that he resumed his place in front of the television.

"What happened with the job?"

"It was boring."

"Lots of jobs are boring."

"Don't worry, I'll get another."

"I'm not worried," I said, and I told him about the sticks. "A stick by itself is easy to break, but it's impossible to break them when they stand together. You see what I mean?"

"Chainsaw," said my son.

"What?"

"Use a chainsaw."

I began rowing for the docks, and my father began to sing. Then he stopped and leaned forward as though he wanted to tell me something. Son, he said, I've been thinking. . . . And just then a gust of wind blew his hat off, and I had to swing the boat around so we could get it before it sank. The hat was waterlogged. My father wrung it out as best he could, and then he settled in against the motor again and started singing.

My best memory of my father was that day on the lake. He lived alone, and, after his funeral, my sisters and I went back to his apartment and began packing and dividing the things as we went. I found his tackle box in the closet at the back.

"Christopher got accepted to university."

"When did that happen?"

"Last week. He said he was going to tell you."

"Good."

"He and Jerry both got accepted. Jerry's father gave Jerry a car and they're going to drive over to Vancouver and see about getting jobs before school starts."

"Vancouver, huh?"

"Not many more chances."

"What?"

"For talking to your son."

Jerry came by on a Saturday, and Alberta and I helped Christopher pack his things in the station wagon.

"Nice car," said Alberta.

"It's a pig," said Jerry. "My father couldn't sell it because of the color. But it'll get us there."

"Bet your father and mother are going to miss you."

"My father wanted me to stick around and help with the business. Gave me this big speech about traditions."

"Nothing wrong with traditions," Alberta said.

"Yeah, I guess. Look at this." Jerry held up a red metal tool box. "It's my grandfather's first tool box. My father gave it to me. You know, father to son and all that."

"That's nice," said Alberta.

"I guess."

"Come on," said Christopher. "Couple more things and we can get going."

Alberta put her arm around my waist and she began to poke me. Not so you could see. Just a sharp, annoying poke. "For Christ's sake," she whispered, "say something."

Christopher came out of the house carrying his boots and a green metal box. "All set," he said.

"Where'd you get the box?" I asked.

"It's an old fishing tackle box."

"I know."

"It's been setting in the closet for years. Nobody uses it."

"It was my father's box."

"Yeah. It's got some really weird stuff in it. Jerry says that there's good fishing in B.C."

"That's right," said Jerry. "You should see some of those salmon."

"You don't fish."

"You never took me."

"My father gave me that box. It was his father's."

"You never use it."

"No, it's okay. I was going to give it to you anyway."

"No big deal. I can leave it here."

"No, it's yours."

"I'll take care of it."

"Maybe after you get settled out there, we can come out. Maybe you and I can do some fishing."

"Sure."

"Love you honey," said Alberta and she put her arms around Christopher and held him. "I'm going to miss you. Call us if you need anything. And watch what you eat so you don't wind up like your father."

"Sure."

Alberta and I stood in the yard for a while after the boys drove off. "You could have told him you loved him," she said.

"I did. In my own way."

"Oh, he's supposed to figure that out because you gave him that old fishing box."

"That's the way my father did it."

"I thought you told me you found the box when you and your sisters were cleaning out his place."

After supper, Alberta went grocery shopping. I sat in the bathroom and imagined what my father had been going to say just before the wind took his hat, something important I guessed, something I could have shared with my son.

War in a Mild Climate

Jennifer Willoughby

T HIS WEEK there is a revolution on the island: the price of lettuce goes up sixteen percent. The food—food is what I do here, I am a hotel cook—begins to rot as soon as the rebels cut the power lines. My precious joints of veal and pork bubble waxy with mayfly eggs. My hotel manager, Sita, tells me just to scrape them and make soup—tourists will eat anything and call themselves adventurous.

I wasn't watching during the actual coup, the violence, the bloodletting. I was in my room peeling eggplant and watching television. *Bonnie and Clyde* was on. I'd turned the volume up high to try and hear the dubbing. I remember Faye Dunaway and her subtitles kept fading into snowy flickers.

Sita tells me the embassy will let students and visitors—I am one of these things—leave without difficulty if they leave this week. Right now there is no narrow-eyed innuendo about what will happen after that. I call my sister Olivia collect. She lives in Portland and has never been restless. She has moved once in her life, like the Westward Expansion, out of supreme righteousness rather than desire.

A friend had given Olivia a baby boa constrictor for her birthday. She tells me how she feeds it bull frogs and gerbils and then asks, how's the work study thing going? I tell her there is a revolution. Oh? says Olivia. Her disinterest prompts me to elaborate.

I think the hotel cats knew it was coming—as though it were a storm or some natural disaster. That afternoon, about three-thirty, eight of them assembled like politicians on the north patio. They sat very still, not cat-like, but like cows smelling a wolf slide in. We heard the sirens two hours later.

Hmmm, said Olivia, well. Are you going to ask me to meet you at the airport? I need a time and gate number and Thursday wouldn't be good for me at all.

I understand, I say, I think I'll have to call you back. Good-bye, Olivia. I hang up and start setting tables for dinner.

After I serve an oily, raisin-studded custard for dessert, Sita tells me the rebels have blown up the city beauty shop. Some people thought they'd made a mistake, trashing the beauty shop, leaving only a solitary upright hairdryer as odd testimony. Why not the mayoral villa, the church, the post office? A gesture, Sita says, a big noise, a big memory. It doesn't signify. Although I didn't actually see it, the hairdryer is the picture I keep in my head to designate that time on the island. My memories always turn into static pictures with captions—I want them that way, I think. Want them to be tidy, biblical illuminations, subject intrinsic to setting. Not a slick magazine layout where the subject can be airbrushed away without damaging the landscape.

I know I had pictures in my head when I came here, pictures of past events, chronologically packaged. The humidity lulls, though, the daytime heat makes me runny inside. The order and importance of the pictures are shifting. I know I came here to be alone, comfortable, with time for new pictures. Stucco hotel with tile floors, red hibiscus, pressed linen tourists. Serving tourists who all look alike isn't debasing. It's like serving dolls who are neither snobbish nor ungrateful; they just don't know how to talk.

Sita looks at the calcified organs of a chick in the yellow of one of my brunch omelets. She says the only thing this revolution need change is our diet—we must eat more green vegetables. I ask her if she will be able to keep the hotel open. She says of course. People always stay in hotels. Some people never like to go home.

You are a foreigner, the taxi-driver tells me on the way to the airport. I feel vaguely pleased, as if Robespierre had just declared me a citizen for the duration of the Terror. Thank you, I say. A foreigner is always better than a tourist.

I have seen too many movies. I expect the airport to be steaming with tension—soldiers with machine guns, ferrety refugees swarming the visa counters, rich white men lounging, bored with playing mensch Hemingway, wanting to be home with familiar accents and stores that are open on Sunday.

I am wrong. Just a lot of thin haired Scandinavian families lugging piñatas, filing neat as spoons into tiny commuter planes. The airport seems cleaner than when I arrived months ago: no pan-handlers and fresh paint at the baggage claim.

I'm at the airport, I tell Olivia. Here? she asks. No, I say, there. Her boa constrictor is fine, as long as the gerbils hold out. Any blood there? she asks, needling. Oceans, I say. I'll be staying on here a little longer. I thought so, says Olivia.

The same taxi-driver is waiting to take me to the hotel. From the taxi window the landscape looks unchanged—perhaps fewer people lingering outside, perhaps not. The events of the war are all around me but like some Renaissance court dance, we only pretend to hold hands — no actual touching. I am the safest person I know.

I am back at the hotel. My hotel. The stucco, the tile floors, mine. Hibiscus, linen tourists, silverware, rancid food, mine. Dear cats who see no elevation in humanity, mine. The stillness of the evening begins to brush along my ears like fur. I go in to set the tables for dinner.

Salt & Pepper

Robley Wilson

"It's offensive," she said, "all these scraggly whiskers in and around the bathroom sink. Can't you be neater?"

"I try," he said. "I really do."

"Try harder."

"It offends me too, you know. All those nibs and nubs, those bits and snips."

"You could at least wash them down the drain."

"Those tiny pieces of brown and gray, black and white. They remind me I have a salt-and-pepper beard. Condiments. Seasoning."

"Don't go on about it. Just be neater."

"On the other hand," he said, "they don't clog the drains—the whiskers, short and sweet and salt and pepper. They aren't like some people's hair I could mention."

"I clean out the drain in the tub whenever it starts to get slow," she said. "Don't start. Don't think that makes the whiskers all right."

"The long brown strands like a spider's spinning, that swirl with the blue water and catch in the traps and slowly build their gossamer dams across the drainpath."

"Enough."

"That catch the innocent ankles of men taking showers and trip them up and hurl them unceremoniously to the slick porcelain floor."

"Blah, blah, blah."

"That catch on the sleeves of sportcoats and ride into the homes of unsuspecting wives . . ."

"God," she said, "don't start me crying again."

"Hey. It's only banter. It's only dander. It's only dead protein."

"It isn't funny now. You never know when to stop. You never know when fun stops and hurt begins."

"Hey."

"Get out of here and let me finish."

"Sure."

"Now."

"Now," he agreed. "But have you noticed the whiskers lately: how much more gray there is? Such quantities of salt? So precious little pepper?"

"I only notice they exist."

"They do. They exist. They announce the passing of the seasonings. They tell the piling-up of years."

"Damn you." She was crying. He had brought her to it for the hundredth time. "God damn you and all your stupid years."

The Time, The Place,
The Loved One

Susan Welch

I SPEND A lot of time alone now. It doesn't bother me. The others took up too much time. I am glad that they are gone. But it is January and now and then I think of January in Minnesota, how in late afternoon a rusty stain appears along the rim of the sky and creeps across the ice. The stain seems to stay there forever, spreading beneath the banked tiers of white sky, until it fades suddenly into the snowbanks and is gone. It is bleak then, as if the sun has just slipped off the edge of the world. Then there is only the ice and the freezing wind on the ice as the sky gets blacker and blacker through the long, deep night.

I hardly ever think of Minnesota now that I am content in Florida. There is a garden with a trellis and orange trees. The branches bend to me as I pluck the fruit, then spring back. As I bite into an orange I can taste the juice of the tree still in it, all its green leaves. The thorns on the rose bushes tear my skirt. The house has pillars and a courtyard; it is not far from the sea. Mal has given me all he promised. When Mal comes home he picks up my daughter at her school and she drinks lemonade while we drink scotch, sitting in the gazebo. By the time my head is clear again we have gotten through dinner and put the little girl to bed and are upstairs, lying on the bed.

So I hardly ever think of Minnesota, how dark and still the winters are there. There was an apartment once, but I don't miss it, I just think about it sometimes when I consider how completely I have gotten out of the cold. From the street you could see a pale lamp shining through the window of the apartment, and the reflection of the lamp in the window; it was high up on the second floor above a store. Signs hung beneath the windows: Grimm's Hardware, Shaak Electronics—and together with the streetlights they cast a white glow into the big room all night long. Sometimes, coming home, we would see the snow falling silently in the beam of the streetlight, as if it were all a stage set.

Across the street was an all-night restaurant and sometimes people would leave there late, and yell to each other before they got into their cars. The first night I saw Matthew he was rushing down the stairs of our apartment building to confront some boys on the sidewalk near the restaurant. If I hadn't pressed against the railing he would have collided with me in his descent. I stood watching him through the glass of the door as he told the boys to be quiet, people were trying to sleep. They hooted and snickered as he turned to leave. As he came in the door, almost in tears, the boys were screaming in a mocking, falsetto chorus.

"They laughed at me," he said, bewildered, shutting the door against them, staring out. We started up the stairs together. He was tall and very thin, stooped even, pigeon-breasted in the t-shirt he wore in spite of the cold. His hair was a mass of ringlets and golden curlicues and it seemed full of its own motion like something alive at the bottom of the sea. For a moment, standing in the hallway, he looked very beautiful and strange.

"I live here now," I told him. "In that apartment, there."

His face was haggard, lantern-jawed, but his eyes were gentle as he stared at me. "Come over and visit me tomorrow night," he said. "I'll bake you some brownies."

All day long I thought I wouldn't go. I stood a long time in the hallway looking from Matthew's door to mine, before I turned to knock on his. When he called "Wait a minute," I thought he was a girl, that's how light and high his voice was.

His apartment was immaculate. The wooden floor gleamed. There was a rug made up of swans' heads and necks, dark and light, facing in opposite directions—the neck of a dark swan provided the relief so you could see the neck of a white swan and so on. It was impossible to hold both the white and dark swans together in your mind at the same time. There was a bed at one end of the large room, a table with two chairs, and windows that faced the street all along the wall. There were no pictures up, just plants on a shelf, purple passion, jade plant, wandering jew, and a bulletin board studded with funny clippings, cartoons, a picture of a bald woman in a long smock.

"I see her all the time at school," Matthew said. "She goes to all the rallies and concerts and just walks around the university."

He was wearing a t-shirt that said "Minnesota" and a pair of jeans that hung on him. I saw that he was not handsome at all. He was bony and long and his joints, his elbows and wrists and probably his knees, were huge, like a puppet's.

"How old are you?" I asked.

"Twenty-one," he said, but he looked sixteen or seventeen. "You?"

"Twenty-five."

"I couldn't imagine what your age was," he said. "People are always drawn to you, your looks, aren't they?"

"My mother was beautiful. She's dead," I said.

I looked out the window and saw how the dark was settling in. When I was eighteen I won a beauty prize, Princess Kay of the Milky Way at the Minnesota State Fair. They sculpted my face in a thirty-pound block of butter, put the bust in a refrigerated glass case and it ran round and round on a kind of a merry-go-round so people at the fair could look at it. I liked it and went every day to see it, standing on the dirt floor near the glass, wondering if anyone would recognize me, but they never did. My father told me I looked like my mother in the sculpture, but he thought it was dumb of me to stand around there all day. He made me come home.

"What in the he world brought you to this place?" Matthew asked, and then I told him how I had come to be there. I must have been lonely, or starved for someone so nearly my own age, I know that's what made me pour out my feelings to him so. I told him how I had met Mal when I took a job in his publishing company, and how he had left his wife and his children for me, and how he had taken me to live with him five years ago, right after my father died. I told him how Mal called me his suburban Botticelli and how he took care of me and taught me all he knew. Now Mal had sold out his interest in the Minneapolis company and we were moving to Florida, where he had a new business. But I had never been out of Minneapolis, my parents had died here, it was all too sudden. I begged him to let me have a couple of months here, work in the business as it changed hands, get used to the idea of leaving as he got our new life settled. I had found this apartment in a familiar area, near the university, where I, too, had gone to school. Matthew was looking at me so hard his jaw hung.

It was late autumn, just before Halloween, and Matthew and I watched out the window as the sky went down from copper to livery red to mother of pearl. The streetlights blinked on and so did the signs above the stores. The room darkened with the sky but the signs and the streetlights shed pools of incandescent light on the bed, on the floor.

"What kind of person would leave his wife and children?" Matthew asked.

I sat with my head in my hands. "I don't know, he felt so awful about it. They'd been married twenty years. He told me not to think about it. He said it was my face; he loved my face." I pressed my fingers into my cheeks. The flesh gave like wax. But suddenly I was asking myself, what kind of a person was Mal, to leave his wife and children. I had never thought of him in that way before.

Then slowly Matthew began to tell me about himself. It was hard for him to talk, he didn't charm me with what he said or the way he said it, not at all. His voice was a whisper and sometimes it cracked as it came out, no, not a man's voice at all. He had been in love with a girl and she hadn't loved him, but still he kept loving her and loving her and finally he had gone crazy.

He told me what it was like to be crazy. Everything seemed to have a secret meaning, cracks on the sidewalk, a phone that rang once but not again, the world was full of hidden messages.

"It sounds wonderful," I said. "I would love to feel that everything had a secret meaning."

He shook his head and his curls bounced. "You don't know what you're saying. No, it wasn't wonderful at all. It was horrible."

"And the girl?"

"She's gone. Gone a long time ago."

It was hard to talk to him, I had to strain to hear him, his murmurs. It was as if he were used to talking in whispers to himself. His father was a doctor, his mother wanted him to be a doctor, but he couldn't do it, his grades weren't good enough, he couldn't concentrate. So instead he was taking this degree in psychology, maybe something would come of that.

I don't know what it was, I didn't want to leave him. After a while he got up and turned on the lamp by the window, then he put on a record.

"I like that a lot," I said. "Mal and I don't listen to any rock, just classical. Bach. Vivaldi. Telemann. A lot of baroque."

"Don't you know any people your own age?"

I looked at him. "Hardly any. There are a few girls at work but I don't see them much."

It was late when I got up to go. I walked along the shiny dark floor to the door. The lamp shone on the green leaves of the plants and reflected white in the window. I could feel the cold on the street below seeping in around the window frames.

Matthew followed me and stood with me by the door. I thought I had never seen such a delicate-looking man. I could almost see the blood beating in his temples. He took my hands in his huge bony hands. I felt it only for an instant but my hands were throbbing where he had touched them.

A few days later I found a copy of the album we had been listening to wrapped and pushed under my door. When I walked over to Matthew's apartment I could hear the bass pounding in the record he was playing. I stood in the hall for a moment but the door opened.

"I heard your footsteps," he said. But how could he have heard me over the music? We stared at each other. He looked gawky and stupid. I wondered why I had come. "Listen, I've got a coupon for pizza," he said. "Do you want to go?"

As we walked he took my hand in his. I couldn't take it back, my own hand trembled so.

"They removed a rat's memory surgically today," he said. And all through dinner we talked about how the rat experienced everything for the first time, every time.

When he himself had gone crazy, Matthew said, he thought about the same things over and over again. He had thought then that he was refining memories, getting down to their essence and their core. Now he realized that was impossible.

His way of talking was innocent and strange. He thought differently from other people and I had to listen carefully to catch his meaning. Neither of us ate much. We pushed the pizza back and forth between us.

"Do you want to come back over?" he asked as we walked out into the bitter cold. He took my hand again. I just wanted to be with him, I don't know why. Perhaps I admired the sculpted, jutting angle of his cheekbones. He made some coffee and got out a box of fresh pastries from the bakery downstairs. He sat across the table from me, staring down at the coffee, his long legs stretched out until they nearly touched mine. The white light enclosed us in a long oval. He shook his head and ruffled his fingers fiercely through his curls.

"You hair is so unusual," I said.

"I was helping my father give EEGs last summer," he said. "One lady saw me and wouldn't let them put the electrodes on. She thought that was what had happened to me."

We laughed. At that moment, I looked at him and he looked at me. I felt a dizziness, a tightness near my heart. I was snug, safe in his apartment against the cold—I'm sure that's what it was. I have thought about it since.

He put a record on and we were silent, sitting in the pool of light.

After a while he came over and knelt beside and me and wrapped his arms around my waist. I could see the top of his head, his bobbing curls.

"Matthew, I have a lover."

He ignored me and put his cheek next to mine, holding my head. I could see the fine grain of his gold skin, how tight it was on the bone.

"Do you want to go lie down with me?" he asked and I nodded, yes.

I looked into his face as he undressed me and saw that his eyes were all pupil. For a long time he stroked the place where my hip met my thigh, running his fingers over the pale blue traceries of the veins.

"I love you," I said. Yes, I remember I said it, and I said it many times, I don't know what came over me. And I thought, this is the most wonderful night of my life, nothing will ever be this sweet again. We stared at each other in the light of the streetlamps and Grimm's Hardware sign and we made love. All night long we looked into each other's eyes. He was so young I could see that his eyes were brand new, just budded in their sockets.

Sometimes even now I fancy I can feel Matthew's tongue, scratchy as a cat's, and the way he wrapped me up in his long, long arms. But I scarcely think of him at all now. In fact, I have entirely forgotten him. If it weren't for the little girl, considering her as much as I do, and the way the days are so long for me here, I doubt that I would think of him at all.

Three days later I went to work again. The phone was ringing as I walked into my office and I picked it up, knowing it was Mal. There had been a short circuit in one of the stereos in the electronics store and all night music from a rock station had pounded up to us through the floorboards. Elton John, Matthew told me they were playing. "Love Song." "Come Down in Time."

"What are you telling me?" Mal asked. "You were walking along, just minding your own business, and you got hit by a freight train?"

Light from the apartment flooded into my eyes and behind them as I held the receiver, the pure light on Matthew's face as he twined me with his legs and arms.

"I never should have left you alone, I knew it was a mistake," Mal said. And when I didn't answer he said: "I'm coming up there."

He was waiting for me in the office the next morning. For a long time he wouldn't believe that I was serious, that I wasn't coming down to Florida.

"I suppose his teeth are all white, not stained like mine," Mal said. "And I suppose he has all his hair and a flat belly, that's what you're thinking when you look at me, isn't it?"

"No, it's not," I said, but now that he'd said it it became true. All I was worried about was that he would kill me, and then I wouldn't be able to be with Matthew.

I wanted to tell him how fond I felt of him, how grateful I felt, how it hurt me to see his eyes glaze as he slumped against the window. But I stood speechless.

"I gave up everything for you. I can't let you go," he said.

For a moment I thought of the filthy warped floor in the hall of my apartment building, the way the brown paint on the floors bubbled and peeled. "I was a child then," I said. "That was for then."

I turned my face away as he held me.

"There's nothing I can do," he said. "I can't live without you." For an instant I prayed, begging that Mal would not die.

Then, miraculously, he was gone. He had me fired from my job but I found another where I just had to type. I bore no grudges. I was walking on love's good side. I had Matthew.

From our first night together Matthew was always in my thoughts. I suppose you could say I lived for him. He wanted us to be twins.

"One consciousness in two bodies," he said. "That's what we are." He looked at me in a way that made me feel holy. No one had ever paid this kind of attention to me, no, never. He painted our toenails the same color, green with silver dust. When I got a pimple, he would often get one himself, in a similar spot. We wore each other's clothes, bought matching shoes. We copied each other, walked alike, talked alike. How I loved imitating Matthew. It was no longer lonely being me. We could be each other.

We had been together two months when I found out I was pregnant. Matthew had told me not to get another diaphragm, there could be no mistakes between us. Anything that happened was right.

When I told him, he smiled. "That's wonderful," he said. "I can't wait to tell my family. Now we'll get married."

We drove out to the suburbs for dinner so I could meet his parents. He had told them about me but they had resisted meeting me, until now. We drove to a ranch house with a swimming pool behind it, big as a gulch. His father was a tall, silent man who left in the middle of dinner to go to the hospital. His mother had Matthew's jagged features but none of his softness. She hated me on sight.

After dinner she took me aside.

"Do you realize what a sick boy he is?" she asked. "You're a grown woman, you should see these things. He's been institutionalized for long periods."

"I love him," I said calmly. "He loves me. He knows exactly what he's doing. And it's medieval to think of mental illness as a permanent condition. You get over it, like a cold."

"What do you know about it?" She stared until I dropped my gaze. "Have you ruined your life the way I have, eating your heart out over him?"

We left before dessert.

"Cheer up, honey. We have to go out and get some sour cream cherry pie, some cheese cake," Matthew said as we sat in the car in his mother's driveway. He started kissing me, digging his fingers into my thighs. "There's a great place near here. You'll love their hot fudge cake," he said. "I can't take my honey to bed until she's had her dessert."

We went to a delicatessen where cakes and pies dipped up and down on little ferris wheels. "It tastes as good as it looks, too," Matthew said. We held hands and fed each other hot fudge and cherries on heaping spoons. The rich goo dripped like wax. We nudged and stepped on each other's feet the whole time, pressing each other's soles and toes till they hurt.

"Why doesn't she like me?" I asked. "Is it because I'm older?"

"She'll get over it, don't worry about her," Matthew said. "All she knows is her Bible. That time when I got sick—she thought it was God's rebuke to her. She's just going to have to get used to it."

I scraped some hot fudge on my plate with my spoon. It dried fast, a sweet cement. "You're so old for your age, Matthew. I'm surprised she can't see it. I've always known I could depend on you."

He fed me the last bite of hot fudge cake. "How about some more?" he asked. "Come on, honey, you know you want it."

"Let's have the hazelnut torte," I said.

"Great," Matthew said. "Great. My mother would die. She believes in minimal sweets."

"Mal too," I said. "Seaweed and spinach. He made us eat seaweed and spinach every stupid day." We both grimaced, wrinkling our noses.

Matthew stared into my eyes and jammed my feet tight between his. "Hi, baby."
I saw his mouth move but no sound escaped his lips. The waitress put the torte
before him. Shrugging and rolling his eyes at me he plunged his fork into the
crest of hazelnut lace.

We got married and I moved all my things into Matthew's apartment. Our lives
went on much as before.

How did those days pass? They went by so quickly I swear I can't remember.
We had everything in the world to find out about each other.

He took pictures of me with an expensive camera his parents had given him
for his birthday. He gloated over the prints. "Look how you're smiling," he said.
"How happy I must make you." He set the time adjustment so that we could be
in the pictures at the same time, hugging or kissing or with our heads together,
staring at the camera. "What a beautiful couple," he said.

He played his guitar as we sang duets of rock songs. He was charmed by my
flat singing voice. He even admired my upper arms which had started to get pudgy
from all our desserts. He flapped the loose flesh with delight. "That's one of the
things I love about you most," he said. "Chubby arms just like a little baby."

One freezing night as we walked home after a movie our boots crunched into
the moonlight on the snow. Our gloved hands fitted into each other like the pieces
of a puzzle.

"What should we name the baby?" he asked.

"I don't know," I said.

"If it's a girl how about Phoebe, after the moon," he said. "The moon is so
beautiful, look how we're walking on silver, baby. And it always seems to have
so many secrets."

"But we don't like secrets, Matthew," I said. "We don't believe in secrets."

"I bet she'll look like the moon," he said. "You'll get round like the moon and
then the baby will come out and look like the moon."

I woke up once during the night. He was sleeping with his arms around my
neck. He slept silently, like an infant. How could he be so quiet? The lights outside flooded his bulletin board, the shiny wooden floors, the carefully arranged
cabinets. The radiators hissed then fizzled to stop. Outside the window the full
moon shared the secret of the shadows on the dark street, his beating heart. I
almost woke him up to tell him. I wanted to say, I could die now. I am so happy
I could just die.

For Valentine's Day he wrote me a song. I sat on the bed while he played it
for me on his guitar. He didn't need to breathe with my lungs filling his, the song
said. He wanted to die from drinking my wonderful poison. I listened, filled with
wonder.

As he played, I watched his hands. For the first time I saw tiny scars on his wrists, fine and precise as hairs. When he finished playing I put my fingers to his pulse.

"Your wrists, Matthew," I said. "Look. Where did all those little marks come from?" He had never told me, yet he said he told me everything.

He withdrew his hands, fixing me with his long stare. "Let's stay in the here and now. Why talk about things that happened a long time ago, things you can't remember right anyway. What did my honey get for me?"

I had forgotten Valentine's Day. The next day I bought him a shirt and an expensive sweater. He thanked me but seemed disappointed. His mother could have given him the same. He had been involved in his gifts, mine were clichés.

The next day I got a valentine from Mal, forwarded from the old office. He loved me, he was thinking about me, he wanted me to come back to him. As I put it in the wastebasket I found the valentine I had given Matthew folded at the bottom.

In the dead of winter it was fifty below for days at a time. We would sit on the bed and watch the smoke rise out of the chimneys in timid frozen curls. When we came home late at night, walking across the huge U of M campus, we would have to kiss and hold each other for twenty minutes before our noses and fingers thawed.

On Sunday mornings we would have breakfast at the restaurant across the street. We sat facing each other, our legs locked, talking about what was happening in our lives. I treasured my separate life for it provided me with stories to tell him. Nothing was real until I told Matthew about it.

After breakfast I walked him to his part-time job at the laboratory where he was working on a hearing experiment. Chinchillas were made deaf in one ear and then trained to jump to one side of a large revolving cage or another, on the basis of certain sounds. If the chinchillas didn't perform correctly they got a shock. That was Matthew's job, running them through tests and shocking them if they made mistakes.

I went with him once and saw the little animals in their cages. They were furry and adorable, bunnies without ears: how could Matthew, the gentlest of people, stand to shock them?

"They have to be shocked when they're not doing their job," he said. "It's horrible, but that's the way life is."

"Since when do you believe life is that way?"

One evening he came home shaking. A chinchilla had died when its eardrum was being punctured for the experiment.

"Matthew, why don't you quit that job?" I asked, looking up at him from where I sat at the table. "Don't you see what it's doing to you?"

"It's not doing anything to me. I'm fine," he said, standing there trembling. "Do you think you're better, that you wouldn't do that job?"

I stood up and rushed to him. "Matthew are you angry at me? Please don't be angry at me. I just want you to be happy." I hugged him tighter, tighter. "Do I give you everything you want?" I whispered into his shoulder. "What can I give you?"

"You're everything I want," he said.

"But is it enough? You're so much better at being somebody's lover than I am."

"Yes, I am good at that, aren't I," Matthew said, and I could feel him thinking about it, there was a hum in him like currents in fluorescent tubes.

Then he held my shoulders and looked deeply into my eyes. "Come here, baby. Let me tell you about this experiment I've been thinking about all day."

We sat down at the table holding hands. "When they fasten electrodes to the pleasure centers of a rat's brain the rat will do nothing but push the bar that activates the electrode. It won't eat, it won't drink, it won't sleep, it just keeps pushing the bar for the pleasure sensation until it dies of starvation and dehydration."

We sat silent. "That's interesting," I said. I watched his hand as it moved slowly up my arm, to my shoulder, then curled around my neck.

"You," he said. "You."

Late afternoons Matthew would go to the bakery downstairs and come back with boxes of sweets. then we would sit at the table, listening to the voices on the street, feeling how the winds lightened and the air became less bitter as spring blew in our windows. We watched the sun on the grain of the table. We cut eclairs with knives and fed them to each other. When Matthew ate chocolate he was in such ecstasy he had to close his eyes. I could see him shudder. It was like when we were in bed. Being around all those sweets made me greedier for them, it was strange. The more I ate the more I wanted. It was like being in bed.

I got fatter and fatter from the sweets.

"If you can't get fat when you are pregnant, when can you?" he asked, feeding me another pastry. Yet Matthew never got fat.

I ate cakes, petits fours, upside down tarts. At the soda fountain around the corner he fed me hot fudge sundaes.

"Eat, baby," he said. "I love to see your little tongue when you lick the syrup."

My breasts became huge. I swelled like an inflatable doll. All night long Matthew would lie in my arms as I lay there puffed with life and the splitting of my own cells. When we woke up he went downstairs and got doughnuts, filled and frosted pastries called honeymooners, pecan rolls.

Before long it was spring verging on summer and we took long walks along the Mississippi, breathing the crisp shocking air that rose from the torrents of icy water that came with the thaw. Sometimes we took sandwiches and stayed out till two in the morning. On one walk a pale, ovoid form approached us. It was the bald woman whose picture was on Matthew's bulletin board.

She stopped Matthew, held onto his arm, mumbled to him. She had been at the zoo, she said, and fed the elephant peanuts. It had lifted them out of her hand with its trunk, she said, holding up her palm, showing it. Its soft trunk had tickled and nudged her hand, gentle, tender. She could feel its hairs.

"Do you know her?" I asked Matthew, watching her as she disappeared. But Matthew wouldn't answer.

One afternoon after a rock concert we followed the path along a cliff near the river; below us the Mississippi glimmered like diamonds. We walked hand in hand but I was waddling fast to keep up with Matthew's long strides.

"Let me catch up," I said, and he stared at me, his eyes hard.

"You know I've been thinking," he said, walking faster. "We're really not that much alike."

I couldn't catch my breath. The air was freezing my fingertips even where Matthew held them.

"Like how so?"

"Like make-up," he said. "Like you wear make-up and I don't."

My eyes watered from the wind. "But I've always worn make-up," I said. "I'll stop wearing it if you don't like it."

"That won't do any good," he said. "And you take up a lot of the bed. It's hard for you to keep up with me when I walk."

"But I'm pregnant, I've got fat," I said, nearly in tears. "If I weren't pregnant and you didn't force all that food on me, this wouldn't happen."

Tears were streaming down my face but Matthew was walking fast, not seeming to notice.

"I don't make enough to support a baby," Matthew said. "It's all going to be different. It seems cruel. Sometimes I think I can't do the job."

"You know I've got savings. And your parents will help." Now I couldn't stop crying. I halted in my tracks, jerking my hand out of his. The Mississippi roared below us. I waited for long moments by a tree, waiting for him to come back. And suddenly I knew that we would never again be as happy as we once were.

Finally he came back, retracing his steps, and looked at me.

"I'm sorry," he said. "I never want to hurt you."

I looked into his eyes and saw how young and frightened he was. I will never leave you, I said to myself. You need me and I will always take care of you.

That night in our room rainy air billowed the curtain inward on our long embrace. There was the smell of skin, warm salt flesh, clean.

"Please baby, whatever you say, never say you stopped loving me," Matthew said.

"Oh, never. I would never say that."

"You would never start hating me, would you? You would stop long before that."

Stop? He had never said anything about stop. "No. I would stop before that."

"We would stop while we still loved each other. And now. . . are you going to hug me all night long?"

The next day, on impulse, I called up Mal from work.

I couldn't even wait for him to get over his shock. I rushed into it. "You won't believe this, but I've just got to talk to someone. About Matthew. It's just interesting, you won't mind? He's absolutely terrified of getting fat. He is the skinniest man you've ever seen, yet he's worried about fat. Once he went on a fishing trip with his father and he ate a whole pound bag of M & Ms and he was so appalled he didn't eat anything else the whole trip. And by summer he had got so thin he could see the sun shining through his rib cage. Can you imagine anything so stupid?

He loves sweets, you know, we live near a bakery, and some times he'll get so many good things and eat them, then do you know what he does? He sticks his finger down his throat and throws up. Really, I've seen him do it."

Mal listened, silent, until I was done. "Why don't you leave him?" he said.

"Because I'm happy, that's why," I said, suddenly desperate to be off the phone. "Besides, I'm very fat, do you think you could like me fat?" He didn't answer. "I was just kidding about him throwing up. Do you believe me?" Mal was silent. "Well, maybe he did it once or twice when he was drunk."

"Do you know why I'm fat?" My voice grew shriller in the silence. "Because I'm pregnant. I'm going to have a baby in two months."

I pressed down the button, hoping he'd think we'd been disconnected.

I came home from work one afternoon and found Matthew lying naked on the bed, his stereo earphone on, one leg propped straight against the wall. He was so absorbed in the music he didn't see me coming up to him, see how I was staring at the long red marks on the inside of his thigh. As I sat down beside him he took his leg down quickly and removed the headset, smiling.

"It's spring," I said. "It's gorgeous out, Matthew."

"It's pretty," he said. "Have a good day?"

"Did you?" He said he hadn't been out and, leaning back again, he pulled me down with him. I moved away.

"Matthew, let me see your thigh." He watched me docilely as I lifted his leg. It was as if it were a specimen we were both going to examine.

"What are those red marks from?" I asked.

"Me."

"How did you do it?"

"With my own little fingernails," he said.

They weren't scratches, they were deeper than that. The gold hairs on his thighs spoked up innocently around.

"Matthew, why did you do it?" He took his leg down.

"Don't worry about it. It's nothing. It's something I do sometimes. I put iodine on it, it won't get infected."

"But why did you do it?"

"Because I was having evil thoughts."

"About what?"

He shook his head. "Don't worry about it." He eased me back down. "Don't worry your little head," he said. "Baby. Double baby. Baby squared." He started moving his hands up and down my body.

I pulled away. "Wait."

"What's the mater, baby?" he asked, touching me all over. I felt his tongue in my mouth and I closed my eyes.

One night he came in late, very agitated.

"There was this guy following me down the street just now for about a mile. He was this weird, juiced-up black guy even skinnier than I am. He was muttering, calling me sweet cakes, doodle-bug, boney maroney. Can they tell about me?" he asked, looking into my face. "Can they tell I've been crazy? Do I give out special vibes?"

I thought of the tense air he always had, the speed of his walk on those long legs.

"He followed me all that way. He kept saying, 'Think you're pretty hot stuff, you creep, you creep.'"

And the bald lady, had he seen her? Matthew wouldn't answer.

"People can't tell," I said finally, but he wouldn't stop looking at me.

"Why are you staring?"

"Because you're so nice and fat," he said, still staring.

Behind that gaze there was intensity that had nothing to do with me. I felt something ungiving in him, the tightness of his skin on the bone. "Stop making me eat," I said. "You're turning me into a monster."

"But honey," he said smiling. "I likes you fat." Then his expression changed. It was a dark look he gave me. "You're eating with your own mouth," he said.

I called up Mal again. "Can you imagine?" I said. "He washes his hair every morning because he doesn't want dirt to accumulate too close to his brain. He's afraid it will penetrate and sink in. and he scratches himself with his fingernails when we have a fight. When I told him to stop buying me so many sweets he thought I hated him and you know what he did? He put a long cut down the top of his arm with a knife."

"He's crazy," Mal said. "Don't you know you've got a mental case on your hands? Why don't you get out before he does something to you?"

"He won't do anything to me," I said, but it was a long time before I could hang up the phone.

When I came home that night Matthew was sitting at the table with a stack of pictures. I sat down beside him.

"What are they of?" I asked.

He looked annoyed but said nothing. I slid the pictures over and started going though them. They were all of him. He had taken twenty-four pictures of his own face: laughing, smiling, stern, pensive, in profile, in three-quarter view, from the back.

"These are really good," I said. "When did you take them?"

"I've really changed a lot," he said. "I've suspected it, but I can tell from the pictures how drastic it is."

"How have you changed?"

"In ways." He put his hand over his mouth, staring at me and then staring at nothing.

"Why are you so indifferent to me?" I said.

"I'm not indifferent." He took the stack of pictures and began looking through them again, humming to himself.

"Why don't you take my picture?"

He continued to sort through the pictures, humming.

"Why don't you take my picture, Matthew?"

There was a long silence. "Sure, I'll take your picture some time," he said, and I saw how his hair flared out in the photographs, like a sea fan.

I remember every detail of the next few days. It was the hottest part of the summer in Minnesota. Night after night I went sleepless in the motionless air, hanging over the side of the bed so Matthew would have more room. I was so huge and moist my nightgown clung to me like a membrane. I had to take it off and lie naked on top of the sheet. When I tried to meet Matthew's eyes he looked away. "It will all be different after the baby comes," I whispered to him, but he pretended to be asleep.

One evening I could hardly walk when I got off the bus after work. With every step my fat thighs rubbed against each other. They had become so sore and chapped they had begun to bleed. As I walked past the bakery the heat rose in waves; behind the window, a sheet of sunlight, I saw wedding cakes, gingerbread men, cookies with faces, shimmering.

I heard music, coming from our apartment. I twisted my key again and again in the lock. Surely Matthew could hear me? I punched my knuckles against he door. I tried the key again and the lock gave suddenly.

The room was filled with smoke. Matthew was sitting on the bed with the bald woman and a short black man who was even skinnier than he was.

"We're tripping," Matthew said. "But there's nothing left for you."

"Who is that?" said the bald woman.

"She lives down the hall."

"I do not live down the hall and you know it, Matthew," I said. "I live here and I'm his wife." I stood there awhile and nobody looked at me. I put down my purse and sat down next to it on the floor.

"These are my friends. They're like me," Matthew said. He looked at me with the eyes of a little animal, eyes that were all pupil, the color black, absorbing everything and giving nothing back.

"He's a cabdriver," Matthew said. "You wouldn't think of having a a cabdriver for a friend, would you? Or a busdriver? I like cabdrivers."

"I would so have a cabdriver for a friend," I said, but I couldn't think of a single friend I did have. Matthew was my only friend.

"You wear make-up and you're fat and you only want to be friends with editors," Matthew said. "Oh, yes, and friends with Uncle Mal." The bald woman edged closer to Matthew on the bed. Her hand brushed my pillow, the pillow I had brought to Matthew from my old bed. She whispered in his ear, moving her hand to his hip, to the front of his pants.

"We're going now," Matthew said, standing up.

"Wait a second, I'll come too," I said.

"Do you want her to come?"

"No way," said the bald woman.

"See? They don't want you to come," Matthew said. "They're my friends and they're like me and they don't want you to come."

I stood still as they passed, stupefied by my pain.

"Matthew, please don't go!" I said. "It's just a tough time now, baby. Isn't it?"

He stopped in the doorway, staring down at me. A vein like a root throbbed in his temple. His face blurred in my gaze and I saw his eyes staring wide at me as we made love on that bed, silver ghosts in the wash of pale neon. I saw the snow falling silently as we hurried home in the cold, looking high up for the glow of the lamp in our apartment.

He put his hands on my shoulders. His palms and fingers cut into me like brackets. "Stay here," he said.

I watched him from the window but he did not turn to look back up at me.

I lay on the bed watching the ceiling change as it got darker and darker. I don't know how long I lay there or when the pains in my back or my stomach started, they blended so imperceptibly with the other things I was feeling, staring at the ceiling, lying on the bed. Then I lay down on the floor, on the rug of swans' heads and necks, hurting so much I imagined I felt them moving under me, nudging me with their bills. I waited and waited there for Matthew to some back, but he didn't come back. It must have been a couple of days later that I called a cab to take me to the hospital.

The baby was tiny. She was born feet first, the wrong way. They gave me a drug that put me in a twilight sleep, that turned everything pink until I saw her after she was born. She came out curled like a snail and stayed calm in her crib sleeping all the time. She fit over my shoulder like a chrysalis, a tight little cocoon.

It was Matthew's father and mother who came to see me at the hospital and who took me home. I wanted to go back to our apartment, but they wouldn't let me, they said Matthew wasn't there and I needed somebody to take care of me. They took me to the house in the suburbs, but Matthew wasn't there, either. He had taken too many drugs and hurt himself, they had to send him away somewhere, they wouldn't say where. His mother gave me the Bible to read.

He came to see me once, I was still lying down most of the time. He came and sat down beside me near the big swimming pool. He had seen the baby. "She wasn't like the moon," he whispered, or did I dream that? He sat down on a chair next to me in the sun for a little while and he cried.

He got up and started walking toward the house, muttering something.

"Matthew, I know you didn't mean to hurt me," I said, but he kept walking, shaking his head.

"He didn't even recognize you," his mother told me later, glaring at my face in the sunlight.

"Then why did he cry?" I asked. "If he didn't recognize me then why did he cry?" Words from her Bible swam in my head, he whom my soul loveth. We could do anything, be anything, with what we had. Hadn't he always told me that?

I rushed into the house, hoping I could still find Matthew, but he was gone. I took the keys to his mother's car off the kitchen table and ran to the garage, before she had a chance to stop me.

Then I went out to look for Matthew. I looked everywhere nearby, up and down the streets, and when I couldn't find him I drove back to our old neighborhood. I parked in front of the old apartment and went upstairs and knocked and knocked on the door but no one answered. I tried my key but it wouldn't fit into the lock. I pushed at the lock until the key had scratched my fingers and made them bleed. Then I sat down by the door on the floor in the hallway and remembered how there had been heaven in that apartment, time had stood still. No matter what he did, Matthew knew. We had made love all night, in the light of the streetlight and the Grimm's Hardware sign. If I put my cheek to the wood I could feel the vibrations of those nights, still singing in the floorboards of the apartment.

Mal came to the house in the suburbs after I called him. He cried when he saw me and I saw how his cheeks were now cross-hatched with tiny red veins. Matthew's mother wanted to keep the baby for herself, but Mal wouldn't let her. He took me, and the baby, and brought us to this beautiful house where we have been so happy. It is not far from the ocean and we go sailing a couple of times a month if the wind is not blowing too hard. I am thin again and Mal has bought me wonderful new clothes. The little girl calls him Daddy and has never known another father.

I thought Mal would ask me to explain a lot of things, but mostly he hasn't.

"I know you've never loved anybody but me," he said. "I knew you'd come back.

That's why I waited." That was four years ago. And more and more I think Mal was right.

Once we were sitting under the trellis and and Mal asked me what I was thinking about when I looked so preoccupied and far away. I told him an apparition gripped my mind sometimes.

"It's a picture of man who looked like a boy and a girl at the same time, a man with hair like a sheaf of golden wires, with eyes as black and shiny as lava chips. You remember, it was a man who confused me, a man who studied the memory and even tried to look into his own head. I must be making it up, don't you think? For no real person could be like that."

Mal was annoyed, he said it was certainly something I had made up. I'd made a mistake and had altered the memory to turn it into something more compelling, so I didn't seem like quite such a fool. It was basic psychological theory, he said.

That was a long time ago. I am content with my life and light of heart. I know how evening rises up in the blue noon and I know every moment by the angle and quality of the sunlight spreading on my lawn and on my courtyard. I stand in the courtyard and watch the days and walk through my garden and wait for my daughter and Mal. For surely, as Mal tells me, I am the happiest of women. But it is always summer here and sometimes I remember how the winter was in Minnesota, how dark and drear. And it is just occasionally, as I watch Phoebe's copper hair growing into tighter and tighter curls with each passing year, that my mind strays back to that time.

Telling Uncle R

Julie Schumacher

for my father

U NCLE R IS the very last relative I have in this world. He is a homely old
man, a pathological liar, and he is selling the house that he and my father
grew up in. He says that anything within its walls is mine. Most of the furniture
is old, and in a week or two the antique dealers will arrive, bidding on tables
and chairs, buying the mirrors where my grandmothers combed their hair for
a hundred years. He says I should buy the house itself, but I tell him no. When
I look at the tilt of the upper floors, the slant of the porch and the footsteps worn
in the stone beneath the door, I feel the weight of too many lives, a century of
habits not my own.

"Suit yourself," says Uncle R. "If you plan to be a jackass all your life, you might
as well start right here at home."

Uncle R is seventy-two and plans to move to a senior citizens' retreat. In the
meantime he has a live-in aide and companion, a woman named Mrs. Becca, who
lives alone on the second floor. She is a high-strung woman with a narrow head,
and with fingers that are small and curled and pinkish, like rows of shrimp. She
seems to be fond of Uncle R and periodically pulls me aside to discuss his
condition.

"He talks about death a lot," she says. "I thought I should warn you. Funerals
all day long, hideous stories I couldn't repeat. He seems to have a very active mind."

"I know those stories," I tell her, just to let her know who's familiar and who's
not. "Shark tanks and prison camps and Indians buried alive. Did he tell you about

the man who got caught in a tuna-pack machine? He came out the other end in a bunch of cans, and they had to open every one to reassemble him."

Mrs. Becca ignores me. She is peeling vegetables, leaving all the eyes in the potatoes.

"What does he say about me?" I ask. "I barely see him anymore."

"He's glad you're here." She shrugs. "He says you'll be taking a lot of things with you when you leave."

Briefly I wonder how deep her interest goes. Does she have her eye on a marble-top dresser, on the sewing machine underneath the stairs?

Uncle R's toes are on the linoleum just behind me, and I step on some of them and turn around. He is wearing a red knit bathrobe and a pair of sweatbands on his wrists. His face is thin, his blue eyes unnaturally bright.

"I didn't hear you coming," I tell him.

"That's because of my invisible slippers." Uncle R is a short man, and now seems frail in a stubborn and aggressive way. "I should be underground already, is that what you're thinking?"

"No."

"I'm going to save the both of you a lot of trouble." He leans back against the cabinets and crosses his legs. "We won't have a funeral. You'll just fold me in half and drop me into the trash. You put a ten-dollar bill in my mouth and set me out on the curb. What are you drinking?"

"Nothing yet."

"We'll fix you a scotch and water," he says, sitting down at the kitchen table. "I'll bet you barely remember this place. You were just a kid when we had holidays here. You don't understand what this house is worth."

"I know what it's worth. Anyway, I was here a year ago, last July."

"Take the table." Uncle R is back to his days as a salesman, when he peddled housewares door to door. "We had card games here that lasted nights and days. Your Uncle Karl stabbed me here, nicked me on the temple with a knife, because I beat him at this table Christmas Eve. You don't remember things like that. You were too young."

"I remember them perfectly. When everyone else was eating dinner you'd be gambling in the kitchen, snacking off the plates when we were done. Everyone said you cheated."

"I didn't cheat," he says. "I won by magic."

Mrs. Becca skins her finger with the peeler.

"That's what's wrong with you," he says. "You didn't stay long enough to find out who we were. You grew up alone. You don't even speak German."

"We lived all over the country," I remind him. "My father was transferred a half dozen times. It wasn't easy to come back."

"He used to visit just enough so he wouldn't feel guilty. So he wouldn't feel bad for having deserted us. He would have stayed here if it wasn't for Winifred."

Winifred was my mother. "I don't see anything wrong with wanting to lead your own life," I tell him. "She didn't want to share a house with her husband's relatives."

"She called us drunks and degenerates!" he shouts. "We were a normal, loving family."

"What about Uncle Karl? And Uncle Edward? I heard he tried to murder his wife."

Uncle R pauses to clean his teeth with a carrot. "Uncle Edward was dead before you were born. Besides, she deserved it."

"This was your father's room." Uncle R insists on leading me through the house as if I have never been here. The ceilings are low and stained with waterspots and the wood floors are buckled.

"We spent years in this room together. Your father and I grew up in this room. You were supposed to be born here, right on this bed. But your mother decided to go to a hospital."

I examine a dust-mouse the size of a dog.

"The *best* thing about this room— " Uncle R's face is flushed like a young boy's " —is the closet. You can crawl through a door in the ceiling and make your way to the roof. Your father and I used to climb up there at night and watch the stars, lying there right on the edge of the roof."

"I've been through that trap door. It just leads to the attic."

He turns and stares at me. "Who's the visitor here, me or you?" But I can tell that he's pleased.

"This was Tante Lena's room." He is breathing hard from climbing the stairs but is trying not to show it. "She used to stand here by the window —right here— " he pulls me by the arm so I am standing in the very spot he's referring to " —and stay here sometimes half the night. She almost never slept. She didn't need to sleep."

"My mother never liked Tante Lena," I offer. "She thought she was too domineering."

"Your mother," says Uncle R with a yawn, "was an idiot."

We check the attic, the seven bedrooms, and the garage. So far I have chosen a silver hand mirror, the sewing machine that might otherwise have gone to Mrs. Becca, and a small embroidered footstool with someone's initials woven all around the sides.

"Now for the basement," says Uncle R. "I've set aside some things you'll want to have." He flips on the light and we descend.

On the basement floor is an enormous heap of furniture and dishes, boxes overflowing with paper, photograph albums, clothing, books and toys. A set of porcelain floor lamps, each with life-size Oriental ladies holding up the shades, flanks the pile.

"You're out of your mind," I tell him. "I live in an apartment. I have three and a half rooms and a closet."

"Is that supposed to be my fault?" he says. "You should get a bigger place."

"I don't want these things, Uncle R."

"It's not a matter of wanting them or not. They can't be sold. You don't have a choice."

I look at the stacks of furniture and clothes, including two fur coats and a row of foxes biting each other's tails. Some of the things are beautiful, in fact, but they aren't mine. The massive dressers have claws for feet and the armchairs have wings: this is the opposite of my life, a heavy, well-endowed existence built on certainty, determination, drive. My own life is reflected more by cotton and rattan.

"Look at this." Uncle R holds up a photograph. It's a sepia-colored woman in a floor-length dress. She stares at the camera intensely, as if rehearsing for the moment when I'll reach down and dust her off.

"You have her nose," he says. "A bump in the middle and little ball on the end. Very unusual. Actually there's quite a likeness."

I hand it back to him and sit down in a velvet chair.

"It's Tante Lena as a young woman," he says. "Nearly six feet tall by the age of fourteen. She could put out a fire with her hands."

"I'll take the picture, Uncle R, if you'll leave me alone about the rest."

"This was hers," he says, patting a roll-top. "This was your Tante Lena's desk."

"I'm going upstairs to take a bath. I'll take the picture if you want."

"You'll take all of it. Every scrap."

I reach the steps and turn around. Uncle R is facing his possessions, gathered there as if waiting for a speech. He spreads out his hands in astonishment. "Do you believe this woman?" he says.

To pass the time we play pinochle. Mrs. Becca has never played but we need a third, so she sits perched on the edge of her seat, tallying points.

"What do you say we raise the stakes?" says Uncle R. "Give the game a little spice."

"What do you mean? A dollar?"

"I had more than that in mind." He tightens the belt of his bathrobe, cracks his wrists. "Let's say we wager my grandmother's desk. You don't have a desk like that at home. Win the round and we take it from the pile; I'll even chop it into firewood myself."

"What if I lose? Why don't we bet that you go to a doctor. He might be able to tell you what you've got."

"My health is fine." He crosses his legs. "Nothing that a few pleasant years below a garden can't take care of. I'll take out the lamps. Double or nothing keeps the lot."

"You don't look well Uncle R."

"Oh, is that your opinion?" He raps my cards with a knuckle. "You should worry about your own life for a change. You live like a hermit. A single window the size of a dime and some naked walls. There's something strange about a person who wants to live in a place like that. It's not fit for a mole."

"Suit yourself." I trump his king with the nine of hearts.

He pauses, then spreads his cards like a fan. "We never used doctors when I was growing up. Not unless we had to get rid of someone in a hurry. Then we called up for a quick injection, the way they kill criminals. That's what happened to your great Aunt Emma. She was fine, perfectly healthy. But everyone said she was just taking up space."

"I'll take the picture and the things I found upstairs. But that's the end."

"She was a witch. A real pain in the ass. I'm not asking you to take it all at once. You start with a chair. A miniature couch for your apartment."

"I don't need a chair."

"Or a doll-sized rug. Maybe a goddamn silver thimble you can use as a bathtub!"

Mrs. Becca jumps up and spills her coffee on the cards. The liquid rolls across the face of a king of spades; then it follows a cleft in the table, seeping quickly toward the edge.

"Great," says Uncle R. "Magnificent." He mops the coffee with the belt of his bathrobe, wringing it out above his cup. "I always knew one day I'd be sitting at a table, just like this, across from a woman with a scorepad in her hand. We'd be sitting around like regular people, except that one of us was nuts and one was a hermit. The nut would have coffee stains on his clothes and the hermit would sit there like a stone, and even if he offered her a couple souvenirs from one of the nicest houses in the state of New York, a goddamn landmark, she'd sit there like a deaf-mute and refuse to answer."

"I can't take the furniture, Uncle R."

He dries the belt against his leg. "You'll come around. I can feel it."

After dinner he tells us a story. Mrs. Becca has dished out ice cream with frozen peaches and is pretending to wash the pots. Bits of rice still cling to the dishes in the drainer.

"We were on our way to a wedding," he says, "your father and your Uncle Edward and I, and your great-grandmother at the wheel. And right smack in front of our car is the Henderson kid, sitting in the middle of the road by the tracks. We hear the train coming and figure he's waiting for freight cars. He used to throw stones at the guys on top, hoping they'd get mad enough to throw down coal in return. Sometimes he'd get enough to heat the house for a week. So we honk at him, tell him to beat it. But the kid stands up— " here Uncle R would usually stand, but now just straightens in his chair " —looks us straight in the eye and walks out onto the tracks. Just stands there with his eyes wide open until it comes up and kills him."

"This is another decapitation story, isn't it?" Uncle R has a number of versions, each one ending with a headless man in the trunk of a car. "Can you hold off on that until I've finished my dinner?"

Uncle R begins cutting his ice cream with a knife and fork. "Weak stomach?" he rasps. "We had to piece him back together right here in the kitchen—right here on the maple table like it was an undertaker's slab! We didn't have time for weak stomachs. We didn't have that *luxury!*"

I can see his next sentence taking shape, his accusations dropping into place. I have had it too easy, my entire childhood I was entertained, I have no idea what hardship means and am therefore yellow, flabby, pale and unformed. But Uncle R seems suddenly tired. He puts his head down on the table, the wisps of white hair on his freckled scalp drifting into the ice cream. "When was it that your father died?" he asks. "Before or after your great Aunt Emma?"

"After," I tell him.

"Sometimes I miss your father like hell. He was my younger brother."

"I know that."

"And when was it that he died? I think I forgot."

"In sixty-nine. October third. You remember that, Uncle R. You went to the funeral."

"And who read the eulogy?"

I have to think back. It's hard to think with Uncle R's head on the table in front of me. "You did."

"And what did I say?"

"You said my father was the finest man you ever knew. You said he was a family man, that he loved his family more than anything else."

He lifts his head off the table. "That's what I thought."

The picture of Tante Lena finds its way into my room. It's on the nightstand, and watches me when I sleep. Such symbols aren't lost on Uncle R. Under his direction I head for the basement once again, selecting several additional items to take home. These are a maple rocking chair, a small oriental rug in red and gray, and the ring of foxes biting each other's tails.

This last choice amuses Uncle R. "I guess those look good with a sweatshirt," he says. It's true I won't wear the foxes, and the idea of animals stuffed or skinned has always seemed to me fairly repulsive, but there's something whimsical in the hinged and furry mouths that I can picture on a wall. Every hour or two we journey to the basement, for lack of anything better to do.

"We're just going to look," he says. "To browse. There's one other thing that you haven't seen." Soon, though, he's insisting that I have to take the object home. "You owe me this," he says. "You wouldn't have been born if it weren't for me. I must have saved your father's life a dozen times."

"Not the last time, though," I say.

He picks up a vase but I shake my head.

"You're deranged. They were right. Tante Lena and Uncle Karl. They always said it was disappointing the way you turned out."

"That's ridiculous. Uncle Karl was nearly blind when I was born, and Tante Lena must have been ninety. They didn't know me. Both of them died when I was small."

"So he was blind," says Uncle R. "He had ears that you wouldn't believe. He heard even better in the dark. And Tante Lena, she was the strongest woman alive. One day it was raining, just like this, but the gutters were jammed full with leaves and the roof was starting to leak. So Tante Lena climbed up the drainpipe herself, shinnied up the side of the house in the pouring rain to dig out those leaves. Your father and I were sitting here playing checkers, on this very board, and we saw her pass by the window on her way to the roof. Like a rabbit," he says. "You can still see the marks from her boot-toes on the wall."

"Uncle R— "

"I wouldn't expect you to be interested," he snaps. "You always hated your own great-grandmother."

"I wasn't old enough to hate her."

"Chocolate-covered raisins," he says. "She used to feed them to you from the palm of her hand."

"Those are stories, Uncle R."

"Well of course they're stories. What else is left?" He puts down the vase and weighs an ashtray in his hand. "What a joke," he says. "That you're the only one left. Out of such a family we should all boil down to you. Do you think you can stay another week?"

"I have things to take care of. I left the cats with a neighbor."

"Cats," says Uncle R. "Nothing to go home to but a house full of cat hair."

"I have other things to go home for."

"Such as?" He turns to face me and I have to concentrate to bring the twelve white walls of my apartment into view. It's true that except for the cats I have cleared out a lot. The more I throw away the better I feel. But this is something Uncle R would not understand. "Organization," I say at last. "Cleanliness."

"I'm overwhelmed," says Uncle R.

He tells stories, one after the next, and wonders why I don't repay them with my own. What could be worthwhile telling Uncle R? When I try to tell him about my job, or about the families in the building where I live, the telling seems pointless to us both.

"Who was the kid? What did he have to do with the lady in green?" Uncle R squints at my narration, impatient with people he doesn't know. "It's in the delivery," he says. "It's like a joke. You learn to build up to the climax, take your audience along. Mostly you have to start with something good."

I could tell him that this is what I love about him most: the authority with which he tells a lie. Instead I ask him for the story of the rosebush.

"You could tell that one," he says. "I'm sure you know it well enough."

"I'll get to the middle and forget."

"Liar," he says. "You could tell that story in your sleep." He cleans his finger-nails with a tweezers. "Just give me the beginning. Start me off and I'll take over."

"I wasn't there. I wasn't born."

"What year was it?" he insists.

"Twenty-two."

"Twenty-four. You're doing fine. And who bought the rosebush?"

"Her husband bought it. Tante Lena's husband."

"Very good. And what happened when he brought the rosebush home?"

I try to imagine the house as it must have been. I have heard this story twenty times. It's meant to illustrate our crustiness, the family's unwavering hostile stance in the face of kindness, persistent sympathy, love.

"They'd been arguing all day, they were out of money. Her husband took the last of his paycheck from her purse and bought a rosebush, just to make up for the things they'd said. He was a gardener and he had a way with plants. Tante Lena thought he'd gone to pay the rent, but he came back with a rosebush and some dirt. She was furious when she saw him coming up the walk."

"What did the rosebush look like?" Uncle R sinks back in a chair and shuts his eyes.

"It was yellow, nearly in bloom. Even my father said it was the most beautiful rosebush he'd ever seen: tiny yellow buds in such profusion it was impossible to count them. He was just a boy at the time but he always said he remembered it perfectly, my great-grandfather trailing up the walk with a rosebush in a yellow bucket."

"Your great-grandfather. What was he like?"

"What was he like?" Uncle R's robe has fallen open to reveal a pale white thigh, slender and almost hairless.

I close my eyes. "His name is Anthony. He's very handsome, with a huge mustache and a red bandanna at his neck. He likes to tell jokes."

"What happens next?"

"He takes the rosebush up the steps of the porch, but Tante Lena sees him coming. She grabs the rosebush out of his hands, straight up out of the dirt so the thorns are cutting deep into her palms. She doesn't feel it, she's got arms like a stevedore and she throws the roses into the street, throws them up over the gate and into the gutter."

"Then what?"

"He left and didn't come back. She planted the roses by the side of the house and they bloomed here for years." We sit with the story between us now. "Is that what you wanted, Uncle R? I still don't feel I have it right. Did I get it right?"

Uncle R sits up and looks at his watch. "When I'm dead," he says. "That's when you'll learn to get it right."

In the middle of the night my uncle falls on his way to the bathroom. When I help him back to bed he refuses to look at me, and in desperation I ask him for a story.

"I don't know any stories," he says, his face turned toward the wall.

"A story about my father. Or about Tante Lena."

He is still facing the wall. "Those are old stories," he says.

In the morning I lift the car keys from the nail. The car is a massive old machine, brown and rounded at the corners, with a huge steel smile between the headlights. In the overstuffed driver's seat I put the key in the ignition, knowing that this is the car that drove us to my father's funeral, and to great Aunt Emma's, and even earlier to Tante Lena's. I can almost picture the old lady in the back seat behind me. I see her deep blue eyes in the rear view mirror, the high black collar of her dress. She nods at me and I see her nose somewhat like mine. I begin to believe that Tante Lena could do anything she wanted. She could climb a waterspout like a spider in the rain, or glide past the window on her way to the moon.

It is almost two hours later that I pull into a garden shop. Although they don't have any yellow ones I find a large, sturdy, white-budded rosebush that might look yellow in the sun. I imagine the look on Uncle R's face when he sees it, and I am surprised at how excited I feel, at how completely satisfied the purchase has made me. As I pull into the drive I see the sun shining on the face of the house, lighting it, and Mrs. Becca standing on the edge of the porch. She catches sight of me and steps down onto the lawn. She is running toward me now across the bright green grass, her handkerchief over her face, and for the first time in my life I feel everything falling into place, the past taking shape all around me.

Sheetrock

Will Weaver

W HAT FIRST ATTRACTED me to "This Old House" was the sound of a circular saw, or "soar," as Norm Abrams says it, which always reminds me of President Kennedy, the way he talked, the long scarves he wore, the way the wind puffed at his hair. Anyway, I was doing dishes when I heard an electric, hand-held 7¼ inch blade circular saw, the kind every carpenter uses. I cocked my head, leaned forward to look through my kitchen window. Up and down the street. Nothing. No one sawing. Just houses, all prefabs like this one, that peter out where the hills begin and a couple of oil rigs sit like black teeter-totters on an empty playground.

My subdivision sits at the west edge of Minot, North Dakota. No construction has ever gone on here. These houses come on trucks. You've seen them on the freeway, half a house on one lowboy, the second half on another trailer behind. The factory staples a big sheet of white plastic over the open middle of each side to keep out road dust and birds, but wind usually tears away the plastic and you can drive alongside and look right into the living rooms, the bedroom. Herb, that's my husband, says hitchhikers are attracted to prefabs. If the plastic doesn't tear by itself they'll cut the sheet, just one razor slit, to get inside and ride. Some prefabs include furniture, like a couch, a kitchen table, a TV-stereo combination, a queen-sized bed. The factory staples the furniture to the floor where they think most people would like it (later, if you want, you can move it) and Herb once saw a bum riding along at sixty miles an hour stretched out sound asleep on the davenport, his hair flapping in the wind. Anyway, when the two sides of a pre-fab arrive at the job site they're slid onto a concrete slab, then power-nailed together whacka-whacka-whacka. Houses like this one, there's nothing to saw.

Still in my kitchen I kept hearing that faraway whine of a circular saw. I let my hands go quiet in the dishwater. Listened. The sound was like the flip side of a siren. When an ambulance or a fire truck wails by you can bet somebody's dead or hurt, their house is burning, their luck's gone bad. When you hear a carpenter's saw—hear that high, steady calling—you know somebody's life is on the ups.

Which made me look around my own kitchen. The dark, wood-grain paneling. The bowed, plastic strips of floor moulding. The muddy white linoleum split here and there, cuts never stitched, from dropped kitchen knives. The cupboard doors with vinyl peeling at the corners like spiked hair. I didn't grow up in a house like this one. Our house was nothing fancy but it was all wood and it didn't come on no trailer.

I grew up in Golden Valley, which is now a part of Minneapolis, on a street with two rows of identical one story houses all built by Mr. Jenkins. He started with one house, sold that and built another. As soon as the sub-flooring was down and the plumbing worked he moved in his family. His kids coughed a lot from the sheetrock dust, but my father said sheetrock was just chalk and paper, the same they use in school. Every night of the summer Mr. Jenkins's saw was the last thing I heard before I drifted off to sleep. Once my mother complained about the sawing. "For crissakes that's the sound of progress," my father said, and rattled his newspaper. It was the 1950s then.

I dried my hands and soon enough tracked that faint sawing sound to the den. There the TV was flashing in an empty room. On the screen was a man cutting plywood; another dark-haired fellow held the sheet steady. Big men, with noses and bellies. They wore leather tool belts, jeans and plaid shirts and scuffed boots that had seen some dust. Two big men working together. Saw horses, sheets of plywood. A silvery circular saw, its blade eating up the thin red line, the yellow sawdust feathering up behind in a golden drift. I turned up the sound. I sat down. For some reason the scene got to me. Choked me up. There was something about it—the tools, the boots, the wood, the two men working. It was all so real. It was something anyone could believe in. After that, Thursday nights it was Bob, Norm, and me.

T-minus twenty-five minutes.

Bob Vila himself picks each house to be remodeled. He drives around looking for older homes for his next project, and these houses could be anywhere in the United States. Anywhere. Sure most of the jobs are out East. That's because Norm and Bob are from out east originally. But they have remodeled houses in

Connecticut, Tennessee, California, Colorado, Wisconsin and more. I know because I keep track.

In our den I have a United States wall map and each red pushpin is a "This Old House." It took some work, I'll tell you, getting all the sites pinpointed. I had to order the tapes I'd missed, then go through them one by one. But I'm glad I did. Looking at the pins it's clear to me now that Bob Vila could show up in anyone's neighborhood.

Once I was driving west in Minot when I saw a shiny blue crewcab Ford pickup, the driver with sunglasses, coming at me from the other way. For a second I froze at the wheel—then I closed my eyes and spun a louie across traffic. Cars honked at me, which was serious because people in North Dakota never use their horns. I made it across the traffic but there were too many cars and I lost him. Afterward I had to pull over. My heart was pounding. I had to catch my breath.

I bowl, and that night at the lanes I told the girls in my league who I just might have seen.

They laughed. Phyllis said, "You sure it wasn't Elvis?"

Anyway, once Bob picks a house—say it was your house—all the remodeling is free. I have thought and thought about this matter and I believe it to be true. Reason number one, Bob is a wealthy man. He has his television show. He has his videos. He has his books on remodeling. Reason number two, even if Bob wasn't rich, he is not the kind of guy who would take money from homeowners who are struggling to make life better for themselves and their kids, even if they offered him the money.

I don't tell people my ideas on the free remodeling. If you know in your heart that something is the truth, there's no need to broadcast. Besides, it would only hurt Bob and Norm. Imagine how people would try to get close to them, to be their friends. Imagine the women, the things they would try.

T-minus fifteen minutes. I'm knitting with one eye on the clock when Herb pokes his head into the room. The top of his head shines.

"Yes?" I say immediately.

"Have I got something for you," Herb says. He is a middle-sized man with a round head and one of those soccerball bellies that truckers get from the constant jiggling, the continual pounding over seams in the freeway concrete, which over the years weakens the stomach muscles. Herb holds up his new *Playboy*.

"There's nothing in that magazine for me," I say. I check my watch against VCR time, keep my needles moving.

"Not even an interview with Bob Vila?"

My yarn snags.

Herb grins and holds out the magazine.

I make a point of unhooking the snag before I set down my wool, my needles. Then I clutch the magazine. It's heavier than I expect.

I look for the right page, making sure to glance away when the pictures flash up pink. And suddenly there it is, "Twenty Questions with Bob Vila." A picture, too. Bob is standing beside a low red car that I read is a Ferrari. A Ferrari his wife has given him for his birthday.

"I could sure go for one of them Ferraris on my birthday," Herb says from behind me. He puts his hands on my shoulders, begins to rub them. I can feel his belly, round and firm, against the back of my head.

"Well we're not rich, you're not Bob Vila and it's not your birthday," I say, and hand him the magazine. I check the time on the VCR, then pick up my knitting. I have to focus on my yarn, concentrate, remember the pattern. I crochet newborn caps for the local hospital. New-born caps are my bowling money.

"My birthday ain't that far off," Herb says softly. He is still standing behind my chair. He takes my head into his hands and begins to run his thumbs slowly over the rims of my glasses and down the sides of my ears.

I keep knitting, which my girlfriends say I could do through a tornado.

"What if I was Bob Vila and I came driving up and knocked on the door?" Herb says. His voice has dropped a note, turned husky. He keeps stroking my ears. He knows what that does to me. And I know that his new *Playboy* has got his batteries charged up.

"Piff to that," I say. It's a nervous saying I have.

"Piff?" Herb says. "That's all?" He laughs once.

"Piff," I say.

Tomorrow morning Herb is leaving for Duluth, Georgia with a load of durum. When he's gone I stay pretty much in the house; in winter you shouldn't leave a house alone, even for the afternoon. Especially this house. When the temperature drops to twenty below and the wind comes in from Montana and ice knocks down a powerline somewhere, it's trouble. Frost grows from the plug-ins, from around the window sills, from the keyhole. It grows like toadstools. I've sat there and watched it move. On those days I wear my parka and one of the newborn caps.

"What if?" Herb whispers. He's leaning down now. His breath is sweet and woody from his Copenhagen, which I'd rather smell than cigarettes.

Summers I stay in, too. I can't take the heat outside so I stick to the den where we have a window air conditioner. I keep knitting. Sometimes if the shades are drawn and the air conditioner is blowing cold I'll forget that it's summer and I'll put on a jacket and one of those wool caps. The caps feel good any time of year really. I can see why black people wear them. And one size fits all.

Herb leans down, whispers in my ear.

For a moment my fingers stop; the needles go silent. I look across the living room, see my reflection in the TV. I am low and round and gray. "I used to be prettier," I say.

"You're pretty enough," he says. He keeps stroking my ears.

"I never weighed this much in my life," I whisper.

"It's all the same by me," Herb says.

I can't say anything.

"Really," he says, his voice softer now.

I set down my hooks, my wool, shut my eyes and lean my head back into his belly. Its firmness, heavy as a ripe pumpkin, always surprises me. There are worse things about a man than a belly. When I open my eyes Herb is smiling at me, hopefully, upside down.

"Say I was Bob Vila and it was my birthday besides."

T-minus three minutes.

In our bedroom Herb is breathing hard. I have my arms around him. "Come on honey," I say. My eyes are on the clock.

The headboard is thumping, thumping, thumping against the wall. It's only half-inch sheetrock. I try to concentrate. "Okay Honey!" I call out to him. His eyes are closed; I don't know if he hears me.

I think of the sheetrock. Sheetrock is really billions of tiny dead fossils ground into powder, then rolled out in wet slurry. Pressed flat. Baked. Papered both sides. Then painted white. I saw the whole process once. Bob and Norm visited the quarry and the factory, which were somewhere along a coast in Canada. From the loading dock there were trucks one after another hauling away the finished product, the 4 x 8 sheets. Which we make into rooms, white rooms, so white we have to hang things on the walls. No one can live with bare sheetrock.

In this room, across from the bed, there's a calendar with a nature picture. A stream with trees and sunlight. There's no water or trees like that around here; it had to have been taken somewhere else, another state. Below the color picture there is a line of twelve little squares. The months. I can't read their names, let alone pick out the days.

Thump and thump and thump.

Across the bedroom the digital clock blinks the time. It's T-minus one. I call out to Herb. He hears me this time, and picks up speed. I start to feel something, but it's too late for me. So much is late for me that my eyes burn and the room begins to tilt and shimmer. I have to close my eyes and keep them shut. I concentrate on the thudding sound. Herb goes on and on. After awhile it's like there's someone pounding, pounding, pounding on the front door.

Biographical Notes

Editors:

JONIS AGEE has published two collections of short stories: *Pretend We've Never Met* and *Bend This Heart*, named a 1989 New York Times Notable Book. Her novel, *Sweet Eyes* has just been published by Crown Press. She teaches creative writing at The College of St. Catherine in St. Paul, Minnesota.

ROGER BLAKELY, who teaches English and art at Macalester College in St. Paul, has edited several books for New Rivers in the past, and served as co-editor of the anthology *Border Crossings* issued by the Press in 1985. He also authored *North from Duluth*, a collection of essays and poems about northern Minnesota published in 1981.

SUSAN WELCH was a Wallace Stegner Fellow in Creative Writing at Stanford University and she received an M.A. in creative writing from Stanford in 1980. She is the recipient of a Bush Foundation grant, a Loft-McKnight grant, and a Minnesota State Arts Board grant. Her fiction has been published in *The Paris Review*, *The Pushcart Prize Anthology*, and in *Love Stories for the Time Being*.

Contributors:

ELEANOR ARNASON was born in the borough of Manhattan in 1942. She grew up mostly in Minneapolis and has lived in Paris, Honolulu, Brooklyn, and Detroit. She sold her first short story in 1973. Since then, she has published nine short stories, three novels and a number of poems. Her most recent novel, *Daughter of the Bear King*, published by Avon Books in 1987, is a fantasy about a middle-aged housewife from south Minneapolis. She is currently working on a new novel, which is about life in the upper Midwest even though it is set on another planet. "The Ivory Comb" is an excerpt from this novel.

CONRAD BALFOUR, never one to do something easy and efficient, wrote three 400-page manuscripts as practice toward his fourth which he submitted for publication. In the past his wife Mary has declined to read his works because she claims that his anger is always evident. Anger at what? Anger at whatever makes the planet remain in its constant turmoil. Although she admires that trait in him she sees no need to read the man she lives with. Balfour currently instructs creative writing classes at the Loft and is an English Instructor at North Hennepin Community College. He is no stranger to New Rivers Press as he was the editor of the acclaimed *Butterfly Tree*.

STEPHEN BARTH grew up on a farm in the boggy dunes of central Minnesota where his father turned sand and rock glacial deposits into cattle feed, groceries and eight rather large sons. Not the wizard he was, Barth gravitated to mind-spells, and currently works at a State Institution as a Psychologist/Supervisor. He lives on an island in a swamp where he is turning an electronic hovel into a shelter machine. "The Broken Dam" is his first short story to be accepted. He is currently working on editing a novel into final draft form, and on a new story.

CAROL BLY was born in Duluth in 1930. Her most recent publications include *The Passionate, Accurate Story* (Milkweed Editions, 1990) and *The Tomcat's Wife and Other Stories* (HarperCollins, 1991). She lives in St. Paul and Sturgeon Lake, Minnesota.

JONATHAN BORDEN is a poet who lives with his wife and their dog Toby in Killarney Lakes, Minnesota, near the southernmost bend of Minnehaha Creek. "The Shoes of Death" is a chapter from a novel in progress entitled *The Shoes of Death: Tales from the Cypress Grove*. An episode from another fictional work in progress, "Sunday Afternoon at the Track," appeared in the anthology *Blossoms and Blizzards* (Rochester, Minnesota: Pegasus Prose, 1986).

NONA CASPERS was raised in rural Minnesota in a German Catholic town surrounded by cows, crosses, blood sausage, and fried potatoes. She now lives in San Francisco where she attends the graduate program in Creative Writing at San Francisco State University. Eight of her stories have been anthologized along with the stories of Julie Blackwomon in *Voyages Out 2*, published by Seal Press. Her first novel, *The Blessed*, was published by Silverleaf Press.

RICK CHRISTMAN, originally from north central Wisconsin, graduated from the University of Wisconsin (B.A.) and Drake University (D.A.). He has published fiction, poetry, and articles in a number of magazines and newspapers, among them, *Indiana Review, Great River Review, Stone Country, Wormwood Review, Z Miscellaneous* and *The Des Moines Register* . He also received a Loft-McKnight Award in Fiction. His first novel, *When I Could Fly*, is in its final stages. He teaches at Des Moines Area Community College, Akeny, Iowa.

GARY ELLER was born and grew up in a farming town — Rolla, North Dakota. After several years in Alaska he returned to the Midwest to study creative writing at the Iowa Writers' Workshop from which he graduated in 1989. Both his fiction and nonfiction have appeared in various publications including *Wellspring, Fireside Companion*, and the baseball anthology, *The Ol' Ball Game*. Although Eller often uses Alaksa as a setting for fiction, his literary heart is, he believes, in the Midwest.

EDIS FLOWERDAY, a native of Nebraska, has lived in Minnesota for the past twenty-five years. She holds a B.A. from Macalester College and an M.A. from the University of Minnesota, both in English literature. She lives in Minneapolis with her husband Laurence Risser. They have three daughters. Although she prefers to write short stories, Ms. Flowerday has completed two film scripts, has been a research writer, and is currently working on longer fiction. In her fiction, she draws substantially from regional elements and historical sources.

DON GADOW grew up in southwestern Minnesota near the Lower Sioux Agency, site of his story "Football." He teaches in the English Department at Winona State University and makes his home in Annandale. One of his humor columns, written for *The Annandale Advocate*, "The Sex Life of the Vegetable Patch," won an award from the National Newspaper Association in 1985. A previous story about Allie, Don's Nick Adams, won first place in a fiction contest sponsored by Mankato State University in 1982 and was published in *Gathering Post*.

DIANE GLANCY after writing for 100 years, in the first half of 1990 won an NEA, Minnesota State Arts Board Fellowship; a Jerome Travel Grant; a Blandin Foundation Fellowship; and NEH Summer Institute Fellowship to the Newberry Library in Chicago; a Diverse Visions Fellowship for Collaboration with Harmonia Mundi for an experimental musical/verbal composition; the Capricorn Poetry Award from The Writer's Voice in New York for *Iron Woman*, a collection published by New Rivers Press; The Nilon Award from the University of Colorado and The Fiction Collective for *Trigger Dance*, a collection of short stories; a letter of acceptance from West End Press for another poetry manuscript, *Lone Dog's Winter Count* to be published in 1991; a Borderlands Theater award for *Stick Horse*; and The University of Nebraska Press Native American Prose Award for *Claiming Breath*, a collection of essays.

ALVIN GREENBERG's fiction has been appearing in a wide variety of literary magazines since the early seventies. He has published three novels and three collections of short stories, including *Delta*, winner of the 1982 AWP Award in Short Fiction and, most recently, *The Man in the Cardboard Mask* (Coffee House Press). New Rivers Press also published Greenberg's first two collections of poetry, *the metaphysical giraffe* (1968) and *the house of the would-be gardener* (1972). A native Cincinnatian but a Minnesota resident since 1965, Greenberg teaches at Macalester College, does most of his writing on the shores of Lake Superior.

JON HASSLER, a novelist, lives in Sauk Rapids, Minnesota, and teaches at St. John's University. Between 1977 and 1990 he published eight novels: *Staggerford*, *Simon's Night*, *The Love Hunter*, *A Green Journey*, *Grand Opening*, *North of Hope*, *Four Miles to Pinecone*, and *Jemmy*. (The last two are books for young adults.) He has received fellowships from the John Simon Guggenheim Foundation and the Minnesota State Arts Board. Hassler, a life-long resident of Minnesota, was born in Minneapolis, lived his first ten years in Staples and his next eight in Plainview. He graduated from St. John's University (B.A.) and the University of North Dakota (M.A.) and taught high school English for ten years before entering college teaching at Bemidji State University. It was at the age of thirty-seven, while teaching at Brainerd Community College, that he began seriously to write fiction. He has been at St. John's since 1980.

DAVID HAYNES lives in St. Paul and writes fiction. His stories have appeared in *Other Voices*. He has just finished his first novel.

JUDITH K. HEALEY lives and works in Minneapolis, Minnesota. Her short stories have appeared in *Studio One, Groundwater,* and *Fallout.* She has published fiction and has authored and edited a number of professional publications. She has just completed her first novel, *Daddy Longshadow.* As soon as her children are finished with college she will retire to the mountains and write wildly.

JACQUELIN HILLMER began writing fiction in 1983 when she took her first class at the Loft. She has had articles and stories published in *The Minneapolis Tribune, Scope Magazine,* and *Plainswoman* and is the recipient of two essay contest awards. She works with children in a chemical dependency prevention program and is doing graduate work in counseling psychology.

DAVID JOHNSON earned a Master of Fine Arts from the University of Arkansas. After a stint working with rehabilitation publications in Hot Springs, Arkansas, he taught at universities in Wisconsin and Minnesota. He is currently living in Eau Claire, Wisconsin, where he works with law-related publications. Mr. Johnson's poems have appeared in *Kansas Quarterly, Beloit Poetry Journal, New Orleans Review,* and numerous other magazines, including *From the Tongue of the Crow,* a *Wisconsin Review* anthology. A chapbook of his poems, *Much Toil, Much Blame,* was published by Red Weather Press in 1982. He would like to thank novelist Tim O'Brien for his enthusiastic and insightful criticism of an earlier draft of this story and short story writer Rick Christman for always being willing to sit down and talk about wild stories.

JEFFREY A. JOHNSON's fiction has appeared in *The Iowa Review, Intro, Minnesota Monthly,* and other publications. He is a former senior editor of *Twin Cities* magazine. He lives in St. Paul.

JUDITH KATZ is a Jewish lesbian playwright, critic, and novelist who moved to Minnesota in 1983 from western Massachusetts. In her life she has worked as a janitor, furniture mover, college instructor, dishwasher, and writer, sometimes all at the same time. Her fiction has appeared in *The Original Coming Out Stories*, *Fight Back! Feminist Resistance to Male Violence* and the journals *Hurricane Alice*, *Evergreen Chronicles*, and *Sinister Wisdom*. She has received numerous awards, including a Minnesota State Arts Board grant, a Loft-McKnight award, and a National Endowment for the Arts Creative Writing Fellowship.

DAVIDA KILGORE was born May 9, 1956, in Chicago, attended Howalton Day School and Francis W. Parker High School. Later, she moved to St. Paul to attend Macalester College and the University of Minnesota. She became a single parent in 1976. She knew from the age of eight that she would become an artist: writer, painter, musician, actor . . . any field where she could share her passions with others. She is a winner of New Rivers' 1987 Minnesota Voices Project Competition for her collection, *Last Summer and Other Stories*. She is currently at work on a novel.

THOMAS KING's short stories and poems have been published in magazines and journals in Canada and the U.S. His novel, *Medicine River*, was published by Viking in 1990 and is being made into a TV movie by the Canadian Broadcasting Corporation. King has edited two collections of short fiction by Native writers in Canada. The latest, *All My Relations*, was recently published by McClelland and Stewart. He has also co-edited a collection of critical essays, *The Native in Literature*. King currently teaches American Studies, Native American Studies, and Creative Writing at the University of Minnesota.

WANDA KOLLING was born in Watson, Minnesota and was graduated from the University of Minnesota with a B.A. in English. Her stories and poems have appeared in various magazines, including *The Carleton Miscellany* and *Shenandoah*. She lives in St. Paul.

MARY LACHAPELLE is the author of *House of Heroes and Other Stories* (Crown; hardcover, Vintage Contemporaries; paper edition). She is the recipient of national awards such as the PEN/Nelson Algren award and the Whiting Writers award. She teaches fiction at the University of Minnesota.

ROBERT LACY lives in Medicine Lake, Minnesota, and is a graduate of the Iowa Writers' Workshop. He received a Loft-McKnight Fiction Fellowship in 1984 and was a winner of the Midwest Voices fiction competition in 1985. His stories have appeared in *The Saturday Evening Post*, *Crazyhorse*, *Ploughshares*, *The Crescent Review*, *Indiana Review* and elsewhere, and have been anthologized in *The Best American Short Stories* 1988 and *The Best of Crazyhorse*.

ELLEN LANSKY was born in St. Paul, Minnesota, and grew up in Overland Park, Kansas. She received a B.A. from The College of St. Catherine in St. Paul, and an M.A. from the State University of New York at Binghamton. At present she lives in Minneapolis, where she writes, teaches, and attends the University of Minnesota.

IAN GRAHAM LEASK was born and raised in London. He moved to Minneapolis in the mid-seventies, started taking extension classes in creative writing and got so hopelessly hooked on the whole shebang that he now holds a master's degree in English with an emphasis on writing and is a dissertation's length away from completing his doctorate in the theory and craft of contemporary prose narratology. He has taught for the University of Minnesota, COMPAS Writers-in-the-Schools and the Loft. He is a 1987-88 Loft Mentor Series winner and is currently working on a book about writing to be published by New Rivers Press. Forthcoming, also from New Rivers Press, is a collection of short fiction, *The Wounded and Other Stories*.

CHERYL LOESCH has lived in St. Paul all her life. She earned a B.A. in English from Macalester College in 1985, and is currently taking writing classes at the University of Minnesota. She participated in the 1987 Emerging Voices Reading Series at the Loft, and has since enjoyed reading aloud to anyone who will listen.

MARY LOGUE was born in St. Paul, grew up in Lake Elmo, and after four years in New York and a stint in Brussels has moved back to Minnesota. She worked at the *Village Vo'ce*, Simon and Schuster, and put in many years in the Minnesota and New York Writers-in-the-Schools programs. Currently, she's teaching at the Loft and at Hamline University. Her poetry and short stories have been published in magazines and anthologies nationwide. Her first novel, *Red Lake of the Heart* was published by Dell in 1987 and her first book of poetry, *Discriminating Evidence*, came out in 1990.

MARIANNE LUBAN was born in Europe and came to Minnesota in 1952 and has lived in St. Paul ever since. Her favorite pursuits are traveling and reading—particularly books on world history and British mysteries. She has visited England eight times. Recently, her collection of short stories, *The Samaritan Treasure*, was published by Coffee House Press.

JOHN KING KAI MING MCKENZIE grew up in Grand Forks, North Dakota, and is a 1990 graduate of Macalester College in St. Paul. He has been a mower of highway medians in the flattest land and a forest fire fighter at high altitudes. In the course of his work he has come to believe that language is a powerful hallucinogen.

WILLIAM MEISSNER directs The Creative Writing Program at St. Cloud State University. He has won four PEN/NEA Syndicated Fiction Awards for his stories, and three others have been selected for syndication by The Fiction Network, San Francisco. Twenty-five of his stories have been published in numerous magazines, including *Twin Cities, Minneapolis/St. Paul, Indiana Review, Mid-American Review, Minneapolis Tribune Sunday Magazine, Chelsea, Louisville Review,* and *Great River Review*. He is currently completing a first novel.

JOHN MIHELIC is a writer who lives and works in the Twin Cities. He makes his living writing and producing film projects for corporate clients.

LYN MILLER is a fiction writer, critic, musician, and theologian. Her family has lived in Minneapolis for five generations.

DONNA NITZ MULLER has lived in South Dakota since her first breath and within easy walking distance of aunts, uncles, and grandparents. She has six children growing steadily into another generation. She is currently working on her Masters Degree from Augustana College in Sioux Falls. Only side trips necessary to the maintenance of her family have interrupted the single goal of writing. The inevitable distance and emptiness between little clusters of persons who have no control over the forces which come often with violence in her fascination. The struggle is so quiet.

DAN NICOLAI is from Austin, Minnesota and now lives in the Twin Cities. He is an organizer with the Association of Community Organizations for Reform Now (ACORN) and writes articles for various rags and periodicals in the area. His mom met Elvis.

KATHLEEN NORRIS lives in South Dakota, where she is working on a book on the Plains. Essays from the manuscript have appeared in *The Hungry Mind Review, Massachusetts Review,* and *North Dakota Quarterly*. Her books of poems include *How I Came To Drink My Grandmother's Piano, The Year of Common Things,* and *The Middle of the World*. She works as an Artist in Residence for the North Dakota Council on the Arts.

JIM NORTHRUP, JR., is the editor of the *Fond du Lac News*. He won the Lake Superior Contemporary Writers Series and his work was included in New Rivers' anthology of Ojibway Prose, *Touchwood*.

LON OTTO has published two collections of short stories — *A Nest of Hooks*, winner of the Iowa School of Letters Award for Short Fiction in 1978, and *Cover Me*, Coffee House Press, 1988. He recently spent a year in Costa Rica, completing a draft of a novel titled *Temper* and beginning work on a new novel, titled *The Flower Trade*. He lives in St. Paul.

ANNE PANNING is from Arlington, Minnesota, and currently resides in Minneapolis. She recently returned from the Philippines, where she taught English for two years with the U.S. Peace Corps. Her first collection of short stories, *The Price of Eggs*, is being published by Coffee House Press in the spring of 1992.

STEPHEN PETERS is a freelance writer, teacher, and storyteller who lives in Minneapolis. His work has appeared in *Prairie Schooner, West Branch, The Christian Science Monitor*, and many other publications.

MARGI PREUS has published stories in *MSS* and other miscellaneous literary journals. She is a 1985 winner of the Lake Superior Writer's Award and a 1987 recipient of an individual artist's grant from the Minnesota State Arts Board. She is currently working on completing a collection of short stories. She lives in Duluth where, in addition to writing stories, she produces, directs, and writes for Colder by the Lake, a satire-comedy theatre. She lives with her husband and son in a little house overlooking the big lake.

GEORGE RABASA lives in St. Paul.

STEPHEN ROSEN's story "The Deerhide" was the author's first published story. He is currently working on other stories. He lives in Cloquet, Minnesota.

MARY KAY RUMMEL is a poet and the story "White-Out" began as a group of poems written after a reunion. Her book of poetry, *This Body She's Entered*, was published by New Rivers Press as a 1988 Minnesota Voices Project winner. She was a Loft Mentor winner in poetry in 1985-86 and began to write fiction after Maxine Hong Kingston told her she thought she was a "closet story writer." Her work has appeared most recently in *Songs of the Earth*, an anthology published by Mesilla Press. She lives in Fridley, Minnesota and works as an educational consultant and in the COMPAS Writers-in-the-Schools Program.

JAMES C. SCHAAP was born and reared on the shores of Lake Michigan in a small Wisconsin town named Oostburg. He is a graduate of the writing program at the University of Wisconsin-Milwaukee and has been teaching literature and writing at Dordt College, Sioux Center, Iowa, since 1976. His work has appeared in many Midwestern journals, including *Kansas Quarterly, Prairie Schooner, South Dakota Review, Great River Review*, and *Minnesota Monthly*. His first novel, *Home Free*, was published by Crossway in 1986. He lives in Sioux Center with his wife Barbara and their children Andrea and David.

JULIE SCHUMACHER was born in Wilmington, Delaware in 1958. She received a B.A. from Oberlin College and an M.F.A. from Cornell University. Her short stories have appeared in *The Atlantic*, the *O. Henry Awards*, 1990, and *The Best American Short Stories*. She teaches at St. Olaf College and the Loft, and is currently completing a book of short fiction and a novel. She lives in St. Paul with her husband Lawrence Jacobs and their two-year-old daughter, Emma.

JANET SHAW makes her home with her husband, Bob, on forty acres of birch woods in rural Ridgeway, Wisconsin. She's published two volumes of poems, three childrens' novels, a volume of short stories, *Some of the Things I Did Not Do*, and a novel, *Taking Leave*. Her short stories have appeared in *The Atlantic Monthly*, *Redbook*, *McCall's*, *Family Circle*, *Triquarterly*, *The Sewanee Review*, *The Missouri Review* and many others, including several anthologies. She has three children, Laura, Mark and Kirsten Beeler.

JOHN SOLENSTEN grew up in a small town in southern Minnesota. His publications include two short story collections (*The Heron Dancer and Other Stories*, *Mowing the Cemetary*) and a novel, *Good Thunder*. He teaches literature and writing at Concordia College, St. Paul, Minnesota.

MADELON SPRENGNETHER has published a book of poems, *The Normal Heart* (New Rivers Press, 1981), and a collection of personal essays, *Rivers, Stories, Houses, Dreams* (New Rivers Press, 1983). With C. W. Truesdale, she has co-edited *The House on Via Gombito: Writing by North American Women Abroad* (New Rivers Press, 1991). In 1988, she was awarded a National Endowment for the Arts grant for creative non-fiction and is currently working on a fictionalized memoir, tentatively titled *Abandoned Love*.

SARA L. SPURGEON is a Kansas native and 1987 graduate of The College of St. Catherine. She has lived in St. Paul since 1982, with a year off for good behavior.

BARTON SUTTER was born in Minneapolis in 1949 and was raised in small towns in Minnesota and Iowa. His latest collection of poetry, *Pine Creek Parish Hall and Other Poems*, was awarded the Bassine Citation by The Academy of American Poets. His first collection of fiction, *My Father's War and Other Stories*, was published by Viking in 1991. The recipient of a Loft-McKnight Award and a Bush Artist Fellowship, he lives in Duluth.

BILL TINKHAM attended the University of North Dakota and the University of Minnesota (both briefly and without distinction). He studied creative writing at De Anza College (Cupertino, CA) and the Loft. He has received a scholarship to the Bread Loaf Writers' Workshop and has published fiction in *MSS, Minnesota Ink, New North Artscape,* and *Lake Street Review*. He's currently at work on a novel, *The Surreal McCoys*.

C. W. TRUESDALE has had seven books of poetry published, has written many stories and essays, and has been Editor/Publisher of New Rivers Press since 1968. He has taught at Macalester College from 1962-7 and intermittently since. His current obsession is with dreams and the unconscious.

MARK VINZ is the author of two books of prose poems, *The Weird Kid* and *Late Night Calls*, and eight other collections of poetry. His short fiction has appeared in such places as *The Antioch Review, Colorado State Review,* and *The Quarterly*, and in several newspapers via the PEN Syndicated Fiction Project. He lives in Moorhead, Minnesota with his wife Betsy.

WILL WEAVER was born in 1950 in northern Minnesota and grew up on a dairy farm. He received his M.A. from Stanford University in 1979. His first novel, *Red Earth, White Earth*, was published by Simon & Schuster (1986) and developed for film by CBS Television. *A Gravestone Made of Wheat* (Simon & Schuster, 1989) was recently issued in paperback by Graywolf Press. He lives in Bemidji and travels widely.

KRISTI WHEELER writes historical films and fiction. She has a special interest in country people and folkways. Her films have won national awards. Her stories have been published in literary magazines and adapted by the History Theatre. She has received Minnesota Arts Board and Bush Foundation Fellowships. Wheeler teaches historical writing seminars for the Minnesota Historical Society and works in the film department of Macalester College. She lives in St. Paul with her sons, Kent, Adam, and Kirk-Erik.

SUSAN WILLIAMS teaches writing and literature courses at the University of Minnesota (Extension) and Metro State University. She reviews books for Minnesota Public Radio's *Weekend* program. Her manuscript *Dying Old and Dying Young* won the 1986 Minnesota Voices Project Competition in poetry and was published in 1987. "And Say Good-bye to Yourself," her first short story, was a winner in the *Minnesota Monthly* 1987 fiction contest. She lives in south Minneapolis with her son Garret and their cat Bob. She has not been back to Europe since 1963.

JENNIFER WILLOUGHBY writes from her home in St. Paul. Her work has appeared in *Paragraph Magazine* and *The New England Anti-Vivisection Quarterly*.

ROBLEY WILSON has lived in the Midwest since 1957, when he left his native state of Maine to study at the University of Iowa. Since 1963 he has taught at the University of Northern Iowa, in Cedar Falls, and he has edited the *North American Review* since 1969. The most recent of his four short-story collections is *Terrible Kisses* (1989); his first novel, *The Victim's Daughter* is forthcoming from Simon and Schuster.